Love Again

A Historical Novel of Key West
1831-1842

SUSAN BLACKMON

With the exception of historical figures, all characters in this novel are fictitious. Any resemblance to living persons, present or past, is coincidental.

Sources for direct quotes can be found in the Author's Notes at the end of the book.

This book contains an excerpt from the forthcoming book *Enduring Love* by Susan Blackmon. This excerpt has been set for this edition only and may not reflect the final content of the forthcoming edition.

Dream Publishing
P.O. Box 464433
Lawrenceville, GA 30042

ISBN: 0988664844
ISBN-13: 978-0-9886648-4-5

www.susanblackmonauthor.com

Cover illustration: John (Jack) H. Morse III

Printed in the United States of America

DEDICATION

To my wonderful and supportive husband for all he does to make sure I have time to write. To my editing crew for reading the drafts, offering advice, and cheering me on: Mom, Lisa Morse, Apryl Bennings, Pam Alteri, and Cathie Brailey. And to my Dad and brother for the gift of their time and talent in creating another beautiful cover.

Thanks to all my fans for encouraging me and patiently waiting four years to read this book. You kept me going even when I was weary of the struggle. A special thanks goes to Teresa Klawitter for letting me bounce ideas off her and sharing her suggestions.

Thanks to Teresa Morato for the Spanish translations and to my proofreader, MaryKay Harman, for her enthusiasm to take on another one of my projects.

Above all, thank you, Lord, for my many blessings.

Chapter 1

It wasn't supposed to be like this...

Theodore Whitmore was exasperated. He ran a hand through his russet hair as he reminded his young son for the third time, as gently as his frustration would allow, to stop playing with the spindle top and find his missing shoes.

They were late leaving the house again. A noon deadline at the newspaper weighed heavy on his mind. It was mornings like this Theodore missed his wife the most. He was having a hard time finding the patience to deal with his five year old son. Granted Henry turned five just this week. Still, Theodore hoped five would bring more independence. He watched as the child half-heartedly searched for his shoes in the parlor only to be distracted by a wooden boat he found in the corner. Interesting how he could find these things now but couldn't see them last night when he was supposed to put away his toys.

Theodore straightened the stack of work papers he gathered from the table and dropped them into his satchel. He then closed his eyes and breathed deeply to control the building frustration. Feeling a little calmer, he walked over to his son and crouched down to his level. Removing the boat from Henry's grasp and tilting his chin up, Theodore waited until his son's light blue eyes met his hazel. "Henry, where did you take off your shoes last night?"

Henry scrunched up his face as if thinking real hard.

Theodore's eyes narrowed. "Hmm." He realized the rational approach was not going to work. Taking Henry by the hand, Theodore walked him room to room visually searching the floor of each and asking, "Did you leave them in here?"

Each time Henry shook his head.

Where in heaven's name could he have hidden them?

Margaret would have known where to find them. Of course, if Margaret were still alive Theodore would have been at work by now, and she would be taking care of their son. A sudden unbidden memory arose of his wife standing on the doorstep holding their baby boy on her hip, teaching him to wave goodbye as Theodore left for the office. His throat tightened and his step faltered.

He missed her so.

It had only been a few months, but it felt like years since he last saw her face or held her to him. They both missed her, father and son. Henry still cried for her at bedtime although it was occurring with less frequency.

Theodore brushed his hand over Henry's blond head, and noticed he was in need of a haircut. It was hard raising his son by himself, but he refused to take the easy way out and turn him over to his cantankerous old aunt or worse yet, strangers, to see to his rearing. And as he so often did since Margaret got sick, he wished his parents were here to help. Ten years ago they decided to relocate to his mother's birth country of Austria leaving their home to Theodore. No other relatives existed from either side of Henry's bloodline. His peers ridiculed him—rearing children was woman's work—still he refused to have it any other way.

Reaching the nursery upstairs, Theodore realized this should have been the first place he looked. The shoes were lying haphazardly on the floor at the end of the bed, as if having been kicked off in a hurry. He would have thought five years old mature enough to manage a pair of shoes, but apparently he was wrong. Sitting his son on the bed, he straightened his socks, slipped his feet into the leather shoes, and buckled them rather than wait the countless minutes it would have taken Henry to do it. Then, taking the trusting little hand in his big one, Theodore waited for Henry to hop off the bed, and together they returned downstairs.

They donned their winter coats to walk the three blocks to his Aunt Agatha's house where he would leave Henry in her care while he worked. The arrangement was made out of desperation in those awful days before Margaret's passing, and now, although he would prefer to leave his son with someone younger and more congenial, his aunt would take it as a betrayal, and so the situation remained status quo.

The morning air filled with the whinny of horses pulling their burdens. The steady sound of carriage wheels against cobblestones underlined with the harsh staccato of hooves emphasized his need to hurry. He desperately wanted to take longer distance-eating strides but necessarily restrained his gait to match the smaller steps of his son. Henry, oblivious to his father's angst, cheerfully waved to the grocer sweeping the walkway.

The aroma of fresh baked bread as they passed the bakery had Theodore wishing, just once, they might have the time to stop. Another block and they turned the corner to pass a cluster of houses before coming to the iron fenced yard of his aunt's abode. He opened the gate and ushered his son through and up the steps to the front door of her brick three story, two chimney house. Theodore impatiently knocked and waited for the aging butler to open it and usher them into the pristine morning room. He unconsciously paused to smooth his russet hair back from his forehead and run his hands down the front of his clothing, making sure all was in place before entering the room. It was a leftover habit from his childhood when Aunt Agatha would chastise him anytime his appearance was less than pleasing.

As usual, his aunt was dressed in black, still mourning the loss of her love over three decades ago; although if asked, she would say it was in deference to her parents whose deaths were more recent. At her throat rested a cameo pendant she had worn for as long as Theodore could remember. A white lace cap covered her gray hair, loosely knotted on her crown. It was an oddity, her loose hair, when everything else about her was straight laced and starched.

She pierced him with a glare. "You're late."

Preferring not to cross words with her, he agreed without speaking. "Hmm."

Her frown deepened with the hated non-response.

Henry cheerfully said, "Good morning, Aunt Aggie," before climbing onto the sofa with a primer in his hands.

Theodore ruffled his son's head and gave his aunt a perfunctory kiss on the cheek before hurrying to the door.

She called after him. "At least your son has respectable manners."

Theodore smiled ruefully as he exited the house. Even at the mature age of twenty-nine, she had the power to make him feel disobedient and rebellious. He continued the additional eight blocks to the office of the *New York Weekly* as fast as his five foot eleven muscular frame could walk.

He arrived at half past nine and paused in the doorway of his editor's office. "Good morning, Bob."

The disheveled man looked up from the galley he was reviewing. "Good morning, Teddy." He waved his hand towards him. "Come on in. We need to talk."

A longtime family friend, Bob Jenkins was like a much older, albeit shorter and heavier, brother to Theodore. He also was the only person who still used his boyhood nickname. Bob got his feet wet in a publishing house as an errand boy. He cut his teeth in journalism at one of the city's largest papers. When he inherited money from his parents, Bob started his own paper and brought Theodore into the fold fresh from his Union College graduation.

Theodore took to it like a duck to water. He worked every position in the production of the newsprint before becoming a writer. Once he saw his first story published, he knew he had found his passion.

Not wanting to get caught in a lengthy conversation, Theodore said, "Perhaps later? I've an article to finish."

Bob waved off his impatience. "I'll not keep you long. Come, have a seat."

Theodore stepped into the cluttered office. He moved some books out of the old wood and leather arm-chair in front of Bob's desk. "What can I do for you?"

"I have an idea I want to share with you." Bob leaned back in his wooden bankers chair giving him more room to gesticulate as he became more enthusiastic about his idea. "I've been thinking of a way to get ahead of the other papers in subscriptions. It's not easy to do when we all share the same circulated stories from abroad. Local stories and political leaning are all that differentiate each paper. We need something to set us apart from the two dozen other newssheets. If we were to get our own stories from beyond this city... Why, we could give a different perspective, a full telling of the story."

3

Understanding the potential, Theodore was infected with Bob's excitement. He leaned forward, enthusiastically adding, "We could define the story and have the ability to share all sides of the situation. So often what we get is only one point of view and a politically motivated one at that."

Bob leaned across the desk, hands out to Theodore. "Exactly. I want to try sending someone to the story to report exclusively for our paper."

Intrigued but skeptical, Theodore asked, "How would you know where to send this person and wouldn't it be expensive for the paper? You would have to be sure there was a story to report to deem the expense worthy."

"The resulting increased circulation and advertisements could well justify the expense. Anyway, my mind is made up. I'm going to try it out. As for where to send this… what shall we call him?" He squinted his eyes searching for an idea, and then his face suddenly brightened. "A field man. No. A field reporter. A field correspondent." He jotted it down on the corner of the closest paper. "I'll keep working on the title, but it should work the same abroad as it does locally. One goes where the lead takes him. Especially if it's one no one else is following." Bob stood up and walked over to a world map hung on the wall of his office. He tapped on the area of water between Cuba and the tip of Florida. "I happen to know Major Glassell's troops are being reassigned to Key West. Why? The major wouldn't say. Congress claims it is to protect the island from Spain."

Theodore's brow furrowed. "Why would they be worried about Spain? We practically stole Florida from them without a fight."

"True. Although, I suppose retaking a small strategic island would make for good vengeance, but that was ten years ago, and Spain isn't going to tangle with the likes of us."

"Perhaps Congress is worried about getting caught in the crossfire between Spain and Mexico."

Bob nodded. "Then again, I also heard John Simonton, the island's founder, petitioned for protection of the salvage courts and claim revenues. He's a rational fellow, which begs the question; protection from what? Maybe the pirates have returned?"

Theodore's was skeptical. "Possible."

"Maybe from local thievery?"

Theodore tilted his head. "Probable. There is a lot of money flowing through the salvage courts."

"There must be a lot of money if they are taking Simonton's request serious enough to send the army. Then again, maybe there is some kind of conflict building we are as yet unaware of." Bob gave him a cocky grin. "Theodore, I want you to follow the army down there and find out what is going on. If there is something brewing in the Caribbean, Key West would be right in the thick of it. It's a good place to test this new idea of ours."

For half a second, Theodore's heart raced at the idea of tracking down the details and writing a full unbiased news story to impress the entire city of New York, maybe even the country, until reality returned pressing down on his shoulders.

Henry.

"Bob, you know I can't do it. I have my son to consider. I can't leave him for that long."

Bob expected his objection. "Take him with you. The paper will pay the hotel room and someone to stay with him while you're working."

"Have you gone daft?"

Bob pretended not to hear him. "A brother of a friend lives down there, William Whitehead. He can assist with all the arrangements."

"It is a generous offer, but you will have to give it to someone else. My son suffers enough without his mother. I'll not take him from the only home he has ever known to live in a hotel on some island while I'm chasing a story."

Bob countered with a ready argument. "A home as full of memories for him as it is for you. A change of scenery will do you both good, and Key West is a booming place. Maybe you'll find a secondary story there too."

Theodore inwardly flinched. His friend struck a nerve. Margaret's presence seemed to linger in every room. But he said no, and he meant it. Theodore stood up, placed his hands on the edge of the desk, and leaned towards Bob to make his point. "I will not take Henry to Key West. I can't and won't leave my son to the care of strangers at the drop of a hat, and I won't leave him here with my aunt. The answer is no."

"I knew you would feel that way so I arranged for my niece to accompany you as his caregiver. You have no objections to her, I assume." Bob had the confident smile of someone about to win his argument. "You could really make a name for yourself as a top reporter in this town." Seeing no change in Theodore's face, Bob played his trump card. "If this endeavor is successful, I'll make you a partner."

The offer surprised him. Bob really knew how to play on his deepest desire for his career, and he knew Theodore wouldn't object to his niece, Annalise. She took care of Henry during those dark days when Margaret first became ill while he kept vigil at her bedside. His mind immediately shied away from the memories. They were still too raw.

Bob added, "It will be good for both you and Henry to put some distance to this city and that house. Some new experiences are just what you need." He opened his desk drawer and took out an envelope dropping it on the desk in front of Theodore. "Here is an advance on the travel expenses. How soon can you be ready to leave?"

Theodore stood up straight and firmly said, "The answer is still no." He held Bob's stare for a moment longer, then turned on his heel and left the office.

* * *

Normally when Theodore made a decision it was cut and dried, firmly made, not to be questioned, not even by him. He certainly never had a decision give him second thoughts like he was currently experiencing. Theodore was in turmoil.

Why was this one so different?

He knew why. It had everything to do with what was best for Henry.

Decisions used to be easy. College, career, and wife were straightforward choices. There was never a doubt when he decided not to follow his father in business. He attended Union College because it was prestigious and close to home. He didn't give marriage a second thought. He knew within three days of meeting Margaret he would marry her and did so six months later. Even after marriage, the decisions he had to make were clear. It was only now that he alone was responsible for Henry's well-being, something he was ill-equipped to handle, was he unsure of his decisions.

As if the opportunity of field reporting and a possible partnership were not enticing enough, the story was of interest to him as well. His wants were juxtaposed against Henry's needs. He would lay aside his wants in a heartbeat to do what was right by Henry. The real reason for the confliction was not knowing what was best for his son. Bob made a good point about getting away from the memories. Maybe it would be good for Henry to experience something new. He wanted to do what was best for his son. If only he knew what that was.

He continued down the hall, deep in thought, passing by the press room where two men worked in tandem printing out this week's edition. He then passed the page-setting room where the compositor and the stoneman put together the next pages to be printed. Finally, he came to his simple wooden desk, similar to five others, in the back office of the *New York Weekly*. Sitting down, he stared at the unfinished pages of his editorial calling for a cleanup of the city's rubbish laden streets. He still had a noon deadline to meet. He tried focusing on his work, but his thoughts refused to cooperate.

Was 'no' really the only answer he could give?

Desire was trying to override logic, and he was having a hard time ignoring it. He couldn't take Henry. He wouldn't leave Henry behind. Therefore, decision made. Nothing else should be a consideration. He told his boss 'no' with good reason, but every other part of him wanted to say 'yes'. If not for Henry, he would have said 'yes' and looked upon it as an adventure.

Indecision was a new experience, and the only way Theodore knew to handle the doubts and conflicting ideas was to approach it with analytical reasoning.

Could he leave Henry? He still wouldn't consider his aunt, but what about someone else? If his parents were here instead of in Austria, he could have entrusted them with Henry's care. No one else came to mind.

Could he take Henry with him? The strong desire to grasp this opportunity had Theodore giving the idea more thought. The first consideration would be safety. He needed more information about Key

West. He heard the island was a hangout for fisherman and wreckers, but Bob seemed to believe there was civilized society in residence. He could start his research this afternoon. Next, would be a caregiver. He trusted Bob's niece, Annalise, to watch Henry, but she was of an age they couldn't travel alone. Assuming her parents would let her go, she would require a chaperone for the sake of her reputation. Then, and most important, he had to carefully consider if it would be good for Henry.

All this weighed against an assignment that could become dangerous and a possibility of a partnership in the paper—something he really wanted. He would have to give it more thought. For now, it was back to the work at hand. With an action plan in place, he was now able to focus on his task.

For the next several hours, all that was heard in the office was the scratching of his nib pen and that of his colleagues as they worked to finish their stories by deadline. Twenty after eleven, Theodore stood up, stretched his stiff shoulders, and flexed his fingers from the constant writing. He picked up his draft and headed towards Bob's office mentally preparing for a replay of their earlier conversation. He knew from history Bob would broach the subject several more times before accepting his negative reply. He was thankful to find the office vacant. He didn't want to give Bob any inkling he was wavering in his decision least he be pressured even more. He dropped the article in the inbox and retreated down the hall.

Theodore picked up his coat and headed to a tavern down the street for a quick bite and ale followed by a meeting with his liaison to the governor's office for a weekly update. Afterwards, he returned to the office to do the required rewrite of his editorial based on Bob's notes before starting on his research project. He handed his final draft over to the proofreader and headed for the file room. The next two hours, he searched their archived papers skimming the stacks of faded dusty pages looking for every article he could find on Florida, and Key West in particular.

By the time he was done, his eyes were strained and dry. Worse, only one article touting the virtues of the island was helpful to his dilemma and it was marginal at best since it was biased to encourage more settlers to move to the Florida Keys. He may not have found what he was looking for, but he did find some pertinent reading.

Since boyhood he held an avid interest in anything Indian related so naturally the article about Andrew Jackson's invasion of Spanish Florida in 1818 and the fight against the Florida Indians caught his attention. Theodore was only fifteen at the time, but he recalled having discussions with his father about the resulting destruction of a fort, many deaths, questionable executions of two Britons, the treaty with the Seminoles, and ultimately the cession of Florida from Spain. Reading of the events again brought back fond memories of his father and empathy for the Indians now restricted to a reservation when once they freely roamed the whole territory.

The opening of the Florida territory afterwards led to the next article of interest which was Key West's founding and early ownership dispute. There were several stories about the first naval occupation and their task of eradicating the last of the Caribbean pirates with Commodore Porter's "Mosquito" patrols. Next, he found articles on Key West's primary industry, ship salvaging. The writers either praised the salvagers or disparaged them depending on the outcome of the wrecks. There were many of these articles due to the local interests of all the New England ship owners, investors, and insurance companies involved in those disputes.

He checked his pocket watch and confirmed it was time to leave. He would have to resume his research elsewhere tomorrow.

Leaving the office just after four o'clock, he followed his usual routine of returning to his aunt's home where he and his son would join her for a quiet dinner—his aunt had a notion conversation was bad for digestion—before returning to his home. These days he dined with his aunt almost every evening, but when Margaret was alive, it was only once a week. He smiled recalling how she would rein him in whenever he would get too grouchy about it.

Aunt Agatha had always been a part of Theodore's life. His father's only sibling and the elder by nearly a decade, the two of them were raised in a wealthy, albeit strict, household. At sixteen, she ran off and married a sea captain against her parent's wishes. Captain Jedidiah Pary's death a few years later brought Agatha back to her father's house where she still lived to this day now having buried first her father and barely a year later her mother. Theodore's father actually inherited the house but having no need of it Agatha resided as mistress of the manor. Theodore knew none of the details of her marriage, not even if she had been happy.

Theodore's father, Lawrence, married a wealthy Austrian girl, Katarina, and then made a fortune of his own. He built a large house in what was then Manhattan's richest neighborhood where Theodore was born and raised as their only child. Although Theodore grew up enjoying wealth and privilege, his father kept him grounded in the important things in life such as taking care of family and strong work ethics while his mother kept him from suffering the same stern upbringing his father had endured.

While growing up, Theodore and his parents would have dinner with Aunt Agatha at least twice a week. Quiet dinners. Afterwards, they would adjourn to the parlor to talk, except for Theodore. In Aunt Agatha's house, children were seen, not heard and were always neat, tidy, and well behaved; just as she had been raised. For the hour or two they were there to visit, Theodore had to sit still and be silent, or he would receive his aunt's annoyed glare and his mother's reproving look to be followed later by his father's lecture on the way home. It instilled in him an intimidation towards his aunt, so deeply ingrained, it still influenced his behavior towards her today.

His son, on the other hand, had a special relationship with his aunt. Henry's first attempt at saying her name came out as Aunt Aggie, and much to Theodore's surprise, she never bothered to correct him, so the name stuck. It astounded and amused Theodore to this day that his son managed to find her soft spot. For though she still had her rules, she was much more lenient with him. In short, his son had a healthy respect, instead of fear, for her. Margaret figured Theodore wore his aunt down in his youth and she no longer had the energy to discipline Henry in the same manner. Theodore rather suspected Aunt Agatha couldn't resist Henry's charm any more than Theodore had been able to resist Margaret's.

After their marriage, Theodore and Margaret lived in the east wing of his father's large estate while his parents occupied the west wing. Three years later, Henry was born and Theodore was working at the *New York Weekly*.

Life was good.

When Theodore's parents decided to move to Austria, his father bequeathed the house to him and reminded Theodore of his family duty to look after his aunt.

He regarded Aunt Agatha sitting regally at the head of her table and wondered who was really looking after whom. When his wife died, it was Aunt Agatha who helped him through the details of burial and adjusting to life without Margaret. She also took over much of Henry's care although Theodore insisted Henry come home with him every night. A few months after Margaret's passing, when Theodore was feeling more in control, he wanted to make other arrangements for Henry, but when he broached the subject with his aunt, she emphatically objected insisting 'family took care of family', so Theodore dropped the idea for the time being.

His aunt always dressed for dinner. Today she wore a black bombazine dress with a high neck and ecru lace covering the bodice. Her ashen hair loosely gathered in a bun. Her only adornment was the black cameo pendant with an ivory rose inherited from her mother. Narrow strait nose, thin compressed lips, chin tipped upward, and a few more creases over the years made her appearance as standoffish as her personality. She disapproved but tolerated his working clothes and ink stained hands at her dining table because it would be more inconvenient to wait for her supper while he stopped at home first to change into fresh clothing.

They exchanged a few pleasantries before dinner was served, and he rarely stayed after their meal. His evening activities varied slightly but always ended with reading a story to his son before tucking him in for the night. Theodore would then pour himself two fingers of brandy and light a cigar while he reviewed the other published newspapers of the day before turning in himself.

Tonight, he followed his son into his room ready to read him a story from *Mother Goose's Fairy Tales*. Henry crawled into bed, and as Theodore tucked him in, he rubbed his eyes and in a petulant voice asked, "Where's mama? I want mama to read to me."

Caught off guard by the verbal dagger to his heart, Theodore replied bluntly. "Mama can't read to you anymore."

Henry's brow furrowed and his lips pursed. "Why?"

Despite having this same conversation more times than Theodore could count, Henry still seemed unable to accept his mother was gone. It broke his heart to see his son's distress, and so he modified his tone in an effort to soothe him. "God called her to heaven."

"Why?"

Theodore was never sure how to answer other than with brutal honesty, so rather than further upset Henry, he avoided it altogether by distracting him. He dreaded the day this tactic quit working. "Do you want to hear *Little Red Riding Hood* or *Puss in Boots*?"

He smiled in relief when Henry clapped his hands. "*Puss in Boots. Puss in Boots.*"

Theodore settled in to read the much loved tale while in the back of his mind he thought maybe Bob was right. Leaving would be better for Henry. A change of scenery may be good for his son. Maybe, it would keep him from asking for his mother and twisting Theodore's insides.

Later, settled in his chair with his drink and smoke, he wished he could ask his mother for advice. He needed a mother's opinion on taking Henry away from the only home he had ever known. He couldn't research a written answer to this question. He would have to feel his way through it, and he felt woefully inadequate to the task. Adding to his misery, he missed being able to discuss such things with his wife, but then, if she were here, he would have told Bob 'yes' and the decision would be whether or not he would take his wife and son as the assignment was sure to last many months. Henry's reaction would not have been an issue.

Another thought occurred to him. Was it right for him to leave his elderly aunt? She was more than capable of taking care of herself, but if something happened to her and he was not here to help, he would be racked with guilt. He could have Bob look in on her every once in a while as a condition of accepting the assignment but would that be enough to ease his conscience?

Sleep was elusive with all the questions circling in his mind. A rarely taken second glass of brandy proved to be the cure. Theodore headed to bed hoping tomorrow would bring some clarity.

* * *

Theodore spent most of the next day doing research. Instead of going to the office, he went to see a friend at the *Saturday Evening Post* who introduced him to Mr. Tighe, the archive curator. He was shown into a storage room with a daunting number of storage crates filled with back issues of the newspaper. It was enough to make Theodore consider abandoning the task until Mr. Tighe handed him a register listing the subject of every article and every paper along with any notable names and places. Now he need only skim the register for key words and find the particular paper rather than go through them all. Mr. Tighe next showed him how to use the listed key code to find the papers in the labeled crates. It was all very ingenious and saved him many valuable hours, perhaps days, of searching every paper otherwise.

He found several articles of interest and easily bypassed the same reprints from the *Niles Register* in Baltimore that he read yesterday leaving only a few papers to pull from the crates. Again, nothing about the current inhabitants of Key West, but he did find a reprint of the 1823 Moultrie Creek treaty he found fascinating. It promised the Seminole tribe twenty years of peace if they remained on the reservation in central Florida. Idly, he noted there were twelve years left and wondered what would happen to the Seminoles when they expired.

Theodore stopped at Mr. Tighe's desk before leaving. "Thank you for your assistance. I have refiled everything."

"Appreciate that. You were looking for information on Key West, weren't 'cha now? Did you find what you need?"

"Not really."

"I recollect my neighbor went down there a few years back. He would be willing to tell ya what he knows. Would you like to speak to him?"

"I believe I would if you could arrange a meeting."

Mr. Tighe looked at his pocket watch. "It's close enough to lunchtime. I'll walk you over and introduce you to Mr. Howe."

"Much obliged to you, Mr. Tighe."

The two men walked the few short blocks to the residence of Mr. Howe. Mr. Tighe preformed the introduction and then left. Mr. Howe turned out to be very helpful. He told Theodore there was a reasonably comfortable boarding house run by a widow and many friendly people on the island, including a few families with young children. More important was the assurance there was a doctor living on the island. Theodore concluded that with the army in residence, he shouldn't have any concerns for safety and could expect to stay on the island in relative comfort.

One question answered.

He also learned Mr. Howe and his wife had seven children and had moved several times while they were growing up. Mrs. Howe assured him children were resilient, and he would probably be surprised how easily his son would adapt to the change in environment. She also added, "Adventure is good for the soul of any age."

Theodore was for once grateful for his aunt's decree of silence during meals. It allowed him to think through all he learned today. Based on location, amenities, and Mrs. Howe's assurances, he felt comfortable making the decision to take the job. He would need to find a companion for Annalise, but otherwise, he didn't have any qualms with his decision. He was once again in control of his emotions. It felt good to put the turmoil behind him.

Aunt Agatha violated her own dinner rule to ask, "Why are you smiling like the cat who swallowed the canary?"

11

Lost in his thoughts, for a moment Theodore wasn't sure she had spoken. "Excuse me?" It took another second for her question to register. "Oh, I have been offered a promotion to field correspondent."

She set down her knife and fork and gave him the fullness of her attention. "And what does one do as a field correspondent?"

He followed suit, laying down his utensils and placing his hands flat on the table. "I will be leaving for Florida to write a story for the paper."

"You think anyone cares about the Florida territory?"

Trying not to get defensive with her he limited his words. "Yes, some people do."

"Humph." She pierced him with her sharp brown eyes. "And what are your plans for Henry while you are gone?"

Not knowing how his aunt would react, he mentally braced himself. "I plan to take him with me." Theodore noticed Henry watching their exchange with wide-eyed interest. He wondered if Henry was following the conversation, or if his interest had more to do with the odd fact they were conversing during the meal.

Agatha wasn't about to let this chance for adventure pass her by. At her age, they didn't come around very often. "Good. I will go too. Where exactly are we going in Florida?"

His aunt surprised him. Once the shock dissipated, Theodore immediately wanted to refuse but common sense prevailed. It would solve the companion problem for Annalise and the guilt of leaving her alone. She stared at him defiantly waiting for an answer. "Very well then, Key West. It's a tiny island just north of Cuba. You are willing to endure the discomforts of travel?"

She gave him a sarcastic look rather than answer his question. "See Captain Blake at the docks tomorrow. He'll recommend a safe ship to take us there." She picked up her silverware and returned to eating indicating the dismissal of the subject.

Theodore grimaced. Leave it to his aunt to take control of his plans. He guessed this Captain Blake to be a friend of her late husband, so it probably would be beneficial to seek him out even if he would rather thwart his aunt's high-handed demand.

On the way home after dinner, Henry walked quietly beside Theodore. Normally, his son skipped ahead of him working off his pent up energy after being contained in his aunt's house all day. He put his hand on Henry's shoulder. "Son, is something bothering you?"

Henry looked up at him with troubled eyes. "I don't want to go away."

His answer surprised and dismayed Theodore. He wasn't surprised Henry understood the conversation, but he didn't expect his son's objection. It naturally didn't occur to him to ask Henry if he wanted to go as a child's wants did not matter, only his needs, and a five year old was not expected to know what he needed. Theodore's first instinct was to dismiss Henry's concern but decided it would be better for both of them to question his objection. "Why not?"

"Because we won't come back."

"We would eventually."

"Mama went away and didn't come back."

Oh! Now he understood. Theodore stopped walking to crouch down in front of his son. "That's different Henry. Mama went to heaven to be with the angels. We are going to another place on earth, and we can come back any time we want." Henry's eyes were still wide and worried. "I promise."

"Why do we have to go at all?"

Theodore kept his manner serious. "Well, Henry, we could stay but we would miss out on an adventure."

Henry's head tilted just a bit. "What's an adventure?"

"Something different and exciting. Usually it involves traveling to a place you have never been before."

"Where would we go?"

"To start, we would sail on a big ship out in the ocean where all you can see is water; no trees or houses or buildings. It will take us to a place where the weather is always warm." He pulled Henry's coat collar a little tighter. "A place where you don't need a coat, even in winter."

"Really?"

Theodore smiled. "Yes, really."

* * *

Theodore knocked on the door frame of Bob's office. He waited for him to look up from his task.

"Come on in Teddy. Does this visit mean you have reconsidered my proposal?"

"It does." Theodore thought it would be a gloating moment for Bob. It was unexpected for him to be graciously happy with the decision. Theodore was aware Bob had partially invented the assignment as a way of helping him and his son heal from their grief. Ruefully, he had to admit it was already working.

Bob's face split into a grin. "Excellent, excellent my boy. If you didn't accept I was going to scratch the whole idea. Glad you changed your mind. Have a seat. Let's talk about the details."

Theodore had to clear the chair again before sitting down. Two days since his last visit found it piled high again in books and papers. "When did you have in mind to start this project?"

"Well, right away, of course. As soon as you can make the arrangements." Bob reached into his desk and pulled out the envelope he tried to hand Theodore before and slid it across the papers on his desk. "This will take care of your travel arrangements."

Nodding, Theodore said, "I suspected as much, so I have already started making arrangements. Do you know when the army will be mobilizing?"

"They should already be in Key West."

"Then I will depart as soon as possible."

The two men continued to discuss the details of the assignment for the next half hour until they had covered every aspect. Theodore stood up to leave. Bob rose and walked around his desk to place a hand on Theodore's shoulder. "As long as you are submitting stories, you should make it an extended stay. I meant what I said, Teddy, a change of scenery would do you both good. Don't come back until you're ready. If you tire of the army, I am sure you will be able to find other interesting items to write about while you are there." He held out his hand to Theodore who shook it firmly.

"Thank you." Those two words were meant to convey his gratitude for the opportunity and for Bob's concern for him and his son.

* * *

Once the decision was made, preparations went surprisingly swift. Even Aunt Agatha and Annalise were prepared to leave three days later.

The hired carriage came to a halt in front of his home. The mismatched mares snorted and stamped in protest to the cold winter morning. The driver promptly informed Theodore, assistance was not included in his service, not for any price, but it mattered little as Theodore and Henry were light on luggage. It was easily loaded and they proceeded to the home of Annalise. His aunt lived closer, but Annalise was furthest from the docks. To limit time spent with his aunt in the confined space of the carriage, Theodore decided to pick her up last. The young lady's luggage consisted only of a small trunk, and with the aid of her father, it was easily managed. Theodore took one look at the large trunks piled in Aunt Agatha's foyer and walked back out. Fortunately, he found two lackeys nearby more than willing to earn a coin.

Now with all the passengers and belongings loaded, Theodore settled back and relaxed for the half hour journey to the South Street Seaport. Those with him were strangely quiet allowing the outside world to be heard. He rested his eyes and listened to the sounds of the other traffic, the shouts of street vendors, people greeting each other, and underneath it all, the soothing rhythmic sound of the carriage wheels and horse's hooves against the cobblestone street. These were the familiar sounds of home. He must have drifted into a light slumber because the cadence of cobblestone giving way to the thump of wood planking on the docks jolted him awake.

"Wait here," he told the others before exiting the carriage to find himself standing in front of the *Pride of Baltimore* making ready to sail for New Orleans with several ports of call along the way, including Key West. It was a handsome, two-masted clipper and looked to be sturdy and dependable. He easily found dock hands to unload their luggage and pile it up on the wharf for loading onto the ship, but he had to insist the impatient driver wait, allowing his family to stay in the relative warmth of the carriage until time to board.

When the captain gave his permission, Theodore opened the carriage door and assisted their exit.

Henry tugged on his father's hand to get his attention. "Are we going on that boat, Poppa?"

Theodore looked down to see the wide-eyed wonder in his son's eyes. "Yes son, we are going to sail on this *ship* to Florida. Remember, I showed you where we are going on the globe."

"I remember, Poppa. We are going to an island at the end of the pencil…"

"Peninsula."

Henry carefully repeated, "Peninsula."

Theodore could tell he was committing the word to memory, and it made him feel proud.

As they walked up the gangway, Henry pulled on his hand trying to get him to move faster. Theodore was about Henry's age the first time he stepped aboard a ship. He remembered how he felt. Looking down at his son, he saw those same feelings of awestruck wonder and excitement in Henry's eyes. It was contagious. Theodore felt it growing within him and lightening the burden he had been carrying since Margaret's death. He didn't realize how oppressive it had been.

They quickly stowed the belongings they were carrying in their cabins, one for Theodore and Henry and another for Aunt Agatha and Annalise, and then returned to the main deck to watch the ship leave the harbour. Henry jumped up and down trying to see over the bulwarks. His son's enthusiasm made him smile—a real genuine smile. The muscles were stiff and unnatural making Theodore realize it had been far too long since he had worn the expression. He lifted Henry up bringing his son's face level with his not only to see the view but to share his son's joy in the moment. Henry's excitement reassured Theodore he had made the right decision for both of them. This trip was exactly what they needed.

Soon the orders were given to cast the lines and haul the sails. The ship moved away from the dock and into the harbour quickly catching on the current of the Hudson River.

As the ship pulled away, Agatha watched her nephew closely. His emotions were always so controlled and rarely revealing, requiring keen observation to discern what he might be feeling. The smile he bestowed on his son was surprising. It was so rarely done, it transformed his face, so she hardly recognized him. It seemed as if there was even a touch of excitement hovering under the surface. These two elements would bear further scrutiny. There was no telling where such hidden passions might lead. As the ship picked up speed, Agatha excused herself from the windy deck to venture to the salon below intending to watch the rest of the shoreline slip by from a port window while she reminisced of a long ago sailing adventure as a newlywed running away with her beloved, Jedidiah.

Theodore committed the scene of his home town to memory as their distance from shore increased. The wood smoke rising from the chimneys of the predominately brick buildings near the waterfront created a drifting haze over the rooftops. He could see the spires of the Second Trinity Church and St. Paul Chapel reaching for purity above the man-made cloud. His family worshiped in the chapel just yesterday. Today would be the last he set eyes on it for six months to a year. The thought did not engender emotion within him, it was merely a passing thought before he turned to point out the ships in the harbour for Henry.

The large number of vessels and variety of sails in the bay always impressed him, the largest of them being his favourites. Theodore was so engrossed in watching the ships, he nearly missed turning starboard to see the new lighthouse recently built on the bluff of Stanton Island near Fort Tompkins. This light tower at the mouth of the Upper Bay was a much anticipated second light making headlines when it opened three years ago. Now the land fell away on either side as they entered the Lower Bay. Sandy Hook Light could be seen in the distance as they finally sailed out of the bay and into the bight and finally out into the Atlantic Ocean. Surrounding ships became more distant with each expanding waterway. With nothing more to see other than open water and Henry's cheeks rosy from the cold wind, Theodore took him below deck to join his aunt for what he hoped would be a very smooth sail down the eastern seaboard and into the Florida Straits.

Chapter 2

Key West, Florida, Spring 1831

It wasn't supposed to be like this...

Most days Betsy Wheeler, a widow these last five years, could not recall her late husband's visage, as if her mind erased his image without her consent. After the long years of grief, it was both a blessing and heartbreaking. She took it as a sign she was ready to find love again, but at the same time, she missed the comfort of his countenance.

However, this morning, Ben visited her dreams in crystal clarity with sweet words of love and devotion. He gently brushed the back of his fingers across her face before curling them around the nape of her neck. He leaned in to kiss her.

She awoke just before his lips touched hers to feel the sharp pain of his loss all over again. She pressed her hand to her pale cheek trying to hold on to the feeling of his ghostly caress.

Now, several hours later, she felt acute loneliness but perversely did not want any company to dispel it. Normally, she would push aside her feelings and focus on her work or distract herself by visiting one of the other ladies living on the island. Today, she wanted to hold onto his memory.

The knock on the front door disturbed Betsy from her melancholy. The petite, twenty-six year old seamstress put aside the shirt she was hemming to cross the front room of her small home and seamstress shop. As it was Saturday, whoever was there had probably come for a social visit. Betsy didn't feel like trading pleasantries this morning. Maybe she could feign a headache and send her guest on their way.

She ran her hands over her shiny coal black hair smoothing it towards her chignon before opening the front door. Thoughts of feigning a headache disappeared at the sight of her friend, Abigail Eatonton, holding her wiggling eighteen month old daughter, Emily Rose. The toddler's enchanting smile as she reached her chubby arms out towards Betsy had the seamstress opening her door wide in welcome. It had been weeks since the two friends were last able to visit.

Betsy eagerly took Emily from her mother. "Good morning, Abby."

Abby answered in her faded English accent. "Good morning to you, dear."

Betsy closed the door, then led them to the sitting room. She noticed the tiredness lurking behind her friend's soft smile and dove gray eyes. "Abby, would you like some tea or perhaps lime water?"

Abby gracefully seated herself on the sofa. "Tea, please, if it would not be too much trouble."

"No trouble at all." Betsy looked a little closer at Abby's face. "Should I add some soda crackers as well?"

Abby grimaced. "Is it so obvious? I thought I was hiding it well."

Betsy transferred Emily to her mother's lap. "We have been friends far too long for me not to notice you are feeling unwell, but do not trouble yourself over others, most would never suspect."

Abby gave her a weak smile as she tried to contain the toddler. Emily wanted to get down and walk, but Abby did not have the energy to chase her around the room trying to keep her out of trouble. Scissors, pins, and needles were too easy for little fingers to find in the seamstress' home.

Betsy quickly exited the back of the house to the outdoor kitchen. She made two cups of tea from the teakettle she kept warm on the wood stove. She stoked the fire, then refilled the copper kettle from the bucket of water drawn earlier from the cistern, and replaced it on the back burner. She arranged the tea cups, a tin of soda crackers, and a biscuit for Emily on a tray and carried it back to the sitting room.

Setting the tray down on an end table next to Abby, Betsy took the squirming baby from her. Abby wasn't the only one who was tired. Betsy picked up a large button the size of the toddlers hand from a container in her workroom and handed it to Emily to play with, then sat down on the ladder-back chair on the other side of the end table and unconsciously began rocking her torso to soothe Emily to sleep.

Betsy sent Abby an understanding smile. "Unless I am mistaken, you are increasing again."

Abby's answering smile brightened her becoming face. "I am. Max and I are trying not to get excited. This early, so much could go wrong, but we can't seem to help it. Neither of us had siblings, and we do not want Emily to be an only child."

Betsy inhaled the delicate scent of babyhood still clinging to the child in her arms. It immediately brought a return of her melancholy. "I am sure all will go well for you. Are you praying for a son?"

"I am sure Max has his hopes, but healthy is all I ask for."

Betsy tried to paste a smile on her face and be a good hostess. "I suppose your condition has changed your plans to visit England this summer."

Abby stopped nibbling on her cracker to answer. "Unfortunately, it does, and I was looking forward to seeing my friends again, especially Elizabeth and Tria."

Elizabeth and Abby grew up together in England, but Victoria, whom Abby affectionately nicknamed Tria, was a former resident of Key West and a mutual friend of Betsy's. Two years ago, she married a duke's son visiting the island and sailed away to his home in England.

Betsy nodded in understanding. "Have you received any letters from Victoria? I have not had one in quite some time."

"I have not received any recently, and the last one was so brief as to be a waste of good paper, but then I am not surprised. Tria is not one to sit still long enough to hold a pen to parchment." Abby noticed her sleeping daughter and couldn't help her sigh of relief. "You have the touch with her. It usually takes me an hour to get her to settle down for a nap."

Betsy looked down at Emily's sweet face and felt the longing in her heart. She would have loved being a mother. She felt her heart constrict. Her emotions were normally on a very even keel. Today they were fragile and too close to the surface.

Abby studied Betsy's oval face framed by dark hair and accentuated with high cheekbones. Her milky skin was marred only by a tiny birthmark on her temple. She knew Betsy thought her forehead was too tall therefore she kept it hidden under bangs, but anyone would agree, her most striking feature was her large round sky blue eyes framed by long dark lashes. Behind those eyes, hidden in the depths of her irises, her normally cheerful friend was struggling with her emotions. Gently Abby asked, "Betsy, what is it? You seem somber today."

The concern in Abby's tone was her undoing. Betsy's eyes welled up. Someone to care about her was what she missed most living alone. It had been five long years since Ben succumbed to yellow fever, and some days, the loneliness became unbearable. She quickly wiped away the unexpected tear as it slipped down her cheek.

As Betsy's silence continued, Abby said, "I am sorry, forgive me for intruding. If you would rather be alone, we could leave."

Betsy swallowed back her tears and looked at Abby. She saw only concern on her friend's face; no discomfort towards her weakness. For the first time, Betsy felt the need to share the feelings swelling in her breast. She had held the grief inside for too long. "No. Please. Stay."

Abby's tiredness fled in the wake of concern for Betsy. They had known each other for three years now, and Betsy had yet to share anything of her past. All Abby knew was she had become widowed after moving to the island. She felt her friend's need to share her story and sought a way to help her start. "What brought you to Key West?"

Betsy smiled to herself. "It was Ben's idea. He was a tailor. A very good tailor. We were married almost a year when he read about the new settlement here. I think it was the adventure that lured him. I hated leaving all of my family in Philadelphia—we both came from large families—but I would have followed him anywhere. As long as we were together, I thought I could handle anything." She looked around the walls of her simple home, her mind drifting in the past. "He built this house for us, and he was going to open a shop closer to the harbour. He needed to buy fabric and notions to get the shop started. So he left for a few weeks, sailing to Mobile."

Once started with her story, Betsy found she couldn't stop. "He returned with yellow fever. Actually, it was your husband who took him there and brought him home. Ben nearly didn't survive the return voyage. Captain Max and Thomas had to carry him home. I nursed him night and day for almost a week with Mrs. Mallory's help, but it was not to be. He died still apologizing on his last breath for leaving me here alone so far from my family and not enough money to return to them. He had spent nearly all of our funds to setup the shop."

Abby said nothing. She waited for Betsy to continue, sensing there was more to her story. She watched the emotionally deep pain intensify on Betsy's face, and the tears release unheeded, and perhaps unknown. Abby handed her the handkerchief from her sleeve which Betsy reflexively accepted. Her eyes returned to the sleeping child in her arms as she continued her story.

"After he passed away, the only way I found to go on was by focusing on the babe growing inside me. I still had a part of him."

A soft gasp escaped Abby, aware of how this story would end. Fortunately, Betsy didn't notice her reaction.

Betsy caressed the hand of the sleeping infant and felt herself losing the battle to maintain her composure. She stood up and walked to Abby, silently transferring Emily to her mother. She moved to the window, arms crossed over her chest, and her back to Abby. "When I lost the baby shortly afterwards, I was devastated all over again."

Abby ached to comfort her friend, but sensed she was not yet ready to receive it.

"It was quite a while before I was ready to face the world. If not for Mrs. Mallory's support, I don't think I could have done it. Having lost her own husband in much the same manner and one of her sons, she understood my situation as no other could."

Betsy became aware of her tears and impatiently swiped the embroidered linen handkerchief across her cheeks. She took a deep breath and lifted her head tall, looking towards the front room of her shop before continuing. "I had to support myself, so I hung up my shingle and started sewing. With so many men and so few women, there was an abundance of work to keep me busy. My earnings were enough to keep going but never enough to get back to Philadelphia. Eventually, I quit trying and accepted that this would be my home."

"What about your family? Could they not send you money?"

Betsy shook her head. "My parent's had my younger brothers and sisters to support."

"Were you not afraid to stay here by yourself? Being a widow would have made you especially vulnerable."

"I think there were only four of us women at the time compared to over a hundred men, but no, I wasn't afraid. He would never admit it, but I believe Captain Max and his crew put out the word I was under their protection."

Abby smiled. It sounded like something her husband would do. "Have you ever considered remarrying? Max mentioned you and Jonathon had once...," she faltered not knowing the exact nature of their relationship.

Betsy shook her head. "After a year of mourning, Jonathon and I had dinner together at the boardinghouse a few times, but I wasn't ready to let go of the past, so we became friends instead. Then he fell head over heels for Esperanza Sanchez."

Abby gently probed. "And now? Are you ready to move on?"

Betsy considered before answering. "I'm not sure. Ben is still in my heart." She ran her finger along the thin gold band on her left hand recalling their wedding day and Ben's nervous attempt to slip it on her finger. "Today would have been our eighth anniversary." When she looked at Abby, her eyes were surprisingly clear. "I think, now, if the right person came along— someone I could at least care for a little—I think I could be ready to consider marriage if for nothing else than to put an end to the loneliness."

She was still fidgeting with her wedding band. The idea of removing it gave her pause. She wasn't ready to do that yet, but surely she could consider her options before she took the next step.

* * *

After her conversation with Abby, Betsy started taking more notice of the men around her. Most were sailors, some drifters, a few lawyers, a blacksmith, ship chandlers, barkeeps and other tradesmen. The men were plentiful, but even if she found one appealing, what then? It was easy with Ben. He had always been there, right by her side; her childhood playmate turned sweetheart. All she did was wait for him to notice she had grown into a woman, realize he didn't want to live without her, and ask her father for her hand. All of which occurred in less than a month's time. She never learned the art of flirtation or how to fend off unwanted suitors. Even if she had, surely the rules and methods were different for widows than for debutantes. For one thing, she didn't have a father's protection, and for another she wasn't a virgin. She feared being taken advantage of by less scrupulous men and there were plenty of them on this remote island. So how did she go about getting a husband now?

While she believed her heart was ready to love again, it was the choice of suitors holding her back. A sad fact considering there were hundreds of available men to choose from, and all she had to do was drop a handkerchief to bring them running. Why? Not because she was so irresistible, but because currently, she was the only unattached female over the age of twenty and under the age of forty. There were several younger women of marrying age—daughters of prominent families—but they were kept under the close guard of watchful mothers. Only the proper young man's attention was allowed for those girls, and those young men were likewise not interested in an older widow. But the other men would no doubt swarm her if she showed the slightest interest.

Betsy's quiet and cautious nature made her carefully consider how she would approach opening the social barrier around her. Thanks to Captain Max Eatonton's protection, the men of this island had kept their distance from her ever since her husband died. Breaking that barrier was dangerous.

She needed its protective shield to survive on her own, especially since her livelihood brought her in contact with these men in her own home. If they in general did not have a healthy respect for her safety, she could find herself in an unsavory situation. She also understood, if she made too bold an advance, she would also risk her safety and reputation. And if she lost her reputation, it would also mean the loss of her livelihood.

So over the last several weeks, she covertly observed the men of her acquaintance and chose as her first candidate, Mr. Aronsdale. She deemed him safe to approach. He worked at the ship chandlers and attended Sunday services. He was a polite gentleman, quiet, like her, and trustworthy. A few Sundays ago, she arranged to brush past him upon leaving the worship service. She begged his pardon and carefully made eye contact hoping to indicate her interest. When he didn't react, she made a point of meeting up with him in the street on his way home from work. A greeting and polite conversation of the weather ensued, but nothing more, so she looked for another prospect.

Twice a month, she would take her supper at Mrs. Mallory's boarding house to treat herself to a meal she didn't have to prepare and eat alone. It was a luxury she shouldn't indulge in with her meager earnings, but she reasoned the benefits of human company outweighed the monetary sacrifice. For her current endeavors, the visit proved worthwhile.

Last week, George Casey sat across from her. He was in his mid-thirties, brown hair, brown eyes, and a good conversationalist. While enjoying their fish dinner in Mrs. Mallory's dining room, they discussed the weather, people they knew in common, and recent events. Afterwards, Mr. Casey offered to walk her home. He left her at her door and behaved like a perfect gentleman. He kept a respectable distance between them and never touched her. A simple nod, a good night wish, and he left. The next afternoon, he stopped by her shop to have a shirt mended and asked to walk her to services on Sunday which she accepted. Again, he was a gentleman with no undue touching. He asked if she would join him for dinner Wednesday at the boarding house, and she accepted. Mr. Casey was pleasant and congenial. He worked as a laborer for Mr. Fitzpatrick at the salt ponds and had hopes of becoming a foreman as the business increased.

Betsy found him pleasant and easy to be with. He would make a good companion, but was it enough? Should she settle for companionship or should she keep looking? She couldn't imagine finding someone she could care about as much as Ben. But could she share her life, share herself, with Mr. Casey? She wasn't sure yet. She needed more time to get to know him better.

And then her careful plan fell apart.

The word was out. Monday morning started the flow of men from every class bringing in orders to mend shirts, hem pants, patch holes, adjust waist bands, or order new clothes, and all of them made requests for her company. As soon as one man left her shop, another would appear. She accepted two offers of escort for Sunday services, one of them from Mr. Aronsdale, but otherwise gently declined the other men. Only one man cancelled his order after receiving her rejection. She had more orders by the end of the week than she had all last year.

Betsy was standing in the doorway of her workroom looking at the pile of orders wondering how she was going to get it all done when she heard the front door open again. Mentally, she prepared herself to deal with another hopeful suitor. She turned around and was relieved to find Mrs. Sanchez and her daughter, Esperanza, on the other side of the counter instead of another man.

Mrs. Sanchez wore a faded red dress covered by a white pinafore. She was a small woman with black hair, as yet untouched by gray, captured at the nape of her neck in a bun. She didn't speak English and despite Betsy's attempts to make her feel comfortable, she always chose to stand near the door and let her daughter speak for her. In this manner, Betsy contracted her services to make lace and tatting for the occasional dresses she was commissioned to make.

Esperanza was as petite as her mother and very pretty. Even wearing a plain serviceable dress and with her glossy black tresses braided and coiled tightly at the back of her head, she was becoming. It was no wonder Jonathon Keats was enamored.

"Good afternoon, Mrs. Wheeler. We have brought you the lace *Mamá* finished." Esperanza laid the paper wrapped package on the front counter.

Betsy opened the wrapping to find the beautiful handmade lace she needed to complete a gown for Judge Webb's wife. As usual, the lace was exquisite. It gave Betsy an idea. She sent a nod of appreciation to Mrs. Sanchez and then spoke to Esperanza. "Thank you for bringing this to me. How are you with a needle, Miss Sanchez? Can you sew?"

"Yes, of course, Mrs. Wheeler. Why do you ask?"

"I was wondering if you would be interested in working here, part time, for a week or two." Betsy gestured to the piles of clothing behind her. "I had a lot of work come in this week and could use the extra help."

Esperanza looked at her with regret. "I am afraid I couldn't, Mrs. Wheeler. *Padre* would not approve. I would like to help, but he would not allow it."

Mrs. Sanchez spoke to her daughter. "*Que te dijo ella de mi, es que mi trabajo no es aceptable?*"

Esperanza answered. "*Mamá tu trabajo está bien.*"

Betsy counted the coins from her box and handed the payment to Esperanza with a sad smile. "That is too bad. I would have enjoyed your company along with your help."

Esperanza shyly admitted, "As would I. Thank you for the offer and for the payment."

Mother and daughter left her shop carrying on a hushed conversation in Spanish. Betsy watched them go and sighed. Somehow, she would have to

23

find a way to get all this work done and keep her social engagements. At least tonight, she was free to work.

After finishing her supper of leftover turtle soup, Betsy picked up a stack of shirts she was mending and her sewing kit and headed for the rocker on her front porch to take advantage of the remaining daylight rather than burn costly candles. While Betsy worked, she rocked gently to and fro and hummed a childhood tune. Singing or humming while she worked was something she had done all her life. It never failed to lift her spirits and always made a task more pleasant. She loved music, and having a sweet soprano voice, her family encouraged it. Now it was an unconscious habit.

As the day faded into dusk, the birds were actively courting their mates in springtime fashion darting to and fro. The light sea breeze from the ocean not far beyond her back door kept the palm fronds swaying and carried with it the delicate fragrance of her potted plumeria. Neighbors greeted her as they passed by on their way home, some even stopped for a moment to talk. A little while later, her next door neighbor, Dr. Waterhouse, could be heard playing his violin as was his wont in the evening. Tonight, he filled the air with the notes of 'Robin Adair'. Betsy joined in singing the story of a lost love. In the distance, faint sounds of carousing could be heard from the grog shops down by the wharf, but nearby the rustle of leaves and bird calls added to the good doctor's melody.

She finished her task just as the sunlight faded. Laying the shirts aside, Betsy continued to rock and sing or hum to the music not yet ready to retire for the evening. She let her thoughts drift as the night turned clear and bright with a full moon. The spring air was comfortably warm. Usually Betsy found peace in her solace, but tonight, she felt only longing for someone to share it. Ben didn't come to mind. Perhaps, it was because even if he was still alive, he would be working on something. He was not one to sit still for any length of time. But neither did she think of Mr. Casey or Mr. Aronsdale. Instead, she longed for a shadowy figure of a man conjured in her mind. Heaven only knew if he really existed, or if they would ever find each other.

In the evening twilight, her gaze traced the familiar faint outlines of the houses across from her on Whitehead Street down towards Front Street and those beyond belonging to Fitzpatrick Street. Light from burning lamps or candles could be seen in a window or two in most houses. Perhaps a dozen or so in all. The boarding house was easy to distinguish in the background between two other houses as almost all its windows had light. Front Street extended the length of the harbour on the northwest side of the island ending behind her house in uncleared land. It wasn't even a half dozen blocks in length but it was the main street of the town and home to all the businesses, taverns, and warehouses. In all, a person could walk from one end to the other in five minutes. To her right was the rest of Whitehead Street with a few more houses, including Max and Abby's lovely, new two story with copula, and a small foot path leading out to the lighthouse on the southern point.

The island had been her home for eight years now. She knew all her neighbors and a good handful of the sailors of the fishing and wrecking boats who stayed in the harbour year round. She not only depended on them to support her business, she depended on them to be her substitute family when needed, especially Mrs. Mallory and the Eatonton's. The boardinghouse matron was her surrogate mother, Captain Max her older brother and protector, while his wife and her best friend, Abby, was every bit as close to her as a sister.

Earlier, she read a long awaited letter from her mother with updates on the events in the lives of her eight siblings and their families. Two more babies were on the way and her eldest brother, a professor at West Point, received another promotion. Her mother's pride in them was clear in the wording of her letter. Betsy also sensed what was not written; her mother wanted more for her.

What would she think of this place?

Betsy was surprised the thought never crossed her mind before. She tried to look at her environs through her mother's eyes. Her home was a simple four room house made of unpainted bare wood inside and out. It was sparse, but it was all hers. Her mother was practical enough to realize it put her in a better position than many other widows. The view from Betsy's porch was innocuous enough to meet with her approval. It was the other end of town she would find fault with, especially the proximity of its inebriated inhabitants. It would no doubt have her packing her daughter on the next ship headed anywhere. Betsy smiled at the conjured image of her mother rapidly tossing her belongings into trunks in a rush to get her to safety.

Her father would love this island, of him she was sure. He would be at home anywhere and had never met a stranger. He easily made friends wherever he went while her mother was quiet and more critical of other's behavior. Her mother's ideas of what was proper for a lady were stricter than Betsy's, but then current circumstances may have influenced her own leniency. For example, before Abby married Max she came to Betsy for help in dressing as a cabin boy to sneak past a devious man and his crew in order to reach Captain Max's ship and warn him of their nefarious plot. Society and her mother would dictate Abby should stay home and not get involved, but Betsy admired Abby for taking action and did what she could to help.

Her mother lamented frequently in her letters over Betsy's situation often imploring her to accept their money and return home. Betsy always refused. Her parents could ill afford the expense, but truth be told, she loved her tropical island home. She had no intentions of trading it for New England winters, not even to return to her family, although, she would dearly love to visit them. Oh, how she would love to walk into her mother's embrace, lay her head upon her shoulder, and absorb the bestowed comfort of unconditional love.

The sound of male laughter reached her ears. Betsy stopped rocking the better to hear, and Dr. Waterhouse stopped playing too, apparently to listen. She soon saw three young men round the corner from Front Street, three houses down from hers. She relaxed when she heard the sound of a fiddle. She couldn't see him for his dark skin, but knew it would be Roberts, and typically, he was in the company of Stephen Mallory with his flute. The third man would be one of Stephen's friends. She resumed her rocking and waited to see which young lady would be serenaded tonight. No surprise they stopped in front of the Whalton home. Miss Whalton was usually favoured with a song or two. Stephen Mallory and Roberts played their tune while the third man, she had yet to recognize, offered up a soft tenor ballad. Dr. Waterhouse, being outdone, retired his violin for the evening. Midway through the second song, Mrs. Whalton came out of the house to send the trio on their way since Captain Whalton was currently away captaining the lightship at Carysfort Reef near Key Largo. Undeterred, the men continued up the street visiting the open windows of Miss Ximinez and Miss Breaker.

Betsy was a little envious of the young ladies. They were courted with songs while she received shirts to be mended. Not that she expected songs, and she was grateful for the extra income. She supposed romantic courtship was only for the young, something you outgrew. She certainly didn't expect to find romantic love the second time around, although, it would be nice. Love and marriage were now a pragmatic consideration for security and companionship with none of the emotional excitement of young love. Even though her practical side recognized this, her woman's heart yearned. None of the men who sought her attentions now generated the kind of fervor she had felt for Ben, but then, maybe Ben was her one and only love. Maybe, love only happened once in a lifetime. The thought made her sad. While she was grateful to have had it for a little while, she felt too young to never experience it again.

Deciding it was getting late, she picked up her mending and returned inside. She left her work on the front counter and without lighting a candle made her way through her front room and parlor to her bedroom in the back. By the light of the full moon she undressed down to her shift, brushed her hair, said her prayers, and crawled into bed. She turned on her right side, pulled the second pillow to her middle, and curled around it. While planning out her work for tomorrow, she drifted off to sleep.

* * *

The next morning was another clear day. Betsy was humming a bright tune while diligently hemming a pair of pants when Mr. Sanchez and Esperanza entered her shop. She laid aside her work and rose to greet them. "Good morning, Mr. Sanchez, Miss Sanchez."

Esperanza cheerfully returned her greeting. "Good morning, Mrs.

Wheeler."

Mr. Sanchez was a very strict looking man. Betsy had never seen him smile although the lines on his face indicated otherwise. He was short of stature, dark of complexion, and very neatly kept. He spoke a fair amount of English, though heavily accented. He inclined his head and removed his hat in greeting to Betsy. "Good morning, Mrs. Wheeler. Did you offer my daughter work?"

Betsy was not sure if he was offended or was here to accept. He was a hard man to read. "Yes, I did. I am in need of some assistance with the extra orders I have received. It would only be temporary work. Maybe a week or two."

"I see." Mr. Sanchez turned to his daughter. "*Tú me vas a prometer que vas a trabajar atrás y que no vas a tener contacto con los clientes. Vas a hacer lo que la Señora Wheeler te mande. Me prometes que vas a hacer lo mejor trabajo que puedas y que nos vas a dar sólo honor a la familia.*"

"*Claro que si Padre.*" Esperanza could not help the excitement in her voice as she agreed to her father's instructions not to speak to the customers, obey Mrs. Wheeler, and do her best work to bring honor to her family.

Mr. Sanchez turned back to Betsy. "Esperanza may work for you. I will bring her in the morning and come for her in the evening until you no longer need her. She is not to leave this shop alone for any reason. Understand?"

Betsy gravely answered him. "Yes sir, of course."

"Very well." Mr. Sanchez handed Esperanza a lunch pail and left the store to walk to his job on the other side of town as manager of Mr. Wall's cigar factory.

Turning to Esperanza, Betsy was baffled. "You said he wouldn't approve. What happened to make him agreeable?"

Esperanza smiled. "*Mamá* convinced *Padre* it would be a good experience for me, and the money would be good for the family. He eventually agreed with her. He usually does."

Betsy laughed lightly. "I am glad he did. I can really use your help. Two more orders came in this morning. Let me show you where I keep everything."

A counter ran across the width of the front room with a section in front of the parlor door that lifted up allowing access from one side to the other. Betsy kept the counter closed while her shop was open giving a boundary between her and her customers, especially the male customers. She now lifted the counter opening for Esperanza to pass through and follow her to the workroom off the parlor. After showing Esperanza where she kept the needles, thread, scissors and notions, and how she organized her work in progress, they returned to the front room and the customer's side of the counter so Betsy could show Esperanza her secret.

"I am sure you have noticed this dressmaker's form before, but I doubt you noticed the markings on the back side facing the counter." She turned the form towards Esperanza.

"No, I never have. What do you use them for?"

Betsy smiled at her own cleverness. When Ben died and she realized becoming the town seamstress was her only option for earning income, and worse, she would have to run it from her home not being able to afford the rent on both the house and the new shop, she devised a way to protect herself as much as possible from the strange men she would be dealing with. "Most of the men are sailors and their clothes are simple in design. A few measurements are all that are required. To avoid direct contact, I marked this form with the height from the floor. When I need to know a man's pants or shirt length I note the measurement of his waist, the top of his shoulders and the length of his inner leg, as best I can tell. I then hand the man this yarn and have him wrap it around his waist and hold the point where it meets when he hands it back to me. I can place it against the counter to get his waist measurement." Betsy showed her the markings on the edge of the counter. "The rest I can usually guess close enough. I rarely get orders for tailored gentlemen's clothing, so it isn't much of a concern."

Esperanza looked at Betsy with new respect. "You are a smart woman, Mrs. Wheeler."

"Please, call me Betsy."

"As you wish, and you may call me Esperanza."

"Well then, Esperanza, shall we get to work?" Betsy picked up another pair of pants to be hemmed and led Esperanza to a chair in the parlour.

The day's work went smoothly. They talked of things in general. Betsy wanted to ask about Esperanza's relationship with Jonathon but decided to wait until she brought it up. Just after four, Mr. Sanchez arrived to walk Esperanza home. Betsy assured him his daughter was an excellent worker which pleased him. He promised to bring her back at nine the next morning.

* * *

Betsy and Esperanza were quietly working the next afternoon when a commotion in the street aroused their curiosity. Walking outside they saw several people rapidly headed towards the harbour. Betsy stopped one of her neighbor's boys. "What is happening?"

The ten year old shared his excitement. "The navy's here! A bunch of ships are sailing into the harbour. Some of them have cannons!" He took off running to catch up to his friends.

Betsy looked to Esperanza. "Do you want to go see?"

"Yes, if you go, I suppose I could too."

Betsy turned her shingle to *closed*, donned her bonnet, and together they walked to the harbour. Most of the townsfolk were already gathered in front of the wharves. William Whitehead, the recently appointed Customs Collector, could be seen at the front of the crowd waiting to greet the officers. Excitement filled the air. It was seven years since the barracks on Front Street were last occupied by the navy.

Standing not far from them was Captain Max Eatonton holding his daughter Emily. Abby stood next to him with his crew nearby. Betsy noticed his former first mate, now a captain, Jonathon Keats' gaze frequently drifted towards Esperanza, and her shy glances cast in return. Betsy wondered how much longer the two of them would wait for Mr. Sanchez's approval before they acted of their own accord.

Murmurs of surprise passed through the crowd when they learned the new arrivals were the army and not the navy as everyone assumed. Brevet Major James Glassell stepped ashore and was immediately met by Mr. Whitehead and Mr. Pinkham, president of the town council. Once the fanfare was over, the elected officials led the officers to the abandoned barracks for an inspection. Most of the islanders wandered off to their own affairs, although a few stayed around to see what might happen next. Betsy and Esperanza returned to their work.

* * *

The arrival of the army was eagerly welcomed by all. They brought money and opportunity to the town and added security. Their arrival also nearly doubled the population of residents on the island.

The former marine barracks were found to be too dilapidated for use. It was decided they would be torn down. The next day, two companies of infantry set up a bivouac on the north beach. John Simonton, the island's founder, agreed to sell the government several lots for military use. Over the next few weeks, barracks and other needed buildings rapidly appeared. Uniformed men were frequently seen about town and eventually the citizens became used to their presence.

* * *

Sunday morning, promptly at ten, Mr. Aronsdale arrived at her door. Betsy was ready. She stepped outside before he even knocked. He was a very tall man, having to duck through entryways, and standing next to him made her feel even more petite than her five foot four inches. She was sure standing together they must make an odd sight. He had an angular face and smiled often. She wouldn't call him handsome, but he had a kind soul and good values.

Mr. Aronsdale shyly offered his arm. "Good Sabbath, Mrs. Wheeler."

"Good Sabbath to you, Mr. Aronsdale. Thank you for your escort."

"It is my pleasure."

They continued the polite and impersonal conversation as they walked. Since a church had yet to be built on the island, services were held in the Custom House located about halfway down on the beachside of Front

Street. The building was one of a few built on stilts in case of flooding. They climbed the steps to the piazza and walked inside to find seats, politely greeting neighbors who looked their way. Betsy felt as though she were on display and being silently questioned. She did her best to hide her discomfort and embarrassment.

There was no clergyman on the island this week so volunteers read their favourite Biblical passages and they sung a few hymns. Afterwards, as they were leaving the yard of the Custom House, they were approached by Mr. Casey.

"Good morning, Mr. Aronsdale." He doffed his hat to Betsy. "Mrs. Wheeler, may I have the pleasure of escorting you next Sunday?"

Mr. Aronsdale, not to be outdone, said, "I was going to ask the same when we returned to your house."

"Gentlemen, neither of you will be able to as I have already promised next Sunday to Mr. Sanderson."

Mr. Casey quickly replied, "Then would you join me for dinner Wednesday?"

Bothered by his forthright and rude approach, Betsy politely said, "I am afraid, I will have to decline your offer. Good day, Mr. Casey." She was thankful Mr. Aronsdale was as anxious as her to walk away.

Over the next few weeks, Mr. Casey, Mr. Aronsdale and Mr. Sanderson rotated Sundays walking her to church. Mr. Casey was always carefully polite after having received her earlier rebuff. She didn't like one man more than the other, so it didn't bother her when eventually only Mr. Casey continued to ask to escort her home. After the second week in a row, they fell into a pattern. He showed up on her doorstep every Sunday morning, and for lack of a better prospect, she let him. She wasn't sure what she would do when he decided to ask for more from their relationship.

* * *

One afternoon, Betsy was working on mending a torn shirt and pondering her situation with Mr. Casey. She felt sure he was going to request a formal courtship soon, and she needed to decide if she was going to accept. Other than the one incident of rudeness when he asked for her company in the presence of Mr. Aronsdale, he had been the perfect gentleman. But try as she might, she just couldn't find any enthusiasm for the idea of marriage to him. She didn't expect to feel the same excitement she had felt for Ben but even a tiny sliver of it would have been reassuring. None of the men managed to incite a whiff of emotion. Maybe, she was too old for such feelings. Maybe being smitten was only for the young. If she accepted that excitement was not to be found, the question became, did she want his companionship, and could she accept sharing the other aspects of marriage with him?

Her mother would tell her a bird in hand was worth two in the bush.

Her father would tell her to be practical, but follow her heart, and preferably do both.

Ben would tell her to choose whichever one would make her happy.

Her sisters would tell her to wait for love.

Could she marry without love? Could she be happy with companionship?

She certainly didn't love George Casey and doubted she ever would. She, of course, would come to care for him. The intimacy of marriage would bring about those feelings.

But was it enough?

George Casey was the practical bird in hand, but she wanted the alluring stranger from her daydream.

Maybe Abby could help her decide companionship versus waiting on the chance of finding love.

Esperanza interrupted her thoughts coming to stand before her with a hopeful smile. Holding out a bolt of fabric she found stashed in the back of the workshop, Esperanza asked, "Could I do some extra work to earn this fabric? I would like to make a new dress to wear for a friend's wedding."

The fabric Esperanza had chosen was a beautifully made sprigged muslin with delicate sprays of embroidered pink flowers. It was one of several bolts in a parcel Betsy had bought on a whim from a salvage auction. There was another bolt of delicate moss green fabric and matching satin ribbon Betsy wanted to use to make a dress for herself.

"Certainly. You can earn the fabric by helping to sew a dress for me too. We can work together to measure and cutting both dresses. We should have plenty of time even with the orders we have now to work on them." Putting aside the shirt she was finishing, Betsy went into the workroom to find the green fabric and bring it to the front counter.

Esperanza laid her bolt on the counter too and lightly smoothed her hand across Betsy's bolt. "How lovely. It will certainly make a beautiful dress." Looking up at Betsy, she said, "I do hope Mr. Keats will be in attendance to see me in this dress."

Betsy smiled confidently. "I am sure he will, and he won't be able to resist dancing attendance upon you."

Esperanza didn't understand her words. "What do you mean?"

"It is an expression meaning you will have his complete attention."

Esperanza gave a sigh. "His attention yes, but we both wish for more."

"Does your father still stand in the way?"

"I am no longer sure of *Padre*'s thoughts, but fear of his rejection keeps Mr. Keats from asking for my hand. Once he asks, whatever *Padre* decides will be the only answer given. There will be no chance of changing his mind. At least he tolerates Mr. Keats' attentions towards me now, but I am unsure if the answer would be favourable if Mr. Keats proposed, and so we wait for a sign."

Betsy didn't envy Esperanza's position. "Then, I will pray you receive a sign. For now, do you have a pattern in mind for your dress?"

"Not really. Do you have a suggestion?"

"I'll draw some ideas tonight. Let's work hard to finish the orders we have today, and we can get a fresh start on our dresses tomorrow."

"Yes, ma'am." Esperanza gathered the bolts and returned them to the workroom, then picked up the next pair of pants to be hemmed.

They worked another hour or so in companionable silence when Betsy suddenly recalled she needed to run an errand.

"Esperanza, can you mind the shop for a while? I need to get more candles so I can continue working tonight."

"I don't mind at all. Take your time."

Betsy decided to take the opportunity Esperanza's offer presented. "Thank you. I would like to make a short visit with Mrs. Eatonton as well."

Esperanza nodded. "Will you return before my father arrives, or should I close the shop for you?"

"I should be back before you leave." Betsy put some money in her reticule, tied her bonnet, and left the shop to walk the two blocks down Front Street to Mr. Patterson's store. She returned the greeting of the two soldiers she passed walking on patrol. She could hear the sounds of progress as a platoon worked to remove the old decayed barracks facing the harbour. Betsy entered the mercantile and immediately turned to the left where she knew the candles were kept. She was pleased to find Abby doing some shopping as well. Abby's back was to her, so she called out a greeting to announce her presence. "Good afternoon, Abby."

Abby turned around with a smile on her face. "Good afternoon, Betsy, such a pleasure to see you."

"And you. How is Captain Max?"

"Quite well, thank you."

The ladies traded pleasantries and shared news while they browsed the notions piled on the table between them. Betsy stood across from Abby and was facing the doorway when she noticed William Whitehead enter in the company of an unknown man. The stranger immediately captured Betsy's attention. She was drawn to him like a moth to a flame. Her eyes followed his broad back as he walked with Mr. Whitehead to the rear counter of the store where Mr. Patterson presided. He looked to be slightly taller than Mr. Whitehead whom she knew to be a good few inches taller than her. He had brown hair, mustache and beard all of which were trimmed short. From what she could tell, his demeanor was serious, his stride deliberate. He carried himself with pride and purpose.

Abby, realizing she had lost her audience, turned to see what had caught Betsy's attention. Noticing the stranger with Mr. Whitehead, she turned back to Betsy full of curiosity. Meanwhile, Betsy, suddenly aware she had been staring, pulled her gaze away from the man's back with an effort and looked down at the bottle of scented orange water she held in her hand.

Abby asked in a low voice, "Have you met the gentleman with Mr.

Whitehead?"

Betsy raised her head, reflexively glanced at the man in question, then looked to her friend. "No." Hopefully, she asked, "Do you know who he is?"

"No. I have never seen him before."

"Neither have I." Betsy put the bottle back on the table and browsed the items next to it, occasionally lifting her gaze to the men in the back.

Abby covertly watched Betsy in amusement. Her friend was smitten with just a glance. *How interesting!* The gentleman seemed to be an upstanding person by appearances. She would be sure to mention him to Max. Her husband would easily be able to learn more about the stranger from Mr. Whitehead.

Betsy squared her shoulders, picked up a box of candles, and started for the counter to pay for her purchase. At the same time, the men finished their conversation and turned to leave. Her footsteps faltered as her eyes collided with the stranger's for a brief powerful moment.

And in that moment, for her, everything changed.

Both men doffed their hats as they passed. Her hope of gaining an introduction was lost as the men passed by at too great of a distance to warrant the courtesy. Betsy's gaze followed the stranger's progress as he exited the shop. The depth of her disappointment over the missed opportunity was surprising. She reasoned with herself that he was probably only a temporary visitor to the island as most strangers tended to only be here for as long as their ship was in port. Betsy continued to the counter to pay for her candles.

Mr. Patterson greeted her with his usual cheerful smile. "Good afternoon, Mrs. Wheeler. Will that be all for you?"

"Yes, please." She so wanted to ask the shop keeper who the stranger was, but it would be unseemly of her to make the inquiry and garner speculation she would rather do without. There were more discreet ways to learn of the man's identity. Finished with her purchase, she turned to Abby to say goodbye.

"I am afraid I must be getting back to the shop before Esperanza's father arrives."

Abby said, "Of course. You must come by for tea one day soon."

"I will. Good day, Abby." She brushed the baby's cheek. "You too little Emily."

Betsy returned to her shop, and by the time Mr. Sanchez arrived to take Esperanza home, she had finally put the incident out of her mind, if only temporarily.

Chapter 3

Theodore and his family arrived in Key West on the 16th of March, just a few weeks after the troops made port. They stood at the railing of the ship anxious to see their temporary home for the first time. Slivers of green emerged on the horizon and swelled into islands as they drew nearer to their destination. A lighthouse could be discerned, tall and white, against the emerald foliage. They sailed around the southern point towards the western shore. Buildings soon appeared; first houses and then businesses. The verdant backdrop gave a picturesque look to the wooden structures.

Theodore knew the island was small, but he hadn't properly imagined just how small. The town, occupying only the western tip of the island, was equivalent to a few city blocks. Why, he lived further from Aunt Agatha than the distance from one end of this settlement to the other. He expected to feel confined in the smallness of the island and the town. It was another surprise to find the expanse of sky and water surrounding the island gave it space, and as he stepped off the wharf and into the heart of the settlement, there was still a sense of openness. The buildings were not crowded in on each other and the streets were not defined by walkways and pavers. Vegetation was everywhere softening the edges and adding charm to the small community. He found the whole of it appealing and soothing to his soul. Life in a small town was going to be a new experience for all of them but maybe not the hardship he imagined.

Acclimating to the warm temperatures was something else again. They were still wearing their winter coats when they left New York. Now, they stood under a tropic sun wearing their lightest summer clothing and feeling the effects of the humidity. If this was only spring…

They took up residence in the only boarding house in town until Theodore could find a suitable private home to rent for the duration of their stay. The Cocoanut Grove Inn was run by Mrs. Mallory, a sweet Irish widow. It didn't take long for Theodore to learn she was the first woman settler on the island who not only cared for her boarders but often helped with the sick and infirm. She was well liked and respected by all.

Theodore wanted to learn all he could about his temporary home and its citizens. In the news business, it helped to have friendly relationships when a story was afoot. The first person he sought out was Mr. William Whitehead with his letter of introduction from Bob in hand.

He was greeted warmly by the young man of twenty-one who was more than willing to share his knowledge of Key West before he even looked at the letter, and he possessed a wealth of knowledge. Mr. Whitehead was not only the collector of customs but also brother of one of the island's founders. He proved to be very instrumental in gaining Theodore introductions to the most prominent citizens. He also became a trusted friend. From him, Theodore learned much about the island and its inhabitants.

Mr. Whitehead proudly showed him the map he had drawn of the island. Theodore was impressed with the details of his work despite his lack of training as a cartographer. From the map, Theodore could tell the island lay at a slant from southwest to northeast, nearly four miles long by one mile wide. The settlement began on the western end of the island where the water formed a deep natural harbour. Front Street followed the harbour. The map showed a city drawn up in neat squares extending inland but it was not yet reality.

Currently, a handful of roads or paths radiated inland as needed. All were nothing more than unpaved limestone used predominantly by pedestrians, some hand carts, and the occasional mule and dray. He had yet to see a horse. A tidal pond bordered the rear of the existing town, another formed along the southern coast and several dotted the undeveloped northeastern side. A rough path was cut to the far end of the island and another one to the lighthouse on the southern point.

Mr. Whitehead carefully rolled up his map. "Do you know what I find most intriguing about this island?" He didn't wait for Theodore to respond. "The people. Due to our location at the entrance to the Gulf of Mexico, we receive goods and travelers on their way between the eastern states and the southern territory as well as from many other countries."

Theodore noticed the eclectic mix of nationalities in the faces he passed on the street. It was something unique to Key West. To be sure, New York was also a mixture, but the immigrants tended to isolate themselves in neighborhoods. Here they co-mingled ostensibly with ease.

Mr. Whitehead gestured toward the door. "Would you care to take a walk around town?"

Theodore consented and the two men stepped out into the eighty degree afternoon. They left the Custom House headed in the direction of the warehouses and wharfs, a short walk away.

As they walked, Theodore asked, "What is the current population?"

"Last year's census was just over 500. We have a mayor, city council, marshal, sheriff, judge and lawyers lending a cosmopolitan air to the class of our citizens indoors. While outside, it is still a rough water frontier and as such has more than its fair share of captains, sailors, and grog shops."

Theodore was taking notes and absently replied, "Hmm." It was all the encouragement the Custom Collector needed to continue.

"Our soil is poor being mostly limestone, so we depend on our closest neighbor, Cuba, for pork, beef, fruits and vegetables."

Theodore said, "I suppose that makes them an expensive commodity."

Mr. Whitehead nodded. "It does indeed; especially fresh beef. The fishermen can add to their income ferrying over a load of vegetables on their small boats keeping the prices down, but fresh meat must be shipped on the hoof requiring a larger vessel."

Theodore nodded. "Thereby making it a luxury item. What is the main food source?"

"Game birds and anything from the ocean; fish, turtle, lobster, conch…"

"Conch?"

"It's a large mollusk or sea snail and a favoured Bahamian dish. You should make a point to try some."

"Hmm. What industries do you have?"

"Wrecking is our main livelihood. One way or another everyone on this island is dependent upon it. Without it, the community would have failed shortly after the military left seven years ago. Fishing and turtling are the other main occupations. Salt and cigars are burgeoning enterprises started just this year. We are anxious to see how well they do. The army's arrival brings in additional revenue, but we have learned to treat it more like gravy on top of the current industries instead of the mainstay of the community. The citizens like having it, but we are grateful not to be dependent upon it."

"Why is that?"

"We suffered financially the last time they left the island. We'll not make the same mistake again."

"Why is wrecking more lucrative here than other areas?"

"You probably know Key West is part of a chain of islands extending from the tip of Florida into the Gulf of Mexico. What many don't know, much to their dismay, is the islands run parallel to a reef and are surrounded by unpredictable currents. They capture ships floundering in storms and the unwary captain who ventures too close."

Mr. Whitehead stopped walking to speak to two men standing in front of the now empty ground where the marine barracks once stood. "Speaking of wrecking, here are two fine examples of our industry leaders. Mr. Whitmore, let me introduce you to Amos and Asa Tift."

The men all shook hands. Theodore found the brothers to be intelligent, cultured men of New England origin.

Mr. Whitehead said, "Theses fine gentlemen run a dry goods store, manage the mail ship, serve as auctioneers, have successfully expanded into the wrecking business, and have just procured this prime waterfront lot." He turned to the brothers. "What is it you gentlemen are about today?"

Asa nodded to the empty space. "We're contemplating what size to build a warehouse to store salvaged goods."

Theodore said, "Aren't there already two large ones?"

Asa grinned. "Yes, but they are not ours."

The men exchanged a few more pleasantries before they parted ways.

Theodore said, "I would guess there to be about a hundred buildings on the island."

Mr. Whitehead nodded. "Something like that, and as you just witnessed, more are being built every day."

"I haven't noticed any made of brick."

"It's too expensive to obtain. If it doesn't originate on this island, it has to be brought in. Lumber is closer and cheaper. With temperatures rarely going below sixty-five degrees, and more often averaging close to eighty, more solid protection is not required except perhaps during tropical cyclones which are rare."

Mr. Whitehead gave Theodore a running history on each of the buildings and their proprietors. When they came to a small seaside shack, he said, "This is known as the 'Sweat Box' which currently serves as a jail of sorts."

Theodore looked skeptically at the building. It was a small single room with a very low ceiling. It either indicated the surprising congeniality of these folks, or the lax arm of the law—he wasn't sure which yet.

Seeing his look, Mr. Whitehead smiled. "A petition has been approved to build a new jail. We are waiting on the funds to arrive."

"Where will it be built?"

Mr. Whitehead pointed towards the lighthouse. "We've designated a block for city use on Whitehead Street just past the pond to hold the jail and a new court house."

Next, they entered the dry goods store. Mr. Whitehead led him to the back to introduce him to the owner, Mr. Patterson. To his left, they passed by two ladies shopping. One was willowy with auburn hair and a baby on her hip. The other, petite and dark-haired, was facing him, but studying something in her hand. Theodore followed Mr. Whitehead to the back counter where they chatted with the jovial storekeeper for a few minutes.

As they were leaving the store, Theodore noticed the brunette had moved closer. She was intently watching their progress. Eyes, the color of a bright summer sky, captured his attention. She was quite comely. It surprised him that he took more than a passing note of the fact. Even more surprising, he didn't immediately compare her to Margaret. It was something he had done to every woman since the day he met Margaret, and he always found them lacking, but not this one. He doffed his hat and continued following Mr. Whitehead out of the door. The image of curious blue eyes lingered with him the rest of the day.

At the next storefront, Mr. Whitehead led them inside. There was no shingle to indicate the business within, but as soon as they entered the front room, Theodore could hear the familiar rhythmic sound of a printing press.

Mr. Whitehead loudly called out, "Dr. Strobel?"

The press stopped, and a young dark haired gentleman appeared from the back room wiping his ink stained hands on a well-used towel. "Good afternoon, Mr. Whitehead. How can I help you?"

"I don't mean to take up a lot of your time. We stopped by for a quick introduction. This is Mr. Theodore Whitmore. He is visiting us from New York. Mr. Whitmore, this is Dr. Benjamin Strobel."

The two men shook hands.

Mr. Whitehead said, "Dr. Strobel is our resident surgeon these past few years. He serves on the town council, and he is the editor of the *Key West Gazette*. The first printing of which ran just this past week."

Theodore had read the paper. The articles were good, albeit a bit verbose. "You must be a very busy man."

Dr. Strobel inclined his head. "Indeed."

Mr. Whitehead added, "The two of you have something in common. Mr. Whitmore is a journalist from the *New York Weekly* here to report on our little island."

Dr. Strobel said, "Really? How interesting. If you'll excuse me gentlemen, I do have a paper to get printed, and I'm afraid my ink is drying."

Mr. Whitehead frowned at the unexpected dismissal. "Of course. Good day, Dr. Strobel."

Theodore wondered at the change in the doctor's demeanor. He was friendly until Mr. Whitehead mentioned Theodore's occupation, and then he couldn't dismiss them fast enough. Was he afraid of competition or perhaps of having his failings pointed out? It was a plausible theory but felt weak. Time would tell.

The rest of the afternoon was spent meeting all the town dignitaries including the mayor, the marshal, and most of the town council. This included Dr. Waterhouse, an aging surgeon from upstate New York. Theodore found him to be a bit eccentric but a congenial fellow who also served a vital role in the community as Postmaster.

Shortly after leaving Dr. Waterhouse, it was with relief, he and Mr. Whitehead parted ways. Theodore couldn't possibly remember another name, and his hand was cramping from recording his copious notes.

* * *

Wednesday morning, Theodore walked into the newly constructed army office and approached the desk of Lieutenant Newcomb. Bob sent him to Key West to learn what the army was doing. Theodore decided to start with the man in charge.

"Can I help you, sir?"

"I'd like to make an appointment to speak with Major Glassell."

The door was open to the major's office. Theodore saw him stand up and approach the doorway. "No need for such formality. Come on in."

"Thank you, sir." Theodore held his hand out to be firmly grasped by the major who appeared to be in his early forties. "My name is Theodore Whitmore."

"Pleased to meet you Mr. Whitmore. Have a seat. What can I do for you, sir?"

"I am a journalist from the *New York Weekly*, sir. I believe my editor, Bob Jenkins, may have written to you of my visit."

"He did. You're pursuing a story a long ways from home."

"Yes, sir."

"What do you hope to learn?"

Judging the major to be willingly forthcoming, Theodore said, "To start with, why did Congress deem it important to send the army to Key West. With the military spread quite thin around all our borders, it must be something important to setup another post."

"I suppose you have asked Congress this question."

"Mr. Jenkins did. They said it was for protection from Spain."

The major chuckled. "I wonder which congressman gave him that excuse. No, we are here to offer protection to the courts but not from Spain. Although, I am to report anything of interest in the area which I suppose would include Spain's movements."

Theodore quickly realized Major Glassell would reveal more if he used his approach of 'speak little, listen much' and by getting him to talk freely. "What threat are the courts under?"

"An imaginary one as far as I can tell. It was argued that the Custom House coffers were so laden as to be ripe for the prey of pirates."

"Pirates?" Theodore was flabbergasted. The theory he and Bob dismissed had actually been used as an argument.

"I kid you not. I believe 'lawless hands of piratical intruders' was the specific term used. So far, the only thievery I've found going on here are the prices the owners are charging the government for land and provisions. If you ask me, Mr. Simonton's motivation seems to be lining his pockets. It's a waste of time and money setting up this base when we are more urgently needed on other fronts. However, that is just my humble opinion."

"How long will the army be in residence?"

"A withdrawal date was not given, hence, the reason we are building permanent structures."

"I see." Theodore sensed the major was ready to end the interview, so he stood up. "Thank you for your time, sir. Might I extend an invitation to you and your officers and of course your wives to dine with my family one evening? Perhaps Friday?"

"How kind of you. On their behalf, I will gladly accept your offer."

As Theodore walked home, he considered all the major had said. Next, he would speak with Mr. Whitehead, the judge, and anyone else who could offer a valid opinion on the likelihood of thievery. Even if Major Glassell's assessment was true and there wasn't much of a story, he might as well enjoy the island as Bob suggested. At least for a couple of months.

* * *

Betsy and Esperanza spent most of Wednesday morning working on their dresses. Mid-morning, Abby, followed by her maid, came by the shop to share some news. Betsy offered to make tea.

Abby sat Emily on the counter and shook her head. "I am afraid I cannot stay for a visit, but I could not wait to tell you what I have learned.

Max met your stranger yesterday."

Betsy cringed at Abby's reference to 'her' stranger.

Abby's tone was giddy as she relayed her news. "His name is Theodore Whitmore. He is a newspaper man from New York. He plans to be here long enough that he is looking for a house to rent. Namely the one across from your shop."

At this, all three ladies looked across the street to the large two-story empty house in question. Betsy's heart fluttered. Mr. Whitmore would be around awhile, and they might be neighbors.

Abby added, "Oh, and he is a widower."

The other two looked to Betsy as if his being a widower meant they were destined for each other. She scoffed at the idea, but secretly it gave her a feeling of connection to this stranger.

Esperanza said, "He sounds perfect for you, Mrs. Wheeler."

Betsy laughed. "Aren't you two putting the cart way ahead of the horse?"

Abby picked up Emily. "That is all I know so far. I have to get home now. It is time for Emily's nap. Good day, ladies." She left as quickly as she breezed in waving a hand in return to their murmured farewells.

Betsy and Esperanza returned to their work, but Betsy's gaze kept straying to the house across the street. The same excitement she felt yesterday infected her now with just the mention of this man. It was absurd. She knew nothing about this stranger whereas Mr. Casey was known to be a solid citizen. It was hard to dismiss her romantic imaginings, but she forced herself to do so. The stranger was only visiting. Besides, Mr. Casey would be a good provider once the salt industry grew, and he was promoted to a manager. As her mother said, a bird in hand was worth two in the bush.

She didn't see the newcomer that afternoon, but over the next few days it seemed whenever she left the house, she would notice him nearby. Unfortunately, it was always from a distance too great to garner an introduction. And, each time her interest in the widower increased, dangerously filling her mind with thoughts of romance. For the most part, she had been content with her life before Abby put the idea in her head of finding another husband. Now, it seemed all she could think about was a suitable mate, and the only one who seriously sparked her interest, she had yet to meet.

* * *

Sunday morning Betsy waited by the front window for George Casey. She had been restless all weekend for two reasons. One, she was anxious to put an end to her doubts concerning Mr. Casey's courtship, and two, she kept vigil on the empty house but had yet to see Mr. Whitmore make a visit. Maybe he decided to rent another house. She started nervously pacing until Mr. Casey arrived a few minutes later.

He kept up a steady one-sided conversation on the walk to services. It did not endear her to him.

The visiting Episcopal minister read from Genesis and preached of God's will for his people to marry and multiply. Betsy felt his words directed at her. Was this God's way of encouraging her relationship with Mr. Casey? Was the man sitting next to her supposed to be the father of her children? If so, why did it not feel right? Was this not God's plan for her? The questions and doubts circled in her head throughout the rest of the service. She silently prayed for God to open her heart and mind to make the right choice for her future.

The final hymn was sung, and they filed out of the building to circulate among friends on the Custom House lawn. George excused himself to speak with the other men leaving her in the company of several ladies. Betsy noticed a stately, elderly lady she had never seen before follow a golden haired little boy in knickerbockers down the steps of the Custom House. She watched the scene play out several yards in front of her while she half listened to the conversation around her.

The grandmother and the boy, who looked to be four or five, seemed to be waiting for someone. The boy was watching some older children playing a game and didn't pay heed to his grandmother's words nor did he notice when she left him and headed around to the side of the building. Betsy naturally assumed the lady was going to visit the outhouse. She turned her attention to the women talking around her but kept glancing towards the boy. A moment later, he became aware of standing alone and started to appear distressed. Betsy immediately excused herself from the other ladies and made her way to the child.

She crouched down to his level in the hopes of soothing him. "Hi sweetie, I believe your grandmother is making use of the privy. I am sure she will return soon."

He gave her a confused look. "My gran'ma lives in Austria."

Betsy was momentarily disconcerted before she made the next logical guess. "Is she your aunt, the lady who was with you?"

He nodded. "She's my Aunt Aggie." He turned his head again to watch the older boy's game.

Betsy moved her head to the side to regain eye contact. "My name is Mrs. Wheeler. What is your name?" He focused on her when she was speaking, then mimicked an answer he must have heard adults use frequently.

"Please to make your 'quaintance. My name is Henry." As an afterthought, he held out his hand to her not yet understanding it was improper to shake hands with a lady.

Not wanting to hurt his feelings, Betsy shook his hand in all seriousness trying to hide her amused smile. "Very nice to make your acquaintance too, Henry." Enchanted with this little man, she sought to continue the conversation. "How old are you?"

He held up a hand with his fingers spread wide. "I'm five years old, ma'am."

"Are you and your Aunt Aggie visiting our island or will you be living here?"

"Poppa has work to do, so we will be living here for a little while."

"And your mother, is she here too?" Betsy looked around her in search of his parents.

"No. Mama is with the angels in heaven."

This statement abruptly ended her search and brought her attention back to his earnest little face.

"She's not with Gran'ma and Gran'pa. She's in heaven."

Again it sounded like he was repeating something he had heard often from an adult. Most likely his father. It dawned on Betsy who his father might be at the same time a set of manly legs came into view behind Henry and large hands came to rest on the boy's shoulders. Her nerve endings hummed in anticipation, excited to finally meet this man in person.

Her eyes traveled up his torso absently admiring the cut of his suit. He had an excellent tailor. His hand reached out to offer her assistance. She placed her gloved left hand in his and felt her pulse quicken. As she returned to a standing position, she lifted her eyes to his face and was immediately drawn into his gaze. Even though his well-shaped nose and full lips were his dominate features, hazel eyes captured her attention. The soul of this man seemed to be openly there for her to see. The sadness she saw within was unexpected until she recalled his widowed state. His presence affected her entire being, heightening all of her senses which were already disconcertingly attuned to him. His musky smell surrounded her like a blanket, igniting desires long dormant. Her attraction to this man was growing out of control, and he had yet to speak. It must be the intensity of his gaze. It was as if he looked straight into her heart.

Afraid she was staring, Betsy quickly looked over the rest of his face. Unlike most men of the day, he had a full beard and mustache, which she assumed to be brown when she first saw him in the mercantile, but now the bright sunlight captured the red highlights. A small scar slashed the end of the eyebrow over his right eye. She was curious as to how he came by it. A hat covered his forehead, but she could tell from the sides his hair was a slightly lighter shade of auburn than his beard.

Her hand still in his, she smiled. "Hello. Welcome to Key West, Mr. Whitmore." The momentary widening of his eyes betrayed his surprise that she knew his name.

He let go of her hand to lift his top hat in greeting revealing a somber forehead and thick, sweat dampened, wavy hair. "Good morning, madam. I am afraid you have me at a disadvantage."

Even his rich voice was soothing to her soul. She tried not to smile, but it was impossible to hide the pleasure she found in finally coming face to face with him. "My name is Betsy Wheeler. I was keeping company with your son while his aunt was indisposed."

Theodore felt his attraction increase for the lady with raven locks and big blue eyes. Much to his chagrin, she was even more appealing up close. "Thank you, Mrs. Wheeler, for tending my son. I am pleased to make your acquaintance."

Betsy's smile broadened as she heard Henry's phrase repeated in the masculine tones of his father. "It was my pleasure, sir. You have a very polite and smart boy."

Pride in his son made him answer more warmly than he intended. "Thank you, madam." Another time and place perhaps... But in this time and place, it was too soon to feel this way about another. It conflicted with his feelings for Margaret, and the respect he held for her memory. Having heard the end of his son's conversation, Theodore added, "As you may have noticed, he is still struggling to understand what has happened to his mother."

"I would imagine it to be normal for his age."

"So I am told."

"If you don't mind my asking, how long ago did she pass?"

"Just before the New Year."

"You have my condolences, Mr. Whitmore."

"Thank you, Mrs. Wheeler." He thought he was immune to the soft look of sympathetic doe-eyed females—looks that would take over as soon as they learned of his widowed state—but the look in Betsy Wheeler's eyes brought unexpected desire. Guilt over his wife made him suppress the odd feeling. "I wonder how long it will take before Henry is able to understand."

He tried not to notice her milky white skin or the lingering soft smile on her kissable lips. He brought his wayward thoughts up short. He was still in mourning for heaven's sake, and she must have a husband somewhere nearby. He was pretty sure he felt a ring under her glove.

Betsy completely lost her train of thought. She felt the visceral pull on her senses and wondered at it. How curious to feel this way now and for this stranger. She had seen the spark of desire in his eyes quickly doused. They both felt the magnetic force drawing one human being to another, and he was fighting it. Newly widowed, it was expected of him, but as it was exactly what she was seeking, Betsy was powerless to resist.

They stared at each other until the timely return of his aunt broke the spell.

Ignoring Betsy in a way only the elderly can get away with, Mr. Whitmore's aunt brusquely said, "Theodore, we must return to the hotel. It is time for my nap. You know how cranky I get without it. Annalise is probably wondering what has detained us and wasn't that preacher a bit long winded."

Theodore took advantage of a break in his aunt's rantings to introduce Mrs. Wheeler. He didn't dare berate his aunt for being rude as the result would further disturb those around them not to mention increase

Theodore's embarrassment when she turned her wrath in his direction. "Aunt Agatha, this is Mrs. Betsy Wheeler. She is welcoming us to the island."

His aunt turned her sharp eyes in Betsy's direction. She looked her over with obvious disapproval. "I hope all women on this island are not as forthright and bold. A lady should not introduce herself to a strange gentleman. It's simply not done."

Flustered by her scolding, Betsy was saved from a response by the timely return of Mr. Casey.

"There you are Mrs. Wheeler. Are you ready to return home?"

As propriety dictated, Betsy made the introductions. "Mr. Casey, this is Mr. Theodore Whitmore, his son, Henry, and his aunt…," she floundered, realizing she hadn't properly been introduced.

Theodore finished for her. "Mrs. Agatha Pary."

George lifted his hat to Mrs. Pary, then held his hand out to Mr. Whitmore. "Please to meet you, sir. Will you be staying long in Key West?"

"The length of time is dependent upon my business."

Because it was expected, George asked, "What business would that be, Mr. Whitmore?"

"A journalist for the *New York Weekly*." Theodore expected that to be the end of the conversation, but the lady surprised him—not just by continuing the conversation but by doing so with real interest.

Betsy asked, "What brings you to Key West, Mr. Whitmore?"

Seeing her companion's irritation, Theodore tried to keep the conversation short. "The army."

Betsy was intrigued. "Why would your readers in New York be interested in the army here?"

He liked the way her mind worked. She didn't ask the obvious question. "They may not be interested. It depends on why they are here."

"And have you discovered why?"

He ignored Mr. Casey impatiently shuffling his feet. He was enjoying this conversation and wanted it to continue. "Partially. I don't have the full story yet."

George had plans for today, and they did not include listening to Betsy converse with this stranger. Hints weren't working, so he took action. He held out his elbow for Betsy. "Mrs. Wheeler, I suggest we be on our way and let these good people enjoy their afternoon." Betsy's mouth thinned. She did not like his peremptory attitude towards her, but rather than create a scene, she placed her gloved hand in the crook of his arm.

Mrs. Pary was in agreement. "Yes, Theodore, let us be on our way. I would like sustenance and rest, post-haste, if you please." She placed her hand in the crook of her nephew's arm and attempted to turn him in the direction of the boarding house.

Theodore accepted her prodding with grace. He lifted his hat and bowed his head to Betsy. "Good day, Mrs. Wheeler." He nodded to George. "Mr.

Casey."

Betsy replied, "Good day, Mr. Whitmore, Mrs. Pary." She peered to the side of Theodore. "You too, Henry." She then allowed George to turn her away. Henry smiled and waved in return.

His aunt's demand to return to the hotel had them following in the couple's wake for a short distance giving Theodore a chance to observe them. He assumed Mrs. Wheeler had a husband, but if so, she was not with him. This man had another name, did not appear to be related, and was much too possessive of her to be a casual acquaintance. Theodore perceived her to be too proper for anything untoward leaving the most obvious answer to his speculation. They were a courting couple. Perhaps he was mistaken about feeling a ring on her hand. He wondered how serious the relationship was, for he noticed her displeasure with Mr. Casey at their parting. Her frown bothered Theodore even though her happiness was none of his concern.

His group turned on Fitzpatrick Street while the couple continued onward around the corner to Whitehead Street. His arrival at the boarding house distracted him from his musings of the lovely Mrs. Wheeler.

On the way home, Mr. Casey kept up a running monologue about his work and the need for a tariff on imported salt. The locals were using the duty free salt rather than Key West salt which kept the business from growing and could keep him from moving into management. As he rambled, Betsy's thoughts returned again to the sermon on marriage and procreation, to having someone to share her life and grow old with, and to starting her own family. She tried to picture having all of this with George Casey, but Theodore Whitmore's face refused to leave her mind.

One meeting with this stranger sparked a flame that threatened to consume her. It was too much to believe he was the man for her. He was still grieving for his wife. But if she could feel this much for him she had to believe she could find the excitement of new love again. She felt more in the few moments of today's encounter with Mr. Whitmore than she had in all the time she had spent with Mr. Casey. So right or wrong, she believed there was a man somewhere in this world that could bring her joy. She was willing to chase the elusive dream now that she knew it could still exist rather than settle for safe. Hardly giving it any more thought she knew she would end her relationship with George Casey.

She was going to dare to dream of love again.

George was planning to propose as soon as they reached the front porch of Betsy's home. Nervousness caused him to speak more incessantly than normal not even giving Betsy a chance to add to the conversation. As they reached her door, he paused to gather his words and his courage giving Betsy the chance to speak first and lay waste to his much rehearsed speech.

Betsy took one step onto her porch and turned around to block his assent. Not wanting to hurt his feelings Betsy tried to phrase her rejection as kindly as possible. "Mr. Casey, thank you for escorting me home. I am flattered by your attentions, but to be honest, I cannot in good conscience continue to take advantage of your time after having come to realize I would not be able to accept the inevitable outcome of such an arrangement."

She waited for him to respond.

George didn't quite grasp exactly the meaning of her words at first, but he did understand their tone and the look on her face. It took a moment to sink in and then he said the only thing he could think of, "Is there someone else?"

"No."

"Then why? You need a husband."

His petulant voice combined with the oft heard admonishment from well-meaning matrons frazzled her patience. "No I don't. I have gotten along just fine without one for years. I can certainly wait a little longer for the right man." She blanched as she realized in addition to her rude vociferation she had just insulted him.

Resigned to her decision, George's tone became forlorn. "And you have decided I am not the right man. I don't have any say in the matter?"

"I am sorry, Mr. Casey. There is nothing more to be said. I've made up my mind."

He didn't want to let her go, but he couldn't force her to want his attentions. He lifted his hat. "Very well. I will respect your decision. Good day to you, Mrs. Wheeler."

"Good day, Mr. Casey."

Betsy turned and entered her house, firmly closing the door behind her. She stood at the window and moved aside the curtain to watch him walk away. She hated having caused the dejected slump in his shoulders, but she certainly couldn't undo it even if she so desired. The deed was done and now she would have to live with the consequences of her impulsive action.

Chapter 4

As the spring of 1831 slipped into summer, Theodore didn't have much to report concerning army activity unless he counted bickering with the island proprietors over their exorbitant land prices. Other than that, the army occupied their time building their buildings and walking their patrols. They had yet to do anything else of significance. To occupy his time, Theodore sent Bob the occasional editorial of life in Key West he thought might engage New Englanders. He also submitted local interest pieces to the *Key West Gazette* although the editor, Dr. Strobel, so far had politely refused them for various reasons.

The slower pace and isolation of island life felt restrictive to Theodore until he realized it was in his best interest to relax and practice patience not only for professional reasons but also personal. After all, Bob made it clear he should treat this time more as a sabbatical with work as a side project. In that frame of mind, he began lounging with the local gentlemen on the Custom House piazza sharing stories or watching the comings and goings of the harbour traffic. Occasionally, he would spend time in the bars talking with the fishermen and sailors or sitting in on court hearings. From these activities, he began to appreciate the rich tapestry of life on Key West. It wasn't all pretty or idyllic, but it was always interesting. The evenings were spent with his family and the other guests at the boarding house, and every night he tucked Henry into bed. Reading his son a bedtime story was his favourite part of the day.

A month after their arrival they were finally able to move into a two story rental on Whitehead Street. Theodore was looking forward to having more space, but he would miss the conversations around the boardinghouse dinner table. Aunt Agatha, on the other hand, was looking forward to the return of quiet digestion.

* * *

It was the Whitmore's last dinner at Mrs. Mallory's table before moving into the rented house. Upon finishing the meal, his aunt excused herself taking Annalise and Henry with her. Theodore declined to join them preferring to enjoy the conversation of the dozen or so guests who lingered around the large dining table. He refused to acknowledge—especially to himself—that it had anything to do with the lovely seamstress who had joined them for dinner. Betsy was seated directly across from him looking lovely in a sage colored printed dress. Her hair was done in a single, heavy, sable braid draped over one shoulder.

The dishes were efficiently cleared from the table and drinks refilled. Several of the men lit their pipes or cigars creating a pleasant earthy aroma.

When the noise settled down, the night's entertainments began in earnest as those around the table shared their amusing tales and anecdotes.

It took very little persuasion for the young and brash Dr. Strobel to relate his tale of buried treasure. Theodore could not determine if the story was fabricated or truth. Dr. Strobel certainly told it as if he truly had stumbled upon a person in the midst of darkness digging up pirate treasure under a certain palm tree. The drunken miscreant was thwarted of his prize, but Dr. Strobel did not accept that to mean it didn't exist. A general round of arguing his theories of where the treasure might be followed until Dr. Strobel gave up in frustration.

On the other hand, Dr. Waterhouse, a gaunt man of sallow complexion, was repeatedly asked to share a taradiddle and repeatedly declined much to everyone's chagrin. A few others made contributions instead. Dr. Waterhouse, believing that to be the end of it, began to relax only to be dismayed a short while later when District Attorney Chandler took up the challenge. The doctor finally succumbed to his request. The delight of all was so obvious, Theodore couldn't help being intrigued. He shared a congenial look with Mrs. Wheeler before turning his attention to the aged sawbones.

Dr. Waterhouse began his story while oddly emphasizing each point by gesturing with his fore-finger from the tip of his nose to the table before him. "I once knew of a thief down on his luck. He had not had a decent meal in weeks and was getting desperate. He also had narrowly escaped several confrontations, so he was more than a little leery of getting caught. One Sunday afternoon, the thief watched as a church emptied of its parishioners, and the clergy man left shortly after on business. He waited a bit then gathered up his nerve and snuck into the church. He looked around deciding on his target when he heard a noise. Quickly, he concealed himself in a dark corner and waited. It was a parishioner visiting for a private prayer. The thief settled in to wait for the opportune moment to abscond with the valuables. Several more comings and goings of laity and the return of the clergyman forced him to wait until well after dusk. When the clergyman finally retired for the evening, he locked the doors behind him."

Theodore and Betsy shared a brief look of confusion unable to determine where the story was headed but none the less enjoying the tale.

"When it was safe to do so, the thief collected his chosen purloined goods then looked for a means of escape. He soon learned his only mode of egress was by an open upper window. He felt fortunate to find a rope hanging in just the right place conveniently allowing him to climb to the window. The thief slung his cache over his shoulder and made the first pull on the rope to haul himself up, but much to his dismay, the rope gave way followed by the loud tolling of the bell in the steeple."

Dr. Waterhouse paused for effect and to enjoy his captured audience.

"Unable to affect an escape the thief was trapped. It didn't take long for the aroused neighborhood to find him and bring about his arrest. As they were leading him away, he turned around and addressed the bell, as I now do you Mr. Chandler," said Dr. Waterhouse, taking his finger from his nose and pointing it at the district attorney. "If not for your long tongue and empty head, I would have escaped."

All present were so caught up in following the story, they were taken entirely by surprise at its close.[1] Laughter rose to the ceiling and increased with Mr. Chandler's sputtering discomfort. Theodore found himself laughing out loud for the first time in longer than he could remember. He had to agree with his fellow guests, Dr. Waterhouse had a gift for repartee.

No one felt equal to following the doctor's success, and so the party ended with residents and guests bidding each other good night. Theodore watched as one of the gentlemen approached Mrs. Wheeler and offered to walk her home. He was surprised to discover he wished to be the one doing so.

* * *

For the past several weeks, Theodore occupied the house across the street from Betsy Wheeler but had yet to have another opportunity to speak with her. Their paths only crossed at a distance. He didn't seek her out, for in truth, he was still in mourning not just based on the calendar but also in his heart. He was very attracted to his bright-eyed neighbor, but if he was honest with himself, he was not emotionally ready to open his heart to another. Thoughts and reminders of Margaret still occurred too frequently. But he had to admit, Bob was right. Moving away from his home gave him freedom to work through his sorrow rather than flounder in it.

* * *

Betsy watched the comings and goings of her new neighbors with interest, but she had yet to find the opportunity to interact with Mr. Whitmore. His aunt, on the other hand, visited on several occasions in essence inviting herself to tea. It took all of Betsy's forbearance to tolerate her frequent complaints. The days she brought Henry and Annalise with her were much easier to bear. Henry's boyish impishness was hard to resist, and Betsy encouraged his interaction with her which brought about the majority of his aunt's criticisms. Agatha Pary firmly believed children should be seen and not heard. Betsy firmly believed a child's spirit was to be encouraged.

* * *

It was a cheerful, sunny morning in mid-May when Betsy learned the monthly mail had arrived. Knowing the islanders would rush to the post office, Betsy waited for the crowd to disperse before making her way to the office in hopes of a letter from her mother or siblings.

She walked through the open doorway of the post office and warmly greeted her neighbor, Dr. Waterhouse, who was also the island's first postmaster. For the last two years, he performed the duties of the office with deliberate attention. He was a gangly, unhealthy looking man for a doctor, and the only person she knew who wore dentures. He claimed they were made from hippopotamus tusk. They gave his cheeks a sunken look adding to his odd appearance as if his eccentric personality was not enough to make him stand out in the community. But he had a gentle soul, and Betsy considered him a friend.

"What can I do for you today, Mrs. Wheeler? I am afraid I haven't any mail for you this time."

Betsy was disappointed but accepted the news with grace. "Maybe there will be two next month." She laid the book she carried on the counter between them and pushed it towards him. "I thought I would return your book."

Dr. Waterhouse, being the only person with an extensive collection of books, was also somewhat of the town librarian. He picked up the book to read the title. "Ah, *Precaution*. And how did you find the writing of James Fennimore Cooper?"

Betsy grimaced. "Not to my liking. The copious cast of characters was tedious to keep up with and the story seemed overly drawn out, but I understand this to be his first novel and that he wrote it because of a challenge issued by his wife. Perhaps he has improved."

"Shall I loan you *The Pioneers* to make your determination of his improvements?"

"Only if you recommend it. I am not impressed enough to deem his work worth the price of another candle."

Dr. Waterhouse smiled around his false teeth. "I understand. Perhaps not then. Have you read Sir Walter Scott's *The Monastery*?"

Betsy shook her head. "I don't believe I have."

The little bell attached to the front door tinkled announcing new arrivals. Betsy turned to see two gentlemen enter and smiled. "Good afternoon, Mr. Whitehead, Mr. Whitmore."

In unison they removed their hats and replied, "Good afternoon Mrs. Wheeler, Dr. Waterhouse."

Dr. Waterhouse said, "I will be with you gentlemen in just a moment." He left the room for a brief moment to retrieve the book. He returned and slid it across the counter to her. "Now, Mrs. Wheeler, is there anything else I can do for you?"

"No. That will be all. Thank you."

His smile faded. "I see. Well, I was hoping to demonstrate the new stamps I just received but perhaps another time."

"You could still show them to me." Betsy noted the suppressed excitement in his manner as he pulled out a box containing the new stamps. She looked from Dr. Waterhouse to Mr. Whitehead. "I am sure our collector of customs must have some important mail requiring the use of your stamps."

Dr. Waterhouse couldn't help the excited grin that spread across his face. "That he does."

Betsy stepped aside so the two gentlemen could join her at the counter while Dr. Waterhouse retrieved William Whitehead's mail. Betsy was as curious of the process as Dr. Waterhouse was excited to demonstrate it. Of course she had stamped letters, but she had never seen the process performed before now. The group stood quietly while Dr. Waterhouse tallied the amount of postage due on Mr. Whitehead's mail.

"That will be fifty-nine cents, sir, for the six letters as two traveled greater than thirty miles by land, and of course it includes the ship fees."

Mr. Whitehead counted out the coins and laid them on the counter. Dr. Waterhouse eagerly selected the appropriate stamp, carefully inked it, and then stamped each letter 'Paid', re-inking in between each one. Next, he built the date on the date stamp, secured it with binding, and then repeated the procedure. He proudly handed them to Mr. Whitehead. "We are getting to be real official now."

Mr. Whitehead inspected the stamps on the uppermost letter. "Nicely done, sir."

"Thank you."

Mr. Whitmore peered at the letter, then to Dr. Waterhouse's box. "What are the other stamps?" He didn't ask out of any real interest in the act of stamping or even in the different stamps. He merely hoped to prolong the moment as he enjoyed observing Mrs. Wheeler's fascination.

"Would you like for me to show you?"

Mr. Whitehead handed him back the top letter. Dr. Waterhouse stamped it twice more and returned it to Mr. Whitehead. It was now also marked 'Ship' and 'Free'.

When he was finished stamping, Betsy looked up in time to catch Mr. Whitmore watching her. She blushed knowing she had been as entranced as a child watching Dr. Waterhouse while Mr. Whitmore, of course, would have seen more impressive stamping in the big city. She expected him, at the very least, to be bored with their amusement, yet as she studied his face, she noted a bit of wonder not unlike what one might feel in the study of a child's innocence. Realizing, she was the sole source of his fascination both thrilled her and furthered her embarrassment. She returned her attention to the letter Mr. Whitehead held out for their inspection. Unfortunately, she had no idea what he just said. She nodded her head and replied, "Nice," which thankfully seemed to satisfy him.

Dr. Waterhouse closed the tin containing the ink pad, carefully cleaned the stamps, and returned them all to the wooden box. He then recorded the transaction in his ledger.

Having embarrassed herself enough for one day, Betsy decided it was an opportune moment to leave. "Gentlemen, I bid you good day." She barely gave them enough time to return the sentiment before turning on her heel and fleeing out the door. Behind her, she could hear Mr. Whitmore speaking as she left the building. "Dr. Waterhouse, have you any correspondence addressed to me?"

Betsy walked briskly toward Abby's house for an impromptu visit while she pondered the meaning of Mr. Whitmore's behavior. Her fourth encounter with this enigma of a man had not helped her. He was a man of few words. One had to study his eyes to know what he was thinking, and even they were often veiled, allowing one to see only that which he chose to show. And today, she amused him with her naiveté but that was all there was to be seen on his face. What else did she expect? Just because she was attracted to him did not mean he shared the feeling. He was a man in mourning. If he loved his wife as she had her husband, then he was not thinking of anyone in romantic terms. Even if his grief abated, it was still too soon to supplant his wife's memory with someone new.

She remembered those early days of grieving; they were lonely, yet it was unthinkable to allow anyone else to fill the loneliness. She could offer Mr. Whitmore her friendship, but it would be fruitless to pine for anything more from him; something easier to tell herself than to make her heart oblige. The heart's desires, once set, cannot be redirected. And her heart was set on him. It happened so fast she had no time to reason with it. Now all she could do was keep her desire hidden and give him the space he needed to heal his. At least it wasn't love. Not yet. But unless something grave came to light, it was only a matter of time. Her feelings were growing stronger each time they met.

Betsy knocked on Abby's door and was quickly ushered into the house by Mrs. Baxley, her housekeeper. "Mrs. Abby will be happy to see you Mrs. Wheeler. She is finding her condition to be quite vexing today and could use the distraction."

Mrs. Baxley showed her to the morning room decorated in soft shades of green and lavender. It was Betsy's favourite room in the house. She rushed to greet Abby in her chair, not giving her a chance to rise.

"Heavens Betsy, not you too! I am getting tired of being treated as an invalid. I was told being with child was taken for granted the second time around, but Max is worse than ever, and I still have three months to go."

"Mrs. Baxley warned me you are having a harder time carrying this child."

"Harder time as in more uncomfortable, not more feeble."

"Of course, Captain Max is attentive. All a man has left to do is worry once he has planted his seed. He cannot carry the burden, much as we women may wish to transfer it."

Abby was a bit shocked by Betsy's frank language. It was out of character for her, but Abby took it as it was meant—a distraction. "True, if I could turn this one over into his keeping for a while, today I would. It must be a son. Emily was a joy in the womb compared to this one. But enough of the complaints, at least I don't have it as difficult as poor Tria."

"Have you a letter from her?"

"Yes and the longest letter too. Have you heard of this new idea of 'confinement'? As if being with child was contagious or too suggestive or risqué for public viewing."

"But it is a natural state, a God given blessing. Why would it need to be hidden?"

"I do not know the reasoning, but apparently, the idea is spreading across England. Tria complained at length of the Duchess trying to impose it upon her to keep her from the theater. She was even more furious with Lord Jason for siding with his mother."

"One would think, Lord Jason, would be more interested in heeding his expectant wife's wishes than his mother's."

Abby gave an unladylike huff. "A man seems to lose all rational thought when his wife is carrying his child. Max would applaud the idea. He thinks I do too much already. He treats me as if I was as delicate as spun sugar." Abby shook her head. "I sure hope this idea does not make its way across the Atlantic."

"I am sure it will eventually, but you needn't worry about it now. Would you like to go for a walk?"

"I would indeed."

Arm in arm, the two ladies strolled around town in comfortable companionship.

* * *

As the heat of summer increased, Aunt Agatha's visits decreased. Betsy had long ago run out of work for Esperanza. She once again toiled in solitude except when she ventured into town on errands or to visit friends. On the days when the heat or her own company became unbearable, Betsy would put aside her work to pack up a snack, a canteen of water, a towel, and a big floppy hat to protect her face from the sun.

Dr. Waterhouse kept a small ten foot sail boat down by the beach which he generously allowed her to use whenever she wished. Betsy marked her initial on the ground to indicate she had taken the boat and then pushed it into the water before climbing in. Taking up the oars, she rowed herself out from shore and raised the square sail. She navigated around the island past the lighthouse until she was sure she was hidden from view by the trees. Only a rare fisherman ventured this way as the water was shallow on this side of the island. She picked a sandy spot that looked inviting, dropped the anchor, undressed down to her chemise, and slipped into the refreshing water.

Underwater was a magical place. Floating on her stomach, she loved to watch the light play across the slender blades of sea grass wafting in the current. She often pushed her lungs to their limit to enjoy the view as long as possible. Many brightly colored fish swam by, sometimes in large schools. She swam a little ways from the boat to float over the coral where the water was a little deeper and the fish a little larger. She always kept a careful eye out for sharks, but they usually weren't a problem in this area. She wished she knew the names of the different fish. Some were a light iridescent blue; others were round and bright blue with a black tail. There were tiny yellow ones and gray and white striped ones. Sleek silver ones were often in large schools. Today a lone green sea turtle swam with her for a while. They were such graceful creatures in the water and so cumbersome on land.

When the turtle swam away she decided it was best she head back. Too much sun was not good. She climbed into the boat and stretched out to dry, placing the hat over her face. Her mind wandered as it often did to Mr. Whitmore. It was probably foolish to daydream of him, but she did it anyway. She would indulge her fantasies for a moment before chastising herself for daring to dream them. She thwarted a perfectly good proposal just to remain alone. Maybe she could have been happy with Mr. Casey. Maybe not. She put a stop to the train of thoughts. It only went in circles.

Realizing she was dry enough, she slipped into her dress and sailed back home.

* * *

Summer passed with few events to break the monotony. Yellow fever broke out on the island, but Dr. Strobel was getting adept at handling it. The days drifted by until the calendar declared it to be fall, although, their sub-tropical climate only had two seasons; wet and dry. They were in the rainy season. It was also storm season which typically lasted until November. All the islanders kept a weather eye on the horizon wary of the harsh tropical cyclones that could bring destruction and death.

* * *

The last Sunday in August, the community welcomed its newest resident. Captain Max and Abigail Eatonton proudly introduced their three week old son, Richard Christoff Eatonton, born August 6th. Abby's father, Richard Bennington, returned from his brother's Alabama plantation just in time for the birth of his grandson and was quite emotional to learn they named the boy after him, in honor of his efforts in bringing the couple together. The baby's middle name came from Max's deceased father.

Betsy received a letter the same week from Victoria announcing the birth of her second lordling. Now that she had provided the heir and a spare, her mother-in-law, the Duchess, was leaving her in peace. As usual, her letter was short and to the point. She didn't even bother to mention the baby's name. Maybe it was in Abby's letter. It was enough of an excuse for Betsy to lay her work aside, wrap up the loaf of cinnamon bread cooling on the kitchen windowsill, and head over to the Eatonton's.

Max answered the door and greeted her more warmly than usual. The sounds of the squalling infant probably explained why. "Is that your famous bread?" He reached for it before Betsy could form a reply and used his other hand to pull her inside.

Betsy's amusement over Max's behavior was suppressed by her concern for the baby. "How long has he been crying?"

"It seems like hours. Would you please try your magic charm and see if you can settle him down? Abby is at her wits end which seems to be making it worse."

Betsy smiled at the desperation in his voice. "I will give it a try but don't get your hopes up. It could be my charm only worked with Emily."

"Please try."

Betsy found Abby pacing the floor of the morning room, looking anything but herself. Her hair was disarrayed, her eyes were tired and weepy, and her clothes were rumpled. Christoff, as they were calling him, had his hands balled in fists, crying as hard as any newborn she had ever heard. Without saying a word, Betsy walked up to her friend and gently took the babe from her arms.

Abby collapsed on the divan while Betsy paced and soothed as best she could. When he didn't settle down, she checked his nappie. It was dry. She then laid him down next to Abby to redo his blanket, which promptly escalated his crying. Betsy made sure the stick pin was secure then quickly swaddled him in the blanket. She scooped him up, cradling him tightly to her chest and resumed her pacing and humming. Both ladies breathed a sigh of relief when he quieted. A few minutes later he was asleep.

Emily entered the room, walked to her mother's side and then turned around to look at Betsy. "Noisy brodder. Take away."

Betsy smiled and Abby scolded.

"Emily, you don't want to give away your brother."

Betsy said, "It will get better, sweetie. When he is not so new, you will have fun playing with him."

Betsy tried to lay Christoff in the basinet but as she took a step back he started crying. She quickly picked him up again.

Emily put her fists on her hips. "Bad baby brudder."

Abby stroked her daughter's tangled hair. "Emily sweetheart, will you bring me your brush?"

Max came in bearing a plate of sliced bread which he offered to Abby. "Betsy, you are welcome anytime when you bring sweet bread and blessed quiet." Max kissed his wife and then surprised Betsy by kissing her cheek before walking out of the room.

Abby said, "As you can imagine, it has been a rough morning. Actually, it has been a rough two weeks. You'll have to teach me how you wrapped the blanket. How did you know to do that?"

"It was the only way my mother could get my brothers to quiet down."

Emily returned to the room and handed Abby her brush. Abby turned her daughter around and began working on the tangles while Emily nibbled on a piece of bread.

Betsy suddenly recalled the purpose of her visit. "Have you received a letter from Victoria?"

"Yes. She had another boy."

Betsy nodded. "She did mention that in my letter as well but she neglected to tell me his name."

Abby smiled. "She did not include it in mine either. How have you been, Betsy? Any news to share?"

She knew Abby was referring to Mr. Whitmore. "No. Nothing has changed." Betsy held Christoff a little tighter to her and couldn't help the unbidden thought, *When would she hold a child of her own?*

"One day it will. Something unexpected will happen and when it does all your dreams will come true. I believe you will find love again. Maybe even with Mr. Whitmore. I have seen him look at you." Abby realized she was having a one-sided conversation. She tilted her head in contemplation. "Betsy, have you heard a word I have said?"

Betsy looked at her as if waking from a dream. "I'm sorry Abby. Did you say something?"

Abby softly smiled. "Nothing of importance."

Betsy sighed. "Some days I wonder if I didn't dream it all."

Abby looked at her in confusion. "Dream what, dear?"

"Marriage, Ben's death, especially the baby. It was so short a time. It was as if it never happened, yet it cut so deep my heart is scarred for life. Can you understand how something can be so real but feel so unreal?"

"I cannot say that I have experienced such a feeling, but I do think I understand what you mean."

Betsy tried again to lay Christoff in the bassinet. Thankfully, he continued sleeping. Feeling too melancholy now to be good company, Betsy decided it was time to leave. "I believe I will be going. You need to try and get some rest while he is sleeping."

Abby nodded. She watched her leave sharing in the sadness that resided in Betsy's heart. She prayed God would show her how to help her friend.

On her way back home, Betsy crossed paths with Jonathon Keats mumbling to himself in Spanish. He was studying Spanish in the hopes it would help him win over Mr. Sanchez so he could marry his daughter. When he noticed her, she asked, "How are the lessons going?"

He grimaced. "Esperanza says my accent is horrible, but the words are correct."

His forlorn expression tugged on Betsy's heart.

He sighed deeply. "I don't know how much longer I can stand to wait. It's been two years of learning the language and four years since we met. When will her father realize I'm not giving up? Perhaps we should elope."

"You could but you would put a rift between Esperanza and her father that might never be repaired and do more harm than good. Stay the course, and when the time is right, find the courage to act on it."

"You don't think he believes she is too young to marry, do you?"

Betsy smiled. "Have you seen how young some Cuban brides are? At twenty, she is in danger of spinsterhood. No, 'tis more likely he considers you too old for her."

"I'm too old? I hadn't thought much about our age difference."

"Nine years would be concerning. Perhaps he is hoping Esperanza will change her mind."

Jonathon's shoulders fell. "Perhaps I should give up. Maybe you and I should consider consoling ourselves with each other."

"Oh!" She playfully swatted his arm with her fan. "How unflattering! No lady wants to be second choice, not even in jest."

He bowed his head low. "My apologies, madam. I'm afraid my frustration is getting the better of me."

"Apology accepted."

Jonathon bowed again. "If you'll excuse me? I should be getting back to the ship. There is much to be done before we sail on the morning tide."

Betsy nodded. "Stay the course Jonathon. I'm sure all will work out in the end."

"Thank you for your encouragement. Good day, Betsy."

Betsy continued on her way home. The talk with Jonathon, focusing on his problems instead of hers, lightened her mood.

Chapter 5

By October, the Army finished constructing their buildings and turned their attention to the safety of the island. In the mainland territory of Florida, tensions were building between the Seminole Indians and the plantation settlers surrounding the reservations. Despite their distance from the area, Major Glassell considered it reason enough to take precautions on the island. He approached the town council with a proposal to clear the trees around the settlement and behind the tidal pond to prevent any kind of sneak attack from Indians. The idea was approved and plans were made. Civilians were encouraged to join the efforts.

On the designated day, Major Glassell was pleased so many men offered to share their tools and their brawn. The soldiers and the civilians were organized into work parties taking different sections to be cleared and further divided into tasks of cutting underbrush, felling trees, cutting logs into lumber, hauling off the lumber, and burning the debris.

The ladies organized the food and drinks. Several barrels were filled with water from the largest cisterns. Betsy was tasked with making switchel and assigning ladies to carry it out to the working men in buckets with dippers. When working in the heat, switchel—a mixture of water, vinegar, ginger and honey—was easier on the stomach than plain water. They were fortunate in having procured honey from a recent shipwreck.

Betsy saved the section Mr. Whitmore was working for her distribution. She worked her way down the line of men, anxious and a little nervous, waiting to reach the object of her affection. It was hot, sweaty work, under a sweltering October sun, and the men were grateful for their turn to pause and drink. Unfortunately, she also had to serve Mr. Casey. He greeted her with more than casual familiarity clearly hoping to renew his courtship. She discouraged his overtures and quickly moved on to the next group of men.

At last she reached him. Mr. Whitmore and another soldier, Private Jones, were using machetes to clear away the underbrush in their section to make it easier for the ones who came behind them to fell the trees.

Theodore sheathed his machete and wiped his hands on his trousers as he approached Mrs. Wheeler. She looked as fresh and sparkling as a dew kissed morning glory, despite the heat. He couldn't help but notice how the blue of her dress enhanced the blue of her eyes. She was as pretty as a picture and twice as enticing.

All of the men greeted Betsy's appearance with smiles, but Mr. Whitmore's was the only one she really noticed. He had a nice smile and as she recalled from the night of Dr. Waterhouse's story, he had a nice, baritone laugh too. Most of the time he wore a serious expression making moments like this one, when he did smile, noticeably striking.

Theodore gestured for the younger Private Jones to take the firs[t] allowing him to linger longer and rest. "It is nice to see you, Mrs. Whe____

"And you, Mr. Whitmore." She handed the full dipper to the soldier. "You gentlemen have made good progress today. I believe you are further than any other team."

The soldier refilled the dipper from the bucket she held. "I am sure that is because Mr. Whitmore, here, doesn't talk much. He is a very determined man in a task." He watched the two of them as he drank the second scoop.

Theodore replied, "I have found you learn more listening to others than by speaking and hard labor gets done faster without talk."

The soldier dropped the empty dipper in the bucket and turned away with an audible huff.

Betsy handed Theodore the dipper. "Why are you helping to clear the land? The soldiers are required to, and the islanders have a vested interest. No one would give it any thought if you did not participate."

Their gloved hands touched as she took the empty dipper from him to refill. Her wide eyes looked to his face for his reaction and that connection affected Theodore more than the physical one. Only when she looked down a moment later to refill the dipper was he able to breathe, and think, again. "My father taught me the value of hard work and to always lend a hand when I was able. He said it was good stewardship. Besides, I do have a vested interest in the safety of the island as long as my family resides here." He took the dipper from her, careful not to touch her hand again. He did not want to encourage any feelings between them. This beautiful lady deserved more than he was able to give.

"Yes, I suppose you do. Although I was referring to the temporary nature of your residency." She watched fascinated as he tipped his head back and drank the final contents of the dipper, admiring the manly contours of his throat and neck.

He caught her regard as he returned the dipper to the pail and couldn't help but notice the unguarded infatuation in her gaze. He decided to put a quick end to their encounter for both their sakes. "Thank you, Mrs. Wheeler." He quickly returned to his work before she could reply.

Betsy watched him for a moment before moving on to the next group of men. An hour later she made her rounds again but Mr. Whitmore took his drink first and said little, as was the case each successive time. She didn't have another chance to speak to him. The men were served dinner first and all ate together in large groups sitting on the ground under the shade of select palm trees saved from the saws.

With so many to help, the massive job was completed in one day. They succeeded in moving the tree line back a hundred yards from the town.

* * *

In November, Theodore was finally able to do some serious

correspondent work. William Whitehead was asked to report on the conditions of the native inhabitants of Charlotte Harbour. He offered Theodore the opportunity to join him which of course was eagerly accepted.

That evening in the parlor, Theodore broached the subject with his family. "Mr. Whitehead told me he is making an excursion to visit an Indian village on the Florida mainland."

Aunt Agatha looked up from her knitting. "Whatever for?"

"The government has asked for a report on them, and somehow it falls to Mr. Whitehead to do so. He asked if I would care to join him."

"And having a strange interest in the natives you, of course, accepted."

"Hmm."

"How long will you be gone?"

"Just over a week. It made me realize I have neglected to inquire as to your wishes for Christmas. Do you desire to return home for the holiday season? We could make arrangements."

"Whatever for? Cold weather and a drafty old house? My bones would just as soon be in this warm climate." *Why in the world would he think I would want to leave this nice island? There are so many men I just might find a salty seaman to my liking. In this magical little spot on the ocean it feels like anything is possible.*

Theodore felt the same. "Very well. We will stay, at least until spring."

* * *

In preparation for his week long absence Theodore made a visit across the street. Walking up on the porch he removed his hat and smoothed his hair before knocking on the door. It was Saturday and the shop's closed sign was out. He hoped she was home. He waited only a moment before the door was opened and he was greeted with Mrs. Wheeler smile.

Betsy was surprised by her guest and couldn't imagine what could bring Theodore to her doorstep. She felt sure if it had been for her services he would have come during normal working hours, but a social call did not seem likely either. "Good afternoon, Mr. Whitmore. What can I do for you?" Propriety and her reputation prevented her from inviting him into her home on the weekend, so she stepped outside onto the porch and let the louvered front door close behind her. She already knew he was a good six inches taller than her, but in the confines of her porch she felt dwarfed by this broad shouldered man.

Theodore unconsciously turned his hat in his hand. "I am here to ask a favour of you, Mrs. Wheeler. If you would be so kind as to offer your assistance?"

"Certainly, Mr. Whitmore, if it is within my means to assist I will gladly do so."

"I am leaving on Tuesday and will be away for a week or so. Mrs. Pary and Miss Annalise are not well acquainted with the other neighbors. They asked if they could come to you if, for some reason, they were in need during my absence. My aunt is elderly and I am not sure how well Annalise would fare in a crisis. It would relieve my mind to know they could depend on you, if needed, and I'm sure if further assistance were required you would know whom best to provide it."

After so many months of only short, terse conversations, his request came as a surprise in more ways than one. "Of course, Mr. Whitmore. I am more than willing to oblige. It wasn't even necessary for you to request it, but I am sure it will relieve you to know they will be looked after."

He nodded once. "Thank you, ma'am. It does give me comfort." He continued turning his hat. "This will be the first time I have ever been away from Henry for more than the work day. I am not sure how he will handle my absence." Theodore wondered what made him share such intimate information with her.

"I am told I have a way with children. If he takes it hard your aunt and Miss Annalise are free to come ask for my help." Her response garnered his first smile in this exchange, albeit a small one. It wouldn't matter now if she was dragged from a sound sleep to help his family, she had earned one of his coveted smiles.

"Thank you, again, Mrs., Wheeler." He took a step back and placed his hat on his head.

"You're welcome, Mr. Whitmore."

Theodore unconsciously tucked the image of Betsy standing on her porch in the soft light of evening smiling just for him into his memory for safe keeping while consciously he made preparations for his trip and tried to explain his forthcoming absence to Henry. He wondered now if he should have done so sooner rather than waiting until the last night as he tucked him into bed.

He cleared his throat. "Henry, we need to have a talk, father to son." Henry immediately stilled, all his attention focused on Theodore with wonder at what could be so important. "I have to go away for a little while. I won't be here to tuck you in at night or to eat meals with you. It's going to seem like a long time, but I will come back. Henry, how many fingers do you have?"

Henry pulled his hands out from under the covers to show him his wiggling digits. "I have ten fingers, five on each hand."

"That's right, son. Can you count to ten?"

Henry nodded. "Yes, sir." He counted as Theodore pointed to each finger.

"Good. That is how many days I will be gone." He planned to only be gone a week but did not want his son to worry if it took longer.

* * *

Early Tuesday morning, November 22nd, Theodore crept into Henry's room. He watched over his peaceful slumber a few minutes before lightly brushing aside the hair on his forehead to kiss it. He then quietly moved downstairs to pick up his canvas sack of clothing and gear and left the sleeping house. The cool morning air was invigorating and the sky was brightening into a cloudless blue. He met Mr. Whitehead at the dock and together they boarded the revenue cutter *Marion* to sail partway up the western peninsula of Florida to Charlotte Harbour. Excitement flowed through Theodore's veins in the hopes that here, at last, were the makings of a good article.

* * *

Wednesday afternoon Betsy left her workroom to see who had come into her shop. She was surprised to find Annalise and Henry. "Well hello there. What can I do for you?" Betsy studied the petite blond as she waited for her to answer. Annalise was a timid girl, no more than fourteen. Betsy thought her to be young for a governess, but she did seem to take care watching over Henry.

Annalise looked hopefully to Betsy. "Mr. Whitmore said to come to you if we were in need."

Betsy smiled. "Of course. What kind of help can I offer?"

"Mrs. Pary is suffering from a headache."

When the girl said no more, Betsy asked, "Does she need medicine?"

"She took her powders and retired to her bedroom, but then she called for me. When I went to see her she told me to take Henry and go somewhere. We were disturbing her convalescence. The only place I could think to go was here."

Betsy frowned. She thought it negligent and cruel of Agatha Pary to cast these children out just because she felt unwell, and then she got the strange feeling Mrs. Pary was taking advantage of her agreement with Theodore. It was easy to see Mrs. Pary intimidated Annalise. It didn't surprise Betsy. From what she had seen so far, it took a strong person to stand up to the cantankerous woman. But now Betsy wondered what she was going to do with her sudden guests.

She lifted the pass-through on the counter and invited them into her sitting room. "Of course, you can stay here for a while." She watched as they carefully seated themselves on the sofa, hands in lap, and looked to her. *What a sad way to spend a nice sunny afternoon.* She didn't have any pressing orders to finish. "Why don't we go walk along the shore and see what we can find?"

They returned a few hours later having walked down to the lighthouse and visited with the light keeper's family. The Mabrity boys and Henry bonded quickly and ran off to play while Annalise and their teenage daughters were content to stay on the porch and talk, allowing Betsy and

Barbara Mabrity a chance to visit. On the way back Henry found several seashells worthy of starting a collection and chased a crab around the shore before it escaped back into the water.

Upon entering the Whitmore home, they were greeted by the housekeeper who informed Annalise, "Mrs. Pary is still under the weather. She said to tell you to eat your supper without her."

Annalise turned to Betsy. "Won't you join us for supper? Cook always makes plenty of food."

The housekeeper said, "Tis true, there is always plenty. Tonight it is snapper with black beans and rice."

Betsy couldn't resist. "I would be honored. Thank you."

Tired from the sun and exercise they spoke little during the meal. Henry yawned several times. Afterwards, Annalise told him it was time for bed and he should thank Betsy.

Henry walked up to Betsy. "Thank you for taking us to the lighthouse Mrs. Wheeler. Will you read me a bedtime story?"

He asked so politely and with such a sweet face, Betsy didn't have the heart to refuse. "You may call me Mrs. Betsy, and I would be honored to read to you, Henry."

"Hooray!" He turned and ran up the stairs. Betsy saw Annalise cringe and assumed it to be the noise he was making in disregard of Mrs. Pary's headache.

"You may call me Mrs. Betsy as well."

"Thank you…, Mrs. Betsy. I enjoyed the day too. It was far more enjoyable than the usual day spent indoors reading and doing needlework."

"And more enjoyable than my typical day of sewing."

"Henry has a hard time playing quietly. Being outside was good for him. I should see to him."

Both ladies ascended the stairs to find Henry already dressed in his night shirt, kneeling by the bed, saying his prayers. He climbed into bed and under the covers then pointed to the book at the end of the bed. Betsy picked up *Mother Goose's Fairy Tales*.

"*Puss 'n Boots*, Mrs. Betsy."

She smiled, enjoying his eagerness, as she settled on the bed and turned to the appropriate page.

She was still smiling as she let herself into her own home an hour later. She thoroughly enjoyed the childhood ritual. She savored the feeling without allowing the thoughts to intrude of what might have been if she had not lost her baby.

* * *

Thursday afternoon Annalise came over to extend an invitation to supper from Mrs. Pary. She was to arrive promptly at half past four. Betsy changed her dress, brushed her hair, walked across the street, and knocked on the door at the appropriate time. The housekeeper led her into the salon where Mrs. Pary, Annalise and Henry were gathered. They all rose and came forward to greet her. Annalise and Henry returned to their game of checkers leaving Betsy and Mrs. Pary to talk.

"How was your day, Mrs. Wheeler?"

"Please call me Betsy. I had a pleasant day. My hands were busy so I cannot complain."

Grudgingly, the gray-haired lady said, "You may call me Agatha. I am sure you are wondering why I invited you over." She barely gave Betsy a chance to nod before answering. "I found myself in need of adult company. You are the only one I know on this island other than Mrs. Mallory, so I suppose you will do."

Betsy's upbringing demanded she allow Agatha's effrontery to pass unchallenged being her elder. She was grateful Henry chose that moment to approach giving her an escape from replying to his aunt. "Hello, Henry. How are you today?"

"I am well, Mrs. Betsy. Will you come play with us?"

"Certainly, what game are we playing?" Betsy could tell by her horrified look, she shocked Agatha with her response. "If you will excuse us, Mrs. Agatha?" Betsy didn't wait for her reply. She followed Henry to the other side of the room. With her back to his aunt, she was unable to keep the smirk off her face. How dare the woman invite her to dine and then insult her. She was not going to allow her to continue. Betsy didn't have to see it. She could feel Agatha's disapproval as she played a simple card game with Henry and Annalise.

Promptly at five, the housekeeper announced supper was ready. Agatha waited by the door for Henry and Annalise to pass, then said to Betsy in an aside, "I insisted on hiring and paying for the housekeeper and cook, against Theodore's wishes, so they would know from whence their pay came and therefore pay heed to my requests."

Betsy continued past her in silence having no idea how to respond to such a statement and, indeed, wondered at her reason for sharing it in the first place. Was Agatha making a point concerning her or Annalise's behavior or was it merely a sad attempt at conversation? She did not know the lady well, but her conversation skills did not seem poor, thereby, leaving Betsy to assume it was meant as a warning of some kind.

They entered the same dining room as the night before, but this time the table bore starched white linen, wine glasses, and more silverware than was necessary. Betsy felt more comfortable last night with the simple cutlery and bare table. Their food was served, and the housekeeper retreated. Mrs. Agatha prayed over the meal. When Betsy lifted her head, she watched as the others began quietly eating.

Picking up her own fork, she said, "Mrs. Agatha, are you enjoying your stay on the island?" Annalise's eyes grew large. Henry gave her a strange look. Her hostess set down her fork and finished chewing.

"Mrs. Betsy, as a guest in this house, I allow that you are not familiar with our custom. Obviously, Annalise and Henry did not acquaint you with it last evening." She sent the two culprits a withering look before continuing. "We do not speak at the table as it interferes with proper digestion. Food should be thoroughly chewed before swallowing and tends to grow cold while one is occupied with conversation. I cannot abide cold food. To answer your question, I do not much care for the heat or the insects. Otherwise, your island is not unpleasant."

Sufficiently admonished, Betsy merely nodded her head in acknowledgement and set to eating her meal in silence. Afterwards, Henry quietly asked her to tuck him in again. Betsy followed him upstairs without looking in Agatha's direction, sure that she would find disapproval. She was not going to give Agatha the opportunity to keep her from such a rare and sweet experience. Henry was asleep before she finished the story. She couldn't resist kissing his forehead before leaving him.

She returned to the salon in dread of keeping company with his aunt, but they conversed peacefully of mundane matters for a half hour before Agatha indicated it was time to end the evening. It was odd, but Betsy had the impression Agatha was more congenial in Henry's absence, as if she felt she could relax her stern influence.

* * *

Betsy spent Friday alone. She couldn't help but wonder how Henry and Annalise were doing. Saturday morning, she decided to rescue them. After making some preparations, she headed across the street at ten in the morning and bravely knocked on the door.

Annalise answered. "Good morning, Mrs. Betsy."

"Good morning, Annalise. Is Mrs. Agatha seeing visitors?"

Annalise stood aside for Betsy to enter. "Wait here while I go ask her?" She went up the stairs and around the corner. Betsy could hear her knock on Agatha's door followed by a whispered conversation before Annalise returned. "She asked for you to wait for her in the salon."

Betsy was surprised when Annalise left her alone to wait. It wasn't long before Agatha made her appearance. "Good morning, Mrs. Betsy. What brings you to my doorstep so early in the day?"

"Good morning, Mrs. Agatha. I thought I would invite your family to go sailing around the island. It is a small boat, only large enough for four. But we will keep close to the shore."

"I have no interest, but you may ask the children."

Agatha led her into the hallway where they found Annalise and Henry waiting for them.

Agatha said in her usual brusque tone, "Annalise, Mrs. Betsy has asked to take you and Henry for a sail. Would you like to go?"

Timidly, Annalise said, "Yes, ma'am."

Henry answered with enthusiasm. "Oh yes, Aunt Aggie. I want to sail."

Sternly, Mrs. Agatha turned back to Betsy. "Be sure they are back in time for dinner."

Betsy smiled, feeling quite congenial for the way her invitation was received. "Yes, ma'am."

The three were off in no time, picking up the items Betsy had gathered before heading to the beach and Dr. Waterhouse's boat. "Annalise, can you help me push it into the water?" She nodded in reply and laid her hands on one side of the boat's bow. Betsy turned to the boy. "Henry, can you draw a B on the ground for me? Make it large, please." Betsy placed her hands on the bow opposite of Annalise and began to push the stern toward the water.

Henry gave them a forlorn look. "Mrs. Betsy, I don't know how to draw a B."

Betsy straightened from her task in surprise. She returned to Henry's side and picked up a stick lying nearby. "I'll show you and then erase it, so you can do it." She crouched down to his height. "Watch carefully." She drew the letter, then stood and rubbed it out with her boot before handing the stick to Henry. He did well for his first try. "Very good. Come now and I'll lift you into the boat." Once the boat was halfway in the water, she had Annalise climb in. She launched it the rest of the way before wading into the water with hiked skirt to climb aboard. Her passengers held on tightly as the boat rocked and righted itself.

Their reaction concerned Betsy. "Do either of you know how to swim?"

Both shook their heads.

"Have you ever sailed in a small boat like this one?"

Again their heads shook.

Sighing, Betsy reconsidered her plans.

She raised the sail, but instead of heading out into deeper water, she kept close to the shore. Instead of her plans of taking them to swim over her favourite coral bed, she stayed close to home, sure that they would be content to look over the sides of the boat. She let them each take a turn at the tiller and shared with them her rudimentary knowledge of sailing. Later, they shared the dried apples and water she packed for a snack.

Clouds began building in the southern sky. The square sail snapped in the increasing wind, so Betsy turned the boat back to shore. By the time they were pulling the boat out of the water the storm was imminent. She led the way back to her home where they spent the rest of the afternoon teaching Henry the first part of the alphabet as the tempest raged outside. By the time she took them home, after the rain had passed, she felt sure Annalise would be able to continue the lessons, and Henry would soon know all the letters.

* * *

Sunday morning, Betsy walked to services with Agatha, Annalise and Henry at Agatha's request. The morning was a balmy seventy degrees making the walk enjoyable. They rounded the corner on Front Street to find an unusual crowd gathered at the docks. By the time they reached the Custom House, Betsy could tell most of the people gathered were unfamiliar to her. Agatha, holding Henry's hand, nearly reached the stairs of their destination when she realized Betsy was not behind them but had continued on towards the crowd. Curiosity made her follow. Annalise and Henry trailed behind her.

Betsy noticed a few islanders on the fringe of the growing crowd of strangers. She was disconcerted by how many people continued to appear from the direction of the wharfs. Betsy approached one of the local ladies she knew would be most likely to have information.

"Good morning, Mrs. Webb."

The judge's wife greeted her with a smile. "Good morning, Mrs. Wheeler."

"Am I right in assuming these are passengers of the latest ship to be claimed by the reefs?"

Mrs. Webb nodded. "Carysfort Reef, so I heard. The ship was carrying nearly 250 souls, and they are bringing them all here." She looked to Betsy with concern. "Good Lord, where are we going to place all these people?" Her eyes returned to scanning the crowd as she shook her head in dismay.

Betsy understood. If the ship was a loss, the passengers were in need of shelter for the interim until arrangements could be made for another ship to take them to their destination. Mrs. Mallory's boardinghouse had room for maybe a half dozen, perhaps more if they doubled up. The army camp did not have enough room either. It would be up to the citizens to provide accommodations. Her eyes followed Mrs. Webb's looking over the gathering of men, women and children, all travel weary from their ordeal of facing storm, reef, and an unforeseen detour in their journey. Many were without their possessions. An odd thought occurred to her; the residents of Key West were close to being outnumbered by transient passengers and military.

Mrs. Agatha reached her side and after introductions said, "Who are all these people?"

Betsy replied, "Shipwreck survivors," but held further explanation as Mrs. Mallory approached them.

The Irish boniface raised her voice to gain their attention. "Ladies! Ladies, please, come hither." She waited for the matrons of the island to gather around her. "Might ye see we have many here in need of charity? For sure more than I have beds ta spare. The army captain has set about providing tents but as ye can see der are families with some wee ones and those more aged dat such living t'would be a burden. Are there not those among ye willing ta open yer hearts and yer home ta provide dem shelter?"

Most of the ladies nodded.

"'Tis good. I knew dey could count on ye good Christian women. We're making a list of those in need of good shelter and of those willing ta provide and how much dey have ta spare, so we can make de best placements. Please see Lieutenant Newcomb over in front of Mr. Patterson's store."

Betsy began to move forward with the other ladies when Agatha's condescending voice stopped her.

"Mrs. Wheeler, you cannot mean to take in strangers living alone as you do? Why it isn't safe, and it would be unseemly if it were a man."

Betsy's eyes narrowed. "I cannot turn my back on those in need, and I know for a fact, Mrs. Mallory would not even consider sending someone my way that would cause even a hint of impropriety."

"Humph. I can see you will do as you will, but that does not mean I will do the same. I have these two children to consider as well as my own concerns."

Betsy pleaded for the victims in a reasonable voice hoping to persuade the old widow. "Mrs. Pary, have you taken a good look at those people behind you? They are well dressed, respectable looking, and I suspect God-fearing people. You have one of the largest homes on the island, and certainly, other than the boardinghouse, the one with the most room to spare. It is your duty as a Christian to provide shelter."

"I have a duty to my grandnephew first and foremost."

"Yes, but do you not also have a duty to not bring shame on your family?" Agatha gave her a quizzical look. "This community is too small to act so selfish. We are interdependent on one another. To refuse aide to those in need reflects badly on your family."

"But having strangers sleep in our home?"

"It wouldn't be much different than staying at the boardinghouse. Besides, it would only be until another ship can be arranged to take them to New Orleans. Surely you can abide a little discomfort for a few days."

The approach of a fine looking older gentleman silenced Agatha's tart response.

The gentleman tipped his hat. "Good morning, ladies."

Betsy turned to the man with a ready smile. "Good morning, Captain Bennington. Abby mentioned you were returning for a visit."

"Aye. I sailed in yesterday."

"How long do you plan to stay?"

"I can only spare a few weeks, I'm afraid." He pointedly looked from Betsy to her companion.

Betsy inwardly grinned catching the true nature of this meeting and curious to see Agatha's reaction. "Captain, this is my neighbor, Mrs. Agatha Pary. She is here on an extended visit from New York. Mrs. Pary, may I present Captain Richard Bennington, Abigail Eatonton's father."

Agatha maintained her outward composure despite her fluttering pulse. She inclined her head acknowledging the introduction. "What kind of ship do you captain?"

Mr. Bennington was aware of Mrs. Pary's widowed state and her salty tone intrigued him. This lady was crusty, and he couldn't resist the challenge of finding her softer side. "At present, none." He watched the interest fade from her eyes before proudly adding, "But I own a fleet of merchant vessels." The corner of his lip twitched when her eyes flared just the tiniest bit. "Do you like to sail, Mrs. Pary?"

"On occasion."

"And if I were to acquire a small sailing vessel would you care to join me on a pleasure cruise?"

Agatha's lips pursed and her eyes narrowed. The man was too bold and forward. She snapped her fan shut. "Not likely, sir." She turned to Betsy. "We should be going if we are to secure our choice of a family to shelter." She gave a barely civil nod to the impertinent man. "Good day, Captain."

Betsy watched the odd exchange, amused by the flirtatious undercurrent of the conversation, and its sudden end. She was also pleased by Agatha's unexpected agreement to aid the survivors. "It was good to see you, Captain Bennington. Please give my regards to Max and Abby."

Betsy and Agatha silently made their way to Mr. Patterson's store to convey their desire to provide shelter for a suitable family. For a man in charge of finding temporary housing for over two hundred souls, Lieutenant Newcomb was amazingly calm.

Betsy willingly gave up her own bed to two middle-aged sisters traveling together. She would take up sleeping on her sofa for the interim. There were several families in need and Agatha accepted Betsy's suggestion of taking in the one with three middle aged children as they were young enough to play with Henry but old enough not to be too much of a disruption. Annalise and Henry would move into Agatha's room freeing up two bedrooms for the family.

After seeing the sisters, Martha Jane and Marilyn Joyce Caldwell, settled in her home, Betsy returned to town to assist Lieutenant Newcomb and Mrs. Mallory with the other passengers. The army set up tents in the newly cleared area behind the salt ponds to accommodate the passengers not placed with residents. Then there was food, water, and bedding to be arranged. It was a monumental task, but they managed it with the help of many volunteers. Betsy was thoroughly worn out by the time she made her way home. It was nice to be greeted by the sisters instead of a quiet house. The three ladies talked over tea for several hours before finally retiring for the evening.

Late Monday morning, Betsy walked over to see how Agatha and Henry were faring with their house guests. As expected Agatha had much to complain about, but Henry was very much enjoying the attention he was receiving from his playmates. The eldest was a ten year old girl and the other two were boys, nine and seven. The boys became fast friends. Henry insisted on moving his sleeping pallet into their room the second night.

Chapter 6

Tuesday morning, a very tired and dirty Theodore trudged up Whitehead Street with visions of a bath, a meal, and a very long nap. The faces of five strangers in the living room made him question for a moment if he had entered the right house until a small blond bundle of energy appeared from behind one of them to launch himself at Theodore's legs.

"Poppa, I missed you!"

Theodore brushed his head and quietly said, "I missed you too, son."

Henry quickly backed away from him. "Poppa, you need a bath!"

Theodore chuckled. "I am sure I do. Where is Aunt Agatha and Annalise?"

"Annalise is taking care of Aunt Aggie. Her head hurts."

Theodore sent Henry off to find the maid with a message to start heating water for his bath. He then turned to his guests. He knew his aunt often feigned a headache to avoid situations she considered unpleasant, but it was odd for this family to have been accepted into their home for visitation if his aunt did not want visitors.

Another thought occurred as he stepped further into the room. These people weren't visitors. They were relaxed when he walked in; it was the reason he momentarily thought he was in the wrong house. They had the casual appearance of being at home together. The father was reading a paper, the boys were playing, and the girl and her mother were looking over a publication of *The World of Fashion and Continental Feuilletons*. They ceased these activities at his appearance; their posture now held somewhere between resident and guest, waiting for his reaction. Theodore walked towards the gentleman. "Hello, sir. I am Mr. Whitmore."

The middle-aged man rose to his feet and firmly shook Theodore's hand. "I am Horace Brooks and this is my wife, Rachel, my daughter, Grace, and my sons, John and Joshua. It's a pleasure to meet you, Mr. Whitmore."

Upon reaching shore this morning and anxious to see how his son had fared in his absence, Theodore had quickly left the company of Mr. Whitehead as he was approached by the head of the town council. He only peripherally noticed something was different in town as he made a beeline for home. He now recalled having seen the army tents, recently replaced by barracks on the north shore, now set up beyond the town proper. He realized two things: there must be many displaced people on the island, and the makings of a story.

"Likewise, Mr. Brooks. What circumstance has befallen your family to bring you to our humble abode?" He saw the man visibly relax as if he had been preparing himself for Theodore's displeasure and was now relieved to find acceptance. Theodore did not have an issue with providing shelter for a family in need, but he was extremely curious as to how his aunt had been convinced to take them in. It seemed so unlike her. She wasn't uncharitable, just overly cautious when it came to letting strangers disturb her peace.

Horace Brooks, a lanky man in his forties, slipped his hands into his pockets. "We were bound for New Orleans. Our ship, unfortunately, struck a reef on Saturday. Fortunately, we were rescued by some 'wrackers', I believe you call them, before she sank. All the passengers were brought to Key West. Your aunt was kind enough to take us in, otherwise, we would be in one of those tents."

"How many passengers were there?"

"I heard tell over two hundred."

Theodore nodded. The excitement he always felt when discovering a lead hummed in his veins now. The need for sleep was forgotten. A bath however was still critical. A week of sea, sun, sweat and hiking the hammocks left him feeling rank and unfit for company. "I would like to hear more Mr. Brooks after I have freshened up from my journey. If you would, please excuse me."

Theodore knocked on his aunt's door before going to his room. Annalise opened it just wide enough to see before stepping back and allowing him to enter. Her tiny nose wrinkled in displeasure as he passed by. He found his aunt fully dressed, lying on the made bed, propped up against the pillows. The curtains were drawn against the sunlight, leaving the room deeply shadowed.

"Hello, Aunt Agatha."

"I would say it was good to see you safe and sound, Theodore, but I suspect that awful odor is coming from your person. You are quite offensive, in case you didn't know. I suggest a bath and change of clothes are immediately required."

"The water is heating as we speak, Aunt."

"If you are here to ask about the strangers in this house, you best go see Mrs. Betsy. It was her doing." Just then the three boys went running past her door to Henry's room. His aunt cringed. "She insisted we take on a family of urchins to keep your son company. Now I haven't any peace."

As a response was not required of him, he didn't give one. Theodore backed out of the room closing the door behind him. Their conversation invoked a lot of emotions within him. He checked on the boys playing in Henry's room before going downstairs to retrieve the tub and the first bucket of water from the outdoor kitchen. He normally would bathe in the family room at night to save the work, but with a houseful of people in broad daylight, he decided to haul his bath up to his room.

As he worked he mulled over his aunt's conversation. For the first time, he noticed behind her harsh words, her feelings were different. Maybe it was because her critique wasn't directed at him that he was able to see she was secretly pleased with the situation, or maybe he was so tired, he was hallucinating. But it was her use of Mrs. Wheeler's Christian name that intrigued him most. There were only a few, very close friends whom she addressed by their first name. How did Mrs. Wheeler slip into such an elite category in a week?

Theodore left his room a half hour later feeling refreshed but famished. He dumped his dirty bath water in the yard and then went to the kitchen in search of food.

While Theodore was eating leftovers in the dining room, Henry entered and climbed up on the chair next to him. Sitting on his knees, Henry placed his elbows on the table and propped his head in his hands in a dejected manner.

Theodore hid his smile at the comical display. "Where are John and Joshua?"

"They went outside to play without me."

"Hmm. They said you were too little to play?"

Henry nodded, his head still perched in his hands. "Uh, huh."

Theodore nodded in understanding. "You won't always be too little. But promise me, when you get big, you won't treat little boys like they are too young to play. You'll remember what it feels like and be nicer, won't you?"

"Yes, sir."

"What did you do while I was gone?"

Henry perked up and smiled, raising his head from his hands. "Mrs. Betsy took me and Annalise to the lighthouse, and to see the fishes, and she played checkers, and she read me bedtime stories."

Theodore didn't know what to think. It seemed Mrs. Wheeler spent a good bit of time with his family over the last week. He wasn't sure if he was more grateful or concerned. He didn't want Henry to form such a strong attachment to a person who would only temporarily be in their lives.

The boys returned indoors and once again claimed Henry's attention. Finished eating, Theodore collected his writing pad and pencil intending to head into town for more details of the shipwreck and stranded passengers. He came across Annalise leaving his aunt's room.

"Did you run into any problems while I was gone other than housing the Brooks family?"

"The second day Mrs. Pary had one of her headaches and wanted peace and quiet. She asked me to get Henry out of the house. I didn't know where to go, so I did just as you said; we went to Mrs. Betsy. She took care of us for the day, and she settled everyone right down that night and the next. Weren't no trouble after that until the folks needed housing. Then Mrs. Pary got riled about keeping strangers. Mrs. Betsy calmed her down and made her see reason."

He nodded his approval. "I see. Well done, Annalise." It was obvious the young lady was impressed by and perhaps even idolized Betsy. It seemed his whole household was enamored with their neighbor.

Theodore spoke with Mr. and Mrs. Brooks again before he left. Even they mentioned the widow across the street. Her name was spoken by everyone in his household, as if he stepped away and somehow gave her permission to invade his home and family. It also kept her foremost in his mind, against his will, so that when he stepped out intending to go to town to learn more about the shipwreck, he instead went to her doorstep first. Her shingle read open, so he walked into the shop. She greeted him from the other side of the counter spanning her front room.

Betsy could not contain her joy in seeing Theodore again. Her greeting was more enthusiastic than usual. "Good to see you, Mr. Whitmore. Was your voyage a success?"

Theodore refrained from returning her smile with some difficulty. Somehow in a week, he forgot how her amazing blue eyes affected him. "Yes, it was. Mr. Whitehead gathered the information required of him, and I learned something of the area and the Indians. I wanted to thank you for taking care of my family while I was away and invite you for supper to show my gratitude."

"That isn't necessary, Mr. Whitmore. It was my pleasure to help. Henry is such a sweet boy."

"Yes, but I know my aunt can be trying."

"Mrs. Agatha means well."

He was surprised she could see past his aunt's words to the meaning behind them. Mrs. Wheeler was indeed a special person. "I would still like you to come to supper tonight." The voices from the room behind her surprised him. "I'm sorry, have I interrupted? You must have company."

She smiled. "I have taken in two sisters from the wreck." Betsy lifted the counter opening and beckoned him into her sitting room.

"Mr. Whitmore, this is Miss Marilyn Joyce and Miss Martha Jane Caldwell. They are sisters from Pennsville Township in New Jersey on their way to visit another sister in Louisiana."

Theodore bowed to each sister. "Miss Caldwell and Miss Caldwell. Pleased to make your acquaintance. I hope your stay is not unpleasant."

Marilyn Joyce was quick to reply first. "Not a'tall Mr. Whitmore. Mrs. Wheeler has made us feel most welcome. She has taken great care to see to our needs and those of your household in your absence."

Theodore nodded. "My family has mentioned her many times already. It is the reason for my visit. I have invited her to supper to express my gratitude. I would also like to extend the invitation to you nice ladies."

The sisters murmured their acceptance together.

"Good. May I look forward to hearing of your ordeal over supper?" When they gave him a questioning look, he added, "I am writing a story on the wreck for the *New York Weekly*."

Martha Jane said, "Oh, of course, we would be happy to oblige."

Theodore nodded his head. "Thank you. I will wish you all a good day and look forward to seeing you this evening." This time he nodded to all three ladies before making his way out of the house, not in a rush, but definitely with purpose.

Betsy suspected he found being alone with three ladies a little overwhelming. She followed him to the front door. "Good day, Mr. Whitmore." She watched him walk towards town. The visit seemed perfunctory on the surface. She hoped there was more underneath. Walking back into the sitting room, the sisters gave her knowing looks as they spoke to each other.

Martha Jane said, "My, he is one handsome man. Didn't his aunt say he was a widower the other day? If I was twenty years younger, I would be smitten too."

Marilyn Joyce dissented. "You would not, sister. You never got over your first beau. If you had, you would have married one of those many swains who tried courting you."

Martha Jane gave her sister a reproving look. "Well you know those boys were there for you. You were the beauty of the town. They only spoke to me because you were too shy to speak to them."

"I was not too shy. I just refused to make a spectacle of myself."

"Are you saying I did?"

Marilyn Joyce sighed deeply. "No sister, you didn't. Forgive me. I didn't mean to imply you had." She deliberately redirected the subject. "Mr. Whitmore seems very serious in nature. He doesn't look like he smiles much but still a charmer if ever I saw one."

Betsy smiled to herself enjoying their sisterly conversation. She was from a large family and can well remember having similar meaningless tiffs with her siblings. Something else she missed living on her own; no one with whom to occasionally argue with.

At the appointed hour of supper according to Mrs. Agatha's schedule, Betsy walked across the street with the sisters reminding them one final time not to converse during dinner. Marilyn Joyce and Martha Jane both murmured their assurances.

After the introductions and greetings were dispensed with Theodore said, "Mrs. Wheeler, I learned I have as yet one more thing for which I owe you a debt of gratitude. According to Annalise, it was you who provided the method for which Henry was able to learn the entire alphabet in just a few days. He recited it for me just a little while ago. I am quite impressed."

Betsy couldn't help the blush his praise generated. "It was of no consequence. I simply shared the method my mother used to teach me."

"Quite effective."

Betsy felt herself blush even more as his eyes warmly lingered on hers before he turned his attention to the Caldwell sisters.

"Ladies, I was wondering if you would share your story of surviving the shipwreck."

Marilyn Joyce said, "I am afraid there isn't much to tell Mr. Whitmore. Sister and I were in our cabin when the ship struck the reef. It was quite frightening the way the ship shuddered all around us as she hit. We immediately went to the forward cabin to learn our fate and there we huddled with the other passengers until help arrived several hours later."

Martha Jane added, "Well, that is other than making a quick trip back to our cabin for our valuables and there was some concern for the rising water in the hull. Captain McMullin assured us the wreckers would arrive in time, and so they did. Captain Houseman was first to arrive and being elderly ladies we were first to be taken off the *Maria*. The sail to Key West was uneventful."

Supper was announced just as Martha Jane finished speaking. It was a quiet group of seven adults that entered the dining room to be seated around the fully expanded table. The four boys, Grace and Annalise had their meal earlier and were now playing quietly in Henry's room. Theodore said grace and silence descended as the first course was served broken only by murmurs of politeness.

Presiding at the head of the silent table, Theodore decided a change needed to be made. "Our cook makes a wonderful turtle soup. I believe our next course is poached fish." Everyone momentarily stopped eating to look his way, but none dared to utter a rejoinder. Theodore looked to Betsy seated next to his aunt in the hopes of finding a co-conspirator. "The weather is quite warm for November. Do you find this to be a normal temperature for this time of year, Mrs. Wheeler?"

Forced to reply but unwilling to be caught in the middle, Betsy regarded him questioningly as she answered, "Yes, it is quite typical."

Aunt Agatha gave him a visual admonishment which only served to ignite his temper. Disregarding the guests gathered around the table, Theodore finally overruled his aunt's wishes. His words were measured and forceful albeit spoken in a moderate tone. "I am head of this household and if I wish to have a conversation with my meal, especially when we have guests, then so be it. We will, however, refrain from speaking with you, dear aunt, in deference to your digestion." He took another spoonful of soup as he continued to hold her gaze. She was first to look away and with a deliberate, sulky dismissal returned to eating her soup.

Betsy was a little dismayed and baffled by the exchange. She had not expected such poor manners from Mr. Whitmore but then maybe it was because he was tired. She cast a glance in his aunt's direction just in time to see the corner of her lip momentarily quirk upward. Was she secretly pleased with her nephew for standing up to her?

After a moment of awkward silence, Theodore realized engaging the others in conversation would be problematic, so he decided to distract them instead. "I have not had a chance to share with you the details of my trip." He looked to each of his guests. "Mr. and Mrs. Brooks, Misses Caldwells, you may not be aware, I sailed last Tuesday with our Collector of Customs, Mr. Whitehead, to visit the fishing villages of Charlotte Harbour on the western side of the Florida peninsula. Mr. Whitehead was tasked with collecting details of the Spanish Indians in residence there. We arrived at Charlotte Harbour last Thursday morning but were forced to wait until Friday for the winds to pick up and for the lieutenants to sound the bar for safe passage. The *Marion* sailed into the harbour only about two miles. From there, we rowed a boat another seven miles to one of the fish camps upriver." He paused to take a spoonful of his soup.

"The bay was quite large and tranquil. No birds, no breeze, even the water was quiet. The solitude was so complete; it was as if nature's domain was invaded by mankind for the first time. When we reached the first camp we were greeted by five friendly hounds yapping a chorus, but otherwise the camp was eerily empty. The lack of gear led us to surmise the Indians were away fishing. Having lost nearly a full day already, Mr. Whitehead did not want to further delay by waiting for their return, so he commenced to inspecting the insides of their housing."

Theodore paused his story to finish his soup so the next course could be served. He noticed the appalled looks of the females around the table just as he had intended except for Betsy, who stared at him in wonder, not as he intended. He knew how she felt. Her feelings were clear to be seen on her face. Another time and place…, but it was this time and this place and not meant to be, and so he didn't linger looking at her. Instead, he focused on his aunt, in defiance, as he resumed his story. He was pleased to note she was listening even though she pretended otherwise.

Betsy barely comprehended the words he was speaking. She was more enthralled with the novelty of his story telling, especially from a man who spent more time listening than speaking, but when he chose to tell a story, he did so with enthusiasm.

Mrs. Brooks was first to speak. "How disrespectful of Mr. Whitehead to enter a person's dwelling uninvited."

Theodore nodded. "I thought so as well, but the others seemed to think nothing of it. They assured me the Indians do not value privacy in the same way we do, so I said nothing. Mr. Whitehead worked his way into the first abode. When he came back out he likened it to Ichabod Crane's Schoolhouse in the *Legend of Sleepy Hollow*. 'One could get in but it was difficult getting back out.'" Theodore was relieved to see smiles appear on the faces of his listeners as they recognized the quote. "He then suggested I take a look so in I went. Their huts are made from palmettos, the largest of which was maybe fifteen feet square. It had a loft for corn, a hanging shelf to store crockery and two or three stools, nothing more and some even had less. I did not expect to find such a meager existence. Mr. Whitehead left his card at the chief's hut, and then we rowed the long distance back to the *Marion*."

Betsy asked, "Did you not find it difficult getting back out?"

"Oh, I did."

"Why is that?"

"The huts are made completely of thatched palms. Going in, you move inward with the palms but to return you must find your way against the pointed tips. The opening is small and easily lost when turned around inside."

Mr. Brooks asked, "How many villages did you visit?"

"Four. I believe that's all there were. The patriarch of the whole area is an old Spaniard named Caldez. He's about seventy years of age, and previously acquainted with Mr. Whitehead. Early morning Saturday, we paddled southward arriving at Caldez's fishery. His village is a little larger than the others with fifteen dwellings, one or two storehouses, about twenty men—some Spanish and some Indian—maybe six or eight squaws, and I lost count of the unclothed children running around, obviously of mixed blood.

"We arrived in time for breakfast. Caldez made obvious efforts to treat us to the limits of his hospitality. A burlap sack was spread out on the ground as a tablecloth. We were offered cold fish, cold potatoes and onions, bread and coffee. Caldez himself served us, carefully inspecting each plate, cup, and saucer. If he found unacceptable bits of debris, he scratched it off with his dirty fingernail."

Unwittingly caught up in the story Aunt Agatha cried out, "Oh my!" Her hand went to her throat, while the other ladies' eyes widened in horrified dismay.

"Oh yes! He then drew his hunting knife from his belt, cleaned it on his less than clean shirt and handed it to us to cut our food. However, we were forced to eat with our hands as there were no forks. Our appetites were such that the delivery mattered little.

"It took us until sundown to reach the next fishery, a great distance away. The trip was miserable with oppressive heat and no wind. We looked forward to supping in comparable comfort. At this camp we had forks for our meal, but alas! the knives were now missing leaving us to find other means of tearing apart our meat.

"This camp had nearly a dozen buildings inhabited by fifty or so men, women and children. We stayed up late sitting on the porch with the head fisherman until Mr. Whitehead satisfied his curiosity about their fishing business through a Spanish interpreter.

"We arose before daylight to make our way to the last fishery lying a mile or so up a river bordered by lush vegetation. The head fisherman was absent so Mr. Whitehead made his inquires as to population and dwellings. We returned to Caldez's camp in the early afternoon and were served much the same meal as breakfast the day before for which we were grateful. Our hosts also generously filled our boat with limes, fish, clams and such. Mr. Whitehead and I took a stroll towards the interior and found ourselves climbing a huge mound, taller than any house I've seen, composed entirely of oyster shells covered in vegetation. The immense number of shells it took to create it is astonishing. Caldez relayed the story—or tradition as he refers to it—of how the long ago Indians occupied their time when not hunting or at war by building the mound. The most curious thing about it, is there are no oyster beds in the vicinity, at least not at present. So how did they get the shells and get so many as to build the mound?"

Theodore looked to his captive audience for an answer not surprised to encounter only silence and shaking heads.

"It is a mystery. Caldez shared many stories about his ancestors with us. The one I found most interesting was in regards to Key West."

This peaked everyone's attention.

"The Indians living in the Keys and the ones on the mainland were of different tribes and as the islanders visited the mainland for the purposes of hunting a feud arose between the tribes. The mainlanders drove the islanders from key to key until they reached Key West and were forced to face a final battle which resulted in almost total extermination. It is said seventeen canoes of survivors were launched upon the waves. Caldez believes Providence guided them to Cuba where their descendants are yet to be seen."

Betsy nodded. "I have heard that story before. It is generally accepted as truth."

Aunt Agatha, finished with her meal, joined the conversation. "You mention their hospitality. Not one of the Indians you met with was hostile? I find it hard to believe. They must have wanted something in return."

"I don't know that it was some*thing* they wanted so much as to be left alone. Mr. Whitehead and I discussed their situation on the way home. The reason for his trip was supposedly due to concerns over fishing rights, but they should not be in question as the Spaniards were residents even before we declared our independence from Brittan. It leads one to think there may have been an ulterior motive. Mr. Whitehead wonders if the Indians have some sense that our government is seeking information for future relations considering the growing tensions with the tribes to the north."

Mr. Brooks said, "Information to use in case of war with the Indians?"

"Possibly or maybe it will be used for gathering them in preparation for the move west."

Betsy said, "They would move these Indians even though they have harmed no one?"

Theodore nodded. "President Jackson has no use for Indians. The Indian Occupation Act is all inclusive no matter the character of the tribe or their location."

Mrs. Brooks asked, "How would they be aware of our government's intentions?"

Mr. Brooks shook his head. "I imagine word travels as rapidly among the Indians as it does among the whites."

Theodore nodded in agreement. "Most likely so."

Agatha signaled an end to the meal by standing which forced the men to stand as well. "Shall we adjourn to the parlour?" They returned to the sitting room to continue a more mundane conversation.

A short while later, Theodore noticed the mantel clock. "My how the time as flown, please excuse me. It is time I put Henry to bed." As he started up the steps, from the top of the stairs came a small voice.

"I want Mrs. Betsy to tuck me in too."

Theodore felt he needed to firmly put an end to his son's attachment. "Mrs. Betsy is occupied; you will have to settle for me." Henry started to protest, but a look was enough to quell his dissension. He left the landing to return to his room. Theodore turned to look towards Betsy and saw her disappointment. "Please wait for my return, Mrs. Wheeler." At her brief nod, he continued up the stairs.

Betsy felt elated by little Henry's request and crushed as Theodore effectively dismissed her from the ritual. She tried to hide her feelings from the others in the room, but failed for Agatha was quick to comment.

"Bedtime rituals are for family."

Theodore returned but didn't enter the room. From the doorway, he gently said, "Mrs. Wheeler, may I speak with you in private, please?"

Curiosity got the better of her, along with a soft spot for his pleading look. She rose and walked across the room.

Agatha spoke to the room in general, but her words were clearly meant for Betsy. "It wouldn't be done in my day. A lady barely spoke privately to a groom before she married him, much less to a man she has no ties with."

Betsy's step faltered with Agatha's comment, but still she continued to the door. Why would she mention groom and marriage? Did Agatha already see marriage in their future? Maybe Theodore had expressed his thoughts in private leading her to such a conclusion. Unbidden, hope soared in Betsy's chest.

Theodore turned away before anger got the best of him in front of company. He mumbled to himself as he led the way to his office set up in the front room. "She's a fine one to talk of propriety before marriage." He stopped at the door to let Betsy precede him, then followed her into the room leaving the door open.

"Mrs. Wheeler…"

"Please call me Betsy. I think this situation," Betsy looked around the room indicating their privacy, "now puts us on terms of familiarity."

Theodore gave her a long look. He intended to limit her intimacy with his family by keeping her from Henry's bedside, but now out of concern for her feelings, he managed to put them in an even more intimate setting. *What was I thinking?* Obviously he wasn't thinking at all. Why did he react so strongly to this woman? He didn't want to. He was still grieving for Margaret. He didn't want to give Betsy false illusions, either. He brought her in here to ease her disappointment. He must not give her more to be disappointed about, so he deliberately ignored her request.

"Mrs. Wheeler, I don't think it is wise for Henry to get too attached to you when we are not here long term. Besides, it is my opinion bedtime rituals should be reserved for family."

His use of her proper name said volumes for how he felt about her. It cut across her heart, effectively dashing her budding hopes as did his reminder of their temporary presence in her life. She looked down for a moment until she was sure her eyes would not betray her disappointment, but her heart was still heavy when she brought her gaze to his. "I understand, Mr. Whitmore. You can be assured it won't happen again."

Her dejected tone made him want to comfort the hurt he had caused. "Mrs. Wheeler, please don't take this wrong. I do appreciate your generous nature and the way you stepped in to help my son and my household while I was away. I am thankful you were there to comfort Henry in my absence. Because of you, he was not troubled by it, but now that I'm back, it must end."

"I agree it would be unwise to continue. I was only momentarily disappointed because I enjoyed taking care of him, and I suppose because, for a moment, I knew what it felt like to be a mother."

Her wistful tone struck him deep in the chest and nearly made him reconsider his mandate. He also had no idea how to respond to such a personal statement without making matters worse, so he sought to quickly end the ill-conceived tête-à-tête. "Shall we rejoin the others?" He held out his arm for her to precede him out of the room.

Betsy led the way back to the sitting room feeling as if her foolish dreams had been ripped to shreds. She was eager to return to the privacy of her own home. When the Caldwell sisters declared it time to leave, she was happy to comply even though she suspected they did so on her behalf. The sisters bid her goodnight as soon as they returned to her house leaving her alone. She heard their whispered conversation behind the bedroom door but didn't concern herself with their speculations. Instead, she pondered how she could have misjudged Theodore's feelings.

She began to feel ashamed of herself when she thought about it from Theodore's point of view. Of course he wasn't ready for a relationship. She knew from experience a year was not long enough to grieve for someone you love. Besides he has his son to worry about and work to occupy his thoughts. He had no room in his life or his heart for another woman.

But then again, his eyes betrayed him. He looked at her with tender feelings, at least until his rational thoughts told him otherwise. Each time they met, for a moment, she would see desire in his eyes. Surely she wasn't imagining it. But if he wasn't ready to accept his feelings what could she do? She was taking a risk waiting on his heart to heal before he decided it was time to return to New England, but what choice did she have? Her feelings for him were already too strong to allow her to reconsider any of the other men on the island. The only thing she could do was pray for him to be ready to love again.

Chapter 7

Friday afternoon, three days after Mr. Whitmore's supper party, Betsy and the Caldwell sisters ventured to the mercantile to pick up some necessities. The sky was overcast but not threatening and the temperature was balmy making for a pleasant walk. They were cheerily chatting with each other as they entered the store and proceeded to browse the shelves, taking their time in picking up the essential items they planned to purchase. A half an hour later, by mutual consent, they gathered at the back counter. Mr. Patterson was in the process of totaling their expenditures when raised voices reached them from outside.

Mr. Patterson's gaze flew to the front window. "Not again!" He came around the counter and made straight for the front door with the curious ladies on his heels. He stopped at the edge of the front steps to watch the commotion across the street. Mr. Patterson explained, "Last night this same crowd had all of us on edge. They were fussing and fighting amongst themselves, but with such fervor, we feared any moment they would start assaulting our property and persons."

Betsy crossed behind the sisters to the front corner of the piazza and shaded her eyes against the sun. She was a few feet elevated from the ground giving her a good view of the events unfolding at Mr. Browne's wharf. The confrontation brought his business to a halt. Betsy had to raise her voice to be heard as she asked Mr. Patterson, "Do you know the cause of their unrest?"

"No, I have not heard any say what the cause may be. My guess is too much drink and free time. Some thanks our guests are showing for our hospitality." Belatedly, he remembered to whom he spoke. "Pardon me ladies, present company excluded, of course."

The sisters murmured acceptance of his apology. Meanwhile, the hostilities of the gathering crowd escalated. They were arguing over each other making it impossible for Betsy to determine what the disagreement was about, but it appeared the displaced shipwreck survivors were the offended party. The passengers were arguing defensively while the warehouse owner, Mr. Browne, tried to wage reason. She wondered what could have ignited such a heated exchange.

From the corner of her eye she saw the measured strides of Mr. Whitmore approaching. He made his way to the edge of the crowd, but did not engage in the argument. He instead took interest in the events as they transpired much as she imagined a journalist would. His keen observation fascinated her. Caught up in watching Theodore, she was unaware anger had escalated to violence until he moved to intervene. Theodore waded into the fray despite the overwhelming numbers and dozens of men involved. He grabbed the collar of a man at least a half foot taller, halting him in his tracks, and placed his other hand squarely against the chest of another. He said only one word, his tone measured, and his voice commanding respect.

"Enough."

He said it loud enough to be clearly heard where she stood, yet he hadn't shouted it. The reaction of the crowd was immediate. They all stopped their arguing to listen to Theodore. He now spoke in low tones she couldn't hear, but she could see the result. He diffused the situation and the group began to disperse.

By the time the sheriff and marshal arrived there was little to be done. She continued to stand there and watch as the sheriff, Theodore, and some of the men talked. When all was said, Theodore moved away in her direction. He spied her on the piazza watching and doffed his hat as he continued walking away. The act was innocent enough unless one saw the intensity of the gaze he sent her way. She couldn't help it. Her heart fluttered and a smile quirked the corner of her mouth. It could have been a courteous gesture, something he would have done to anyone he made eye contact with, but somehow it felt as if they made a deeper connection. Then again, she supposed she could have imagined it from her desire and not from reality. She cleared her face of the evidence of her reaction, then glanced to the side to see if the others had noticed.

The sisters moved to either side of her.

Martha Jane said, "That's a fine man. Lucky is the woman who catches his fancy. He'll take proper care of his lady."

Marilyn Joyce peered intently at Betsy's face. "You have set your cap on him."

Betsy was embarrassed her feelings were so easily discovered, but one look at Marilyn Joyce and she knew it was pointless to deny it.

* * *

Saturday the ladies took a walk into town to stretch their legs and discovered the army was heavily patrolling the streets. It was the same on Sunday when they walked to church. Visiting with neighbors before the service, they learned many islanders had written letters requesting protection resulting in the army being called in after the disturbances of Thursday night and the one they witnessed on Friday. It had been quiet around town since then.

Today's service was a special one as Captain Max and Abby were baptizing their son. Betsy and Jonathon were Emily's God-parents and were honored to be chosen again for baby Christoff. Now four months old, he liked to move about, a lot. Betsy had trouble keeping a secure hold of him as he squirmed in her arms. At least he was quiet. Even when the minister baptized him with water and oil, he didn't utter more than a whimper, only waved his arms and kicked his legs vigorously in protest. Half way through the proceedings she briefly looked out over the congregation. As usual she was drawn to Theodore. His head was down as if in prayer. A small fist to her chest brought her attention back to the moment at hand. When she was finally able to return the infant to Abby, she found her back and arm muscles were tight from the strain.

After the service, Theodore and his family paid their respects to the minister and to the Eatonton's. They greeted Betsy too but did not linger to talk as Mrs. Agatha was in her usual hurry to return home. Betsy and the Caldwell sisters were invited to dinner at the Eatonton's to further celebrate the special occasion.

* * *

Wednesday, Betsy sadly waved good-bye to Martha Jane and Marilyn Joyce as they and the other passengers from the *Maria* continued on their journey to New Orleans. For half a month her home held conversation and companionship. Returning afterwards, she was greeted with silence. Unable to bear it after only a few hours, Betsy went to the boardinghouse for supper. On Thursday, she didn't even make it to midday before she wandered into town on the pretense of picking up a copy of the *Key West Gazette*. Finding a captive audience gathered near the Custom House she read aloud the story of the shipwreck. Theodore approached from nearby to listen.

> On Thursday last, after a rather free indulgence to Bacchus, they, from some imaginary cause, became dissatisfied and threatened the lives of Captain McMullen and some of his crew. They evidenced their feelings that night, by the most boisterous behavior; in consequence of which the inhabitants at the lower end of the town were prevented from sleeping and were in momentary expectation of having their homes assaulted. On Friday afternoon they collected in such numbers on Browne's wharf that the proprietor was obliged to suspend business. Here a general battle ensued among them, in which it was difficult to tell who or how many were engaged, and a disfiguration of eyes and noses followed, which by no means added to the engaging appearance of the party.

Betsy made eye contact with Theodore recalling his involvement in the scuffle. She continued reading.

> The citizens generally became alarmed for the safety of their property. Under these circumstances letters were addressed by the proper authorities to Major Glassell, commandant of the post, and Captain Shubrick, of the United States sloop of war Vincennes, then in port, requesting them to co-operate in protecting the citizens of Key West from

aggression. These calls were promptly answered; a detachment of marines under the command of Lieutenant Engle, from the Vincennes landed and remained during the night at the warehouse of Pardon C. Greene, whilst a detachment of United States troops under the command of Lieutenant Manning, patrolled the streets. As soon as it was known that steps were taken to prevent or suppress any riotous conduct, the mob dispersed and remained perfectly quiet, up to the time of their sailing on yesterday for New Orleans.

Had not these steps been taken, it is more than probable that some serious mischief might have resulted, as the individuals composing the mob were generally under the excitement of liquor during their stay here.

We understand that in consequence of this occurrence, and the prevalence of unfavourable winds, the Vincennes has been detained at this place longer than was contemplated on her first arrival.

Since the above was in type, we have been informed that the disturbance originated with a Mr. Smith (one of the contractors), who had illegally exacted money from some of the unfortunate individuals. Upon the interference of some of our citizens he was compelled to disgorge.[2]

Finished with the story Betsy folded the paper. Her listeners dispersed.

Theodore approached her before she could turn away. "Please allow me to escort you home, Mrs. Wheeler."

"If you like, Mr. Whitmore."

He fell in step beside her. She looked his way but said nothing. Although she was secretly pleased he sought her out, she didn't want to get her hopes up again. He pulled away from her several times before; she did not expect this time to be any different.

"How have you been, Mrs. Wheeler?"

"Fine, Mr. Whitmore, and you?"

"I am well. How does your business fair?"

"I am thankful to have a few dress orders for the Christmas season to keep me moderately busy."

They descended into silence for a moment before Betsy said, "Did you know the fight you broke up was a disagreement over money?"

"Hmm. I was in the bar Thursday night when the argument started. Afterwards, I informed Mr. Whitehead of Mr. Smith's actions. I was with him and the marshal when they confronted Mr. Smith. I also informed Dr. Strobel." Theodore grimaced. It was unlike him to brag about his work.

She smiled. "So then it was your doings that brought an end to the disagreement not to mention the article would have been incomplete without your contribution."

"I suppose that is true." Unbidden, her smile reminded him of last Sunday. She was holding the Eatonton baby and he saw a flash of what the future could be. His mind conjured an image of her smiling at him while holding their child. Instant guilt made him shy away from the idea. He was a man torn. He had a growing desire to have Betsy in his life, but he still loved Margaret, still missed her every day, and wanted to honor her memory. Even though the anniversary of her passing was only a few days away, and socially he would be free to remarry, he was not ready to make any serious overtures.

Betsy felt as if she read his thoughts. Walking side by side she wasn't able to see his features, but she was so attuned to his being, she felt the flashes of interest closely followed by guilt and grief. She understood and respected them, but what if he were to leave before he was able to move past his mourning? Where would it leave her besides another year older and alone? She put aside a secure future with Mr. Casey in the hopes of what might could be between her and Theodore. She prayed her decision wasn't in vain.

Theodore interrupted her thoughts. "I don't believe I have ever asked how you came to live on this island?"

She welcomed the distraction. "Did you know my husband was a tailor?"

"Yes."

"Ben first heard of this island in his uncle's shop. John Simonton was in New York on business when he stopped by the shop to order a new suit. Mr. Simonton, of course, extolled all the glories of the island and casually mentioned there was need of a good tailor. We had been married a year and while Ben dreamed of opening his own shop, he lacked the faith or conviction of being successful. In New York, he would have been just another tailor in town. But on this island with its growing community of professional men, he would be the only tailor in town."

They arrived at her home.

As Betsy climbed the front porch steps, she said, "Six months later we opened shop in this house. Another six months later, he was putting in motion his plans to open a shop in town so we could have more room to start a family. In the meantime, we were hopeful and happy."

Her sad reminiscent smile tugged at Theodore's heart in several ways. He wanted to erase her sorrow. She was a woman who deserved joy in her life. But was it fair to make her wait until he was ready and was he the one who could make her happy? When it didn't seem as if she would continue, curiosity made him prompt her. "What happened to your husband?"

Betsy was brought back to the present by Theodore's question. She had to push aside the image of her sick husband lying on his death bed to answer. "Yellow Fever."

When he realized she wasn't going to elaborate, Theodore doffed his bowler and turned to walk to his porch. He felt remorse for having stirred up her painful memories, but there wasn't anything he could do to fix it.

* * *

Two weeks before Christmas, a choir was started from a casual comment about wassailing made during dinner at the boardinghouse. In a matter of a few days a group of interested citizens gathered for their first rehearsal. Betsy was thrilled with the idea and impatiently waited for the appointed evening. It also gave her something to dwell on besides Theodore.

They had several musicians: Dr. Waterhouse and his violin, Roberts with his flute, and when they occasioned to be ashore, Jonathan Keats played a harmonica, and Tim Sudduth played guitar. The men were able to harmonize well enough for the group to practice four songs. One of them was Betsy's favourite; *What Child is This?* The group had fun caroling during Christmas week and the other residents seemed to enjoy their performance. It helped a little in making their tropical home feel more like a New England Christmas.

Theodore especially appreciated the carolers' visit. He was feeling displaced and out of sorts with the holiday. He hadn't expected to miss the season; especially the way New York wrapped itself in the wonder of Christmas. The decorations and the good cheer of the people transformed the city into something magical.

The choir was honored to be asked to perform during the Christmas Eve wedding reception for the light keeper's third daughter, Nicolosa Mabrity. She and William Bethel were married by Judge Webb in the early evening followed by a potluck supper in front of the Custom House. Afterwards, the men played music for dancing.

The wedding party was quite festive with pleasant weather, a starry sky, good music, and plenty of drink. The bride and her very proud father, Michael Mabrity, started the dancing and were soon joined by others. Captain Max asked Betsy to dance as the third song was starting. They noticed Jonathon standing on the perimeter watching Esperanza and her family, as they whisked by for the third time.

Max said, "Is he ever going to have enough confidence to ask for her hand?"

Betsy's smile was wry. "He has learned Spanish and made friends in the Cuban community for her sake. It seems all that is left is to ask for her hand. I understand his hesitance. Esperanza told me he will only have one chance. If her father refuses, he will never reconsider. That kind of pressure is enough to make anyone hesitant."

"True, but he also runs the risk of appearing weak by delaying so long in asking. If she were my daughter, four years is too long."

"Oh, you would allow Emily to marry at the tender age of sixteen to a gentleman almost twice her age who doesn't speak your language?"

Max looked down at Betsy in shock. "Well, when you put it that way..."

"Esperanza was sixteen when they met. She is nearly twenty-one now.

And Jonathon, how old is he? Thirty, I think."

"I believe so."

"So you see, he had to wait for her to prove to her father she was set on having him. Plus, he needed you to advance him to captain to be able to afford a wife. and it took him two years to learn the language which was Abby's idea if I'm not mistaken."

"Yes, it was."

Betsy saw him look towards his wife, nod and smile. She was sitting with a group of other matrons rocking a sleeping Christoff. Two year old Emily was not far away being twirled in the arms of Fish, one of Max's crewmen. They were a happy family, and Betsy was happy for her friends, but it still gave her a twinge of jealousy. In the next turn, she noticed Theodore standing next to his aunt's chair... watching her. The resulting nervous flutter caused her to miss a step, landing on Max's boot.

"Hey there, what happened to Betsy, full of grace?"

"Must have been a tree root." She pretended to search the ground they had just passed.

"Sure it doesn't have something to do with Mr. Whitmore?"

Her head snapped up in surprise. "What do you know of Mr. Whitmore?"

"From the look of him, he is smitten with you. What has been going on between you two? As your self-appointed protector, should I be concerned?"

"Not at all. He is still in mourning for his wife."

Max looked down at Betsy with a quirky grin. "And when he is done mourning, will you have him?"

The music ended and they broke apart to applaud. Max leaned toward her to whisper, well aware Mr. Whitmore was watching from the other side of the yard. "How do you feel for our dear, Mr. Whitmore?"

Betsy knew Max was half teasing her, the other part was brotherly concern, and so she answered him honestly. "Cautiously, hopeful." She gave him a small curtsey. "Thank you for the dance."

"My pleasure."

"Why don't you see if Annalise will mind the baby so you can dance with Abby?"

"I believe I will."

Max left her side with purposeful strides. She turned to seek out Jonathon. She had an idea. He was so intently focused on Esperanza, she approached his side unnoticed. "You should ask her to dance."

Jonathon looked to Betsy in surprise. He wondered how long she had been standing there. "Pardon me? You want to dance?"

"No, you want to dance," she nodded towards Esperanza, "with Miss Sanchez."

"You don't think her father would consider it improper?"

"Not if you ask her father if she may dance. I think it would be a good test to find out how he feels about you."

Jonathon had been looking for a way to do that very thing; how to test Esperanza's father's reception to his proposal of marriage without risking outright rejection? Betsy was right. Tonight was his opportunity. He was feeling daring, and it appeared as if Mr. Sanchez was in a good mood.

Betsy smiled as she watched Jonathon walk directly to Mr. Sanchez. They exchanged greetings and she assumed Jonathon asked his question. There was an assessing pause from Mr. Sanchez, long enough to cause concern for all involved before he reluctantly gave a slight nod. Esperanza, who had been watching her father closely, nearly squealed in delight before checking her reaction. Betsy watched her recover herself and politely thank her father before walking away with Jonathon. They kept a few inches of proper distance between them as they joined in the country dance that had already begun.

A few moments earlier, Agatha spoke to her nephew from her seated position while her eyes remained focused on the dancing couples. "I don't know what you see in that girl. She is nothing more than a flirtatious hussy."

Theodore pulled his gaze away from Betsy and Jonathon to look at his aunt. "Whatever do you mean, Aunt?"

"Mrs. Wheeler. First she practically drapes herself all over Captain Eatonton, and then when he walks away in disgust, she moves on to the next man she finds standing alone."

"Aunt Agatha, you are mistaken in your observations. Mrs. Wheeler has not done the least thing improper in the eyes of these islanders."

"Exactly. Here propriety might as well not exist. I'm surprised they aren't dancing naked in the streets."

Annalise, sitting in the chair next to her, gasped in shock. She had never heard anyone use the word 'naked'—ever—much less in public.

"Aunt Agatha!" Theodore was appalled, just as she intended. His forehead creased in consternation. His aunt was up to something. She was intentionally trying to shock him. He didn't know what she was about and he really didn't want to stay in her company long enough to figure it out. His gaze went to the last place he had seen Betsy. She now stood alone watching something off to his left and smiling. He couldn't follow her gaze as he was forced to respond to the Eatonton's greetings.

Captain Max held out his hand to Theodore. "Good evening, sir"

"Good evening to you."

Abby shifted the child to her hip. "We were wondering if Annalise would be willing to watch our children for a few moments so we could enjoy a dance?"

Agatha looked to Annalise. "It is fine with me so long as you are able to keep your eye on Henry too."

Annalise nodded. "Certainly, ma'am."

"I have no objection. Would you excuse me, please?" Theodore nodded to the group and took the opportunity to leave.

Abby heard Mrs. Pary's disparaging remarks of Betsy as they approached and would like nothing better than to set this woman straight on her poor opinion of her friend. She watched the old lady as she carefully chose her words. Max laid a hand on her arm in restraint, knowing too well what his wife was intending. She handed him the squirming infant. She turned back to Mrs. Pary and discovered a fleeting smile before her face returned to its usual petulant expression. Curious Abby turned to see what amused her from across the yard. It was Theodore asking Betsy to dance. She looked back at Mrs. Pary in shock. "You approve of them!"

Agatha turned to Abby, who was still gaping at her. "Close your mouth, dear. Of course I do."

"Then why the ruse?"

"My nephew has been in mourning for a year. I am afraid he needs a push to realize it is time to move on and forbidden fruit is the sweetest."

Abby was forced to revise her opinion of this woman. She was not merely cantankerous; she was also a skillful manipulator. "Careful you do not underestimate how much he respects your wishes. Your plan may go awry."

"Nonsense, he is his own man. I am merely a family nuisance he puts up with out of respect for his father."

"I pray you are correct."

Max took Abby's arm and placed it on his leading her away before any more was said. "Come sweetheart, let's have our dance."

Jonathon and Esperanza gracefully danced past the Eatonton's.

Esperanza was enjoying the momentary freedom from her parents and the nearness of the man she loved. "I am proud of you. Your Spanish was nearly perfect even if your accent was not. *Padre* was impressed. I am sure that is why he consented."

"I care little why, I am only grateful that he did." Their hands touched as they traded places in the dance. He wished he could grasp her hand and walk down to the beach in private. He could feel her father's eyes following his every move, but despite it, he would enjoy this moment. It didn't stop him from wanting more and now her father's consent to a dance gave him hope for more. He smiled as he gazed into her coffee colored eyes. She was the most beautiful creature he had ever seen and time only enhanced it.

The song ended too soon. When Jonathon stood still looking at her, Esperanza cast a nervous glance towards her family. "Jonathon, you must return me to my father immediately, or you will lose all you have gained this evening."

Jonathon pulled his mind away from his wayward thoughts. "Of course." They turned and walked back, perhaps an inch closer than before but still not touching.

"Maybe my father is coming to accept I love you. He has stopped bringing home other men for me to meet. I believe it is time you should practice your proposal in Spanish."

Jonathon smiled inwardly and kept his eyes focused ahead. "I have done so every day since I started taking lessons. I am ready."

"But not tonight."

"No, not tonight. We will watch for the right moment. Once we are engaged, may I kiss you?"

Esperanza's heart leapt at the thought, but kisses would have to wait. "No, not until we are married. You know this."

"And if I steal a kiss?"

Her eyes grew wide with alarm. "You had better not. At least not unless it is in private. And we will not be allowed to be private."

More rules. He prayed it was a short engagement, almost as hard as he prayed her father would consent to the marriage.

Theodore stopped in front of Betsy and bowed. "May I have this dance?"

Betsy was speechless. It was every girl's dream to have the man they were smitten with make a beeline in their direction and ask them to dance. He must have read the answer in her eyes because without a word from her, he gestured for her to precede him into position with the other couples. She expected to feel his hand touch the small of her back but to her disappointment it did not. Of course, he wouldn't. It was an intimacy reserved for established couples, still she hoped.

They now stood facing each other in line with the other couples as the music started. The first turn in the dance allowed their hands to touch. The warmth of his grasp radiated up her arm. It was a good thing he had to let her go or she would never have been able to concentrate on the steps of the dance.

She hadn't given much thought to hands before but within his firm clasp her hand felt dainty. Theodore's fingers were thick, making her wonder how he managed to hold a writing pen. Ben's hands had been long and tapered with nimble fingers. Fine hands for a tailor. But they had certainly never provoked the feeling of femininity generated by Theodore's clasp.

The dance did not give them time to speak. When it was over they clapped for the musicians and the other dancers then turned to each other.

"Thank you for the dance, Mr. Whitmore."

"Thank you for the pleasure of your company, Mrs. Wheeler." When the musicians started a reel, Theodore pulled her to the side near Henry and Annalise but away from his aunt. "I am not much of one for these lively dances."

Betsy looked up at him and smiled. "I have noticed you seem to prefer all things quiet, controlled, and orderly."

He whispered close to her ear in his deep voice. "Is that a character flaw?"

Betsy felt the sound vibrate in her being. It was more intoxicating than the wine. "No, but it does leave room for improvement." Betsy noticed the children behind Theodore and gestured for him to look. Henry and Emily were dancing, doing their best to mimic the adults' movements. They watched them until the dance ended and then clapped for their performance. Henry bowed to them just as he had seen other adults do and Emily bowed following Henry's lead.

Betsy and Theodore couldn't help laughing.

All good things must come to an end and tonight was no exception. Betsy thoroughly enjoyed the evening. She walked home in the company of Theodore and his family and even his aunt's sometimes bitter remarks did not bother her.

* * *

Betsy awoke Christmas morning and wondered what was going on in the house across the street. Did Saint Nicholas visit Henry?

She wished she could be part of their family gathering. Instead, Betsy celebrated Christmas and New Years the same as in years past, in the company of those gathered around Mrs. Mallory's table. It was pleasant enough to pass the time with others who did not have family of their own. Still she dreamed one day…

Maybe 1832 would be her year for love.

Chapter 8

Key West, January 1832

Theodore folded the *New York Weekly* he received in the post from Bob. The cover story was the same as the one he read in the *Niles Register* describing the horrible flooding, winter storms, and starvation plaguing the Choctaw Indians on their forced pilgrimage from their southern homelands to the Arkansas territory. Only the most hardened could read of such things and not feel pity for the natives. The *Arkansas Gazette* quoted one of the chiefs describing their ordeal as 'a trail of tears and death'. This was only the first of the tribes to be moved west. Was there any chance the others would be any less tragic? And what of the Florida Indians? How long would they be allowed to stay before President Jackson forced them to move? He knew without a doubt, they would be forced to move; it was only a matter of time.

He laid down the paper staring straight ahead as a startling idea occurred to him. Perhaps here was the story he needed to follow.

Indians fascinated him. They had ever since his father took him to visit a Lenape village when he was a child of six or seven. He couldn't recall why they had gone but the impressions of seeing the tribe for the first time were clear, especially of the boys his age running around barefoot with loose clothing and bows and arrows. To him they were having great fun while he, in contrast, was covered neck to toe and expected to stand quietly beside his father.

Eventually, his father took pity on his wistful looks and allowed him to play with the native children for several hours. Despite the language barrier, they communicated well enough to get along, and he was welcomed into their activities. By the time he returned to his father, Theodore had discarded his jacket, shirt and socks, and he was covered in dirt. He tried running around without shoes but his feet were too tender to keep up with his new found friends. He expected his father to chastise him, but he merely shook his head with a smile and herded Theodore down to the river where he took out his handkerchief to wash off the dirt and redress him. Theodore sadly waved goodbye to his new friends.

On the return trip home, he excitedly shared his experience with his father and the other men in the carriage. They, unlike his aunt, tolerated the non-stop chatter. He then asked dozens of questions about the Indians which his father patiently answered as best he could until twilight descended. He then asked Theodore to kindly give their ears some peace and quiet. For days after, Theodore continued to plague his father with questions. Then one day, his father brought home some books for him to read. Theodore had been studying Indians ever since; from the first attempts to indoctrinate them to the current efforts to move them, and the politics Congress used over the years to achieve their goals. He occasionally visited the various tribes of New England before he was married. He wrote many articles, first for his school paper, and later for Bob. Theodore admired the Indians' stoic nature, dedication to family, and reverence for the land. Of course, they weren't always peaceful and when they behaved with savagery, he tried to understand their motivations.

The more Theodore thought about the Florida Indians and their situation the more certain he became this was what he was meant to do. Some would say it was his fate or his destiny, but Theodore believed God brought him to this place and time to serve His purpose, and He had just revealed it.

Excitement flowed through his veins. Not just for the sake of a newsworthy story, but also for the possibility he could build sympathy for the plight of the Indians and their desire to keep their homeland. If he could bring enough public sentiment to bear for them to stay, then maybe there was a chance Congress would leave them be. Not only could this be a good story, there was a noble purpose to pursue. He had the power to tell both sides of the story and doing so just might change the opinion of the populace enough to change the government's course of action. Wouldn't that be something amazing?

Inwardly, he laughed at himself. It was an unlikely outcome, but it was a goal worthy of pursuit.

His knowledge of the Seminoles was limited to the articles he read before leaving New York. He would start with learning more about them, and the best way to do that was to visit them. If he was seriously going to pursue this story, he should meet the people involved, see where they live, and what kind of life they would be forced to leave. Making travel arrangements to central Florida would be his first task. A visit to the army commander seemed the logical place to start since he would need permission to be on the reservation.

An hour later, Lieutenant Newcomb ushered him into Major Glassell's office. The major painfully stood to greet him before collapsing back to his seat and returning his feet to a well-worn footstool. Theodore learned on his last visit that the officer suffered from dropsy. It was apparently bothering him more than usual today.

Major Glassell greeted him cordially. "What can I do for you today, Mr. Whitmore?"

Theodore was not one to waste words on small talk if he could avoid it. He knew from his last visit the major felt the same way. "I understand there is an Indian Reservation in Central Florida."

"Yes. That is correct."

"Could you direct me to the person I need to speak with to arrange a visit?"

"Why ever would you want to visit the Indians? I was happy enough to be reassigned from that God-forsaken outpost."

"You've been there?"

Major Glassell grimaced. "I was previously stationed at Fort King Cantonment after personally supervising its construction in 1827. Are you familiar with the location?"

"No sir."

Major Glassell instructed Theodore to retrieve a rolled up map from the corner of the room. He did so and unrolled it across the major's desk. Glassell put his feet on the floor, scooted his chair closer, and then reached for his spectacles. The map was a crudely drawn depiction of the Florida peninsula with sparse details. The major pointed to Tampa Bay above Charlotte Harbour half way up the western coastline. "Fort Brooke is here at the mouth of the Hillsborough River." His finger traveled northeast into the upper center of the interior. "About a hundred miles this way through unsettled country is Fort King, positioned just north of the reservation." He then pointed to the upper right coastline. "Saint Augustine and Fort Marion are located here."

Major Glassell sat back in his chair and lit his pipe speaking around the bit as he did so. "I spent two years as the commanding officer of Fort King before it was closed." He puffed on his pipe to get the draw going and then added, "Glad to leave, I was. Too much heat, mosquitoes, and conflict for my taste."

Theodore thought the heat and mosquitoes must have been bad if Glassell considered them worse than Key West, but he didn't ask about it. The last part of his statement begged further questioning. "What kind of conflict?"

"Every kind. White settlers making claims on runaway slaves, accusing the Indians of harbouring fugitives, or accusing them of leaving the reservation to raid their cattle. The Indians, of course, claimed rightful ownership of the slaves and cattle, and the Negroes declared they were free men. Not to mention, the infighting and politics of those in charge. The War Department and the military are expected to work together but when you mix military and civilian leaders you have problems."

"What kind of problems?"

"Well, for instance, Colonel Clinch gave me orders to build a strong and comfortable—his words— fort near the Indian Agent, but the supplies were authorized by the War Department. The War Department deemed it a cantonment and a waste of funds to build permanent structures. My material requests were denied. I was instructed to use logs and clay to build the chimneys and use tents for housing. We built the barracks anyway, but unable to procure bricks, the chimneys were built with logs. It was no surprise we had a fire that was quite difficult to put out despite being prepared for it."

"Is that why it was closed?"

"No. The fire happened about a year before the closure and the damage was quickly repaired. It was closed because the Secretary of War decreed it despite Colonel Clinch's protests, but I'm sure you did not come here to hear my complaints. To answer your question, you will need to get approval from Agent Phagan to visit the reservation; a man nothing like his predecessor."

"How do you mean?"

"Gad Humphreys was a good man doing his best at what must be the most thankless job in the whole territory. Citizens, slave catchers, and local politicians standing against the Indians he was there to protect. He could never do enough to satisfy them and whatever he did for them made the Indians feel betrayed. I guess he ended up feeling like the enemy of both sides." The major stopped to take a few good pulls on his pipe, filling the room with the aromatic smoke.

Theodore was rapidly taking notes thinking Gad Humphreys would make a good side story. Title ideas were running through his mind: Lone sentinel. Caught in Between. A Man Alone.

Glassell continued without prompting. "He didn't deserve what happened to him. Governor Duval dragooned him out of his job because they thought he wasn't doing enough to retrieve runaway slaves. Never mind that his job was to protect the rights of the Indians." He paused. "Why are you interested in this?"

"I think readers are interested in the deeper stories of people behind the headlines. Colonel Humphreys sounds like a very interesting man. Please go on."

"Very well. Humphreys was the first, official Indian Agent in the Florida territory. He served the Indians well. He was charged with handling the claims, and he often sided with the Seminoles. He kept them from starving the first year on the reservation when the drought ruined all their crops. He ordered more rations and earned Governor Duval's wrath in doing so, although Duval eventually conceded Humphreys had done right."

"If I understand correctly, the Indian Agent reports to the Governor making Duval Humphreys' superior."

"Correct."

"Hmm." Theodore could see why Major Glassell held such high regard for Gad Humphreys; a man willing to put his job on the line to defend his rightful actions. "What are the duties of an Indian Agent?"

"He is expected to protect the rights of the Indians from those that would take advantage of them and at the same time protect the white settlers from any depredations by Indians. Not an easy task to begin with and Humphreys often complained about not having militia support to help. He was expected to accomplish this by influence alone."

"Why was there no militia?"

"Cutbacks for one, but what military there was in the territory, including my command, were reluctant to take orders from Duval being a civilian. Still, Humphreys ran the Agency with his conscience and tried to do right by the Indians even when it angered everyone else around him. You've got to admire a man with that much integrity. He even stood his ground in front of a grand jury investigation."

"For feeding the Indians?"

"No, for mishandling slave claims."

"And what was the conclusion?"

"They found in favour of Humphreys. However, the issue eventually led to his dismissal."

"Why was Humphries involved in slave claims?"

"You see, the white plantation owners from Georgia, Alabama, and Florida were making claims that the Seminoles were harboring runaways and in some cases alleged they had actually stolen their slaves. Ha! In several cases Humphreys discovered the whites sold the slaves to the Indians without papers and then filed a claim of theft demanding the return of their property.

"But I digress. Initially, Governor Duval stood firm that what the Indians had prior to the Moultrie Creek Treaty could not be taken away from them. However, based on an article of the treaty, the governor demanded the Indians turn over any runaways. It took some strong arming to accomplish. His favorite tactic was threatening to withhold their annuities even though he was advised by the Secretary of War he had no right to do so. Duval eventually got the Indians to turn over a good number of runaways, but that wasn't enough. The claims continued to pour into the agent's and the governor's office demanding satisfaction.

"In the beginning, it was up to Humphreys to determine ownership and persuade the Indians to comply in turning over the runaways, but he often discovered the settlers and plantation owner's claims to be fraudulent. Over time, Humphreys grew to respect the Indians more and the white's less. Duval on the other hand was more willing to believe the whites' claims over the Indians' claims. He thought the best way to solve the conflict was to remove all blacks from the tribes. It didn't matter to him that some were free men or if they were married into the tribes."

Theodore scowled. "So now Duval and Humphreys are at odds with each other."

Major Glassell grimly nodded. "Quite so. Around 1827 a changing of the guard in the War Department and the plantation owners turning to Congress for assistance with their claims led to a decision to settle the claims in court. Initially, everyone was in favour of this, except the Indians. Part of the process was the claimant would put up a bond for his property to the courts, and the Indians were expected to surrender said property until the outcome of the trial. If found in the Indian's favour, the white man was expected to return the slave."

Theodore said, "I assume the Indians believed the slaves belonged to them, so I can see why they would take issue with this expectation of handing them over their property until the case was decided."

"They also didn't believe the slaves would be returned even if the ruling was in their favour, but out of respect for Humphreys, the Indians complied— at first. As the number of claims grew so did their refusal to do so. While the courts were being established, Governor Duval was getting pressure from the settlers to get the claims settled, so he in turn made demands of Humphreys to turn over the slaves. Humphreys, of course, refused, and the new judge supported him saying the slaves could only be removed by treaty, by Indian consent, or by the decision of the courts. But it didn't matter. In the end, the complaints, real and contrived, became overwhelming. An investigation was launched in 1829 to verify the accusations. Lieutenant Newcomb and I both gave testimony disputing one of the charges against Humphreys."

"What charge was that?"

"For not turning over a slave to the proper owner. It was a false claim. The slave, Sally, was captured with the aid of my command and turned over several months prior to the charge being filed."

Theodore was aghast. "Are you saying a claim was filed against Humphreys for a slave you personally returned to the owner?"

"Yes."

"What a sham!"

Major Glassell exhaled a ring of smoke, satisfied with Theodore's outrage over the injustice of it all. "I agree. When the investigation did not find enough fault to warrant Humphreys' removal, Governor Duval started a political campaign to get him removed. By then Fort King was closed, and I was reassigned, but I did send one last letter to the new Secretary of War, John Eaton, promoting Humphreys' character. Alas, Governor Duval's repeated attacks held more weight with President Jackson. Humphreys was dismissed in March of 1830. President Jackson appointed subagent, John Phagan, as his replacement. Even worse, Governor Duval convinced Secretary Eaton to return the power of deciding the slave claims to his office removing Judge Smith from the decision process and thereby leaving the Indians defenseless. And adding insult to injury, the War Department finally assigned Governor Duval the military assistance Humphreys repeatedly requested and never received.

"The situation is disintegrating. The poor Indians are being accosted on all sides especially now that they have lost their one champion. With no avenue for justice, it's only a matter of time until hostilities break out. I think the Indians showed remarkable patience in their dealings with the government due to their faith in Humphreys, but now with Phagan in charge, their patience is gone. Over the last two years, the Indians have grown more restless, often leaving the reservation and clashing with the white settlers. I've also heard rumors Phagan is swindling government money from those involved in reservation business. He's certainly not doing right by the tribes."

Theodore's interest perked up. "Rumors from what source?"

Major Glassell's lips pursed around his pipe. "Can't say as I recall." He had gone and done it again; said too much to this man. It had to be the way he listened so intently. It made a person willing to say more than they should.

Theodore suspected Glassell was being less than forthcoming. He decided to change the subject rather than further discomfort his informant. "What is the best way to get to the reservation from here?"

An hour later, he left the major's office with a letter of introduction for the commander at Fort Brooke and the fortuitous advantage of traveling with the mail carrier as escort if he could be ready to leave in the morning. His mind was churning with all the new information Major Glassell had given him.

He secured passage on the same ship as the mail carrier and procured the items he would need for the journey. On the advice of Major Glassell, he purchased a bedroll, a large piece of oilskin for protection from ground moisture, and heavier boots for the overland journey to the reservation. He already had a canteen and a rifle he bought in New York before coming to Key West.

Now on his way home, Theodore impulsively decided to make one more stop. He called himself all kinds of a fool as he walked through the open front door of the seamstress' house. He had done well avoiding her for more than a month, but today, having an excuse to do so, he was unable to resist the pull to see her. This certainly wasn't a necessary errand. If something happened while he was gone, his family would naturally turn to Mrs. Wheeler. There was no need to stop and specifically ask her to watch over them, and yet, he now stood inside her threshold for that very purpose.

Betsy, having heard his tread across the wooden floor, appeared from the doorway of her workroom to stand behind the counter. She was naturally surprised and happy to see him, and curious. "Good afternoon, Mr. Whitmore. What can I do for you?"

The smile she bestowed on him was positively radiant. His step faltered. The image of Margaret on their wedding day with a similar smile momentarily supplanted Betsy's face. In less than the space of a heartbeat, he was awash in memories of the past followed by guilt. Mentally berating himself for walking into the room in the first place, he changed the tone of his response from social to business. "Good afternoon, Mrs. Wheeler. How are you?

"Well, thank you."

"I find I am leaving on another trip tomorrow. Would you mind checking in on my family? They are more familiar with the island, but still I would like to know they have someone to turn to for assistance."

"Of course. How long do you expect to be gone?"

"A couple of weeks at least. I apologize for the suddenness of my request."

Betsy saw the change of emotion in his eyes. Theodore could convey more in a look than Ben would say in an hour long conversation. She saw the flash of awareness between them turn inward to memories and understood friendship was all he had to offer. He was still in mourning, and while she respected his barrier of grief, it was disappointing. "Do not concern yourself with extemporaneousness. You know I am happy to help. May I ask where you are going?"

"To Fort Brooke and then, hopefully, I will be able to join a military group headed for the Indian reservation."

"Are you going to write about the Seminoles?"

"Learn about them for now. There is a storm brewing between our government and the Indians. When it breaks it will help me to report a full account if I can understand the Indian's side of the conflict."

"Because you will learn more from them as their friend than as their enemy."

"Yes." He was impressed with how astutely she perceived his mission.

"Even though we are not at war with them, it is still dangerous to travel near the reserve, is it not?"

He heard the concern in her voice. It weakened his resolve to keep his feelings in check. "So I have heard, but I should be safe enough in the company of soldiers or militia men."

With every encounter, Betsy learned more of his character and found more to like about this man. On the other hand, she was developing a case of jealousy for a dead woman. She turned her thoughts in another direction. "I wish you safe travels, Mr. Whitmore. May the good Lord watch over your journey."

"Thank you, Mrs. Wheeler. Please let me know if there is anything I can do for you in return for your kindness. Good day." Theodore nodded farewell and quit the house. Finally returning home, he set to work on all the tasks he needed to complete in preparation for tomorrow's departure.

* * *

Good fortune found Theodore approaching the Seminole reservation two and half weeks later. He was fortunate in only having to wait a few days in Fort Brooke before being able to join a patrol dispatched to monitor and maintain the Fort King Road. His journey from Key West to Fort Brooke at Tampa Bay and was uneventful. The fort commander was accommodating, even supplying him with a bunk in one of the barracks strategically located under huge oak trees. He enjoyed the amenities knowing the next trek in his journey would likely be the most uncomfortable of his life.

Leaving Fort Brooke behind, he joined a patrol of ten soldiers. The next six days they walked over a hundred miles to reach the reservation. The road was a twenty foot wide path mostly bordered by tall, thin pine trees, palmettos, and stately oaks heavily draped in Spanish moss. The pace of their travel was laborious for a man who typically worked behind a desk. The mosquitoes were annoying. It was of no comfort to Theodore to be assured they were more aggravating in the summer. The ravenous insects were feasting on him now. Nor did he like spending nights sleeping on the ground, but it was a sacrifice he was determined to endure.

During the day, the men walked in formation, two by two, keeping vigilant for attack from predator or foe and clearing debris from the road as they moved along. More than once they came across the ominous black presence of an alligator sunning in their path, usually in the morning. One of the soldiers proved to be adept at encouraging the reptiles to return to the water. However, a particularly large and stubborn one refused to give ground. His large jaws snapped at the soldier many times, while the lad nimbly side-stepped the threat to his legs. Growing impatient with the beast, the lieutenant stepped forward and without warning aimed a perfect shot between the eyes, startling many of his men. It took four of the strongest soldiers to remove the carcass from the path.

At night, after their meal, there was time for talk and a chance for Theodore to get to know these men. Private Randolph from Virginia was a frequent companion. His loquacious company and observant nature provided a wealth of information for Theodore especially his insights into the character of the army's leaders, the topography of Florida, and what he knew of the Seminoles.

The second night Private Randolph stood to refill his coffee and returned to the fallen log he and Theodore were sharing. After contemplatively staring into the fire for a few moments he spoke without looking at Theodore, picking up a thread of yesterday's conversation as if the intervening time had not occurred. "The Seminole are not really one tribe. They are a mixture of several tribes. I would say the majority of them are Creeks who migrated south to escape the whites or fled here after their tribe lost in the Creek Wars. These Creeks mixed with the few remaining native tribes; the Apalachee, Timucua, Calusa, and others."

Theodore was intrigued. "Why were there numbers low?"

"Mostly from diseases brought by European settlers and warring with each other."

"I've not heard of tribes mixing like that. Why would they?"

Private Randolph shrugged. "Don't know really. Safety in numbers, I suppose. Do you know what Seminole means?"

"Hmm?"

"Runaways, on account of the Creeks and slaves and other Indians they've taken in."

From across the fire another private said, "You're wrong, it means 'person from distant fires'."

"All of you are wrong." They looked to another private wearing spectacles and reading by the dim light of the fire. "Seminole is a derivative of 'cimarron' which means 'wild men' in Spanish."

Theodore said, "I find it strange the word would have a Spanish meaning if it is of Creek origin."

The man shrugged. "Just repeating what I read."

Private Randolph changed the subject. "What are you bringing for a gift?"

Theodore looked questioningly at him.

"White man always brings gifts to the red man. It will be expected."

A gift hadn't crossed his mind, and it should have. He knew the tradition, and it especially applied when one wanted something from them. A quick mental assessment of his backpack found nothing acceptable. "I do not have one." He hoped explaining his cause would give him allowances for the oversight unless he could come up with something before they reached their destination. It didn't seem likely. The Indians lived in these woods. There was nothing here he could possibly find that they couldn't provide for themselves.

Randolph shrugged. "Mayhaps they won't notice."

Theodore could only hope.

The trek continued. Occasionally, they passed open grassy fields or skirted around black water swamps studded with the pleated trunks of cypress trees. Their passing set alight the beautiful white egrets. Theodore hated going around the swamps and even more so going through them, but he did appreciate the wild beauty they offered.

They crossed several rivers, some with bridges, others were shallow enough to wade across. In many areas, the trees were shrouded in leafless vines which the soldiers would cut back to keep the road clear. As they moved further north, the brush and trees became more open. Although not fearful of an attack, Theodore could tell the tension among the men lessened as they passed into this more open area where it would be difficult for an enemy to approach unnoticed.

Theodore was relieved they did not have to contend with rain, but the journey was still tedious. His pack, which seemed manageable in the beginning, now weighed heavily upon his back. They were coming to the end of another prairie. On the other side, the tall, sparse, leafless trees nearly strangled by moss and vines looked much as he felt: old, weary, gaunt and weighed down. Theodore groaned in relief when the lieutenant called a halt to make camp on the final night before reaching their destination.

Shortly after supper, Private Randolph approached with Private Miller. "Mr. Whitmore, I believe I have a solution for your problem."

Theodore looked up at the two men in confusion. "What problem would that be, sir?"

"A gift for the red man."

Interested, Theodore stood up.

Randolph held his hand out to his companion who held forth a green bottle. "Miller, here, has an unopened bottle of his Kentucky family's finest. He is willing to offer a trade."

Unsure, Theodore asked Randolph, "You believe alcohol would be of interest to the Seminoles?"

"Absolutely. One bottle may be a token gift, but it will be acceptable."

Theodore looked to Miller. "Did you have a trade in mind?"

Miller's chin lifted towards Theodore's middle. "I seen you looks at a pocket watch. Always wanted me one of those."

Theodore pulled the watch from his coat pocket. Fortunately, he left the one he usually carried, given to him by his grandfather, in Key West. This was a relatively inexpensive one with no sentimental value. It was an easy decision to make. He held out his hand to Miller. "Deal."

The two shook hands and exchanged items. Theodore turned to Randolph laying a hand upon his shoulder. "Thank you."

"No need."

Later another soldier approached him. "I heard you are using Miller's bottle as a gift for the Seminoles. It is against the law to trade spirits with the Indians. Take heed of whose presence you are in when you bestow your offering." He drifted off into the dark before Theodore could question him further or express his gratitude.

Rising at dawn, as usual, Theodore was happy to learn they would reach their destination in a few hours. He was anxious to meet these Indians. After crossing another river and passing through yet another forest of pines and palmettos, they finally turned from the road leading to the abandoned Fort King to follow a smaller dirt path to the reservation. They were now in the Cove of the Withlacoochee. Glimpses of the erratic shoreline of Tsala Apopka Lake could be seen through the trees. They eventually came to an area of cleared land with two large open air structures made of pine poles and thatched roofs with raised platforms underneath. Nearby were signs of tribal gathering areas. They had reached the village of Chief Micanopy.

Private Randolph approached his side. "They're called chickees. The larger structure is their dwelling and the smaller one is for their food stores." Several men walked out from the village to greet them. Randolph whispered, "I see several chiefs from different tribes in the area. A runner was probably dispatched to bring them in as soon as our patrol was spotted."

It gave Theodore an eerie feeling to know these people had been watching them, undetected. Around the camp, he noticed many warriors, the elderly, and the very young. "Where are the women and children?"

"Most likely in the fields. The women plant and tend the crops. The young warriors guard the new crops at night from deer but otherwise leave the gardening to the women."

Lieutenant Graham called a halt to the patrol. He led Theodore to meet the group of Indians. As they approached, a tall and slender middle-aged black man stepped forward. The lieutenant introduced Theodore to Abraham who acted as interpreter and advisor to the chiefs. Abraham, with surprisingly courtly manners, introduced Theodore to Chief Micanopy, the second most powerful chief of the Seminoles.

Micanopy was short of stature and plump, especially when compared to his interpreter, but he commanded the respect of those around him with ease. Behind him stood several other Indians assumed to be lesser chiefs and warriors. Their dress seemed quite formal to Theodore as it was obviously impractical for day to day life. They wore knee length skirts and loose shirts with decorative embroidery. Elaborate leggings covered their lower legs and many sported turban-like head coverings with bird plumes or other decorations.

Theodore asked Abraham to explain to the chief his purpose in visiting the tribe. The chief's reaction was encouraging. He smiled at Theodore, then spoke rapidly to Abraham in Muscogee. Theodore thought it a musical language with soft tones and a soothing cadence.

Abraham turned to Theodore. "Chief Micanopy wishes for you to stay as a guest in the village."

Theodore could not be more pleased with this turn of events. Since boyhood, he had occasionally visited some of the local tribes although not as often as he would like; school, marriage, and a job prevented more interaction with the Native Americans. Never before had he been invited to stay for longer than a few hours. He felt honored to be asked to do so now even though he suspected the invitation was issued in the hopes he could be an advocate for them. Theodore agreed to stay.

The patrol did some reconnaissance of the area and left soon after. Abraham gave Theodore a brief tour of the village and showed him where he would sleep for the night.

The rest of the day Theodore was mostly left alone to quietly observe life in the village. He made notes in his journal of all he witnessed and wished he had a talent for sketching. He would love to capture the images of the chief's dress, the children playing, or the squaw preparing food for his readers. Alas, his sketches were poor by a child's standard much less an adults. He would have to do his best to paint a picture with his words.

On the surface their life seemed peaceful and ideal, but of course it was far from it. Besides being limited to a reservation, Theodore soon discovered sustenance was still a concern. He saw firsthand their meager food supply which they willingly shared with him. It was not enough to last until harvest. He was no farmer, but even he could tell their crops were doing poorly. If it was this bad now, he wondered how much worse it must have been when Humphreys ordered more rations.

The next morning, on his way to join the tribe for breakfast, he passed a picturesque dark water pond dotted with lily pads and surrounded by trees on three sides. A multitude of birds flew back and forth across the expanse reminding him of a child's game of chase. He stopped for a moment to enjoy the view.

Abraham and Micanopy approached wanting to talk. He was more than willing. The chief didn't seem to know where to start, so Theodore offered the bottle of whiskey to Micanopy. To Abraham he said, "A gift for your chief to thank him for his hospitality." Abraham translated and Micanopy accepted it gracefully. He opened the bottle and sniffed the contents, then took a tentative sip. His smile grew, but he put the cork back in and set the bottle aside.

Micanopy, with Abraham interpreting, began speaking of his desire for peace between the white and red man. He asked Theodore if he believed it was possible. Not sure what to say, Theodore gave a noncommittal answer. He asked the chief about the new agent, John Phagan. The immediate response was displeasure from both men. They believed Phagan was encouraging the theft of their slaves. Abraham was bitterly vocal about the slave raiders visiting their camp almost weekly now making claims they knew to be falsehoods. They asked Theodore what could be done to end the false allegations. He could give them no answer.

They were interrupted by the return of a hunting party with a large kill. Micanopy was clearly distressed and angry with the warriors. Theodore asked Abraham for an explanation. He replied they had been gone too long. Theodore didn't believe that to be the reason. He suspected their kill was a cow from outside the reservation, why else would badly needed food bring the chief's displeasure.

Later that afternoon, Abraham led Theodore to another area of farming mostly run by colored families. Abraham introduced Theodore to his wife, a Seminole woman who was the widow of Chief Bolek, Micanopy's predecessor and great uncle. They had several children of mixed blood. Theodore realized he must be in Abraham's village. Women and children from the field and several black warriors approached to speak with Abraham although Theodore suspected they were curious about his presence. Past the fields, he saw more dwellings and many more blacks going about their daily lives.

Alarm shivered along Theodore's skin. Land was the motivating factor with all of the Indian removals. White man coveted the red man's land, but here in these Florida tribes resided another, darker motivation. The southern planters viewed blacks as valuable property with a high price tag and in high demand after the act of 1807 prohibited the importation of slaves which limited the sources for replacing the labor pool. These factors meant that in the eyes of the slave owners, what Theodore saw in front of him—hundreds of healthy dark skinned men, women and children—was a valuable commodity. The Seminoles didn't stand a chance of being left alone.

Theodore did his best to hide his growing concern from his hosts. He wasn't going to be responsible for starting a war. Besides, he and Bob both believed it was their job to report a story not become involved in it. So he kept his thoughts to himself. He left Abraham's village to return to Micanopy's in time for the evening meal. On the way, he passed a freshly cleaned cowhide on a drying rack. The mark of a branding iron could be seen on the hide confirming Theodore's earlier suspicion.

Without Abraham to interpret, conversation was minimal that evening.

The following day Theodore awoke early. It was his last day with the tribe. He was disappointed not to have learned more about them. They were understandably reticent to share too much but the language barrier was the main problem. Although his observations gave abundant insight, he had many unanswered questions. He decided he would have to seek out Abraham and persuade him to spend more time interpreting. He was on his way to do so when a disturbance distracted him. Children ran past him towards the road. He was afraid it might be the soldiers returning early. He turned around and was relieved to discover a white man in his mid-forties approaching the village. A young boy ran past Theodore in the opposite direction likely dispatched by Chief Micanopy to bring in Abraham.

Theodore started walking towards the newcomer. He waited until the man greeted Chief Micanopy and the tribe before he stepped forward with his hand extended. "Theodore Whitmore of Key West."

The gentleman firmly shook his hand. "Gad Humphreys, at your service."

Theodore's surprise was so great he knew it showed on his face. "I'm very pleased to make your acquaintance. I've heard a lot about you from Major Glassell."

"That's right; he's posted in Key West now. How is the old buzzard?"

"He is well."

"Do you mind my asking, what you are doing here? Not too many white men visit the reservation. Most of those who do so are up to no good."

"I assure you my intentions are honorable. I am a journalist for the *New York Weekly*. I came here to learn more about the Seminoles and their current situation. I'm surprised you are still here after being forced to leave the agency."

"My, Glassell did tell you a lot. I opened a trading post just outside the reservation. Someone has to stand up for these people against the jackals surrounding them."

"Major Glassell filled me in on some of the background of their plight. Would you mind giving me more of the details?"

Abraham arrived and Chief Micanopy became impatient. Colonel Humphreys said, "Let me speak with the chief, and then we can talk."

They moved to the council area. Theodore followed. No one seemed to mind. A long pipe was lit and passed around the group. Most of the talk centered on the tribe's current legal troubles. It was no surprise there were several cases of runaway slaves. Humphreys gave them advice. He seemed to be acting in the Seminoles' best interest while attempting to maintain some neutrality; a difficult balance to maintain. Theodore suspected he would not be able to walk such a fine line much longer. Two of the claims Humphreys advocated they turn over the suspected slaves until the cases could be settled in court. A young warrior answered for the tribe claiming the runaways could not be located. Humphreys told him to keep trying.

An hour or so later, Theodore had Humphreys' undivided attention. The two men strolled away from the camp walking down the path that led to the Fort King Road.

"I can see you have many questions."

"So many I hardly know where to begin."

"Just pick one."

"Who is the young warrior charged with finding the runaways?" Theodore noticed the young man several times. He was reserved and gentlemanly in manner. His features very aquiline and almost feminine, but his eyes revealed a steel resolve not to be trifled with. There was something about him that stood out from the other young warriors. He drew attention and respect.

"Ah, that would be Powell, Micanopy's tustenuggee."

"Tustenuggee?"

"A high ranking warrior appointed by the chief. He is the leader in times of war. His birth name is Billy Powell. He is of mixed blood so his rank is awarded by merit not heredity."

"How did he get such a Christian name?"

"I believe his father is Scottish. His mother is Creek. Mother and son fled here in the wake of the Creek war. Upon adulthood, Indians receive another name. Powell's is Osceola (Asi-ola). I was told its meaning is taken from Asi, the ceremonial black drink they make from the yaupon holly, and Yahola, meaning "shouter" because of his unique war cry."

"Interesting." Theodore held his pencil to paper. "How do you spell it?"

"I've seen it two ways 'Osceola' and 'Asi-Yahola' but since they don't write, I don't suppose it matters one way or the other."

"If Micanopy is the second highest chief, who is the first?"

"Tuckose Emathla, also known as John Hicks. He replaced Nea Mathla. Actually, Governor Duval declared Nea Mathla replaced by John Hicks when he discovered he was encouraging the tribes not to move to the reservation."

"Why would the tribe allow Governor Duval to replace a chief? Isn't that something the they should decide?"

"Yes, but I think they accepted it because they were upset with Nea Mathla for receiving lands to get the other chiefs to sign the Moultrie Creek Treaty which confined them to the reservation. He was shamed for his weakness. I suppose he was trying to make amends by shunning the treaty afterwards. In the end, Duval's declaration humiliated him into leaving the tribe. There were actually six chiefs that made land deals, but Nea Mathla suffered the most for it."

"How many Seminoles are there?"

"A census was taken in 1822. I believe the number was close to 4000, with 800 Negroes."

Theodore recorded the numbers, then asked, "Who are some of the other important Indians?"

"Jumper, Alligator, Charlie Amathla, Sam Jones, Black Dirt, Billy Bowlegs…"

"And their Indian names?"

"Um, let me think. Sam Jones is Ar-pi-uck-i. Billy Bowlegs is Halpatter-Micco. Black Dirt is Fuch-ta-lus-ta-Hadjo."

Theodore smiled. "That's a mouth full."

Humphries smiled too. "There's young Caocoochee known as Wild Cat. He's the nephew of Chief Micanopy. His father is another chief, King Philip or Emathla. Mad Wolf is Yaha Hadjo. He is known throughout the territory to Indians and whites as the best hunter. Alligator is Coa Hadjo." He paused for a moment. "I'm afraid I don't remember the others off the top of my head."

"Are they all in Micanopy's village?"

"Most of them have their own villages scattered about and not all are on the reservation. As I mentioned before, a few chiefs managed to keep their land in exchange for convincing the others to move."

"Major Glassell hinted that Agent Phagan is swindling the Indians. Do you know how he is doing it?"

"I suspect mostly by hoarding tribe allowances and by turning in receipts for reimbursement to the Indians and pocketing the funds. Sutlers are complaining they have not been paid. Although there may be other ways. Are you planning to expose him?"

"It is one of many stories I am contemplating. You are another."

"Me?"

"What Glassell told me about you is interesting. I think my readers would like to learn of a man of your integrity, that is if what Glassell says is true."

"Likely so. I have never known him to embellish the truth, but I hardly think what I have done is extraordinary. Why, any honorable man given the position I was in would do the same."

"I am not so sure. Would you be willing to share your history?"

Colonel Humphreys gave it due consideration before agreeing to allow Theodore to write about him. The next two hours he gave accounting of his service as the Indian Agent and then patiently answered Theodore's questions. By the time the patrol returned and Theodore had to leave, he felt like he had enough information to write a book much less an article. Perhaps it would be a series of articles. He also planned to write Bob and suggest he work on the opposing side of the story from the War Department.

All in all, Theodore headed home feeling like he accomplished more than he set out to achieve. He had the makings of three different stories and enough information to keep him busy for weeks. Humphries promised to write him if anything interesting happened. He also felt like he made a good step towards establishing relations with the Seminoles. They didn't trust him yet, but in time he believed they would.

Chapter 9

Betsy was sitting in Abby's parlor with a steaming cup of tea feeling the need to unburden her heart. She waited a moment, inhaling the fragrant vapors, while Abby finished giving directions to a servant. Once she had her friend's attention, she became hesitant to share her feelings. Instead she asked, "Where is Emily?"

"Taking a nap. Now tell me what is bothering you."

Betsy smiled inwardly. It was just like Abby to go straight to the heart of the matter. "It's Henry. With his father away, Annalise and Henry have been visiting nearly every day. Mrs. Pary visits at least once a week too." Betsy took another sip of tea then carefully set the cup and saucer aside.

Abby patiently waited for her to continue.

"Mind you, I like their visits. It's just that… Well… Henry's becoming attached. I'm afraid he may be too attached to me, and his father will be angry when he returns."

Abby nodded. "And?"

"And…" Betsy looked at her clasped hands in her lap. *Why is it so hard to admit my feelings?* She took a deep breath and looked up to her friend. "And I've grown attached to Henry too. If Theodore forbids him to visit…"

"Theodore? You are on a first name basis with him now?"

Betsy blushed. "No. He is Theodore only in my thoughts."

Abby smiled. "And you have been thinking about him often?"

Sheepishly, Betsy nodded several times.

"What is going on between the two of you?"

"Nothing. I'm sure I've seen flashes of interest but then his eyes become shuttered. He's fighting the attraction because of love for his wife. He's still in mourning."

"When did she die?"

"Last December."

"So it has been a year, and he still mourns her. Do you mean to wait until he is ready to move on? It could be years before that happens."

Betsy grimaced. "I know. Worse, he could decide to leave at any time and return to New York. It is bad enough I am attracted to Theodore, but its Henry that scares me. I look forward to seeing his smiling cherub cheeks and laughing blue eyes every morning. And some of the things he says… He makes me laugh. He has such a bright mind and so eager to learn. So innocent and trusting. And thoughtful. He's always bringing me something; a flower, a rock, a shell.

"And he has gotten into your heart."

Softly she added, "And I into his."

"I see only two options. You either cut the ties now or enjoy him while you can."

"If I cut them now, he won't understand. If I wait for his father to return and forbid his visits, he will be upset with his father. I would hate to be the cause of strain in their relationship. I know it's what I should do; I'm just having a hard time making myself do it."

Abby inhaled sharply, amazed by her sudden revelation. This was more than her friend's usual caring nature. Betsy was in love with Theodore.

* * *

In late January, when the town council proposed a celebration of George Washington's centennial birthday, Betsy was quick to volunteer; thus giving her something of significance to occupy her time and a valid excuse to limit Henry's visits. She threw herself wholeheartedly into the planning and preparation of the event. She and Esperanza spent many long hours working on decorations for the town. They used the leftover material to make rosette corsages which quickly garnered favour with the women. Daily she sold out as the men scrambled to buy them for their wives, daughters, or favoured girls. Betsy often fell into an exhausted sleep making the days pass quickly.

The 22nd of February, 1832, dawned bright and beautiful. As she walked down Front Street, Betsy checked that every building boasted the American Ensign, the first of her many tasks today. Out in the harbour, the ships displayed their colors adding to the festive nature of the day. She hurried along to the Custom House lawn anxious to begin her next task of setting up the tables for this evening's banquet. The large number of guests expected to attend forced the dining to be set up outside. It took days to acquire enough promises of loaned tables and chairs to seat everyone. They were to be delivered this morning giving her and the other volunteers time to arrange them.

First to arrive at the Court House, she gave a cursory inspection of the grounds, pleased to find the boys had done a good job clearing the debris yesterday. Mrs. Webb and Mrs. Fielding soon joined her and while discussing how they planned to arrange the tables, Esperanza and her mother approached. They stopped at the edge of the yard staring down the street.

Esperanza waved them towards her. "Come and look. You have to see this."

Betsy and the other two ladies hurried to the street to find a parade of men and boys carting tables, chairs, and crates of tableware and linens all headed in their direction. It was a sight to behold. Betsy was filled with pride for how her community came together to celebrate the birth of a great leader. Preparing for the flood of furniture headed their way; Betsy quickly gave the ladies their assignments.

It wasn't long before all the furniture was in place. The largest rectangle table was set up at one end for those leading the ceremony. Several makeshift tables of planks laid across framework were set up at the other end to hold food and drink. In between were all the other tables of various shapes and sizes for the guests. Next, they dressed the tables with linen, place settings, and simple floral decorations of garlands made from the compact branches of a pigeon plum tree chosen for its shiny dark green leaves and red tinged leaf sprouts. The greenery was festooned with red, white and blue fabric bows.

At noon, their work was disturbed by the loud report of the thirteen gun salute fired by Major Glassell's company of U.S. troops. Focused on putting the final touches on her tables, Betsy was unaware of the time. Despite knowing of the planned activity, she flinched at the sound dropping the branches she held. Based on the number of surprised cries from the other ladies, she was not the only one startled. It was a good thing they were working with the florals and not the china.

They were finished with the decorations shortly after the salute. Betsy stood back to view the results. She was pleased with their work and being done ahead of schedule. Mrs. Mallory and Mrs. O'Hara had the difficult task of heading up the food preparation. Betsy was able to take a break until it was time to serve the meal. She took advantage of the respite to go home, freshen up, and get something to eat.

Upon returning to the banquet area, she gave her volunteers assignments starting with placing the first course of turtle soup on the tables covered with cloth to protect it from insects. Meanwhile the guests began to gather and converse on the fringes of the yard, dressed in their finest. Betsy noticed many women and some men sported her handiwork. Pride was quick to surface although she checked the feeling not wanting to succumb to one of the seven deadly sins.

Rain was the central topic of conversation. February had been drier than usual. They had not had a drop of rain in weeks. Cisterns were beginning to dry out. Some of the larger families had run out of water. It was one of the reasons the tables were decorated with tree branches rather than vases of flowers that would require water. For an island very much dependent on Mother Nature to resupply such a basic need, the weather was foremost on everyone's mind and was the primary topic of conversation. When would there be rain? How much longer could the water last? The latest cistern to run dry. Remembrances of other dry spells. No one could recall it being worse. If this continued, how would they survive till the summer rains? Many ships were dispatched to other islands with all the water barrels they could carry to procure what to them was becoming a highly valued commodity.

Every time the clouds built it brought hope only to be shattered when the skies cleared again. Rain was sometimes seen on the horizon falling over the ocean waters. It was grim torture for an island starved for water. The situation was getting so dire she doubted anyone would be upset if the event, so long planned, were to be called off on account of rain. In fact, rain would probably turn it into an even bigger celebration than now anticipated.

Promptly at four o'clock, Mr. O'Hara, as president of the day, took his place at the head table, followed by Mr. Fielding Browne as vice-president, Mr. Chandler, and the other dignitaries. Gathered for this prestigious event was the veritable crème of Key West society seated at the tables while many more stood around the perimeter to witness the festivities.

A few opening remarks were made by Mr. O'Hara, followed by a well said blessing to start the meal. Then Mr. Chandler rose and made a few appropriate remarks before reading George Washington's Farewell address. Over the next hour, it was hoped that equal attention was given to Mr. Chandler's oration as was given to the roasted flamingo, fish, and vegetables.

The serving staff cleared the last of the meal from the tables and ensured all the glasses were full for what was sure to be very numerous toasts following the address. Now all Betsy's volunteers had to do was keep the cups full and relax on the sidelines, while a group of the eldest girls washed and repacked the dishes and silverware. Betsy found a comfortable spot under a buttonwood tree to the side of the main table.

It wasn't long before Mr. Whitmore joined her with a notepad in hand and the serious expression befitting a working reporter. She was surprised to see him. The last few days were so busy with preparations, she wasn't aware he had returned from his trip.

Theodore spent the better part of the day avoiding the young widow, but now like a moth drawn to a flame, he couldn't resist the rare opportunity to engage her in a private conversation within a respectable public setting. She earned his respect this morning in managing the details and the volunteers with cheerfulness and efficiency. "Good evening, Mrs. Wheeler. Do you mind if I share your tree? I believe I will be able to hear better from this vantage point."

"Not at all, Mr. Whitmore. Are you making note of everything said or only the parts of interest?"

"I fully expect Mr. Whitehead to engage in recording every toast made. It is in his nature, so I am free to absorb the highlights. You could be of assistance in identifying the speakers I am not familiar with."

"If you like but you seem to be familiar with most of the town. I have noticed you engaged in conversation with almost everyone here at one time or another."

"Hmm. I have made a point of meeting people. One never knows who may be the key to the next big story."

"In a sense, then, you are always working. It must be hard on your family at times."

He was reminded of the night Margaret stayed up to the early hours of the morning waiting for his return from a fire. One of the factories had turned into a raging inferno at the end of a shift with workers trapped inside. The survivors had to be rescued from upper story windows. Margaret was with child at the time, and he hadn't realized how his delay would affect her.

She ran into his arms crying when he returned. He ended up holding her to his chest in bed until they both had fallen asleep. He hadn't been in any danger, but Margaret had no way of knowing, and so she worried. "Yes, it has been on occasion." The reminder of his wife had Theodore turning his attention back to Mr. Chandler in time to hear the last lines of the address.

Betsy wondered at the change in Theodore's demeanor. She had been thinking of his aunt and son when she referred to his family, but the look on his face made her realize he was reminded of his late wife. Out of respect, she refrained from continuing their conversation.

Mr. Chandler finally finished his reading and left the podium to stand behind his chair. Mr. O'Hara came to the front and gestured for the guests to stand before beginning the toasts. The opening toasts would have all the solemnity, dignity, and patriotism the occasion required but would quickly disintegrate into a contest of sorts to see who could out toast the other. Mr. O'Hara raised his goblet high and solemnly declared, "To the Memory of General Washington—may his example be the star that guides our destiny."[3]

The silent crowd raised their glasses in salute and drank.

"The Day we celebrate—may our remotest posterity hail its approach as did the shepherds of old tho' Star in the East."

Again the toast was saluted in silence.

The next toast, he uttered with vigor. "To Our Country—the Independence guaranteed to us by the blood of our ancestors, should never be forgotten by their descendants."

Mr. Browne added, "Three cheers. Hip! Hip! Hip!"

The guests answered with a rousing, "Hooray!"

Mr. O'Hara's voice rang out gaining strength with the momentum of the celebration. "To the Union—an inheritance to us from Washington and his associates. Let the trifling cause burst the holy band." Three robust cheers followed from the crowd.

"To Patrick Henry—His doctrines he left as a legacy to his country. May these times find them as fearlessly and eloquently supported."

The guests toasted. "Hear! Hear!"

"Our Statesmen—May they remember the principles of '76—think less of *self* and more of their country."

"Hear! Hear!"

Indicating the importance, Mr. O'Hara raised his voice. "To the President of the United States." His toast was followed by six vigorous cheers.

"To the Army and Navy of the United States—Ever ready in the cause of freedom." Three more cheers.

Betsy missed hearing the next two toasts as she checked the drinks at her assigned tables. She resumed her place under the tree as Mr. O'Hara built up the energy for his final opening toasts.

"One Hundred Years Ago! A period from which to date a Nation's gratitude; may the next centennial recurrence of this anniversary find our countrymen in the enjoyment of the privileges secured by our Fathers—found wise by the experience of more than fifty years' trial, and rendered sacred by the association therewith of the name of George Washington."

"Hip! Hip! Hip!"

"Hooray!"

"Hip! Hip! Hip!"

"Hooray!"

"Hip! Hip! Hip!"

"Hooray!"

"The People, May posterity never blight the fair fruits of their virtue and intelligence and to our fair land—America!

"Hip! Hip! Hip!"

"Hooray!"

"Hip! Hip! Hip!"

"Hooray!"

"Hip! Hip! Hip!"

"Hooray!"

Mr. O'Hara stepped aside and the guests as a whole returned to their seats for the start of the volunteer toasts. Many present had anxiously awaited this portion of the evening. It sometimes was turned into a game of who could make the better toast. Betsy made another round of refills then returned to her spot under the tree. Letters were read from Major Glassell and General Parker both of whom were unable to attend.

Betsy covertly watched Theodore work. She secretly thought of him as 'Theodore' in spite of his refusal to use given names. It was a dangerous habit that fed her feelings for this man. Just being near him brightened her day and made her pulse leap. The firelight from a nearby torch played across his features, accentuating the bold lines of his nose and chin. His face reflected the solemnity as his demeanor, but every once in a while, she caught a tantalizing glimpse of lightheartedness that kept her intrigued waiting for its reappearance.

The next toast caught her attention. "To the City of Key West—No section of the United States has so delightful a winter climate; and no city so great a proportion of intelligence and hospitality in its population."

"Hear! Hear!"

Judge Webb stood up next. "Washington—May those principles of heroism, patriotism, and virtue, which have rendered him immortal, be ever diffused through our land."

As the toasting became more vigorous, Betsy made another round of refills.

William Whitehead stood up as she returned to her post. "To Our National Flag—May the stars that compose its union forever remain united and as brilliant as they are now."

"Hear! Hear!"

Betsy resumed watching Theodore watching everyone else and let herself wonder what it would be like if he did return her feelings; to have his undivided attention focused on her. The idea was exciting. It made her heartbeat quicken and her breath grow shallow leaving her a bit lightheaded.

Dr. Strobel raised his voice to a near outcry making sure everyone heard his salute, momentarily drawing Betsy's gaze away from Theodore. "To the Union—its best safeguard—the virtue, intelligence and patriotism of the people."

Theodore caught Betsy's gaze as it returned to him and promptly lost interest in the toasts. There wasn't anything in this event of interest to his readers in New York. It was a local piece and plenty of others around to record it for posterity. Mr. Whitehead was diligently taking notes and Mr. Bertram and Dr. Strobel where both paying close attention allowing Theodore the luxury of being a casual observer. The speakers faded into the background as he studied the feelings reflected in her irises. The sun was dropping towards the horizon allowing long shadows to play across her alabaster skin. This woman caused him so much confliction. He wanted to be able to let go of the past and be free to explore his feelings for her, but love for Margaret kept him from acting on those desires. He struggled to keep Betsy at a distance, but at the same time his attraction would not allow him to completely forsake her company.

He tried breaking the spell she wove around him with conversation. "How long do you expect they will continue?" He indicated the group of men engaged in toast making.

"Till long past dark if allowed."

"What is there to stop them?"

Betsy looked over the crowd and smiled. "Their wives." It pleased her immensely when her rejoinder earned her a slight uplifting of the corner of his mouth revealing his amusement. He kept his emotions close to his vest. It took a discerning eye to read them on his face. "Do you think New Englanders are having similar events? Sometimes I think we islanders use any reason to celebrate to break up the monotony of island life."

Theodore absorbed her smile, then glanced to see who had stood to make the next toast before returning his attention to her. "Yes, I believe they are, and I think celebrating is common to all. Your island is not the only place that feels the need to break up the mundane. Is there anything else planned after the toasting?"

"No. I realize in New England it is common to have fireworks but we don't have any today. We had a fireworks display a few years back. I believe it was a Fourth of July celebration. They were part of a salvaged shipwreck Mr. Browne generously shared with the town rather than sell them off. Some were ruined by the water, but there was still plenty to put on a nice showing."

When it appeared Theodore did not have a rejoinder, Betsy said, "How was your trip? Were you able to visit the reservation?"

"Yes."

"Were you not afraid of visiting those savages?"

As usual, the term 'savages' angered Theodore. He was aware most of his race considered Indians to be savages because of their simple living or misconstrued history. Betsy was not racist. She treated not only Esperanza Sanchez as a friend but also counted many free blacks living in Key West as friends. He knew her assumptions were fueled by sensationalized newspaper reports and gossip. He could do something to convey the facts.

"I would not call these tribes savage. They only want to be allowed to live on their land in peace. Their current housing is not much, but I have learned that before we forced them onto a reservation they had a very civilized community with log cabins. It was communal living, but I would still call it civilized. They are a noble people given to farming and hunting, but now there is little of both. They are near starving and all they ask is to keep their land."

Betsy's brows drew together. "Yes, but that is how they live. What about how they fight? I have heard many stories of the Indians attacking ships and leaving all for dead, taking scalps, and brutalizing bodies. Is that not an act of savagery?"

"I would guess those attacks were made by a different tribe altogether. The Seminoles are living peaceable, most of them on the reservation, suffering for it, but peacefully nonetheless. The tribes are different just as races are different. Consider this: French, Scotch, German, English, all white men but they are all distinctly different with different beliefs and different ways of fighting their enemies. Some are more peaceful than others. Not to mention, every race has a number of men who are born troublemakers, but that does not mean the whole race should be discounted."

Betsy nodded in agreement realizing she had made an assumption about all Indians.

Theodore nodded his head towards the tables. "It appears you are being summoned."

She turned to find Mrs. Webb gesturing with her empty cup. *Oh no!* Her conversation with Theodore was supposed to be discrete. By nightfall, the matron matchmakers will be calling Theodore her beau.

Betsy made her rounds. Thankfully, the table conversation kept Mrs. Webb from speaking to her as she refilled her wine. Her task complete, she then faced a dilemma; return to Theodore and risk further conjecture or find another place to stand and risk offending or hurting his feelings. She couldn't decide until their eyes met and consequences no longer mattered. His gaze pulled her to him as surely as if he had taken her hand and led her back to her position under the tree.

Theodore turned his head to her. "I apologize if what I said sounded like a lecture. I tend to react strongly to perceived prejudice against Indians."

"There is no need to apologize. You did make me realize I am guilty of judging all Indians by the actions of some. I will not make that mistake again. What are the Seminoles like? You said they are peaceful."

"As I said, they are farmers and hunters, and from what I understand, they used to live in log cabins before they were moved to the reservation. The tribe I visited now live in open huts called chickees."

"What do they grow?"

"Corn, squash, beans, pumpkins and such. Or at least, they are trying to. Their crops are not doing well."

Betsy's lips thinned knowingly. "Not enough rain."

"That and the soil is poor."

"So we not only take their lands and force them to live in restricted areas, but the land we leave them is poor. What an outrage!"

She was getting worked up the way he used to. It made him smile. "Yes, it is."

Her eyes flashed when she noticed his grin. "How can you smile?"

"I assure you I am not smiling about their situation. It is you that makes me smile."

Her eyes softened at the unexpected comment. "Me? Why?"

"Your passion for the injustice of it is the same as mine."

"Oh." She liked having something in common with him.

The celebration going on around them faded into the background as they continued to speak of all Theodore had seen and heard on his trip. They were both surprised by the dispersing crowd signaling the end of the event.

"Please excuse me, Mrs. Wheeler. It has been a pleasure conversing with you." Theodore left her to speak with the departing guests.

She and the volunteers had cleaning to do. They gathered all the glasses and desposited them on a table set up as a washing station where four volunteers washed, rinsed, dried and repacked them to be picked up by the owners. The soiled linens were collected in a basket to be cleaned tomorrow by another lady and her daughter. Most of the furniture was removed as soon as it was cleared but some would be left to be picked up the following day.

When all the guests departed, Theodore returned to Betsy and silently began helping to remove all evidence of the celebration. She was touched by his gesture and smiled her appreciation when he caught her looking his way. They worked in companionable silence with only the torch lights to guide them. Others were nearby but Betsy's awareness was limited to Theodore. Once finished, the other volunteers said their goodnight. Being head of the committee, Betsy was last to leave.

After putting out the last of the torches Theodore turned to Betsy. "May I walk you home, Mrs. Wheeler?"

"I would like that, Mr. Whitmore."

They slowly walked along in silence until they reached Clinton Place. Betsy was contemplating the wisdom of her impromptu idea. With a burst of spirit, she decided to throw caution to the wind. "Would you and your family care to go sailing tomorrow?"

Her excitement was palpable. Theodore felt the jump in his pulse and chose to answer based on reaction rather than reflection. "I can't think of a better thing to do for Henry's birthday. He thoroughly enjoyed the first time you took him."

"Oh yes, I forgot its Henry's birthday. And you? Do you love sailing?"

"Yes, I do."

"Do you have any other plans for his birthday?"

"No"

Betsy teased him. "Not even a special meal?"

"I suppose a supper could be arranged. Will you join us?"

"Of course, I would."

"When would you like to meet for sailing?"

"Come to my house in the morning."

They reached Betsy's front porch. Theodore stopped at the foot of the steps and spoke to her darker shadow in the doorway. "Thank you for the invitation. Sleep well, Mrs. Wheeler." He was looking forward to spending more time with the cheerful widow tomorrow.

Betsy smiled at the intriguing man bathed in moonlight. "Good night, Mr. Whitmore."

Chapter 10

Morning dawned bright and beautiful. Betsy awoke early in a buoyant mood. She dressed quickly, first donning a newly made soft pink cambric bathing costume she fashioned from a picture she saw in a French magazine. It consisted of a shift covering her from neck to knees and trousers with leggings going down to her ankles. Over this she slipped on a loose fitting dress. She wore her usual kid boots.

She took one last glance in the wall mirror over the dresser to check her appearance and used her left hand to tuck in a stray tendril. A flash of gold caught her attention. She brought her hand down and held it out in front of her. She hadn't thought about her ring since the day she told Abby about Ben. In all these months it had not crossed her mind to remove it, but now, today, it seemed a lie to continue wearing it. She wanted something to happen between her and Theodore. She supposed she still wore the ring because it gave the illusion of a barrier between her and the other men, especially George Casey. Today, she no longer wanted or needed that barrier. It was time to remove this last vestige of mourning.

She slid the ring over her knuckle and off her finger. She looked at it for a moment, recalling a few cherished memories of Ben and silently thanking God for the blessing of their marriage and for what time they had together. She lifted the lid on her simple wooden jewelry box and laid the ring inside next to her grandmother's red onyx cameo broach of Madonna and child she only wore on Christmas day. Betsy closed the lid and ran her hands over the smooth surface, pausing to look at the indention on her now bare ring finger. She wondered who would be the first to notice its absence. She inhaled sharply and turned away, ready to face the day.

Next she went to the kitchen to pack everything she had portable to eat for snacks along with canteens of fresh water.

A knock sounded on the door promptly at nine. Betsy opened it to find Theodore in a loose fitting shirt and pants and Annalise looking fresh as a daisy in a white dress and straw hat. Henry was standing in front of them nearly bouncing up and down in his excitement. He looked adorable in his knickerbockers and a little sailor hat.

"Mrs. Betsy, Poppa said we are going to see the fishes today 'cause it's my birthday."

Betsy returned his big smile. "That's right Henry. Happy sixth birthday to you! Let me gather my things and we'll be ready to go." She handed the bag of food to Theodore, the canteens to Annalise, and then picked up her big floppy hat and some towels. She closed the door behind her and led the way to the beach. Theodore helped her push the boat towards the water while Henry proudly made a 'B' in the sand where the boat had been. Theodore helped Annalise aboard and then picked up Henry and placed him into the boat. He held out his hand to the beautiful widow. "Let me help you in Mrs. Wheeler. I can launch the boat into the water."

"I don't mind helping."

"Of course, but there's no sense in both of us getting our shoes wet."

She conceded and placed one hand in his and gathered her skirt with the other, intending to climb over the side as gracefully as she could with both hands detained.

Theodore realized his intent to help was really making the transition more difficult. Rather than let her struggle he chose a more forward method of assistance that was likely to earn her displeasure. The idea was not entirely unpleasant. He glanced around to make sure no one was watching then placed his hands on her waist and lifted her into the boat.

Betsy's body stiffened in shock from the unexpected sensation of strong hands encasing her waist. It had been a long time since she experienced such intimate contact and the subsequent feminine awareness. It was followed by embarrassment which ruled her emotions. *How dare he take such liberties!* She turned around to face him; her eyes sparking with feeling while her voice remained controlled not wanting to concern the children. "Thank you, Mr. Whitmore."

The corner of his mouth lifted. "My pleasure, Mrs. Wheeler."

She thought she heard a hint of familiarity in his tone. She sought his gaze to confirm, but he turned around leaving her to wonder if she had imagined the verbal caress. Was he flirting with her or was it wishful thinking on her part? Perhaps, the day would reveal his intent.

Between the two of them they got the boat quickly under sail. Theodore worked the jib while Betsy took the tiller to guide them around the shallows to her favourite place. Henry and Annalise were perched in the bow enjoying the passing underwater scenery of alternating sand, grass, and varying sea life. They sailed around Whitehead Point, then followed the coast northeast to Betsy's favoured spot over the coral reef.

The day was turning beautiful. The temperature was pleasant and warm. The bow cut smoothly through the sparkling turquoise water. Betsy could not ask for a more perfect day for their excursion.

As the boat passed between clusters of the distinctive red mangrove with their long reaching aerial roots, Henry pointed to one, "Poppa, look at those bushes in the water. The roots aren't in the ground."

Betsy laughed. "Those are red mangroves. We call them 'island makers'. Debris gets trapped in the roots and builds up. More mangroves take root and grow sending out more roots to trap more debris and eventually you have an island. It's also a good place to find bait fish."

Henry frowned. "What are bait fish?"

Theodore replied. "They are small fish you use to catch bigger fish."

Henry's frown deepened. "Fish eat fish?"

Betsy gave him a smile before returning her attention to their course. "Some do."

Just then a gray-brown hump broke the surface near their boat. Annalise jumped away from the side of the boat in surprise, briefly rocking them. Theodore looked to Betsy. "What was that?"

"A manatee. Some call them sea cows."

Theodore's first thought was the children. "Are they dangerous?"

"I assure you they are quite harmless. They eat plants and move very slow. Watch, you'll see him come up for air again soon." She steered the boat to stay parallel with the mammal for a few more minutes so they could get a closer look. When Henry began to look bored she veered off towards their destination.

Betsy suddenly remembered something. "Mr. Whitmore, I forgot to ask if you can swim."

"I do, but Henry doesn't."

Betsy knew Annalise didn't either from their previous sail. "We shall anchor in the shallows. Theo... Uh, Mr. Whitmore, let's head for that lighter colored area just over there. It will be a sandy bottom and only about knee-deep."

A few moments later, Betsy directed Theodore to drop the anchor, then disconcerted him by unbuttoning her dress. He politely turned away.

Betsy's cheeks bloomed as if she was doing something wicked. She may be decently covered in her bathing costume, but she still felt exposed. Quickly, she dropped into the water.

Theodore felt the boat rock and heard the splash as she landed in the water. He instinctively turned to look and discovered Betsy in a very proper bathing costume.

Annalise said, "Your bathing dress is very becoming, Mrs. Betsy."

"Thank you, Annalise."

Theodore normally swam naked when the occasion arose which previously only occurred in the presence of other men. Neither he nor Henry owned a bathing costume never having the need for one before. Today they would have to settle for swimming in their clothes. He removed his socks and shoes and slipped into the refreshing water. Henry didn't need encouragement to follow suit. He tossed them aside and reached out his arms. Theodore lifted Henry from the boat and placed him in the cool water reaching to the little boy's chest before turning to Annalise.

She leaned away from Theodore. "I believe I'll stay in the boat, if you don't mind."

"Are you sure? You can stand in this water."

"I would rather stay dry."

"Very well. If you change your mind call to me and I will help you out."

Betsy noticed her companions were both wearing their clothes. She had also seen pictures of male bathing costumes and decided she would surprise them by making some for next time. At least she hoped there would be a next time.

They played for a while, chasing fish, hunting shells, and gradually getting into deeper water just over Henry's head where Theodore began teaching him the fundamentals of swimming. When he showed signs of tiring, they returned to the little boat. Theodore placed Henry in the boat then turned to Betsy. "What do you want to do now?"

"We can sail over to the reefs or we could leave the boat here and swim over. They are just a little further out."

"I think I would rather have Henry closer to me."

"I understand." She turned to the boat prepared to pull herself aboard when she was suddenly removed from her feet. "Oh!" Theodore picked her up with one arm under her knees and the other supporting her back to place her in the boat. It was quickly done but left her flushed and flustered.

Theodore climbed into the boat well aware he took her by surprise. It was the gentlemanly thing to do, to assist her into the boat. He enjoyed the momentary pleasure of holding her close, but it was the clinging fabric and the hint of what lie beneath that now left him feeling uncomfortable. He forcibly banned the image from his mind as he pulled the anchor and they sailed out to the edge of the reef.

As the wind whipped against her wet cossie, Betsy became aware her choice of fabric was unwise. The costume in the magazine was made from a dark colored wool but she decided against the heavier fabric thinking it would absorb too much water and make swimming difficult. Unfortunately, she chose to make hers from cambric which now closely clung to her skin revealing her shape to any who cared to notice. She hoped it was not also transparent but feared otherwise by the way Theodore carefully avoided looking in her direction. Not wanting to end the outing just yet, she bravely held her form erect pretending all was well while keeping behind the sail as much as possible for modesty. When they reached the reef, she directed Theodore to drop the anchor while she quickly returned to the gently undulating water without assistance.

She held the side of the boat and spoke to Theodore. "Before you get out would you mind retrieving the bucket under Henry's seat and fill it half way with water?"

Theodore did as requested then carefully exited the boat to keep from routing the younger occupants.

Henry leaned over the edge. "Is the bucket of water for us to play in?"

Betsy smiled. "If you like, but don't spill it. I'm going to bring you something later that needs to go in the water."

Henry's curiosity grew. "What is it? What are you going to bring me?"

"You'll have to patiently wait and see." She nearly laughed out loud at the dramatic fall of his face.

Theodore said, "Son, you understand this water is deep, right?"

"Yes, Poppa."

"I want you to stay in the boat with Annalise. We'll come up and check on you every few minutes. Be careful looking over the edge so you don't fall in."

"Yes, Poppa."

It was just over three fathoms or roughly ten feet deep where they were anchored, so a breath of air could easily see them to the bottom to look around. Betsy pointed out many interesting fish and coral. One particular coral she pointed to while vigorously shaking her head. Theodore easily understood her meaning. That particular coral was dangerous. She led him to an area over a bed of waving sea grass on the other side of the boat.

They came up for air and Betsy said, "I love to watch the play of sunlight and shadow across the bottom, especially in the grass."

They went under again and he could see what she meant. 'Play' was a good word for the shifting light over the grass caused by the movement of water. He liked watching the fish hunting for food. There were so many in number and variety making their home amongst the coral and grass.

On the next dive, he watched Betsy gracefully swim to the bottom and pick up what looked to be from his point of view a pile of sand and barnacles. It took two hands for her to lift it but she was able to hold it in one as she swam up to him. They surfaced together, and he turned to her in curiosity.

Betsy brushed her hair back and asked, "Do you like conch?"

Theodore could now tell by the shape it was a large shell and he could see the foot of the muscle peeking out from the opening. "I don't know. I haven't had the opportunity to try it yet." She turned the shell over, the muscle retreated, and he could now see the polished pinkish-white lip of the shell opening.

Betsy's smile widened. "Then let me be the first to serve it to you tonight. It is a true Caribbean delicacy."

"I look forward to it." At least he would look forward to enjoying more of her company. He wasn't sure he was going to like conch in any dish.

Betsy held the shell out to him. "Please put this one in the bucket. I'm going to go look for a few more for us, and I always bring one back for Dr. Waterhouse as a thank you for the loan of his boat."

Diving under again Betsy searched for her prey. Theodore handed the conch to Henry and then followed her. She pointed to one. Theodore nodded and swam to retrieve it while she found another. They surfaced with their prizes then dove again for two more. This time, knowing what he was looking for, Theodore was able to find one on his own. Betsy decided five would be enough; one for the doctor and four to share with Theodore's family.

Henry was fascinated with the sea creature. Every time the slug made an appearance he would cry out in delight as he tried to grasp it, but each time it eluded him by slipping back into its shell.

"Mrs. Betsy, I want to see it. How do you get it out?"

"I'll show you when we get back."

Being in deeper water, this time Theodore insisted on getting in the boat first and helping Betsy by pulling her aboard. She barely avoided landing in his lap, then immediately turned her back to him and donned her dress over her wet cossie. With modesty returned, she took her place at the tiller while Theodore again managed the sail for their return trip. As they sailed past the lighthouse, they waved to the keeper's children playing along the shore having finished their morning chores.

Upon their return to the beach, Theodore leapt from the boat to pull it out of the water. He helped the others disembark. Again, he gathered Betsy to his chest, before dropping her feet to the sandy coral. Unbalanced, she wobbled and instinctively reached out for support. Her hand closed around the solid muscle of his upper arm. Unexpected desire swept over her. She lifted her gaze to his and in the depths of his hazel eyes saw the same. Everything within her tightened in reaction. Then his eyes shuttered, he stepped away, and the spell was broken.

They gathered their items from the boat and walked the short distance to Betsy's outdoor kitchen. Theodore carried the heavy bucket of conch. Betsy picked up another bucket she kept by the door and turned to Theodore. "Would you mind filling this with sea water?"

"Hmm." He placed the bucket of water and conch beside the table, took the empty bucket from her, and walked back to the water.

Betsy watched him walk away. She noticed he often made that sound and its meaning varied greatly. In this case, it seemed to be more of an acknowledgement of her words. She didn't believe he meant to be insulting or rude it was simply his frugal way of communicating. He was more thoughtful than verbose while his eyes spoke volumes—and were quite distracting. She pulled her gaze away from him to focus on the task at hand, first retrieving a hammer and small knife from a drawer.

Theodore returned a few moments later, placing the second water bucket next to the first one.

They all gathered around the kitchen work table so Betsy could show Henry how to divest a slug of its shell. "Henry would you bring me one of those conch?"

He approached the table carefully holding the dripping conch in front of him. Theodore lifted him onto a stool across the table from Betsy, so he could see what she was doing.

Betsy pointed to the center of the table. "Sir, would you kindly place it right here for me."

Henry set the shell on the table then pushed it towards the center. He watched with avid interest as Betsy turned the shell so the spirals were pointed toward Henry and waited for the slug to find its grip. She used the hammer to make an elongated hole under the third crown and then she picked up the knife and inserted it in the hole feeling around till she found the muscle. Deftly she cut it.

"Henry, do you want to pull it out?"

He nodded his head in excitement as he reached for the shell. Betsy held it for him as he tried to grasp the creature. It took him a few tries, but he finally got a good enough hold to pull it with both hands. Theodore stood behind him to make sure he didn't fall backwards when the snail released. Henry studied the creature in his hands with the inquisitive nature of a young boy not afraid of getting messy. Annalise quietly watched with furrowed brow and wrinkled nose. When Henry was done with his examination he offered it to Annalise. She vehemently shook her head. He turned his head to look at his father.

"I see it. You can return it to Mrs. Wheeler."

Betsy accepted the meat from Henry. She prepared the conch by removing the non-edible colored parts. She used the second bucket of sea water to rinse off the slime. She then tenderized the remaining white meat with a hammer before cutting it into pieces. The process was repeated with the other three. However, Henry lost interest before she finished the second one, so Theodore took Henry and Annalise home. Betsy finished harvesting the meat, then set about adding the rest of the ingredients to the conch in her large stew pot.

While the chowder was simmering on the stove, Betsy rinsed the salt water from her hair as best she could with her limited water and changed clothes. Gathering clouds dimmed the sunlight filtering into the house. Betsy stepped outside to take a look, daring to hope they might bring rain and the answer to their prayers. The bucket touched bottom in her cistern this morning. Some families were already forced to buy imported water. She was going to join their ranks if rain didn't come soon. The clouds did not look promising.

She took the last conch waiting in the bucket of water to Dr. Waterhouse. Conch fritters were his favourite, and he was always grateful for the gift. She was standing on his doorstep when she heard a faint sound of thunder. She glanced at the sky again, but rain still didn't seem likely. Maybe she only imagined the sound. The doctor answered the door, and she handed him the bucket accepting his profuse appreciation.

She returned to her kitchen preparing to take the conch chowder across the street for dinner when she heard another distant rumble. She knew she hadn't imagined that one. Gathering up the pot, she stepped outside planning to walk around her house and across the street with her burden. A sudden flash of lightening startled her causing some of the soup to spill. Fortunately, the hot liquid did not land on her. She continued on her way. The clouds were marginally darker than before, that is to say they were a light gray with a darker edge. Certainly not menacing, and if they did produce anything it was still likely to miss them. It was such a tiny island to rain upon under the vast sky.

Theodore greeted her at the door. He took the heavy pot of soup from her and lifted it towards his face. "It smells wonderful." He stepped aside allowing her to pass. "Please come in, Mrs. Wheeler."

He left her standing in the parlor while he took the soup to the kitchen to be served with supper. Aunt Agatha soon joined her. They greeted each other cordially.

Theodore called to them from the hallway. "Come quick! It's starting to rain!"

Betsy would have flown to the door if not for Agatha's presence. She impatiently held to a brisk walk instead. As soon as she reached the door, she could smell the rain. An excited thrill rushed through her. She gave little thought to appearances as she passed through the door close on Theodore's heels. Agatha stopped under cover of the upper porch. Theodore and Betsy continued out into the yard.

Betsy tilted her face skyward with childish delight, then raised her hands. "Praise God." She turned in circles enjoying the feel of the drops on her face while laughing with joy. Theodore watched her with a grin. She stopped to study the rare appearance of mirth on his countenance. Agatha watched in disapproval, but it mattered naught to Betsy. When the sprinkles increased to a sudden downpour, she ran for the porch with Theodore on her heels. Their laughter brought Henry and Annalise downstairs to investigate. Betsy didn't care about her wet clothes. She was too grateful for the rain.

Supper was a success. Everyone, even Agatha, enjoyed the conch chowder. Betsy did her best to conceal her pleasure when Theodore requested a second bowl. High praise, indeed! The rest of the meal consisted of Henry's favourite dishes: beef pot roast and potatoes in a rich brown gravy with biscuits followed immediately by dessert of rice pudding. Betsy knew it was nothing short of miraculous their cook had been able to procure all the ingredients needed at the same time. One of the downsides to living on an island with limited food sources was only having ingredients recently imported.

The meal included lively and pleasant conversation. This was likely due to Theodore's encouragement of Henry to lead their dialogue. It started with a recap of the events of the day. His favourite part was seeing several green sea turtles swim past their boat on the way back to shore. This led to a vivid, albeit imagined, story of the life of a sea turtle.

The most joyful part of the evening was the rain continued in a steady downpour. The only mar was Agatha's obvious dislike of conversation during the meal, but at least she held her tongue.

It seemed too soon when Theodore declared it to be, "Time for bed, son."

Annalise immediately stood up from her place to lead him upstairs. Henry paused beside Betsy. "Thank you for my birthday sailing, Mrs. Betsy."

Betsy's heart warmed at his thoughtfulness. She laid her hand against Henry's cheek. "You are welcome Henry. Sweet dreams."

Silence descended on the table in the wake of the children's departure. Since her companions seemed content in their own thoughts, Betsy did not try to interrupt the quiet.

A few moments later, Henry's voice called from the top of the stairs.

"Poppa, I'm ready for my story now."

She watched as Theodore stood up and placed his napkin on the table. He made eye contact with her and in his gaze she read 'wait for me'. As soon as he quit the room, she wondered if he had really conveyed the message or if she was seeing what she wanted to read in his eyes.

Agatha interrupted her pondering. "Let us adjourn to the sitting room."

Betsy obediently followed allowing her to have first choice of the seating. She settled into a wingback chair so Betsy chose the divan. "Did you enjoy your day, Mrs. Agatha?"

"It was pleasant enough while the house was quiet."

Betsy tried to think of another question but became distracted listening to the footsteps upstairs followed by the faint sounds of Theodore's deep voice drifting into the easy cadence of the nursery story. She really should mention to him it was time for Henry to learn to read the stories to Theodore. Her attention was brought back to the room when Agatha rose from her chair.

"I believe I have had enough excitement for one day and will retire. Good evening, Mrs. Betsy."

Betsy stood also. "Good night, Mrs. Agatha." She watched as the elderly lady disappeared and wondered what to do next. She was not asked to leave but propriety dictated she should. It would not be proper for her to be alone with Theodore, but it would be rude not to wait for his return. Betsy resumed her seat. Was his aunt testing her morals? Perhaps she should leave. She stood up again, and then she heard Theodore's heavy tread leaving Henry's room. She recalled the compelling look in his eyes when he left the table and decided she wanted to know if her interpretation was correct. Foregoing decorum, she resumed her seat once again and folded her hands in her lap.

Theodore entered the room, hesitating at the threshold. He held her gaze for a moment before noticing she was alone. "Where is Aunt Agatha?"

"She retired to her room."

He gave a single nod. "Hmm." He turned to the side bar across the room from her. She heard the clinking of the brandy decanter against the glass tumbler and considered again if perhaps she should leave. She heard more glass clinking and realized he was fixing a drink for her too. She wondered what he would present to her since he hadn't asked her preference. Theodore crossed the room with the two drinks. Hers was a goblet of sherry; exactly what she would have requested. *Should I be flattered he knows my taste or insulted by his assumption?*

He handed her the glass. "Thank you for today, Mrs. Wheeler. It meant a lot to my son… and to me. It was the most enjoyable day we've had in a long time."

Flattered. She was definitely flattered. The piercing look and earnest appreciation in his voice left no room for ill thoughts. "It was my pleasure, Mr. Whitmore." He took the chair opposite the one his aunt vacated and immediately to her left. Reaching for any topic to start the conversation, she asked, "Have you found much to write about our little corner of the world?"

"Some. Not as much as I anticipated when coming here."

"Does that mean you will be leaving soon?" His answer was more important than she cared to admit.

"Not necessarily. Our stay is still open ended."

They lapsed into silence. Theodore stared at the drink in his hand. Betsy did so as well. He had large hands. She recalled the feeling of them around her waist earlier in the day. The thought unsettled her in a way she hadn't felt in a long time. Dangerous feelings to be having, alone as they were.

Theodore knew he should have escorted her home as soon as he discovered his aunt had retired. It was the proper gentlemanly thing to do. He should have, but he didn't. He didn't want to drink alone tonight. One of the things he missed most about his wife was their nightly ritual of sharing a drink and their thoughts after Henry was put to bed. It was their time alone. She would ask him about his day and let him bore her to the point of nodding off to sleep. Some nights he would scoop her up and carry her to the bedroom, and if she woke up...

He shook himself out of his reverie. They were dangerous thoughts to be having, alone as he was, with a woman who was not his wife. Especially as it was a woman he admired. Besides her pleasing looks, she was intelligent, resilient, steady and strong. She displayed surprising strength and leadership today during their sailing excursion. Instantly, images of holding her to his chest in her wet bathing costume flooded his mind. Really dangerous flesh and blood thoughts. He shifted to ease his discomfort.

Betsy broke the awkward silence. "Were you born in New York?"

It took a moment for her question to register in his mind. "Yes."

She didn't allow his short answer to discourage her. "How long have you worked at the newspaper?"

"Since I graduated from Union College in 1825."

"Did you plan to work at the paper after graduation?"

"No."

When it appeared he would not elaborate she prompted him. "What did you plan to do?"

Theodore pulled his mind away from his musings to focus on her questions. "I had no plans. It was assumed I would enter my father's business, but I had no interest in textiles."

"Then how did you get into the news business?"

"A family friend offered me a job. Newly married, I needed one at the time, so I accepted."

"Did your father approve?"

"He was disappointed at first."

She sensed he didn't want to elaborate so she changed direction. "How did you meet your wife?"

Her question surprised him. "At Union College."

She looked at him shrewdly. "Women are not allowed to attend college."

"Margaret was the daughter of one of the deans."

"And?"

He listened to the spring storm outside and allowed the memories he had avoided for the past year to surface. "I discovered her one rainy afternoon hiding in a corner of the library surrounded by a vast array of books. It was obvious I was searching for a book I needed for my thesis. She asked if she could help me find something. I refused, but she persisted until I told her what I was looking for which she handed to me a few minutes later. She then offered to help with my paper. I scoffed at the idea, probably even insulted her intelligence which challenged her to prove me wrong. She ended up spending the next few weeks helping me proofread and improve my work. We were married six weeks later."

Her eyes flared. "Oh!" He did not strike her as an impetuous man.

He could see her doing the mental math of Henry's birth. "It was nothing like that. Margaret didn't want a long engagement, and I certainly had no reason to delay the inevitable."

"Oh." The quietness of the room and the solitude of the moment emboldened her. "May I ask you a personal question?"

"A little late for asking permission. You have already asked several personal questions."

"True. Perhaps I should rephrase my request. May I ask you an intimate question?"

"Hmm."

How was she to interpret that sound? It could mean yes or no. His gaze was steady, as if daring her to ask the question, so she did. "What do you miss most about your wife?"

He pondered long enough she started to think he wouldn't answer but then he did. "Our nightly talks, much like this one. Her care of Henry. It's hard for a father to take the place of a mother. And having someone to share the burdens of life." He suddenly realized how much he had said. It was her turn to share. "And you? How did you meet your husband?"

She set her empty glass on the table and clasped her hands in her lap. "We were childhood playmates."

"Hmm. What do you miss about him?"

"The way he made me feel secure and cherished."

"I can imagine it is hard for a woman to make her way on her own. From what I can tell, you are doing so remarkably well."

His affirmation meant a lot to her. Softly she said, "Thank you."

Theodore decided it was time to bring an end to the intimate conversation. He casually stood up and took the two steps necessary to offer his hand to assist Betsy to her feet. "Perhaps it is time for you to return home."

"Yes, I suppose it is."

They were both surprised to discover it was still raining. They were so focused on each other, they didn't notice the low patter until he opened the door. Theodore didn't think it was the gentlemanly thing to do to send her home in the rain. "Perhaps you should wait a bit longer." Or he could let her wear his coat.

Betsy smiled, "A little rain never hurt anyone."

He looked back at the falling water and found the solution. "Wait a moment, please."

Betsy thought he was making too much fuss. She could quickly dash across the street and hardly be wet at all. He soon returned carrying an umbrella. She followed him out on the porch where he opened it, then offered her his arm. They walked across the street attempting to avoid the milky puddles of standing water mixed with limestone dust. When they reached her porch, he closed the umbrella. She turned to him and waited hoping to have a few more minutes of his company. The curtain of water enveloped the porch in privacy. She was disappointed when he opened the door for her and stepped back.

"Good night, Mrs. Wheeler."

"After such intimate conversation, you could call me Betsy."

"I could but what would others think? I'll not do anything that might harm your standing in the community, Mrs. Wheeler."

She curled in her bottom lip realizing he was firmly avoiding further familiarity. "I suppose you are right. Good night, Mr. Whitmore."

He nodded once and waited. She had no choice but to enter the lonely house. She quietly closed the door and listened to his tread as he exited the porch. She retreated to her bedroom to prepare for bed. As she reposed waiting for slumber, she replayed the evening's conversation, especially his response to what he missed about Margaret. The things he mentioned were were actions, not emotions. It made her wonder and gave her hope for their relationship. Perhaps he did not care as deeply for his wife as she assumed and therefore, perhaps, his heart would open soon for another. The confessions didn't really change the status of their relationship, but they gave her hope for the future.

Chapter 11

It was a pleasant Friday afternoon, the beginning of May, when Theodore stepped up to the piazza of the Custom House to join Judge Webb, William Whitehead, William Wall and Dr. Strobel. It was a custom of the educated men of the island to share their thoughts and the news of the day. "Good afternoon, gentlemen."

All the men warmly returned his greeting except for Dr. Strobel who still maintained a reserved distance.

Mr. Wall stepped forward with cigar box in hand. "We are celebrating the first run of cigars from my new factory. Would you care for one, Mr. Whitmore?"

"Congratulations, Mr. Wall. Thank you." He lifted one of the aromatic cigars from the Spanish cedar box and ran it under his nose, inhaling deeply. He then made use of the cigar scissors Mr. Wall handed him to cut the cap, followed by a strip of Spanish cedar Mr. Wall lit from a nearby candle on hand for just that purpose. The cigar lit with a few short puffs. The first taste of smoke gave hints of sweetness to enhance the rich tobacco. Theodore blew out the smoke and said, "Sir, you are to be commended for a very fine cigar."

Mr. Wall's eyes brightened with pride but otherwise he maintained neutral politeness. "Thank you, Mr. Whitmore."

William Whitehead said, "Our city has come a long way from its start not so many years ago. And with enterprising men like you, Mr. Wall, I look forward to seeing how much more we can grow and prosper."

Mr. Wall said, "As do I, Mr. Whitehead." He picked up his bowler and placed it on his head. "Gentlemen, I'm afraid I must leave you. The misses will be most grievous if I am late for supper. Good evening."

Judge Webb rose to his feet as Mr. Wall passed by. "Aye, mine as well. Good evening, gentlemen."

The two men left the piazza and Theodore claimed the Judge's vacant chair on one side of Mr. Whitehead. Dr. Strobel remained on the other side with his back towards town, so he did not see the runner until the boy was half way up the stairs. The doctor rose to meet him. "What news is there?"

In between panting breaths the boy said, "The *Marion*, sir, she's entered the harbour. I came as quick as I could, just like you asked."

Mr. Whitehead asked, "The revenue cutter, *Marion*?"

The boy nodded vigorously. "Yes, sir."

Mr. Whitehead rose to his feet. "Duty calls gentlemen. The custom collector is never free from his offices."

Theodore watched as Dr. Strobel pulled a coin from his pocket for the lad. Noting the doctor's underlying excitement, curiosity made him ask, "Are you expecting someone, Dr. Strobel?"

Mr. Whitehead blew out the candle and straightened his clothing.

Dr. Strobel unconsciously straightened his shirt as well. "I have reason to believe Mr. John James Audubon is aboard the *Marion*."

Theodore was too surprised to hide it. "The famed ornithologist?"

"Yes, indeed! I have been charged with greeting him upon his arrival."

Theodore was delighted with the news after weeks of nothing new to report to Bob since finishing the Indian and Humphries articles. Dr. Strobel and Mr. Whitehead headed straight for the docks. If the ship was just entering the harbour, he should have time to gather his son and meet up with them. He wanted to share the opportunity to meet a famous person with Henry. Theodore nearly ran to the house on Whitehead Street and flew through the front door.

Betsy was humming to herself as she hemmed a shirt while sitting on her front porch. She was startled to see Theodore run into his house as if something had gone terribly wrong. She laid her work aside and walked to the front railing straining to listen for sounds of duress. Perhaps he was just late for supper. Not that it should matter to her. Over two months had passed since the evening of Henry's birthday supper; months in which there was little contact between her and Theodore despite their intimate conversation that night. He was clearly keeping her at a distance, so his comings and goings should not concern her... but they did. There didn't seem to be any indications of trouble next door. She was about to return to her seat when the front door opened.

Theodore and Henry stood on the threshold. Theodore leaned back into the house. "Hurry Annalise, we don't want to miss him." The two of them then walked down the steps and into the street to wait. Theodore happened to look Betsy's way. "Hello, Mrs. Wheeler. Would you care to join us? We are headed to the dock to meet Mr. Audubon, the famous painter of birds."

Betsy dropped her work in her chair and stepped down from her porch into the streaming sunlight of late afternoon. "John James Audubon is here? Yes, I would like to meet him. Thank you for the offer." She hoped her excitement of meeting the painter disguised the pure joy she felt to be included in his company again.

Annalise came down the steps and the four of them walked briskly towards the docks, except for Henry who was nearly running to keep up with them.

Betsy asked, "Your aunt did not want to meet him?"

"She said she would wait for a more civilized opportunity."

As usual on a small island, word spread fast. There were people following behind them and many others already waiting with Mr. Whitehead and Dr. Strobel. Theodore took up a position next to Mr. Whitehead to make sure he would have an opportunity to speak with the famous woodsman. Dr. Strobel cast a look of annoyance his way.

The cutter was anchored in the harbour, and the rowboat had just reached the shore. Five men and a very large canine disembarked. Captain Day approached Mr. Whitehead and the two shook hands. "Good to see you again, sir. Here are our papers and assignment. I am sure the rest of our business can wait a moment. I have passengers anxious to make their acquaintance with your island."

Mr. Whitehead agreed. "Of course, we are anxious to meet them as well."

Captain Day gestured to each man as he introduced them. "May I present Mr. John Audubon and his assistants, Mr. Henry Ward and Mr. George Lehman. Gentlemen, this is Mr. William Whitehead, the collector of customs and your host, Dr. Benjamin Strobel."

Theodore noted Mr. Audubon's attributes already thinking of how he would write them.

Aquiline features of a six-foot gentleman, wavy light brown hair flowing past his shoulders with large observant gray-blue eyes. A man courteous in deportment and congenial in spirit.

Audubon stepped forward, clearly pleased to be greeting the surgeon. "Ah, Dr. Strobel, I have a letter for you from our mutual friend, Reverend Bachman. It is always a pleasure to meet a fellow enthusiast. The specimens you sent to the good reverend were intriguing."

Obviously pleased by the compliment, Dr. Strobel generously shook the hand of the taller woodsman. "He has written in advance of your arrival, as well, and I am looking forward to showing you around the island."

During this exchange, Henry had taken a great interest in the white-spotted Newfoundland, obediently standing next to his master, whose head was taller than his. Henry approached the huge stocky animal without fear, intending to pet his muzzle. Theodore's hand flew out to restrain his son by the shoulder. "Henry, no! You must ask first."

Audubon turned his attention to the pair and smiled at Henry. "His name is Plato." He then lifted his eyes to Theodore. "And he'll do no harm."

Encouraged to do so by dog and owner, Henry placed his hand on Plato's silky black muzzle as he stood eye to eye with the huge canine.

Theodore kept a wary eye on his son while he held his hand out to Mr. Audubon. "I am Theodore Whitmore, with the *New York Weekly*, pleased to make your acquaintance, sir. It would be an honor if you would grant me the privilege of an interview while you are here."

"Certainly, I would be happy to, but tell me, you are not here on account of my arrival? I could not be so famous as to warrant such a journey."

One could not resist this Frenchman's jovial spirit. Theodore's lips tilted upward before he answered. "Nearly famous enough sir, but no, other concerns brought me to this island a year ago. It is fortuitous that our visits coincide."

Dr. Strobel cast Theodore an irritated look as he interrupted them. "I am sure Mr. Audubon is weary from his travels." He then turned to their guests. "Will you be staying on the *Marion* or moving to accommodations on shore? Mrs. Mallory has a fine establishment just down the road."

"We will remain with the *Marion* for the time being, however, I was hoping to take up some of your time this evening gathering information, if you don't mind?"

Dr. Strobel's pleasure was apparent to all. "I am at your service, shall we go to my home? I have a few specimens I have not yet sent to Reverend Bachman I could show you."

Strobel led Audubon away from the gathered crowd much to the disappointment of those who were not given an opportunity to speak with him. Mr. Whitehead resumed his business with Captain Day while everyone else dispersed to their own dwellings. Betsy and Theodore started walking back with Henry in between them and Annalise trailing behind.

Betsy said, "He seems like a very nice man."

Theodore nodded. "Yes, he does."

"I think Dr. Strobel was a little miffed you were first to ask for an interview."

Theodore's mouth tilted. "He did send me a rather pointed look."

Henry piped up. "That was the biggest dog I have ever seen. Have you seen a bigger one Poppa?"

"No, son, I haven't. And you should have asked to pet the dog before you did so. He could have hurt you."

"No he wouldn't. I could see in his eyes he wanted me to pet him. He was looking right at me. Besides, you always say 'a child is to be seen and not heard' so how was I supposed to ask for permission and even if I could be heard adults never give a child a chance to speak."

Theodore was at a loss as to where to start unraveling Henry's logic let alone admonish his insolence.

Betsy smiled in sympathy at Theodore's conundrum.

"Poppa, can I have a dog?"

Theodore turned to his son in dismay.

Betsy couldn't help laughing at the look on Theodore's face. It slipped out before she could catch it. Fatherhood seemed to be getting the better of him at the moment. When he looked her way, she offered him an apologetic smile

The magical sound of Betsy's laughter caught Theodore by surprise. He found it pleasing to his soul and it eased his tension allowing him to reply to his son without the harshness he would have used a moment ago. "We'll discuss it later."

They reached their houses and Henry went running ahead up the porch steps.

Theodore turned to Betsy. "Good evening, Mrs. Wheeler."

"Good evening, Mr. Whitmore." She walked up her steps and paused to pick up her discarded needlework from earlier before returning inside.

* * *

Theodore discovered catching Mr. Audubon for an interview was not an easy task. The Woodsman's nickname was well earned as he was typically out hunting for specimens and observing birds in their habitat by three in the morning. He returned for a light dinner and then spent the rest of the afternoon and evening painting and journaling. Theodore tried to interview him during this time but the man was too distracted by his work. Theodore solved the problem by inviting himself along on the next excursion.

Two thirty in the morning, Theodore joined the group at the northernmost end of Front Street where two boats and the necessary gear awaited them. Their group consisted of the pilot, Mr. Eghan of Indian Key, several hands to maneuver the boats, Dr. Strobel, Mr. Audubon, George Lehman—the Swiss landscape painter, and Henry Ward—a young Englishman employed as taxidermist.

As the men were dividing into two boats Dr. Strobel kept close to Mr. Audubon obviously wanting to share transport with him. He also kept a conversation going with Ward and Lehman in an attempt to have a full boat and force Theodore to the other one. Although Theodore hoped to have time to interview Audubon before the bird hunting started in earnest, he felt it would not bode well to irritate Dr. Strobel and risk making an unfavourable impression with Mr. Audubon. Besides, he was sure to have other opportunities.

Mr. Audubon turned to Theodore. "Shall we ride together, sir? Now would be a good time to commence your interview."

Theodore couldn't help feeling a little guilty pleasure over Strobel's thwarted maneuvering. He was also heartened the Woodsman remembered his request. Mr. Ward graciously moved to the other boat making room for Theodore to join them. The two newspaper men occupied one seat facing the Woodsman and his artist companion. Plato settled on the bottom between them while rowers took up the other seats fore and aft.

Darkness still enveloped the island as they pushed off from shore. Theodore heard the humming wings of insects, the rustling of leaves and palm fronds stirred by the salty breeze, and the gentle lapping of water against the shore. These were the never-ending heartbeat of Key West. Their presence may be subtle but they encompassed the soul of those who embraced the island's charm.

In the predawn quiet, the two boats made their way out of the harbour headed for the darker presence of mangrove keys lying north of the island.

Theodore questioned Audubon in a near whisper. "What are you searching for today?"

"I hope to find flamingos, but I'm also looking for the breeding grounds of the other birds to study their nesting habits in more detail."

It was so dark Theodore could not put pencil to paper and have anything legible to show for his efforts. He hoped he would be able to remember the details of their conversation later. "Have you made any new discoveries?"

"Oh heavens, yes! Just yesterday, while searching the interior with Sargent Sykes, I discovered what I assumed to be a Zenaida Dove was in truth not. What's more, I have only seen this species on this island. I am contemplating naming it the Key West Pigeon in honor of the hospitality everyone has bestowed here."

One couldn't help sharing Mr. Audubon's excitement. "What makes this pigeon unique?"

"It is the most beautiful of cooers I have ever found. So beautiful, I sincerely doubt I can do it any justice at all in transferring it to paper. One cannot duplicate the metallic sheen of its wings."

All of a sudden Audubon grew quiet and listened intently. Theodore, at first could not hear anything though he listened as intently as his companion.

"There!" Audubon's face brightened.

Theodore heard it too. Birds. But he was sure one or two calls in particular had captured Audubon's attention. They were also nearing their destination.

The boats did not stop until they brushed the arching mangrove roots. Theodore expected Audubon to look at the island from the boat, but this was apparently not close enough. The man picked up his rifle and he and his dog were overboard in rapid succession. Theodore watched as he pushed his way from knee deep water into the woodsy thickness of the mangrove and soon disappeared from sight. It was not easy to climb through the twisted aerial roots of the island makers. Theodore and Strobel looked at each other but neither one felt inclined to follow into the verdant tangle, especially in the darkness with only a half-moon and a few lanterns to light the way. Sunrise was still hours away. They could hear thrashing in the brush but no other sounds until, moments later, their companions returned with nothing to show for their efforts except wet and dirty clothes. They explored the next two islands with the same result.

The boats were pushed off the islands but soon bottomed out on a sandy shoal. Theodore and Strobel were left no choice but to follow suit as all exited the boats which were then lifted and walked across the sand bar. Even Audubon helped. When they again found water of some depth their burden was set afloat and seats resumed. They rounded the island intent on passing through the narrow waters between Key West and Stock Island. It wasn't long before another flat was reached. This time they had to carry the boats nearly a mile, the strain of which kept talk to a minimum.

Streaks of dawn began to mar the night sky when their guide decided to put ashore on the eastern most bank of Key West. Birds could be heard calling but Audubon showed no interest as they were known species. Instead, he was intrigued by the variety of seashells. It wasn't long before all were involved in their collection. After an hour of this enterprise, their guest took note of his surroundings and proposed leaving the shells and unnecessary items in the boats in order to explore the interior, especially the salt ponds located on this end of the island. Hours were spent wading through mud and muck in search of the flamingo and other elusive prey. The sun rose, steadily heating the moist air to a humid stickiness. Still the Woodsman carried on exploring the fauna surrounding every patch of water in the hopes of finding his quarry and their breeding grounds.

Nearly two decades Theodore's senior, the indefatigable Woodsman kept pushing forward when many of the others were beginning to lag behind. Theodore was feeling the strain of the expedition. He supposed it would have been easier to bear if they at least found something of interest, but Mr. Audubon did not allow his disappointment to dissuade him. They continued on despite sweltering heat, burning sun, and swarming pests. He saw Strobel stop to rest in the shadow of a seagrape and decided to do the same until he realized the lack of movement increased the annoyance of the mosquitoes and sandflies.

It was a short lived relief when they returned to the island's edge to be greeted by the mild trade wind for the cooling effect did not last long as they absorbed the sun's reflected heat from the coral beach. At ten a.m., all were relieved to reach the lighthouse on the southern point. Mrs. Mabrity, the light keeper's wife, provided them with some much needed switchel to replace their lost fluids. Strobel, feeling more fatigued than the rest of the party, accepted use of the Mabrity's donkey to return directly home. The rest of the party soon resumed their journey.

Half way back to town, walking along the coast, they met up with Mrs. Wheeler, Annalise and Henry making their own exploration. An excited Henry ran to Theodore, anxious to show him his treasure only to find himself intercepted by Plato. The big dog nearly knocked him down in the excitement of his greeting. Henry laughed it off and, standing nose to nose, he pet the dog as it so obviously desired. When Theodore reached them, Henry held out his hand. "Look what I found Poppa. Isn't it wonderful? Mrs. Betsy said she has never seen the likes of it before."

Theodore picked up the cream colored, brown speckled shell to examine it closer and realized it wasn't like any he had seen this morning. He returned the shell to Henry. "You should show it to Mr. Audubon. He had us hunting for shells earlier this morning." His eyes drifted of their own accord to Mrs. Wheeler. She looked lovely in a blue dress with her wind-kissed cheeks and escaped tendrils of silky hair streaming in the coastal breeze.

Mr. Audubon approached them. "Hello young man, I don't believe we have been properly introduced."

Theodore said, "This is my son, Henry."

Henry straitened his shoulders and held out his hand which Mr. Audubon politely shook. "Nice to meet you sir."

"Likewise, young man."

Henry then held out his other hand with his treasure. "See what I found this morning?"

"May I?" asked Audubon gesturing toward the mollusk.

Henry nodded and Mr. Audubon picked it up for closer scrutiny. "I believe you may have found a Junonia. It is a rare shell. A prize indeed! Would you allow me to make a drawing of it? I promise to return it in a day or two."

Henry's chest swelled with pride for having found something rare. He looked to his father for guidance and receiving a nod, reluctantly agreed. "You promise to return it as soon as you are done?"

"I promise, Henry."

He carefully placed the shell on Mr. Audubon's open palm. "May I play with Plato?"

Mr. Audubon smiled. "Yes, you may."

Henry clapped his hands. "Come, Plato." The boy and canine went running towards the water's edge in joyful exuberance.

Mr. Audubon's gaze turned nostalgic. "He reminds me of my son, John, when he was that age."

Theodore asked, "And how old is he now?"

"Twenty."

"How many children do you have?"

"Two sons living." Quickly changing the subject he said, "Is this your wife?"

Theodore glanced at Betsy before answering Mr. Audubon. "I'm a widower. This is our neighbor, Mrs. Betsy Wheeler." He turned back to Betsy. "Mrs. Wheeler, this is Mr. John Audubon."

Betsy executed a proper curtsey as best she could on the uneven limestone. "Pleased to meet you Mr. Audubon."

"I am charmed to meet you, Mrs. Wheeler." While they talked the rest of the party continued onward. Now one of them called for Mr. Audubon's attention to something they found just around the bend of the shoreline. "I would love to visit more, but it seems we are being summoned." He whistled and Plato immediately responded by leaving Henry to return to his master's side.

Theodore would have preferred to stay with Henry and Mrs. Wheeler. He wasn't sure he had the energy to keep up with the woodsman, but he still had an interview to finish. "Good day, Mrs. Wheeler." He tipped his hat to her and waved to Henry before catching up to Mr. Audubon.

Betsy watched the two men walk away, then gathered Henry and Annalise. It was past time for all of them to get out of the sun. They took the path through the woods to return home rather than follow the men on the more circuitous route along the shoreline.

Later that afternoon, she made a visit to Abby instead of finishing the hem on a dress order. She wasn't normally one to procrastinate, but this time work could wait till later. A visit suited her mood.

* * *

Later that afternoon, Theodore left Mr. Audubon at the home of Captain Geiger, hard at work shaping his birds in preparation for drawing them. Theodore was on his way to speak with Captain Max when he crossed paths with Major Glassell. "Good afternoon, sir. What have you there?"

"Good afternoon, Mr. Whitmore." He held up his hand to display the dead bird with palpable excitement. "A cuckoo for Mr. Audubon shot by one of my soldiers this morning."

The bird, slightly larger than Major Glassell's fist, was mostly brown and black but had two striking features; a beautiful yellow chest and unique black tail feathers with large white circles on the tips. "I am sure Mr. Audubon will be most appreciative of your efforts." They parted ways and Theodore smiled to himself. It seemed the anthropologist was infecting many to enthusiastically advance his endeavors.

Theodore fortuitously learned of Mr. Audubon's plans for later this week and found he was in need of transportation. His first thought was of a friendly wrecker he met upon his arrival. Several conversations since then allowed him to build a solid friendship with Captain Max Eatonton. Having noticed his ship in the harbour, he was now headed to the captain's home further down Whitehead Street to enlist his aid.

Mr. Baxley bid Theodore to enter and escorted him to the study.

Max was making an entry in his personal journal when Theodore arrived. He set the book aside to finish later and eagerly rose from his desk to greet his visitor. "How are you, Mr. Whitmore?"

"Fine, and you, sir?"

"Well as can be on dry land. What can I do for you?" Max gestured to a padded arm chair in front of his desk for Theodore while he resumed his seat.

Theodore was glad Max did not require small talk. He could get straight to the point of his visit. "Would you be interested in sailing for the Dry Tortugas?"

"Possibly. What's your interest?"

"It seems Mr. Audubon is planning to sail there. I would like to continue working on my article about him which requires following him on his many jaunts."

"A curious fellow. Can't say I understand his fascination with them, but there are a lot of birds to be found in the Dry Tortugas. The sound of them is deafening at times. But why do you need my services? Why not sail with Audubon?"

"Alas, I am not allowed to travel aboard the *Marion*."

"Ah, tis true, a government vessel would not allow civilians aboard without due cause. I wonder how it is Mr. Audubon travels with them."

"It is my understanding he obtained special permission from several authorities."

"Ah. Well, I suppose I can take you out on one of my ships as long as an eminent storm does not require us to be elsewhere. When did you want to leave?"

"Thursday morning. You have quite a dangerous occupation; sailing into storms when others are apt to avoid them."

Max smiled hugely. "So I have been told."

Theodore smiled in return. "I suppose you have. As for my request, I am willing to pay for your time and expense." The men negotiated a fair price and discussed details for another half hour before Theodore stood to leave.

He offered his hand to Max. "Thank you."

"Certainly," Max walked Theodore to the foyer. Upon hearing his daughter's non-stop chatter from the stairway, he picked up Emily and swung her into the air loving the sound of her laughter. "There's my lil' sweetheart."

Theodore watched the interaction of father and daughter before looking toward the stairs to greet Abby. His heart skipped at the sight of Betsy, two steps above Abby, holding nine month old Christoff in her arms. An odd sensation of looking into his future overwhelmed his senses. His mind saw a vision of Betsy holding his child. Until that moment he wasn't aware he wanted more children. Or was it the woman he desired? He liked Betsy; even admired her. She was intelligent, honest, and trustworthy. She had an inner strength enabling her to survive and even thrive on her own. It would take a strong man to equal her in marriage.

Marriage?

No. Surely he wasn't thinking of marriage. He wasn't ready to put aside Margaret for another. But if he was... His eyes met Betsy's. Her luminous gaze was steady... and questioning. It seemed to him as if a momentous moment hung in the space between them. He deliberately let the moment slip away. He wasn't ready. Margaret was still there in his heart and even contemplating another felt like a betrayal. He was grateful when Abby interrupted his thoughts.

"Mr. Whitmore, will you stay for dinner?"

Betsy's heart, suspended while Theodore stared so intently, now rapidly resumed its beating leaving her lightheaded. She shifted the baby to her side so she could grasp the hand rail for support. Had she truly seen it? A fleeting glimpse of desire so powerful she was left breathless by the strength of it. Before hope could settle in her breast, the ghost of his wife sailed between them, and his eyes shuttered. Her mother's words came to mind: 'careful what you wish for.' If a half felt emotion on his part affected her so strongly, could she withstand the full measure of his desire? She bit her bottom lip to keep from smiling. She sure would like to find out. His steady deep voice drew her from her musings.

"I am afraid I cannot. My aunt is expecting me home shortly."

Abby tried again, not wanting to let go of this opportunity to interrogate him on Betsy's behalf. "Of course the invitation includes the rest of your family."

Theodore nodded in understanding but held firm. His feelings of a moment ago still lingered and were too raw to ignore if he remained in Betsy's company. "Another time, perhaps." He made good on his escape *post-haste*.

Max closed the door behind Theodore and turned to the ladies. He noticed Theodore's reactions and looked to its source. "Aye, you've anchored his attention, Betsy-girl, but he'll not let go of his heart."

Betsy felt her sliver of hope shatter. She knew Max was right. "So it is just as I feared." His heart was still tied to another. How long would it take for him to let Margaret go? Would he return to New York before she had a chance to win his affections? Or what if she did win his affections? Was she willing to live in New York? She didn't need to ponder the question. For love, absolutely!

Abby sent her friend a compassionate smile. "I hoped you were mistaken, but it seems as though you have read the situation correctly."

Chapter 12

May 10th, 1832

As agreed, Theodore met Max on the wharf in the pre-dawn of Thursday morning. Stars were still bright in the dark sky. He left his household in the middle of their nightly rest but still he noticed the *Marion* was already gone. They silently rowed the gig out to Max's three-masted barque, the *Abigail Rose*, riding gently at anchor in the harbour.

Theodore nodded to the empty anchorage of the *Marion*. "Can you catch her?"

Max smiled. "No, she has a two hour head start on us but really there is no need. We will likely beat her to the Dry Tortugas as she will be detained by her duties, first of which is to pick up the light keeper at Sand Key."

The *Marion* brought to mind the conversation Theodore had yesterday with Ben Strobel.

Theodore crossed paths with the doctor on his way home from the Eatonton's. At first glance the man seemed upset or disgruntled but he hid it behind a courteous greeting. Theodore was a bit surprised by his address. The doctor usually continued walking past with only a brief nod. Propriety made Theodore ask, "How are you today?"

The doctor's lips pursed briefly in displeasure before he gave a non-committal reply. "Fine. And you sir?"

"Well, indeed sir." Theodore wondered at the reason for this conversation.

"I see you have been to visit Captain Eatonton. Might I suppose you were seeking passage to the Dry Tortugas?"

Theodore unconsciously gave a single nod at an angle confirming the doctor's assumption but also revealing his discomfort with the doctor's preoccupation with his movements. "Hmm."

"Whilst working together on his latest specimens at my home yesterday evening, Mr. Audubon issued an invitation for me to join his excursion to the Dry Tortugas on the *Marion*." He emphasized the last as if to impress Theodore with his importance and being allowed to travel on the revenue cutter. "Naturally, I had to regretfully decline. While I could spend a day following the good man around the island, I could not so neglect my duties as army surgeon and town doctor to take leave for several days on such a lark as chasing birds. However, you must allow, my position as editor of the paper makes me very keen to follow him." He paused waiting for Theodore's response.

Forced to say something, Theodore replied, "Of course."

Strobel's brow furrowed when he said no more and then smoothed as he drew forth a congenial smile. "You'll, no doubt, be writing the story for your paper." Again, the doctor waited for a reply.

Theodore was by nature a listener rather than a talker; when engaged in an interesting conversation he rarely did more than ask questions as needed. He refrained from offering his own experiences or opinions preferring to absorb those of his companion. He found a well asked question was all that was required to get a person talking. It was not often this tactic was turned on him. It was even more unusual for his movements to be scrutinized. He found it discomforting. "Yes."

"I was wondering if you would be willing to share your writings with the *Gazette.*"

Theodore relaxed. So this was what he was after, collaboration for his paper. Knowing how much Strobel admired Audubon, he knew the doctor would dearly love to be in Theodore's shoes and his commitment to his paper would make it doubly hard for him to ask Theodore to submit the story in his place. Theodore, from their first meeting, had pegged the doctor as a shallow, jealous man caught up in his own self-importance. In the year since then his interaction with Strobel was rare leaving his opinion unchanged. Now he considered if perhaps he had misjudged him.

Before Theodore could answer, Strobel added, "Of course a customary recompense would be made depending on the content."

Even if his first opinion was correct, Theodore was not a petty man and besides it was likely he might have use of Strobel as a source once he returned to New York. With that thought in mind, he answered, "I would be willing. Shall we discuss the details upon my return?"

Dr. Strobel gave a half nod. "Of course. I hope you have a pleasant trip."

Theodore returned the nod and continued on his way.

* * *

Theodore boarded the barque with Max and was introduced to the crew. The ship was neat and tidy and the crew worked well together. In no time they were sailing rapidly across the turquoise water of the Florida Straits towards the Gulf of Mexico.

Max noticed Theodore closely watching his men work the lines and sails. By the time the sun made an appearance on the horizon behind them they were in open water and well away from the reefs. They could safely put on more sails so Max decided to issue Theodore a challenge. He nodded towards the lines. "Why don't you give it a try?"

"Seriously? Wouldn't I be in the way?"

"Not at the moment." He raised his voice. "Men! Let's show him how it's done. Prepare to make sail."

The crew lined up on the rope. Theodore wasn't about to ignore the gauntlet. Besides he could use the exercise. He took up a place in the line.

142

Max called out, "Haul away!"

The crew started pulling the rope to raise the sail. What looked like a reasonable pace from the sidelines was in reality too fast for Theodore to keep up. His first attempt was pathetic. Some of the men ridiculed his efforts fueling his determination to succeed. Max issued more commands. Theodore's second attempt hauling rope went much better, earning him a slap on the back. Max gave a few more commands for Theodore's benefit before allowing the crew to rest. Theodore took up a spot at the rail on the starboard side of the helm.

Morning light gave way to pure blue skies sprinkled with fluffy clouds and a fortunate freshening wind. A beautiful day for a voyage. He leaned over the balustrade and became entranced watching the whitecaps on the passing water. Wildlife was in abundance if one bothered to keep vigilant. He saw turtles, large fish, jelly fish, and what he thought was a dolphin until Max informed him it was in fact a shark. Even above, birds trailed the wind with the ship.

A few hours after dawn, Max pointed out islands on the northern horizon. "Those are the Marquesas." Theodore remembered seeing them on a map in Max's cabin. They were a ring of islands not quite half way between Key West and the Dry Tortugas.

The second half of the trip, Theodore's thoughts turned inward. His encounter with Betsy was pushed aside in deference to the things he needed to get done. Now he had nothing to occupy his time or his hands and so the memory of her on the stairs came unbidden to his mind and once there could not be dislodged so he gave way to analyzing it with rational thoughts.

It had been a year since Margaret's passing. An acceptable amount of time by society's standards for mourning. Yet he wasn't done grieving. His heart was lighter now. The gut wrenching sorrow subsided leaving a vague emptiness in its place. He realized it was the hole Margaret used to fill. He still missed his wife. Every evening when she wasn't there to hear about his day and every morning he didn't wake up to her smile.

The practical side of him recognized that Henry needed a mother. It was clear in the way he cleaved to Betsy whenever she was near. Maybe it was time for him to put Margaret's memory aside for the sake of his son. He could see the logic in such an idea. Besides he may never be able to love another woman. It made sense to look for a wife to be a mother to his son and to provide more children. Love didn't have to be a part of it. Many married for reasons other than love. He could consider it. At the moment no candidates came to mind. Betsy wasn't even a consideration. She needed someone to love her in return. Something he couldn't give her. Her friendship, on the other hand, he enjoyed very much. And she was good with Henry. So patient with all his questions. She was going to be an excellent mother one day but not for Henry. Theodore would look for someone who was willing to settle for a loveless marriage and he would start as soon as he returned to New York.

His time here in the Keys seemed to be coming to an end. His purpose of reporting on the army's movements had come to naught. The Indian situation, while tenuous, was at a status quo. The Moultrie Creek Treaty gave them twenty years on the reservation of which eleven remained. While he did have plenty to write about on the topic, he didn't see a reason for it to keep him in Key West. Audubon's visit was the most newsworthy event to happen but once he left the island, there would be nothing to keep Theodore from leaving.

His secondary purpose of finding solace after Margaret's passing was fulfilled. He felt strong enough now to face returning to his home and Henry had grown so much over the last year, Theodore felt certain he would be able to adjust as well. Yes, it seemed it was time to end this respite and return to New York.

Early afternoon they passed expertly through the southeast channel and around to the north side of Garden Key before dropping anchor. The deeper draft of the barque did not allow them as close as the schooners occupied by the wreckers. Once the ship was secured, Max waved to his friends on the other ships before joining Theodore at the rail to await the arrival of the *Marion*. The ship's bow pointed southeast toward the lighthouse and outbuildings on Garden Key, the largest of the islands. The next largest was Loggerhead Key which could be seen in the distance off their stern. Both supported some trees but they were short, gaunt and gnarled from constant abuse by the trade winds. The waters around them reflected many different shades of blue due to the varying depths of water over the shoals and the changing sand, coral and vegetation found beneath the surface. What Theodore found odd was the absence of red mangroves that copiously surrounded the other Keys. Here sand and water merged uninterrupted by vegetation.

Ahead of them, Bird Key appeared to be covered in brush and an overwhelming number of birds filled the sky above it. The sound of them permeated all, even from their distance of several hundred yards. This place attracted large quantities of birds for breeding. They were everywhere; nesting on the islands, flying in the air, and floating on the water. Many were feeding on fish. Theodore noticed they had several methods of catching their dinner. Some floated on the surface and ducked their heads under water to snatch a passing fish, some skimmed the water's surface while others dramatically dove straight in to the surf. Before they were even settled at anchor, birds were perched on the spars of the ship. No wonder Mr. Audubon was so anxious to visit this place.

Max leaned back against the balustrades. "I would have preferred sailing the *Mystic* into these waters but she couldn't be spared from her duties patrolling the reef in the upper keys."

"No matter. I would not be this close without your aid."

"You'll soon learn the disadvantage when you tire of rowing in chase of this bird man. You do mean to follow him around?"

Theodore again looked at the distance from their position to land and began to understand Max's warning. He brought his gaze back to Max's, "Yes."

"Then you'll need a boat." Max gestured toward the hull of a small boat stored above the cookhouse. "There's an old row boat we can tie to the side of the ship for your use. You should be able to manage it on your own if need be."

Max turned to lean over the stern rail and nodded past Theodore towards the southwest, "Loggerhead Reef is over that way. It's where I first met my wife on this very ship. She and her father were sailing for New Orleans when this ship hit that reef. I was the second wrecker to arrive. The wreck master, an oily man by the name of Captain Talmage, assigned my crew to remove passengers." Max's grin deepened at the recollection. "I found Abby in the hold trying to rescue the family jewels all by herself." Max shook his head, "She is stubborn when she has her mind set but so am I and I had cargo to unload and she was keeping me from it. I got her out of the hold but Talmage ended up with the chest of jewels. We had to fight him in court to get them back which brought Abby and I together." Max paused and a look of wonder passed across his face, "Hum, never thought about it quite that way before; guess I owe that old bilge bucket a debt of gratitude."

"How long have you been married?"

"Nearly four years."

They were interrupted by Max's crew, now finished with their duties. "Captain, do we have permission to use one of the jollies?"

"Aye." He slapped Theodore on the back. "What do you say we join them for a little fun?"

"Hmm." Theodore wondered what kind of fun they had in mind. He hoped it wasn't fishing for shark in a small boat. He assumed the crew was teasing him when they suggested as much earlier but now he wasn't so sure it was a jest as he noticed a tell-tale fin pass under the shadow of the hull. He grimaced as the vision of Jonah and the whale came to mind.

Max and Theodore lowered the small rowboat to the water while the rest of the men piled into the larger jolly boat. They headed toward Garden Key to do some exploring in the shallows in somewhat safety from the sharks patrolling the deeper water. The men amusingly would dive under the waist deep water like a duck and bring up a prize, collecting the oceans odds and ends; shells, coral, mollusks and the like.

In the distance, Theodore could see swarms of birds over the land while many flew over their heads and others were diving into the water for fish. They were everywhere and their cries blended into the cacophony of sound enveloping him.

The afternoon grew long and having grown tired of the water their group joined a crew of wreckers for a drink aboard the *Siren's Song*. An hour or so before sunset their host lifted his spyglass to an approaching ship.

Theodore walked over to the rail to watch in anticipation. They had been waiting several hours now for the *Marion* to arrive.

The *Siren's* captain announced, "Aye, 'tis *The Lady of the Green Mantel* come to join us."

Theodore looked to Max in disappointment as he came up beside him. Noting his expression Max clapped him on the back. "He means the *Marion*. The other is her nickname."

Relieved to hear this, Theodore returned his gaze to the ship now making its way carefully through the deep but intricate channels between the islands. While still several hundred yards distant, Theodore could discern Audubon's palpable excitement. The man nearly couldn't wait to get overboard. It surprised him naught when no sooner had they anchored, a yawl was lowered and headed in the direction of Bird Key. Following suit, Theodore bid a hasty farewell to the wreckers, intent on returning to his rowboat. He was surprised when Max joined him in pursuit of the ornithologist.

Max and Theodore easily rowed the short distance to Bird Key, arriving only moments after Audubon's crew clambered ashore. Thousands of black and white swallows rose in protest like a swarm of bees. The air filled with the sound of their distress. Theodore intended to join the invaders on land but as they began immediately firing upon the winged birds he felt safer observing from the boat. The angry birds attacked the men making known their displeasure. Undeterred, Audubon and his followers fearlessly made their way into the brush. Some of the men used sticks to procure specimens for the eccentric naturalist's work. In less than a half hour, they killed hundreds of birds and collected baskets full of eggs. This was obviously more than he needed for study and drawings which concerned Theodore until Max mentioned both were also good eating.

Audubon called a halt to the melee as twilight descended. They gathered the birds in buckets. Plato could be seen running here and there in search of the hunted prey. Theodore had never known a dog as disciplined as Plato. He was the perfect companion for the woodsman. On the return to the *Marion*, they pulled alongside Max and Theodore and issued an invitation to join them for a feast of roasted fowl which was eagerly accepted.

While dinner was prepped, Theodore welcomed Audubon's invitation to see his works in progress below decks. Before descending the ladder, Audubon paused at a water barrel to soak his handkerchief which he then used to clean his bloodied hands. At Theodore's questioning look he proudly showed him the battle wounds received from beak and claw in defense of raided nests. Even this discomfort gave the tall woodsman pleasure for he had learned something about sooty terns in the process.

Below deck, Theodore was shown the many drawings completed and in process from Audubon's travels since leaving Charleston. Carefully preserved specimens and detailed journals littered every corner of his cabin. Audubon took him into the hold to show him the many cages of birds he was trying to keep alive. Theodore was beginning to appreciate how much effort was supplied in producing the works of this master ornithologist.

Later, Audubon and the crew celebrated their success with drink. It was at this time, Theodore learned the *Marion* had been commissioned to bring the Sand Key light keeper to inspect the Garden Key light in order to provide a legitimate excuse for transporting Mr. Audubon to the Dry Tortugas. He also was regaled with how the marines of the revenue cutter *Marion* had boarded the sloop *Paragon* just prior to her arrival at Garden Key. Captain Noyes produced papers declaring the ship to be carrying only ballast but a search of the hold revealed it was laden with cotton. Captain Day promptly dispatched a letter to the Key West Customs office reporting the violation of customs.

An hour or so after dark one of the crew members alerted them of a new interest. Turtling. Loggerhead sea turtles were spotted in the water headed for land to lay their eggs. Audubon was not about to miss this opportunity for discovery. In no time, the boats were full of men rowing for shore, including Max and Theodore. They met the wreckers from the other ships onshore who were eager to supplement their shares with money to be had from turtles.

Theodore observed Audubon who was carefully observing the turtles' journey from water to land and noting how far inland they traveled before choosing their nest site as if oblivious of their audience. Audubon was fascinated, watching by lantern light, as they used their legs to shovel sand out from under their body in a most efficient manner, piling it up on either side of them. Once the hole was deep enough the eggs were deposited and unknowing to the turtle, carefully counted by her observer. The sand was then efficiently pushed back into the hole, covering her progeny but not before a few eggs were stolen for research. When the turtle was done she tiredly worked her way back to the water; her nest expertly covered and hard to detect.

Over and over Audubon watched and recorded the details of the turtles before turning his attention to the wreckers. These men were collecting the nests of eggs and capturing some of the animals for sale. Audubon now watched these men work. Once a turtle began the process of digging a nest and laying eggs she did not allow anything to disturb her, thereby making her an easy target. The men would choose a side and putting their shoulder between her legs use their strength to heave her over onto her back where she became helpless. A rope was then tied around her and she was dragged to the boats to be hauled back to their ship. The turtles were kept and sold alive to preserve the meat for market. Eggs were also gathered for sale as food.

Audubon wanted to capture some turtles for study. Men from the *Marion* were eager to put their strength to the test in turning over the creatures. Theodore gave it a try as well soon learning it was not as easy as the wreckers made it look. These animals were very large and some likely weighed over five hundred pounds. They did manage to flip a few and Audubon skillfully used his knife to kill and then dissect them. Dictating notes for his assistant as he went along.

Theodore decided he had seen enough after the first dissection. He and Max wearily rowed back to the *Abigail Rose*. They had not slept in twenty-four hours and Theodore was anxious to reach his bunk with the delightful anticipation of sleeping late in the morning. He wondered how Audubon was able to continue. He had likely been awake even longer.

Dawn was coloring the sky when Theodore heard the knock on his door. He asked to be alerted when there was movement from the *Marion* but this was too soon. He rolled over in disgust wishing he could ignore the summons. Hoping perhaps there was another reason for the intrusion he lifted his head to ask, "Yes, what is it?"

Muffled by the door he heard the reply, "Mr. Audubon is on deck, sir. He looks to be preparing to leave ship."

"Thank you." His head dropped back to the pillow for a moment before summoning the energy needed to get up.

Over the next few days, Theodore learned firsthand to what lengths John James Audubon was willing to go to study birds. No inconvenience was too great. No suffering too much. Nothing bothered him; not smell, not water, not discomfort or difficulties. Not even a shark would deter him from his quest for long. Thursday, Theodore watched from shore as the woodsman made his way through a channel in pursuit of his quarry. He was so engrossed in his work he wasn't aware of the danger stalking him below the water's surface until Theodore pointed out the tiger shark sending Audubon to shore with all due haste.

The trek they made around Key West on Monday, while difficult, was not to be compared with the discomforts Theodore experienced on Friday. He rowed from the *Abigail Rose* to the *Marion* long before dawn to join the day's excursion. Mr. Audubon commissioned one of the wrecking vessels the night before to take him and his party some eight miles distant to Booby Key; so named for the large nesting of booby gannets. Theodore pressed Captain Max to offer his services so he might enjoy a little extra sleep while they sailed but was informed a ship of lighter draft was required.

To Theodore, initially, the birds were too similar to discern the differences which fascinated Audubon. They all seemed to be black, brown, white or some combination thereof, mostly of a medium size and they flew by much too fast for his observation. But as he participated in the collecting of specimens and listened to Mr. Audubon enthusiastically point out the different flight patterns, color distinctions, tail shapes, nesting habits and methods of catching fish he began to distinguish the differences between a sooty tern, a noddy tern, a booby gannet, or a frigate.

Theodore wasn't sure what he expected of Booby Key but certainly more than a sand bar of only a few acres barely above the water's surface.

The yawl was launched and they approached the key in the hopes of bringing down a few specimen before disturbing the birds into flight. The birds were engaged in pluming themselves or basking in the sun but still their plans were thwarted when fifty yards from the beach their prey flew off in all directions. The pilot advised landing to wait for the birds' return, to which Audubon was very agreeable. Little did Theodore suppose this would mean laying upon one's back on the dung covered sand while the nasal passage was assaulted by the pungent droppings scant inches away from one's face.

The pilot moved the boat away and soon the birds returned although they refused to alight. The white chested, brown birds with webbed yellow feet presented easy targets. Guns were brought to bear as they hovered above the invaders. Still it was difficult to shoot them and harder still to catch them if the wound was not lethal for many of the birds would rapidly make their way to the water and secure their escape. It took several hours to procure thirty specimen.

From there they sailed on to Noddy Key. Theodore stood near Audubon as he catalogued their cache looking for the best specimen to later use as models for his artwork. The rest were carefully dissected, studied and journaled. Theodore already understood the tortures the man was willing to endure, what great lengths he was willing to go to get a specimen. Now he was beginning to appreciate the details the man was collecting; the science of it all. For example, the unique aspect of this species were their webbed feet and long pointed beak. Both ideal for their manner of catching fish which was to dive straight into the water. Theodore was fascinated by the strangely odd sky blue feet of some of the birds. Audubon believed these to be juveniles of the same species. Theodore found himself growing as anxious as Audubon to make the next discovery.

Audubon looked up from his journal to the other occupants of the room. "Would you say their cry was somewhat like that of a strangled pig? *Hork, hork*. Is that about right?"

Theodore and the others nodded in confirmation and again he was struck by the man's attention to detail. Theodore *heard* the birds but Audubon *listened* to them.

They arrived at Noddy Key in the evening. It was thickly covered with bushes and small trees of which few were taller than a man allowing them the unique perspective of looking down on the nests much to Audubon's delight. These birds were the opposite of the elusive booby. They allowed them to get several yards inland before the greater part began to take flight as they approached and land again as soon as they passed. Many flew so close as to be caught by hand. Theodore thought the noddy tern brazen with a menacing look in their eye. He preferred the boobies with their colorful feet.

On the return to Garden Key, Theodore made a point of asking the

Woodsman any other questions he could think of to finish the interview. Max had to return to Key West in the morning so this was likely his last opportunity to have the man's attention—distracted as it may be with all his new discoveries.

Theodore finished making the last of his notes, then quietly watched Audubon work the latest tern specimen into a desired pose using wire. For a moment he thought it would follow the last four into the rubbish pile but suddenly the woodsman stood back with a smile on his face and then looked to Theodore to share his triumph.

The man was never still for long. Done with one task he moved to the next in rapid succession. He cleared the space of all his previous appurtenance to set up his easel and pencils and begin capturing the still life. As he explained once before to Theodore, time was of the essence. The bird's plumage lost their vibrancy after death, some more rapidly than others. Theodore was surprised he would do such delicate work while they were sailing but he seemed to have developed a stance to compensate for the ship's movements.

When Audubon was done drawing the subject, his artwork often would go to his assistant to add background interest. The collection, when they were done, would go to an engraver to make copper plates which would then be stamped on very large paper called double elephant folio and hand colored. Audubon had approval on the final outcome before it would be reproduced to fill the subscriptions for his 'Birds of America' book.

But in this quiet moment, Theodore wasn't thinking about the man's work. He was pondering the sacrifices made by him and his family. "May I ask a personal question, for my sake, not for the paper?"

He received a distracted nod from Audubon.

"How does your family cope with your long absences? I ask because I am now gone days and weeks at a time for work and wonder how it will affect my son."

Audubon paused with paintbrush held in mid-air. "I am fortunate my wife is understanding and supportive. She has had much of the responsibility of the home and children these many years and she has also done much to help get my first works in print. Without her support I would have given up long ago."

Audubon returned to his work with such concentration that for a moment Theodore had the curious notion he imagined his reply. Feeling he had taken up enough of the man's time he chose to remain silent for the remainder of the voyage content to watch the artist work while he outlined his story and pondered his situation with Henry. A new mother for his son was definitely in order but it must be one who would tolerate his long absences. A strong woman willing to accept an unromantic but not platonic relationship. He would marry this time using his head and not his heart.

Sunset was upon them by the time they returned to Garden Key. The sheets were dropped and the ship was soon anchored while Audubon packed up his belongings in preparation of returning to the *Marion*. Theodore returned his work to his satchel then approached his companion with outstretched hand. Audubon grasped it with both of his.

"Mr. Audubon, it has been a pleasure learning about you and your work. Thank you for allowing me the opportunity to join your excursions and interview you."

"It was my pleasure, Mr. Whitmore. I wish thee safe journey."

They parted ways and Theodore went above deck to bid farewell to the wreckers. He made quick work of rowing back to the *Abigail Rose*.

On deck, a sailor noticed the bucket of dead birds he held. "I see you brought some back. We'll be eating good tonight!" He took the birds from Theodore. "We call these noddies." He drew Theodore's attention to the yard arm. "'Cause once it turns dark they perch there to sleep."

Exhausted, Theodore could barely keep his eyes open through supper, despite the jovial company. Gratefully, he turned into his bunk. When he awoke the next morning they were already many miles from the Dry Tortugas. Theodore broke his fast, then strolled on deck for a few minutes to stretch his legs before settling in to work at the galley table. Having a full story to write felt good. His thoughts flowed freely onto the paper. His scrawling words rapidly filled the page. He was little disturbed by the mild storm they were sailing through nor the swaying lantern casting shadows across his writing.

By the time they docked in Key West, the article was complete and ready to send to Bob plus a copy for Dr. Strobel. His readers should delight in learning of a day in the life of John James Audubon. He was proud of the results of this trip and happy to have been able to take part in Audubon's exploration of the Dry Tortugas but he was also glad to be returning to the comforts of home and a bath.

Chapter 13

The *Abigail Rose* returned to Key West harbour Monday evening with the sun sinking behind her. Theodore helped the crew secure the ship. Anxious to get home, he thanked Max again for accommodating him then joined the first group of sailors headed for shore in the rowboat. Supper that night was a lively affair as he regaled Henry and Annalise with his exploits in the company of Mr. Audubon. Agatha pretended not to listen but every once in a while he saw the corner of her mouth twitch in amusement.

The next day he was catching up on his mail before visiting Dr. Strobel to hand over his story when a letter from Private Randolph gave him cause for concern.

> *Sir, you asked that I inform you if the situation here changed in any way. I deem it prudent at this time to inform you of the arrival of General Gadsden with several other men in his company. At least one of them is an interpreter. I do not yet know the role of the others. I leave it to you to decide your course of action but I believe something is afoot in regards to the Indians.*

Theodore's first instinct was to repack his bags but after giving it more rational thought he instead made his way to Major Glassell's office for advice.

After reading the contents of the letter, Major Glassell folded it and handed it back to Theodore. "I have no word of anything out of the usual. It is likely nothing more than a routine inspection by the war department."

"Hmm." Theodore wasn't convinced but decided it was prudent to wait for more news.

Audubon's party returned from the Dry Tortugas a few days later and stayed another five days on the island. It was enough to distract Theodore and allow him to temporarily put aside thoughts of returning to the reservation. Not long after Audubon said goodbye to their community and sailed for Indian Key, Theodore was summoned by Major Glassell. He approached the army encampment full of curiosity as to the reason. Although the major, so far, was very forthcoming when asked questions, he was not likely to voluntarily share information with a civilian. So why was he summoned?

Major Glassell stood to greet Theodore. After shaking hands he got right to the point. "It seems, sir, I owe you an apology."

"How's that, sir?"

"Your informant was correct. Colonel Gadsden wasn't visiting the reservation for an inspection. I've received word there was a meeting held at

Payne's Landing with the Indians. Apparently it was a secretive, unexpected meeting led by General Gadsden and the new Indian Agent, Major John Phagan."

"For what purpose?"

"To negotiate a new treaty."

Theodore's brow rose high. Glassell's news dismayed him. The new treaty most likely did not benefit the Indians and he was keenly disappointed to have missed a monumental event. Also, the major's inflection on the word negotiate told Theodore there was cause for concern. "You think they coerced the Indians into a new treaty?"

Glassell sidestepped the question. "The details are unknown but the intent is to move them out of Florida."

"We knew it was only a matter of time. Why the secrecy?"

"From a military strategy, when expecting resistance you don't give the enemy a chance to plan and act. You want to catch them by surprise."

It was a good answer but Theodore had a hunch it was not the full answer. The major suspected more than he was telling but being an honorable man he wasn't willing to share more than the facts. Theodore knew what he had to do. "Is anyone headed to the interior?"

"Not at this time."

Theodore was going to have to make his own way to the reservation.

Frustrated by the delay of finding transport, Theodore couldn't help but think if he was on the mainland, he could climb on a horse and gallop off at his discretion. He could have been halfway there by now. Instead, it took several days to find a ship headed to Fort Brooke and every day that passed he worried over what else he might be missing. He was sure this latest treaty was meant to validate moving the Seminole tribe to the western territory. He wondered how fast the Government would act on it. Was it possible he could get there and find them all gone? He doubted the move could be accomplished so quickly but it wasn't impossible and therefore his anxiety grew. While he waited, he sent a letter to Bob informing him of the treaty and suggested he reach out to his contacts in Washington for details of the document and the reasoning behind it.

Henry took his leaving again in stride. Theodore was grateful since he didn't want to upset his son. Of course, on the other hand, it gave him concern over the lack of closeness in their current relationship. He vowed to spend more time with him upon his return. Aunt Agatha curiously had little to say of his departure. This time, there was no point in visiting Betsy. His family made regular visits across the street. If they needed anything, she would be the first to know.

He tried to keep his distance from her not wanting to inadvertently encourage her feelings when he could not reciprocate them. He knew she would accept his friendship but it seemed cruel to leave her hopelessly wanting more. As long as Margaret's spirit was still with him he felt it was best to maintain a barrier between them.

June 7th, 1832

It was with great relief Theodore approached Micanopy's village in the golden hour before dusk. The smell of food cooking and the sounds of children playing were comforting after the days of isolation on his solitary walk from Fort Brooke.

He arrived at the fort six days ago to discover no one was headed toward the reservation, no mount was to be found for hire or purchase, and General Gadsden and the others involved in the treaty had already departed the territory. Not wanting to delay any longer, Theodore decided to walk on his own. It was a risk but fortunately the only threat he encountered was the alligators sunning on the road. They were daunting to walk past but none seemed interested in him. Although one did twitch his tail and turn as Theodore was passing. It gave him such a fright, he ran flat out for several yards before he dared to look back relieved to find the reptile had not given chase.

He probably should have gone to the Indian Agent's office first but he did not expect Agent Phagan to be forthcoming with information nor did he believe the man would welcome him so he decided to see Chief Micanopy first. Besides, he was tired, the village was closer, and it was growing dark. He did not care to spend another night sleeping with one eye open for wild animals.

As soon as the children recognized him, they surrounded him with excited chatter and escorted him to the chief. Theodore wished he understood what they were saying. Micanopy came forward to greet him with several warriors trailing behind. Theodore was welcomed with reservation. He expected as much.

A black warrior was summoned forward and Theodore was introduced to Cudjo, another one of the tribe's interpreters. Through him, Micanopy asked the purpose of his visit.

Theodore replied, "I have heard of the meeting at Payne's Landing but do not know the details. I came to ask you what transpired."

Cudjo translated the chief's reply. "Why not ask your people?"

"I will, but there are two sides to every story and I want to hear yours." Theodore waited patiently for Cudjo to interpret.

Micanopy said, "Come by the fire and share a meal. Later we will speak with the peace pipe."

Theodore nodded in agreement, thankful for his consent. The tribe's feelings were an important part of the story. Theodore remembered to bring gifts this time. He presented several knives and other trinkets easy to carry on his long walk to the chief before their meal. They were accepted with appreciation.

Later that evening the men gathered, including chiefs and warriors from neighboring villages. Abraham acted as interpreter, relaying Micanopy's retelling of events.

Theodore learned in early April, General Gadsden told Micanopy they needed to talk. When asked the subject he said it was moving west. Micanopy immediately objected but Gadsden was insistent so the chief asked for a month to gather the other chiefs. On May 8th they met at Payne's Landing and argued for days. The tribe couldn't understand why they were being asked to move when there was still time left on the Moultrie Creek treaty. Gadsden knew this, he negotiated that treaty too. They also objected to being reunited with their former enemy, the Creeks, on the new reservation in Arkansas plus there was concern their slaves would be stolen by white men and Creeks. But the tribe was starving and the White Father knew it. They were told rations would not continue unless they agreed to move. Finally, it was suggested they send a delegation to see the land. If found acceptable, the tribe would agree to move. With this stipulation added to the treaty, fifteen chiefs and sub-chiefs agreed to sign the paper.

Theodore's brow drew tight. Surely the last part was a misunderstanding. Had the government really given the Seminoles a way out? They had to know it was most likely the delegation would find the land unacceptable.

As soon as Micanopy finished, a debate arose among the tribesmen. General Humphries told Theodore this was a common practice with the Seminoles. All opinions and ideas could and were offered freely within the council but ultimately the chiefs made the decisions for the tribe. Abraham did amazingly well interpreting the flying conversation. Theodore was able to conclude that some of the seasoned warriors, including Micanopy and Charlie Emathla, were willing to relocate rather than risk starvation or war. The younger warriors couldn't bear the injustice. They wanted retaliation for mistreatment and deceit.

Observing the tribesmen in the council, Theodore noticed a change in Micanopy's tustenuggee. Osceola, was standing across the circle from Theodore. The firelight cast his features into harsh relief. His eyes flashed as much fire as the flames that danced between them. The last time Theodore was here, the warrior was obedient and respectful to the chief. He did as he was asked even when it included turning over his own tribesmen to the whites to hold for trial. While still respectful, he now seemed agitated and restless like a caged animal. Anger sparked in his eyes whenever the treaty was mentioned.

The back and forth discussions would likely have continued into the night but after an hour or so Micanopy put a stop to it. Abraham interpreted, "Brothers we will discuss this no more until the delegation returns from this land in the west."

A rain shower hovered over the village for several hours the following morning. Theodore didn't mind. The rain was light and it not only cooled the temperature, it also kept the mosquitos at bay. He walked over to the main chickee and found Abraham sitting alone. Theodore had been looking for this opportunity. He hoped to find this intriguing man willing to be interviewed. He wanted to know more about the lanky black man with the lazy right eye and how he came to hold the role of 'sense-bearer' to Micanopy. Theodore entered the sideless abode, brushing the water off his shoulders. He gestured to the empty place next to Abraham on the raised platform who in turn gestured for Theodore to join him. For a moment they watched the rain in silence.

At length, Theodore asked, "How did you come to be part of this tribe?"

"I was captured and made a slave of Micanopy before he was chief, when he was known as Sint-chakkee."

His answer was not what Theodore expected. "Were you a free man before being captured?"

Abraham smiled. "Not exactly. I was a runaway slave of a Spanish doctor in Pensacola."

"Why did you run? Were you abused?"

"No. The British offered freedom to any slave that took up arms against America."

"So you joined the war of 1812 to gain your freedom."

"Yes, except the British lost so I suppose I was still considered a runaway. Are you familiar with the Negro Fort?"

"Yes." Theodore remembered reading about it in the articles he studied before leaving New York. It was a fort built on the Apalachicola River in Spanish Territory. After the war of 1812 ended, Spain left it in the hands of the black populous. Even though it meant passing through Spanish territory, Andrew Jackson ordered supply ships to use the river to resupply Fort Scott on the other side of the Georgia border. The Negro garrison attacked the supply boats killing all but one of the sailors. Jackson then sent a gunboat to retaliate. It fired heated cannonballs at the fort; one of them happened to land on the powder magazine. The resulting explosion was massive, destroying the whole fort. "I thought the few that survived were captured?"

Abraham nodded. "Most were. I escaped their patrols and wandered to the east, not sure where I was headed except away from all the death and destruction. I was close to the Suwannee River when I was caught off guard by a band of warriors and taken prisoner."

"But you are not a slave now?"

"No." Again he smiled, adding modestly, "I am good with languages so Micanopy took me to Washington with him. Upon our return, he granted me freedom for my service."

"How long ago was that?" Theodore was coming to realize what Micanopy knew, behind his appearance, Abraham was a very intelligent man.

"About six years ago. He has trusted my council ever since."

The rain slowed to a bare drizzle and soon the children were out playing in the puddles. The two men naturally drifted into conversing about their offspring with a shared sense of fatherly pride. When they parted ways, Theodore felt he had a deeper understanding of Abraham. His loyalty to the Seminole tribe was strong. His love for his family ran deeper still and concern for their future weighed heavy on his mind.

Theodore left the following day headed for the Indian Agency. He approached the home of Major John Phagan with some trepidation. On his previous visit, he briefly met Major Phagan at Fort Brooke. It was a mere five minute meeting to request permission to visit the reservation. He would be surprised if the Agent even remembered him.

Major Phagan greeted Theodore with all the warmth of an iceberg. "What brings you here? It certainly isn't to ask permission to visit the reservation since you have come from there."

Theodore hid his surprise. He didn't anticipate Major Phagan being aware of his movements. If he could, he would ignore the remark altogether but he needed information from this man so instead he was going to have to smooth the agent's ruffled feathers. "I apologize. I was not aware I would need your permission each time I visit. I assumed the first would suffice. As for my purpose, I heard you have successfully negotiated a treaty for the removal of the Seminoles. Would you care to share the details?"

Pandering to the man's vanity worked. As soon as Theodore mentioned the treaty his whole demeanor changed. "Come have a seat in my office you must be weary from your walk. Would you care for something to drink?"

For half an hour, Agent Phagan relayed to Theodore the events of the negotiations and the detailed contents of the treaty drafted in Washington for General Gadsden to present to the Seminoles. His admiration of General Gadsden was abundant with one exception.

Phagan's chest puffed out with pride. "General Gadsden may have been leading the negotiations but he never would have gotten it done without my help."

Theodore's lips twitched. The man certainly wasn't lacking in modesty. "How did you help?"

"I could see we were getting nowhere after days of arguing. It's no secret, Abraham has Micanopy's ear and could make the whole proceeding easier. I simply offered him encouragement to point things in our favour."

"You bribed him? With what?"

"Two hundred dollars each for him and Cudjo. Of course, it won't be paid until they reach the Arkansas territory."

Theodore found it hard to believe Abraham would betray his tribe by taking such a bribe. Abraham had more to lose by moving than he stood to gain, especially since it was unlikely he would reach the reservation and maintain his freedom. If the slave catchers didn't capture him before he left, the Creeks would once he arrived. Then it occurred to Theodore, Abraham may be deceiving Agent Phagan and purposely stirring conflict to avoid both outcomes. Clever. Behind that crossed right eye was a cunning mind; a very cunning mind, indeed.

"When are they to move?"

"There is a clause to be met first before the treaty is binding."

Theodore pretended he wasn't aware of the treaty's contents. "A clause?" Phagan's hesitation gave Theodore the impression he was ashamed. Could he be personally responsible for adding the loop hole?

"The tribe will send a delegation to inspect the land. The treaty becomes binding once they approve the land."

Theodore's eyebrows shot upward. So it was true. The government was giving the Seminoles an opportunity to refuse to move. It didn't make sense. "Who are 'they' to be satisfied, the delegation or the nation as a whole?"

Again, Phagan hesitated. "The chiefs make the decisions, do they not?"

Interesting. He answered with a question not really stating one way or the other. "Has the delegation been appointed?"

"Yes."

"And they would be?"

"Seven chiefs including Jumper, Charley Emathla, Holata Emathla, Alligator, Sam Jones, Black Dirt, and Mad Wolf."

An interesting group. Theodore knew at least three of them were favourable towards moving. "When is this visit to take place?"

"It has not yet been decided."

"In other words, this clause has not been approved by President Jackson."

"Something like that."

Phagan must have grown weary of Theodore's questions for he suddenly rose from his chair declaring an end to the interview. "I'm afraid I must excuse myself. I have duties to attend." He ushered Theodore all the way to his front door. "Good day, sir."

Theodore had to smile, so much for southern hospitality. He had certainly gotten underneath the agent's skin. He now stood on the agent's front porch in the late afternoon sun wondering where he should sleep for the night. Hearing laughter in the distance, he recalled the friendly sutler, Erastus Rogers, who lived on the other side of the hammock. As expected, there he found a hot meal and shelter for the night.

Theodore spent a few more days with the tribe before he began the hundred mile trek back to Fort Brooke. As he walked he considered how to write his article on the treaty. The tactics used to obtain the treaty were questionable at best and downright deceptive at worst. He couldn't write an article that painted the government as the villain. Yet, if he was to include both sides, he should include his concerns. But would they be unbiased?

And so he trudged the miles torn between loyalty, patriotism and his beliefs.

In the end, he chose to write only what he knew to be fact and let his reader's make what they would of it.

Chapter 14

July 1832

Betsy greeted the warm July morning with enthusiasm. Flowers were profusely blooming, birds singing, and the temperature was pleasant, at least until the sun climbed higher. She stretched her limbs and began her morning ritual. First a cloth dipped in the basin of cool water to wipe her face, neck and body before dressing. Next she picked up the silver handled brush, a wedding gift from Ben, and began working the tangles from her dark hair. She could almost hear her mother chastising her for not sleeping with it braided but Betsy's preference to have her hair loose during slumber made her willing to endure the morning chore. Once her tresses were smooth she made two long braids then twisted them into a coil at her nape. Next she pulled back the mosquito netting to neatly make up her bed and fluff the pillows. She took the basin outside to water the plants on her front porch. She returned it to the bedroom and carried the pitcher out back leaving it in the kitchen while she visited the outhouse. Upon returning, she drew water from the cistern to refill the pitcher and for the kitchen, then stoked the fire and started some water to heat for tea and oatmeal while she returned the pitcher to her bedroom. All of this was done efficiently and with an economy of motion to be admired.

Returning to the kitchen once more, she made her breakfast which she ate sitting on a stool at the table. The same stool Henry used when they were preparing the conch. The memory made her smile. Afterwards, she cleaned up her breakfast and set out on her usual morning walk along the coast to the lighthouse and back, before settling into a long day of sewing.

Today she stopped at the graveyard. She stood in front of the cross marking Ben's resting place. He was so comfortable and easy. Life with him was pleasant. Now she was in limbo waiting for something to happen and daring to dream of love again. Her heart was ready. It felt as if Ben approved. She kissed her fingers and touched them to the cross. She turned and finished her walk enjoying the familiar sounds of lapping water, rustling palm fronds, and crunching sea shells underfoot.

She made a second cup of tea to enjoy while she worked, turned her shingle, and spent the next few hours in earnest sewing and serving the occasional customer. Betsy barely started mending a shirt when her front door was opened with a flurry. She walked into the front room surprised to find Abby waiting for her on the other side of the counter and curiously without her children in tow. It usually meant someone was under the weather and in need of her care.

"Good morning, Betsy."

"Good morning, Abby. Could I offer you a cup of tea?"

"That would be lovely, thank you dear."

"Come, have a seat in the parlor. I'll be but a moment. The water is already heated."

Betsy left the room returning a moment later with teacup and saucer in hand. "Is someone sick?"

"Yes, I am afraid so. Mr. Mabrity has been bed-ridden for a few days. They sent one of the boys to fetch me at dawn. It appears to be yellow fever. Poor Mrs. Mabrity has been working the lighthouse and trying to keep up the household. Faustina has been helping to care for her father during the night along with her daytime chores and schooling. I worry about them succumbing to the illness being so worn down. When I left, Nicholosa— pardon me, Mrs. Bethel—had just arrived to help care for the boys and her father so her mother and sister, Mary, could get some rest. I plan to return tonight to relieve them."

Betsy could well understand the exhaustion of the Mabrity women having given her husband weeks of around the clock care. The work alone was enough to wear out a soul but it was the constant worry that could bring down the strongest of caregivers. "You have your family to take care of not to mention any others that might become sick. We both know there is never one case of fever before there are many. I will make some food to take over later and offer to stay the night tending Mr. Mabrity."

Abby started to object. "There are others...."

Betsy nodded. "Yes. Other married women with families to care for and unmarried ladies who cannot tend to a grown man. Mrs. Mallory has her boarders to care for so that leaves me. I have no family and my work can be taken with me."

"I can't let you take on such a burden."

Betsy lips compressed in mild irritation. "It's not a matter of letting me. I insist. If you must feel useful you could make arrangements for the others to take turns bringing food."

Realizing she had offended Betsy, Abby quickly agreed. "Of course, you are right." She embraced her friend placing a kiss on her cheek. "There is none other like you, Betsy. We are all blessed to count you as our neighbor. Take care and I will come by tomorrow to relieve you if need be. I pray to God I am wrong about the fever and he will be better by then. Nevertheless, word was sent to Dr. Strobel. He promised to stop by this afternoon to offer his opinion."

"Abby, you know the symptoms as well as any doctor. It's not likely you are wrong."

"I know. I have heard of three other cases already. It appears as if we are in for another bad year of it."

Their visit moved on to more pleasant topics for a brief spell until Abby finished her tea.

After Abby left, Betsy gathered together as many sewing projects as she could make ready to take to the Mabrity's. She knew from experience there were many vigilant hours ahead while the disease progressed. She stopped a moment to send a prayer heavenward for the health of everyone on the island.

Next she went to see the grocer. She would make a fish dinner for herself and the Mabrity family.

Mr. Patterson looked up from his counter as she crossed the threshold of his store. "Hello, Mrs. Wheeler. Fine morning, isn't it? What can I get for you?"

"Good morning, Mr. Patterson. I was thinking of some fish to make a stew. Enough to feed about twelve."

He gave her a curious look that turned to knowing. "Aye, you're planning to feed one of the needy families."

She looked over the meager remains of yesterday's catch in disappointment. "Yes, the Mabrity's."

"If you are interested, I do have a few pounds of beef left. Mr. Hansen had to slaughter one of his milking Jerseys. The good cuts sold real quick like, but what I have would make a fine stew. Since it's for charity, I'll sell it to you for half price."

Betsy smiled. "That is a generous offer, Mr. Patterson." Even at half price it was more than she would have paid for the fish and would put her over budget for the month. On the other hand a hearty beef stew would be good for Mr. Mabrity. "Very well then, I'll take the beef."

Betsy returned home and began preparing the food. A simple meal of fresh bread, sliced cheese and beef stew using the last of the root vegetables she had on hand. Coming from a large family proved useful in this task and it felt good to cook for more than just herself. She counted ten people total but she made enough for more just in case.

It was nearing evening when she lifted a drawstring sack to her back containing her work and a change of clothes. She picked up the basket laden with food and walked out the front door pausing to turn her shingle to *closed*. She made a brief stop to let Dr. Waterhouse know where she was going in case anyone came looking for her then made the near mile long trek to the lighthouse. She arrived damp with perspiration and more tired than expected from carrying the heavy basket. She set down her burden with a grateful sigh before knocking on the door.

Faustina's elfin face appeared in the opening and seeing Betsy she opened the door wide. "Please come in, Mrs. Wheeler."

"Thank you, Faustina. Would you mind getting the basket? Take care, it's heavy and mind you don't spill the beef stew."

Faustina looked to Betsy in delighted surprise. "Beef stew?" she asked, wanting to confirm what she heard. Her family rarely had anything other than fish or turtle.

Betsy smiled. "That's right." She watched the nearly full grown girl take the basket to the kitchen with as much care as if it contained dozens of eggs;

admonishing her rambunctious brothers to move out of her way. Her older sister, Nicholosa, heavily burdened with child, approached from the sickroom down the hall.

"Hello, Mrs. Wheeler."

"Hello, Mrs. Bethel."

"Please, Nicholosa is fine."

"As I am here to offer my help to your family in this time of strife, please, call me Betsy."

She nodded. "I'm sure you could use a cool drink after your walk." She led the way into the main room, poured a glass of water with lime slices from a tray kept on the sideboard and handed it to Betsy.

Betsy accepted the refreshment with relish. "Thank you."

Nicholosa carefully took a seat in a straight back chair with a hand pressed to the small of her back. "You're welcome. Mother is resting in the boys' room. She will likely rise soon as the lamps will need to be lit in a few hours. I left father sleeping fitfully in their room."

"I brought some food for supper. Afterwards, you should go home and get some rest. I'll stay the night and help your mother cope. I can always send Francis to get you if anything changes."

"I'm afraid I won't be staying for supper. Joseph will be here soon to walk me home. Did I hear you say you brought beef stew?"

"I did and there's plenty for you and Mr. Bethel to stay and eat or at least take some home with you."

Nicholosa smiled. "You are so kind."

The sounds of stirring could be heard from one of the bedrooms. Nicholosa turned to listen. "Mother is awake."

From her vantage point, Betsy saw Mrs. Mabrity walk from the boys' room into her room. Murmurs indicated she was speaking to her husband. A few moments later she made her way to greet Betsy with graying hair freshly brushed and pulled back in a bun, spectacles in place, and a fresh apron atop her hastily smoothed dress.

"Mrs. Wheeler, what brings you all the way out here?"

"I've come to help for the night, if that's alright with you." Betsy waited for Barbara to accept or decline her offer. She really wasn't sure how the woman would feel about someone else helping to care for her husband. Abby and Mrs. Mallory were given allowances for their nursing skills. She may consider Betsy unsuitable.

Barbara wanted to refuse. She was proud enough to want to care for her own family and if it was just her family to tend to she would have but there was also the very demanding job of keeping the light. She and Faustina were both worn out and in need of reinforcements. Her two eldest daughters had families of their own to care for and Nicholosa was in too delicate a condition. The boys, Francis and Miguel, while helpful with the lighthouse chores were not much for nursing. She really did need another woman and Betsy was familiar with the disease, including its sinister possibility. Barbara lost her breath at the dark thought. What would she do if she lost her husband? She suddenly felt much older than her fifty years. Pulling on her inner strength she took a deep breath, straightened her shoulders, and walked over to the sideboard to get some water.

Betsy carefully watched Barbara. Seeing her straighten her shoulders she thought her offer was about to be refused. Before either lady could say more the front door was opened by Joseph Bethel, at the same time Faustina entered from the back door carrying dishes and utensils to begin setting the table.

Betsy looked to the congenial young man. "Good evening, Mr. Bethel."

Joseph removed his bowler and set it on the table by the door. "Good evening to you Mrs. Wheeler, Mother Mabrity." He walked over to his wife and leaned down to kiss her cheek. "How are you fairing wife?"

Nicholosa looked to her husband with adoration. "I'm fine."

"Good, are you ready to walk home?"

"Actually, do you mind if we have supper here? Betsy brought beef stew; enough for all of us."

Faustina stuck her head into the room. "It tastes wonderful. You should stay."

Joseph looked to his wife. "If you wish then we shall certainly stay." He turned to Betsy. "Thank you, Mrs. Wheeler, for your generosity."

Betsy was impressed with the young man's consideration of his wife's wishes. "You're welcome."

Barbara moved forward. "Yes thank you, Mrs. Wheeler, for the meal and we are blessed by the generous offer of your time." She turned to her youngest daughter. "Faustina, after supper, would you please put fresh sheets on your bed for Mrs. Wheeler. You and I will take the boys' room. They can sleep on the floor for tonight." Barbara looked out the window to judge the amount of daylight left. "Is supper ready to be served?"

"Yes, ma'am." Faustina returned to the kitchen.

Betsy moved towards the doorway. "I'll see if she needs help."

Betsy and Faustina put the meal on the table as the boys came in fresh from scrubbing their hands and faces. Once all were seated, Mrs. Mabrity blessed the meal and for a moment all were quiet as they began eating. Joseph was the first to praise Betsy's cooking. The others quickly agreed. After supper, she helped Faustina do the dishes while Mrs. Mabrity fed Mr. Mabrity and made him as comfortable as she could for the night. When the dishes were done, Faustina set about remaking her bed. Betsy knocked softly on the sick room door.

Mrs. Mabrity held the door wide for Betsy to enter. Mr. Mabrity lay prone and feverish. He barely responded to her intrusion in his private quarters. His wife leaned down and gently shook his shoulder to rouse him. "Michael, Mrs. Wheeler has come to help care for you." His eyes opened for a moment, unfocused and weary, before dropping shut. Barbara turned to the dresser to show Betsy the medications Dr. Strobel had left in the afternoon and explained how to dispense them. "Mrs. Wheeler, thank you for offering to help."

"Please, use my Christian name and I am only doing the Lord's work. No need to thank me."

"Just the same, I do." She looked to her husband and Betsy could easily read the concern on her face.

"I am sure he will be fine. It's only been a few days."

"Four days now." Barbara closed her eyes for a moment, and then looked to Betsy. "How long was Mr. Wheeler sick before..." She floundered, unable to finish the sentence.

Betsy's answer was matter of fact. "Just over two weeks."

Barbara nodded. "Time will tell." She breathed in deep and straightened her shoulders. "I had best see to my chores. Please let Faustina know if you need anything."

"Of course." She almost told the poor woman not to worry but refrained knowing it to be useless advice.

The night passed quietly enough. In a chair placed by the bed, Betsy worked on her sewing alternately with replacing the cool cloth on Mr. Mabrity's fever heated brow, or piling on extra blankets when he was racked with chills, all the while humming or sharing stories of her childhood in a soft-spoken voice.

Mrs. Mabrity joined her for several hours in between her other duties. Twice during the night she had to climb the lighthouse steps to clean the lamps and windows and replace the oil and wicks in order to keep the lights burning throughout the night.

The next morning, Mr. Mabrity seemed to be making a turn for the better. He was able to sit up in bed and demand more to eat. Betsy prayed for his health. She feared the return of the disease as was so often the case but kept the fear to herself. She didn't want to needlessly worry Barbara.

Betsy helped Faustina prepare and serve breakfast. Barbara's eldest daughter, Petrona Wall, arrived shortly afterwards with her seven year old daughter, Elizabeth. Petrona would watch over the household for the day allowing Betsy to go home for a little rest before returning for the night watch if needed.

During the night, Betsy suppressed the memories threatening to surface. Now on the walk home, in her exhaustion, she was unable to keep them at bay. She shuddered as she relived the devastating progression of the disease and the deterioration of her husband's body. When he relapsed, the fever returned with intensity. He couldn't hold down any fluid, his skin yellowed, and she often found him doubled over with abdominal pain. But the hardest part was when the bleeding started. He bled from his eyes, mouth and nose. All the while, the vomiting continued, turning black with blood. By the time he passed away, Betsy was sure they both believed it to be a relief to his suffering. If Mr. Mabrity relapsed could she do it again? Could she sit with him until the end?

Betsy halted in her tracks, shutting her eyes tight. *Lord, please bestow Your healing on Mr. Mabrity. But if Your will is for him to die please give his family the strength to bear the burden.* She opened her eyes and resumed walking home. She had done all she could for now. It was time for her to rest.

Theodore was about to enter his home, having just returned from visiting the reservation, when he noticed Betsy approaching from the opposite direction. He waited for her at the foot of his steps. She was preoccupied with her thoughts and hadn't notice him yet. She looked weary and burdened with a basket and sack. He dropped his travel bag on the front porch and walked towards her. A few yards away, she finally noticed him.

"Mrs. Wheeler, can I help you with your basket?" He reached out to take it from her, not waiting for her reply.

Betsy was grateful to relinquish the basket. She forced herself to concentrate on conversation as they walked together to her door. She was so tired even that small task was difficult. "Thank you, Mr. Whitmore. Was your trip successful?"

"If success is measured in traveling to and fro safely or if it is considered a success to have spoken with the tribe the answer would be yes. However, since I have returned with more questions than answers I would not necessarily deem it a fruitful endeavor."

"Oh, I see."

Her rejoinder further enforced his opinion; she was tired.

She stopped and turned to him at her front door, clearly expecting him to hand over the basket. "Thank you Mr. Whitmore."

"You're welcome, Mrs. Wheeler. You go on in; I'll walk around the house and drop this basket off in the kitchen for you." He was curious as to why she was in such an exhausted state but did not want to prolong her misery by asking. He also wanted to tell her to get some sleep but such a comment would be presumptuous and likely insulting. "Good day, Mrs. Wheeler." He walked away before she could form a reply.

He deposited the basket in her outdoor kitchen and returned to his porch. He picked up his bag and entered the house in time to hear Aunt Agatha berating the maid over her perceived lack of cleaning skills. This was the third maid in as many months. There were not any more to be found on the island. If this one quit, his family would be on their own. Perhaps he should intervene. He dropped his bag at the foot of the stairs and headed toward the voices in the parlor.

Agatha noticed him as soon as he reached the threshold. "Theodore, you're home." She turned back to the chastened maid. "Millie, please bring us some refreshments and mind you don't forget to add coffee for my nephew."

Theodore stepped aside allowing the maid to pass. "Thank you, Millie."

She bobbed her head in acknowledgement and continued out the door.

Theodore walked into the room. "Aunt Agatha." She was seated in a wing back chair looking as regal as ever in her starched black dress, white collar, and cameo pendent with nary a hair out of place despite the ninety plus degrees outside.

"Theodore, I am so glad you have returned and not a moment too soon. We need to discuss leaving this island—immediately. Don't you think it is time we returned home?"

It was supposed to be a question but she said it as a statement and fully expected him to comply. "No, I don't think so. I have work to do here."

"What do you mean you have work? Haven't you done enough work? I thought this was a sabbatical. We have been here over a year now and I have not complained but enough is enough. The summers here are horrendous and I can't take much more of this heat, not to mention the sickness. Three people already sick with yellow fever on this street alone. It is time to go home." She vigorously fanned herself to make her point.

"This trip was always about work. I am following a good story with the Indians. Perhaps we can leave in a month."

"A month will be too late if one of us gets this fever."

"No one's going to get sick, Aunt. We made it through last summer just fine. Now if you'll excuse me I'd like to see Henry."

Conceding the battle but not the war she made her parting shot to his retreating figure. "Just remember when it happens, I warned you."

Betsy woke up refreshed after sleeping most of the afternoon. She dressed in a simple shirtwaist and skirt over her chemise with stockings and serviceable shoes. She then performed all the needed chores around her house, repacked her work for the night along with the other loaf of bread she made yesterday. She hummed to herself as she walked to the Mabrity's, all the while hoping she would find Mr. Mabrity continuing his recovery.

Faustina opened the door at her gentle knock with a strained look on her face. Before Betsy could utter a greeting she heard the sounds of retching from the sickroom and knew they were all in for a rough few days. The dreaded second phase of the disease had taken hold. Betsy crossed the threshold and gave Faustina a bracing smile. "You're father is a strong man, I'm sure he will pull through. Is your sister still here?"

The distraught girl could only nod in acknowledgement of Betsy's hopeful prediction. "Petrona and Mother are tending Father. Mrs. O'Hare brought us dinner. I will have it on the table shortly."

Betsy reached into her bag for the sourdough loaf. "Here, I brought some bread to share. If not for supper, then for breakfast."

"Thank you." Faustina retreated to the kitchen.

Betsy left her belongings in the sitting room and made her way to the sickroom. She gently tapped on the door left slightly ajar.

It was opened by Petrona to reveal Mr. Mabrity lying on his side facing away from the door and Mrs. Mabrity wringing a cloth to put on the back of her husband's neck. Petrona ushered Betsy back into the hallway, closing the door behind her.

"Mother has been with him all day. She won't let me help." Petrona lifted her dark eyes to Betsy's sympathetic blue ones unable to control the welling tears. "He is so weak and sick." Her voice left her for a moment before she could continue, "What will Mother and the others do without him?"

Betsy embraced the weeping young woman. "You must not give up hope. He still has a fighting chance to pull through this and you must be strong for your mother."

The two women stepped apart. Petrona dried her tears. "I'm glad you are here, Mrs. Wheeler. Thank you for coming."

"You're welcome." She looked to the closed door. "Has your mother had any rest today?"

"No. I'm worried about her taking care of the light tonight."

"She will find the strength, at least for tonight. It's what we women do. The boys will help her get through the chores in the morning. Hopefully she will get some rest tomorrow. Are you staying?"

"I have to return home. Mary and Faustina are taking turns watching the children and taking care of Father. Mother insisted Nicholosa stay home since she is nearing her time."

"I agree. Nicholosa doesn't belong here."

Faustina entered the house and placed a tray of food on the table then entered the sitting room. "Supper is ready. I'll call the boys in."

"I'll tell Mother." Petrona returned to the sickroom. A moment later she came out alone. "Mother doesn't want to leave him."

Betsy became even more concerned. "Has she eaten at all today?"

The two daughters looked at each other, both shook their heads. Faustina said, "I don't think so."

Betsy walked to the sickroom with determination and again gently knocked on the door. "Barbara, may I come in?"

"Yes."

Betsy entered the room and closed the door behind her. "Supper's ready."

Barbara was seated in a chair by the bed, holding her husband's hand and smoothing the hair from his forehead. "I told Petrona you should start without me."

"I know you did but I also know you need to eat. You have to take care of yourself in order to continue caring for your husband. I'll stay with him while you go eat with your family. I'll bet the boys haven't seen you all day."

Barbara acknowledged the truth of her statement.

Mr. Mabrity opened his eyes and weakly spoke to his wife. "Go. Eat." Barbara had to lean down to hear him. "Eat."

"Okay, dear." She looked to Betsy. "You'll call if I'm needed?"

Betsy's lips curved at the needlessly spoken request. "Of course."

167

Barbara rose from her chair and leaned over to kiss his forehead before leaving the room. The door was left open. Betsy walked around to the chair. She saw Mr. Mabrity shiver a little so she paused to pull another quilt over him. He mouthed 'thank you' then closed his eyes. Betsy sat in the chair and said another prayer for the return of this man's health. Petrona's worry was real. If Mr. Mabrity died, how would Barbara support herself and her three children still living with her?

After supper, Betsy convinced Barbara to take a nap before beginning the night's work on the light. Petrona sat with her father so Betsy could take her meal. Twenty minutes later, Barbara was once again at her husband's side being unable to sleep. Betsy reentered the room at sunset to find the couple much as they were earlier except Barbara appeared to be lightly sleeping. Mr. Mabrity, as if on instinct, opened his eyes to peer towards the window then looked to his wife. He squeezed her hand and in a voice marginally stronger than earlier said, "Lighthouse."

Barbara opened her eyes and reflexively looked to the window to check the time. She smiled at her husband. "Of course, dear. I'll take care of it."

During the night, Betsy tended Mr. Mabrity's needs and encouraged his wife to sleep in between her duties. Come full light of morning, Barbara extinguished the lamps and began the arduous task of cleaning the lamps, reflectors, windows and floors of the lighthouse.

Betsy, knowing Barbara had to be well past exhaustion, woke the two boys and sent them to help her. Faustina was already busy making breakfast. Mr. Mabrity slept fitfully through the night, tossing and turning in pain. Betsy gave him as much laudanum as she dared. This morning he was lightly sleeping when Barbara entered the room.

"How is he?"

"Alright for now. Not improved but not worse. I gave him a dose of medicine about an hour ago."

Barbara only nodded in response as she drifted to the chair Betsy vacated on the other side of the bed.

Betsy paused at the door. "I'll see if breakfast is ready." She found Faustina in the kitchen and helped her finish getting the food ready then she went to the lighthouse to see if the boys were finished sweeping out the dead bugs. They promised to be done in a few minutes so Betsy returned to the kitchen to help Faustina carry in the food.

It was a quiet meal and when it was over Betsy and Faustina cleaned up while Barbara cared for Michael and the boys took care of their other chores. Mary arrived a short time later. Betsy tried to convince Barbara to get some sleep before leaving. She wasn't sure the matriarch would heed her advice but there was nothing more she could do about it.

This became the pattern of days to come while Mr. Mabrity continued to decline in health. As his symptoms worsened it became harder for them to hold out hope. Betsy wasn't sure if it was better or worse that the family kept their emotions at bay following Barbara's example. By the end of the fourth night, Betsy didn't think she could take much more of the stress. She trudged home already dreading her return that night.

Hours later, Betsy awoke from her slumber and doggedly prepared for another night at the Mabrity's. She was nearly ready to leave when Dr. Strobel knocked on her door.

"Good evening, Doctor. Is there something I can do for you?"

"I've just come from the Mabrity's. Mrs. Mabrity asked me to stop by and let you know Mr. Mabrity passed away a few hours ago."

Her hand went to her chest. "Dear Lord." She was torn between sorrow and relief and guilt over her relief. Just as she felt when Ben passed and much the same as she imagined Barbara was feeling right now. "Did she say if she wanted me to come over?"

"I got the impression when she asked me to stop by that they wanted time alone to grieve."

"I understand. Thank you for letting me know."

"Good evening, Mrs. Wheeler."

"Good evening, Dr. Strobel."

* * *

Michael Mabrity was buried in the beachside graveyard the following day, leaving behind his grieving widow, seven children and three grandchildren. Nicholosa gave birth to his fourth grandchild a short time later. Little Michael Bethel brought a measure of joy to the grieving family.

Chapter 15

Betsy slipped back into her daily routine but it was unsettling at first. It wasn't surprising she would miss the comradery of being part of a family. She expected to feel the loneliness of returning to her solitary life. What she didn't expect was to feel at loose ends not having the constant worry and responsibility of tending Mr. Mabrity. Throwing herself into catching up on her backlog of orders soon worked to relieve those feelings of desolation.

One afternoon a few days later, Mrs. Agatha walked into her shop. It was obvious something was wrong. She never left her house without a hat or bonnet but here she was without either and her normally composed facade registered panic. Betsy opened the walkthrough counter and approached the elderly lady. "What's wrong, Mrs. Agatha?"

Her hands fluttered with her agitation. "It's Henry. He's burning up with fever. He's got the yellow jack, I just know it. I told Theodore we must leave this place. I knew this would happen."

"Where is Mr. Whitmore?"

"He's gone to town on business."

Betsy guided Agatha out the door and flipped her shingle to *closed*. The ladies hurried across the street. "How long has he been ill?"

"Just now. He was fine when he got up this morning."

"Then it's likely too soon to tell what is ailing him."

Agatha abruptly stopped and turned to Betsy forcing her to halt as well. "If you don't know then we should ask Mrs. Eatonton or better still, send for one of the doctors. You have two on this island, don't you?"

Knowing Abby was expecting again and suffering in the early stages and Dr. Strobel was likely busy with other patients, Betsy held her hand toward her next door neighbor's house. "Yes ma'am. If it would make you feel better we could summon Dr. Waterhouse."

Agatha brushed past her without a word. Betsy followed her into the house. She found Annalise reading to Henry who was tucked in bed. "Hello."

Henry came out of the cover and up on his knees in the middle of the bed. "Hello, Mrs. Betsy. You have to take care 'cause I'm sick. Aunt Aggie said so."

Betsy couldn't help her grin. "Is that so? Do you feel sick?" Betsy pressed the back of her hand to his forehead. He did feel a little warm.

"Not now. I felt really hot when I came in for lunch."

Ah, likely it was too much heat. "Did you do a lot of running outside?"

"Uh huh." Suddenly recalling his lessons, he said, "I mean, yes ma'am. I was chasing the older boys. They run fast."

Betsy sagely nodded to Henry then turned to Annalise. "Please bring Henry a glass of water with lime or lemon if you have it."

Annalise left to do her bidding. Not seeing a basin in his room, Betsy walked across the hall to what appeared to be Agatha's room. She peered inside and seeing a pitcher and basin pushed aside any concern for invading Agatha's private space to pick up a clean cloth, soak it, and wring it out. She returned to Henry's room and made him lie down so she could place the cloth on his forehead. Annalise returned with Agatha and Dr. Waterhouse following behind.

Betsy stood aside to allow the doctor to examine Henry. The first thing he did was remove the cloth and feel his forehead. Heavy footfalls were heard rushing up the stairs just before Theodore burst into the room, out of breath.

"What is going on here? Is Henry sick?"

Dr. Waterhouse turned to the group of adults. "The boy feels fine to me."

Agatha said, "Well of course he does now, he's had that cloth on his head."

"Ma'am, if he truly had a fever he would be warm despite the cloth."

Betsy interrupted before Agatha could say any more. "He said he was running this morning and felt hot when he came in. I think it was too much activity in this July heat."

Dr. Waterhouse nodded. "I believe you're right, Mrs. Wheeler." He saw Annalise standing next to the door holding the glass of water. "Make sure he drinks the whole glass of water, and I'm sure he'll be right as rain. If not, you can call for me again."

Theodore walked the doctor to the front door. The two men shook hands.

Noting Theodore's high color Dr. Waterhouse said, "And you sir, would be wise to drink a whole glass of water too."

Theodore nodded. "Thank you Doctor. What do I owe you?"

"Nothing. Mrs. Wheeler did more doctoring here than I did."

Agatha sent Annalise to the kitchen on an errand but apparently wasn't concerned with Betsy's presence. She barely waited for Theodore to enter the room. "I told you he would get sick. It is time we packed up and returned home."

Betsy's heart dropped. They were thinking of leaving? She knew the day would come and realized it would probably be soon but still it surprised her. The ache in her breast let her know, despite guarding against it, her hopes for a future with Theodore had grown well beyond her control.

Theodore noticed Betsy's discomfort and attributed it to being present for a private family conversation. It had been weeks since he last saw her and he was now forced to realize he missed being with her. His gaze locked on Betsy as he brushed his aunt's concerns aside. "We'll discuss it later."

His quiet emphatic tone brooked no argument. Agatha quit the room without another word but she would continue the campaign later. In her mind, Key West had turned deadly and home couldn't be reached soon enough.

Feeling uncomfortable in the sudden absence of Agatha's presence and under Theodore's brooding stare, Betsy turned to speak to Henry with a lightheartedness she was far from feeling. "Are you feeling better now, Henry?" She checked his forehead again and found it cool to the touch.

Henry moved from his prone position to his knees again with typical childlike ease. "I am. Can I go play now? I promise I'm not sick."

Betsy smiled at the seriousness of his pledge. It was so endearing for his tender age. "I believe you may." When he raced to get off the bed, she cautioned, "But do so quietly." She raised her voice to call after his retreating back. "No running!"

Alone now, she was forced to turn her attention to Theodore. His attention barely wavered from her, creating a nervous tension in her middle. She waited for him to speak, desperately wanting to know what was on his mind.

Theodore was conflicted. Here he was a year later, questioning another decision... no, two decisions. In May, he decided it was time to remarry but did not consider Betsy a candidate for a loveless marriage. His attraction to her at the moment was cause to reassess his feelings. Her wholesome milky complexion and blue eyes brightened the room like a sunny afternoon, and her dew-kissed lips... well, it was best he not follow that line of thought. Most appealing of all, she was beautiful inside and out. Here she was helping his family again as she had done numerous other times. He was also well aware of her recent sacrifice for the Mabrity family. She volunteered for community events, sang in the choir, and those were the things he knew about.

Then again, maybe she was too good for the likes of him.

The other questionable decision was in opposition to pursuing these feelings. He told his aunt they would be staying so he could work on his story. Seeing the doctor rush to his house on Henry's account scared him more than he wanted to admit. Even though he was rationally aware no harm had come to his boy, he was irrationally still shook up over the event. Enough so, he was considering what information he might need to collect for his story before their departure.

Betsy would have retired from the room by now but Theodore, lost in thought, stood between her and the door. "Mr. Whitmore?"

Betsy's voice brought him out of his thoughts and made him aware he had been staring. "Please, forgive me. I didn't mean to make you uncomfortable." Realizing they were alone in the bedroom, he stepped aside and gestured for her to precede him out the door and followed her to the parlor. He hoped she would visit for a while but instead she bid good day to his aunt and continued on to the front door.

Betsy waited for him to open the door for her. "Make sure Henry gets plenty to drink and he should be fine. Good day, Mr. Whitmore."

He was left with no choice but to let her go. He could not think of a single valid reason to ask her to stay. "Thank you for your assistance, Mrs. Wheeler." It was best he let her go. He needed to sort his thoughts and he didn't want to inadvertently toy with her feelings.

"You're welcome."

She turned toward her home and Theodore closed the door. The house felt curiously empty with her departure. Head down, lost in thought, he returned to the parlor.

Agatha looked up from her needlepoint. She spent these last few months nudging her nephew towards the seamstress but now continuing to do so would be counterproductive to her plans of returning to New York. So where she would have admonished Theodore for not walking Betsy home, instead she asked when they would be leaving.

Theodore's thoughts were broken for a second time this hour by a female. He looked to his aunt. "Pardon me, what did you say?"

She gave him a withering look. "I asked, when are we leaving? We must leave, you know."

"Hmm."

She hated his habit of making that sound rather than a full reply. One never knew what it meant exactly. Was he in agreement or simply humoring her for the moment? She waited in vain for more as he turned and left the room. She decided it might be best to wait until tomorrow to push him for an answer when he was done thinking through whatever was bothering him.

Theodore spent the next few hours mulling over his feelings and his plans. His main concern was Henry and his aunt's well-being. Those moments when he feared his aunt's prediction had come to pass were still with him. On that basis alone, he already decided they should return to New York but there were other things to consider. His next concern was being able to continue following the Indian story if he left. The Seminole situation was at a status quo until the chiefs visited the western reservation. He could join them on the trip as easily from New York as he could from here. The last to be considered were his feelings of earlier. With time and space between them, he could easily attribute his attraction for Betsy to a physical response due to his long abstinence and not real emotions. All in all, he really had no reason to stay any longer.

He spent a few moments jotting down a list of things to do to prepare for their departure. By then it was time for the evening meal. He arrived at the table feeling much calmer. When the meal was over he made the announcement knowing his aunt would be pleased. Henry was quiet as was expected of him.

When Theodore tucked Henry into bed later, he asked, "How do you feel about returning home? I was thinking we could get you started in school? Would you like that?"

Henry frowned in thought. "I don't know if I'll like school. I've never been."

"You will. You liked learning your letters and numbers from Mrs. Wheeler."

His frown deepened. "I'll miss her. Can she come with us?"

"No son."

"I didn't think so. Will you be home every night when we go back, like you were before?"

Theodore didn't think now would be good time to mention he would likely be gone for several months sometime in the near future. "I won't be traveling without you for a while."

"Good. I miss you when you're gone."

His heart constricted. He kissed his son's forehead and ruffled his blond head. "Good night, Henry."

"Good night, Poppa."

Theodore set in motion his decision to leave the island forthwith. He discovered William Whitehead was also planning to head north and both decided it would be enjoyable to travel together. A few days later the two men were walking together down Front Street finalizing the details.

William said, "So it is set. We leave in two days on the..." He stopped mid-sentence and mid-stride to watch the rather large group of women walking towards them. "It may be my imagination but those ladies appear to be making a beeline for us."

Theodore studied the group. They all seemed to have eyes on Mr. Whitehead. "It is not your imagination. They mean to speak with you, sir."

William shook his head. "The women of this island have to be strong to survive here. When they all have their mind set on something, together they are a force to be reckoned with. I don't mind saying, it's a little unnerving when all that energy is directed at you. It's enough to make a man shake in his boots."

Theodore counted more than a dozen bonnets and hats but he was only aware of one face. Betsy was in the front of the group looking as radiant as ever, despite the midday heat. He realized he had not told her of his plans. She deserved to hear it from him after all she had done for his family. He would have to make a point of doing so soon.

William and Theodore doffed their hats. "Good afternoon ladies."

The group came to a halt in front of the two men, half a second later several of them started speaking at once. William was able to gather from the broken bits he understood that they were making a plea on behalf of Barbara Mabrity. He held up his hand for their attention, "Ladies. Ladies." He reached into his breast pocket. "I have already drafted a letter petitioning the Coast Guard to allow Mrs. Mabrity to continue running the lighthouse as she has already demonstrated to be fully capable of the task over the last two weeks. I was on my way to mail it. As far as I'm concerned the position is hers."

His announcement was followed by a lot of head bobbing and thank yous as the women dispersed. Betsy gave Theodore a searching look before turning away.

Mr. Whitehead breathed a sigh of relief. "How fortunate I was one step ahead of them. I best get to the post office. Dr. Waterhouse will be bundling up the mail to send off soon."

Theodore said, "Very fortunate indeed. I believe our plans are set. Send word if you think of anything else to be considered." The men parted company and Theodore headed home. Betsy's shingle was turned to open so he decided to see her first.

He was glad her front room was devoid of customers. He wanted to get this done quickly and privately. She appeared from her work room smoothing down her skirt. She smiled when she looked up to see him. It made him feel good. He refused to dwell on the emotion. "Mrs. Wheeler, I know I have said this many times before but I want to thank you again for all you have done for my family. We have met a lot of nice people here but you will be remembered most fondly."

Betsy found it hard to hold her smile but she did. "You really are leaving then. When do you sail?"

"Thursday morning."

It hurt to try and keep the facade so she let her face fall. "So soon. May I come over tomorrow to wish you well on your journey?"

"Hmm."

She hoped that sound meant yes.

The timely entrance of Mrs. Ximenez and her daughter was a relief to Theodore. He bid the ladies good day and made his escape.

Betsy was left reeling with her emotions and forced to put them on hold to take care of her customers. When she was alone again, she suppressed the building sorrow and instead focused on ideas for a parting gift basket. Ship's rations were not always dependable so food items would likely be welcome.

She couldn't afford to buy crackers so she made some hardtack. She pulled an unused basket down from her top shelf, wiped it clean and placed the hardtack wrapped in cloth inside. She added a jar of pigeon plum jelly, a wedge of cheese and looked around for anything else to include. She didn't find anything in her kitchen but the tree outside gave her an idea. She hoped to find a few cocoanuts on the ground but to her disappointment there were none but several were close to falling. It was not a very old tree so she tried pushing on the trunk in the hopes of shaking them loose. Fortunately she was looking up as she did so or one would have landed on her head. She barely managed to move out of the way of Mother Nature's cannonball as two of them fell to the ground.

She removed the green husks and placed the brown fibrous cocoanuts in the basket which sufficiently filled it. She took it inside and covered the contents with a scrap piece of fabric she trimmed into a neat square. Her next thought was to make some conch chowder to share with them tomorrow. Henry declared it to be his favourite dish on the island. Then she thought making it a last outing might be fun too.

Before she gave it too much thought, she walked across the street and knocked on the door. Annalise answered and invited her into the foyer. From the sounds around her, she realized they were busy packing. Too busy to go sailing. Before anyone else noticed she was there she told Annalise to disregard her visit and withdrew from the house. Her disappointment nearly made her scrap the whole idea but then her normal even nature returned. She would do this much for them.

Alone, she sailed out to her favourite conch grounds. The harvest was easy. Deciding to make the soup tomorrow, she left the conch in the buckets overnight.

Wednesday turned out to be a rainy day. She made the soup in her little kitchen despite the occasional wind driven spray of water. It was ready in time for the noon day meal. Fortunately the rain slacked off while Betsy carefully carried the pot of soup across the street. She knocked and again, Annalise let her in. Betsy walked around the stacked trunks packed for their voyage to deposit her burden in the dining room.

Theodore saw Betsy from the top of the stairs and followed. "Conch chowder? It smells wonderful and I'm starving."

"I made plenty." Betsy set the table and served the soup while Theodore called the others to eat.

For the last time she sat at this table to share a meal with this family. Theodore said the blessing and included a request for their safe travels and thanks for the blessing of good friends, especially her. Betsy was touched by it. When they were done eating she bid them wait a moment before returning to their work. She dashed back to her house for the basket and returned to the dining room to present it to Mrs. Agatha.

"As a token of my enjoyment of our time together. I hope it eases your journey."

Agatha removed the cover and inspected the contents and tartly asked, "What kind of jelly is this?"

"Pigeon Plum. You'll find it's similar to apple jelly."

"We shall see."

Betsy noticed she appeared less than thrilled and sought to defend her choice. "The hardtack should last nearly your entire voyage if need be and that was all the cocoanuts I could find. They'll keep unopened for a few months."

Agatha grimly said, "Thank you, Mrs. Betsy."

Theodore smiled to offset his aunt's ungratefulness. "It was a thoughtful gift."

Now came the part Betsy was dreading. She was going to have a hard enough time saying goodbye to Theodore. She wasn't sure she could say goodbye to Henry without crying but for his sake she had to find a way. He couldn't know how much this was hurting her. He was too young to deal with those emotions from an adult. She was spared the ordeal for the moment when Theodore suggested she take Henry to her place for the afternoon. Betsy eagerly agreed.

The rain ended while they ate and now the coastal breeze and the sun worked in tandem to dry the porous land. As she and Henry gained her front porch she asked, "What would you like to do?"

They were playing chess on her front porch when Abby came to visit with her children. The game was put on hold while Henry and Emily took off to play under the seven year apple tree in her backyard. Abby carried Christoff inside, following Betsy. She set him down to walk in the parlor keeping a close eye on him. "I came as soon as I heard. Is it true they are leaving tomorrow?"

"Yes, tomorrow morning."

"How are you taking the news?"

She wanted to brush it off, but Abby knew her too well. "For now, I'm not thinking about it."

Henry came running in the house with three year old Emily trailing behind in tears. Betsy was first to reach them. "What happened Henry?"

"She's such a baby!"

"Henry! What an unkind thing to say. You need to apologize to her."

"But she wouldn't touch the bug. She ran off crying cause..."

Betsy interrupted his explanation. "It doesn't matter. You owe her an apology." She was aware of Abby standing behind her with Christoff and hoped she was handling the situation correctly.

Henry didn't understand why but he knew Mrs. Betsy would not be happy until he did as she asked. He turned to Emily. "I'm sorry." He looked back at Betsy. "Can I go back outside?"

Betsy nodded. Henry turned on his heel and promptly left the house. To the surprise of both ladies, Emily abruptly stopped crying and took off after him.

Abby laughed. "Maybe it's a good thing they are leaving if my three year old is already smitten with him. Shall we sit outside and keep an eye on them?"

"I think that would be a good idea. How are you feeling?"

"Today is a good day. The sickness is tapering off."

"That is a good sign, isn't it?"

"Yes."

They spent an hour talking, watching the children play, and helping Christoff practice walking. When Abby left, Betsy and Henry resumed their chess game. As time crept forward she became more and more distracted. She planned to let Henry win the game but he may have in truth.

She took Henry back home when it was time for supper and was invited to stay for the meal. She agreed, again prolonging the inevitable. It was a silent meal. Betsy did not feel like conversing and the others were obviously tired from the day's occupation.

Afterwards they moved to the parlor. Agatha was nodding off after only a few moments. Suddenly she rose from her seat. "I believe I will retire for the evening."

Theodore and Betsy both got to their feet. Betsy was shocked when Agatha walked right past her without even a glance. She did turn at the doorway to say—as if she had only known her for sixteen minutes instead of sixteen months—, "It was nice to meet you Mrs. Wheeler. Come along Annalise, Henry. We have an early start in the morning."

Annalise bravely defied Agatha's example by going to Betsy and embracing her. "I will miss you."

Betsy squeezed the young girl's slight frame. "I'll miss you too." She let her go and knelt down in front of Henry. "I enjoyed spending the day with you." She had to take a few breaths before she could continue. "I hope you have a safe journey home. Will you write to me?"

"You want me to write you a letter? What would I put in it?"

Betsy laughed lightly. "Whatever you want. Tell me about the things you do and the people you meet and how your family is doing."

"Alright, I'll write you."

She opened her arms and he walked into them, wrapping his arms around her neck tightly. She nearly didn't wipe away the escaped tear before he let her go. "Good night, Mrs. Betsy."

"Good night, Henry."

Her eyes wistfully followed him as he left the room.

The way Henry hugged Betsy gave Theodore a vivid flashback of Margaret. It was exactly the same way Margaret used to come to him, often when he was seated in a chair, and wrap her arms around him. He felt the ghost of the sensation now and wondered at it.

Betsy returned to her feet to find Theodore looking at her but not seeing her. It gave her a strange feeling. It was as if she could feel Margaret's spirit in the room. It passed quickly and his eyes once again focused on her.

"I'll walk you to the door."

Betsy was left with no choice but to follow him to the foyer. Her hopes of having a last conversation dashed.

He turned toward her with one hand on the door knob. "It has been a pleasure knowing you, Mrs. Wheeler."

Betsy tolerated his aunt's arctic farewell but she was not willing to walk away from Theodore without giving them both something more to remember. She acted on a moment of sheer bravery, rising up on her tiptoes to place a kiss on his cheek. Her chin brushed his short whiskers. She pulled back so quick she caught the flash of surprise in his eyes. Bravery instantly fled replaced by the urge to escape the impending heartache. Unintentionally, she placed her hand atop his on the knob. He pulled away as if her hand held some danger to him. She turned the doorknob and he stepped away on reflex allowing her to open the door.

"Good bye, Theodore." She walked out and didn't look back; her concentration solely focused on making it inside her front door before the tears started falling.

Betsy
1832-1833

Chapter 16

Betsy closed the door behind her. She couldn't help going to the window to see if he was still watching. The sight of the closed entry brought home the finality of their leaving. One by one she brought them to mind: charming Henry, handsome Theodore, quiet Annalise and even dour Agatha. They had become an integral part of her life, especially Henry and Annalise. Some weeks they had visited her nearly every day becoming a surrogate family of sorts.

Her eyes remained dry.

The tears were there, she could feel them burning behind her eyes, but they wouldn't come even though she craved their healing release. She could feel the pain of loneliness stealing around her heart and she trembled, knowing how it would swell in the days ahead.

She rubbed a finger across her bottom lip in an attempt to chase away the prickly sensation of brushing against his closely cropped chestnut beard. She wished now she had been brave enough to wait for his reaction. She knew she surprised him but was it followed with anger? Aversion? Uncaring? If it had been an emotion she wished for, he would have followed her.

Betsy left the window to walk through the deepening shadows inside the house to her workroom. She really should light the lamp and work on some of the orders piling up. She wasn't sure how long she stood in the doorway before giving up on the idea. Her mind was too numb and unfocused to accomplish anything. Instead she walked out the backdoor and kept walking until she reached the beach then followed it in the direction of the lighthouse. The sun had already set but the moon was high and nearly full casting enough light to guide her path.

When she reached the cemetery she hesitated. Perhaps it would help. She weaved her way around the gravestones by memory to the simple wood cross containing only a name and dates. At the time she thought she would replace it with a stone one later. Reality had taken away that wish too.

Ben Wheeler

1803-1826

Now that she was here, the words wouldn't come. How do you tell your former husband about the man you wanted to take his place? She knew Ben would understand, still the words wouldn't come. All she could do was feel. Emotions warred within her and depression threatened to consume her.

She wanted to collapse on the ground and lean against his headstone and weep for what might have been. She needed to weep. But the cross was not stone and wouldn't support her, the ground was too rough, and the tears wouldn't fall. Frustrated, she turned back to the house Ben built for them. She crawled into the bed she once shared with him, still dressed, and waited; waited for tears, waited for sleep, waited for the peace that normally surrounded her.

Nothing.

She sat up again. And then she knew what she had to do. She got down on her knees and silently prayed, first the *Our Father* and then the *Hail Mary*. She said her usual prayers for those around her before asking for her needs. When she prayed for Barbara Mabrity and her family she realized her problems were not so grave. Finally, she prayed for peace and grace and strength.

Feeling better, she got up and performed her nightly rituals, then crawled into bed. Slumber followed not long after.

Betsy woke up later than usual the next morning. Too late to see her neighbors one last time before they left for the ship. The house across the street looked empty. Sad. Hollow. Just like her. Not feeling like eating, she dressed and flipped her shingle to *open* and threw herself into her work. The day slipped by quietly with no customers and no visitors. She snacked on a few things during the day; finally making a decent meal long after supper time. She worked late before finally going to bed.

Friday and Saturday followed much the same pattern except for customers. Many of the ladies stopped in on the pretense of requesting sewing. Really, they were probing her emotions. Some asked outright what her plans were now that Mr. Whitmore had left without an offer of marriage. Others offered sympathies for the loss of her perspective groom and soothing words like, "I am sure he will return as soon as he realizes he misses you." Saturday afternoon, when she found herself ready to physically push the well-meaning Mrs. Webb out the door, she turned her shingle.

Sunday, Betsy arrived at the Custom House just before the start of services to avoid any more uncomfortable conversations. She took her seat in the choir and looked up to a sea of faces all looking at her in sympathy as if she had lost her family. Then she noticed the empty row usually occupied by Theodore's family, as if everyone planned to save it for their imminent return. She spent the next few minutes controlling the irrational anger flowing through her veins before she could trust her voice to join in the hymn.

After the service, a concerned Abby was quick to reach her side to shield Betsy from further distress. "How are you doing?"

"Not so well. They all look at me as if I lost someone but they were never mine to lose."

Abby said, "True, but you lost the dream of having them and that's worth mourning too." She indicated the other parishioners with her head. "They mean well even if they are careless in expressing it." She gave her friend a critical look. "I insist you join us for dinner. Your God-children will entertain you and lighten your spirits."

Betsy wanted to say no, but knew Abby had her best interests at heart. Maybe she understood it was sometimes easier not to eat than to fix a meal for one. From that day on, it became part of the pattern of her life to have dinner with the Eatonton's every Sunday and she resumed eating at the boarding house once a week too.

Life returned to normal on the surface but underneath was an emptiness she did her best to fill with visits to friends. And in the quiet moments when memories haunted her, she sought comfort in prayer.

* * *

While Betsy felt stagnant, life continued on for those around her and the town.

Barbara Mabrity was officially named keeper of the Key West lighthouse, allowing her to support her family. The women of the island congratulated themselves on saving one of their own even though Mr. Whitehead deserved the credit.

William Whitehead spent the summer visiting his family in New Jersey leaving deputy-collector, Mr. Pinkham, in charge of executing the duties of the custom office. The poor man became quite overwhelmed during the busy summer wrecking season. It was mostly due to his lack of experience to handle the complicated matters presented to him. He muddled through as best he could but there were those who were less than understanding. Mr. Whitehead returned in the fall to multiple complaints and demands for disciplinary action; Dr. Strobel being the most vocal of Mr. Pinkham's detractors.

Mr. Whitehead reviewed each complaint but found Mr. Pinkham clear of any wrong doing. In the case of Dr. Strobel, the deputy-collector acted on assumption rather than fact. One of Mr. Pinkham's duties was keeping roll for the Marine Hospital. He saw one of Dr. Strobel's patients walking about town and assumed he was discharged from the hospital so he removed his name from the roll without consulting Dr. Strobel. When it was brought to his attention it was corrected but Dr. Strobel continued complaining and asking for his dismissal. In a particularly heated conversation Dr. Strobel even suggested he should be removed from office on the grounds of unpopularity. Mr. Whitehead refused, as fidelity to the government and not popularity were the qualifications needed for the post. The situation should have dissipated. Instead it festered for many months.

* * *

In December, one of the island's four original owners, Mr. John Fleeming, and his wife returned to Key West. The community welcomed their return, none more so than Mr. Whitehead. Mr. Fleeming hoped to take up salt production and expand the burgeoning market for Key West salt. He studied the industry well and was looking forward to turning his knowledge into reality.

The family stayed as guests of Mr. Whitehead and the two men were often seen about town, deep in their own conversation about everything from meteorology to philosophy; two birds of a feather, despite the decades between their ages. Mr. Whitehead was not alone; most of the islanders liked the congenial Mr. Fleeming. His sudden death, presumably from heart failure, brought great sorrow. As was the island custom, all businesses along Front Street closed for his funeral procession. His was a great loss to the community.

In honor of her husband's memory, the Widow Fleeming donated a plot from his holding to be used for the church although it would be years before construction was started.

Early the previous year a committee was nominated to start a church and school. The people of the island were of many different faiths so after much deliberation it was decided an Episcopal minister would best please everyone. And so the search began; something else that took many frustrating months to accomplish. Finally, on December 23rd, Reverend Sanson Brunot arrived from Pennsylvania and services were now held with confidence in its spiritual guidance. The first service of St. Paul's Protestant Episcopal Church was held on December 25th in the custom house. Many were in attendance and afterwards signed the register officially joining the church including the island founders; John Simonton, John Whitehead and Pardon Greene.

* * *

January 1833 brought a young German botanist by the name of Edward Leitner to their shores. He spoke English amazingly well after only a year of study in the States and he was already gaining fame in his field. He was pleased to be the first botanist to visit the island and the residents were beginning to feel very cosmopolitan having first Audubon and now Leitner choose their island as a destination.

Betsy shared Mr. Leitner's love of plants and his visit helped pull her from her despondency. They spoke of horticulture at great lengths. He spent hours helping her expand her small kitchen garden and the plantings around her house. He generously shared some of his acquired seeds and seedlings with her.

She was aware some Islanders speculated on their relationship but theirs was a simple friendship based on a shared interest in botany. His departure soon came and she returned to quiet living.

* * *

Betsy continued on mostly as she had done before meeting the Whitmores except now every month she waited anxiously for a letter from Henry. She did not receive any mail the first month, not that she really expected one so soon. Fortunately, there was a letter from her sister the second month to stem her disappointment. It mostly contained news from home and how the others were doing but one line did bring a smile to her face.

> *If you would but allow it I would send our brothers to exact punishment for the grievance Mr. Whitmore has caused. You say you know not his address, but dear sister, knowing you as I do, I feel you are protecting him, even in your distress.*

She was protecting him from her sister. Theodore may not have made her happy but he certainly didn't deserve to be on the receiving end of her sister's scorn.

The third month brought a single folded paper bearing a New York stamp. She tore open the seal in nervous excitement to see what Henry would send her. The neatly written script inside was a disappointment. It was a brief note from Mrs. Agatha letting her know they had returned home safely. Betsy supposed courtesy demanded a reply but it would have to wait till she recovered from her jilted excitement.

Another change in the pattern of her life affected her slumber. She suffered from a recurring dream. It began with the sweet comforting persona of Ben only to be supplanted with the brooding mysterious face of Theodore leaning in to kiss her. She would wake before their lips touched leaving her bewildered, bothered and melancholy. She thought maybe she would have an easier time moving on emotionally if only the dreams would leave her to sleep in peace.

Otherwise, her life was as it was before.

Day in and day out, week in and week out, she did the dishes, the laundry, her work, visited with friends, picked up the mail, but it was hollow.

It was all so hollow.

She dearly missed the sweet little boy who brightened her days but mostly she missed the exciting sparks of emotional connection she felt for Theodore. She might even call it love. Obviously he must not have felt the same or he wouldn't have left her.

She received sporadic letters from Mrs. Agatha, but they never mentioned Theodore. They were usually about her and Henry. The little urchin, on the other hand, only wrote her one brief letter but he did include a drawing of their house. It was quite good for his age and if it was close to true, he lived in a very large traditional three story. If they were so well off in the city, why would Theodore ever want to return? There was nothing here for him.

Now what? She was pining for something she couldn't have and the pining was only bringing her misery; worse misery than she felt before his arrival. So in the end, was she back at the beginning? Was she ready to accept a relationship without love for the sake of having a relationship? To have something else to focus on other than loneliness and her broken heart?

He was still there in the background; patiently waiting. George Casey knew he had been close to having her before and she suspected he felt like he was close again. And in truth, he was probably right. All it would take was a look from her after church and he would be by her side escorting her home. She would be exactly where she was before Theodore ever set foot on the island with the same tough decision in front of her. Should she sacrifice one desire in order to achieve another?

Could she do it?

Having felt the spark of love with Theodore's arrival she thought for sure she couldn't but now the drudgery of loneliness consumed her even more. Still, she was not yet at the point she could let go of hope and desire to settle for less.

Betsy often visited Abby over the winter months of the island's dry season. It was harder some days than others not to be jealous of her growing children and increasing middle. Betsy ached for a family of her own. One particularly somber day, Abby commented, "I found volunteer work helped me to get through my dark days."

Betsy's brow furrowed wondering what Abby would refer to as dark days.

Abby noticed the concern on Betsy's face and smiled. "I was miserable in the early days of marriage. Max was gone most of the time and during his brief visits home we argued. So I volunteered to help nurse the sick with Mrs. Mallory to keep from dwelling on my problems. Focusing on others may help you move past your melancholy."

Betsy's complexion blanched with chagrin. "Is it so obvious?"

"Most days you hide it well, but on some, like today, you seem unable to mask your feelings. Although anyone can see you are not as cheerful as you used to be. Mr. Whitmore took your heart with him, didn't he?"

Betsy's mouth thinned. "I guess so, because I sure haven't been able to give it to another."

Abby was suddenly curious. "Have you been trying to give your heart away?"

"No."

"Do you want to?"

Betsy considered her feelings. She knew pining for someone she couldn't have was no way to live so she was forcing herself to face an alternative. The passage of time also concerned her. Her child-bearing years were slipping by and she felt the need to settle before another year was lost.

On the other hand, Abby asked if she wanted to give her heart away and the truth was it was still attached to Theodore. It was hard to let go of her heart. "No."

Abby sagely nodded. "There will come a day when you will be ready. For now, focusing on others will help."

* * *

January was coming to an end. Six months had gone by since Theodore's departure and Betsy finally found her way past the heartache. She took Abby's advice. When she wasn't sewing for her clients she volunteered at the Marine Hospital doing mundane tasks like rolling bandages and serving food. The little bit of free time she had was spent gardening. She found that nurturing plants helped fill the void, at least for a little while.

One sunny afternoon, Esperanza and her mother came into Betsy's shop. It was obvious the young girl was bursting with joy. She was hardly able to contain her emotions. Betsy had the feeling she would have ran to the counter and jumped up and down in excitement if not for her mother's controlling presence. "Oh Betsy, I have the most exciting news!"

"Hello, Esperanza, Mrs. Sanchez." Betsy braced herself, having a good idea what was coming.

"It finally happened! We're getting married! Jonathon asked for my hand. *Padre* made him wait ten whole minutes before he gave his blessing. We are getting married in six weeks and I want your help to make a special dress for the occasion."

Betsy walked around the counter to embrace her friend and kiss her cheek. "Congratulations. I wish you both great happiness."

They spent the better part of the next hour discussing patterns, material and costs for the dress and other needed items for her trousseau. It was agreed Esperanza and her mother would do the majority of the sewing to help defray the expense. While in her presence, it was easy to share in Esperanza's excitement but as soon as she left it faded. Betsy focused on drawing different dress designs to present to the bride-to-be in an attempt to keep her mind occupied. It didn't help very much. She found herself drawing the dress she would want to wear if marrying again and daydreamed of what it might have been like to stand in front of Theodore wearing it.

* * *

February and half of March flew by in a flurry of wedding preparations. Mostly, Betsy kept her thoughts on the happy couple but sometimes, in the quiet moments of simple sewing, she would think of them and wonder what they were doing now. Was Henry in school? Did he do well in his studies? How much would he have grown? Was Theodore courting anyone? Or was he already remarried?

* * *

The 16th of March finally arrived. One could not have asked for a more beautiful day for a wedding. Fluffy white clouds floated on gentle breezes across the sapphire sky. The wedding procession moved through the streets to the custom house where the happy couple was joined as one.

Esperanza's dark complexion was the perfect complement to her cream dress made of silk net over a satin undergown with netting overhanging the short puffed sleeves. Her mother's delicate embroidery along the edges of the netting gave the gown an appearance of being draped in gossamer lace. A wide satin ribbon adorned her waist and topped the two flounces circling the bottom of her dress. The three of them created the best wedding dress Betsy had ever seen, in person or in a magazine. Esperanza wore a long veil of the same embroidered netting and satin ribbon to cover her silky dark hair.

Betsy made Jonathon's long black jacket, fitted at the waist, with white trousers and cream vest. She copied it from a fashion plate in one of her French magazines. With the tall black top hat he borrowed from Max, the groom was quite a dashing figure.

The wedding party also consisted of a cousin to bear witness for Esperanza and Max stood up for Jonathon with Reverend Brunot officiating. The ceremony was simple but it was followed by the biggest reception the Islanders had ever seen with lots of Cuban food, music and dancing.

Betsy knew Abby regretted not being able to attend but the imminent birth of her baby kept her home. Max promised to bring her some cake as consolation while Betsy promised to share all the details on the morrow.

As the wedding vows were exchanged, Betsy's feelings were a strong mixture of joy for her friends, fond remembrances of her wedding day, followed by sadness for Ben, wishes for what might have been and contemplation of her choices for the future.

George Casey sat nearby. He looked handsome today in his dress clothes and clean shaven. He must have felt her regard for he turned her way. Catching her stare he offered a questioning smile. She gave a friendly nod of greeting and returned her attention to the ceremony to avoid tendering further encouragement.

George sought Betsy out during the reception and stayed by her side through the receiving line and while they ate dinner and for the first few dances. She finally asked him to get her some punch just to have a moment alone. He was kind and attentive to her. He still worked for Mr. Fitzpatrick at the salt ponds so he was steady and dependable. All in all, he was an agreeable man and would likely make a good husband.

"Will you be tying the knot next?"

Betsy's hand flew to her chest. She turned to Jonathon, surprised to find he was alone. "You startled me."

"My apologies madam." He nodded in George's direction. "He'll still have you, you know."

"Yes, I know."

"So the question remains, will you have him?"

"So it would seem."

"What's holding you back?"

"I'm not sure anymore."

"He's likely the best offer you will receive."

She looked him up and down. "You are so happy in this moment, you wish for all to feel the same. While Mr. Casey could make life more," she searched for the word to use, "companionable, I'm not sure it would be enough—for either of us."

"He believes it will be enough for him."

"And I must decide the same; hence my dilemma." She sought to redirect the conversation. "Are you ready for married life?"

"Getting married was a dream for so long I never considered the reality afterwards. Did you know I will be moving in with her family?"

"No."

"It is a Cuban custom, especially as she is the only daughter. I am far more nervous about living under Mr. Sanchez's roof than I ever was asking for his permission to marry."

"My goodness, that says a lot. But you'll be fine. Just remember you both love Esperanza and it is not forever, right? You do get to move into your own place at some point, do you not?"

"Yes. It shouldn't take too much longer to save enough for land and to build a house as far away as we can go and still be on the same island."

"Have you thought of moving to another key?"

"I don't think my bride would be willing, but we'll discuss it when the time is near."

Betsy laid a hand on his shoulder. "You two will do well together. I pray you have a long and happy and fruitful life."

"Thank you. I best return to my bride."

"A good idea." She laid a hand on his arm. "I am truly happy for you Jonathon."

He covered her hand with his. "I hope you can find your happiness, Betsy."

Jonathon turned and walked away. George was headed towards her when Max appeared and swept her into the next dance.

"I know I should probably stick to dancing with the married ladies but you look as though you need to be rescued."

"Perhaps."

"You could do worse than George." The dance sequence spun her away. When she returned, he said, "You don't have to be in love to benefit from marriage."

"True, but if love can be found is it not preferable?"

"I suppose so but 'a bird in hand is worth two in the bush'."

"My mother would agree with you. How is Abby doing?"

Max accepted the change in subject. "As poorly as she felt this morning, I am guessing the babe will arrive before the week is out. Actually, I should head home. Likely Mrs. Baxley is ready for me to take over with the children."

Betsy was in shock. "You take care of the children?" It was unheard of, or at least Theodore was the first she had ever witnessed a man caring for his children.

He laughed off her disbelief. "I can do well enough for short spells."

The dance ended and Max wished her goodnight. Betsy wandered back to where George waited with cup still in hand. He held it out for her.

"Thank you."

"You're welcome. Would you care to dance the next set with me?"

Betsy put a congenial smile on her face. "Yes, of course. Thank you for asking." She set her cup down when the music started again and put her hand in the crook of his arm. They lined up with the other couples. After dancing two long dances, George led her to some empty chairs under a tree. They watched the others dance for a few moments in silence.

George turned his head and shoulders towards her. "Mrs. Wheeler, would you allow me to escort you home?"

She looked at him in surprise. "Now?"

"Well, a little later, of course, when the festivities are over."

Betsy knew where the answer to this question would lead. She would be returning to the path of courtship with this man. Walking home tonight would lead to walking home from church and eventually a proposal. Now was the moment of decision. Should she refuse him or was she willing to encourage him? She pondered her feelings so long he began to nervously twitch and then turned away to face the dancers. It wasn't easy but Betsy made the decision. It was time to bring an end to the loneliness. Marriage meant she could have children, and that dream made her say, "Yes."

To his credit, George didn't openly rejoice. He merely nodded while he continued to watch the other couples. Did he have some idea of how she felt? She was a little ashamed of her selfishness. He had feelings too. Betsy made an effort to be more encouraging for the rest of the evening.

Their walk home was pleasant. He left her at the door with a simple. "Goodnight." The invitation to walk her to church didn't come. She spent the rest of the night pondering the significance of it. She could only conclude her hesitation in accepting his offer had caused offense. She may have even lost him. If George was no longer interested she may even have lost her last chance at a decent marriage and children. *Oh, what have I done now?*

* * *

As promised, Betsy visited Abby the next day. They enjoyed tea on the porch while the children played in the yard. Abby placed a pillow behind her back and absently rubbed her heavily rounded abdomen while Betsy relayed all the details of the wedding and the wedding guests. Both of them were very happy for Jonathon and Esperanza having both had a hand in bringing the couple together. Betsy wanted to tell her about George until she noticed the pained look crossing Abby's face for the third time.

Betsy's surprise was too great to hide. "Abby, is the baby coming?"

Abby winced and nodded at the same time. "Betsy, would you mind gathering the children?"

"Of course." Betsy walked to the steps. "Emily, Christoff, it's time to go inside."

Four year old Emily grasped her little brother's hand and brought him up the steps.

Abby told her children, "Go play quietly in your room, please."

Emily obediently said, "Yes ma'am," which Christoff mimicked in his adorable toddler way.

Betsy let the children in the house and turned to Abby. "What do you need me to do?"

"Help me to the bedroom." She took a deep breath and slowly released it. "Then go to Mrs. Baxley. Her husband will send word to Max and the midwife."

Betsy helped Abby out of the chair. They paused at the door while another contraction gripped her. She nearly crushed Betsy's hand with the pain of it. When Abby could breathe again, she said, "Something's wrong. It feels different this time. Tell Mr. Baxley to send for Dr. Strobel too."

It must be serious for Abby to ask for the doctor. Betsy could only imagine the fear Abby must be feeling. "I will."

Abby paused to implore. "Please take the children home with you."

"Of course."

Betsy helped Abby change and climb into bed. She checked on the children then quickly ran the short distance to the Baxley's house. She delivered her message and rushed back with Mrs. Baxley who immediately went to tend Abby. Betsy found a sack and put in a couple of changes of clothes for the children then took them to see their mother.

Abby stoically did her best not to let them see her in pain. "Children, you are going to stay with Betsy for a little while. I know she will take good care of you."

Emily wanted to ask why but knew better than to question her mother. "Yes, ma'am."

Christoff looked from one to the other in confusion but obediently followed his sister's lead.

Abby kissed each of her children on the forehead before Betsy ushered them out of the room. Mrs. Baxley promised to send word when the baby was born.

Betsy sent a silent prayer heavenward for the mother and child.

She was a little nervous, this being the first time she had full responsibility for children since her younger siblings were babies. Her first thought was the need for food so they walked past her house and down Front Street to Mr. Patterson's grocery. She picked up a few things Emily was familiar with and then walked back to her house. Christoff gave up walking halfway each trip. The unusual burden of carrying a toddler and a basket of groceries left Betsy exhausted by the time they reached her house.

The three of them played games to while away the afternoon. Betsy made supper and tucked them into her bed then set about doing some of the sewing work she had neglected for the past two days.

It was now ten hours since Abby's labor started. Betsy knew she delivered her first two rather quickly, in just three to four hours. Abby's foreboding of something wrong must have come to pass. Sleep seemed elusive with so much worry for her friend but knowing the little ones would be up early Betsy forced herself to lie down on the sofa and try to sleep. It was sometime later before she fell into a restless slumber.

Thankfully, Betsy awoke before her charges and went to the kitchen to put some oatmeal on the stove to soak. She returned to the house to hear Christoff whimpering. She found him wandering the hall crying for his mother. She scooped him into her arms and headed for the nearest chair to rock him. She did her best to soothe him but her own anxiety hindered her success. Fortunately, Emily appeared shortly after. Her presence gave her brother the comfort Betsy could not.

Betsy cleared the parlor of any sewing items then closed and barred her workroom door. She left the children playing in the parlor after admonishing Emily to watch her brother while she went to the kitchen to make the oatmeal. She walked back and forth between the house and the kitchen, checking on them as often as she could leave the cereal. She well remembered how fast her little brothers could get into trouble when they were toddlers.

The three of them ate their breakfast and then continued playing games like ring around the rosy and hide and seek. All the while, Betsy worried over the lack of news from their parents. Her mind was conjuring all the possible tragic scenarios.

Late afternoon, Max arrived to collect the children. One look told her something horrible had happened. She didn't think it was Abby. He was grief stricken but she imagined he would be much worse if he had lost his wife. Fortunately the children were napping so they could talk for a moment.

"The baby?"

His voice was lifeless. "A girl. Stillborn."

"And Abby?"

"Sleeping. The doctor gave her a heavy dose of laudanum."

"You could leave the children with me for a while longer. You look as though you need rest."

"No. I'll take them home. Abby will need to see them, hold them, as soon as she wakes up."

She couldn't keep the tears from welling. "I'm sure she will."

Betsy led the way to the sleeping children. While she gently woke Emily, Max picked up Christoff, deciding it best to let him finish his nap. She stood at the door and watched them leave; her heart heavy in grief. Emily turned around to cheerfully wave goodbye. Betsy smiled and returned the wave. She wondered how much Max and Abby would tell their daughter of today's tragic loss.

* * *

Betsy visited Abby the next afternoon. She found her sitting in her bed staring out the window. Her hair was brushed and curled about the pillow, she wore a freshly laundered gown, and the covers were neatly arranged around her. She turned to her friend and offered the tiniest of smiles. The best she could do under the burden of her broken heart. Betsy fully understood and sympathized. She sat in the chair next to the bed, leaned forward and squeezed Abby's hand but didn't say a word. She knew there were no words of comfort to be offered. Instead she waited for Abby to indicate what she needed. It wouldn't matter if it was a shoulder to cry on or if she wanted to be left alone, Betsy would do as she asked and understand.

Abby blinked and her eyes welled again. "I am drowning in sorrow." She squeezed her eyes shut against the pain and tried to swallow the lump in her throat. When she opened her eyes again, Betsy noticed her normally dove gray eyes were dark and stormy and in desperate need of comfort. "The cord wrapped around her neck. She died as I...."

Betsy shook her head and rushed to Abby's bedside to grasp her hand. "You know it's not your fault. You couldn't prevent it from happening."

Abby's brow furrowed and her chin wobbled with heartbreak. "I know, but I still feel guilty. I am her mother. I am supposed to protect her." Betsy sat on the bed and opened her arms, giving Abby her shoulder to cry on. The ensuing flood of tears lasted several minutes. It was not a ladylike cry but the deep wracking sobs of a mother's heart in mourning. Betsy rubbed her back and soothed as best she could.

When the worst of it passed, Abby pulled away. She blew her nose with her sodden handkerchief. "I am sick of crying. I am not the first woman to lose a child and certainly will not be the last. I can bear this burden."

Betsy remembered crying when she miscarried until it felt as if the tears were hurting more than helping. "No you are not the first nor the last but you are the *only* mother who lost *this* child." Abby convulsively swallowed to check the next rush of tears. Betsy continued, "She was your blessing you waited and longed for. A child you named."

Abby nodded. "Catherine Ann."

"It is a beautiful name."

"I think she would have had my red hair."

"You're hair's not red."

Abby smiled the first true smile in what felt like ages. "It was when I was a child and it vexed me so...."

The faint sounds of the children playing and laughing downstairs drew Abby's attention. She turned serious. "We decided to say as little as possible to the children. We will leave them with Mrs. Baxley tomorrow morning while we lay Catherine to rest. Max was going to have her buried this morning but I insisted on being present so he decided to wait another day."

Her tears would have started again but she held them in check when she heard Max's unmistakable tread on the stairs. He stuck his head in the door. "May I come in?"

Abby lifted her hand to him. "Of course, husband. You need not ask. You are always welcome for you have my heart."

The tenderness in Abby's voice and Max's affectionate gaze had Betsy backing away from the bed and towards the door. Max assumed her vacated position holding Abby. Feeling the need to leave them alone, Betsy said, "I'll see you in the morning." She left, closing the door quietly behind her without waiting for them to answer.

* * *

Clouds banked the October morning sky as Catherine Ann Eatonton was laid to rest with only her parents, Betsy and Reverend Brunot in attendance per Abby's request. The tiny box nearly brought Betsy to her knees in sorrow. She didn't know how Abby was able to hold herself together. Betsy was sure she would have been in a sobbing heap on the ground in her place. Afterwards, they went their separate ways. It was oddly surreal. Normally there would be food and socializing and condolences after a funeral. It seemed wrong to return home and to the normal chores after such a momentous event.

Chapter 17

Tragedy struck the island again the following week.

Mrs. Graham and Mrs. Reynolds came into Betsy's shop one afternoon in unusually high spirits. Often they would take turns employing Betsy with a small order as an excuse to visit and share the latest gossip. For some reason they never considered just visiting as friends and, as a businesswoman, Betsy couldn't afford to suggest it.

Mrs. Reynolds barely sashayed through the door before saying, "Mrs. Wheeler, did you hear the news?"

Mrs. Graham was right behind her. "It's tragic."

Mrs. Reynolds said, "Mrs. Mabrity saw it all while she was cleaning the lighthouse this morning."

The two spoke back and forth like magpies not even giving Betsy a chance to greet them. The news must be extra noteworthy if they weren't even going to make the pretense of placing an order.

Mrs. Graham said, "Dr. Strobel wouldn't let the offense rest, even though Mr. Whitehead cleared Mr. Pinkham of any wrong doing."

Betsy realized she must be referring to the trouble between Strobel and Pinkham last fall. She too had heard Dr. Strobel berating Mr. Pinkham in public months after the incident.

Mrs. Reynolds laid her reticule on the counter and leaned towards Betsy. "Mr. Pinkham was forced to demand satisfaction for his honor. And what do you suppose happened?"

Mrs. Graham leaned even closer to share her offended sensibilities. "It was a duel, Mrs. Wheeler. The second one in this town. And here we are trying to present our island as a civilized place."

Mrs. Reynolds was more dramatic. "I'll tell you what happened. Ben Strobel put a bullet in his chest."

Mrs. Graham ruefully shook her head. "Mr. Pinkham was so nervous he didn't even fire a shot."

Betsy's attention swung from one to the other as they continued the back and forth relay.

"What was he thinking; demanding a duel when he had never fired a gun in his life?"

"Why his honor, of course. Dr. Strobel carried his dissatisfaction way too far."

"Now our dear Mr. Pinkham lies near death in the Marine Hospital."

"And where do you think Dr. Strobel is now?"

"We just saw him boarding the *Marion*."

"He means to leave town rather than face what he has done."

"And for what? An honest misunderstanding, I tell you. Mr. Pinkham was only correcting what he believed to be a ledger error."

Finally taking a breather in their repertoire, Betsy was able to ask, "And Mr. Pinkham, will he live?" A man these two ladies cared little about otherwise was made to sound like family.

Mrs. Graham answered, "One of the new doctors at the hospital is operating on him now to remove the bullet. We won't know for some time if he shall live or die. It would be such a tragedy to lose our dear Mr. Pinkham, such a fine person as he."

Mrs. Reynolds said, "We must be going. Good day, Mrs. Wheeler."

The two left her domicile as rapidly as they had appeared; off to share the news with anyone else who hadn't heard. Betsy was left alone to think. It was a sad day when grown men resorted to violence to resolve their differences with little concern for those who would bear the consequences of their actions.

* * *

Mr. Pinkham fought to stay alive for two weeks. At one point it was thought he might pull through but alas he succumbed to eternal slumber. Typical for Key West, the coffin was carried through town to the accompaniment of musicians before being interred in the graveyard on the southern beach and another grieving widow was left to fend for herself.

Mr. Whitehead fell in step beside Betsy on the walk home.

Betsy asked him, "What will become of Mrs. Pinkham?"

"I believe Reverend Brunot will be taking up a collection on Sunday to send her back to Kentucky. It is my understanding she has friends there who have offered her shelter.

Betsy felt for the widow but she also had compassion for Dr. Strobel's wife. She was forced to leave the island under a cloud of shame. "Mrs. Strobel leaves soon as well to join her husband in Charleston."

Mr. Whitehead grimaced. "Such a shame. Two homes broken by one man's bitterness. 'The tongue is an unruly member full of deadly poison.'"[4]

Betsy recognized the biblical verse and thought it appropriate. "Yes. Yes, it is."

* * *

The weeks following the wedding, George Casey made a point to speak to her every Sunday but offered nothing more. Betsy came to realize he was waiting for a sign from her; one she did not yet have the courage to make. She may have decided at the wedding reception she would accept his courtship, but it was easier to accept if he pursued her. She found it much more difficult to initiate the change in their relationship.

Perhaps this Sunday she would find the courage to do so.

But she did not.

The following Sunday, when George approached, Betsy made herself ask, "Mr. Casey, would you mind walking me home?"

George smiled as if she had given him the best gift ever. "I would be honored, Mrs. Wheeler."

He offered his arm and she accepted it. She would have preferred to keep her own space but since she intended to marry him, if he would still have her, she would have to learn to accept his intimacy as well.

They spoke of the weather, Reverend Brunot's service, young Stephen Mallory's appointment as custom collector and other town events. When they reached her door, she expected George to ask to escort her to church next Sunday and she was prepared to say yes. Instead he asked her to join him for dinner at Mrs. Mallory's on Wednesday. Again, she was finding it difficult to take the next step. Rather than risk losing him altogether, she graciously accepted, while inside, her heart screamed it was too soon.

And so as April drifted into May, their routine became established and accepted if not comfortable. He walked her to church on Sundays and home again, after the second week he asked to sit with her as well. Wednesdays they dined together at Mrs. Mallory's and one or two nights a week he would visit with her on her front porch in the evenings. He would come by after work and tap on her window to let her know he was there, then wait for her to join him. They would talk of random everyday things. Nothing of significance. Sometimes they argued but not for long as he would usually concede to her. Differences of opinion became less and less too as he yielded to her ideas making conversations rather dull.

Betsy was aware everyone around them assumed they would wed and there would be one less widow in their community. She was growing to accept it too. She knew there would come a day when he would ask for her hand and she would put aside her hesitations and accept.

* * *

Reverend Brunot came to them in poor health hoping the sub-tropic environment would help. Unfortunately, it did not. He continued to deteriorate and finally decided to return home in May leaving the islanders to once again manage as best they could with only the occasional visiting clergy that happened upon their shores. The search was immediately taken up again but it would be many more months before it was fruitful.

In her weak moments, Betsy felt as if disappointments and tragedies were becoming a way of life.

* * *

It was a sunny day, the end of May, dry, hot and humid, with little breeze coming from the water. A terrible day to be doing laundry, much less ironing. Betsy hated the task with a passion. She wished she could afford to hire out the arduous chore. She did too much of it in the course of her business making her personal ironing that much more distasteful.

Betsy returned the flatiron to the stove to heat again, shifted the dress on her work surface and wiped her sleeve across her perspiring brow. Carefully she adjusted the towel around the handle and removed the iron from the burner to run it across the hem of the skirt.

Her thoughts returned to the letter she received this morning. It was from her eldest sister and full of praise for her children's accomplishments and her husband's recent promotion. The letter made Betsy feel even worse than usual for her own situation of no husband and no children. It brought to mind, Henry, and his daily visits last year which never failed to bring to mind Theodore and the hopelessness of those thoughts led to George.

"Ow!" She jerked her hand away from the iron and put the side of her finger in her mouth to soothe the mild burn. One small rational part of her brain was thankful the iron had cooled down but the rest was too focused on all her emotional hurts and this added physical pain was the final straw. She placed the iron safely on the stove top and left the rest. She returned to the house in search of Abby's burn ointment. She sat down at the table to apply the soothing gel. Remembering how Ben would have done this for her made her feel even more forlorn.

In the sweltering house, her misery complete inside and out, she shut her eyes as the scorching tears flowed down her cheeks. She gave herself a moment to wallow in her wretchedness before going to the basin in the bedroom to splash tepid water on her face. She heard George tapping on the front window as she picked up the towel. She blinked hard. His timing was vexing. Hastily she dried her eyes and checked her appearance in the mirror. She tried smoothing her hair frizzed by the heat and humidity. Her face was flushed and her eyes were red rimmed. Hopefully he wouldn't notice in the shadows of the porch. She contemplated donning a fresh dress but in this heat it would be in the same state soon enough and unnecessarily add to her laundry which was the ill that started today's misery.

As always, George stood up from the chair as soon as the door opened to greet her in his customary manner of grasping both of her hands with his and complimenting her. Today he continued to hold her hands after their greeting. She was grateful he didn't make contact with the burned skin but his intense gaze made her a bit uncomfortable.

Instead of a compliment, George asked, "Are you ill, Mrs. Wheeler?"

She grimaced, her pride stung by his observation. "No. I'm not ill, just overly warm from this heat and a little somber I suppose. It has been a trying day." She would have shown him her burned finger but he still held her hands captive. "I received a letter from home."

Concern washed over his face. "Was it bad news?"

She had to admit, his interest felt good. "No. It was all good news, but it made me miss them."

He looked at her with such intensity it was clear he was contemplating something serious. She felt a touch of panic build around her ribs. Was she ready to answer if he asked the question?

George used her hands to gently guide her to a seat, then he dropped down on one knee.

"I've never done this before and I've waited so long... I'm a little nervous."

Do I want this? Can I accept him? She had to make the decision now. One she would be honor bound to keep. There would be no turning back from her answer. If she said no, there would not be a third chance with George. If she said yes, her future would be sealed.

He cleared his throat and braced his shoulders. "Betsy Wheeler, would you do me the great honor of becoming my wife and put an end to your loneliness and mine? I promise I will cherish you always."

Tears welled. She pushed aside all the doubts, worries and unrealistic dreams. She bit her lip and tried to empty her mind to the moment and the kind and considerate man in front of her. If he was willing to propose at a moment when she surely looked her worst, it must be a sign from God.

"Yes."

She was shocked by the weakness of her voice, it was barely a whisper. But the sky didn't fall and her heart didn't crack. She could do this. So she strengthened her voice and said it again, "Yes."

He sprang to his feet pulling her with him and into his embrace. He danced a little and made her laugh. The laughter eased the tension in her shoulders.

"You have made me the happiest man."

It took him a few minutes to calm himself enough to sit down and talk of wedding plans. Betsy felt drained. The emotions of the day were too much. He mentioned something about traveling to Charleston soon and marrying when he returned. Knowing she would have months instead of weeks before the event was of some comfort.

George got up to leave. He leaned down and kissed her cheek. "Thank you, Betsy, for agreeing to be my wife."

She could only offer a partial smile in return.

He walked down the steps and continued down the street whistling a happy tune. Betsy remained where she was, waving a fan to cool herself. Her mind blank. The ironing forgotten.

Eventually she became aware of something different across the street. The windows were open and there was activity in the house. It was being aired out for new tenants. It gave her an ominous feeling. She put it down to the stress of the day and fanciful thinking.

Theodore
1832-1833

Chapter 18

Theodore and Henry stood at the rail of the ship enjoying the welcome sight of the New York waterfront. The ship smoothly rode the morning tide through the harbour ending their uneventful journey home. Agatha and Annalise kept to the cabin for much of the voyage while Henry was rarely far from Theodore's side and as often as not they were in the company of Mr. Whitehead. Theodore enjoyed conversing with the intelligent young man especially since they shared many interests, including journalism. It made the journey pass quickly.

After the long days on board the ship, Theodore was ready to return home and to his daily routine at the paper. Mr. Whitehead soon joined them to watch the approach to the dock. New York was their first port of call since leaving Key West. The ship would return to Mobile, making several stops along the way. Next was Hoboken, on the other side of the Hudson River, and Mr. Whitehead's destination. From there he would travel overland to Newark to visit his family for a few months before returning to Key West.

The first hint of looming trouble appeared in the form of yellow flags. The two men noticed them on several anchored ships they were passing in the harbour. Theodore looked to Mr. Whitehead and found the same concern in his eyes. Quarantine flags did not bode well. They may very well have sailed from one yellow fever epidemic into another or something worse.

Around them, the sailors efficiently worked the lines from long practice, approaching the dock with precision. The sails were sheaved and the boat secured in preparation for debarkation. They watched from the rail, as two men from the city approached to speak with the captain albeit from a curious distance. They surmised them to be health officials. Theodore hoped, whatever the affliction, it was not so bad as to turn them away from the city. Both men and the crew intercepted the captain as he returned to the ship anxious to learn the news.

The captain addressed his audience. "The port is closed. The city is struck with cholera." He turned to Theodore. "They will let you disembark since this ship has no sickness and has not been to infected ports but it would be ill advised to return to the city now. If you mean to do so, then hurry. We sail for Hoboken within the hour."

Mr. Whitehead asked, "How far has the disease spread? What of New Jersey?"

The captain shook his head. "They couldn't say for sure, but it is believed New Jersey is as yet unaffected."

Theodore said, "Excuse me gentlemen. I must go speak with my aunt. Mr. Whitehead, would you mind keeping an eye on Henry?"

"Certainly."

Theodore knocked on Aunt Agatha's door. She opened it promptly. "Is it time to debark?"

"Not quite yet. There is a matter I wish to discuss with you." He looked over her shoulder at Annalise. "Privately."

Agatha entered the companionway closing the door behind her. She followed Theodore to the galley.

The heat below deck was intense. Theodore had no idea how Agatha could tolerate it. He used his handkerchief to wipe his brow. "It seems we have left one contagion only to return home to one more sinister. Cholera has reached New York. We are being advised not to return home just now."

"How bad is it?"

"Bad enough they have closed the port."

"What do you propose we do?"

"I am not sure. We have no other home to go to. Although we don't know how far the disease has spread, we could remain aboard this ship and debark in the next port free of the disease and stay in a hotel until it passes."

"It could be months before the danger is gone."

"True, and although we have funds it would quickly deplete them. Another option would be to find passage to Austria to stay with my parents."

Agatha said, "We could take our chances here. According to the news from Paris, the disease affects the destitute and depraved, of which we are not. If we limit our travels outside our home we should be fine."

Theodore was skeptical. "You are willing to take the chance? I've read the news too. The elderly and very young are most susceptible. You and Henry are most at risk."

"We'll be cautious and take care not to interact with any unsavory individuals. If it gets too dangerous we could always leave later. Besides, Annalise's family is anxious for her return."

He thought it irritating and odd that Aunt Agatha would willingly enter a cholera quarantine after insisting they flee from yellow fever in Key West. He supposed she must feel an overwhelming desire to be home. If that were the only reason to stay, he would refuse but Annalise's parents were expecting her and there was no time to send them a message and wait for a reply. Their last letter was clear, they were eager for her return. They hadn't mentioned the disease and Theodore wondered now if the possible arrival of the disease was behind their urgings for her return. "Very well. Gather your things. The captain means to promptly leave port."

She laid a restraining hand on his arm when he turned to leave. "I am sorry."

"For what?"

"For insisting we leave Key West which led us into this predicament."

Theodore's lips thinned. She should feel contrite. This was her fault but he wasn't angry. He patted her hand. "You were trying to protect Henry."

Agatha watched him walk away with a frown. Men could be so obtuse. He had no idea she had an ulterior motive for insisting they leave. She thought leaving would force Theodore to recognize and act on his feelings for Mrs. Wheeler. When it backlashed, she ruefully regretted her actions but her nephew's swift action gave her no opportunity to reverse her request.

Theodore returned to the deck to make arrangements for their baggage and to hire a hackney to take them home. He said farewell to Mr. Whitehead who generously offered for them to stay with his family if they found cause to flee the city. He thanked the captain for the pleasant voyage then ushered his family to the docks. Their belongings were loaded on a cart to follow behind the coach but not before Theodore scrutinized the drivers and the laborers for any signs of sickness. He gave the coachman directions to the home of Annalise.

The sound of the coach wheels changed as they left the wooden docks for the cobblestone streets. Theodore expected the cadence to be welcoming instead he was surprised to find it a bit annoying. Perhaps it was worry putting him in an ill humor. As the carriage moved further into the city the buildings rose up on either side of the street making Theodore feel confined as he never had before and then he noticed the rubbish piled up on the sides of the street worse than he remembered. His soul beckoned him to return to the tropical breezes of Key West. It was unexpected to be repulsed by a place he had called home his whole life.

At least the number of houses marked for quarantine in their section of the city was minimal. The poorer wards would show a different fate.

They arrived at the home of Annalise's parents who were grateful for the return of their daughter. They planned to leave the city immediately fearing the spread of the disease. From them, Theodore learned most of the affluent had fled raising his concerns for his family's safety. It was believed at the onset of the disease some sixty thousand residents evacuated in just three days.

They passed through an impoverished neighborhood on the way to his aunt's house. Here the street debris was significantly worse. The horrendous stench of death and decay permeated the carriage. A high number of houses were quarantined. The carriage swerved to go around a man pushing a cart full of corpses. The grayish blue cast to their skin was eerily morbid.

The man called out. "Bring your dead."

Theodore and Aunt Agatha shared a look of dismay mixed with disgust. Theodore was glad Henry wasn't able to see the cart. He hoped Henry wasn't paying attention until his son said, "Poppa, what did he mean, bring your dead? Is he collecting rats?"

He wouldn't lie to Henry, but he sure hoped he wouldn't have to explain this either. "No son."

Henry's face puckered. "It smells bad here. I liked the smell of Key West."

Theodore quickly changed the subject. Speaking to his aunt, "May I leave Henry with you for the afternoon? I would like to go to the paper for a while."

Agatha spoke through the handkerchief held over her mouth and nose inhaling the lingering perfume in an effort to combat the pungent smell. "Yes, of course."

They reached her home and paid the men to unload her trunks. It was obvious the majority of homes on her street were empty giving the neighborhood an ominous feeling.

Theodore looked to his aunt and found the same anxiety he felt portrayed in her countenance. "I will return soon."

* * *

Bob heartily greeted him in the office. "Glad to have you back." The two men shook hands. "Your timing is terrible. I sent a letter of warning after I received yours telling of your plans even though I was sure it would arrive after you sailed. Here, I have something for you." Bob pushed some papers aside and picked up the cheque buried underneath which he passed to Theodore. "Your stories from the Florida territory were very well received. Subscriptions increased so advertisements increased. I'm giving you a bonus based on those increases."

Theodore was shocked by the substantial amount. "Thank you."

"Almost hate to see you back here. Just say the word and you can leave again."

"Hmm."

Bob smiled. It had been too long since he heard that irritating non-committal answer. He hadn't realized he missed it.

The two men talked for a while, mostly of the current cholera epidemic, before speaking of what was next for Theodore.

Bob handed him last week's paper with his treaty article. "I thought you should know, my inquiries into the reason for the Payne's Landing Treaty revealed a possible conspiracy between the government and land speculators."

"How so?"

"As you know, the treaty was written before Gadsden left Washington and the Indians are to be moved over a period of three years starting as soon as the treaty is ratified. Did Phagan tell you the first group to be moved is from the Big Swamp area, the land most coveted by the speculators?"

"No, he didn't." Theodore frowned. "Goodness, and I thought this treaty was already corrupt..."

Bob looked at him askance. "Your article cast a shadow on the means of the treaty, but it gave no indication of corruption."

"I felt it best to print only the facts. Painting the Government in a bad light is one thing, making accusations is quite another when there is no proof."

"I see." Bob tapped his finger on the desk, something he did when he was deep in thought. "I couldn't get any proof either. There's finger pointing but no evidence. Copies of the treaties will verify the wording but never reveal the authors."

"Will your contacts let you know when the treaty is presented to Congress for ratification?"

"They said they would."

Theodore sighed. "It appears as though this story is at a standstill—for now."

* * *

He returned to Aunt Agatha's house for an early dinner. A new cook was hired through a service in preparation for their return. Agatha made several complaints about her before the meal was served but not a word crossed her lips after. Their welcome home dinner included many of their favoured dishes served to perfection. Theodore couldn't remember when he had a better meal or a more pleasant one in her house. His aunt was apparently cured of her need for quiet digestion. It was by no means lively but there was conversation initiated by her.

By tacit agreement they waited until after dinner to quietly discuss what each had learned of the cholera situation. Agatha learned the symptoms of the disease from the maid and cook, both of whom lost members of their extended families to the disease. Abdominal pain and watery diarrhea leading to dehydration were most common. Bob told Theodore no one knew what caused the cholera outbreak. Miasmas and God's wrath were the predominate beliefs. It followed here as in Paris that mostly the poor and wretched were stricken although outflow of the affluent likely skewed the numbers. At any rate, they felt a bit more confident in their ability to insulate themselves from the disease. Both the maid and cook agreed to reside in his aunt's home to help minimize exposure.

The fatigue in his aunt's faded eyes echoed his own exhaustion. He called Henry from his play and bid his aunt good evening. It seemed slightly odd to leave her for his home after living under the same roof for a year and a half.

They made their way on foot to their house. Thankfully this street was recently cleaned of debris. Still, Theodore was considering purchasing a carriage or curricle so he could limit even this exposure to the filth and to not be dependent on public transportation which would hopefully limit contact with the disease. The city was trying to clean up the waste but it was a long process and required citizen cooperation not to continue adding to the problem.

Theodore also hired a new housekeeper; employed before their arrival so the sheets would be freshly laundered and the furniture uncovered and polished. He opened the door to the sweet smell of lemon oil and felt the first true smile cross his face all day. He immediately shuffled a protesting Henry off to bed so he could follow. Traveling always left him feeling weary.

* * *

Returning to his old life was more difficult than Theodore imagined; mainly because it no longer suited him. The day to day routine of going to the office, he found trying. Henry, it turned out, was more adaptable. He was usually up and dressed before Theodore. His son was growing up and while one part of Theodore was proud of the self-sufficient boy he was turning into another part missed the exploring toddler to whom all things were a new discovery.

* * *

Theodore navigated his newly acquired two-seated polished black chaise and gray nag to Aunt Agatha's house. They both were sold off by the former owner for a ridiculously small amount so Theodore was able to purchase them at a fraction of the normal cost.

He couldn't help missing the fresh ocean breeze of the island and the wide open spaces allowing the salt air to flow through the town. The ever-present sound of the wind was preferable to the clamor of the city streets. He felt uncomfortably confined and crowded in this city even though it was larger than the entire island of Key West. Oh how he wished he had not listened to his aunt.

Mentally, he was restless and uncomfortable. The local city politics he used to cover could not hold his attention beyond the immediate threat of the plague to his family. Every paper in the city was covering the cholera epidemic and anything related to it and since anyone else of importance had fled the city there was little else to cover. All non-essential business had come to a halt creating further stress on the inhabitants. It wasn't that he didn't care about the plight of the city and its indigent bearing the brunt of the epidemic. He was aware and concerned for his fellow New Yorkers but the three other journalists in his office were writing those articles. He needed a different story and perhaps their subscribers did too.

* * *

A few days later he received an interesting letter from Illinois governor, John Reynolds. Because of his interest in Indian affairs, over the years Theodore collected many contacts in many different walks of life both sympathetic and antagonistic towards the Natives, one of them happened to be the Illinois governor who was decidedly against because his family was harassed by Indians during his childhood in Tennessee. The governor's letter said a skirmish broke out between Indians and settlers when Black Hawk and his followers tried to reclaim their homeland in Illinois. Governor Reynolds planned on personally taking the field to push the band of Indians back to the Iowa Indian reservation.

Desperate for a distraction from the epidemic, not to mention having a deeper interest in the conflict, Theodore convinced Bob to let him investigate for the paper. It was not hard to do since his Key West reporting produced such effective results. Theodore left Henry in the care of his aunt not trusting anyone else to keep his son safe from cholera.

Theodore arrived in Illinois on August 6th, just four days after the decisive Battle of Bad Axe effectively ended the small war. He wasn't the only one to arrive late. General Winfield Scott led a relief force that began as 950 soldiers. By the time he reached Illinois, only a third of the men made it to the battlegrounds. Most died of cholera during their trek to Illinois although some deserted. They were a ragtag group marching into the field. It was probably a good thing the field commander, General Edmund Gaines, claimed their services were not needed. The declaration led to a heated exchange between General Gaines and General Scott before cooler heads prevailed.

Undiscouraged that he missed the battles, Theodore interviewed many of the military participants including an interesting young captain by the name of Abe Lincoln. It did not surprise Theodore to discover a disputed treaty to be a root cause of this latest conflict. It was a recurring theme between the white and red man. Seventy-seven white settlers, militiamen, and regular soldiers died during the extent of the war. The Indian casualties were much higher. It was estimated Black Hawk lost half of the 1100 tribesmen who followed him into Illinois. At least a hundred of those were victims of drowning as they tried to retreat to Iowa by swimming across the Mississippi River.

On August 27, Black Hawk and White Cloud surrendered at Prairie du Chien to Indian agent Joseph Street. Theodore was present when Colonel Zachary Taylor took custody of the prisoners dressed in beautiful newly made white deerskin tunics. They were sent by steamboat to Jefferson Barracks, escorted by Lieutenants Jefferson Davis and Robert Anderson.

Theodore followed them. He hired an interpreter so he could interview the Indians. Even behind bars, Black Hawk extolled the look of a fierce warrior with his scalp lock, angular features, and proud bearing. Surprisingly, the warrior was openly willing to speak with Theodore and he was unusually inquisitive of Theodore's profession.

Theodore would like to have interviewed more of Black Hawk's Sauk, Fox, Meskwaki, and Kickapoo followers but they were forced to flee back across the Mississippi River. So as August came to a close, Theodore decided he had all the information he could get for an article and was unlikely to gain more by staying longer. He also had been too long away from his son. It was time to return home.

* * *

It was late evening when Theodore returned to New York so he waited until the next morning to make his way to his aunt's house. Henry came running into his arms as soon as he walked through the door, warming Theodore's heart. At the breakfast table, Henry was chattering a mile a minute updating Theodore on all the things he missed while he was gone. Realizing his son needed his attention, he said, "Henry, be quiet and finish your breakfast so you can go with me to the harbour."

Henry's face brightened as if he had been handed a present. He loved watching the tall ships sail in the harbour. "Yes sir." He stuffed the last of his oatmeal in his mouth, mumbled his request to be excused and went in search of his shoes.

Aunt Agatha gracefully lowered her teacup to the saucer then gave her nephew a steady searching look. "He missed you. All these trips you take, leaving him behind, are difficult for him."

Theodore held her gaze. "I am aware of his needs. Hence, the reason I plan to spend the day with him."

"As well you should, but I fear it will not be enough."

Theodore's reply was brusque. "And what would you have me do, Aunt?"

"Stay home."

"Hmm."

Agatha picked up her teacup. It was his typical non-answer when he chose not to answer or didn't have one. She wondered which it was this time but dropped the subject knowing she would make little difference in his thinking. She could only hope she had impressed upon him the needs of his son.

Theodore was a little ashamed of his outward display of his inner turmoil. He knew his work was hurting his son but he also felt the need to give voice to the Indians. Their plight would go unnoticed if men like him did not write of it. Something he felt he had to do by experience and not by relaying word of mouth which was so often prejudiced or censured. President Jackson and Congress were determined to rid the east side of the Mississippi River of Indians no matter the cost to those being displaced. If the newspapers did not publish their sufferings who would know of their hardships? What he did turned fears of unprovoked Indian attacks into empathy for a vanquished people.

It was important work but was it more important than his son? Easy to say 'of course not' but harder to act in that manner. The question then always turned to how he could take care of his son and do his work which inevitably led to the same conclusion. He needed to take a wife to be a mother to his son. How did one go about finding a wife who was not a simpering debutante? It was a hard enough question to answer when times were good, in the middle of a cholera epidemic—impossible.

Henry's return to the dining room put an end to Theodore's uncomfortable thoughts.

Father and son walked to the nearby livery stable to retrieve the carriage. The stable hands were busy so rather than wait Theodore decided to take the opportunity to teach Henry how to hitch a horse to a carriage. It having been some time since Theodore had managed the task he was a bit rusty. The nag had another agenda as well. She was perfectly content to munch on hay in her stall and protested the idea of being put to work by refusing to stand still while Theodore attached the harness and reigns. Concerned for Henry's safety he sent him to watch from the carriage seat. It took longer than it should have but Theodore finally accomplished the task just as the stable hand arrived. Theodore was glad he didn't have to suffer the indignity of turning the task over to another when he was trying to teach his son.

They spent a few hours watching the ships at port and the ones under sail on the Hudson River. Theodore pointed out the different masts and sailplans of the passing vessels. There were brigs, barques, merchants, schooners, clippers, sloops, smacks, yawls and many more. Henry quickly learned to identify them and soon it became a game as to which of them could spy a different ship first.

The rumbling of Henry's stomach finally forced them to leave in search of sustenance. Theodore would have liked to take Henry to his favourite tavern for a meal but its proximity to an area besieged with cholera made him decide to return to his aunt's domicile instead. Afterwards he assumed Henry would take a nap but his son soon set him straight.

"Poppa, I stopped taking naps weeks ago."

Theodore looked to Aunt Agatha. She angled her head and gave him a look that said 'your son is growing up without you'.

Now Theodore was having a hard time coming up with something else for them to do together. The arrival of an afternoon rain shower further limited his ideas. Henry solved his dilemma by leading him to the chess board set up in the drawing room.

"Let's play chess, Poppa. I'm old enough now."

Theodore smiled and ruffled his son's hair. "Good idea Henry. Do you know which color moves first?"

Henry nodded. "White. Mrs. Betsy taught me to play."

Theodore's breath caught as the image of her face after she kissed his cheek floated in his mind; her cheeks flushed with embarrassment and her blue eyes reflecting the longing she tried to hide. The recollection was an unconscious reaction made all the more potent by his conscious efforts not to think of her. For the first time, he wondered if his feelings for her might be more than a physical attraction, but he couldn't dwell on it now. His son waited expectantly to begin their game.

Theodore picked up a rook of each color and put his hands behind his back. He then swapped the pieces around a few times before presenting Henry with a closed fist holding one piece. "If you can guess the color I'm holding you can choose which color you want to be."

Henry gave it some serious thought before guessing. "White."

Theodore opened his palm to reveal the white rook. He smiled at his son. "And which color would you like to be?"

Henry tilted his head, again carefully considering his decision. "Black."

Theodore's right eyebrow went up.

Henry shrugged. "White has the advantage, but I would rather see what you do first."

The sensible reasoning behind Henry's answer amazed Theodore, exciting his desire to share this favoured pastime with his son. They played until supper time when both were reluctantly pulled away and returned soon after their meal until Theodore noticed Henry's drooping eyes.

"Come Henry. Time for bed." He intended for them both to return home but decided it would be best to let his son sleep at Aunt Agatha's one more night.

Henry slid off his chair without protest. They skipped the bedtime story since Henry could barely keep his eyes open long enough to change into his night clothes. Theodore brushed the hair from his forehead and kissed his son goodnight.

Henry whispered, "Thank you, Poppa."

Theodore tilted his head. "For what, son?"

Henry took a deep breath, turning to his side. "For the best day ever."

He was fully asleep before Theodore could answer around the tightening of his chest. He tucked the covers tighter around Henry's shoulder. Love for his son filled his heart, blessing him.

Theodore returned to the drawing room to bid his aunt 'good evening' and then drove the carriage back to the livery leaving it in the keeping of the overnight stable hand. Once home he headed straight for his office, poured his favoured two fingers of brandy, and settled in at his desk to go through the stack of mail accumulated in his absence.

He made a point of keeping correspondence with Major Glassell in Key West, Gad Humphries, the former Indian Agent, Colonel Gadsden, the commander at Fort Brooks, and a few other officers, enlisted men and residents allowing him to keep tabs on the situation in Florida. It was through these men he received word of Indian Agent, John Phagan's plans to travel west with the delegation of chiefs in October to inspect the western reservation. The delegation would report back to the tribe for approval of the move so the treaty could be ratified.

Theodore saw a whole lot of problems with this plan, especially if the delegation or the tribe found the reservation unsatisfactory. He knew the men in Washington would not tolerate anything less than their agreement to move. Sending the Indians to inspect the land was an idea originally conceived by Agent Gad Humphries years ago with honest intentions but wasn't embraced by the government until this latest treaty. It seemed to Theodore as if the constructors of the Payne's Landing treaty included it as a means to an end; a ploy to get signatures with no intention of adhering to the true results. Now being a stipulation of the treaty the terms must be carried out before the treaty could be ratified.

Plans were immediately swirling in his head of joining the delegation. It was sometime later when the thought of telling Henry he was leaving again brought him up short. He would likely be gone for months this time after being home for less than a week. The conversation with his aunt was not going to be any more pleasant. He wouldn't consider not going. This was his story. He may not truly understand them but he knew these people. He had to see the story through to its inevitable conclusion. As hard as that was going to be on his son and on him, it was a temporary hardship. The Seminoles were facing much worse.

* * *

Bob used his contacts in Washington to help Theodore make arrangements to meet up with the delegation headed to Fort Gibson in the Arkansas Territory. Once again he closed up the house, sold the nag and carriage, and did his best to reassure Henry before leaving on a ship bound for New Orleans. If he was lucky he would catch up with the delegation there but if not he would take a steamboat up the Mississippi River and journey overland to Fort Gibson, located in a bend of the Neosho River north of where it joined the Arkansas River, arriving shortly after the delegation.

Henry became fretful and withdrawn as soon as Theodore told him he was leaving again. Aunt Agatha said not a word. She didn't have to; her frequent looks of disappointment and head shaking were enough to inflame the guilt he was already feeling. Rather than displacing Henry twice he left him at his aunt's house for the week he was home. He spent every evening there until Henry's bedtime. They played chess when Theodore wasn't occupied with work and correspondences.

The day of his departure was emotionally distressing. At breakfast, Aunt Agatha announced they would not see him off at the dock as she did not feel up to making the journey there and back. Theodore conceded in understanding but for Henry it was one more disappointment to miss seeing the ships.

A hansom cab waited out front as the small family gathered in the foyer to say goodbye. Theodore knelt down in front of his son making him the taller one. *When had he grown so much?* The last time he did this they were eye to eye. He brushed the hair from Henry's forehead and straightened his collar then ran his hands across his shoulders and down his arms before pulling the reluctant child into his arms. "I'll miss you son."

"No you won't. You'll be too busy with the Injuns to care about me."

"Henry!" Theodore was angered by his outburst and his choice of words. "Where did you hear that word? Don't use it again. They are Indians or Natives. Do you understand?"

Henry meekly nodded.

It was then Theodore realized the meaning of Henry's words. He softened his look. "I truly will miss you. I have enjoyed spending time with you this week. Will you practice playing chess while I'm gone?"

"Who will I play with?"

Theodore looked to the lady behind him. "Did you know Aunt Agatha is an excellent chess strategist?"

Henry turned to look at his aunt in awe, then turned back to his father in surprise. "But she's a girl!"

"Yes son and you'll find some girls are every bit as smart as men. Some even more so." Theodore returned to his feet. "Do you promise to practice?"

"Yes sir."

"And you'll be a good boy for your aunt? You promise to listen and obey her? No playing outside or wandering down the street. There are still a lot of sick people out there."

"Yes sir."

"I promise I'll write. Will you promise to read your aunt a bedtime story every night?"

Henry rushed up and hugged him. "I promise, Poppa."

He ruffled the already tousled blond head then turned for the door before they could see the moisture gathering in his eyes. Leaving had never been so hard.

Chapter 19

Arkansas Territory, Fort Gibson, 28th March 1833

Theodore sat astride his borrowed horse, enjoying the crisp clear morning as he looked west across the Neosho River. Fort Gibson stood a hundred yards behind him. He could faintly hear the drill calls of the military practicing formations. It was close confines in the fort and this morning Theodore sought refuge in the solitude of the leafless oak and hickory sentinels along the bank of the river. He huddled in his deerskin coat against the breath of cold air from the north.

Spring was coming but he sincerely hoped he wasn't here to see it. He left Henry over six months ago. It never crossed his mind it would take this long to inspect the land but then he hadn't considered the Seminoles would be caught up in negotiations. The Government and the Creek Nation expected the Seminole tribe to amalgamate with the Creeks. The Seminoles demanded their own section of land due to concerns of representation, mistreatment and stealing of slaves by their former enemy, the Creeks.

He and the seven chiefs; Jumper, Black Dirt, Charley Emathla, Holata Emathla, Alligator, Sam Jones and Mad Wolf, along with Abraham, toured the entire Creek reservation and had several meetings with their chiefs. They now waited for Washington to answer their quest for separate land. Hopefully a favourable answer would come soon. Spring in New York was calling to him. He was ready to return home to his family.

The sound of galloping hooves reached his ear. He turned in the saddle to watch the horse and rider approach. It was the stocky Private Kinsley Dalton he befriended.

"Hullo, Theodore. Want some company?"

"Good morning Kinsley. Are those fishing poles?"

"They sure are. I have leave today and thought you might like to join me."

Theodore didn't have any plans with the Seminoles today. "Sounds good."

The two men spent a relaxing and pleasant day fishing returning well after the noon day meal with a mess of fish for the cook. Not enough for the entire fort but plenty for Private Dalton's unit to enjoy.

Theodore was headed to his quarters in good spirits when he left his companion until he discovered the entire Seminole delegation was nowhere in sight. He made a few inquiries expecting to learn they had ridden off somewhere. The first few soldiers he asked claimed ignorance. Fortunately he ran across the twins, Fred and Rod Drake. Theodore liked the friendly red-heads though their bright blue eyes eerily reminded him of Betsy's. Though in their mid-twenties they looked younger and had a reputation for being camp pranksters and honest to a fault. Without guile, they revealed the Indians were sequestered in a private meeting with Major Phagan and under no conditions were they to be disturbed.

And then the treachery became clear.

Theodore thought it strange the delegation had to wait here for Washington's reply when it could just as easily be sent to the reopened Fort King. It was really an excuse to wait for the arrival of President Jackson's commissioners to obtain approval of suitability. Theodore should have known something was afoot when he was introduced to the new arrivals yesterday afternoon. After assurances they didn't have the awaited reply, Theodore didn't give their presence another thought. That was his first mistake. The second was taking this morning's fishing trip at face value. The gullible young Private Dalton was sent to keep him out of the way. Obviously, Gadsden and Phagan did not want a witness to this meeting.

All he could do now was wait and fume. He wondered what Major Phagan was discussing with them. The trip was meant as an inspection of the land to be reported back to the tribe. It was the acceptance of the tribe, specifically King Micanopy, which would satisfy the conditions of the treaty.

Or was it?

Phagan said 'they' would approve the land but evaded Theodore when he questioned who 'they' were. It was clear now; to him 'they' was the delegation. But the delegation knew it did not have the authority. Likely another reason for the secret meeting, Gadsden and Phagan were determined to finalize the treaty. How far were they willing to go to do it?

Hours later a somber group of delegates returned to their quarters. Theodore was not welcomed among them being considered one of the enemy, at least for tonight. He did learn from a satisfied Major Phagan that the second part of the treaty, finding the land acceptable, was signed by the delegation. While not as openly jubilant as Phagan, Colonel Gadsden was pleased to have his task complete. Plans began immediately for their return to Florida. While Theodore welcomed the latter news, he was distressed by the former but all involved refused to discuss the day's event. He only hoped the journey home would loosen their tongues.

Theodore planned to obtain passage on the same ship as the Indians. The captain informed him his ship was full with a smirk. Phagan standing behind him made Theodore realize he was purposely thwarted again. It took him two more days to find passage to follow but this captain was more than willing to catch up to the slower vessel allowing them to arrive at Fort Brooke at the same time. The walk to Fort King gave Theodore time to learn of Phagan and Gadsden's deeds at Fort Gibson.

The closer they came to their destination, the more vocal and concerned the delegation became of the impending reunion with the rest of the tribes. Abraham eventually revealed to Theodore that coercion, bribery and finally the threat of not returning to Florida were used to make them sign the treaty despite not having the tribe's authority to do so. Now they would have to face the tribe and report on the unacceptable situation.

As soon as they returned to Fort King, the delegation wanted to call the nation together to report their findings. Agent Phagan brushed aside their request. "There's no need for a meeting. The terms have been met. The treaty is signed. Now we wait for it to be ratified."

In the days that followed their return, the delegation found itself ridiculed by other tribe members for succumbing to the white man's trickery. In self-defense they began denying their actions. Division soon became evident within the tribe. The higher chiefs having not signed the last two treaties vowed to refuse removal while some of the older chiefs were willing to capitulate fearing bloodshed. The young warriors were becoming more vocal against leaving their land. Theodore could see the building resistance within the tribe. It was very likely to lead to war.

Knowing formal action to begin removing the Seminoles from Florida would not take place until the treaty was ratified; Theodore made plans to return to New York. He knew he would have to decide if he was going to continue following this story from Florida or New York. He wasn't sure he would have an answer by the time he reached home.

He sent a letter of inquiry to Key West thinking it wouldn't hurt to know if the same house was available to rent. He wished he could visit the island again but he was departing from St. Augustine this time. As close as he was, it was too far away. The detour would take weeks and he had three letters in his pocket from Aunt Agatha urging him to return home to Henry.

Big blue eyes and ink black hair surfaced in his mind. He hadn't expected to carry her memory with him but at odd times over these past months it was there—her face, her smile, her laughter and the graceful way she moved. He wondered, as he so often did, if she was married now. She was too much of a treasure to remain alone for long. It was mentioned to him several times that she had nearly married George Casey before his arrival. With his departure, it was likely the courtship may have resumed. His chest tightened. He often tried to remind himself of all the reasons he had not offered for her. The strength and validity of his arguments lessened with each recollection while his regret redoubled. He refused to allow his mind to consider if only....

New York, end of May 1833

Theodore opened the front door of his aunt's house expecting Henry to run into his arms. He was disappointed to be greeted only by the new butler. He found his aunt sitting in a chair by the fire even though the day was warm enough not to require the supplement heat. He leaned down to kiss her cheek. "Are you feeling well, Aunt?"

"I am fine. It's these old bones having trouble adjusting. They tell me there'll be snow tomorrow."

"Snow? Why, it's well over fifty degrees today."

Her lips pursed. "You mark my words, nephew. It will snow."

Theodore dismissed her silly notion. "And where is Henry?"

"He and his tutor have left on a jaunt. They will likely return soon. You will not believe how much he has grown." She gave him a reproachful look. "You were gone a long time."

"Much longer than expected."

He heard the front door open and waited restlessly for Henry to find him in the room, hoping to surprise him. Henry stopped short in the doorway of the drawing room when he spied Theodore.

"Hello, Father."

Father? Henry had never called him father before. "Hello, son."

Agatha saw Theodore's pained look. "Don't mind him. He is picking up airs from the other children he's been socializing with thanks to that tutor."

Henry ignored her remark but his back stiffened and his tone was dry. "Welcome home." He then addressed his aunt. "I'll be in my room studying." He turned and walked up the stairs.

Henry's aloofness made Theodore feel like he had been gone much longer than seven months. What happened to his sweet little boy?

Supper was a quiet affair. Theodore tried to break the silence by asking after his son's activities. He received short answers in reply. His aunt soon claimed a headache and departed for her room. Theodore gave up on social conversation and resorted to practical matters.

"I'll have our house reopened tomorrow. You'll need to pack your belongings to return."

"How long will you be home?"

"I don't know, son." Theodore had not yet made up his mind to stay or return to Florida.

"Then why should I move only to move back again."

Theodore didn't want to discuss it with Henry until he had made a decision. "It is not for you to question my decisions."

"Yes, sir."

Not wanting to end the evening on such a sour note, Theodore tried another tact. "Shall we play a game of chess?"

"If you like, sir."

His tone left something to be desired but Theodore would take what he could get of his son's attention. They played a quiet, civil game. Henry had learned much in the way of strategy during his absence. Walking home Theodore noted how much had changed while he was gone. The streets were cleaner. The cholera epidemic thankfully faded in December. A new streetcar railway was started along the Bowery and Henry no longer worshipped him.

In hindsight, the Arkansas trip was a complete disaster. The hardship on Henry was more than he anticipated. Somewhere in the last seven months, he lost his little boy.

A cold wind blew against his back causing an involuntary shiver adding physical discomfort to his mental misery. The discomfort ended when he reached his hearth; the misery plagued him into slumber.

The unexpected and unusual thunderous snowstorm hit the city overnight. Theodore was so tired he slept right through it. Waking up to the city covered in white caught him by surprise even though his aunt had predicted it. He trudged through the fresh snow on his way to the office pulling his coat tight against the chill.

Unbidden came the image of Betsy playing in the turquoise water under a warm tropical sun; of lifting her into the boat and seeing more than she meant to reveal. He wondered which he was pining for more: the warmer latitude or the comely modiste? Why could he not be aware then of what he clearly felt now? She would have been good for him and his son; so patient with Henry and all his questions. Theodore was so sure at the time he could never love again, that he closed himself off to the possibility. And now it was too late.

* * *

He entered Bob's office depositing his article of the Arkansas trip on his desk. Bob looked up from the draft he was editing. "Back again, eh?"

"Hmm."

Bob noted Theodore's distraction. "Take a seat, Teddy."

Theodore did as he asked.

"What's on your mind?" Theodore looked at him blankly and Bob stared back, waiting. "Must be a lady."

The accurate assumption startled Theodore. "What?"

"On your mind, it must be a lady. Who is she?"

He had no intentions of sharing his thoughts of Betsy with anyone, least of all, Bob. "There's no lady."

"Then what's bothering you?"

Knowing Bob would not let it go, he answered, "It's my son."

Bob's eyebrows drew upward. "Is something wrong with Henry?"

Theodore looked out Bob's window. "He is resentful of my recent absence."

"He's a child. Aren't they known for being resilient? I'm sure it won't last long."

"I hope not."

"Millicent asked me to invite you over Friday evening. Just you. She's putting together some kind of dinner party and needs another male to round out the numbers. Will you come?"

Theodore preferred to decline. He did not get along well with Millicent's friends. The last dinner party she had her guests nearly came to blows over politics.

Seeing the forthcoming rejection, Bob pleaded, "Please don't make me tell her you're not coming."

Theodore grimaced. "Fine, I'll be there but you'll owe me a bottle of scotch."

Bob smiled. "Done."

Two days later the snow was almost completely gone. Theodore arrived at his aunt's for supper and discovered she had company. Agatha's friend Mrs. Tolliver and her youngest daughter, Penny, came to visit for tea and were invited to share their meal. The situation appeared innocent enough but Theodore had the feeling he was the target of a matchmaking mother. The Tolliver's lived a few streets down from his parent's house so he and Penny knew each other from childhood. He had seen her occasionally while Margaret was alive but the last time was at Margaret's funeral. As he recalled, her cheery disposition had grated on his raw nerves.

The passing years failed to darken her spun gold hair and her blue eyes still held a youthful sparkle. He wondered why she never married. Even tempered, intelligent and friendly; certainly she would make someone a good wife. Her father passed away in her teen years. Perhaps, in her grief, Mrs. Tolliver had been unwilling to let go of the comforting presence of her daughter and may have thwarted any suiters. Mrs. Tolliver may desire marriage for her daughter now but little did she know Penny's pale blue eyes reminded him of another and in comparison Penny came up short.

Agatha called for supper to be served as soon as the greetings were completed. While they ate, Penny and Theodore shared updates of old school chums while Mrs. Tolliver and his aunt discussed more current matters.

When they ran out of conversation, Penny turned to Henry. "How are you doing in your studies? I'll wager you do quite well, just as your father did."

"Yes ma'am."

Unabashedly, Mrs. Tolliver said, "My Penny adores children and she has inherited my strong hips, good for childbearing."

Penny's face turned scarlet and she dropped her chin to her chest in an attempt to hide it.

Wanting to ease her embarrassment, Theodore cast about for something comforting to say then wished he hadn't. "A good wifely quality, I suppose."

Theodore noticed Mrs. Tolliver lean towards his aunt to whisper, louder than intended. "See? I told you they were perfect for each other."

Penny squirmed.

Theodore shared a commiserative grimace with her. He then redirected the conversation to a safer topic. The rest of the meal passed well enough until he caught his aunt's speculative gaze upon him. He at first supposed their guests were her idea of helping him find a wife but now he wasn't sure. Mrs. Tolliver seemed to be the instigator while Aunt Agatha appeared to be studying his reactions. He wondered at her conclusions.

As for Penny, she was likable, nothing more. But should he not consider her anyway? She could hold an intelligent albeit dry conversation. He wondered how she felt about cigars and brandy. He seemed to recall her being a member of a temperance society. On the positive side, her interactions with Henry were promising.

They adjourned to the parlor for a spell after dinner. Conversation was mostly of feminine interests. Theodore had his usual after dinner drink. The ladies all declined his offer of sherry. While he noted Mrs. Tolliver's look of disapproval sent in the direction of the glass of amber liquid in his hand, Penny seemed to be pointedly ignoring it. He announced his desire to return home a short while later effectively ending the evening. It was only proper he escort the ladies home, especially since it was only a slight detour in his path. Mrs. Tolliver chatted the whole way and clearly showed her disappointment when he excused himself as soon as she opened the door.

* * *

Theodore knew as soon as he crossed the threshold of Bob's home Friday evening, his wife was also on a matchmaking mission and he was the sole target. Her dinner party included three other females of her acquaintance.

Bob shook his hand in greeting and whispered, "I'm sorry my friend, I swear I didn't know."

Theodore looked him dead in the eye and whispered, "A case of scotch or I walk."

"Done." Bob turned to the room as his wife, Millicent, approached.

She effusively greeted her guest of honor. "Mr. Whitmore, how good of you to come."

"Thank you for the invitation, Mrs. Jenkins."

"Come with me." She placed her hand in the crook of his arm, stealthily leading him, the prey, to her chosen predators. At least none of these women could be described as debutantes although two of the three had questionable reputations.

"I would like to introduce you to Miss Daphne Parker..."

He gave a gentlemanly bow to the dark haired vixen. "Miss Parker."

"...and Miss Georgina Alexander..."

Another bow to the buxom blond daughter of one of the most successful lawyers in the city. "Miss Alexander."

"...and Miss Sarah Treadle."

This mousy creature must be the famous merchant's daughter known to be a recluse. He wondered how Millicent enticed her to this gathering. She was clearly a shrinking wallflower. He sympathized more than pitied her. Of the three, this one he understood. "Miss Treadle." She blushed under his gaze and dropped her eyes to the floor.

Theodore was forced to revise his thinking; two predators and one bait.

Millicent clasped her hands together, gleefully smiling. "Dinner is ready. Shall we adjourn to the dining room?"

Theodore offered his arm to the timid Miss Treadle. She lifted her hand to accept, pulled it back, then placed it so lightly on the top of his forearm he wasn't sure she was even touching him.

Millicent was proud of her dining room. The table was set with the full complement of her best china. Two ornate silver candelabras, passed down from her father's family, graced the center of the table with five candles each, providing just enough light to enhance the beauty of her guests. Too much light might reveal their waning youth, too little would be uncomfortable. A silver vase on the buffet held a profusion of white roses standing elegantly in front of her gold wallpaper. The hot house flowers cost her a pretty penny. It wasn't often she was able to entertain so she was making the most of the occasion.

Having given careful thought to her seating arrangement, she directed Theodore and Sarah to one side while Daphne and Georgina faced him on the other. She did this for many reasons but the strongest was she believed neither one of those two could be trusted to keep their hands to themselves which would surely have Theodore headed for the door. He was not a man to be trifled with.

Once seated, she clapped her hands twice to the side of her head signaling the butler to enter with the first course of lobster bisque. She had to call in several favours to get the recipe from a friend's French chef. She hoped her cook was able to faithfully reproduce it.

Theodore knew conversation to his left would be difficult, but he tried anyway for encouraging the two beauties across from him was asking for trouble. "Miss Treadle, how is your father's business? Have you recovered from the bleak days of the epidemic?"

Sarah jumped at the masculine voice so near, dropping her spoon in the bowl. She self-consciously dropped her hands to her lap and began wringing her napkin. Her gaze fixed on her soup as she meekly replied, "Yes, he is doing well now, thank you." She risked a glance across the table in time to see her companions smirk at each other before quickly dropping her gaze again. *Oh why did I ever let Millicent talk me into coming?*

Theodore expected shyness but was ill-equipped to deal with skittishness too. He shot Bob a look sure to impart his discomfort. His eyes then traveled to the other side of the table and encountered openly coquettish flirtation. *What have I gotten myself into?*

Miss Alexander batted her eyes at him and gushed, "I hear you went out west to visit the heathens. What are they like?"

Theodore's jaw clenched. "Civilized."

Bob interrupted, "He means they live in very structured societies. Each of the tribes has their own piece of land."

Miss Parker was more suave than her companion. "Did you find the region agreeable, Mr. Whitmore? Was the land fertile enough for them? I read your article on how the Indians in Florida are starving on their reservation. You would think they would be eager to relocate if food was more plentiful."

If she hadn't ended her sentence by seductively licking her lips he would have felt more inclined to take her seriously. "Yes, the land in Arkansas is something to behold. Much the same as our countryside only not as dense. Hills and trees, many of the same varieties we have, but with less undergrowth. Or at least so it seemed. It was winter when I was there."

A timid voice entered the conversation. "Do you believe the government will force the Seminoles to move there, even though they are against living with their former enemy?"

Theodore glanced at the bowed head beside him. He addressed the table in general to keep from adding to her discomfort. "It's nice to know people are interested in what I write. Yes, I believe even if it comes to war, Congress and President Jackson mean to make them move."

Sarah looked up at him, passion blazing in her eyes. "But it is their land! What right do we have to take it?"

His eyes widened in surprise, but he kept his voice low as if speaking to a skittish colt. "We have no right, but we will take it from them just the same, no matter the consequences."

The second course arrived and with it Millicent and Georgina redirected the conversation to the latest *on-dit* which occupied half the table for the rest of the evening. Bob, Theodore and Sarah did not feel the need to participate or the desire to redirect; instead they were content to finish their meal in silence. Afterwards, Millicent insisted the men join them in the drawing room to be entertained by Miss Parker and Miss Alexander.

It was with no small relief, Theodore closed the door behind him some three hours later. Those three ladies did not give him much confidence in finding a wife, let alone a mother for Henry. Sarah was the best of the three but she was scared of her own shadow. She would be no match for his son.

He hoped they were not the best the city had to offer for none of them could even hold a candle to *her*.

The following afternoon, Bob placed a crate on his desk. Upon inspection Theodore found six bottles of Bowmore. Bob slapped him on the back. "You earned them."

"Thank you, and I tell you now, I will not be accepting any more dinner invitations."

"I understand, but in Millicent's defense, she did mean well."

"Hmm."

* * *

219

Theodore walked home alone in the warm spring evening with only the occasional rider or carriage passing by. The brick buildings towered over him on either side while light from the windows cast a dim glow into the night breaking up the pitch dark. Gas street lights had yet to be installed in this ward. They were mostly found closer to the Battery.

Despite the nice evening and pleasant walk, discontent weighed upon Theodore's mind. He longed to be somewhere else. He tried to return to his former life in this city but he found little satisfaction in doing so. And so far, he met four women this week and instead of opening the possibilities of a wife they only reinforced what he was coming to realize. He made a huge mistake. They all paled in comparison to Betsy's spirit, strength, and resilience.

His main reason for walking away from her was because she deserved to be loved. A bitter smile twisted his lips. More the fool was he. By now she had probably wed another and most likely without love while he was realizing with every step how much he really cared for her.

His false charity likely condemned them both unnecessarily to lackluster marriages.

Later that evening, he downed a dram of his bribery before opening a letter from his Key West landlord. The house was currently available. He made his decision, right then and there. Even if it was too late to have Betsy, he wanted to make the island his home. He could convince Bob to pay for the story of the Seminole removal giving him an excuse to return.

The practical side of him insisted he look for a wife to take with him. To that end, every unattached female he met was considered for the position but ultimately none were found suitable. Still he kept looking right up to the week before their departure.

It took two months to confirm the house rental and to get everything in order but finally it was time to break the news to Henry and Aunt Agatha.

Theodore put down his fork after taking the last bite of succulent pork roast. He looked from Henry to his aunt still considering his choice of words. His relationship with his son had mellowed since his return but it was still not as open as before he left for the Arkansas territory. He worried over Henry's reaction to his news.

"I have an announcement to make."

Agatha put down her fork. "I thought you had something weighing on your mind."

He said it in the only way he really knew how—direct and to the point. "Work requires I return to Key West. It will be for an extended stay so I want you both to come with me. I was able to secure the same house we rented before."

Aunt Agatha gave him a probing look. "Mrs. Wheeler doesn't have something to do with your decision, does she?"

He avoided a direct answer. "You made your feelings clear about her."

"I am afraid I didn't. If I had she might be here now."

It was Theodore's turn to give her a probing look.

Agatha huffed her impatience with his ignorance. "I wanted you two together. I know I made you believe I didn't like her, but I was trying to encourage you."

One eyebrow rose as he continued to question her with his intense gaze.

With a touch of exasperation and guilt, her voice took on a defensive tone. "Well, it always worked with your father, and with my husband, and even with your grandfather. I certainly did not expect you would heed my wishes so keenly."

Theodore had no idea what she meant. "What, exactly, worked with them?"

"If I let them believe I objected to something, they would do it anyway. So I was trying to encourage your pursuit by discouraging it."

"Hmm." Frustration surfaced and was suppressed. "It hardly matters now. I am sure she has wed another."

Agatha squinted at her nephew. His response was monotone but did she detect a note of resignation in his voice? *He really does care for the girl.* Agatha tried to hide her knowing smirk. "She has not."

Another probing look.

"I correspond with Mrs. Mallory and others just as you have correspondence with Mr. Whitehead and Major Glassell. They would have mentioned if she had wed. I would know from the girl herself if she would return a letter with anything more than dull drivel and rarely even that. I believe she only writes to inquire of Henry. She must not be one to write although I don't understand why. Her penmanship is excellent, obviously she's well-educated for a girl, and her writing skills are acceptable."

Theodore felt hope take wing in his chest. Betsy's face appeared in his mind smiling just for him.

He was ready to love again.

He suspected he was already in love with Betsy Wheeler and likely had been for some time.

Theodore looked to Henry. "How do you feel about returning to the island?"

Agatha was more direct. "Would you like to see Mrs. Betsy again?"

Henry's face lit up like Theodore hadn't seen since before they left Key West.

"Oh yes, I had grand adventures with her and I'm older now. Perhaps I can learn to swim and retrieve conch just like she taught Poppa."

In a manner completely out of character, Theodore surprised them all by standing up and saying, "Let's go pack our things. We will be on the first ship sailing towards the Keys."

Henry jubilantly shouted, "Hooray!"

Now that Theodore made up his mind to return to the island, his plans could not be executed fast enough. Not even returning in the midst of the summer heat could dampen his spirits. Once they were finally underway, his impatience grew faster than they sailed. Most days he stood at the railing silently urging the ship onward while running through his head scenarios of what might happen when he arrived. How soon could he seek her out? Was she still available? What would she say? He needed her to say she loved him just as he loved her. He knew that now. He loved her. And he would tell her he was sorry for leaving and for making her wait. He should have recognized his feelings for her a long time ago.

Could he outright ask her to marry him? He would probably have to woo her first. He tried to remember how he courted Margaret but then decided it didn't matter. It would be different with Betsy. It was a second marriage for both of them. They knew what marriage was about and he believed they both wanted it so wooing would likely not be necessary. He was sure she was interested in him so maybe he could ask her straight out.

He patted his breast pocket, checking again to make sure his grandmother's wedding band was secure. On her deathbed, a year after his marriage, his grandmother pressed her ring into the palm of his hand and closed his fingers around it. Her feeble hands shook his fist, "You save this for your bride." She drew a painful breath and added, "Promise." And of course he promised assuming her feeble mind had forgotten he was already married. He offered the ring to Margaret but it didn't fit and she preferred the one she had so Theodore put his grandmother's ring away. Recalling her words now he wondered if somehow she had known he would have a second bride.

Chapter 20

August 1833

Theodore held an excited welcoming feeling of coming home as the ship sailed into Key West harbour. He and Henry anxiously waited at the balustrade for the moment they could debark. They were both scanning the people walking nearby looking for familiar faces and noticing what had changed and what was still the same since their departure nearly a year ago.

Henry pointed to a female in the distance, making her way to the fish market at the end of a nearby dock. "There she is! Can you believe it, Poppa? Mrs. Betsy is right there."

Theodore couldn't look away, especially once he confirmed her identity.

The ship's gangway was now in place. Henry tugged on his sleeve. "Can I go to her?"

Realizing Henry would make a good buffer for their reunion, Theodore gave his consent. Henry took off like a whip, running down the wharf and through the street. He stopped a few yards short of Betsy to walk more sedate and gentlemanly, amusing Theodore. He watched his son wait politely behind Betsy until the person she was conversing with noticed and nodded in the boy's direction. Betsy turned around and even from this distance Theodore could see her delighted smile and hear her excited greeting.

Betsy turned around to find a familiar boy behind her. "Henry!" *Dear sweet little Henry. My how he's grown.* She jubilantly embraced the boy, embarrassing the seven year old, then carefully looked him over for all the differences a year had made; his new front teeth and a few inches in height being the most obvious.

"Mrs. Betsy! I saw you from the ship."

She couldn't help looking in the direction he pointed, immediately spotting Theodore helping Agatha disembark. She forgot how strikingly handsome he was even at this distance. Joy went winging in her heart and the full smile on her face was completely unconscious.

Until insidious reality erased it.

Oh heavens! What have I done?

In a moment of weakness, she promised to be another man's wife. A promise made three months too soon because of her lack of faith in the Lord's timing. Her future was walking towards her. A future she could no longer have. Her spirits dropped to the ground at her feet.

Henry's excited chatter went unheeded.

Theodore approached the woman who had unwittingly consumed his every thought and action over the last few weeks. The woman he hoped held his future in her heart. Hope winged from his soul at the sight of her until he watched her disposition change from utter joy in greeting Henry to reserved politeness for him and his aunt. Her eyes were on him but the light behind them dimmed. Perhaps it was due to the public scene. He certainly hadn't expected her to embrace him the way she did Henry but it seemed as if more than polite reserve was holding her in check. Clearly he was going to have to work harder than anticipated to win her favour. It made sense. He probably hurt her deeply with his sudden departure. He would willingly woo her, if that's what it took to win her heart.

Betsy noticed the looks of those passing by and could well imagine their thoughts. When Theodore left before, they gave her grief asking questions she couldn't answer about his return and why she didn't go with him. Some of those same people were aware her fiancé was due to return any day now and her wedding would soon follow. She could well imagine all the speculating questions running through their minds.

Few knew she would be leaving the island after the nuptials if George found work in Charleston. She pushed the disturbing thought aside. She would deal with it when the time came, for now it was only a possibility. Right now she had a different heartbreak to face.

Betsy pasted a smile over her turmoil. "Welcome back, Mr. Whitmore, Mrs. Pary. It's good to see you again. What brings you back to our island?"

Theodore held her gaze intently. "I cannot speak for my aunt, but Henry and I have returned to make Key West our home." The color drained from her face so fast he feared she might faint. *What did it mean? Was she happy to see me?* He couldn't imagine her having such a strong reaction against his return.

Betsy's knees went weak. She couldn't believe this was happening. The man she wanted returned to claim her home as his while she pledged her life to another who was likely making plans at the very moment to uproot her. Such a cruel twist of fate. *Or was it the devil testing her?* Tempting her to break her promise. "It is hard to resist the charms of this island. Many others have succumbed before you."

Theodore held her gaze. "More than the island drew me back."

Betsy felt her cheeks heat. He wanted her too. She glanced toward his aunt to escape the intensity of his gaze and found Agatha staring at her nephew, mouth agape. Was she unaware of his ulterior motive for returning? Their previous departure was at his aunt's insistence. Betsy had felt her censure of their growing relationship. *Does she still harbour those feelings now?* Betsy stopped the flow of her thoughts. It didn't matter what his aunt thought nor did his feelings matter. She was betrothed to another. A promise made must be kept.

She drew a deep breath as she returned her gaze to his face. Any response she gave to his declaration would encourage him. Her only option was to disregard his words as if he never spoke. "Will you be residing in the same house? I couldn't help noticing it was aired out again in preparation of new tenants."

He felt hope flutter briefly in her blush followed by gut twisting disappointment as she brushed aside his admission. It was absurd to expect her to fall gushing at his feet and in truth he would have lost respect for her if she had. During his previous visit he purposely kept their relationship from developing and then he abruptly left the island. Two things she was sure to have keenly felt. Now it was her turn to deny him. Not out of malice, it was only natural for her to do so to protect her heart. He would have to find a way to move past his natural reticence to woo her properly. A part of him even looked forward to the challenge. "Yes. We are to be neighbors again. We would be honored if you would join us for dinner this evening to celebrate our return."

Her heart's survival dictated she avoid him. Contact could only lead to further heartbreak and she was already suffering enough disappointment in her predicament. "I'm afraid I already have plans for this evening." Hopefully Abby wouldn't mind an unexpected guest for supper to give truth to her lie. "Another time, perhaps."

Theodore thought her denial lacked conviction. *Was she avoiding him?* He would let her have her way; give her a day to adjust to his return. But tomorrow—he intended to pursue the lovely widow for his own.

Abby eagerly accepted Betsy's request to share their meal. It was six months since the tragic loss of their still-born daughter and at least on the surface her friends seemed to be handling it well. After supper, Max played with the children giving her and Abby some time alone.

Abby watched her husband on all fours in the living room letting the children take turns riding his back. She smiled absently. "We've decided we're ready to try again." She turned to Betsy. "I still grieve for Catherine, but it's time to look toward the future."

Betsy pulled in her bottom lip and nodded. "It will be good for you to have another baby to focus on."

A crash from the other room turned both their heads. Hearing laughter they decided it was nothing of concern, Abby turned back to her friend. "I hear Mr. Whitmore has returned. What are you going to do about it?"

Betsy's brows drew together. "You know as well as I, there's nothing I can do." She wasn't surprised Abby knew he had returned. Word traveled fast in their small community.

"What if he shows signs of having feelings for you?"

Betsy grimaced. "He already has."

Abby sat up a little straighter. "When did you see him?"

"Earlier today. I was nearby when he came ashore." A reminiscent smile bloomed on her face. "Sweet Henry came rushing up to me. He has grown so much this past year."

"And what did his father say to betray his feelings?"

Her smile disappeared. "I believe his exact words were: More than the island drew me back."

Abby's hand flew to her chest. "Oh my!"

Betsy's brow lifted. "Exactly."

"And when does George return?"

"Soon."

"I thought I was only teasing but you really are dealing with heartbreak."

"All because of an iron."

Abby's eyebrows quirked. "What does an iron have to do with this?"

"If I hadn't been having such a bad day topped off by burning my finger on the iron I probably wouldn't have been so melancholy and susceptible when George arrived. He wouldn't have proposed. Or if he had, I would have been better able to thwart it. He caught me in a weak moment."

"Oh Betsy, I am so sorry. You are living your own Shakespearean tragedy."

"And there's nothing to be done about it. I will honor my promise to George." Betsy felt the tear slip down her cheek and quickly brushed it away.

"And move to Charleston?"

"And move to Charleston."

"What did Mr. Whitmore say when you told him?"

"He doesn't know about any of it. And it gets worse. He has decided to make his home here. Permanently."

They lapsed into silence, each lost in contemplating the sadness of the situation.

* * *

Theodore darkened Betsy's doorway the following afternoon. He wanted to come sooner but the details of establishing his household took longer than expected this morning. Betsy appeared from the back room wearing a pale pink dress covered with a snow white apron. His heart skipped a beat at the sight of her unbound tresses falling loosely about her shoulders; the hitherto unseen length beguiled him. Her incredible blue eyes widened in surprise sending her brows winging under her bangs, charming him even more.

He wanted her for his own.

She stepped to the counter. "What can I do for you, Mr. Whitmore?"

Spellbound, it took Theodore a moment to acknowledge her words. He approached the counter and leaned across it to take her hands, gently pulling them to rest within his in the center. He would have preferred to walk around and swing her up in his arms but the wariness upon her countenance dictated his actions. She allowed him to hold her hands, but her rigid posture gave rise to a niggling fear of doubt he worked to ignore.

"Mrs. Wheeler." He glanced at their hands and then back to her face while he searched for the right words. "Betsy. I've been a fool. I thought I was protecting you when I left because I wasn't ready. I am now, if you'll have me." Her tears pooled then spilled. He let go of one hand to wipe her checks but she beat him to it. Surely they were happy tears. "I know I stayed away too long." He was so nervous he kept speaking, not giving her a chance to reply. "Please forgive me for making you wait. I should have come in April."

Unable to contain her profound sorrow, she burst into tears.

Theodore was at a loss. This wasn't going the way it was supposed to and darn this counter between them. He wanted to pull her into his embrace and put a stop to her tears. She pulled her other hand from his to retrieve a handkerchief from her sleeve. He tried to make eye contact, but she wouldn't look up. "I'll do whatever it takes to win your heart. I love you, Betsy." Her tears increased. "I was a fool before, but I'm not going to leave you again. I promise." Her tears made him feel helpless, and he didn't know what else to say.

Betsy finally lifted her watery eyes to his, so full of sadness. Her voice tightened as she said, "It's too late."

Theodore's face fell and his heart plummeted. Words failed him. He could only wait for her to explain.

Her tears continued to fall unheeded. "I've promised to be another man's wife. Mr. Casey proposed in May and..." She paused to prevent the wobble in her voice. "...and in a weak moment I accepted."

If someone else had been in the room, he would have sworn they gut punched him.

May kept ringing in his mind.

If he had only come in April....

May.

This was his fault. He was to blame for her unhappiness. His decision to rush home at Aunt Agatha's urgings now condemned her. His shoulders sagged and moisture gathered in his eyes. Sorrow and regret filled him for the fate they now faced because of his poor decision.

She placed her hand over one of his, now pressed against the counter between them, oddly noting the crooked little finger of his right hand. "I'm sorry, Theodore. If I had any indication you would return, I would've," her breath hitched, "I would've waited."

They stood there in momentous silence both staring at their touching hands upon the counter as the seconds ticked past.

Theodore turned his hand beneath hers, grasping her fingers as if to lift her hand to his sensual lips. She waited but he didn't. When he finally raised his eyes to hers there was a profound sadness in them. "I..." His lips compressed. He looked to the window for a moment before he could find the courage to look her in the eyes. "I am sorry. This is all my fault. I was a fool to leave you in the first place. And then again in waiting too long to return."

He held her gaze as he finally kissed her hand. He reluctantly released her to back up a few steps before turning to stride out the door. Betsy's hand drifted back to the counter as she absently stared after him. She felt numb inside and out.

It was several minutes before she roused from her trance and returned to the work room. She moved by rote, doing, more than thinking. She sat down in her rocker and picked up the skirt she was hemming. Twenty minutes later the numbness wore off.

He loves me. I love him. But I am promised to George.

Tears welled and fell. Unable to stop them, she laid her work aside to cover her face with her hands, leaning over as the sobs came to wrack her body. She cried until weariness replaced the tears, then she climbed into bed, curled into herself, and welcomed the escape of slumber's embrace.

Agatha looked up from her knitting as her nephew paused in the doorway. His bleak expression and bowed shoulders were telling. She leaned forward. "Theodore?"

His hollow response trailed behind him as he continued onward. "She's engaged to another man."

Shock, guilt, and sorrow flowed through Agatha one right after the other in a heavy onslaught. A niece she would have followed and gotten the whole story and they would have commiserated and consoled each other but a nephew...

* * *

Theodore didn't know what to do with himself. He wanted to punch someone, but he was the person to blame. He didn't want to give up without a fight but there was no fight to be had. Unless George or Betsy broke the engagement there was nothing to be done. Betsy would never breach her promise and he would never ask it of her anyway. He didn't know George but if he was George he wouldn't let her go. *The lucky...* Theodore couldn't bring himself to finish the thought. George hadn't done anything wrong. He could only hope George would be a good husband to Betsy.

Then it occurred to him how wretched his situation really was. He set himself up right across the street to witness firsthand his own undoing.

He needed something to take his mind off of her. He walked out the front door without saying anything to anyone, making a beeline for the barracks in search of Major Glassell or Major Dade for an update on the Seminoles. Unfortunately, Major Glassell was away and Major Dade was busy drilling the troops.

On his way home he passed by the closed shop of the *Key West Gazette*. Since Dr. Strobel's departure the town had been without a newspaper. Here, Theodore saw an opportunity of not only providing an income but also a project worthy of providing a sufficient distraction from his thwarted love.

Buying the business was easily accomplished. His days became consumed with cleaning and organizing the office, getting familiar with the workings of the press and ordering needed supplies of ink, paper and missing or faulty type face. When not working in the office, he was busy collecting subscriptions.

Learning how to actually produce a paper was a challenging task. Being the writer, editor, copywriter, pressman and distributor kept him busy from before sunrise to long past sundown but at least it kept thoughts of *her* at bay.

By month's end, the *Key West Weekly* was in production.

* * *

Betsy was surprised when Agatha invited herself to tea the next afternoon. The meddlesome old lady was bound to get involved at some point. Betsy poured fragrant tea in her last unblemished cup and passed it to Agatha. She poured another cup for herself then took a careful sip and waited for Agatha to speak.

"I came to apologize."

It was the last thing Betsy expected her to say. The shock of it had her lowering her teacup to the saucer and returning them both to the table least she spill it. "For what do you feel the need to apologize?"

"For parting you and Theodore last summer. If we had stayed you would not be engaged to another."

"True, but who's to say he would have come to recognize his feelings."

"I believe he was close to letting go of Margaret. He just needed a little more time."

Betsy spoke with the bitterness of anger. "Then you do owe us an apology." She softened her tone. "But your heart was in the right place. You were protecting Henry. Of course, I forgive you."

Agatha bowed her head to hide her feelings. "Thank you." In another moment she was herself again. "As it turns out, leaving was a poor decision. I'm sure you read about the cholera epidemic in the northern states."

"Were you truly in danger?"

"It was all around us. We isolated ourselves as much as we could to limit our exposure. Half a year we lived in constant fear. In hindsight we would have been better off to have stayed here. The dead of winter finally brought an end to the disease but it was spring before most of our neighbors returned."

"I'm glad no harm came to you."

Agatha finally asked the question that brought her over. "Where is this fiancé of yours?"

"He is looking for work in Charleston. I expect him to return any day."

"I would like to meet him."

The disconcerting idea dismayed Betsy. There was no telling what Agatha might say. "Perhaps."

Agatha smiled. She would get her way when the time came. "Now tell me all that has transpired in my absence."

* * *

Theodore worked hard to avoid Betsy but three weeks after visiting her shop their paths coalesced in the place where he first saw her so long ago; the mercantile shop. He approached her just as she turned from the counter ready to leave with her purchases, startling her. He reached out to steady her, placing a hand on her elbow. The resulting shock made them both jerk apart.

Offering a weak smile, Theodore said, "Good afternoon, Mrs. Wheeler."

Her reply was stilted. "Good afternoon, Mr. Whitmore. Is your family well, sir?"

"Yes, in good health. And your fiancé? Have you word of his return?"

"He has been detained. He found work and a place to stay with friends. He hopes to come for me before the New Year."

"I wish you both well." He couldn't think of anything else he could say in public and in their situation, nor could she. If only he had returned to Key West in April... "Good day, Mrs. Wheeler."

"Good day, Mr. Whitmore."

Theodore struggled not to turn around and watch her leave. The sadness in her eyes haunted him for days afterwards. It was likely a mirrored reflection of his own eyes.

* * *

Betsy suspected Theodore was avoiding her when only Agatha and Henry were seen attending Sunday services. She didn't object. As much as she wanted to see him, it was better she didn't. The same longing she saw in his eyes, ached in her breast. She wished George would hurry and come for her. Leaving the island was now a means of escape.

* * *

Months drifted by, summer storms came and went, thankfully none of them hurricanes. Yellow fever was minimal; it's victims all surviving. October turned into November without much fanfare slipping quietly into December.

* * *

Theodore leaned back in his chair enjoying one of Mr. Wall's fine cigars in the company of Major Glassell and Major Dade. It was his habit to visit the officers once or twice a week to keep up with the military news. It was Thursday afternoon and while he was there a dispatch from Fort Brooke arrived for Major Glassell. The seal was broken and the contents read in silence while the other two waited. Five pages and some ten minutes later, the letter was refolded and placed aside.

Glassell rose and retrieved three glasses which he set upon his desk then poured a generous portion of cheap whiskey in each. He slid a glass to each of his companions then raised his own.

"A toast, my friends, to the demise of Agent Phagan."

Theodore and Major Dade looked to each other with confused curiosity.

"The scoundrel has been officially relieved of his post. His replacement is a Georgian, General Wiley Thompson."

Major Dade said, "I've met him. He served with Andrew Jackson in the Creek War. Quite an imposing figure but I found him to be an honest man. He'll certainly serve the Indians better than Phagan."

Theodore asked, "Do you think Joseph White ousted him as a political vendetta even though he was found guilty of pocketing tribal funds?"

"Without a doubt. He was merely ordered to pay back the funds as a result of the investigation. Mr. Whitmore, you would also be interested to know the head chief, John Hicks, passed away last month. Wasn't he in favour of removal?"

"Yes although I'm not sure how much influence he really had. He was ostracized by the tribes for signing both treaties. It made him weak, especially in the eyes of the young warriors. If I'm not mistaken his death advances Micanopy to head chief."

Major Dade asked, "Any word on the treaty ratification?"

Theodore said, "No, sir. It should happen soon. Perhaps when Congress returns in the New Year."

Major Glassell nodded. "I'm sure you're right. Agent Thompson had better get familiar with the chiefs and gain their trust. Once the treaty is ratified the troops will be sent in and reason will be hard to come by with all parties involved."

Major Dade said, "I pray it doesn't come to war. We know these people. It will make it hard to execute orders."

Major Glassell added, "But our duty will come first."

Major Dade gave a single nod. "Yes sir."

Theodore rose from his seat ready to take his leave. "I would like to meet Agent Thompson. He would make a good interview subject. Will you let me know when you have the next courier headed to Fort King? I should like to accompany him."

The officers rose from their seats as well to shake hands.

Major Glassell answered, "I will, if you can promise to be ready at a moment's notice."

Theodore nodded. "Not a problem, sir. Thank you. Gentlemen, good day."

* * *

Betsy wasn't sure if she was relieved or disappointed when she met George Casey at the wharf in mid-December. His return meant their wedding day was finally at hand and she would soon leave the island removing her from the torment of seeing Theodore and Henry not that she had seen much of Theodore. He carefully kept his distance. Henry, however, visited her almost daily. It was bittersweet. On one hand she loved spending time with him. He was so smart and chipper; a balm for her aching heart. But on the other hand, it hurt knowing how close she had come to being able to claim him as a son.

She smiled and waved for her betrothed and hoped he didn't notice it was forced. When he reached her, he dropped his luggage and grasped both her hands, then kissed her cheek. She blushed profusely, embarrassed by the public display of affection. "I can only stay for a few days. I have to return to work after the first but I just had to see you. It's been so long, my dear. Have you missed me?"

Betsy could only nod.

"I'm afraid I can't bring you back with me just yet. I need to save more of my wages before I can buy a house for you. I wouldn't even be here now but I worked out a trade for passage on the ship. I'm hoping I can stay with a chum and save the boarding expense as well."

"And I hope you will." Again she felt relief and disappointment. She was relieved not to be married this week but her tortuous proximity to Theodore would continue.

"Let me deposit my things at your place and then take you to a nice dinner at Mrs. Mallory's to celebrate my arrival. Afterwards, I'll leave you to see if I can find suitable accommodations. How does that sound?"

"Very well."

* * *

"I believe I would like to take a stroll."

Aunt Agatha made this unusual announcement as the maid cleared the last of the dishes from the table and intentionally before Theodore stood to leave the room. He heard the command behind her words. She expected him to escort her. The oddity of it was she rarely went for a stroll and as far as he knew she had never done so after supper. He wonder what she was up to now. Resigned to his fate, Theodore rose from his chair and walked around the table to pull out his aunt's chair and offer his arm for her to rise. "Where do you wish to stroll to?"

Breezily she said, "Nowhere in particular. I just feel the need for a little exercise."

"Hmm."

Henry walked ahead of them out of the room.

"Son, do you want to join us?"

Before Henry could answer, Agatha said, "He wouldn't want to walk at my pace. I'm sure he has better things to do. Don't you, Henry?"

Quick to accept the offered escape, Henry said, "Yes, Aunt Aggie."

Theodore had the distinct impression he was being manipulated but sheer curiosity had him going along with her plan. He helped her with her shawl and they left the house. At the foot of the stairs he paused to see which direction she wanted to take. She was on his right side and gave his arm a slight tug. Obediently he turned to the right, toward town and the golden hour of dusk. She kept their pace slow, much slower than she normally walked and made occasional remarks to pass for conversation. It was an agonizingly slow pace for Theodore. She managed to make it take a full two minutes to reach Front Street which was less than a hundred paces from their front door. They made the turn and on they shuffled, for it certainly couldn't be called walking. He expected to continue towards town and so it was a bit of a surprise when she tugged his arm again to make the right turn onto Fitzpatrick Street.

A few dozen steps later, Theodore's heart skipped at the sight of Betsy in a royal blue dress exiting Mrs. Mallory's boarding house. Her face was adorned with a light smile. Something he hadn't seen in quite a while. The pull of her had him moving forward to speak to her despite his self-imposed avoidance and his aunt's presence. The gentleman exiting behind her stayed his progress. Theodore recognized George Casey; a working class man, with some education, he spoke with good diction and only a faint hint of a southern accent. Betsy turned to smile at something her companion said but froze when she noticed Theodore. The smile slowly slipped from her face. Mr. Casey followed the line of her sight to him. He said something to her in a quiet tone then placed his hand upon her back guiding her forward in his direction. The situation demanded Theodore move forward to greet them. He would have preferred to avoid it and in that moment he realized this meeting was the purpose of his aunt's stroll.

Deciding to lead the conversation rather than follow, he proffered his hand. "Mr. Casey, Mrs. Wheeler, nice to see you this evening."

Betsy looked up at her fiancé. "Mr. Casey, you remember Mr. Whitmore. He is now the proprietor of the *Key West Weekly*."

George shook his hand firmly. "I have had the pleasure of reading your paper. A copy is circulated in Charleston on occasion."

"And this is his aunt, Mrs. Agatha Pary."

George lifted his bowler. "Pleasure to meet you ma'am."

"The pleasure is yours, I'm sure, young man."

Her tone was so polite the words didn't register at first and when they did, all three of them tried to hide their surprise. Momentarily stunned, George could not think of a rejoinder.

Agatha continued in her polite tone. "And what do you do, Mr. Casey?"

Deciding perhaps her first sentence was an elderly slip, he dismissed it and answered her proudly. "I am the foreman of a large shipping yard in Charleston."

Agatha gave him a pasty smile. "A respectable occupation to provide at least the essential needs of a wife and family."

Though her tone was still polite, George was aware of the insinuation in her words. "It will provide for more than just their needs."

Theodore tensed his bicep squeezing Agatha's hand against his chest in warning. To Mr. Casey, he said, "Do you find the weather agreeable in Charleston?"

"Most days are pleasant enough."

Agatha turned her attention to Betsy. "You look lovely Mrs. Wheeler. Doesn't she Theodore?"

Her words drew his gaze to the lady in question. Lovely was an understatement. Theodore did not want to get dragged into his aunt's game but on the other hand he didn't want to insult Betsy either by not responding. "Yes, she does."

Betsy, too, wondered at Agatha's intentions. "Thank you."

Agatha looked from Betsy to her nephew as they stood facing each other. "Why Theodore, with your height and breadth you two would make a striking couple."

It was obvious to Betsy the scheming lady was trying to insinuate Theodore between her and George. Her lips twitched as she tried to hide the humorous effect Agatha's audacious tongue was having on her. First the old lady tried to keep her and Theodore apart, now she was trying to breach her engagement to bring them together. She felt George stiffen beside her and knew she should be offended for him, but she couldn't summon the emotion. She was just too tickled to care.

Theodore could find nothing wrong with the man. His manners were good, he treated Betsy well, and he was gainfully employed, so at least she wouldn't be living in squalor. There was, in short, nothing to build his dislike upon but dislike him he would. The man had the right to touch Betsy in public; a fact Theodore was currently having a hard time ignoring. But he needed to diffuse his aunt's interposition by changing the subject, and the only one he could think of was the very subject he was sure brought about this encounter. "I believe congratulations are in order, sir."

George gave him a quizzical look. "Pardon, sir? Congratulations for what?"

Theodore looked to Betsy. "For winning the fair lady's hand in marriage, of course. When do you plan to consecrate your union?"

George smiled proudly. "Thank you, sir. We haven't set the date. Likely, not for a few months yet. I was thinking mayhap April."

April. Betsy blanched at the word. Her eyes met Theodore's and saw the same haunting pain. She may come to hate that month. She turned and gave George a hollow smile.

Theodore could tell the date was news to Betsy. "Be sure to give notice to my office so I may post the banns in the paper."

George looked confused for a moment. "Oh yes, the banns. Of course."

Wanting to draw a close to the awkward meeting, Theodore said, "Good evening, Mrs. Wheeler, Mr. Casey."

The pair looked relieved by his abrupt end to the encounter. They bid

234

them goodnight and moved past. Theodore guided his aunt to Mrs. Mallory's porch rather than follow behind the couple all the way home. He could not endure the torture. He was weak in that regard. Those few minutes of conversation were long enough to watch her stoically stand beside a man she didn't love. He knew he couldn't endure another five or ten minutes of walking behind them and seeing George's hand upon her back or her hand on his arm. Theodore's guilt was ever-present when they were not around, in her presence it consumed him.

News of their postponed wedding discomfited Theodore. The delay in nuptials would also delay her departure for Charleston. He hoped the chance to leave for the reservation came soon. He needed a break from the emotional strain of having her unattainably near.

His mental discomfort made his voice sharp as he turned to his aunt. "What was that about?"

Agatha calmly shrugged her shoulders. "Just making a point."

He looked at her askance. "I think I missed the point."

"It wasn't meant for you."

He waited for her to elaborate. They climbed the porch steps. Theodore held her hand supporting her as she took a seat in one of the rockers.

"My intention was to make Mr. Casey question his worthiness."

"And what do you expect to come of it?"

She waited until he was seated before responding. "They are mismatched. He is too weak in mind and spirit for her. We both know Betsy will not break her promise so I am planting the seeds of doubt in the hopes Mr. Casey will have the sense to end this ill-fated betrothal."

"Humph. I wouldn't if I were in his shoes."

"Then we are fortunate he is nothing like you."

Her emphasis at the end made him wonder if he should consider her words a compliment or an insult to his character.

Chapter 21

A week after his arrival, George returned to Charleston with the promise to return for Betsy before summer. Four more months of living in limbo loomed ahead of her.

The following week was Christmas. Her family sent their annual gift of a large barrel filled with food and topped with letters from all of her relations, even her youngest nieces and nephews. Betsy looked forward to it all year although it was more fun when she had someone to share it. She approached it with a small crowbar in hand to pry the lid off. As Betsy set the lid aside, the sweet grassy lemon scent of her mother's verbena soap filled the room. It was Betsy's favourite smell, instantly taking her back to childhood and helping her mother mix the lemon verbena oil and other ingredients into the hot tallow and lye under the late summer sun. Beneath the letters lay a large cake of the soap; enough to last her all year if she was frugal. Next, she removed a sack of nuts, another of dried apples, and one of dried corn for popping, several butternut squash, a pumpkin carefully packed in straw, and an old flour sack filled with white and sweet potatoes. At the bottom were several jars of her mother's strawberry preserves, one of honey, and two dozen large jars of canned vegetables. It was a wonderful blessing but as usual they sent her more food than she could consume before it spoiled in the heat. It was nice sharing the excess with her friends.

The letters, though cheerful, made her homesick. Especially the paper with her ten month old nephew Aiden's handprint. It brought a smile to her face and tears to her eyes. She had nine nieces and nephews and she had only met one of them when he was a baby. He was going on eleven now. Maybe she and George could find a way to visit her family next Christmas. She smiled—if she wasn't in the family way by then.

Betsy joined Mrs. Mallory for Christmas dinner at the boarding house the same as she had done the last eight years since the two of them shared their Catholic faith as well as widowhood. The meal was a lively affair shared with her son, Stephen Mallory, and the boarding house guests.

She looked upon the arrival of 1834 with a mixture of hope and despair. She held onto the dream of motherhood as a way to assuage the pending loss of her home and friends. For the most part she tried not to think about what lie ahead and only live in the moment. She vowed to enjoy every day she had left in Key West. Knowing it was short, she made the most of precious time spent in the company of her friends.

* * *

One day in March, Henry came to visit. He walked in the front door and peered over her counter waiting for her appearance from the work room.

"Good morning, Mrs. Betsy. How do you do?"

She couldn't help smiling at his use of adult formality. She answered in kind. "Very well, thank you, Master Henry. And yourself?"

She opened the walkway through the counter to allow Henry into the parlor. Like a miniature gentleman he waited for her to enter the room first before following then waited for her to be seated before he perched on the edge of one of her brocade chairs. "Mrs. Betsy, I was wondering if you would teach me how to catch conch."

His request was at such odds with his formal behavior; Betsy had to press her lips together to keep her grin from surfacing. She played along with him. "I could sir but I must ask if you know how to swim."

His expectant face fell. "No, ma'am, I do not."

Betsy gave him an encouraging smile. "Not to fear, I can teach you to swim as well."

His whole body perked up in excitement and the formality disappeared as fast as a startled sand crab. "Could we start today?"

"I suppose we could. We will need to get your father's permission of course."

His shoulders drooped. "Poppa went away again. It will take a long time for a letter to reach him and be answered."

Betsy wasn't aware Theodore had left town. "Where did he go?"

"To see the Indians."

Was that a touch of petulance in Henry's tone? "You miss him when he's gone, don't you?"

Henry nodded.

"Well, I think we can ask your Aunt Agatha for permission in the meantime."

Henry's eyes bloomed with hope. "We could?"

At her nod, he hopped off the chair, racing for the door.

Betsy called after him. "Henry, where are you going?"

He barely paused to answer. "To ask Aunt Aggie if I can go swimming."

Betsy rose to follow. She was sure his aunt would have questions for her.

An hour later, they walked to the coastline behind Betsy's house. She wore a dark blue swimming costume and Henry wore his regular clothes, minus his shoes and socks. Henry stopped at the little sailboat which belonged to Betsy now.

Dr. Waterhouse and his son moved to Indian Key last week at the urgings of the island's proprietor, Captain Jacob Housman, who was trying to establish a community there to rival Key West. Dr. Waterhouse procured a larger boat for the move and generously gifted Betsy with his old one as a token of their friendship. She missed her neighbor. The evening breeze was hollow without the sound of his violin.

"Henry, we'll take the boat out next time. You can learn to swim from here." The water was calm and shallow for a long way out on the southeast side of the island. The force of the Atlantic Ocean was absorbed by the reef several miles out from the Key. Most days it was as calm as lake water making it ideal for swimming lessons and crystal clear so it was easy to see what lurked beneath the surface.

They waded a long distance from shore and still the water was only up to their knees. At eight years old, her companion was now only about a foot shorter than her. "Henry, you must always exercise caution when in the water; many dangers abound. There are sharks and eels and even some fish bite. Jellyfish, Sea Urchin and Fire Coral can sting." Playfully she added, "Crabs will pinch you if they get the opportunity," as she demonstrated gently on his arm to lighten the mood. "You must also watch where you step. Sting rays and sharks hide in the sand."

"I thought sharks swam in the water."

"They do but some sharks also like the bottom."

"That's a lot of things to watch for. It's a good thing I really like conch or I don't think I would do this."

"You may find you like swimming too. Let's keep going till it gets just a bit deeper."

Henry glanced behind nervously noting the distance to the shoreline before following her.

* * *

Theodore momentarily stopped walking to admire the picturesque scene of Fort Brooke nestled at the mouth of the Hillsborough River. The log fort and support buildings were built underneath several ancient live oak trees with new spring leaves. Visible just beyond the fort was an Indian mound thought to be built by Tocobaga Indians many centuries ago. A huge hickory tree grew on top. He wondered if the Indians planted the tree or if a wayward seed somehow managed to find such a perfectly centered spot to root.

He left Key West four days ago in the company of his friend, Private Kinsley Dalton, who was now serving as mail carrier. He received a mere two hours' notice to join Dalton. Major Glassell meant it when he told him he would have to be ready to leave at a moment's notice to catch the ship commissioned for the carrier's run from Key West to Fort Brooke and back. It left him no time to say goodbye to Betsy. It was just as well, he supposed. The encounter could only be painful for both of them. He hoped to return before her fiancé whisked her away. He hated to think there was a possibility he may never see her again.

He also left in such a hurry he was forced to send a message with Henry to advise his new apprentice at the paper of his departure. Right after requesting the trip of Glassell, Theodore sought out someone who could run the business in his absence. It took a while to find the right person, forcing him to turn down the first two opportunities he had to travel to the interior.

He considered it very fortunate when, Robert Mason, a recent arrival to the island from Delaware answered his help wanted sign. Despite having no knowledge of the business, Robert proved himself to be capable, talented and loyal. He even enjoyed doing the typesetting; a task that frequently gave Theodore a headache. He found building words backwards to be a mental trial and dealing with the tiny typeset too challenging for his large fingers. Robert earned his keep simply in taking over the tedious task of building pages to print. It was a bonus to learn he was also an eloquent writer. His editing skills needed strengthening but all in all he was a perfect match to the needs of the business. Theodore had no qualms leaving the paper in his capable hands.

The hundred mile trek from Fort Brooke to Fort King was accomplished in three days on horseback although Kinsley told Theodore allowances had been made for him. Kinsley would normally be expected to make it in two days. Theodore was thankful for the leeway and the companionship of the likable private he used to fish with at Fort Gibson. Being unused to the exercise, his backside could not take riding fifty miles a day.

Fort King came into sight long after sunset. Theodore did not expect accommodations and had planned to sleep in his bedroll on the ground, nor did he expect the latest Indian agent to greet them in the courtyard. Theodore dismounted to stand next to Private Dalton who introduced him to General Wiley Thompson. He towered over Theodore with a solid wide chest. 'Imposing', Major Dade had called him. It was an apt description. The two men shook hands. Theodore pulled a letter from his breast pocket and presented it to the agent. "A letter of introduction from Major James Glassell, and Major Dade sends his regards."

"Thank you. My assistant will lead you to our spare accommodations."

Private Dalton handed the agent his mail and was excused to deliver the rest of his post. An enlisted man was summoned to care for their mounts.

Before walking away, General Thompson said, "Come see me after you've settled in to share a drink."

Theodore nodded. "Thank you, I will." Even as travel weary as he felt he wouldn't turn down a possible opportunity to interview the new agent.

An hour later, Theodore was seated in General Thompson's office with a cigar and brandy after enjoying a hearty stew for supper. They talked of politics, Indian policy, where they were from and how they got here but most important, he received permission to visit the reservation.

"I don't mind you visiting them, as long as you abide by my conditions."

"And what would those conditions entail?"

"No alcohol or firearms of any kind and do not discuss moving west. Until the treaty is ratified, I do not want it mentioned so we may maintain the peace."

Theodore reluctantly agreed for the latter request made him

uncomfortable.

It was late when Theodore finally turned in for the night.

The next morning, he strolled around the fort taking in the comings and goings of its inhabitants. It wasn't unusual for Indians to visit and today was no exception. Micanopy's tustenuggee, Osceola, arrived with several of his warriors to obtain supplies and visit the agent. He nodded to Theodore in aloof recognition.

Theodore intercepted the party when they were ready to leave. "Osceola, my friend, it is good to see you."

Theodore suspected Osceola understood at least some basic English words; still he let the interpreter relay the message.

"Theodore Whitmore, you have returned from the North. Micanopy will be pleased to see you."

"Please tell him I will visit tomorrow."

Osceola nodded in reply to Cudjo's translation but said nothing more.

The next day, Theodore was welcomed into Micanopy's village. The chief's concern was great. He wasted no time in asking if General Thompson could be trusted.

Theodore decided to answer him honestly. "I do not know. I have just met him, but I have been told he is honest."

"Nothing more has been said of the treaty they say we signed last spring. It is good we stay here."

Theodore frowned. He felt the need to make the chief aware of things to come, but he gave his word not to discuss it; something easier said yesterday than abiding by today. To temporarily elude the subject, Theodore retrieved his saddle bag and removed the gifts he brought his friends. Material, buttons, tobacco, and corn meal purchased from the sutler. He was glad to be done lugging around the heavy weight.

He spoke more with Micanopy on general topics and then decided to leave before the next meal so the tribe would not have to share their meager supplies.

* * *

Over the next few weeks, he visited the reservation at least once a week, had several meetings with General Thompson and played a lot of cards with the enlisted men. He also had a lot of time to think which is how he came up with a new plan for obtaining a wife.

This idea meant he wouldn't have to socialize and she wouldn't expect more from him than he was willing to give. He spent days working on just the right words to use. Finally, he had it. A simple, direct and to the point advertisement for a bride. He mailed it to the *Florida Herald* in St. Augustine. He chose the city as being close enough to Key West the woman would likely be more acceptable to the move and because the available women in the other Florida cities was nil. Even so, he still expected it to take some time to find a bride. It came as quite a shock when he received more than a half-dozen letters on the next mail run after the ad's appearance and more than twice that the following week.

April afternoons were spent reading letters from all kinds of ladies but he found fault with every one of them. None could measure up to *her*. He was considering recruiting unbiased help to pick one when word of the treaty ratification spread through the base like wildfire. Theodore soon forgot his quest for a bride in the swirl of activity surrounding him.

Speculations of when the Indians would be forced to move abounded. General Thompson received word reinforcements were being sent and he should arrange a meeting with the tribal elders to prepare them to move to the embarkation camp setup at Fort Brooke pending relocation west.

* * *

Abby rushed to Betsy's house with the St. Augustine paper before she even finished reading the notice. The first few lines had been enough. Now she quietly waited while Betsy read it.

Betsy stared at the paper in her hands in disbelief. When she finally looked up, fire brewed in her eyes. "How could he do this to Henry? There is no telling what kind of woman would reply to such an advertisement."

Abby said, "You don't think he would wed someone without getting to know her first, do you?"

"I should hope not, but the way this is worded, I'm not so sure. Oh!" she tossed the paper on the sofa and began pacing the room. "What do I care? I have my own commitment to deal with. He is free to make his own muss."

"True. Speaking of yours, I noticed your fiancé has returned."

"Yes, two days ago. He is pressing me for a date. I haven't been able to make myself consider one. It is so final. Being engaged—well in truth—with him gone, being engaged was no different than not. But marriage...," Betsy's breath hitched. "I don't think I can do it, Abby. I don't want to leave Key West. I could content myself with marrying George and living here but to move elsewhere makes marrying him a daunting proposition."

Abby embraced her friend. "Have faith. God will provide if you keep your trust in him."

Betsy nodded. "You are right. Forgive me, it was a momentary weakness. There have been many brides in history to marry sight unseen and survive it. I should be grateful. I at least know what kind of man I'm marrying."

"It's only natural to feel as you do. I would feel the same in your shoes." Abby smiled at a distant memory. "Actually, I almost was in your shoes and I ran. So while I know how you feel, I don't have the strength you have to see it through, but I know you will. You'll make new friends in Charleston. At least it's on the coast. It would be worse if you were landlocked after living here for so long."

"The silver lining in my dark cloud, I suppose. Well, that and children."

Abby smiled. "You will make an excellent mother."

"Speaking of motherhood, how are you feeling? Has the morning sickness passed?"

Abby's smile grew. "Yes, it's been over a week now since the last episode. I feel wonderful. Same as I did carrying Christoff."

"Perhaps, this one will be a boy also."

A shadow by the door, slipped away, unnoticed.

* * *

A few days later, military activity dramatically increased. Orders were received for the army to vacate Key West and move to the mainland. Talk was they were preparing for Indian resistance. Many gathered near the general store to learn the latest news. Betsy grew concerned for Theodore. He was at Fort King and she learned Major Glassell was ordered to move to the same fort. *Was Theodore in danger of an Indian attack?*

She was soon joined by Mrs. Agatha with the same concern. "Is Theodore in harm's way?"

Betsy shook her head. "I don't know for sure but it would seem possible."

When it was evident there was nothing new to be learned, the two ladies walked home together. George Casey intercepted them.

"Mrs. Wheeler, I've been looking for you. How do you do, Mrs. Pary?"

"Not so well, it seems my nephew has managed to put himself right in the Indian warpath without a concern for what could happen."

"Now, Mrs. Pary, I am sure the army's move is merely precautionary. The Indians should move peaceably enough, after all, they signed the treaty agreeing to it."

Betsy kept her disagreement to herself not wanting to further upset Agatha. They walked her to her door, then George ushered Betsy to her house. She expected him to remain on the porch, but when she turned at the door, he said, "May I came in? I would like to speak privately."

Betsy allowed him to follow her across the threshold but she turned to face him in the front room. "I'm sorry George, with all the excitement of the last few days, I still haven't chosen a date for our wedding."

He stood in front of her turning his hat in his hand, silent for so long, she began to grow nervous. Finally, he lifted his head. "I have a confession to make. I heard you speaking with Mrs. Eatonton the other day. You care greatly for Mr. Whitmore, much more than you care for me."

Betsy opened her mouth to speak, not sure if she should confess, defend, or deny his accusation, but he held up his hand to forestall her words.

"I must admit, I was selfish enough to overlook your feelings, which by the way dear, were clearly visible when last we saw him together. I had your promise, and I wanted you for my own, so I looked the other way, but I have since found someone else as well. She is not your equal, but she does care for me, and she needs me. I have come to appreciate being needed." He took a step closer to her. "Betsy, I am releasing you from your promise. I sincerely hope you can find happiness with Mr. Whitmore." He took a few steps backward. "Goodbye, Betsy." He turned and walked out her door.

She stood there for some minutes sorting out his words and her emotions. She wasn't sad, but she wasn't happy either, at least not yet. She mostly felt ashamed of herself and very relieved. She didn't have to leave her home. She turned and walked into her sitting room, removing her bonnet and gloves. She put them away and walked into her work room, looking around blankly, unsure what needed to be done. Her thoughts still jumbled. Slowly one thought finally surfaced and took wing in her soul.

She was free!

She took a deep breath and let the smile bloom on her face.

She was free to love again.

Oh, insidious reality! Now he may not be. What if Theodore accepted one of the applicants from his advertisement? Panic swelled in her breast. How could she find out? Abby would tell her to write, but she couldn't do that. It was too improper, especially if he was engaged. She would have to do something else, but what? Of course! She could ask his aunt. Surely, his aunt would know or could find out.

Not caring who was watching, Betsy ran across the street and forcefully knocked on the door. When the maid answered, she rushed past her. "Agatha! Agatha! Where are you?"

Her voice came from the parlor. "In here dear."

The elderly lady was walking toward the door when Betsy entered the room nearly colliding with her. "Slow down. What is it child? Has something happened to Henry?"

Betsy vehemently shook her head. "No. Oh no, no, I'm sorry, it's not Henry. It's Theodore."

"What about Theodore? What have you heard?"

"I want to know what you have heard. Oh, I hope it's not too late. You don't know, do you? Has he accepted anyone yet? I need you to write him, straight away! We mustn't wait a moment longer."

"Slow down, dear. What are you babbling on about?"

"Theodore's advertisement." Betsy's face fell in horror. "He hasn't married already, has he?"

Agatha was at a loss. "What advertisement? I received a letter dated a month ago. He didn't mention anything about an advertisement. Why would he be married? He's in the middle of the heathen jungle, for heaven's sakes."

Betsy's smile returned in full force. "Oh, never mind. You must write to him and tell him my engagement has been called off." Betsy spun around, impatiently searching the room. "Where do you keep pen and paper?" Propriety had never been so inconvenient as now when it kept her from writing to him herself. "We can send the letter with Major Glassell. He will see that Theodore receives it."

"Slow down, child. Very well, if you insist on the here and now, bring my lap desk to the table. It's over there in the corner."

Betsy picked up the portable table and placed it in front of Agatha. With arms crossed and foot tapping, she watched the slow progress as Agatha lifted the lid to remove her writing supplies, close the lid, smooth the paper, dip the pen, and set it to paper. Betsy's patience was worn thin as she waited the twenty minutes it took for Agatha to write the brief message to her nephew. She began pacing as the letter was sanded, folded, and sealed with wax.

"Here you are, and Betsy..." Agatha held out the letter to the agitated girl.

"Yes ma'am?"

"Mind you don't run in the street in your haste."

Taking the letter, Betsy impulsively leaned down and dropped a kiss on Agatha's papery cheek before fleeing the room.

Agatha called after her retreating figure. "It would be very unbecoming of my future niece."

Betsy walked as rapidly as she possibly could all the way to the army barracks uncaring of what anyone thought of her behavior. She found Lieutenant Newcomb directing men in the removal of office items.

"Where might I find Major Dade?"

Lieutenant Newcomb shook his head. "I'm afraid I don't know ma'am. Is there something I can do for you?"

She studied the Lieutenant for a few moments before deciding she could trust him with the most important letter of her life. "I suppose. Are you being sent to Fort King with the major?"

"Yes, Ma'am. Pardon me." He redirected one of the privates, then returned his attention to her.

Betsy tried to remain calm. "I apologize for interrupting your duties. Mrs. Pary asks for this letter to be delivered to her nephew. It is an urgent message. He is currently at Fort King."

"Who is this nephew?"

"Theodore Whitmore."

"I'm acquainted with him. I would be happy to assist Mrs. Pary." He held his hand out to receive the missive.

Betsy closed her eyes and sent a quick prayer heavenward before releasing the letter to the lieutenant. "Thank you, sir." She watched him tuck it into his breast pocket. "It's a very important letter."

"Yes ma'am."

Betsy still hesitated.

"Is that all, ma'am?"

She swallowed hard, then gave a nod. "Yes, thank you. Good day, sir."

"Good day, ma'am."

She turned away and walked a little less hurriedly to Abby's house, too keyed up to delay sharing the news with her best friend. At the very least, she would not be leaving the island any time soon but her hopes and dreams and prayers were for so much more.

Fort King, six days later

The arrival of troops from Key West disrupted the encampment. Theodore waited on the sidelines knowing the majors would have business to attend to before they had time for a social visit. Therefore he was surprised when Major Dade sought him out as soon as he entered the wooden barricade of the fort. They greeted each other with a warm hand shake, and then the major reached into his breast pocket and withdrew a letter. "From Key West."

"Thank you, sir."

The major excused himself and Theodore, recognizing his aunt's handwriting, wasted no time opening the folded paper concerned it may contain bad news. He read it twice to be sure he had not misunderstood and wondered at the words. He looked around, unfocused on the activity in front of him, his mind spinning at the implications of his aunt's words until one thought settled. *I have to go. Now.* Absolutely nothing else mattered. He would not make the same mistake again.

He left the courtyard headed for Agent Thompson's office. He felt fortunate to find him at his desk reading mail.

"General Thompson, I find I must leave your company forthwith. I was hoping you would be so kind as to send word of any occurrences or planned activity of interest so that I might return to witness or at least conduct post interviews."

The agent hesitated. "If the occasion arises, I could have word sent to you if it doesn't violate government protocols."

"I would appreciate it."

"Are you sure you want to leave now? With the treaty signed and reinforcements arriving, it would seem the momentous event is imminent."

"I realize that but a personal matter has become more pressing at the moment. I must return to Key West promptly."

General Thompson gave him a probing look. "You mean to leave *now* without an escort?"

"Yes sir." His conviction left no room for debate.

"Take care, then. Leave your address with my lieutenant."

After leaving Thompson's office, Theodore packed all his belongings in record time, loaded his rifle, procured some meager provisions from the kitchen sergeant and carried it all to the stable. He saddled and loaded his horse and nodded to the stable master as he walked the mare outside. He climbed into the saddle and guided the horse toward the fort gate. Major Dade stopped him midway.

"Leaving so soon? I hope it wasn't bad news I delivered."

Theodore smiled. "Quite the opposite. Will you send word if the situation here warrants my return?"

"Of course. Are you intending to leave alone?"

"Yes sir."

"That's not wise, my friend."

Theodore gave a single nod. "I am aware of the danger, but I will not delay my return a moment longer."

"Is your weapon ready?"

"Yes sir."

"Very well, Godspeed, Mr. Whitmore."

"Thank you, sir."

Theodore made it through the gate without further delay and kicked his mount into a gallop. He had every intention of reaching Fort Brooke in less than forty-eight hours. He could nurse his aching backside on the sail home.

* * *

The first day he rode until he could no longer safely see what was in front of him, only stopping when necessary to rest and water his horse. He chose a spot well away from the water to spend the night. He had no intentions of waking up to find an alligator nearby. He hobbled his horse near some tall grass and put his back to a tree with the gun across his lap. Being alone without someone else to help keep watch, every odd sound would jerk him awake, and there were many strange sounds in the deepest dark of night. The overcast sky blocked the moon's light, robbing him of even that much comfort.

He could not have slept more than two hours when the ink black sky began to change to navy. Anxious to be on his way, he mounted up and headed out. Covering distance was more important than coffee. The dark blue sky brightened to the blue-gray of morning as dawn approached on his left. The sun's progress marked the hours, and the clip-clop of the horse's hooves the seconds, as the day passed. Theodore kept himself awake by constantly searching in the trees for danger, his head swiveling to the right and the left and back again. A few times he thought he heard something and brought his mount to a sudden halt, the better to listen. Each time it proved to be his imagination. He wasn't too worried of an Indian attack feeling fairly confident they would recognize him as a friend. He was more concerned with Mother Nature's predators.

He had no idea how many miles he had traveled by the time darkness settled in but he was fairly certain he was two-thirds of the way there. He spent the night much the same as the one previous and by dawn he was feeling the strain. He needed coffee but the brightening sky beckoned him onward. He climbed on his horse thankful she was doing better than him. It was all he could do to stay in the saddle today. He stared trance-like ahead only occasionally able to rally the energy to scan the trees. By mid-morning he gave the horse her head. She knew a clean stall and rest was not far away. Just holding on was a challenge. He hadn't been this sleep deprived since Henry was a baby.

He perked up when they finally reached the outskirts of Fort Brooke just after midday. The weary horse and rider cantered through the encampment some forty-six hours after leaving Fort King. Theodore tipped the stable hand extra to rub down and feed his hired mount, and notify the owner of the horse's return. He then headed off to find a bed for the night, clean some of the travel dirt from his personage, and fill his stomach with warm food. The latter he was forced to wait till the supper hour to procure.

Afterwards, he sought out the base commander to determine when the next ship would be sailing for the Keys only to learn there would be none since the military was no longer in residence on the Island. Theodore would have to wait till morning to find a civilian craft able to accommodate him.

He slept late the next morning. It was embarrassingly after eight when he finally roused himself from slumber. After a meal of cold breakfast leftovers he headed down to the wharf to search for a means of getting home only to meet with disappointment.

Four frustrating days later he was finally aboard ship sailing towards his love. He prayed nothing else would stand in the way of their union.

Chapter 22

May 7th, 1834

Theodore finally set foot on the Key West wharf anxious to wash off two weeks' worth of grit and grime. He made a beeline for his house not stopping to talk to anyone. In truth, he only wanted to speak to one person, but first he needed to make himself presentable. Walking up to his door he glanced over his shoulder at the house across the street. Soon. Very soon, he would seek her out.

Agatha greeted him in the foyer and promptly agreed his first priority was a bath. While the water heated, she updated him on Henry's activities, surprising Theodore with the news his son now swam like a fish and almost as much as one. Even now, Henry was at the beach with some of the other boys.

Theodore gratefully sank into the tub of warm water. It didn't matter he preferred it to be hotter; it was enough to ease his travel weary body. He would have liked to relax for a few moments before getting to the business at hand but the water was rapidly cooling. After his bath, he trimmed his beard and whiskers, combed his wet hair, put on his best suit, and then allowed his aunt to pass judgement.

Agatha straightened his cravat. "You look handsome enough to woo a princess, but I suppose a seamstress will do." The jovial light in her eyes took the sting out of her words.

"Hmm." The sound was filled with disdain for her biting attempt at humor. He was too nervous to appreciate it.

He stepped outside the front door and faced the house across the street with anxiety and trepidation. He shut down his negative thoughts. There was only one outcome he would accept. He took a deep breath and braced his shoulders.

Reaching her door he saw her shingle was turned to 'closed'. Good. He didn't want to wait for her to finish with a customer or to be interrupted by one. He knocked on the door and waited.

No answer.

He glanced in the window beside the door. The house seemed empty so he walked around to the back. She was not in the kitchen and he didn't hear any sound from the privy. He checked the beach relieved to see the boat was still there. Where should he try next? The mercantile and the Eatonton's came to mind. They were in opposite directions. Which to try first? Eatonton's. It was closer.

Nerves gripped his insides as he knocked on Max and Abby's entry. Mrs. Baxley's friendly smile greeted him as the door was opened.

"Hello Mr. Whitmore, what can I do for you?"

"Is Mrs. Wheeler here perchance?"

She opened the door wider. "Please come in. She is visiting the Missus in the parlor. Please wait here a moment while I announce you."

Mrs. Baxley turned from him to find Abby and Betsy peering from the parlor doorway.

Theodore's gazed locked on the object of his affection. The joyful smile appearing on Betsy's face made all the hardships of getting to her worthwhile.

Betsy left the doorway to walk straight toward him, trying not to assume too much meaning in his presence. "Mr. Whitmore, what a pleasure to see you again."

He looked to Abby behind her, then back to Betsy. "Is there someplace we can speak privately?"

Mrs. Baxley was quick to admonish. "Young man, you'll do no such thing. It's highly improper."

Abby's smile quirked. "Please feel free to use the parlor." She stepped aside and with a look dared Mrs. Baxley to contradict her.

Betsy turned and led the way, giving Abby a hopeful look as she passed. This had to be the moment. Butterflies fluttered in her belly. She wiped her moist palms down her skirt hoping it wouldn't leave a stain and prayed her instincts were not leading her astray.

Theodore closed the door behind them. She drew her lower lip between her teeth and then, realizing it probably didn't look becoming, let it go. Anticipation and excitement hummed through her being. Every part of her was focused on him. As he drew near, she was forced to tilt her head back to maintain eye contact. How had she never before noticed the breadth of his shoulders?

Leaving two feet between them, Theodore considered what to do next and suddenly realized he was assuming she was still free. It had been weeks since his aunt wrote her letter. The situation could have changed. "Mrs. Wheeler, is it true you are free of your engagement? There is not another, is there?"

This close she could tell her head came just up to his chin. As if his nearness wasn't affecting her enough, his question sent her pulse skittering. *Is he going to propose?* "No."

"Good." He breathed a sigh of relief and started to smile, but then he realized she may have answered the first question, instead of the second and his brows drew together in consternation. "No, you're still engaged?"

Betsy shook her head. Unconsciously she ran her tongue over her dry lips. Theodore's gaze dropped to follow the movement, increasing the awareness between them. "I'm not engaged and there is no other."

The urge to kiss her was so strong. Theodore wasn't sure how much longer he could resist her lure. He had to secure her for his own.

Now.

He dropped down on bended knee before her.

Betsy gasped in surprise. Even though she had thought it, she didn't really believe it. Looking down at him in supplication to her, the love she felt, finally free of restraint, blossomed and grew until it felt bigger than the room.

"Betsy..."

It was the first time he used her Christian name, and the sound was a silky verbal caress.

He reached for her hands needing something to hold on to as he gave his heart into her keeping. "I know I am not your first love, but I want to be your last. Will you marry me?" When she didn't immediately answer, he added, "I need you. I need you for my wife and mother to my son."

His choice of words was more practical than romantic but she felt the raw emotion behind them. The telltale word 'need' instead of 'want' gave her confidence in her decision. She pulled her hands from his and placed them on either side of his face as she took a step closer. His warm hands came up to hold either side of her waist enhancing the sense of her femininity. She looked deeply into the eyes of her beloved and gave the only answer there was to give. "Yes."

Theodore's hands slid up her back as he rose to his feet and pulled her tight into his embrace. Hers dropped to rest on his hips. He then brought his right hand up to caress her cheek before sliding around the back of her neck. He used his thumb to gently tilt her head as those lips Betsy secretly dreamed of for the past year finally descended to claim hers. Her lips parted on an indrawn breath and her eyes drifted closed of their own accord to savor the moment. It was more wonderful than anything she dreamed.

Joy filled Theodore's heart again. The last thing he saw was her black eyelashes fanning her porcelain cheeks before closing his eyes to savor the feel of her petal soft lips. His hunger demanded he ravish her mouth but decorum demanded he wait. Even though she was experienced in the ways of love, the timing was not appropriate, and he would respect her enough to pull away.

Betsy's eyes questioned his withdrawal. Already he knew, he would deny her nothing. His first kiss was tender. This one revealed the edges of the passionate fire burning in his soul.

He gave her support when he felt her legs weaken; his primal side relishing the conquest.

Her bold exploration of his lips encouraged him to deepen the kiss further, tongue sweeping her mouth, dueling with hers. Breath no longer mattered as the hunger quickly consumed them.

The second knock on the parlor door finally registered in his mind. He reluctantly created a little separation between them to allow their ardor to cool. The third knock registered with Betsy. She took two steps away from him, running her hands over her hair and dress. Little did she know her swollen lips gave her away. It made him smile.

Realizing he didn't intend to, Betsy opened the door to find Abby on the other side. Her friend peered over Betsy's shoulder, her eye on Theodore, her words for Betsy. "I thought I should make sure you did not need to be rescued."

"No need but would you mind giving us a few more moments?" Betsy closed the door without waiting for Abby's reply.

She turned and leaned against the carved wooden panel and faced her betrothed. The passion of a few moments ago lingered, and dearly would she love to fan the flames, but now was neither the time nor the place. "I do have one concern."

"Hmm?"

"Why did you write the advertisement for a bride?"

He shrugged. "It seemed sensible. Henry needs a mother. You were out of reach. It didn't matter much to me anymore which woman I married as long as she was good for Henry."

Her instincts told her he cared deeply for her, but he had yet to declare his love. It was only being prudent she question his motives; question if Henry was the main reason he proposed to her. She didn't intend to escape one loveless engagement for another. Passion was wonderful, but it was not enough. "You were looking for a replacement for me as Henry's mother?"

"Yes. You are the perfect mother for Henry."

"Thank you. I am looking forward to taking on that role." She took a step away from the door. "What about as your wife? Is that role to be a consequence of the other? Is it only for Henry's sake you have proposed?"

"Eh gads, woman! I thought I made my sentiments clear a moment ago."

"Oh, I understand you desire me, but if that is all, it could fade. I want more."

"More?" He frowned. "But you've already said yes."

"True, but I could take it back."

Horror crossed his face. "What is it you want, Betsy?"

"I want to know you care more deeply than you say. I need to hear the words."

"Love?"

She nodded.

"Did I not already say it?"

She shook her head.

"I do." He closed the distance between them. "I love you." He lifted both his hands to cup her face. "I love you. I need you. I want you to be my wife."

She looked deeply in his eyes and found that which she sought, and her heart responded. "I love you, Theodore." She smiled. "I love you so much it doesn't matter where we live. I couldn't imagine leaving this island before when George asked it of me, but I will gladly follow you to the ends of the earth if need be."

He smiled. "You'll not be leaving this island. I came back intending to make this my home, but there is something you should know. Betsy, I promise to be a good husband to you, but it is only fair I warn you I will have to be away for long periods of time. I fear war is eminent with the Seminoles, and there is none to tell their side of it. I have come to know these people and respect them. I want to finish what I started. It is the other reason I returned. Mr. Audubon told me his wife suffers in his absence. It would be the same for you. Are you willing to make the sacrifice for a cause more worthy than birds?"

She could deal with the occasional month or two without him and by all accounts the war would be short. She had been surviving on her own for nearly a decade. Now, she would have his name for protection, and the homecomings would be their own sweet reward. It was not much of a sacrifice to have to make for all she would gain. "It is a burden I am willing to bear. I will marry you, Theodore."

The speed with which she found herself again in his embrace was astounding. The momentum of it pushed her back against the door. He supped on her lips and she allowed herself a moment to relish in his desire before pushing him away. They stood there looking at each other while their breathing returned to normal.

Betsy asked, "Shall we share our news with the others?"

"I'm sure Mrs. Eatonton and Mrs. Baxley have guessed by now."

"Even so, I should still like to tell them, and then we must immediately seek out your aunt and Henry."

"Hmm."

Betsy smiled. *Reluctant agreement.* She moved aside as Theodore reached for the door handle. He allowed her to exit first and wasn't surprised when they found the other two ladies hovering nearby with hesitant smiles. A simple look conveyed the news and their hostess rushed forward to embrace her friend. "Congratulations, Betsy. You deserve every happiness." She then moved toward Theodore. "Congratulations, Mr. Whitmore. Thank you for making my friend happy."

"You're welcome, Mrs. Eatonton."

"Please, call me Abby."

"As you wish."

Abby looked from one to the other. "When is the ceremony?"

Theodore looked to Betsy. "How long must we wait?"

"Only as long as you say. We could marry tonight as far as I am concerned, although finding someone to perform the ceremony is more likely to be the issue."

It had been a year since Reverend Brunot left and the church was still in search of a replacement for despite the assistance of the Missionary Society of New York. Visiting clergy was often few and far between.

Abby grabbed Betsy's arm in excitement. "Max is expected home tomorrow. You could be married aboard *The Abigail Rose,* the same as we were." Her smile widened. "I even have something 'borrowed' for you to wear."

In mere moments the date was set for the day after tomorrow and Abby would come early to help dress the bride. Abby offered her a dress to wear, but it would need too many alterations for Abby was tall and willowy compared to Betsy. She would have to find something else.

On the way home, Betsy and Theodore were met by several people who couldn't help noticing the change in their relationship. Betsy knew those few would tell others. By the time the sun went down, most of the island would know she was finally getting married. She was too happy to care.

Aunt Agatha and Henry were ecstatic over the news. They insisted Betsy stay for dinner. The conversation centered on upcoming nuptials and when to move Betsy's personal belongings to their house. She would keep her shop in her former home for the time being while a shop closer to 'town' might be considered later.

It was well after dark when Theodore walked his fiancée home. She stopped and turned at her front door.

Taking advantage of the darkened porch, Theodore leaned down to give her a chaste kiss. "I am glad I must only wait forty-eight hours before it is my right to follow you through any door."

Her eyes widened. "You're *right*? Somehow I didn't think of you as one of *those* husbands."

"My *right* so long as you allow. Is that better?"

She mimicked his typical non-committal reply. "Hmm."

"Now you're teasing me."

She grinned. "I am. You're not charming, are you?" She paused in mock consideration. "Ben was charming. I suppose I could get used to a serious husband."

He gave her another quick kiss. "I'm sure you'll find a way."

He lingered as he kissed her again.

Betsy put a hand against his solid chest and gently pushed to break the contact. "Tomorrow will be a busy day. I think I should get to bed."

Reluctantly he allowed her to push him back a step. "I agree. There are many things I need to attend to as well. I suppose we'll have to wait for supper to see each other again. You will come dine with us, of course."

Her brows drew together. "Depends. Is that a question or a command?"

"I apologize. I didn't mean it as a command. Only an assumption you would have the same desire as I to share the meal together."

Betsy nodded feeling a little contrite for being so sensitive. "I do desire the same. I suppose I have been on my own for so long it bothers me to be ordered about. I promise to try and be less sensitive to your words."

"I promise to try and phrase my requests better."

She tilted her head. "Was that our first fight?"

"I believe so and as such it demands a kiss of apology."

She lightly giggled. So far this marriage boded well for wedded bliss. She lifted her face to receive his kiss, not surprised when he soon deepened it.

She waited a moment before pulling back. "Good night, Theodore."

"Good night, Betsy."

* * *

Betsy awoke early the next morning. She was too excited to sleep in. Her first activity was to peruse her wardrobe for something suitable to wear. As expected none of her gowns were worthy of the day. They were all well-worn, serviceable clothes. There was no time to make a dress so she would simply have to choose the least worn which of course was the mustard one—her least favourite.

As soon as she turned her shingle to open, Theodore appeared in her entry. "I couldn't wait till this evening to see you again."

"Theodore, this is a small town. Word of this will get out. There is no such thing as sneaking around." She passed through the counter intent on shuffling him back out the front door but almost there he turned to capture her, reducing her to a puddle of mush in his hands. This time it took the front door hitting Theodore in the back to break them apart. Fortunately, they were close enough to keep the door from opening all the way, giving them precious seconds to regain composure.

From the other side came Esperanza's voice. "Oh, pardon me."

Theodore opened the door partway, keeping Betsy hidden from view. "Forgive me, Mrs. Keats, for being in the way. I trust no harm came to you?"

"No, I am fine. Congratulations, Mr. Whitmore."

Betsy squirmed behind the door. Esperanza knew they were getting married and as a married woman she probably had a good idea what she interrupted. Betsy stepped into view. "Thank you, Mr. Whitmore. I'll see to your request. Good morning, Esperanza."

Theodore looked down at his soon to be wife, surprised she was so concerned with appearances. It didn't matter to him, but since it did to her, he went along with it.

"Thank you, Mrs. Wheeler, I appreciate your efficiency and thank you, Mrs. Keats. Good day, ladies."

He left the shop, placed his hat on his head, and walked down the street whistling. Never having heard him do so before, Betsy stared after him in wonder. When she finally looked away she encountered Esperanza's knowing smile. "Good morning, Esperanza."

Her grin widened. "You said that already."

"Oh, quit teasing me. What can I do for you, today?" Betsy noticed the paper wrapped package she carried. It wouldn't be mending. Esperanza could fix anything she could. Perhaps she needed help making a new dress.

"It is more a case of what I can do for you." She placed her burden on the counter and began pulling back the protective covering to reveal her wedding dress. The one Betsy had designed. "Papa brought home the news last night. My guess is you do not have a dress to wear on such short notice. We are of the same size." Her hand drifted to her stomach. "For a little while longer at least. I thought you might wish to borrow it."

Betsy was touched. "Esperanza, I don't know what to say. It is such a generous offering."

"Why don't you try it on? I have a little time to help you alter it this morning if needed."

They had to let out the seams in the bodice just a bit for the dress to fit perfect.

Betsy embraced Esperanza. "Thank you, I'll feel like a princess wearing such a beautiful dress."

"You're welcome."

"You and Jonathon will be there, of course?"

"Yes, of course we will. I am glad you have found your happiness since you were so instrumental in helping me find mine."

May 9th, 1834

Abby arrived at Betsy's house as planned and began helping her dress. When all was complete she turned Betsy to the mirror to study her image.

"You are beautiful. I love the contrast of your dark hair and the cream of your dress. I know the dress is borrowed but I insist you have one more borrowed item. You'll be double blessed for having borrowed items from two happy matrons." Abby removed her treasured headpiece from its velvet bag.

Betsy turned to see what Abby held. She recognized the delicate gold and gem encrusted tiara her friend wore on her wedding day. "No Abby, it's too much. This is a second wedding. There is no need for such ornamentation."

"There is every need. It doesn't matter that it is not your first. You should still feel special on your wedding day." She placed the headpiece in Betsy's hair. "Perfect. Are you ready to go?"

Betsy couldn't help stepping to the mirror one last time. She felt blessed to have such generous friends. God was truly gracious to her.

They walked to the dock in the slanted sunlight of late afternoon to where the *Abigail Rose* was berthed. Betsy's nerves began fluttering as she climbed the gangway. Jonathon and Max were there to assist her aboard. Both looked splendid in their ship uniforms. She scanned the deck in search of Theodore surprised not to find him.

Esperanza came up to greet her. "You are prettier than a princess."

"Thank you." She turned at the sound of lines being removed in preparation of sailing. "Have you seen Theodore?"

"Max gave him orders to stay below deck. It's bad luck for the groom to see the bride before the ceremony."

Betsy offered a weak smile. "Of course."

Abby said, "We should sit over there out of the way of the sailors."

They were soon joined by Aunt Agatha from below deck. She took a seat next to Betsy and picked up her hand. "I want you to know I am thankful you will become my niece. There is not a better woman for Theodore."

Betsy's eyes blurred. She had grown fond of Theodore's aunt and it meant a lot to have her blessing on their union.

The afternoon was warm but the wind cooled them. Fortunately it was blowing gently so that even as they crossed outside the reef and into the Atlantic Ocean the waves were mild. Max called for the anchor and moments later the party began taking their places. Betsy knew the moment Theodore arrived on deck. She felt the heat of his gaze upon her and turned her head seeking out his presence. His eyes adored her and made her feel like the most special person in the world.

Theodore was followed by Henry, looking rather smart in his suit even if it was a bit small from his most recent growth spurt. She would be sure to make him a new one with added material in the seams so she could let it out as he grew. She smiled to herself when she realized she was already thinking as his mother.

Captain Bennington, Abigail's father and owner of the ship, came to escort Betsy to her groom in place of her father. Betsy's parents would have come if she had asked but she didn't want to burden them with the expense, nor did she want to wait the many months it would have taken to get them here. She was well aware any significant Indian activity would pull Theodore from her side and she wasn't taking any chances of that happening before the deed was done. She had waited long enough. She supposed Theodore felt the same way about his parents.

Betsy's eyes remained fixed on her beloved. The passion she saw burning in his gaze made it hard for her to focus on anything else. She had no idea what Max's opening words were nor was she aware he started the vows until Theodore began speaking.

He repeated the words after Max, his eyes widening slightly upon hearing her full name for the first time. The rich baritone of his voice wrapped around her. Other than the sound of Max's voice, she was only aware of Theodore.

"I, Theodore Finnis Whitmore, take thee, Betsafina Drake Wheeler, to be my wedded Wife, to have and to hold from this day forward, for better for worse, for richer for poorer, in sickness and in health, to love and to cherish, till death us do part, according to God's holy ordinance; and thereto I plight thee my troth."

She almost missed her cue. "I, Betsafina Drake Wheeler, take thee, Theodore Finnis Whitmore, to be my wedded Husband, to have and to hold from this day forward, for better for worse, for richer for poorer, in sickness and in health, to love, cherish, and to obey, till death us do part, according to

God's holy ordinance; and thereto I plight thee my troth."

Max whispered to Theodore, "Do you have a ring?"

Theodore nodded and reached into his breast pocket for his grandmother's simple gold band. Betsy lifted her left hand to him and he slipped the ring on her third finger amazed to find it was a perfect fit. He solemnly vowed to Betsy, "With this ring I thee wed, with my body I thee worship, and with all my worldly goods I thee endow: In the name of the Father, and of the Son, and of the Holy Ghost. Amen."

Theodore then lifted her hand to his mouth and kissed the ring. His lips brushing her skin sent anticipation rushing through her.

Max declared them "man and wife" finally allowing Theodore to do what he had wanted to do since coming up on deck—kiss his beautiful bride. Their guests cheered and then rushed forward to congratulate them.

Max took his time sailing back to Key West while the wedding party watched the sunset from the open deck.

The newlyweds stood at the balustrade enjoying the view and each other. Theodore enveloped her in his warm embrace. Betsy snuggled into her newly discovered favourite place in the whole world with her head tucked under his chin and her ear against his beating heart.

She said, "You're not as tough as you look Mr. Whitmore. In fact you're just a big 'ol teddy bear."

"Hmm." The sound was a cross between amusement and guarded agreement.

"My teddy bear." She pulled back to thoughtfully look him in the eye. "May I call you Teddy?"

The nickname he shunned after childhood now brought pleasure when uttered by his adorable wife. "If it pleases you."

She smiled. "It does." Joy swelled in her heart. "I love you, Teddy."

"I love you, Betsafina." He leaned his head down to tenderly kiss his new wife, bringing his hand up to cradle the side of her face.

The kiss was interrupted by Henry. They parted to pull him between them.

He looked up at Betsy. "May I call you Momma now?"

"I would like that, Henry."

He smugly said, "I told Emily you were my momma now."

Henry broke away from them to run back in her direction.

Theodore pulled Betsy close and kissed her temple. "Are you happy, love?"

She turned to look up to him, her face even more beautiful in the warm golden glow of the descending sun. "Perfectly so."

The newlyweds had eyes only for each other and while the other guests watched the sun's descent, Richard Bennington and Agatha Pary disappeared for a time below deck.

Mrs. Mallory insisted upon giving the joyful newlyweds a wedding supper. The party arrived to find their meal ready to be served. Turtle soup, sautéed snapper, rice and roasted vegetables. She even made a sugared cake. Betsy couldn't thank her friend enough for the generous gift.

She and Theodore were seated next to each other, allowing them to frequently touch hands under the table while sharing smoldering glances above. She was enjoying her wedding supper and the sweet anticipation of the night to come. How different it was from her first wedding. Then she had been unable to taste her food for the nervous suspense consuming her over the night ahead. This time, she thoroughly enjoyed her succulent meal and knowing what to expect afterwards, she was looking forward to its conclusion. Not only to sharing her bed but to sharing her life again. And she felt blessed for it to be with a man she loved. How different this day would be if it was George Casey by her side.

When it was time for the Eatonton's to leave, they found the children in a side room. Henry and Emily, a doily on her head, were pretending to be married with Christoff officiating. They arrived just in time to witness the kiss, or rather, Henry's brush across her cheek as Emily skittishly averted her face. It was a mixed moment of hilarity and disbelief. Max was the first to break it up, whisking Emily up to his shoulder. "You are too young, little lady, to contemplate anything other than being my little girl. Weddings, pretend or otherwise, will have to wait." He tickled her in punishment.

Emily's laughter filled the room. "Stop tickling, Daddy."

Meanwhile, Henry scooted closer to his father afraid he was in trouble until Theodore tousled his hair.

Max scooped up Christoff as well and wished everyone a good night. The rest of the party followed suit. Betsy leaned heavily on Theodore as they walked home. She was feeling the effects of too much wine but she also was simply enjoying the feel of him and the right to cling to her husband.

Her husband. She looked up at him with a smile. The reality of it still amazed her.

* * *

After undoing the buttons down the back of her dress, Betsy sent Theodore to put Henry to bed, allowing her a few moments of privacy. He returned, shutting their bedroom door with relief. They were finally alone.

Betsy walked to him from across the room, barefoot in a demur nightgown, her long hair loose and glistening in the candlelight. The reality of her was more beautiful than he ever imagined in his dreams.

She pressed her hands to his chest tilting her head in anticipation of his kiss. They indulged in the play of lips and tongue until they both were feeling lightheaded.

"It's been a long time." Betsy worried her lower lip as she looked up at her new husband.

Theodore's gaze didn't waver. "For me too."

"There hasn't been anyone since Margaret?"

Theodore lightly brushed back the tendrils of hair at her temple but his eyes remained steadily fixed on hers. "No one."

She felt the warm glow of his emotions spread through her being while nerves fluttered in her belly. "It has been much longer for me... almost a decade. I may not do well at this. What if having been so long it's as painful as the first time?"

His fingers lightly caressed the outer contours of her face from her forehead around to her chin. "It's like riding a horse. It will come back to you."

Her laughter made him pause but helped relieve some of her pent up nervousness. "But I've never ridden a horse."

"Hmm." He leaned in to kiss her, pausing before their lips met. Their breath mingled. "Then you'll have to trust me." He sensually rubbed his closed lips against hers. The sensation stoked the flames of their desire.

When he moved his lips along her cheek, she whispered, "I do." She tilted her head encouraging his pleasurable exploration. "With all my heart." He nuzzled her ear and her knees went weak.

He gently tugged her sensitive earlobe before whispering. "And I'll have to trust you to let me know if anything is uncomfortable."

The sensations stirred by his warm breath against her ear slowed her thoughts. It took a moment for his words to register. When they did her heart swelled. This tender man really cared for her. She turned her face to his and murmured against his lips. "Thank you Teddy."

He tenderly returned her kiss sealing their trust. He kissed her again more deeply while guiding her backwards away from the door and towards the four poster bed draped with mosquito netting.

Betsy helped him undress, taking pleasure in the wifely ritual.

They tried to savor the moment but passion, too soon, carried them to consummation.

The second time was slower.

They lay side by side on their backs, Betsy's head pillowed by his arm, her body humming with the afterglow of their lovemaking. Holding each other's right hand, their fingers entwined softly, slowly exploring the sensitive tactile sensations.

Betsy had never felt this content or cherished. She soon fell asleep cradled in his arms.

At sunrise, he woke her with kisses in the most sensitive places, then took her to heights of passion she never even knew existed.

Sometime later, Betsy lay halfway across his chest with his arm resting lightly across her back. She propped her chin on her arm to study his face.

She lifted a finger to trace the scar that dissected his left eyebrow. "How did you get this?"

"Hmm, a school yard disagreement at the age of fifteen."

"What about?"

He paused, "I don't recall."

"And the other participant?"

"Much worse."

She smiled. "So you can take care of yourself in a fight."

"I can defend my lady, if needs be."

"Good to know." She ran her hand over his right one with the crook in his little finger. "And is this from fighting as well?"

"No. It has always been that way for as long as I can remember."

"A birth defect then." She grinned. "Perhaps, I should toss you back and find another." Secretly she looked forward to learning many more things about her husband.

He growled and tightened his hold. "Don't even consider it. I'll bash the head of any other. You're mine, Betsafina."

She grinned widely. "I like the sound of that."

She gave him a firm quick kiss then another and another before pushing herself off his chest and out of the bed to wash at the nightstand. She was conscious of Theodore's gaze following her. She supposed a proper miss would have donned a dressing gown but Betsy felt being missish after the fact was vacuous. Theodore, on the other hand, coming to the basin to bathe with her in all his glory was a bit distracting, although she found pleasure in taking the cloth to his skin, even noting a few ticklish spots.

* * *

It was late morning by the time they made an appearance in the dining room, so they broke their fast alone. Afterwards, Betsy went to her shop to do some work and Theodore headed to the paper to attend to his business.

Betsy made a trip to the mercantile after lunch to pick up more thread. She passed Mr. Whitehead on the way home walking with Mr. Marsilios, an artist visiting for a few weeks. It gave Betsy an idea she presented to Theodore during supper.

"I met a French painter this afternoon, in the company of Mr. Whitehead, who does portraits. I know it would be expensive, but I thought we could have one done of the three of us as a gift for your parents."

Theodore was touched by her thoughtfulness. "I think it is a wonderful idea. We'll need two paintings, of course. One for your parents as well. Tomorrow we shall seek out this artist, mister..."

"Monsieur Marsilios."

"Monsieur Marsilios, and commission his work to commence right away."

It took a week of long sittings for Monsieur Marsilios to complete the large portrait. Betsy wore Esperanza's dress returning it once the portrait was done. It turned out even better than Betsy imagined it would. Theodore was so impressed he requested a third one be made for their home. They were keeping the little painter busy, for unbeknownst to Theodore, Betsy requested a miniature portrait of her and Henry for Theodore to carry with him when he traveled.

Their lives flowed in newlywed bliss for many months. Even news from the interior forts was quiet, allowing Theodore more time with them.

* * *

One evening the family was gathered in the parlor. Agatha occupied the Queen Anne chair, knitting a blanket. Henry was working on his studies at the table in the corner. Betsy and Theodore shared the sofa. She was reading a Ladies Magazine borrowed from Abby while Theodore was reading copies of the *New York Weekly* he received from Bob.

Betsy broke the silence of the room. "How extraordinary!"

Theodore looked to her. "What is?"

"A French tailor invented a sewing machine and used it to open a factory producing machine-sewn French army uniforms. Amazing. I wonder how it works. Unfortunately, the workers were fearful for their employment. They burned the factory down."

"A bit short-sighted of them, even machines require workers while burning down the factory employs no one."

"I agree, but I was thinking of how nice it would be to have a machine like that. Why I could sew a long seam or a hemline in minutes instead of hours."

"Then we shall buy you one."

"I'm sure they are exorbitantly expensive. I don't have enough work in the shop to justify the cost." She let out a sigh and flipped the page. "I'll just have to keep sewing by hand."

"Or you could quit sewing all together. You don't need to work."

Betsy frowned. "I thought you weren't the kind of man threatened by a woman working. Besides I need something to keep me busy and this town needs my services."

He placed his finger against her lips. "Shh, I didn't mean you couldn't work. I simply want to make you happy."

"Oh." She pressed her lips together. "I'm sorry. I jumped to a conclusion again." She gazed at him in wonder realizing she had it all with him. He was her partner, her friend, her champion and her protector. How did she deserve to be so blessed?

* * *

Betsy loved being Theodore's wife and Henry's mother. She was surprised how easily she fit into their lives and the companionship of being part of a family nourished her soul. It took her and Ben quite a while to get used to the finer points of being husband and wife. She and Theodore rarely clashed. Maybe being older they worried less over the little things. Mostly she enjoyed no longer sleeping alone. That part of marriage was going so well three nights passed before they realized they both liked sleeping on the same side of the bed.

Theodore argued, "The left side is closest to the door and as your protector, should the need arise, I should be closest to intercept a possible intruder."

His argument was thin, and they both knew it, but Betsy ceded the battle and learned to adjust to the other side.

Marriage was even better this time. Theirs was more of a partnership. She had someone to lean on and care for and who valued her opinions.

One of the unexpected perks of being married to Theodore was letting someone else do the laundry. Upon his return to Key West, Theodore rehired the same laundress he used before since Aunt Agatha could not handle the task. Betsy assumed he would let her go once they were married but he insisted Betsy had more than enough to do and didn't need the added burden of laundry for four. She accepted his decree after a token argument.

Once the newness of their marriage faded and the sweltering heat of mid-summer was upon them, Betsy announced at dinner one Saturday it was time they moved their bedding to the sleeping porch. Three puzzled faces stared back at her. "Do you mean to tell me in all this time you have never taken advantage of your porch?"

Since the day Betsy moved into the house she looked forward to using the open room built into the second story on the front side of the house. It was designed to catch the breeze and offer a cooler place to sleep during the over-warm months of summer when the nights were barely ten degrees less than the afternoons. Her little house didn't have one.

Theodore's face was considering. "I have never heard of a sleeping porch. That explains the empty bed frames out there. I thought it was a storage place."

Agatha huffed. "Sleeping outside, all together? It isn't proper."

Betsy laughed. "I assure you, here it is considered quite proper."

Agatha huffed again. "Well I for one will not be joining you."

Henry said, "I want to sleep outside."

Theodore decided he would try it before he dismissed the idea. "Henry and I will help you move the bedding when we finish our meal."

Betsy smiled. "Lovely."

An hour later, the mattresses were moved outside with fresh linens and mosquito netting draped from hooks in the ceiling. That night as Theodore felt the soft caress of the breeze across his exposed skin he had to admit the move was worth even the temporary loss of privacy. He was motivated enough to find ways to get around that little problem.

* * *

Only one thing marred Betsy's happiness. She had yet to conceive. She felt time slipping away and by September, four months into her marriage, she was seeking advice from matrons. Some told her she was a fool for trying, she was too old. She dismissed them. At twenty-nine she wasn't too old to have children, just too old to be starting a family. Others told her of old wives tales for conception but most she disregarded as too pagan. Abby advised her not to worry. It would happen in God's time and not hers. Betsy knew Abby was right but still she fretted as each month brought disappointment. It also hurt to see Abby, Esperanza and one of the Mabrity girls increasing with pending motherhood. For now, she held onto hope but if she had to come to terms with not being able to conceive, she thanked God again for not being married to George. Without children marriage to him would have become burdensome.

Feeling her sorrow, Theodore tried to placate his wife. "If it is God's will then Henry may have to be enough for us."

Betsy turned away from him to face the window. "I love Henry, I do, but I want to experience carrying our child. I want to hold *our* baby." She silently began crying.

Theodore wrapped his arms around her waist and pulled her back tight to his chest. He whispered in her ear. "Then we'll keep praying and doing our part." He kissed her neck and then turned her around to kiss away her tears. "I want our child too." He lifted their hands between them, placed together in prayer, hers bracketed by his, and bowed his head. Betsy closed her eyes and bowed her head at his first words.

"Heavenly Father, thank you for the beautiful day you have given us and for giving me this wonderful woman to cherish as my wife. May your teachings guide us in our daily life and may you bless our union with progeny. Let thy will be done. Amen."

Even in prayer, her husband was a man of few words.

Their joining afterwards was deep and reverent. Betsy felt sure God must have seen the goodness in their hearts and answered their prayer.

And then it came... the news she had been dreading.

Chapter 23

Late September 1834

Two letters arrived from Fort King for Theodore. They waited on the table in the foyer. Betsy eyed them with trepidation every time she walked past. When Theodore arrived home from work, he took them into his office to open in private. Betsy waited anxiously to learn of their content. Theodore didn't emerge from the office till he was called for supper. By then her nerves were on edge.

The meal was served, eaten and Henry excused before Theodore shared his news.

"Major Dade and General Thompson have written to tell me the Indians have been called to a meeting in October to discuss how they will proceed with the removal process."

Betsy took a deep breath knowing what he would say next.

"It's not likely I could get there in time to witness the talks and it will take months to prepare for the actual move. I believe I'll wait till after the New Year to visit the reservation."

Betsy released the breath she was holding. The dreaded moment was postponed. She couldn't help the smile playing on her lips.

In truth, Theodore wasn't sure it would take months to prepare the move. Ships could be available for transport in a matter of weeks. The problem was, as much as he felt the need to witness this important event, he felt more compelled to stay home. His wife needed him. Perhaps a few more months would bring them the blessing for which they prayed. Time was not on their side and every month of disappointment cut a little deeper into their hearts.

* * *

Saturday afternoon, Theodore was playing ball with Henry in the yard but seeing Dr. Waterhouse's old boat gave him an idea. An hour later he called a halt to their game and went in search of Betsy. He found her in the kitchen removing fresh baked bread from the oven.

Betsy placed the hot pan on the counter to cool and brushed her forearm across her forehead to absorb the beaded moisture. Now that the last loaf was done she could finally be free from the oppressive heat in the kitchen. She turned toward the door surprised to find Theodore there wearing a mischievous grin.

He took her hand and tugged her towards the house. "Let's go for a sail, just the two of us."

Betsy laughed at this rare display of boyish enthusiasm but pulled her hand from his. "Wait, I have to cover the loaves and bank the fire."

"You cover, I'll bank," he moved around her with haste to the stove. When they were done, he took her hand again and hastened to their bedroom to change causing Agatha to gasp in surprise as they raced past her, laughing like children.

Betsy pulled out her navy bathing costume and tossed Theodore a matching one-piece she made for him. He walked up behind her and took hers from her hand sending chills down her spine when he whispered, "I want you to wear the pink one you wore the first time we sailed."

She blushed then leaned back to look at him. "Just what are you planning, Mr. Whitmore?"

He grinned. "A very private sailing party, Mrs. Whitmore."

They donned their swimwear and covered it with their regular clothing for the walk to the boat. Watching him undress and redress made her wish they could skip the sail but privacy in this house didn't exist.

They made a quick stop by the kitchen to pick up water and snacks and they were off to the boat. Theodore also grabbed an empty bucket. Her questioning look prompted him to say, "We can bring home supper."

Theodore and Betsy sailed to a secluded cove surrounded on three sides by emerald mangrove islands and shallow sandbars ensuring anything larger than a row boat would have to keep distant. They removed their day clothes and slipped into the cooling waters for a swim, splashing and frolicking, until Theodore caught her up against his chest and their play became that of lovers.

The thin lawn of Betsy's chemise drew Theodore's smoldering gaze and heightened her feminine desire. When the need became too strong to be denied, they returned to the little sailboat. Theodore lifted Betsy into the boat. She moved to the tiller seat and watched with avid interest as Theodore removed his suit, tossed it into the boat, and then climbed aboard *au naturel*. He sat on the center bench and beckoned her to him. She carefully moved to stand in front of him without tipping the boat over and then looked around to assure they were still alone as he reached under her chemise to pull down her pantalets. Her breath was ragged and her heartbeat rapid as he calmly pulled her to him and ran his hands up her calves to her thighs, lifting her skirt. He pulled her closer still and then he pulled her hips down manipulating her willing body to kneel on the bench one leg on either side of his. The provocative position made her feel like a wanton woman.

Theodore immensely enjoyed encouraging his proper wife into acts of impropriety. He couldn't help the flood of desire enhanced by her flushed cheeks and the saltwater taste of her lips. He pulled her even closer creating delicious friction everywhere their bodies touched until he could no longer resist the urge to mate.

Betsy relaxed contentedly in his arms afterwards, her body and mind too languid for thought.

Moments later, Theodore dropped a kiss on her forehead. "Off with ye wench, it's time to catch our supper."

"Am I to assume by your tone, you expect me to do the catching by myself?"

"Aye. I must recover the energy you just took from me, lass."

She playfully punched him on the shoulder. "Oh, we'll see about that." She carefully moved to stand just out of his reach, untied the bodice of her chemise as he warily watched, then lifted it over her head and draped it over the side of the boat. She stood there for a moment absorbing the sun's rays on her bare skin and watching his eyes darken. Just as he started to reach for her, she turned and dove into the water.

Theodore grinned. He was captivated by his playful wife. Unable to resist her siren's call he dove in after her. Being the more experienced swimmer, she thwarted his attempts to catch her. Then offering herself as a bribe, she enticed Theodore to catch their dinner. He did his best to do so quickly.

When he surfaced with the third conch, Theodore discovered they were no longer alone. A jolly boat was headed their way with four men from a larger ship likely anchored in nearby Hawks Channel. His thoughts rapidly changed from lover to protector as he moved between the approaching sailors and Betsy to hide her from their view. Betsy surfaced a few feet behind him laughing, until she noticed his diverted attention, and the other boat. She immediately went underwater, swimming for the far side of their boat and her costume. She struggled for a moment trying to work her way into the wet material before she gave up and wrapped it around her middle as best she could manage. She peeked around the boat. Theodore was only a few yards from their boat. She grew alarmed to find the men were now within shouting distance from him.

"Ahoy there."

Theodore glanced behind him to make sure Betsy was keeping out of sight before answering. "Ahoy." Now they were close enough for him to see they were middle-aged deck hands, but Theodore was unsure yet if they were trustworthy men.

The man at the bow of the boat called out to Theodore. "We've come in search of fresh water." He nodded toward the small island behind them. "Do you know if there is any to be had on this land?"

Theodore saw their inquisitive looks and could only hope Betsy was hidden from view. He had no weapon to defend her honor if these men became aggressive. He held his ground hoping to discourage them from coming any closer. "There is no water on this island. Key West is not far south from here. You can procure water there."

"We would rather not pay for it. Besides we are headed north."

Betsy loudly whispered to Theodore. "Indian Key"

Theodore said to the men. "Then you'll want to head to Indian Key."

One of the men in the middle smirked at him. "We would however pay handsomely for what you got hidden behind that boat."

Even though she knew they couldn't see her, Betsy sank to her chin in the water.

Theodore drew as forceful a presence as he could muster treading water naked. "I'll kindly thank you to respect my wife."

"Your wife, eh?"

From the rear of the boat a man said, "Lay off, Carter. Sorry to bother you and the misses. Men, get this boat turned around."

Theodore waited till they were well away from them before he swam to Betsy. She gave him a grim look. "I'm sorry, Teddy."

It was not what Theodore expected her to say. "Whatever for?"

"The situation would not have been so dire if I was properly dressed."

"I doubt they ever knew you weren't. I didn't see any of them with a spyglass and you were out of sight by the time they were close enough to discern anything."

"But what about you? They likely assumed I wasn't dressed since you aren't."

She had a point but he wasn't going to worry over it now. It was done and no harm had come to them. "All's well that ends well."

Betsy smiled lightly. "You're right."

Theodore glanced back to make sure the intruders had disappeared from sight and then turned back to Betsy. "Let's go home."

"Not yet, we need two more conchs."

"You seriously want to stay?"

"Yes. We still need our supper. Besides, they're not coming back. If we each get one it won't take long."

"As you wish, madam." His wife was anything, if not practical.

Twenty minutes later, he helped Betsy into the boat, unable to resist playfully swatting her bare buttocks as she went over the side. She turned to help him aboard returning the favour when he bent to retrieve his dry clothes. He jerked upright in surprise and turned to her. "You'll pay for that later."

"Promise?"

He gave his best lusty pirate look. "Aye."

Conch fritters were served for dinner.

When Henry saw them on his plate he looked to Betsy in despair. "You went conch fishing without me?"

Betsy felt contrite knowing how hard Henry had worked to learn to swim so he could catch conch. She had promised to take him soon.

Theodore frowned. "Henry, it is not for you to question the actions of your elders."

Henry's head sunk in submission. "Yes, Poppa."

He lightened his tone. "You can go next time, son."

* * *

Mid November, Theodore received word the talk with the chiefs did not go well and they were seen buying arms and ammunition with their annuity. The situation was escalating. Theodore felt he needed to get there soon to speak with the Indians. Once war broke out, he was sure they would consider him the enemy and be less likely to give him their side of the story.

He waited till they were preparing for bed to speak with Betsy. His decision to go hinged on her acceptance. She still had yet to conceive and Abby was due any day now. He wouldn't leave her unless he felt she could handle the emotional burden.

"I've had word from Fort King today."

Betsy stopped brushing her hair to turn toward Theodore. Her chest tightened. Time had run out.

"The Seminoles refuse to acknowledge the new treaty and I think Congress is ready to take action to enforce it. I want people to understand why they refuse and why they may fight." He sat on the bed beside her. "But I won't go, if you need me to stay."

Realizing he was giving her the choice gave her the courage to release him. "No. You should go. Maybe your words can save their homeland."

He smiled thinly. "I wish I could." The smile disappeared. "I'm afraid removal is a given. The only question is how many will die in the process." He looked deep in her eyes. "Do you need me to stay until after Abby gives birth?"

Something about the way he asked made her realize he loved her so much he was concerned with her ability to cope with her barrenness. It also made her wonder about his decision in October. She was so happy he wasn't leaving; she didn't question it then. He may have waited because of her. She did not want to be a burden that prevented him from taking up his cause and doing what no else could do for the Seminoles. *I will never hinder him again.*

She smiled to reassure him. "You should go. I will be alright. I can hold her baby and dream of ours until you return. How long will you be gone?"

"Likely a few months."

"Would you mind showing me where you'll be?" He looked at her blankly. "You have a map in your office. I want you to show me on the map where you are going."

"Of course." He picked up the candle from the nightstand and held his hand out to her. Together they walked downstairs through the darkened house to his office. He unrolled the map across his desk using the pewter candlestick, an ink bottle, a brass compass and his left hand to hold down the corners. Candlelight flickered across the roughly drawn outline of Florida. Much of the land was uncharted territory.

He pointed to their island at the end of the Florida Keys and then moved his finger to a large harbour half way up the western side of the peninsula. "I will first sail to here, Fort Brooke, then I will walk or ride the hundred miles to Fort King." His finger drew a line to a spot in the upper center area. "Located here near the reservation." His finger drew circles in the space below the fort indicating the reservation lands. "The fort was built as a buffer between the settlers and the Indians."

Betsy pointed to the markings at the top of the eastern coastline. "And this is St. Augustine, correct?"

"Yes." Theodore pointed to places on the opposite side of the map. "The territorial government resides here in Tallahassee and over here is Pensacola. Not much is known of the area south of the reservation down to Key Biscayne."

"Will you be traveling much in the interior?"

"I only plan to go to Fort King and the reservation," he placed his hand along her cheek, "and then return to you." He kissed her. "You're not to worry about me. I have already traveled this way several times."

"It seems to me it would be easier for your work if we were to live in Tallahassee or St. Augustine."

"Perhaps, but it is not where I want to live when this business is over, and it will eventually be done. The Seminoles will be forced to move and I will settle for writing only news of this place."

"I look forward to that day."

He gestured to the map. "Are you satisfied?"

"Yes. Thank you."

Theodore picked up the candle. "Then let's go to bed."

* * *

Theodore was ready to leave a few days later. As he finished packing his carpetbag, Betsy presented him with the miniature painting of her and Henry. "Something to remind you to come home safe."

Theodore stared at the painting, awed by the gift. He pulled her into his embrace, tucking her head under his chin; he held her tight. "You are such a blessing. Thank you." He pulled a well-worn travel Bible from his bag and slipped the painting between the pages. He kissed the book and returned it to the bag and then kissed Betsy.

Together they descended the stairs to join Henry and Agatha in the dining room for breakfast. Theodore blessed the food and they ate and talked and tried to pretend for a moment it was an ordinary day. When the meal was cleared Betsy said, "Henry, would you bring the Bible from the parlor, please."

Henry scooted out of his chair and left the room, returning a few minutes later with the heavy book and placed it on the table between Betsy and Theodore. Betsy put a hand on his back. "Will you pick something for us to read?"

Henry's brow furrowed. "How do I do that?"

Betsy gave him a gentle smile. "Have faith son. Open the book and turn the pages until you find something you feel we should read."

Agatha, Betsy and Theodore watched Henry do as she instructed. After flipping a few pages he stopped at the beginning of the Book of Joshua and looked to Betsy.

"Is that what you want me to read?" He nodded so Betsy read chapter one, her right hand remained on Henry's back, keeping him beside her, and her left rested on the top corner of the page. When she read verse nine she stopped and looked to Theodore. "This shall be our family verse to repeat every day while you are gone." She read it again. "Have not I commanded Thee! Be strong and of a good courage: be not afraid, neither be thou dismayed: for the Lord thy God is with thee whithersoever thou goest."[5]

Theodore covered her hand resting on the Bible. "It is a good verse. Joshua 1:9. I will read it every day and in doing so I will be with you."

Betsy's lips trembled with emotion. She was blessed and humbled, anxious for Theodore's safety, concerned for how long he would be gone and how she would maintain the family without him, but mostly overwhelmed with the sorrow of letting him go. She hid it all behind a smile and returned her attention to finishing the first chapter. She knew whatever happened, faith would see her through it.

When Betsy finished reading, Theodore led them in a family prayer and then said goodbye to Aunt Agatha and Henry. She walked him to the ship and waved from the dock until he was out of sight.

And now she waited, her world suspended until his return.

* * *

That afternoon, Betsy took Agatha and Henry for a sail to a nearby reef and grassy area where she often found conch. It was meant to keep them from moping about the house and to keep a promise made to Henry. While Agatha stayed in the boat under her umbrella, Betsy showed Henry how to hunt for conch by looking for the wavy trails in the sand and the telltale lump where they buried in the sand during the day. He caught on quick, finding three of the four they took home. He then insisted Betsy teach him how to harvest the meat.

Henry was working on the third one by himself while Betsy was doing other things, when he suddenly called out, "Sakes Alive!"

Betsy turned to him in a panic, afraid he might have cut himself. "Henry?"

"Look at this, Momma." He held his palm up for her to see his find.

"Why, Henry, you found a pearl." She picked up the delicate looking pink treasure. "These are very rare. I once found a tiny brownish-orange one but never one like this." She handed it back to him. "You must be sure to keep it safe. It could be very valuable."

"In that case, would you hold on to it for me?"

"Of course. I'll put in my jewelry box later for safekeeping." Betsy pulled her handkerchief from her pocket and tied the pearl securely in the center.

Henry finished the conch and Betsy set to work making chowder.

* * *

A week after Theodore left, Betsy was wishing she could share her news with him. Her menses was late; something that only happened once before in her life. Now three days late, each passing day hope grew stronger. She wished Theodore was here to share her secret for it was too soon to tell anyone else.

* * *

A church picnic was held on Sunday to welcome William Whitehead's new bride, Margaret Elizabeth. Abby stayed home. With her time near; she did not feel like attending but insisted the rest of her family enjoy the day. Max left her in the care of her friend and former maid, Maria, while he and the children joined the town gathering. Betsy, Agatha and Henry shared their blanket with Max's family. Following lunch, the adults visited while the children played hide and seek in the nearby trees.

At eight years of age, Henry was usually friendly, outgoing and athletic but since his father left he had turned moody and was showing signs of aggression during the game. Betsy made a mental note to speak with him later.

They were both missing Theodore. It brought to mind her precious secret. *Would Theodore prefer a daughter or another son?* Betsy eyed Max speculatively. "Boy or girl?"

Max turned from watching the children to look at Betsy. "Do you mean what is Abby having?"

She nodded.

He answered with conviction. "Boy."

Betsy grinned. "Oh, you're sure are you?"

Max's grin deepened. "Absolutely."

"And why is that?"

"Just a seaman's hunch. Besides she's carrying this babe much the same as with Christoff."

"Ah. We shall see if you are right. Very soon I expect."

Max's face instantly sobered. "I'll not be surprised if he makes an appearance before week's end."

Agatha chimed in. "And if it's a girl?"

Max looked at her confidently. "It is not but if it was I would love her just as much."

"Humph."

271

Max let her grunt of doubt pass without comment. He returned his attention to the children playing tag.

Betsy couldn't help admiring Max and Abby. They both had amazingly positive outlooks on this birth considering the tragedy of the last. She sent a fervent prayer heavenward for the health of Abby and her baby, adding one for her baby as well.

* * *

Betsy missed the old bedtime ritual of tucking Henry in for the night. It was something she thought marriage would give back to her. She was mistaken. Henry decided he was too old to be tucked in and determined from the start she would get a kiss on the cheek while still in the parlor before he took himself off to bed.

Now she stood on the threshold of his room debating on speaking with him now or waiting until tomorrow. She imagined her mother's voice saying, "No time like the present," and made her decision. She entered his opened door to find him reading by candlelight.

"Henry, could I speak with you?"

"Yes ma'am." He politely closed his book and sat up a little straighter against the pillow.

She was proud of the little gentleman he was becoming. Now that the moment was at hand she wasn't sure how to broach the subject. "You miss your father, don't you?"

"Sometimes."

Betsy sat on the edge of the bed facing him. "You were missing him today, at the picnic."

His jaw dropped. "How did you know?"

Her lips compressed and eyes softened. "I was too."

"Why can't he stay here to write? A person can write anywhere. Why does he have to be away a long time to write?"

"Well." She searched for a way to explain it so he could understand. "Could you describe for someone what it was like to swim underwater before you learned to do it?"

He gave it some thought. "I suppose not."

"But now that you have experienced it you could, right?"

"Yes."

"It's like that for your father. He has to experience the events and meet the people in order to share the story with other people. And it is by writing articles for the paper that he is able to share it."

"But why would anyone care what Indians are doing?"

"They probably wouldn't care if they didn't know about them. But there are some really important things happening to the Indians, and because your father is writing about it other people do care. They may or may not agree with him, but they know what is happening. If he didn't write, they may never know."

"So what Poppa does is important?"

She smiled. "Yes, it is. We should be proud of him. I know I am. And Henry, the only reason he would leave you is because what he is doing is important. He loves you very much."

Impulsively, Henry reached out to hug her. For a moment they held the embrace.

"But Henry, when we are feeling sad because we miss him, we shouldn't let it affect how we treat others."

He leaned back to look at her. "What do you mean?"

"Today, when you were playing with the other children you were not always kind."

She could tell he was thinking it through. She felt like she had made her point so she stood and leaned down to kiss his forehead. "Good night, Henry."

"Good night, Momma."

Her heart still soared every time he said it.

The following morning, Max brought his children to stay with her. He barely said hello and thank you before rushing off to return to his laboring wife. The lightheartedness of yesterday was gone, replaced by a shadow of fear.

It was well into the afternoon before there was another knock on her door. She opened it to find Mr. Baxley standing on the threshold with hat in hand. Betsy braced for the worst.

Mr. Baxley said, "Mr. Eatonton asks if you will keep the children for another day."

"Of course. He needn't have asked." Frightened of the answer, Betsy first looked behind her to make sure the children were not near. "How is Mrs. Eatonton?"

"Resting."

She waited, but he said nothing more. She couldn't believe she was going to have to drag the information out of him. "And the baby?"

"A wee one, but he is a fighter."

Betsy felt faint from relief. She had to put a hand to the door jamb for support. "Thank you, Mr. Baxley."

It was a more lighthearted Betsy who played with Henry, Emily and Christoff the rest of the afternoon. She didn't have any trouble with them until bedtime, when Christoff began crying for his mother and even Emily was a bit homesick. It took some doing but with Henry's help she finally got them settled down for the night.

Just after breakfast the next morning, Max came for his offspring. He gave Betsy a jovial smile when she answered the door. "I told you it would be a boy."

She returned his smile. "Congratulations, Captain. And what is to be the lad's name?"

"Hawthorne Michael."

Hearing her father's voice, Emily came running. Betsy stepped aside for Max to catch her up in his embrace. Henry came to stand next to Betsy while Christoff followed after as fast as his chubby legs could carry him. Max leaned down and swept him up too. "How would you like to meet your little brother?"

Emily pouted. "I don't want another brother."

Max gave his daughter a stern look. "Emily Rose, it is not about what you want. We are thankful for God's gift of a healthy baby."

Her mumble was barely discernable. "Yes, Poppa."

Betsy hid her smile. "Do you think I could come see them later?"

"You may come now, if you like."

"Are you sure? I wouldn't want to intrude, and is Abby well enough for company?"

"Betsy, you are closer to family than company. Come. Abby will be happy to see you."

Henry stayed behind with Aunt Agatha having no interest in babies. They walked the short distance up Whitehead Street, except Christoff who happily rode upon his father's shoulders, to the two story Bahamian style house with a cupola. They entered the door to the mewling cries of the newborn. Betsy saw Emily grimace and Christoff put his hands to his ears just as the sound suddenly ceased. Betsy had a good idea what made the infant suddenly quiet.

Max said, "Could you hold them down here while I assess the situation upstairs?"

Betsy nodded and he took off up the stairs, two at a time. He returned a half hour later. "You can come up now." Betsy led Christoff to the stairs, followed by Emily. The toddler's slow pace up the steps dragged out Betsy's anticipation. They finally entered the room to find Abby sitting up in bed holding the swaddled infant. Betsy hung back while the children went running towards the side of the bed. Max lifted them up and sat them, one on either side of their mother. Abby lowered the bundle to her lap so they could see his face. Betsy felt uncomfortable witnessing such a private family moment.

Christoff yawned. Abby looked to her husband. "Max will you put Christoff down for his nap?"

Max picked up his son, cradling him so he could bury his face in his son's belly, making him laugh as they walked out of the room. Betsy turned back to see Abby shaking her head.

"He gets him laughing and then wonders why he will not go to sleep." She turned to her daughter. "Would you like to hold your brother?"

Emily vigorously nodded her head.

"Scoot up here by me." Emily moved up next to her mother. "Hold out your arms." She dutifully lifted both arms to receive the bundle. Abby grimaced a little in pain as she turned to place the baby in her arms. "Hold his head up. Good girl."

Emily carefully followed her mother's instructions.

Abby smiled at Betsy. "Thank you for keeping my children."

"You're welcome. I'm guessing there was some difficulty."

Both ladies kept their conversation low and vague in difference to the little ears listening.

"Yes. Forceps were needed."

"All is well now?"

"Just some extra tenderness for me, and he has some bruising around his temples."

Emily interrupted them. "Mommy?"

"Yes, dear?"

"May I go play now? All he wants to do is sleep."

Both ladies were tickled. Abby said, "Of course, sweetheart." She retrieved her youngest and watched her eldest scramble from the bed and race from the room. "No running, Emily." She held the baby towards Betsy. "Would you like to hold your newest God-son?"

Betsy couldn't help her eager grin. "I thought you would never ask." She took the sleeping child and seated herself to enjoy the peaceful moment. The next time she looked up Abby's eyes were closed. She watched over the precious bundle while mother and child both slept, enjoying the feel of the newborn in her arms. A secret smile appeared. Perhaps in nine months she would hold her own sleeping babe.

* * *

Betsy awoke in the middle of the night from a bad dream. Despair gripped her as she realized the cramping pain proved to be reality and not part of her slumber. She crawled out of bed and dropped to her knees on the wooden floor in prayer.

"Please Lord, let me keep this child." She said it over and over again rocking back and forth until lack of circulation forced her to get up.

She longed to feel Theodore's comforting arms around her.

In the hour before dawn, she knew hope was gone. She wasn't sure if her menses had arrived late or if she miscarried but either way the result was heartbreaking. She took care of her needs then returned to bed and curled around Theodore's pillow. Strangely enough she couldn't cry.

She drifted into a light sleep until the sounds of Agatha and Henry rising forced her to get up lest they worry about her.

Arriving in the dining room to Henry's happy chatter the tears suddenly rushed to the surface. She turned around to leave again, tossing over her shoulder to Agatha, "Will you mind Henry? I'm going for a walk." She didn't give Agatha a chance to respond in her rush to be alone to allow the tears to flow. Behind her she heard Henry protest he was old enough not to need minding which only increased her sorrow.

A brisk walk on the beach helped to clear her head if not her heart. She returned to the house better able to face the day.

Theodore's insistence on household help freed her to focus her efforts on her business and giving school lessons to Henry. It was a pleasant change from the struggle she had before marriage of maintaining the house and the business. It also provided a healthy distraction for her sorrow.

It was a good thing she was used to surviving on her own because even though married she was doing it again. Only it was harder now that she had lives depending on her other than her own and another's wishes to consider.

She spent the mornings in her shop and afternoons with Henry. He loved to learn, making the task enjoyable for both of them. He did well in all subjects, but ciphering was his favourite. He took it in faster than a meal and he put those down pretty well these days too. He was growing fast these last few months.

Business was good. Her orders increased to the point she was keeping two other women steadily employed. As the island's population increased so did the number of unfamiliar customers, along with the requests for men's suits. Soon it would be enough to support the trade of a tailor. In the meantime, she was thankful to have enough to keep her busy. The alternative would be unbearable.

* * *

It was the first week of December when Theodore reached Fort King. The deciduous trees, newly leafed when he left in spring, were now bare allowing more sunlight to shimmer on dewy branches heavily laden with Spanish moss and covered with tiny ferns. Many species of bright green palm kept the winter landscape from appearing dreary. Theodore dismounted and walked his mare through the palisades. Many of the soldiers greeted him with familiarity and he had not gone too deep into the confines before he was met by Brigadier General Duncan Clinch out for an afternoon stroll. The stocky Georgian warmly welcomed his return. They spoke for a few minutes standing in the mottled sunlight under the leafless branches of an oak tree.

"Ah, Mr. Whitmore, you finally leave the comfortable bosom of your bride to return to our humble company."

"Good afternoon, General Clinch." The two men shook hands.

"We saved your bunk for you. Feel free to make yourself at home."

"Thank you. I was hoping I wouldn't have to pitch a tent."

"Glad to have you. It's nice to have visitors from the outside world."

"I expected more troops to be here considering the resistance shown at the last council."

General Clinch frowned. "There should be in my opinion."

"How is the morale of your men?"

"About what you would expect. We're all a little weary of sitting here waiting for action. We are pawns in between the Indians and our government, waiting to see who makes the next move."

"Any idea what the next move might be?"

"None whatsoever. I just hope it's ours and not theirs. You planning to visit the reservation again?"

Theodore nodded once. "Yes, sir."

"I would recommend going sooner rather than later. I can't say what your reception might be. The warriors who come to visit are aloof at best, insulting at worst. I can see if anyone wants to volunteer as escort."

Theodore grimaced. "Not sure that is wise. If they are hostile toward the army an escort would hurt my reception. Perhaps I should go alone."

"I wouldn't recommend it but I certainly can't stop you. Your previous visits with them may protect you. They are aware you champion their cause?"

"I, sir, do not seek to champion them. I am simply collecting facts from both sides."

"Sooner or later, you will be forced to choose a side but for now let's hope they consider you a friend."

He and the general parted ways. Theodore stowed his gear in his bunk and then headed for Wiley Thompson's office.

The Indian agent also greeted him warmly.

"Welcome back, Mr. Whitmore. I assume your presence means you received my letter. Why else would you leave your bride?"

"Why else, indeed."

"Would you like a drink?"

He gave a nod, "Hmm."

"I trust your journey was uneventful."

"No concerns but it doesn't get any easier to make the trek does it?"

"Not for me but I've only been that way twice. My normal travels take me to Tallahassee."

"Hmm. The seat of the territorial government."

They traded more pleasantries before getting to business.

"Your letter didn't go into much detail concerning the talk last month, only that it did not go well. Might you tell me its objective?"

Thompson sat up straighter in his chair. The relaxed posture of a moment ago vanished to be replaced by recalled frustration. "I was instructed to reiterate the agreements of the Payne's Landing and Fort Gibson treaties and to get answers to questions concerning their upcoming move."

"What were the questions?"

He ticked them off on the fingers of his burly hand. "First, will they accept the invitation from the Creeks to settle promiscuously among them?

Second, do they prefer cattle or money in exchange for the cattle they must give up here? Third, would they prefer to travel by land or water? And fourth, should the next annuity be paid in money or in goods to be provided at their new home? I gave them the night to discuss it."

"And how did they answer?"

"They didn't." Thompson pushed away from the desk and got up to pace the side of the room. "With the exception of three or four chiefs, they informed me they are of a mind to stay. They insist they do not have to move for nine more years; the time that is left on the Fort Moultrie treaty. General Clinch and I assured them troops would be used to affect the move and I explained the outcome of staying. They would be subject to white man's laws and likely deteriorate into poverty. I think I nearly had the majority convinced but those darn young warriors are urging their resistance, especially Osceola. He was whispering in Micanopy's ear the whole time I was speaking."

Thompson's frustration showed as he ran his hands through his hair. "Three days of talks and we are still in a stalemate. I also fear we've lost credibility with them since congress is taking so blasted long to ratify the treaty and our numbers are still so low. They laugh at the idea of the handful of men at this post being able to compel to move. They have no reason to believe they couldn't take us out if it came to war." His jaw firmed making his voice tense. "Convincing them otherwise will mean bloodshed."

"Surely you've requested troops."

"I have. And so has General Clinch and Governor Eaton. But, Secretary of War Lewis Cass, replied, under the current situation, there is no need for additional support. We have maybe two hundred and fifty men between the two forts and more than half are stationed at Fort Brooke. The ones here on the front line are mostly out on patrol guarding the boundaries of the reservation and the trading houses. A surprise attack could have disastrous results."

"I would have thought Congress to have sent more, given the growing concerns of war."

Thompson stopped his pacing. "Many, especially President Jackson, do not believe heavy numbers will be needed to suppress a rebellion. They perceive the Seminoles to be too peaceful—even cowardly—and will eventually concede to moving rather than fight."

Theodore grimaced. "Their belief may prove to be costly. The chiefs are friendly only to a point."

"I agree. I also believe the traders are interfering; convincing the Indians to stay for their own nefarious purposes. Business with military and Indians is good for them. However, I have not been able to prove the theory let alone put a stop to it."

Theodore could well imagine Gad Humphries was one of those traders encouraging them to stay although he was likely the only one not motivated by profit. "So what happens next?"

Thompson sighed heavily. "We wait. I've sent my reports, and we trade letters back and forth until I'm told to take action."

"You mentioned they used their annuity to buy arms and ammunition."

"Yes, I personally witnessed a keg of powder being carried off by the chiefs and I've been told they have purchased many."

"Shouldn't the traders be under strict orders not to sell to the Indians?"

Agent Thompson grimaced. "I haven't given that order yet. I didn't want to risk escalating the situation to violence. The Indians would not take well to such a restriction. Besides, forbidding them to purchase weapons would indicate our apprehensions. Perhaps given time they will capitulate peacefully."

Theodore did not understand this argument, but it was not for him to debate the issue only to report it. "Can you tell me who sold to them? I'd like to get more details of their purchase."

Apprehension suddenly dawned on Thompson that a newspaper report could be unfavourable for him, so he denied knowing who sold the means for war. Then he diverted the subject. "You have to feel sorry for them. If the tribe is moved west they likely will become enslaved by the Creeks, and if they remain in Florida the black Seminoles will be enslaved by the whites and the red Seminoles confined to a worthless piece of land."

"That does seem to be the gist of it. White man's slave or red man's slave."

Thompson tilted his head. "Are you planning to visit the reservation?"

"Yes. Do I have your permission?"

"Usual gifts?"

Theodore nodded. "Trinkets and such."

"Likely wasting your time, but I'll not stop you."

"I appreciate it."

Theodore left Thompson's office in time for the evening meal. When he finished he took a stroll around the compound. When Abraham and Osceola appeared he noticed the increased tension in the soldiers and even the civilians. He witnessed firsthand Osceola's insulting treatment towards Agent Thompson. Considering all that had been done to the Indians it was not surprising they would develop a hatred for whites but that was not the case. Osceola's feelings did not encompass all. He next spoke with Lieutenant John Graham and his attitude was as friendly as it had always been with the lieutenant. His path crossed with Theodore's next. He and Abraham were guarded but friendly. Abraham agreed to escort Theodore to Micanopy's village the next morning.

Theodore left his mount in the stable choosing instead to walk with Abraham. He carried his shotgun, a few provisions, and the gifts he brought for the chiefs. He soon realized, although Abraham was friendly towards him, he was disinclined to talk and so they walked most of the way in silence arriving on the reservation late in the morning.

"*Istonko*, Chief Micanopy."

The great chief greeted him openly. "*Istonko*, Theodore Whitmore."

He motioned Theodore toward the squareground to talk. Abraham followed. Some pleasantries were exchanged before Micanopy opened the conversation to Theodore's desired subject, relieving him of finding the right words to broach the topic. Abraham interpreted his words for Theodore.

"Agent Thompson tells us we must move to the other side of the big river now, not at the end of the Moultrie Creek treaty as we believe was promised. We have no desire to move. You were with us and have seen with your own eyes, the land is not good. Why should we leave these familiar forests and waters for strange prairies and cold weather? The graves of our ancestors are here. What is there for us? You saw the other tribes nearby. The Pawnee are not peaceful.

"And now Agent Thompson suggests we should put ourselves under the control of our enemy. We went to war with the White Sticks almost a century ago. We, of the Red Sticks, would be mistreated and our slaves would be claimed by them. If we gathered to remove, many of our Negroes might be taken by slaveholders demanding the return of their property. Even those who have been legally purchased, or those who are free, could be taken from us; men like Abraham who has been free since the last big war."

Feeling the need to respond in some way Theodore said, "I am sure Agent Thompson will abide by the terms of the treaty to protect your slaves."

"Agent Thompson called me a liar. He said I signed the treaty at Payne's Landing. That is not the treaty I signed. He speaks with forked tongue. We shall not move. This is our home."

Despite his resolve not to get involved, Theodore felt he must warn them. "You will not be allowed to stay. They will send men to force you to move."

"We can defeat their numbers."

Theodore added, "They will send many more."

Micanopy's chin was firm as he spoke and Abraham interpreted. "And we will fight them."

It was clear to Theodore the line had been drawn. War seemed inevitable.

Theodore visited several other villages but his reception was met with reserved politeness and restraint. He did notice the black and mixed women and children were not in the villages. After much probing and prodding, Abraham finally revealed they had gone into hiding in fear of imminent removal. Theodore couldn't imagine all the hardships they must be enduring to live in such constant fear.

He returned to the fort two days later and spent an afternoon writing a news article from his notes. Theodore stared at the last line praying he was wrong.

Forceful removal of the Florida Indians appears to be a foregone conclusion.

If only the white man could live in peace with the red man. He folded the papers and sealed it with wax then addressed it to his business partner. Robert Mason would print it in the *Key West Weekly* then forward a copy of the paper to Bob to reprint in the *New York Weekly*. It would also be sold for reprint to other interested papers around the Nation and the world.

Later, he visited the Indian agent. Thompson casually inquired as to the number of warriors Theodore had met with and what his general perception was of the village. The agent's questions previously seemed innocuous but this time his return was met with more direct questioning. Theodore realized they were taking advantage of him and information he could get that was hidden from them. Specifically, Thompson and Clinch were using him to gauge the enemy's numbers. It made Theodore feel as if he was spying on friends. He did his best to avoid their questioning altogether although he feared not answering at all could be considered treasonous.

* * *

The winter of 1834 to 1835 was the coldest anyone remembered in Florida. Families huddled around the fire in their uninsulated houses. Cattle suffered and died from exposure. Crops perished. It was hoped the starving Seminoles would have a change of heart, but rather than bring them to submission the added hardship served to stiffen their resistance.

Chapter 24

Fort King, January 1835

Survival was the order of the day as the bitter cold winter continued. The Florida army who generally suffered in the heat now appreciated their heavy wool uniforms. Civilians and volunteers wore every piece of clothing they possessed and some even walked around with their blankets as makeshift coats. Hot coffee was kept in constant supply.

Curious as to how the Indians were faring, Theodore made a solitary trip to Micanopy's village. He found the very old and the very young huddled around the large central fire. The others wore clothes to cover more skin but continued with their work as if impervious to the temperature; although he did notice they occasionally came to the fire to warm up. Theodore sat with Abraham and Micanopy for a spell talking about things in general. Of course the cold was mentioned. The great chief could not recall a colder winter. Theodore did not stay long. Their food supply was meager at best and so he made sure to leave before they asked him to share their meal.

Nothing lasts and eventually the cold retreated back to its northern roots. The balmy winter of central Florida was welcomed by smiles turned upward to absorb the warmth of the sun.

Many times Theodore would decide to return home to Betsy only to have his preparations halted by some news or rumor of interest to keep him in place. In three months there had only been two mail runs but in them he received dozens of letters from his darling wife while he managed to send her half that number. Mostly their missives contained daily events they would have shared over supper and often closed with something they missed about the other. The letters were bittersweet. He needed the contact with her and cherished every word she penned but they also made it harder for him to stay. Especially the one he now held in his hand.

Key West, December 25th, 1834

Dearest Theodore,

I sit here on the porch watching the colors of sunset bloom across the sky over my little shop and recall standing by your side watching the same on our wedding day, safe in your protective arms, feeling loved. I miss being held next to your heart.

Your aunt is doing well. She is as feisty as ever though she did take a tumble the other day. She missed her footing on the bottom step coming down the stairs one morning. I do believe her dignity suffered more greatly than her person. It took some doing but she finally consented to let Mrs. Mallory look her over. Fear not, love, other than some purple bruising she is fine.

Henry is doing exceptionally well in his studies at Rev. Bennett's new school. However, if not for meals, I would see precious little of him. When not at school or doing his studies he is usually running wild about the island looking to earn some coin at odd jobs or playing with friends. Abby tells me Emily, and sometimes Christoff, often tag along with him and as always he shows great patience with the younger children.

Rev. Bennett gave a wonderful sermon this morning on the meaning of Christmas. It is so nice to have regular Sunday services again. I hope he will stay for a long while.

We shared Christmas dinner with Max and Abby today. It was delicious as always. I sat and talked with Abby while she fed Hawthorne. She handed him to me to burp when she was called away to handle a domestic issue. He is a healthy growing five week old, but still he feels so tiny in my arms. I really enjoyed rocking him to sleep.

Did I tell you the family has taken to calling him 'Thorn' on account of that is how little Christoff says his name?

I hope your work is going well. Please keep safe, my love.

Yours always,

Betsafina

It was what she left unsaid in her letter that pulled at his heart. It was enough to have him packing his bags tonight if not for the news Agent Thompson shared with him earlier. He was calling another meeting.

Some of the Indians were starving. Expecting to be the first to move after returning from Fort Gibson, the Big Swamp village didn't plant crops and those villages that did plant reaped a poor harvest. They also lost cattle to the freezing winter. The desperate situation resulted in more pillaging from their white neighbors. Agent Thompson, in an effort to stop the brewing trouble, requested permission to distribute some of the food on hand.

Thompson received approval to bribe the Indians to another meeting with 800 bushels of corn. It also came with a letter from Secretary Cass accompanied by a letter from President Jackson to be read to the Indians.

Theodore and General Clinch were visiting with the agent earlier in the afternoon. Thompson handed the secretary's letter to the general.

Clinch read a portion aloud for Theodore. "Let them be reasoned with and if possible convinced. Let every measure short of actual force be first used. Let them be made fully aware of the consequences and then, if necessary, let actual force be employed, and their removal effected."[6] The general looked to his companions. "So the time has finally come. He includes detailed instructions for facilitating the move."

Thompson nodded. "It would seem the time is finally upon us. Were you aware Governor Eaton sent a letter to Secretary Cass questioning the validity of the treaty in one last attempt to avoid war?"

Clinch asked, "On what grounds?"

"The delay in ratification and the political influence on Congress by the land speculators seeking the Big Swamp area."

Theodore asked, "And how did the secretary respond?"

"The question was submitted to Attorney General Butler and he deemed the treaty valid."

Clinch's mouth thinned. "And so we move forward."

Agent Thompson nodded. "I have called the chiefs of Big Swamp for a meeting in March. I have also submitted my recommendation to move the tribe as a whole instead of in three groups as specified in the treaty. It has been approved."

Clinch nodded. "A wise decision."

Theodore wondered if they really believed it could be so easy.

* * *

Over the next thirty days noticeable preparations for moving the Indians were underway and obviously had been in the works for some months already. There could be no mistaking the government's intentions to begin removal. A disbursing agent arrived with enough funds to facilitate an expeditious move of the entire tribe as Thompson requested. General Clinch's forces were increased to seven hundred men in the likelihood force would become necessary. Transport waited at Tampa Bay to convey the estimated three thousand people to New Orleans and for the final stretch of the journey, Captain Jacob Brown had wagons ready to move them from the mouth of the Arkansas River to Ft. Gibson.

During this time, Theodore made one last visit to Micanopy's village. His reception was cordial but obviously unwelcome. He was met at the edge of the village and politely blocked from moving any closer. The activity he could see looked to be preparations for moving making him curious as to what they didn't want him to see. It was well known they had weapons and stockpiled powder. Were they preparing to resist? And if so, should he mention it to General Clinch? These people were defending their home, and in Theodore's humble opinion, they were in the right. But wasn't it considered treasonous not to report planned hostilities against his government? On the other hand what did he actually know for sure to report?

Theodore puzzled over his dilemma while he walked back to the fort and for a good part of the evening before coming to a decision. He was a journalist. It was his job to report facts and in the end, not having any facts, he decided to say nothing. Besides, Clinch and Thompson already knew the Seminoles meant to resist.

* * *

In March, only the most desperate of the Indians arrived as requested in the hopes of receiving food. This included several chiefs with over a hundred and fifty tribe members. Thompson was disappointed by the low turnout and discouraged that the most influential chiefs were missing. Still he pressed forward with his agenda. He read them the letter from President Jackson urging them to comply with the terms of the treaty or force would be used against them.

Jumper was nominated as spokesman for the group. He argued that such an important decision affecting the interest of all required more representation of the nation. He asked for thirty days to respond. Thompson argued against the delay but in the end he agreed to one more talk in the hopes he could get the tribes to leave peacefully. They would meet for another talk on April 22nd.

Theodore walked back to his bunk to write to Betsy, frustrated his return was delayed yet again. Now he would have to stay another month to wait for the outcome of this latest meeting with the Indians. He didn't want to think about what the results of April's assembly could mean for his return home. Their first anniversary was fast approaching. He would have to leave right after the next council to make it home in time to celebrate with Betsy. She mentioned it in several letters so he knew it was important to her therefore it was important to him.

Micanopy's Village, April 22, 1835

Before leaving for the meeting at Fort King, the old chief gathered his sub-chiefs and warriors around him for last minute instructions.

As the morning sun struck his face, the great chief spoke. "We must refrain from hostile action. Make Thompson believe we are willing to move but we must force him to specify a time distant enough to gather our crops and remove our families; when the season is far enough advanced to allow us to carefully plan our attack."

Micanopy was satisfied with the loud vocal agreement he received from his tribe. He turned and led his men to the designated meeting place with Agent Thompson.

* * *

A short distance from Fort King, Theodore stood behind Thompson's shoulder on one side of the open area designated as neutral ground for the talks. Great oaks draped in Spanish moss surrounded them standing guard like Mother Nature's sentinels. Clinch stood beside Thompson, waiting to greet their guests. Behind him soldiers lined up standing at attention with muskets in hand. Before him an empty field waited to be filled. The only sounds to be heard were the birds and the occasional shuffle of feet or weapon.

A few moments later faces materialized in the surrounding trees. Silently chiefs led their bands of warriors into the council area. Theodore was astounded by the sheer number rapidly filling the space before him with hardly a sound to be heard. He guessed there to be over four hundred in attendance.

Thompson was obviously pleased with the turnout. He leaned toward General Clinch and excitedly whispered, "I count fourteen chiefs—a strong representation of the Seminole nation."

The chiefs were seated on the ground in front with the sub-chiefs behind them and the warriors fanned out beyond the trees. General Clinch looked over the solemn faces of men he had come to know. Their strange dress, now familiar. The faces that once smiled in greeting now stared vacant. Not long ago, his orders were to protect these people. Now his orders were to remove them from all they held dear. Their understandable opposition was going to force him to assess them as enemies. "I count fourteen, as well."

General Clinch checked the soldiers behind him. He was pleased to see them standing at attention as requested. He ordered all the available men at the Fort to stand outside the council area, a hundred and thirty in all, to impress upon the Indians the seriousness of his intentions. He would prefer to have three times as many for he feared his meaning was lost in the number of faces on the other side of the table.

When all were finally settled in place, Theodore slipped off to the side of the gathering, the better to view all who participated. A table stood in the center between the two sides. General Thompson stepped forward to dispense with the opening business of the meeting and express his hopes the chiefs would act as honest men. He then asked Cudjo to translate a statement summarizing the treaty of Payne's Landing and Fort Gibson. Finally he opened the letter from President Jackson.

To the Chiefs and Warriors of the Seminole Indians in Florida.[7]

My Children: I am sorry to have heard that you have been listening to bad counsels. You know me, and you know that I would not deceive, nor advise you to do anything that was unjust or injurious. Open your ears and attend to what I shall now say to you. They are the words of a friend, and the words of truth.

The white people are settling around you. The game has disappeared from your country. Your people are poor and hungry. All this you have perceived for some time. And nearly three years ago, you made an agreement with your friend, Colonel Gadsden, acting on the part of the United States, by which you agreed to cede your lands in Florida, and to remove and join your brothers, the Creeks, in the country west of the Mississippi. You annexed a condition to this agreement, that certain chiefs, named therein, in whom you placed confidence, should proceed to the western country, and examine whether it was

286

suitable to your wants and habits; and whether the Creeks residing there were willing to permit you to unite with them as one people; and if the persons thus sent, were satisfied on these heads, then the agreement made with Colonel Gadsden was to be in full force.

In conformity with these provisions, the chiefs named by you, proceeded to that country, and having examined it, and having become satisfied respecting its character and the favourable disposition of the Creeks, they entered into an agreement with commissioners on the part of the United States, by which they signified their satisfaction on these subjects, and finally ratified the agreement made with Colonel Gadsden.

I now learn that you refuse to carry into effect the solemn promises thus made by you, and that you have stated to the officers of the United States, sent among you, that you will not remove to the western country.

My Children: I have never deceived, nor will I ever deceive, any of the red people. I tell you that you must go, and that you will go. Even if you had a right to stay, how could you live where you now are? You have sold all your country. You have not a piece as large as a blanket to sit down upon. What is to support yourselves, your women and children? The tract you have ceded will soon be surveyed and sold, and immediately afterwards will be occupied by a white population. You will soon be in a state of starvation. You will commit depredations upon the property of our citizens. You will be resisted, punished, perhaps killed. Now, is it not better peaceably to remove to a fine, fertile country, occupied by your own kindred, and where you can raise all the necessaries of life, and where game is yet abundant? The annuities payable to you, and the other stipulations made in your favour, will make your situation comfortable, and will enable you to increase and improve. If, therefore, you had a right to stay where you now are, still every true friend would advise you to remove. But you have no right to stay, and you must go. I am very desirous that you should go peaceably and voluntarily. You shall be comfortably taken care of and kindly treated on the road, and when you arrive in your new country, provisions will be issued to you for a year, so that you can have ample time to provide for your future support.

But lest some of your rash young men should forcibly oppose your arrangements for removal, I have ordered a large military force to be sent among you. I have directed the commanding officer, and likewise the agent, your friend, General Thompson, that every reasonable indulgence be held out to you. But I have also directed that one-third of your people, as provided for in the treaty, be removed during the present season. If you listen to the voice of friendship and truth, you will go quietly and voluntarily. But should you listen to the bad birds that are always flying about you, and refuse to remove, I have then directed the commanding officer to remove you by force. This will be done. I pray the Great Spirit, therefore, to incline you to do what is right.

Your Friend,
A. Jackson
Washington, February 16, 1835

Thompson folded the letter and looked over the sea of faces before him, "You have heard the words of the Great Father in Washington. The time has come to be resolute and honest. Now confer with each other. We will wait to hear the decision of the nation."

The chiefs looked to each other, most conveying their sentiment with nod or grunt to Micanopy who in turn nodded to Jumper. He rose and stepped forward to address Agent Thompson and General Clinch. He spoke eloquently objecting to the treaty and removal but out of friendship he was also averse to a hostile resistance should force be used to make them move. He was followed by Micanopy, Charley Amathla, Arpiucki, Coa Hajo, Holata Mico, Moke Is She Larni, and others saying more or less the same thing.

Theodore noticed the growing frustration of Thompson and especially General Clinch at the passing day with no answer, only more talk. Finally, General Clinch stepped forward. "Too much has been said and nothing has been done. Pledges have been solemnly made and now it is time to act. The question now is whether you will go of your own accord, or by force? You will return tomorrow all of one opinion on removal or force will be used to bring you to submission."

Theodore observed the varying reactions of the Indians as Clinch, Thompson and the officers left the assembly. It was a mixture of firm resolution and trepidation. The tribe was not in agreement.

The tribes who traveled some distance were camped outside the open area. When the council convened the following morning the sky was overcast and the smell of cooking fires hung in the misty morning air. It was some time before the sun's rays penetrated the cloud cover. The assembly gathered much the same as the day before with two notable exceptions. Black Dirt was now present having arrived after yesterday's meeting on account of illness. Thompson approached today's meeting with high hopes that this chief's firm support for removal would help sway the rest of the tribe to conform. They were soon diminished when he learned Micanopy, the highest ranking chief, was absent due to pain in the stomach. Thompson's disparaging remarks left little doubt of his lack of faith in the absent chief and his illness.

Theodore returned to his position up front and to the side of the group as Thompson stepped forward and asked the chiefs for the results of their deliberations.

Jumper and other leading chiefs repeated what they said yesterday; in essence giving no answer at all. Black Dirt then gave a long speech encouraging the tribes to act in their best interest and to abide by their agreement in signing the treaty. Despite being interrupted by those opposed to his words he bravely ignored them and continued speaking for removal.

When Black Dirt finished, General Thompson placed a new agreement on the table set in front of the chiefs. This document stated they acknowledged the validity of the Payne's Landing treaty and Fort Gibson treaty. He hinted at more annuities to help the starving tribes if they signed the contract. When none approached of their own accord he ordered them to come forward one by one starting with Black Dirt.

The chiefs consulted with each other. In support of Black Dirt, eight other chiefs came forward to sign. Four adamantly refused. Thompson asked

Jumper where Micanopy stood. Jumper tried to evade answering but was finally forced to reply Micanopy was firmly against removal.

Thompson let his temper get the better of him. He upbraided the dissenting chiefs for infidelity and total disregard for truth and honor. When they still dared to look at him in defiance, he declared, "Then you are no longer chiefs." To emphasize his meaning he took up the pen and made five slash marks across the paper as he said their names as if striking them out. "Jumper, Sam Jones, Alligator, Coa Hajo, Micanopy."

All were momentarily stunned, including Theodore. Thompson had no right to interfere with tribal affairs. It was an insult to the tribes and a gross overreach of his authority resulting in a retaliatory outburst from the chiefs. The council was in an uproar. Heated accusations flew too fast for the interpreters to keep up and they soon quit trying.

General Clinch stepped forward as the voice of reason to calm the fray. First, he ordered Thompson silent, then he turned to the Indians. He said not a word but with outstretched arms, palms pushing downward, he succeeded in calming tempers and they finally returned to their seated positions. He then appealed to the chiefs to use their good sense urging them to fulfill the treaty and at the same time quietly assuring them he was prepared to use his troops if necessary to gain their compliance.

The friendly chiefs held a private conference. The result was a request to postpone the move to allow them time to harvest their remaining crops. Thompson reluctantly agreed to delay the move until the first of January. The agreeable chiefs vowed to assemble at Fort Brooke at the appointed time. Attention was then turned to the four dissident chiefs. They made a small show of resistance before agreeing to the delay of movement. Having accomplished Chief Micanopy's objective, they stepped forward and signed Thompson's paper.

Their perceived betrayal was too much for one warrior. Osceola strode forward past the chiefs to the table. Eyes grew wide as he removed his hunting knife from its sheath. He lifted his arm over his head as all present collectively gasped unknowing of his intentions. He spoke to his tribe as much as he did the generals. "This is the only treaty I will make!" Down came his arm plunging the knife through the hated paper and deep into the table. "There remains nothing worth words. If the hail rattles, let the flowers be crushed—the stately oak of the forest will lift its head to the sky and the storm, towering and unscathed."[8] He then pulled his knife and walked away from the council. The warriors followed in his wake. One by one the chiefs turned to leave as well.

The ashen look of Thompson's complexion attested to his fear of harm though his relief quickly turned to impotent rage. Silently he stewed, merely tilting his head to acknowledge the friendly chiefs as they reaffirmed their intention to gather at Fort Brooke in January before following the rest out of the council area.

Agent Thompson returned to his office irritated and agitated, not even sure he really accomplished anything other than another delay. He would have to trust the chiefs who signed to sway Micanopy and Osceola and not the other way around. He should be preparing to ship Indians west so he could finally be free of Florida, not writing letters to inform all involved of yet another delay.

Feeling the need to vent his frustration, he penned a new order forbidding any further sale of arms, powder and lead. Not even to himself did he admit this was a vengeful retaliation. He justified it as necessary. He could not allow the Indians the possibility of further preparations for war.

Theodore knocked on the agent's open door frame to announce his presence. Thompson greeted him with distraction, waving him to a chair as he walked past him to the doorway and called to his assistant who appeared with haste, "See that this message reaches the sutlers and trading posts right away." He then returned to his desk. "What can I do for you, Mr. Whitmore?"

"I am set on leaving tomorrow."

"I don't blame you. It looks like things may be quiet here until the New Year. But if you care to wait another day or two the mail carrier is due in and you can return to Fort Brooke in his company."

Waiting to leave was the last thing he wanted to do. "I suppose it would be a wise decision."

* * *

Private Dalton arrived the following day as expected. Knowing his departure was imminent put a spring in Theodore's step. Later that afternoon he was making his farewells around camp when Osceola and his interpreter made an appearance. The warrior's rigid features and blazing eyes gave warning of pending trouble. Theodore discretely followed them to Agent Thompson's office.

Thompson stood to greet his guests but hardly started to speak when Osceola began voicing his complaint. He held aloft in his hand the crumpled notice forbidding the sale of arms. "Am I a negro? A slave? My skin is dark, but not black. I am an Indian—a Seminole." Osceola then slammed the paper down on Thompson's desk. "The white man shall not make me black. I will make the white man red with blood; and then blacken him in the sun and rain, where the wolf shall smell of his bones, and the buzzards live upon his flesh."[9]

Thompson tried to reason with the warrior. "Brother, you have no need of arms. You are under the protection of the Great Father in Washington."

Theodore thought Thompson's reasoning to be as faulty as his tactics. Apparently Osceola felt the same. He cited recent incidents in which the Seminoles were not protected as promised while Thompson's impotent rage boiled over and soon the two were in a shouting match. Theodore heard the warrior insult the agent on numerous occasions previous to this argument but this time he went too far.

Thompson called the attention of two nearby sentries. When they appeared in the doorway he pointed to the warrior. "Put this man in irons."

Osceola fought back pulling against them and forcing two more guards to lend assistance. Theodore and the interpreter could only stand by and watch as the warrior was restrained and dragged away to the guardhouse.

Theodore wondered if Thompson knew the full detriments of his action. No man likes restraints but to an Indian it was unthinkable. Incarceration did not exist in tribal culture and for a warrior like Osceola confinement would be the worst form of degradation. And this would make it the second time Thompson humiliated Osceola. A few weeks ago, he removed liquor from the warrior's possession. A ban was placed on the sale of alcohol not on the consumption, making the act unjustified as well as insulting. It was fully understandable to Theodore why the warrior would harbour such animosity towards the agent.

When the cell door was closed on him, Osceola let loose the full force of his fury, very much giving the impression of a caged wild animal. He tested every opening for escape while shouting and presumably cursing his captors until his energy was spent.

Thompson ordered a guard to stand watch at the cell door then spoke to his prisoner. "When you can promise to control your behavior I will let you out." He then turned smartly on booted heel to return to his office.

The interpreter walked cautiously towards the cell, his head hunched low. He glanced towards the guard as he approached the door but was not rebuffed. He spoke Muscogee in low tones to his fellow tribesman. An infuriated Osceola muttered a reply. The interpreter nodded and backed away from the cell.

Theodore asked, "What did he say?"

The interpreter hesitated but a slight nod and defiant look from Osceola made him answer. "That man shall suffer for this, but the time is not come."[10]

The guard and Theodore looked to each other, eyes wide in reaction. It was a personal threat against the agent and indicated possible plans of an attack were being made.

Osceola refused to say more so the interpreter left the fort to most likely consult with his chief.

Theodore walked away from the cell, crossing the compound in pursuit of Agent Thompson. He looked inside the open doorway to find the agent pacing behind his desk, his head bowed in thought. A light rap on the doorframe was enough to draw the agent's attention.

"Yes?"

Theodore entered the room. "As you know I planned to leave on the morrow."

"But now you are not sure."

"It would depend on you sir."

Thompson stopped his pacing to look at Theodore. "How so?"

"If I may be so bold as to ask, what are your intentions with the warrior?"

"Hold him a few days, I suppose, until his temper cools."

Theodore waited for him to say more.

Thompson resumed pacing, his body tensing more with each step. "His behavior will no longer be tolerated. If I am to maintain any authority with these Indians, especially the chiefs, then I must stand firm with this warrior."

Theodore acknowledged his words with a single nod. He quietly said, "You should know he threatened you."

Thompson's pace halted abruptly and his eyes drilled Theodore for more information.

"He said you would suffer, but the time has not come."

"He did, did he? Well, we shall see whose time has come. You mark my words, come January, he and his tribe will be rounded up, loaded aboard ship, and sailing into the sunset. No more delays. I will not let them talk me into another delay."

"You are not concerned they may attack this very fort rather than submit to transport?"

His chest puffed up. "Just let them try."

Theodore left the agent's office more uncomfortable then when he entered. Thompson very likely may have sparked the war they were all desperate to avoid. There was no help for it now. He was going to have to stay a little longer to see how this turn of events played out. He sought out Private Kinsley Dalton to advise him of the change in plans. Kinsley was sorry to lose the company. Theodore hoped the situation would be resolved before the mail carrier returned. The window of time to reach Key West by May 9th was closing. He penned a letter of explanation and apology to Betsy, pressing it into Kinsley's hand the following morning as he set out south. Theodore felt like he was being left behind as his heart so desperately wanted to leave with the mail carrier.

A few hours later, two chiefs arrived to speak with the imprisoned warrior. It appeared from Theodore's observations that Osceola rebuffed them for they did not stay long and left disappointed. The warrior spent the rest of the day in deep contemplation ignoring his food and all who approached his cell. The following day brought a surprising change.

Jumper and the two chiefs from yesterday approached Osceola while a black interpreter hung back waiting to be needed. Theodore approached this man hoping to gain more insight. After exchanging greetings, he asked, "What are they saying to Osceola?"

"They encourage him to make peace. It does no one good for him to be locked up."

"Do you think he will listen?"

"The message comes from Micanopy. He respects his chief so he will do as he asks."

The two men fell into silence as they observed the others conversing. Osceola seemed to argue with them for a time before finally capitulating. Jumper motioned the interpreter to his side. He was then sent to Thompson's office. Theodore waited where he was sure the interpreter would bring Thompson to Osceola.

A few minutes later the two men approached the cell and Theodore moved closer to hear what was said. Osceola spoke firmly and appeared contrite. He promised to agree to move west in January and as a show of friendship, if released, he would return in five days with seventy of his warriors. Thompson was overjoyed and easily accepted Osceola's change of heart. He signaled the guards to release the warrior.

Osceola stepped from the cell with dignity. He responded to Thompson with overtures of friendship giving the agent high hopes that the warrior would keep his promise as they watched the group leave the confines of the fort.

Five days they waited and wondered. Five days of hopeful expectations tempered with realistic contemplations of what should be done if the warrior did not remain true to his word. Everyone shied away from considering the results any retaliatory action would invoke. Five days ensured no possibility of Theodore making it home in time for his anniversary. Five long days everyone in the fort waited in trepidation.

The afternoon of the fifth day following the tustenuggee's release, great relief rapidly spread to every corner of the fort. All came out to witness the arrival of Osceola with his promised band of warriors. Agent Thompson could barely contain his giddiness. General Clinch stood stoically beside Theodore who could only imagine how grateful the general must be not to have to take military action. They counted seventy-nine warriors in attendance. True to his word, Osceola signed the Fort King agreement. He and his warriors agreed to gather at Fort Brooke in January with the rest of the tribes. To further show his friendship Osceola invited the agent to visit his village known as Powell town.

Osceola's capitulation freed Theodore to leave for home, but first he couldn't resist the chance to visit Powell Town having been turned away previously when he tried to visit on his own.

Thompson, Clinch, Theodore and some of the officers and soldiers followed Osceola to his home. His people poured forth from the circle of cabins and chickadees to greet the warrior like a returning hero. They were made welcome with food and drink served around the large fire in the square-ground at the center of the village.

As soon as they were seated on logs a little girl came running from behind her mother's skirt wearing a frock of Anglo origins. She ran straight towards one of the officers. Theodore watched with open curiosity as Lieutenant John Graham spread his arms to greet her. Later he asked Graham about the child and learned she was Osceola's daughter. Theodore knew Graham and the warrior were good friends so it came as no surprise the officer had gifted the dress to the child.

Agent Thompson made a show of presenting Osceola with a silver-plated Spanish rifle as a gift for his renewed friendship. Theodore thought it was an ironic choice considering it was Thompson's order to forbid the sale of firearms to the Indians which started this whole incident and there was still a possibility he could be giving a future enemy a weapon far superior to the muskets issued to the army. Definitely not a gift Theodore would have chosen in his place.

After the meal they were led to an open field with a tall pole in the center made from a tree trunk. Theodore was thrilled to realize he was about to witness something he had often heard about—the Seminole ball game. The players, mostly older children, took to the field with some adults including Osceola. The boys used sticks with woven catches on the end while the girls were allowed to use their hands. A ball was played from one side to the other keeping the pole between them. A team scored when their ball hit the pole. It was a lively game and played quite seriously. More than one player received minor injuries which seemed to be expected. Osceola proved to be a very agile and formidable opponent, quite skilled in the intricacies of the game. His team won and the victorious warrior approached his guests in jovial spirits. It was the first time Theodore witnessed such emotion from him. He could well imagine after two days of incarceration the freedom of the game must have felt invigorating.

Shortly after, their group bid their hosts farewell so they could reach the fort before darkness fell. Clinch, Thompson and Theodore rode their horses while the rest of the party traversed the miles on foot. As they were preparing to leave, Theodore overheard Thompson say to Clinch, "I have no doubt of his sincerity."

Theodore was not as sure of the warrior's feelings. His actions of today appeared sincere in every way, but obeying Chief Micanopy and keeping his family safe could be reason enough to maintain friendly terms with the military. His words of three days ago rang in Theodore's mind; *That man shall suffer for this, but the time is not come.'* Theodore may not be as well acquainted with Osceola as the Generals but he was sure the warrior was not as forgiving as he appeared. He had not betrayed even a hint of anything unfriendly by word or look today. Theodore had nothing to base his opinion on; still he was sure they had not beheld Osceola's true self. Thompson did not listen to his warning before; he would scarcely believe him now. So Theodore decided he would mention his concerns to General Clinch and leave with a clear conscience.

Peace existed for the moment so Theodore had every intention of leaving in the morning. He would likely pass Private Dalton on the road between the forts but Theodore would rather take the risks of traveling alone rather than wait two days for the mail carrier to arrive and depart again. He intended to leave this place before anything else could possibly detain him.

May 5th, 1835

At the break of dawn, Theodore climbed into the saddle and turned his horse toward the gate of the palisades. Finally he was headed home to his family. He nodded to those he passed but didn't stop to converse with any. He was determined to make his way outside the fort. It was four days till their anniversary and it would take two just to reach Fort Brooke. Now that he was finally on his way, Theodore was anxious to travel quickly. Nudging his mount into a gallop he soon left the fort behind entering the shady tree covered road that would lead him to Fort Brooke.

As horse and rider traveled the easy pine needle strewn path leading away from Fort King, Theodore let his mind wander ahead to seeing Betsy again. He hoped she wouldn't be too disappointed with him for being late. He never actually said the words but he felt as if he had broken a promise to her. If she felt the same, he would be begging for her forgiveness before they could celebrate his homecoming. He hoped it would be the last time he disappointed her.

Theodore covered a good distance the first day. It felt like half way to him. He bedded down for the night laying his oilcloth on the smoky side of the fire to help ward off the blood-sucking mosquitoes. There was nothing to be done for the ants and other crawling insects intent on joining him in his slumber. Sometime during the night, he woke up, unsure of the sound he heard. He listened for a spell before drifting back to sleep only to be awoken again a short time later. Knowing he was on his own made him more uncomfortable than he was willing to admit and he found it impossible to return to his rest.

At first light he broke camp, eager to be on his way. It wasn't a mile later he met up with Private Dalton who had just left his camp. They laughed to have missed each other's company by so short a distance. Neither lingered long over conversation but wished each other well and moved on. Theodore rode on past dark to reach Fort Brooke. He left his weary mount in the good hands of the stable boy tipping him extra for the late hour. He wearily stumbled into the nearest tavern with his saddlebags to get a hot meal and something to drink besides stale water. He silently toasted to being done with the first leg of his journey and to the post commander for allowing him once again to sleep in the bunkhouse.

Now the hardest part was waiting for transport from Fort Brooke to Key West. The next day brought disappointment. He couldn't find a ship headed south. Theodore absently rubbed his beard contemplating how to find transport. He already exhausted all the usual means. He growled under his breath in frustration. The only idea he had left was to try asking around the docks again. On his way outside the fort, he caught sight of his reflection in a window. He hardly recognized the hairy stranger. He couldn't return to Betsy looking like a reclusive backwoodsman. He continued outside the fort but instead of heading to the docks, he headed to the barber.

An hour later he rubbed the smooth sharp angles of his jaw while his damp hair, now several inches shorter, clung to the nape of his neck. His head felt lighter and he was in a better mood. While waiting his turn at the barber's he struck up a conversation with a fellow patron who knew of a captain who might be willing to sail to Key West.

Finally, a few hours later, he came to an agreement with Captain James who charged him twice the usual fee but Theodore willingly, nay, cheerfully paid it, to be sailing home tomorrow morning.

They sailed for two days making little headway against a strong current when the ship was unexpectedly becalmed. Theodore paced the deck trying to contain his frustration towards Mother Nature as he watched them drift backwards in the current despite the anchor. Having lost another twelve hours the wind finally freshened in the wee hours of the morning.

Standing at the balustrade, watching the ships bow cut a path through the current, Theodore began to think of the situation he left behind. The months between now and January would be tense between the white and red man as the time for removal drew near. Theodore knew he was likely to miss an important event or two but he needed to return home, even if it was only for a few months. He could return a month or so before the January deadline. He, like every other citizen of the territory, prayed it would be a peaceful process. As for the Indians, they surely longed for a way to be left in peace.

He put aside the depressing thoughts and looked south to his destination. In just a few more days he would be reunited with his family. He was especially looking forward to time alone with his wife.

Chapter 25

May 9th, 1835

Betsy stared at the letter in her hand, not really seeing it. She didn't need to; she knew every word it contained having read it dozens of times. It was the last letter she received from Theodore, dated the twelfth of April, from Fort King. He told her he was impatiently waiting for the next council meeting set for the end of April and how he couldn't wait to be headed home immediately afterwards. Betsy couldn't wait either. If nothing delayed his plans again he could be here any day now. But as she knew from the previous months, all too often something happened to keep him. She dared not get her hopes up too high but she couldn't help wanting him to be here to celebrate their first anniversary together.

Throughout the day, she stopped every time she passed a window facing west to look for him and she must have purposely passed those windows at least a dozen times but all for naught. She stood there now, staring across the harbour, hoping he would be on one of those ships. She looked to the sky noting the sun was already well past its zenith. The day was dwindling.

When he left she hadn't expected him to be gone so long, perhaps two or three months. Certainly not six months. She also thought having been on her own for almost a decade she wouldn't have any trouble handling his absence. But she was wrong about that too. It was amazing how quickly she adapted to having a husband. Today marked the first year of their marriage and only the first six months were spent together. In that time she had come to treasure his companionship, talking before they fell asleep, snuggling, and the hundreds of little ways he had of touching her heart. She had no idea there would be days she missed him so much, it was a physical ache. A different ache than when Ben died. The sorrow of losing Ben left a hollow emptiness, this pain was feverish and needy, and likely more intense for knowing there was an end to it.

Hours later it was a quiet trio around the supper table. She had the cook make a celebratory dinner in the hopes Theodore would arrive today. Now she wished she hadn't made the request as she, Agatha and Henry tried not to waste good food even though none of them felt much like eating.

Betsy tried to smile brightly for Henry. "Perhaps he will be here tomorrow. Any number of things could have delayed his return." Henry said nothing as he continued pushing food around on his plate. Agatha gave her a sympathetic smile. Betsy conceded. "Henry, you may be excused if you like." The boy fled the room without a word or glance in her direction.

Three more long vigilant days passed. Betsy tried not to let worry get the better of her. She wished she had another letter to be sure he had been delayed in leaving again. It would make it easier to not think of all the ways he could come to harm traveling back home.

Staring out her bedroom window for perhaps the hundredth time that week Betsy was so focused on the ships it was some minutes before she noticed the figure walking towards the house from Front Street. It was too far away to be sure. She held on tight to her hope lest she was wrong. As the figure moved closer, she could tell it was a man—trousers rather than a skirt. Hope began to float like a hot air balloon she once saw taking off at a fair. He looked to be carrying a carpetbag. Only a traveler needed a carpetbag and a stranger would have turned toward the boardinghouse rather than continue on Whitehead Street. Hope floated a little higher. He was too far away yet to see his features but she was sure now by the way he moved. Hope sailed skyward in abandoned flight.

It was Theodore!

She could hardly believe it was finally really him. Giddy schoolgirl excitement rushed through her. She spun away from the window, flew down the stairs in reckless abandon, and kept running down the street, caring naught for watching eyes. She didn't stop but ran straight into his arms.

Theodore dropped his bags and ran to meet her part way. He caught her up and swung her around and around in lieu of kissing her senseless as he desperately wished to do. He couldn't recall ever seeing a prettier woman than his wife. "Happy anniversary darling."

Betsy nodded, her throat too thick with tears to speak.

Henry came out the door and walked towards them. Theodore put Betsy down. Not wanting to let him go, Betsy moved to his side wrapping both her arms around his left bicep. Theodore held his hand out to his son. Dignity kept them from hugging in public. Henry shook his hand like a proper gentleman. Theodore, still wanting to show his affection, ruffled Henry's hair. The nine year old pulled his head back and gave his father an offended look, objecting to the childish treatment. Betsy hid the quirk of her lips by turning her face into Theodore's shoulder, not wanting to further insult the boy's dignity.

Theodore was amazed how much Henry had grown in the last six months, at least several inches. "Son, would you mind retrieving my bags? I seem to have lost the use of one of my arms." He smiled down at Betsy and placed his free hand on one of hers to reassure her he didn't mind in the least.

"Yes sir." Henry jaunted to the bags, picked them up, and trailed behind his clinging parents.

Agatha waited for them on the porch. Betsy reluctantly released Theodore to greet her.

"Hello, Aunt Agatha."

Gruffly, she replied, "Missed you boy."

It was the deepest emotion Betsy had ever seen Aunt Agatha display. It made her own eyes mist over again and her smile tighten.

The family visited in the parlor while the cook prepared dinner. They spoke of all Theodore missed while he was gone and he shared some of what he saw while away.

Betsy asked, "How did the meeting go with the Seminoles?"

"As expected for the most part. It was an impressive group with the chiefs and warriors in their formal dress." He looked at Henry. "Did I tell you Seminole men where skirts?"

Henry wrinkled his nose. "Skirts are for girls."

"It seemed strange to me too the first time I saw them but then I remembered reading that Scotsmen wear a short skirt called a kilt. Seminole chiefs and warriors wear skirts down to their knees with leggings wrapped around their calves. They also wear a headdress something like a turban decorated with feathers."

Henry sneered. "More girl clothes."

Theodore smiled. "I assure you they did not look like girls; especially not four hundred of them."

Betsy's jaw dropped. "Four hundred?"

Theodore nodded. "It was a very impressive turnout. Unfortunately, the meeting did not go as General Clinch and General Thompson planned."

Betsy grimaced. "So the Indians are resisting the move. Does that mean war will start soon?"

Theodore gently squeezed her hand. "No. For now, they have still agreed to move, at least some of them have, but not until January, after they harvest their crops."

Betsy's brows drew together. "Some of them agreed. What of the others?"

"I believe for now they will wait till January to resist, unless Osceola has a say in it. He raised his knife and stabbed the signed agreement, swearing he would fight rather than capitulate."

Henry looked at Theodore with brows drawn. "Why did he do that? I thought they agreed to the treaty. They signed it."

"Not all of them signed it and those who signed the Fort Gibson treaty did not have authority to speak for the nation. Osceola and some of the chiefs believe the first treaty is still good, and they have at least eight more years."

Henry's frown deepened in confusion. "But even if they wait, they will still have to move. Why should he be so angry over a few years?"

Betsy nodded. "Yes, why indeed?"

They all looked to Theodore waiting for the answer.

"Principal, for one, I suppose, and they probably hope in time we will go away and leave them in peace."

Henry said with youthful confidence. "But we won't go away."

Theodore replied with somber resignation. "No, son, we won't."

Henry asked "Did we buy their land with the treaty?"

"We traded their land here for land out west, and we have given them money for food. We will give them money to move and more food when they reach the new reservation until they can harvest their first crops."

Henry thought it sounded like a fair trade. "Then why is Mr. Osceola upset?"

"Why indeed?" Theodore considered how best to make Henry understand. "What if I decided to sell something of yours?" Theodore nodded to himself, thinking he had a good analogy. "Suppose I made a bargain to trade something of yours for something the family needed. I didn't ask you first because I made the decision as head of the family and for what was best for the household. But you really cherish this item and you believe I should have asked first. How would you feel?"

Henry's mouth puckered. "Angry."

Theodore nodded. "And?"

"Hurt."

"And betrayed?"

Henry nodded. "Yes."

"Now does Osceola's anger make sense?"

He nodded again.

The cook stuck her head in the doorway. "Are you ready for your meal?"

Theodore smiled. "Absolutely. You have no idea how I have longed for one of your good meals."

There was not enough time to prepare anything elaborate but the simple fare was served on the good china with fine linen and candlelight even though it was not yet dark. Theodore stood to make a toast to his wife. "To our first year of marriage; may we be blessed with many more. Cheers."

"Cheers," echoed Betsy and Agatha.

The meal was enjoyed with relish and conversation. Theodore could not recall ever having a better one. It was amazing he even saw what he was eating. He couldn't keep his eyes off Betsy. After dinner, when they adjourned to the parlor, he would have sworn the clock was ticking slower the more he urged it onward. His heated gaze kept colliding with Betsy's sultry one. Guess he didn't need to worry about apologizing first.

When Agatha had to ask a question for the third time before she got her nephew's attention, she lost her patience with them. "Oh for heaven's sake! Why don't you two call it a night? Off you go now. Henry and I can entertain ourselves."

Betsy and Theodore looked at each other, grinned, and raced for the door as fast as decorum would allow. As they fled the room they heard Henry ask, "Why are they going upstairs so early?" Neither really cared how Aunt Agatha chose to answer him.

Theodore barely shut the bedroom door behind them before he proceeded to show Betsy just how much he missed her. She welcomed him home as only a wife could, before they even reached the bed.

* * *

Henry found his father in his study the following morning. "Poppa, can we go for a sail? I want to show you how well I can swim now."

Theodore was reading one of the letters in his accumulated mail when Henry interrupted him. Distracted he answered, "Perhaps tomorrow, son."

Betsy overheard from the hallway. Theodore looked up when she breezed into the room, a bright smile on her face. "Perhaps today is a good day to spend time with your son. After all, he has waited patiently many months for your return."

"But I have so much here I need to attend to and I really need to finish the story for the paper while it is fresh."

Betsy moved behind him and placed her hands on his shoulders. She leaned down to speak quietly in his ear. "I understand you feel obligated to your work, but you must ask yourself in this moment, which is more important, the dry paper on your desk or your flesh and blood standing before you asking you to spend a little time with him."

Theodore's gaze met the wistful blue eyes of his son while his wife's whispered words chased across his soul rearranging his priorities.

"Have you noticed how much he has grown? Do you realize he is halfway through his childhood? Don't take these moments for granted. They are precious."

He cast his eyes to her and lightly said, "Alright, you have made your point."

Betsy stepped back to allow Theodore to get up from his chair. He walked around the desk to look down at Henry. "Let's go for a sail. Do you mind if your mother comes along?"

Betsy didn't want to intrude on Henry's time with his father. "I have other things to do. You two should go without me."

Theodore knew why she demurred and wondered if he was reluctant to be alone with his son or was it reluctance to be away from his wife that prompted him to include her. Likely it was both reasons.

Hours later, Theodore and Henry returned to the house with windblown hair, reddened cheeks, a bucketful of crab and conch, and jovial spirits. Theodore had to admit it was time well spent with Henry.

After supper, Theodore excused himself from the family to return to his desk. He read and sorted all the mail then pulled out his notes from the last few weeks at Fort King. He reread them all, added a few more, then sat back to think about how he wanted to convey the events to his readers.

Even now with some distance to the situation, he remained convinced Osceola's capitulation was incongruent with his capture. A leopard doesn't change his spots. The warrior was putting up a good cooperative front but Theodore was sure he was planning resistance. The question was when and how it would play out.

Noting the late hour, Theodore pushed away from the desk. He could write tomorrow. Tonight he was more interested in tucking his wife into bed.

* * *

Sunday they walked as a family to the Custom House for services.

Betsy said, "I haven't had a chance to tell you; Reverend Bennett left us last month. We are without clergy again."

"And what has become of the school and Henry's studies?"

"Judge Webb's son-in-law, Mr. Alden Jackson, has taken over the school. He seems to be competent."

Theodore turned to Henry walking behind him with Aunt Agatha. "Do you get on well with Mr. Jackson?"

"Well enough, I suppose."

Theodore gave Betsy a questioning look.

"His studies are progressing fine."

Theodore nodded. Content for now, he would make a point of quizzing Henry later to check his progress.

Service was attended and afterwards in the yard, Theodore was surrounded by friends and acquaintances welcoming him home and asking a myriad of questions showing their concerns for possible Indian attacks on the Island. He did his best to allay their fears.

Betsy was finally forced to rescue him. "Come Theodore, we mustn't keep your aunt waiting for her meal."

Many were aware of Mrs. Pary's temperament and easily allowed Betsy to pull Theodore away.

He leaned close to whisper, "Thank you." His breath sent a delicious shiver across her skin.

* * *

After dinner, the family gathered in the parlor. Agatha was knitting in her favourite Queen Anne chair. Henry sat on the floor studying. Betsy was embroidering. Her shoulder occasionally brushed Theodore's as they shared the settee. He was catching up on back issues of his paper published by Robert Mason in his absence.

Theodore suddenly dropped the paper to his lap and turned to Betsy. "I just had the most wonderful idea."

Betsy lifted her head from her work, eyes wide with curiosity.

"I think it's time I met your family."

Her brows furrowed. "How do you propose to do that? Do you want to write them a letter?"

He shook his head. "I mean in person."

Betsy frowned. "I can't ask them to visit. They don't have the money."

"I was thinking we would visit them."

Betsy gasped while Henry and Agatha both looked to Theodore in surprise.

"We could call it a delayed honeymoon."

Betsy was touched but concerned. "Really? But you have just returned home. You would want to travel again, so soon?"

He grinned. "It would be a different kind of travel and most important, we would be together."

Betsy let the idea sink in and as she thought about it her frown melted into a smile. "I would love to see my family again. I have nieces and nephews I have never met." She looked to Theodore. "My mother will love you."

Theodore suddenly had misgivings. He forgot she came from a large family. Meeting so many of her relatives all at once would be intimidating and what if they didn't like him... trepidation colored his voice. "And your father?"

"He will too—once he sees how much I love you. It's my older brother you should worry about. He and Ben were best friends. He took his death very hard."

Theodore did not feel reassured but the die was cast. He would cut off his right arm before he would remove the excited glow from Betsy's eyes. "Going now would be best and we could stay until fall."

A shadow grew in Betsy's eyes.

"What are you thinking, dear?"

She never really asked him about money before and wasn't sure how he would react to her questioning it now. "This trip will be awfully expensive. Are you sure we can afford it?" She drew her bottom lip in, waiting for his reply.

Theodore smiled. "I have income from the paper here and more from the articles sent to Bob, and earnings from my inheritance. You needn't worry about funds. We cannot be frivolous but neither must we be frugal."

Betsy's lips relaxed into a closed smile. "I'm not sure I know how not to be frugal." She leaned over and kissed his cheek. "I will write my parents immediately. The mail leaves the island tomorrow." She left the room to get her writing desk.

Theodore turned to his aunt. "You have been quiet."

Aunt Agatha lifted her eyes from her work to look at her nephew. "There was no need to speak. I will not be joining you on this trip. I have seen Philadelphia, and I have no desire to wear myself out making the journey or meeting all those people. I will be content to stay right here and wait for your return."

"As you wish."

Agatha bowed her head over her sewing to hide her secret smile.

Chapter 26

For the next two months they focused on plans for their upcoming trip. Betsy worked on sewing travel clothes for all of them. Letters were sent, received and answered with her family settling the details of travel arrangements and when they would arrive.

Theodore was hard pressed to say who was more excited—mother or daughter. The letter they received from Betsy's mother in reply to their announcement was three times its normal length; full of her ideas and plans for their upcoming visit including an elaborate party to bring the whole family together and as many of Betsy's old friends as she could find. She also dropped a not so subtle hint that they should consider moving to Pennsylvania. Betsy lightly brushed the suggestion aside but the idea clung to Theodore. He wondered; if she was free to make the choice, would Betsy want to return to the bosom of her family? He decided to observe her during this visit and if there was any indication she would be happier living there, Theodore would give her the choice. Above all, he wanted to make his wife happy.

One afternoon, a week before they were to leave, Theodore and Betsy had a rare moment alone in the house. Henry was spending the afternoon with the Eatonton children and Aunt Agatha was having tea with a friend. Theodore looked over the top of the paper he was reading to watch Betsy diligently working to finish a new dress for their trip. He knew if she could she would have made a whole new wardrobe for each of them but limited time and having to complete her business orders first prevented it. So far she had finished a new suit and light coat for Henry, smallclothes for he and his son, new undergarments for her and a cape for cooler evenings, and now she was working on a dress.

He noticed the tension in her shoulders as she bent over her work. They must surely ache but he knew she wouldn't stop until she ran out of daylight. He rose from his chair to walk behind her and lay his hands on her shoulders. He rubbed his thumbs down the sides of her neck and across her back feeling the expected tightness. Betsy moaned her pleasure so he repeated the movement. She put down her sewing and leaned her head forward to enjoy the caress.

Theodore continued his ministrations while he sought her relief for something that was bothering him. "It feels wrong to leave Aunt Agatha behind. Are you sure she will be fine?"

"Yes. She's perfectly capable of taking care of herself. Besides, the maid and the cook will be here daily."

"But they are only here for a few hours each day? She had live-in help in New York. What if she gets lonely or worse, something happens to her?"

"Abby promised to check on her but I have a feeling she will not be entirely alone."

His brows drew together. "What do you mean?" Then it occurred to him. "Oh yes, tea with friends, I suppose."

Betsy hid her smile. "A certain friend, I'm sure."

Theodore could hear the smile in her reply. He dropped his hands and walked around the chair to see her face.

Betsy decided it was time she enlightened him. "She and a certain sea captain have been secretly visiting each other." She thought he might have had some clue as to what was going on but judging by his widened eyes and slack jaw her news came as a complete surprise.

"Who?"

"I do not have proof, but I believe it is Abby's father, Captain Bennington. I think your aunt is looking forward to having the house to herself."

Theodore's look of horror made Betsy laugh.

He frowned. "This is serious!"

She put her sewing aside to stand up and place her hand along the bearded edge of his cheek. "No it isn't."

Theodore's eyes narrowed. "What are his intentions?"

"I don't know. Perhaps they are merely enjoying each other's company. I asked your aunt once if she ever considered getting married again. I believe her exact words were, 'I'm too old to tolerate being a wife.' When I recently tried confronting her about Captain Bennington, I was told to mind my own business. I voiced my disapproval for the sake of her soul, but ultimately it is her sin to commit."

Theodore nodded sagely. It sounded just like his aunt. She may appear all prim and proper to the world, but her actions had always been her own. "What if they are discovered?"

Betsy stepped forward to wrap her arms around his waist. His arms naturally completed the embrace. She leaned back to see his face. "I suppose it will depend on who discovers them. The gossips could turn it into an ugly situation but aren't they old enough to worry about their own consequences?"

His lips compressed. "Hmm."

Reluctant agreement. She echoed his, "Hmm," and received a crooked grin and an escaped grunt of laughter in response.

"You're teasing me again."

She looked up into the hazel eyes of her beloved. "Yes, I am."

He squeezed her lightly in response, then his eyes lit up. "I have an idea, Mrs. Whitmore."

"What might that be, Mr. Whitmore?" The impish look on his face told her she was going to enjoy his suggestion.

"Why don't we take a private sail to our secluded little cove?"

Betsy grinned while her stomach churned. She hadn't felt like herself since sometime yesterday, but she wasn't about to let it keep her from a rendezvous with her husband. Besides, the cooling wind on the water might help. She probably just ate something disagreeable. It would pass. Meanwhile, she was going to enjoy the unexpected outing with Theodore. "A wonderful idea."

They didn't bother with swim costumes, only drinking water, bread and dried meat before hurrying to the little boat, hand in hand, like young lovers. They launched the boat together and as it rocked in the calm water before Theodore hoisted the sail, Betsy felt the slight queasiness grow stronger. She valiantly tried to ignore it but each moment grew more difficult. They were sailing smoothly and still the weakness grew until Theodore's chance glance and subsequent move to reach her rocked the boat in such a way she was forced to lean over the side and retch. Her hat fell into the waves. She didn't care.

Theodore placed a hand on her back. "Darling, what is it?" Spying her hat, he returned to the tiller intending to steer the boat towards it.

Another spasm hit her. "Leave it." Her voice was weaker than she expected. Betsy looked to Theodore and tried again. "Leave it. Get me to land."

Theodore heard her first words but not the rest. The pallor of her skin was enough to convince him to turn the boat around. She heaved again and he debated heading for the closest point of land. Carrying her home wasn't likely a good idea for either of them, so he headed the boat for their beach wishing all the while he could make it go faster.

Betsy closed her eyes in relief but quickly opened them again as it made her feel worse. She had never experienced seasickness before and vowed to be more sympathetic the next time she encountered a victim. Looking up, she watched the passing shoreline. Land. If she could just reach land maybe her stomach would settle down. Another spasm hit her. She wiped her mouth and gave Theodore a beseeching look to go faster.

All of Theodore's attention was focused on getting his wife back to their beach. He felt so inadequate watching her back arch as she heaved and he was unable to comfort her.

Land! As soon as the bow scraped against the shore, Betsy scrambled over the side uncaring of how undignified she might look or of the salt water staining the hem of her dress. She splashed ashore before the weakness brought her to her knees. Solid ground did not help as much as she hoped.

"Betsy, wait there. I'll help you to the house as soon as the boat is secure."

She had too little strength to do otherwise.

Theodore was soon there to help her stand. His arm circled her waist in support. She leaned so heavily on him he decided it best to carry her. He scooped her up in his arms. His strides quickly covering the distance to the back door of her former house now used solely as her workshop. The bedroom was converted to storage so he continued to the parlor placing her gently on the divan. He retrieved the water pitcher and basin, a cup, and a rag. He wiped her face and neck before pouring a glass of water. He noticed

306

a slight tremor in her hand as she accepted it. "What happened?"

"I don't know. I wasn't feeling well before we left but I didn't think I was this sick."

"Should I get the doctor? Perhaps you would prefer Abby or Mrs. Mallory?"

She shook her head. "It seems to be passing. Just take me home, please."

He helped her to stand and kept his arm around her for support as they crossed the street and climbed the steps of their house. As soon as they reached their room, Betsy collapsed on the bed, the little energy she had was long spent. She was asleep before Theodore reached the door.

When she awoke, she felt only marginally better. Theodore refused to let her get out of bed, except to relieve herself. He served her evening meal in bed and even held the bowl while she spooned the nourishing beef broth. After her meal, it was late enough, they turned in for the night.

A few hours later, Betsy woke from a nightmare, soaked in perspiration and her stomach recoiling from the imagined motion of the boat. She barely found the chamber pot before she hurled the contents of her supper. Theodore was instantly awake at the sound to light a candle and fetch a wet cloth. She wiped her face and he rinsed the cloth. Returning to kneel on the bed behind her, he lifted her hair and placed the cool cloth against her neck. After a moment, she took it from him and laid back down, placing it on her forehead.

Betsy could tell Theodore's worry was increasing and she sought to reassure him, "I'm sure it returned because I was dreaming we were still on the water. I will be right as rain tomorrow. You'll see. And if not, I'm sure Abby will have a remedy."

Theodore prayed she was right. His first concern was yellow fever and several times he checked her forehead. Her skin was clammy but cool to the touch. He was relieved to discard that worry.

They settled back into bed. Betsy turned on her side facing away from him. Theodore pulled her close and began running his flattened palm from her brow to her crown hoping to soothe her back to sleep.

Betsy felt the tension leave her body with his caress and soon slept.

The next morning Betsy awoke sure today she would feel better. She placed her feet on the floor and stood up only to sit back down from lightheadedness.

The movement woke Theodore. "Betsy?"

She fought to control the nausea. "I'm fine."

Instantly he was sitting behind her for support. His responding, "Hmm," close to her ear, conveyed skepticism and something else. She turned her head, squinting at him, one eyebrow lifted, not sure what he meant this time. It sounded like more than just disagreeing with her.

Another wave of sickness sent her reaching for the chamber pot to give in to her body's demand to purge. She forgot all about questioning what he was thinking. She lay back on the bed and closed her eyes, exhausted and hurting. She was grateful for the cool cloth Theodore used to clean her face before he left the room. Downstairs, she heard Theodore call to Henry and instruct him to bring Abby to the house.

A short time later, Betsy opened her eyes. The sound of footsteps on the stairs had her sitting up. She fluffed her pillow and leaned back just as Theodore stepped around the door.

"Abby is here to see you."

Betsy ran her hands over her head in an attempt to smooth her hair. She hated being sick and indisposed and really didn't want anyone to see her like this. Abby appeared in the doorway, her smile radiated across the room lifting Betsy's spirits despite herself.

Abby crossed the room to sit on her bed. She squeezed Betsy's hand lying on the coverlet. "Hello."

Betsy dipped her head in embarrassment. "Hello."

Abby tilted her head. "There is no need to be ashamed. We all find ourselves under the weather at one time or another. Your color is good. What is bothering you?"

Betsy shrugged her shoulders. "It seems to be a lingering malaise."

Abby cut her eyes from Betsy to Theodore looking for an explanation.

Theodore shook his head. "I thought it was seasickness at first but discarded the notion as ridiculous nor is she running a fever which eliminates every other sickness I am aware of except one."

Abby guessed where Theodore's thoughts led him but Betsy's next words made it clear she had not reached the same conclusion yet.

Betsy shifted impatiently. "I must have eaten something that disagreed with me. I'm feeling much better now so perhaps we are all worrying over nothing."

Abby hid her smile. "Um hum, and if this nausea returns you may need to consider another reason." She watched as Betsy's look of confusion turned into understanding, and then to self-questioning before finally dawning recognition.

Surprise and wonder colored her voice. "It is possible."

Abby patted her hand. "Let us see what tomorrow brings before you go getting your hopes up. Rest awhile longer then move about as you feel able. I'll send over a special blend of tea I found to be helpful with nausea."

Theodore walked Abby to the door then returned to find Betsy out of bed and getting dressed. "What are you doing?"

"I feel fine now and I cannot abide lying abed one more minute. Besides I have work in the shop that needs tending."

Theodore reached for her hand with a sense of wonder. "What if..."

Betsy shook her head. "No. Not till tomorrow. We'll see what tomorrow brings." She wasn't ready to handle the disappointment if they were wrong.

She pulled her hand from his and turned her back to him lifting her dark tresses. "Would you mind buttoning me?"

He did as she asked, brushing aside a tendril to place a kiss at her nape when he was done. "As you wish, dear. We'll speak of this tomorrow."

Betsy was able to do a few hours of work before the metallic taste of bile gave warning of the returned sickness. She quickly gathered some sewing she could do at home then closed up her shop. She made it across the street, through the house, out the back door and to the outhouse before retching in a most undignified manner.

Theodore decided to work from home so he would be close at hand if Betsy needed him. He was right behind her as she exited the back door and waited helplessly outside the privy. When she opened the door, her face was pale and the hand she held against her mouth was shaky. Without a word, he helped her into the house and up the stairs. Now as she sat on the edge of the bed, eyes closed, trying to breathe normally, he approached with a wet cloth in hand.

She opened her eyes, revealing the misery she felt but her tone was light and wry. "I have never heard of evening sickness." She picked up the glass of water from the bedside table and rinsed her mouth spitting it into the chamber pot he held for her. He handed her the cloth and she wiped her face.

He smiled. Even in her misery she still kept her sense of humor. It touched his heart. He carefully sat beside her, gathering her in his arms, wishing he could take the suffering from her. She laid her head on his shoulder. For many long moments, she was so quiet; he thought perhaps she had fallen asleep. He leaned his head forward to check just as she spoke.

"I would be ecstatic if I weren't so miserable."

"I thought we were waiting until tomorrow to acknowledge you are in the family way."

"I have come to the conclusion it is the only reasonable explanation for this heaving. I suppose being so focused on preparations for our trip I missed the signs."

"Did you feel this way before?"

"No." She sighed. "I lost both of them before this stage."

She felt him stiffen and inwardly cringed at her slip.

Theodore leaned away from her. His eyes burned into her soul. "Both?"

He knew it only happened once with Ben. The second was his.

Anger engulfed him like the dark of a wicked storm swirling in his mind. He stood abruptly. He was angry with himself. *I left her with child?* And angry with her. *Did she know before I left? Why didn't she tell me?* Then sorrow thickened in the air around him. He stood motionless by the door, his back to her. He hadn't been here to share it with her; to share the brief joy she must have felt and to comfort her through the pain of loss. She must have needed his comfort for he knew how badly she wanted a child. And finally, he felt hurt that she kept it from him. Even if she hadn't wanted to write of such news, she hadn't spoken of it since his return either. *Why? Was she protecting me or herself?*

He turned to ask but the shimmer of her tears turned his quest for answers into one of comfort. He gently pulled her into his embrace. Stroking her hair, he whispered, "Oh Betsy, forgive me darling. I should have been here for you. I won't leave you again; especially now." He squeezed her tighter. "I'll find someone else to take my place."

Betsy leaned back to look in his eyes touched by the passion in his promise. "You would do that for me?"

"Yes." His eyes traveled down to the flatness of her stomach and back up to meet her gaze, maybe pausing briefly to admire the rounding in between. Wonder now flooded his heart. He kissed her forehead. "You're going to have my baby." A grin touched with pride spread across his face. He kissed her lips. "You are going to be a great mother."

He kissed her again and again, a series of playful pecks on the lips, in joyful celebration, until Betsy suddenly pulled away placing a hand over her mouth. She dove for the chamber pot effectively ending the emotional moment.

Theodore supported her until the worst was over then rinsed the cloth in the basin before handing it to her again. "Climb back into bed and I'll have someone bring you some tea."

Fire flashed in her eyes. With quiet firmness she said, "I don't need to be coddled." He took a reflexive step back and she was instantly contrite. "I'm sorry; I don't know where that came from."

Theodore gave her a wry smile. "I do. Margaret was highly emotional during her time."

Being compared to his late wife unexpectedly piqued her anger again. Betsy swallowed hard and counted to ten.

Aunt Agatha fortuitously entered the room in that moment with a tray. "I thought you might be ready for some tea and crackers. You have to keep up your strength now; after all, you are feeding two."

Realizing it was useless to fight against both of them; she allowed herself to be tucked into bed like a toddler and plied with herbal tea. One good thing, at least now she could empathize with Henry's aversion to the practice.

Aunt Agatha paused on her way out the door to turn and say, "I suppose this means you will be postponing your trip."

Betsy and Theodore looked to each other. Their thoughts had not gone past the novelty of the discovery.

Theodore's gaze held his wife's. "Will you be too disappointed?"

Betsy wanted to protest that they could still go. She was looking forward to seeing her family again. But after yesterday, she wasn't willing to take the chance of being seasick the entire voyage. If it was just her discomfort she would gladly make the sacrifice but the chance of harming her child by not being able to provide nourishment was not a risk she was willing to take. "How could I be disappointed? I will be awaiting our child."

"We will postpone the trip until he is old enough to travel. It will make the journey that much sweeter to introduce your family to our offspring."

Betsy's smile was genuine and full. "He?" Theodore likely used the pronoun in the generic term, but she couldn't resist teasing him. "Already planning on another son?"

Theodore grinned. His wife was anything if not resilient. "A passel of boys would suit me fine."

She smirked. "A daughter it shall be then."

He paused for effect, as if considering the idea, then reached for a ringlet of her hair lying against her shoulder. "Well, maybe one with black curls who looks just like you would be acceptable."

Her eyebrows rose in mock offense. "Acceptable?"

Theodore turned serious. He took a seat on the edge of the bed facing her and picked up her hands. "He, she, it matters not, as long as you both are well." He kissed her forehead. "I could not go on without you, Betsafina, for you would truly take my heart with you." He placed his hands on either side of her face and kissed the tip of her nose before pressing the warm mug of tea in her hands. "Drink."

She carefully sipped the brew taking so long it turned cold but thankfully the liquid settled and soothed her empty belly.

Theodore stood to leave but then turned, his expression thoughtful. "It didn't occur to me to ask before we married." He planned to use the trip to observe his wife with her family, to see if she had a desire to move back to her roots. He made his decision to settle here, but Betsy, for all intents and purposes, was never given the choice. She followed Ben here as a wife should. Would she want to move to Pennsylvania or New York? He had no desire to spend winters in the north, but he would do it for her.

Betsy's brow creased in confusion. "What should you have asked?"

"If you would prefer to live closer to your family. We could if you desire it."

Her lips curved into a soft smile. "You would do that for me." It was a statement of awe and a reminder of how wonderful a man she married. She shook her head. "No. I am happy here, on this island, with you. There is no other place in the world I would rather live than here."

"Hmm."

Agreement. And do I detect a hint of relief too? She mimicked him. "Hmm."

His wolfish grin made her weak—in a good way.

Betsy awoke the next morning feeling better. Not wanting to tempt fate she kept her breakfast light. Theodore tried to get her to stay home insisting she needed to rest. She finally convinced him she was doing no harm going to the shop and seeing customers and would return home at the slightest hint of sickness. It was mid-morning when the queasiness returned but she kept working, thankful it wasn't as bad as the previous days.

Not an hour later, Theodore arrived with the news of several residents sick with yellow fever. Not wanting to take chances he insisted Betsy return home immediately. Frustrated and embarrassed by the knowing looks of the ladies working for her, she turned on Theodore as soon as they entered the house. Unfortunately, her argument was silenced before she could speak by the ignominy of running to the outhouse. Being with child was not as wonderful as she imagined it would be. Still piqued by Theodore's coddling, she refused his assistance in returning to the house and refused to return to her bed. Instead she chose to take a seat in the parlor by the front window and began fanning herself; the July heat annoying her every bit as much as her overbearing husband.

Theodore ignored his wife's uncharacteristic belligerence. He could forgive her anything knowing she was carrying his child. Something they both desperately wanted. Once she was settled, he said, "I'll be in the study if you need me." He felt the weight of her stare as he left the room.

The downstairs study welcomed him with the musk of leather bound tomes lining the shelves on two walls of the room. He eagerly picked up the mail from the corner of the heavy oak desk taking up the center of the room. Mail only once a month was the hardest sacrifice he had to tolerate living on the remote island. He walked around the desk to a simple wooden office chair while perusing the contents. One of the letters was from Gad Humphries, the former Indian agent he met at the reservation. He opened it first, anxious to hear news of the Seminoles. He skimmed over the greeting to get to the substance of the letter.

> Two incidents occurred in June in which I perceived you would have a shared interest. The first was Major General Call sent a request to President Jackson which was granted, to purchase the Seminole slaves in the hopes that removing them would ease the Indian's departure. Agent Thompson denied the request. Speculation abounds he did so in the hopes of keeping the slave profits for himself. However, the agent has sworn he was only upholding his duty to protect the interests of the Seminole people. He often sights the Treaty of Payne's Landing in his defense. I myself am not sure which I believe and you will likely come to your own conclusions.
>
> The second incident occurred on the 19th of June and has become known as the skirmish at Hickory Sink. The details, as I know them, are some Indians slaughtered a cow and some white men found them sitting around a campfire cooking the meat. The whites, finding them off reservation and assuming the cow to be stolen, attacked them. They took their rifles, went through their belongings, and then brutally whipped them. Four other Indians arrived and fired at the whites in defense of their brethren. A firefight ensued and when it was over three whites were wounded, one Indian was dead and another wounded.

Settlers filed a complaint with the agency so the militia was sent out to rebuke the tribe. Some Indians came to the fort to complain to Agent Thompson but he was forced to take the side of the militia and so they left dissatisfied. Many believe pressure from the settlers and military will encourage the Indians to forsake Florida for more peaceful lands in the west.

I am sure you and I see it ending differently.

The rest of the letter contained odds and ends but nothing else of import. Theodore mulled over the two incidents. Thompson knew as well as he did the Indians would not consider selling their slaves. His refusal had everything to do with protecting the Seminole's interests and not personal gain which was a good thing for the tribe. Theodore didn't see much in the way of a story other than to vindicate the agent. The second incident was certainly news worthy but he had no way of verifying the facts other than to write letters of inquiry which could take months to receive answers and by then it would be old news. His hands were tied. He either had to write a second hand retelling or forego the story all together. Neither option was appealing, especially with all the questions swirling in his mind.

Theodore was also concerned there would be an overreaction to the skirmish on one side or the other. It was more than likely the Indians would want retaliation for the slight to their honor. There was no doubt the next event could break the precarious peace and jeopardize any attempt to relocate the Seminole people.

As he was considering all of this, Betsy entered his sanctuary.

"Am I interrupting you?"

He lightly shook his head as he refolded the letter.

"I wanted to apologize for my behavior."

"No need." His look indicated she was being silly to even suggest it.

"There is a need. I was rude and unappreciative and I apologize."

He stood up from his desk with a compassionate smile. "And I forgave you as you were speaking."

She dropped her head in humble gratitude and then she noticed the unopened letters waiting on his desk. "I'm sorry. I have disturbed you." She looked up in time to see the frustration on his face, his gaze fixed on the opened letter. "What is it? More bad news?"

Theodore cleared his features. "It's nothing for you to worry about."

Her lips firmed. "Perhaps, but I would still like to know what is concerning you."

Theodore walked around the desk and kissed her. "It's just boring politics."

He was deceiving her. Something more was bothering him, likely the Indians, but he wasn't going to share it with her. For now, she said nothing. He was being overprotective again and while it frustrated her she also appreciated that he cared enough to do so. She kissed him. "Very well. I'll be waiting for you in the parlor when you are done."

* * *

As July progressed into August so too did the number of cases of yellow fever turning it into one of the worst years ever for the dreaded disease. No one knew how it spread, so fear kept Betsy homebound. She did not want anything to happen to her baby especially now that the sickness passed and she was feeling more like herself again. In between caring for the sick, Abby came to visit as often as she could.

August turned into September and the heat and sickness continued. It was a miserable month. Betsy did more sitting and fanning than working. Life seemed to have a drudgery about it brought on by lethargy and her self-imposed quarantine. She did a lot of letter writing, Bible reading, praying, and fanning in between the sewing to get through the days.

Meanwhile, Theodore kept busy with local stories for his newspaper and keeping up with correspondences. Bob kept him updated with the happenings in New York and Washington while Private Dalton, Gad Humphries, the sutler at Fort King, and others fed him information concerning the military movements and the Seminole.

It was mid-September when he received distressing news from Agent Thompson.

> *Private Kinsley Dalton, the mail carrier, was on his run between Fort Brooke and Fort King, near the Hillsborough River crossing, when the darn Seminoles attacked him. I am told he was shot, scalped, disemboweled and thrown in a pond. Shot his horse too. Such violence tests even my loyalty to the Indian cause. We have lost a good man.*

It was disturbing, the bestiality beneath the Indians' seemingly docile and debonair demeanor. Theodore knew it existed but it had been a while since he experienced it. He took the news of Kinsley's death to heart. He knew this man. They talked and fished while at Fort Gibson with the Indian delegation. They spent many hours discussing the Indians' plight, the possibility of war, and once they even spoke of family and their plans for the future. It was often in the company of Kinsley that he made the long trek between Fort Brooke and Fort King.

The cruelty of his death led Theodore to believe the act was in retaliation of the Hickory Sink incident. It also further increased his desire to return to the front. If only the yellow fever outbreak would end, he would feel better about leaving Betsy for a few months.

Theodore was careful to let Betsy believe what everyone else wanted to believe; that the Seminoles would leave in January without a fuss. He wanted her not to worry in her condition. But each month's passing and with every letter he opened, he grew more convinced war was inevitable. Apparently, President Jackson and Congress believed the same, for the army was deployed once again to Key West. While the community rejoiced in their return and the benefits it brought to the island, it only deepened Theodore's concern.

Chapter 27

Tuesday morning, the 15th of September, an approaching storm darkened the skies to the point Theodore was forced to light oil lamps in his shop. He was putting together a page of typeset while Robert Mason cleaned the printing press in preparation for this week's run. They were both startled from their labors by the sudden gust of wind rushing through the front door with an unexpected visitor.

Max Eatonton pushed the door closed then turned to face the room. He ran his hands over his head to sweep the blond curls from his face, reminding him it was time for a haircut. "Good morning, gentlemen. Fine weather we are having."

Theodore stepped from behind his desk to greet his friend with a firm hand clasp. "Fine weather if you like wind and rain. Good morning Captain."

Max smiled. "Since stormy weather is good for business, I do happen to appreciate a good gale and we look to be getting a doozy this time."

"Then I must ask, what brings you here on such a blustery day when you should be racing to the reefs?"

"I've come to ask a favour, my friend."

Theodore inclined his head. "I'll be happy to oblige. What do you need?"

"Captain Keats is laid up with a leg injury, so I'm taking the *Mystic* out wrecking. If the storm does hit hard here, I wanted to ask you to look in on my family afterwards."

"Of course. If you would prefer, they could stay with us till it passes, or us with them, if needs be, though my aunt would protest."

Max grinned. "Thank you for the offer, but having been through many of these, I'm sure Abby will be too stubborn to leave the house. We have it pretty well secured. I would feel better knowing if it did get bad someone was looking out for her."

Theodore shook his hand. "I promise, I will." The journalist in him took over. "Max, do you give any credence to the British navy man's prediction that the coming appearance of Halley's Comet is the cause of all these storms we've had of late? I hear the islanders talking about it being an unusually active season."

"Hard to say. Halley only comes around once in a lifetime. What do we really know about it? I suppose it could." They heard the howling wind brush by the building again, louder than before. "The winds are picking up. I must be going and you may want to get home and batten down."

Theodore walked Max to the shop door then turned to Robert Mason. "Shall we close shop?"

Robert lifted his chin towards Theodore. "You should go home and see to your house and family. I can take care of the shop."

Theodore looked to the typeset he was working.

Robert said, "And I can finish that too."

Theodore gave his partner a probing look before consenting. "Very well." He donned his coat and top hat, then bid Robert farewell. He stepped out the door and nearly lost his hat and his balance by the gust of wind rushing past the building. He steadied himself, then holding hat to head, pushed forward into the invisible force. Once he turned the corner onto Whitehead Street, the houses buffered him from the gale which had grown stronger during the hours he worked in the shop. Only an occasional light spattering of rain accompanied the wind for now. He supposed even that would get worse before it was over.

Recalling Max's warning, Theodore wondered how strong the winds could become in a cyclone. He and his family had never experienced one. His steps quickened. The house would need to be secured and he had a strong suspicion he would find his wife trying to do so on her own.

Theodore arrived to find Betsy on the front porch studying the cloud movement.

She nodded towards the sky. "See how the clouds move from southeast to northwest?" Her eyes were grave when they met his. "This is more than just a thunderstorm."

Theodore climbed the porch steps and came to stand beside her. "Max said so as well."

"Could you help me with the storm shutters?"

He turned his head to the side, at the same time gently pulling her hand so she faced him. "I would rather you go inside and send Henry out to help me."

"Henry isn't back yet."

His brows drew together. "Where is he?"

"He went down to the turtle kraal this morning."

Theodore turned toward the steps to head back to town.

Betsy placed a hand on his arm to detain him. "You needn't go. They'll send him home soon. I am sure he is helping secure the pens before the storm. He'll be all right, Teddy."

Theodore was skeptical but she knew the ways of the island better than he. "What will happen to the turtles if this becomes a hurricane?"

"It depends on the owner. If he tries to keep them in the kraal, they could drown which would mean more work for the cannery. If he lets them go, the turtlers will have more work restocking the pens. He just rebuilt the kraal with a higher deck so I think he'll take his chances this time so Henry should be sent home soon. Meanwhile we have things to do with two houses to prepare."

"My dear, you are going inside. I'll take care of the houses. What needs to be done besides the shutters?"

"Bring in anything loose."

He handed her his hat so the wind wouldn't take it and left the porch.

Betsy went inside and recruited Aunt Agatha's help to bring in the bedding from the sleeping porches and haul it downstairs to the parlor.

The rain started coming down in sheets while Theodore toiled. Two houses and two kitchens later, he returned to the front porch, his clothes soaking wet. He was relieved to see Henry heading home. He waited, watching him struggle as the storm tried to knock him off his feet. Together they entered the darkened house. The closed shutters blocked out what was left of the meager daylight.

They joined the ladies in the candlelit parlor. Theodore asked, "What do we do now?"

Betsy smiled. "We wait and pray we don't get flooded."

Theodore voiced his surprise. "Flooded? By rain?"

"The rain is only one culprit. These storms tend to raise the sea, sometimes high enough to flood inland."

Betsy nodded toward Aunt Agatha who was settled in the heavy Queen Anne chair by the front window. "Theodore, would you please move her chair closer? We are safer gathered in the center of the room, away from the windows."

Theodore did as she asked then joined her on the sofa. Henry took up a position on the floor in front of the coffee table with pencil, paper and oil lamp for light. Betsy idly watched him work as a turtle began to take shape on the page. For many moments, none of them spoke but the silence was overwhelmed by the varying sounds of the wind.

Theodore had to speak a little louder than normal to ask, "How long do these things last?"

"A few hours at least. Depends on how big the storm is."

"How bad can it get?"

"I've heard tell of some really bad ones in the East Indies. We've not had one here. At least not yet."

The eerie howling of the wind had them all on edge. Betsy decided to lighten the mood. "Why don't we play a game? Do you know *Minister's Cat?*"

Agatha and Theodore both gave her sour looks but Henry perked up. "I like games. How do you play?"

"It is a game of adjectives. We each take turns ascribing an adjective to the minister's cat that begins with the letter A. Once around we then use the letter B, so on and so forth. If you can't think of an adjective or fall out of rhythm, you're out of the game. We won't worry about the rhythm for the first round. I'll begin and we'll go around to the left." Betsy clapped her hands as she rhythmically said, "The minister's cat is an *agile* cat." She looked to Theodore.

"The minister's cat is an *awful* cat."

Betsy grimaced at Theodore's choice of word before turning to hear Henry's.

"The minister's cat..." Henry paused to find a suitable word, "... Is an *angry* cat."

Next was Agatha with a smug smile. "The minister's cat is an *antique* cat."

They made it to E before Henry fell out, unable to come up with a word. Betsy failed to find a word with I and Aunt Agatha stumbled at R leaving Theodore the winner. They played another round at Henry's insistence with the same result.

By the end of the day, they played every game they could think of and still the storm raged, growing in intensity, with no sign of wavering. They skipped the midday meal hoping the storm would wane by evening. Unfortunately it was quite the opposite. Theodore finally decided to brave the elements to retrieve anything edible from the kitchen. Despite the covered walkway between house and kitchen, he was soaked.

They had an impromptu picnic dinner of bread, cheese and preserved peaches. Fortunately, there was enough so everyone could have their fill.

They passed the night huddled in the parlor. The storm continued to rage outside, while the occupants managed sporadic sleep at best. The following day was spent confined much the same way except they were foregoing the lamps to conserve the oil and the detainees were more restless, often wandering the room to get some exercise. They played charades and sang songs. Betsy taught Henry the *Wrecker's Song* that Max taught her long ago.

In the early afternoon, soft snoring from Aunt Agatha proved she was napping while Henry was playing fort under the dining room table. Tired of listening to the howling wind and with a few moments of semi-privacy, Betsy decided to broach the subject weighing on her mind. She had to speak directly in his ear to be heard over the storm. "Teddy, are you keeping something from me?"

Theodore looked puzzled. "Whatever do you mean?"

"You've been distracted and restless of late. I know you've received letters with news of the Seminoles. You want to leave but feel you must stay because of my condition."

Theodore was surprised she knew so much. He looked to his sleeping aunt. "You want to discuss this now?"

"Now is as good a time as any and I could use the distraction. My head grows weary of this constant noise."

"It's been more than a day now. You said hurricanes normally pass in a day."

"I did and this one hasn't. And you're changing the subject."

"Hmm."

Betsy's anger burst catching them both by surprise. She wanted to yell but not wanting to wake Aunt Agatha, she hissed, "Don't dismiss me with that sound. I told you when we married I wanted a husband who shared the burden." Her emotions had never been so volatile and uncontrollable. "And you may think you are protecting me by keeping the burden but you are not." She took a deep breath and tried to calm down. "The weight on your shoulders concerns me more than the outside world, so please, talk to me."

Theodore stood his ground. "There is nothing to discuss."

The crashing sound of something breaking through one of the upstairs windows made them both jump.

Henry came running into the room. "What was that?"

Betsy said, a little harsher than she intended, "A reminder to stay away from the windows."

The noise of the wind was louder now that it was whipping through the upper story. Theodore went to investigate the damage. Not being allowed to go with, Henry resumed his play under the table. Theodore returned, confirming a loose shingle crashed through the window and after cleaning up the shards of glass he stuffed a quilt in the opening. He hoped it would hold through the storm.

Agatha awoke briefly during the bit of excitement but soon dozed again leaving Theodore and Betsy facing each other in a silent battle of wills.

Betsy prompted him. "What news have you received?"

"It matters not what is happening with the Indians. I am not leaving; this household is more important."

Again, anger swept over her in a rush, unexpected and potent. Anger that he was denying her an answer, anger that he was coddling her because of womanhood and motherhood, and angry with a storm that didn't know when to quit. Recalling her mother's advice, she took several cleansing breaths until she felt more in control. "What is happening with them?"

Theodore decided to admit defeat. His feisty little wife was not going to let the matter drop and he was trapped in her presence until the storm passed. "The latest letter said a group of chiefs agreeable to the move met with Agent Thompson to request they have their own agent in the new territory and to request they be given land separate from their former Creek enemies."

"So they are agreeable to moving west. That is good news as so many fear they will not." She noticed the bare flicker of disagreement pass over his features. "They are not agreeable?"

"Some are."

"But others still are not?"

"No."

"And how does the army plan to deal with the dissension?"

"I don't know, other than eventually they will use force."

Betsy resumed her seat on the sofa. "I suppose it is inevitable. President Jackson will not allow them to stay. What else has happened?"

Theodore sat next to her. He needed her comfort and, lulled by the deeply shadowed room and temporary privacy, Theodore put his arm around her shoulder nestling her close to his chest. "Thompson put Osceola in jail for a few days and some Indians were whipped for stealing a cow."

"Did they steal it?"

"I'm not sure. My information is incomplete."

"Do you think the Indians could be guilty of stealing?"

"It's possible. If they are guilty, it is because they are starving."

She drew in a breath. "I see now why you have been so agitated. These incidents are enough to incite the warriors to retaliation and easily start a war."

"They have already."

Startled, she turned to look at him. "The war has started?"

"No, at least not as far as I know, and Major Glassell has not received word of such." He hesitated. Even weeks later it hurt to think about it. "I meant the Seminoles have taken their revenge."

Betsy sensed his pain and patiently waited for him to continue. She lifted her right hand to entwine her fingers with his right hand draped across her shoulder. She gently squeezed them.

He swallowed hard before speaking. "They killed a soldier."

Snuggled as she was against his chest, she felt him tense as he spoke the words. She knew he had been keeping news from her but she hadn't realized he was hiding something so painful. "Someone you knew well."

"Hmm."

She waited, hoping he would say more.

He didn't want to say more but he could tell she wasn't going to let it go. His beautiful stubborn Betsafina wanted to share his burden and he loved her for it. It was both frustrating and heartwarming. He kissed her head nestled under his chin. "I have mentioned him to you, Kinsley Dalton, the mail carrier." He picked up her left hand in her lap and began caressing it as well as the right in the hopes of distracting her.

He was making it hard to carry on a deep conversation while stirring tenderness with his touch but she pushed onward. "Does his death change your feelings for the Seminoles? Is that why you are hesitant to return?"

Theodore laid his hand over the place where their child grew, still barely discernable to the outside world. "This is why I am not returning."

She laid her hand atop his with a gentle caress. The moment was tender and poignant. Softly she said, "You didn't answer the first question."

"It is hard to reconcile the dignified and docile image they portray with the brutality of the warriors' actions." He recalled the gruesome image his mind created from the words in the letter telling of Kinsley's demise. He inhaled the scent of her and focused on the caress of her hands to banish the thought. It was one of those things he wished he had never read in the first place. "But they are protecting their people in the ways of their people. I don't like it or agree with it but I can understand it."

Selfishly she would rather he didn't go, but she knew he needed to for the greater good of the country. So with false bravery she said, "You should go." She felt the protest he was mounting. "Our child isn't due until spring. If you head home the end of January, you'll be here in time for the birth. Until then, I'll be fine."

She could tell he wasn't taking her seriously so she stood up and turned to face him. She held her hand out to keep him from rising. She knew she had to ignite his passion to get him to make the hard choice. "You started this to tell their side. They need you to; otherwise, the only story to be told is that of the military and the slave traders. No one will understand the reasons behind their savagery because no one else cares enough about them to make the sacrifices that you make to get their side of the story nor have they the forum you have to tell it. *You* must make the nation care."

"But I can't leave you. Not now. Maybe after you have given birth."

Aunt Agatha momentarily stopped snoring as she adjusted her position, putting a hold on their conversation. They both watched and waited until the sound resumed.

Quieter but with no less force, Betsy said, "Afterwards, I will need you. Right now all we do is wait and there are plenty here who will look out for us. Besides, by then, either war will have started or the Indians will be beaten into submission and it will be too late for you to tell what happened. You've told me you don't know the details of the events already unfolding and it bothers you—greatly." She leaned down to put her hands on either side of his face and stare into his beloved hazel eyes. "You need answers." She paused to make her point. "More importantly," she enunciated each word, "you need to be there to ask the questions."

He couldn't speak. He was amazed by her selfless understanding. He reached his hands up to her face to bring her sweet lips to his. Theodore's comport was spiritual more than sexual. It was passion for the sacrifice this woman was willing to make for a people she didn't know. The sacrifice she was willing to make so he could finish a story he started. And it was passion for the strength of his mate, for her honor, her dignity, and the love she generously shared with him, his son, and his aunt, and for her love of this town and her country. At the moment, his wife overwhelmed him. How could he not kiss her? Their closed lips met again and again, both cherishing the deeply felt emotions.

One last pull on her bottom lip and he broke the contact. Pressing his forehead to hers, quietly he said, "I'll think about it."

She didn't know what else to say. She allowed him to pull her back down beside him and they lapsed into silence.

Betsy whispered. "I'm sorry."

She baffled him. "For what?"

"For losing my temper earlier. It's not like me."

"Likely it is being with child that has shortened your patience."

"I suppose."

Henry's sudden return to declare his hunger ended their conversation. Theodore made another run to the kitchen. The storm continued but the winds, noticeably lessened from his sojourn of yesterday, now spun from the south. Betsy told him it was a good sign that the hurricane would soon be past.

They picnicked again sharing smoked fish and the last loaf of bread while listening for any sign of waning wind and rain. They all were suffering the ills of confinement and constant noise and doing their best not to let it show in their interactions with each other. They slept again in the parlor as best they could.

The near silence in the early hours of morning awoke them. It continued to rain and the wind occasionally gusted but the roar was gone. As the sun rose, the sky lightened, chasing away the oppression of the last thirty six hours.

With the storm's departure, Theodore donned coat and hat to keep his promise to Max and to see what damage was left in the storm's wake, while Betsy donned hers to make her way to the kitchen to prepare a much needed meal. Thankfully they did not get much of a storm surge saving them from serious flooding.

Betsy was glad her kitchen had a wood floor. While wet, at least there wasn't any standing water from the heavy rain. Her old kitchen was a dirt floor and likely filled with water. She stoked the fire in the cast iron oven to cook some eggs and started a fire to heat the beehive oven so she could bake bread. She planned to make a few extra loaves to share with any neighbors who may be in need. She made use of the fallen cocoanuts she found in the yard to add to their meal, saving the milk to use later for fish soup.

It stopped raining by the time she finished making their breakfast. She checked the fires, and then carried the tray of food to the house. Henry opened the back door for her so she handed him the tray to deposit on the table while she hastily removed her sodden footwear. Betsy left her boots by the back door and hoped they would dry before she had to wear them again. She went upstairs to change her skirt and put on a pair of satin dress shoes, the only other footwear she owned. As she returned downstairs, Theodore came through the front door. Betsy smiled, "You are just in time to eat while it's warm."

"Good. I'm famished."

"How did you find Abby and the children?"

"All is well in the Eatonton abode. There is a lot of debris strewn about but no one seems to be hurt."

"Praise God."

They walked together to the dining room where Henry and Aunt Agatha waited for them. After prayers Theodore reported what he had seen. Some houses, like theirs, suffered broken windows and missing shingles but all in all the islanders were fortunate. At the wharf, a few pilot boats looked to be damaged and although hard to be sure in the rain, he thought a few ships in the harbour may have grounded on the shoals. Some of the men he met in town told him they thought the heart of the storm passed through the Upper Keys. It wasn't said but both Betsy and Theodore worried about Max and the other wreckers patrolling the area.

After their meal, Theodore and Henry spent the better part of the day cleaning up the storm's destruction around their property, piling up palm fronds and limbs, and helping the neighbors to do the same. By the time Theodore stepped into the dry goods store to pick up glass for the broken window, he wasn't surprised to learn they were sold out. He placed an order for the glass, hoping it wouldn't take months for it to arrive.

The following day was Friday. The sky was bright and clear as if freshly washed by the storm. Occasional puffs of white clouds drifted across in whimsical fashion. Theodore left the house anxious to get to work. He arrived at the shop to find Robert Mason already hard at work on their next edition, picking up where Theodore had left off on Tuesday. They lost much of the week for gathering news.

Both men welcomed the appearance of William Whitehead with an article in hand. Robert immediately went to work setting it to type, as Mr. Whitehead's submissions were always well written.

Theodore and Mr. Whitehead walked together down to the wharf to hear the latest news of the sailing fleet. As soon as they reached the bight they found a gathering of sailors and tradesmen discussing the storm. Theodore listened to them intently.

"Worst storm I ever seen."

"We've pulled at least a dozen ships off the shoals in the harbour. No telling how many more up the reef."

"I heard tell Cap'n Smithe and his crew spent all day yesterday digging a two hundred foot canal to get his ship back in the water after being left high and dry."

"Has anyone heard from Captain Whalton?"

"Word just came in the *Florida* is bad off but nobody's hurt."

This news perked Theodore's attention. "Isn't *Florida* the light-ship at Carysfort Reef?"

An old sailor he knew by sight but not by name replied, "Yeah, that's the one."

"How bad is the damage?"

"Her lanterns will have to be replaced and they got lots of decking to repair, but she's still afloat. The same can't be said for her tender they use to get water. That schooner slipped her line and tis likely lost."

Theodore looked to Mr. Whitehead. "Isn't that the same light you told me the first ship was wrecked on the way here from the shipyard, had to be purchased as salvage, repaired, and then replaced shortly after commission due to a rotting hull?"

"It tis. And this ship has only been in service for four years. Now, I have to requisition new lamps and a new tender."

"It has been quite an expensive venture putting light on that particular reef. Is it worth it?"

"The merchant vessels sailing these waters would agree it is. I pray Congress concurs."

The men soon dispersed to go about their business. There was much to do to put their homes and businesses back in order and clean up the town.

Day after day more ships arrived with news of those stranded, salvaged or lost and tales of heroic men each more incredible than the last. And each day that went by without the return of loved ones became harder to bear for those who waited, which included Abby. Betsy knew she was worried more this time than ever before. For the last few years, Max captained the *Abigail Rose*, a merchant vessel, requiring him to avoid storms much to Abby's relief. It had been a while since he captained a wrecker. Out of practice and out of sync with the crew, Max sailed straight into the heart of the strongest gale any of them could ever remember. They all prayed for his safe return, none more so than Abby.

Four days after the gale's departure, the *Mystic* finally returned to port. A more pitiful looking ship, Theodore had never seen. With both masts jury-rigged and an old gun serving as anchor it would seem the *Mystic* was the salvaged ship, but as it turned out, Max's crew was unloading cargo from another ship. His fellow captains gave Max a hard time but Theodore knew they were duly impressed and respected his fortitude and resilience.

The Whitmore's were invited to dine at the Eatonton's to celebrate Max's safe return. Max shared his tale; downplaying it for the sake of the women and children, but at the same time embellishing it for their entertainment.

"After beating it up the keys to Tavernier, we intended to ride out the storm in the Straight but the tempest was fiercer than expected. The *Mystic* was lifted and tossed about," he ruffled his son's curly head, "similar to the way Christoff, here, likes to play with his toy boats in the bath. We were dragged from our anchor, pushed this way and that, twisted and spun till we were no longer sure which direction was home. Both masts snapped, our rigging was lost, and the anchors broke away. The storm tried its best but the *Mystic* never failed us. She's a stout ship and when it was all over, we put her back together as best we could, intending to sail home. But what do you think we found? Other ships in need of rescue. So what did we do?" Max paused for an answer.

Emily shouted, "You saved them too!"

"That's right, Em. I told the crew, we have nothing else to lose so we may as well do what we came here to do. And so we did."

It didn't take long for the island community to recover and life to resume its normal pace. The arrival of another letter from Fort King turned Theodore's mind once again to the Seminole's strife and reminded him of his conversation with Betsy held against the backdrop of swirling winds.

Chapter 28

September 1835 was quickly coming to a close. Theodore had to decide now. He stood at the front window of his shop but he wasn't seeing the bustle of Front Street, Key West. His mind was on the inhabitants of middle Florida. The letter he held spoke of a council meeting held in August between Agent Thompson and the chiefs agreeable to moving. The chiefs asked the agent to request they be given an area of the reservation separate from their former Creek enemies plus their own agent thereby retaining their sovereignty and rights. Theodore understood their reasoning. They feared the Creeks would likely try to subjugate them and sell the Black Seminoles to slave traders. At least, the chiefs were trying to resolve some of the issues with moving. Perhaps there was a chance all could end peacefully. He wanted to believe it just as much as all the others involved, but he couldn't get past the conviction that the young warriors were not going to concede.

Another letter lay open on his desk from Bob in New York. Regiments were being moved and state militias called up. President Jackson was preparing to meet resistance. He had also been told Governor John Eaton was calling for a Florida volunteer regiment.

The coming conflict needed a storyteller. He spent months already laying the groundwork to be able to do just that. He knew of no other willing to consider the motivations behind the Seminoles' actions while there were plenty to report on the military's actions from near and afar; from the field and the decision rooms. It was as if everything he had done up to this point—studying the Northern tribes, becoming a reporter, being present for the Black Hawk War, visiting the reservation, moving to Key West, befriending the Seminoles—it all led to this moment. He felt the call to duty and an urgency to return to the heart of the conflict. And his wife supported the idea so it should be an easy decision.

Except...

His heart's desire was to stay; to see his wife grow heavy with their child; to welcome his son or daughter into the world and to be the father Henry needed.

But...

Such desires, except in the case of Henry, were a want, not a need to stay. As Betsy pointed out, he could leave for a few months and return before her time was due.

There were other reasons to return. Theodore closed his eyes against the recollection of the brutal killing of his friend. He also thought of Chief Micanopy; a man torn between his desire to avoid bloodshed at the cost of his people's freedom and the desire of his people to hold on to what was theirs no matter the cost. He was a man faced with a much harder choice than Theodore's.

And in the end, neither of them really had a choice. They would do what they must when the time called for it. And right now, Theodore conceded, he was being called to return to Fort King.

The night before Theodore was to leave, Betsy lay awake in their bed on the sleeping porch—alone. It was hours later and still Theodore had yet to turn in. She finally placed her bare feet on the floor and parted the mosquito netting. She carefully tiptoed out of the room not wanting to disturb Henry and Aunt Agatha. Dressed only in her thin chemise she went downstairs in search of her husband. The house proved to be empty but she spied candlelight through the open back door to the kitchen. She only hesitated a moment over her lack of dress before quietly walking out the door and through the walkway to the open kitchen doorway.

Theodore was so involved in his task he didn't hear her approach. She leaned against the door jamb with folded arms to watch him methodically cleaning his rifle. She tried not to think of him having to use the weapon or of how much she was going to miss him. A few moments later she was surprised by a strange flutter in her belly. Reflexively, her arms dropped and she stood up straight. It took a moment to register its meaning.

Theodore caught the movement out of the corner of his eye. He turned to find Betsy, her hands moving to her stomach, with a look of wondrous joy on her face. He put down the weapon, wiped his hands, and walked towards her, "What is it?" She lifted her face to his and the maternal glow took his breath away. Tears shimmered in her eyes.

Betsy whispered in awe, "The quickening."

Theodore's eyes widened then dropped to her middle. He slid his hand under hers to press his palm against the gentle slope of her abdomen, needing to share the moment physically. She pressed the warmth of his caress against her and closed her eyes to savor the moment. The unexpected feel of his lips against hers made them flutter open before closing again.

Fighting the desire that consumed them, he pulled away and kissed her forehead. "I'm almost done here."

Betsy walked past him to perch on a stool by the table. "I'll wait for you." She kept a hand pressed to her middle hoping to feel the flutter of new life again. It helped raise her spirits which were low with Theodore's pending departure.

When he was done with the task, he packed his haversack with a canteen, mess kit and other essentials. It still held his Bible and the small portrait of Betsy and Henry from his last trip. He left the bag and his tent by the front door, ready to take with him in the morning. Betsy led the way upstairs, past the sleeping porch, to their bedroom. He approved wholeheartedly, quietly closing the door behind him. Betsy walked to the window, opening it to the cool night air. Moonlight bathed her in its glow revealing her slender outline beneath the chemise. Theodore's gaze wandered from her ebony crown down to her bare toes.

Betsy paused to enjoy the cool air long enough for Theodore to approach from behind. He moved her silky hair to the side to kiss her neck then wrapped his arms around her pulling her to his torso. She wrapped her arms over his, absorbing the encompassing feel of him. His warmth, his strength, the feel of his breath, the sound of his heartbeat, the musky male smell of him—all of this she committed to memory.

Theodore squeezed her even tighter, inhaling the verbena scent of her hair. He didn't know if he would have the strength to leave her tomorrow. Tonight it seemed impossible.

Their lovemaking was tender and poignant each knowing it would be the last time for many months to come. Afterwards they lay beside each other, their hands entwining between them, caressing the sensitive skin of each other's palms.

She felt weak asking it of him, but couldn't help but do so. "Teddy, promise me, you'll come home safely before my time."

He kissed the back of her hand. "I promise." He prayed it would not be another promise he was forced to break.

"I will miss you terribly."

Moonlight touched the foot of their bed. He turned to her and ran his index finger down the side of her temple, drawing her hair away from her face. "Maybe if you consider the same moon shines down on both of us and every time we see it we will recall this moment, I won't seem so far away."

One corner of her mouth lifted in a smile. "I like that."

He hungrily kissed her smile uncaring if they got any sleep this night.

* * *

A week later Theodore was sailing into Tampa Bay aboard the schooner, *Liberty*. He was standing at the railing watching their approach to land when unusual ripples in the water caught is attention. Hundreds of gray creatures swam just beneath the surface. Their shape was that of a diamond with the motion of two sides flapping like wings of a bird in flight giving brief glimpses of the white underside. They were as far as the eye could see and a walk around the ship proved they were on all sides. Theodore stopped a passing sailor and pointed to the water. "What are those?"

The young lad shrugged his shoulders. "No idea. You should ask the captain."

Theodore followed his advice, making his way around the busy crew and over and under ropes to the helm. He changed his mind when he noticed how preoccupied the captain was with their approach to shore so he returned to his original post at the rail.

An older crewman approached curious to see what was holding Theodore's attention. "Ah a fever of stingrays. Wouldn't want to fall into that mess."

"Why not?"

"They have a venomous barb on their tail."

He walked away leaving Theodore to continue watching the rays, fascinated by their incredible numbers spreading out wide across the water as well as their graceful movement.

A short while later he debarked in Tampa to find a landscape vastly different than the one he left in April. The ravaged town suffered the full effects of the recent hurricane adding proof that the storm had merely brushed by Key West. After striking the upper keys it circled back to hit Tampa straight on then crossed the land to strike St. Augustine and continue up the eastern coast. New wood appeared on many repaired buildings while others were so badly damaged they were beyond repair. With the increase in troops and decrease in buildings there was no room in the fort this time for civilians. Theodore was forced to pitch his tent outside the palisades.

He was able to travel with a patrol early the next morning for Fort King and three days later he was greeting Agent Thompson. They spoke extensively of recent events and the plans in place to facilitate the tribe's removal. Thompson lamented the loss of Kinsley Dalton during this critical time. "None of the replacements travel the territory as fast as their predecessor." It saddened Theodore that the agent did not feel Kinsley's loss as personally as he did, to the agent his loss was more an inconvenience.

The following day Theodore made the trip to Micanopy's village and found little had changed from his last visit. It made him wonder why he had felt the urgency to return.

Key West

October passed into November. It was a bright clear day, in the upper seventies, with hardly a cloud in the sky. Betsy was working in her shop, making over another of her dresses to accommodate her increasing middle, while the other hired seamstresses chatted and worked on the orders. Her dress shop was doing well enough to keep three ladies busy.

Sewing aggravated the heartburn she frequently felt due to her delicate condition so she could only work in short spells. Betsy laid her hemming aside, stretched her shoulders, and announced her intention of visiting the postmaster as the mail was due in any day now. She anxiously waited for news from Theodore. His first letter, received last month, was hastily penned to let her know of his safe arrival. A longer letter would be a most welcome distraction to her day. The others nodded without concern as these days she frequently left the shop in their care.

The short walk into town made her feel better, as it often did. For the most part, she enjoyed being *enceinte*, especially now when she often felt the baby move. Once her condition was noticeable, a few of the old biddies told her she was too old to carry a babe. She dismissed them out of hand reminding herself she may be too old to be having her first, but she certainly wasn't too old to have a child.

At the post office, she was disappointed to learn the mail sloop had not arrived. She stood outside the door debating walking further or returning home when Frances Gardiner, one of the army officer wives, approached her. She was holding one year old George with four year old Julia hiding behind her skirts. After greetings, Betsy asked, "Do you have any news from the mainland?"

Mrs. Gardiner nodded. "My husband just received orders to prepare for departure. The troops leave next month to support the forts. Mr. Whitmore is currently at Fort King. Have you heard from him?"

Betsy shook her head. "The mail has not arrived yet this month."

Mrs. Gardiner grimaced. "My husband assures me it is only precautionary, but I know from experience he rarely tells me how bad it is under the mistaken impression it will keep me from worry."

Betsy smiled. "It is a common misconception among men. Mr. Whitmore practices the same false wisdom."

Mrs. Gardiner's look intensified. "Mr. Whitmore is familiar with the Indians. Does he believe they will resist?"

The shoe suddenly being on the other foot, so to speak, Betsy better understood their husbands' intentions. She hated adding to Mrs. Gardiner's worry by telling her the truth. But how could she not? "He does."

"I feared as much. We must pray for our husbands' safety."

"Yes, we must." Until this moment, Betsy had not been too concerned but knowing troops were headed his way changed her perception of Theodore's safety.

They were interrupted by the arrival of an errand boy carrying the newly arrived mail. Betsy impatiently waited for it to be sorted but the wait was worth it. She was handed four letters, all addressed in Theodore's masculine script. She hurried home arriving out of breath and in high spirits. Entering the parlor, she handed Aunt Agatha her letter, then took a seat in the opposing Queen Anne chair.

Aunt Agatha said, "Slow down, missy, you are no spring chicken and in a motherly way. It is not good to be out of breath."

Betsy laughed off her sage advice. "What would you know of spring chickens?"

Aunt Agatha raised her brow at the retort but said nothing. They both lapsed into silence as they read their letters. Betsy sorted hers by date to read them in order.

The first was truly a love letter. It made her heart melt. He didn't mention anything outside of their relationship which led her to believe there was nothing to report. The second was the same. The third wasn't much different other than it mentioned an upcoming meeting in October to go over the immigration plan. The fourth told of the disastrous meeting.

My dear, I'm sorry to say, resistance is now a certainty.

Agent Thompson conducted the meeting as if there was no opposition. He outlined the plans set forth for their removal. They are to sell their cattle and travel to Tampa to await transport to Arkansas. He then asked in a very friendly voice, if they wished to travel by land or sea. The chiefs asked for a recess to discuss. Before they reassembled, a spy, recruited by Agent Thompson, reported Osceola not only rallied them to resist but threatened to kill anyone who tried to leave. When the chiefs returned to council, Charlie Emathla was the only one who dared to defy the young warrior. Thompson closed the meeting with the reminder they would move come January 8th, by force if necessary. He didn't even bother to mention that President Jackson denied their request for sovereignty.

In visiting with Thompson afterwards, I realized he is weary of his post and has little concern which way the pendulum swings. He looks forward to leaving the whole business behind him. Without his support, the Indians have no proponent left in the Government. It will be up to me to rally the voice of the people to demand fair treatment for them.

Knowing you stand by me and support this cause makes it easier to bear being parted.

As for baby names, I wholeheartedly agree with taking from both our fathers. I think James Lawrence is a fine name for a son. As for a girl, I have no strong feelings on the matter and will defer to whatever name you favour. All of your suggestions are acceptable.

My love to you and Henry,
Theodore

His letter left her feeling uneasy; a feeling that lasted for several weeks until the next chain of events brought the possibility of war into stark reality.

Mid-December, disturbing news was received and spread rapidly through town that on November 26th, Osceola kept his promise to kill any tribesman who tried to emigrate. Chief Charlie Emathla supported the move west not wanting to take any part in the blood to be spilt by refusing to leave. He sold his cattle and moved his tribe to Fort Brooke to await transport. Osceola considered the act a betrayal of the tribe and he and his warriors carried out his threat. Charlie Emathla's body was found with the coins from the sale scattered on the ground around him. The warriors also cut communication lines between Fort Brooke and Fort King. The latter news hit too close to home for Betsy as it also cut off her connection to Theodore.

It came as no surprise when the troops promptly left Key West for Tampa aboard the *Motto*. Mrs. Gardiner stopped by Betsy's shop to tell her she would be traveling with her husband to Tampa and offered to carry a letter to Theodore. Betsy appreciated the thoughtful gesture and promised to send one over before nightfall.

That evening she poured her heart and soul onto paper, then balled it up and started over not wanting to burden Theodore more than he already was. The next one was too stiff and formal. It took several more attempts before she was satisfied with her words. As she was finishing her letter, Henry came to her with a drawing in hand.

"Please send this to Poppa."

Betsy took the paper from him expecting an animal of some kind. The image made her gasp and her cheeks burn.

"You don't like it?"

The hurt in his voice tugged at her heart. She pushed past her first reaction to reassure him. "Your drawing is excellent; a mirror could not have been more faithful. I am sure your father will love it."

He smiled his pleasure. "Good. I heard him tell you he wished he could see you grow heavy. I didn't know what he meant then but I do now. He was talking about the baby."

He ran off to play before she could begin to think of a suitable response. She was left alone staring at an intimate moment captured by the hand of childhood innocence. She hated it at first, but as she considered Henry's gesture and how it would please Theodore, she found the beauty in it. She positioned it carefully so the folds of the letter would not crease the image and then sealed the letter with wax. She called Henry in to run it over to Mrs. Gardiner along with a letter from Agatha and a thank you note for her generosity.

Christmas was quietly celebrated and a few days later the *Motto* returned with Mrs. Gardiner and her children. Betsy made a point of calling on her as soon as she was settled.

Mrs. Gardiner had taken ill on her voyage to Tampa but now feeling somewhat improved she welcomed Betsy's visit. A maid brought them tea. Mrs. Gardiner suggested Betsy serve as she was still weak from her ordeal. While Betsy poured, Mrs. Gardiner finished her story.

"By the time we arrived in Tampa, I truly was not myself. Captain Gardiner was assigned to lead a detachment to Fort King. He was understandably very concerned about leaving me behind. Major Dade is such the gentleman. He generously offered to take Captain Gardiner's place so that he could see to my needs. The proposal was accepted and Major Dade left for Fort King. By then I was feeling better which made the Captain feel as if he abandoned his men so when he discovered the *Motto* was ready to set sail we agreed I should return here and he should return to his men. So here I am back in Key West with my father. Oh and don't you worry about your letter. Major Dade is carrying it with him to Fort King."

Betsy smiled. "I wasn't worried. What a harrowing experience. Are you staying here to recuperate?"

"We plan to stay for the time being."

"I see. And how did you find Fort Brooke? Is it well fortified?"

"My yes, there were soldiers and militia everywhere with more due to arrive. With the forces we have, this war will not last a fortnight."

Betsy prayed she spoke the truth. She made her way home from her visit mostly deep in thought. The separation was hard enough, adding worry made it unbearable. It was all she could do to hold back the tears while she was in public. She hugged her arms tight around her body, uncaring that it emphasized her middle. Walking past two ladies huddled together in conversation, Betsy recognized them as the wives of prominent lawyers, newly arrived from Boston. She greeted them politely. They returned her greeting with lofty glances. She heard their whispers as they passed.

"I would never parade myself about in her condition."

"Obviously she has not heard of 'confinement' and has no concern for her ill-becoming presence."

Betsy's brows drew together trying to remember where she read about confinement. Oh yes, Victoria mentioned it in one of her letters and there was an article in one of her ladies magazines. Betsy discarded it as some fancy English practice but apparently the silly notion had made its way to Boston and now here. Oh well, she was a working woman and essentially head of the household while her husband was away. She had more important things to worry about than the offended sensibilities of ladies with nothing better to do than speak ill of others.

Fort King, December 28th, 1835

Theodore's spirits were melancholy as they often were when he finished penning a letter to Betsy. He folded the parchment, sealed it with wax, and placed it in the outgoing mailbox. It was Monday afternoon and he was working at the spare desk in the Indian Agent's office outside Fort King. He pulled out a new sheet of parchment and dipped his pen in the ink to start an article for both the Key West and New York papers. His letter to Betsy mentioned the events he was about to write of but he didn't tell her how he planned to join General Clinch's campaign on the morrow.

War had indeed begun. The death of Charlie Emathla was the final catalyst. Theodore knew the title he would use: INDIAN KILLS INDIAN–STARTS WAR. It was no surprise the death of an Indian would open the conflict, but how odd it should come at the hand of another Indian. Theodore wondered if Osceola acted on his own as tustenuggee or if his action was sanctioned by Chief Micanopy. One thing was sure, the other chiefs willing to move west wouldn't risk doing so now.

In the month since Charlie Emathla's death the Indians moved from their villages to the swamp lands in the Cove of the Withlachoochee in the hopes of being out of reach of the military. The warriors then spent the better part of December attacking plantations and farms in the middle of the territory and along the St. John's River on the eastern coast, burning, pillaging and butchering without mercy. Next, they boldly struck a military baggage train leaving many soldiers dead and wounded.

To the residents of Florida, it seemed as if the enemy was suddenly everywhere and the weakness of the military's defense brought about panic. Settlers fled their homes for more fortified places and safety in numbers, often bringing nothing with them. The burden put a strain on the meager supplies of the forts, including this one. It was said, the citizens of St. Augustine went to bed wearing their shoes in fear of imminent attack.

The militia tried to fight back but had trouble attacking an enemy who refused to stand and fight once the advantage of surprise was lost. It was a bloody month of humiliation for General Clinch, but the worst was yet to come.

His answer was to take the fight to the enemy's camp and tomorrow he was launching his campaign from Fort Drane—his plantation turned fort just north of Fort King—to the enemy's stronghold. He had two hundred and fifty of his men, plus Brigadier General Richard Call arrived a few days ago with five hundred mounted volunteers from St. Augustine. There was urgency in the timing of this mission. The volunteers' service expired at the end of the year, so Clinch planned to lead an attack against the Indians now while he had the numbers.

Clinch might wish for more men, and in fact Governor Eaton requested more troops in a plea to ensure the war was short, but President Jackson scoffed at the idea. His experience told him a heavy defense wasn't necessary. Besides, the Nation's military was small and already spread thin from Canada to the Florida Keys and westward. Secretary of War Lewis Cass was more concerned with building a defense against a possible war with France than against a handful of savages. General Clinch would have to make do with what he had.

Despite this concern, Theodore knew it was the perfect opportunity to report from the frontline of battle, not that he had any intention of being on the front line. He planned to observe from a safe distance. It was also likely to be his only chance to witness war firsthand because he promised to return home in a month and it wouldn't take more than a few months to bring about an end to Osceola's resistance.

With most of the soldiers at Fort Drane, Fort King was left with a defense of only forty-six men so General Clinch sent orders to Fort Brooke to send reinforcements. By Theodore's reckoning they were late arriving but he supposed the canon they were bringing could be the reason for the delay.

Needing a break he stood up to stretch his shoulders and back. He walked to the window in time to see Agent Thompson and Lieutenant Smith exiting the main gate of the fort walls presumably for an afternoon stroll. He nodded in greeting as they passed by the building headed towards the sutler's store. It was a nice day for a walk. Theodore returned to his desk deciding to quickly finish his report so he could enjoy one as well.

His head snapped up at the sound of a rifle shot and a blood curdling yell unlike any he had ever heard before or hoped to ever hear again. It was followed by a volley of shots not far away. It took a moment for his mind to register what it meant. He looked out the window to see the main gates of the fort being closed. It didn't occur to him that he might be in danger outside the fort. He considered himself friendly to both sides.

Leaving the building, he turned in the direction of the firing. He walked just beyond sight of the fort to find a war party scalping their victims. In horror, he couldn't take his eyes from the scene. The bestiality of the act made him aware of his vulnerability having foolishly left the building unarmed, but still he didn't flee. He recognized Osceola as he held aloft the scalp of Agent Thompson and in the crook of his arm lay the silver Spanish rifle, given to him by the agent not long ago. Theodore startled to notice Osceola had made eye contact. He froze in place only to be startled once more as the warrior again gave his shrill yell signaling his men to mount up and retreat on their nearby ponies.

As if in a trance, Theodore slowly moved forward stopping at the edge of the trampled and bloody grass surrounding the mutilated bodies. Their grotesque forms left no doubt of their fate. Even though he heard Osceola threaten to do just what he did, Theodore still couldn't believe he had carried it out. Even though Theodore warned the agent, he still felt guilt and remorse for not doing more to convince Thompson to heed the warning.

The acrid smell of smoke drew him deeper into the woods in the direction of the sutler's store. He began running toward the burning buildings not sure what he expected to find. He was met on the pathway by those escaping to the safety of the fort. He was assured there was nothing to be done to help those left behind and so he turned to follow the refugees back to the fort offering his assistance to an old black woman he recognized as the sutler's cook.

They had to pound on the fort gate and wait for Captain Lendrum to authorize their entry. The captain sent out a command of soldiers to give chase to the marauders, then interviewed each of them. Theodore summoned enough presence of mind to find pencil and paper to take notes. The sutler's family was at dinner when the attack occurred. The cook hid behind a water barrel in the empty store, all of the goods having been moved to the fort weeks ago. She said one of the Indians came in there tossing furniture, clearly upset to not find any supplies.

Next, Captain Lendrum ordered two men, by different routes, to take news of the attack to General Clinch at Fort Drane. Theodore volunteered to be one of them. Captain Lendrum turned him down out of hand. He could not condone a civilian to carry a military dispatch. Theodore argued that he not only knew the way better than the private assigned the duty but he had his own horse and the captain needed every man he could spare. Lendrum finally conceded.

Theodore quickly packed up his belongings, armed his rifle, and saddled his horse. The dispatch was passed to him as he rode out the gate. The other courier had a head start, taking a direct route. Theodore was to take the indirect route in the hopes it was less likely to be watched.

The sun was sinking as he started out with twenty miles to cover. Theodore felt exhilarated by the rush of adrenaline and the need to be vigilant. Man and rider flew beneath the moss laden oaks past all endurance to reach their destination in the wee hours of the morning.

He rode through the gate and dropped from the saddle leaving his mount in the care of a stable hand to walk him and brush down his sweaty flanks. A weary Theodore was immediately led to an audience with General Clinch and was more than surprised to learn he arrived ahead of the other dispatch.

They feared the worst until he arrived sometime later having narrowly missed being captured. Three warriors lay in wait on the side of the road. They burst from the brush as he approached, startling his mount. The horse reared and the attackers jumped out of the way of the flailing front hooves. When his horse returned to the ground the soldier spurred him into a hard gallop for the next quarter mile until he was sure there was no one in pursuit. He slowed his mount to a walk so they could both catch their breath but concern of another ambush made him leave the main path for a time. He rode into Fort Drane as weary as Theodore.

General Clinch ordered his men to be ready to leave Fort Drane an hour before first light. He was not going to wait any longer to face his enemy.

Chapter 29

It wasn't supposed to be like this....

For the second time in as many days, Theodore questioned his decision to follow the army into the wilds of Florida. He expected to suffer and he expected it to be grueling. It was the reason he chose to join the mission; so he would have firsthand experience of a soldier's life. He didn't expect to question military tactics or his patriotism.

He was exhausted. There was no time to rest from his overnight ride as messenger. General Clinch ordered them to leave Fort Drane in pursuit of the enemy just hours after his arrival. Impatient to do battle before the volunteers' hitch expired, Clinch pushed them at a merciless pace. There was little sleep to be had last night followed by another brutal day as their *friendly* Indian guides and a black interpreter led them on a narrow path through swamp and hammock. They finally came to a halt about three miles from the Withlacoochee River. General Clinch decided they should bivouac for the night with the orders to keep quiet and no fires. As much noise as seven hundred and fifty men made getting there, Theodore thought it was useless to try and conceal their position now. Adding to his exhaustion, he was on foot with the regular soldiers, having to leave his tired mount behind, and like them his feet were wet and sore. Without fire to dry them, he expected another miserable night with little sleep. The best he could do was change his socks for his last pair of dry ones. The possibility of being attacked meant they couldn't risk leaving their boots off to air out or sleep under mosquito netting and risk entanglement if they had to suddenly move. It was going to be a long night.

The men were emotionally exhausted as well. They were all on edge having walked for two days in difficult and unfamiliar terrain where behind every palm and bush a warrior could lurk waiting to attack and trying bravely to march ahead as if the knowledge didn't concern them. At least they were making enough noise to keep the rattlesnakes, alligators and panthers away and being winter there were fewer mosquitoes.

Clinch's order for silence kept the men from freely talking in camp but Theodore knew from listening to them today what they might face tomorrow was on the minds of all the men. How far would they have to travel before they met the enemy? How many Indians would they face? How would General Call's mounted volunteers do in action? The volunteers were essentially citizens of St. Augustine and the St. John River area scripted for a month of service and tomorrow was the last day. Could they be trusted not to turn tail and run?

No one was worried about getting across the Withlacoochee River. The guides were supposed to lead them to a shallow crossing before sunrise.

As the dark of night descended on their bivouac, Theodore leaned his back against a tree, balancing his journal on his raised knee. His pencil made a slight scratching sound as he took advantage of the dwindling daylight. His thoughts were interrupted by his companions.

The private on his left whispered. "You're riding a fine line, my friend."

Theodore finished his note and looked up. "How is that?"

"You are with us but sympathetic to them Injuns. How do we know we can trust you if it came down to us or them?"

Several others nearby nodded in agreement.

Another private asked, "How do they know you are on their side if you are with us?"

Theodore had been around these men for weeks at a time over the past year. He even bunked with many of them at Fort King. He didn't expect a question of trust to arise but on the other hand he could see their point— that was peace, this was war. "I am not here to fight with either side, only to observe the events."

The first private looked to the ground at Theodore's side. "You have a rifle. At whom will you point it?"

Theodore's gaze was steadfast. "Preferably no one, but if it comes to a matter of defense and my shot is needed, have faith it will be against the enemy." The words were hard enough to say, Theodore hoped he never had to put them into action, because he wasn't certain in the moment whom he would consider the enemy. Perhaps these men did have good reason to question him.

Lieutenant Graham stepped in to his defense. "Do you question my loyalty?"

The first private flushed. Everyone liked Graham. "Of course not."

"I am well acquainted with our enemy. I have given gifts to Osceola and his family, yet you would not question my motives. Mr. Whitmore is no different."

Lieutenant Fanning walked by admonishing them to be quiet, ending the conversation.

Theodore contemplated answering anyway but what could he say? He could reassure them he was a patriot but somehow he didn't think that would be enough. And in truth, if needed, could he pull the trigger against an enemy he didn't consider an enemy?

Theodore tried to get some sleep. He felt as if he had just dozed off when the bugle sounded reveille at four in the morning. The dogs howled and the men stirred. Theodore opened his eyes to see the shadowy figure of General Clinch running across camp under the moonlight with his arms waving wildly in an attempt to stop the bugler from announcing their position to the enemy.

It was a comical start to what promised to be a tedious day. With no fire, breakfast was hard tack, jerky and water. Within a half hour they were on the march again. The plan was to cross the river before sunrise and surprise the

Seminole in their camp.

Because of their slow movement through the heavy vegetation and swampy ground, it was past sunrise when they reached the place where they were to cross the Withlacoochee. Tall cypress trees with large ruffled trunks guarded both sides of the river intermixed with leafless deciduous trees. Between them mist rose like a gossamer veil softening nature's harsh edges. The smooth surface of the tranquil dark water reflected the soft morning light and black silhouette of the tree limbs hanging over the river. The scene was far too peaceful for the business at hand. All eyes nervously scanned the opposite bank for signs of danger lurking behind trees and fog.

Without the dark for cover, they lost their last chance at surprise. Even worse, the guides failed to bring them to the promised shallow crossing. Instead, they were now faced with water that was wide and deep. Their side of the bank only rose about a foot. On the other side, an open field spanned out several feet above the water.

Theodore maneuvered past the line of soldiers to reach the circle of officers discussing the situation. He stood behind the left shoulder of a lieutenant and blatantly eavesdropped.

The guide was speaking defensively. "I am sure the place could not be more than a few miles from here."

General Clinch asked, "Upstream or down?"

The guide studied the river and tentatively said, "Upstream."

General Clinch threw his hands up in disgust. "We do not have time to search any longer. We must reach the enemy today. We will cross here where we have the advantage of seeing what is across the river."

Theodore could well imagine what the general was thinking. It could take hours to find an easier crossing and he only had today to accomplish his mission before the script ended for the volunteers and his troops would drop in number from seven hundred and fifty men to two hundred and fifty.

Lieutenant Fanning pointed with his one good arm to the opposite bank. "We could commandeer that old canoe."

All heads turned to look where he pointed. It was a ragged looking vessel that had certainly seen better days.

Clinch grimaced and said to Fanning, "Send two of your men to retrieve it. Let us hope it still floats."

The lieutenant turned smartly and left the group to do his bidding.

General Call spoke matter of factly to General Clinch. "I have a man testing the water depth and strength of current to see if the horses can swim it. I also sent scouts a short way in either direction to see if there is a better place. If the first option fails I am going to put the rest of my men to work building a temporary bridge as I expect the second option will prove unviable."

General Clinch gave a bare nod of acknowledgement and General Call left the group as well.

Clinch spoke to his remaining officers. "Line your men up, weapons ready."

Within a half hour the back and forth grating of two-man handsaws filled the air punctuated every once in a while by a fallen tree. The two men returned paddling the canoe. It was so full of water it nearly sank before they made it to shore. It was emptied and six men climbed aboard to be ferried across bailing water as they went. New oarsmen took over for the return trip. The one in front did most of the paddling while the one in back alternated between paddling and bailing water. The process repeated over and over slowly moving the soldiers across, six men at a time.

If asked, Theodore wasn't sure which group he would bet on finishing first. Call's volunteers were making fairly rapid progress of felling trees. Meanwhile the group of regulars on the other side of the river was growing. Theodore watched as the latest group climbed the bank and dropped their haversacks. He frowned when he saw them lean their muskets against each other in a stack and join the other men milling about the open field. A few sentries were keeping watch on either side of the clearing. It was believed the Indians had a stronghold close by and they were certainly making enough noise cutting down trees to alert any scout in the area. So why, on God's green earth, would Lieutenant Fanning allow any of his men to put down their arms?

Theodore turned his furrowed gaze on General Clinch. Did he believe his enemy would wait for him at a battlefield or perhaps he was thinking he could march right up to their camp? Surely, he knew something of Indian war tactics. They would not wait to line up on an open battlefield and at a given signal start an orchestrated attack properly lined up across from their enemy. Goodness knows we used their tactics to win our Independence. Were the lessons so soon forgotten? Indians attacked with stealth and surprise as they so clearly demonstrated in recent months. If they have rules of engagement, it certainly didn't correspond with the white man's 'civilized' fighting.

By noon, the majority of the regulars were across the river and the bridge was fairly underway. Theodore waited at the water's edge for the canoe to return. It was his turn to cross. Watching the men struggle to row and bail at the same time he wished he could wait to cross the bridge with the volunteers. Unfortunately, that was likely to get him left behind which would certainly be worse than having to swim for shore.

One of the sentries called out a warning from the far side of the open field. "Indians! Indians!"

His voice was drowned out by a blood curdling war cry Theodore recognized from four days ago. Osceola and his warriors had arrived. A chill raced down his spine and his head snapped up in time to see a volley of rifle fire explode from the trees surrounding the open field. Soldiers dropped in agony as bullets found their mark. While the Indians were reloading, the soldiers still standing rushed to grab their stacked rifles.

It wasn't till the second round of firing that Theodore realized the precariousness of his position and ducked for cover. He crouched behind the closest tree and held his rifle at the ready as he observed the events playing out on the other side of the river. A glance behind him found General Call lining up his troops to defend against an attack from the rear. Theodore, General Clinch, the remaining regulars, and the river were now in the center of the circle with all backs turned to Theodore. So far the enemy was only across the river but they surrounded that field on all three sides. The water was the only means of egress for the soldiers from an enemy that was firing on them in rapid succession.

On the far side of the field, the short, one-armed, Lieutenant Fanning, bravely pulled together an offensive line. Several times they pushed forward only to fall back and he would rally his men again. Closer to the river, the Indians were sneaking in trying to flank the troops on the right, the side closest to Theodore. He could see a young warrior approaching behind the regulars just on the other side of the bank. He took aim, surprised at how steady he was, and fired at the Indian. He was pleased he hit his target and at the same time thankful it wasn't a fatal wound. General Clinch and the remaining regulars took up firing on both flanks.

As Theodore reloaded his weapon, a bullet grazed the tree just above his head sending a small shower of wood shavings down on his head. It was too close for comfort. He collapsed to a seated position at the base of the tree to gather his wits. A short distance in front of him, General Call, satisfied there was no further danger on their side of the river, turned his men towards the flanking Indians. Theodore mustered his bravery to turn around and face the battlefield in time to see, with five hundred guns now pointed at them, the Indians retreat away from the river.

General Clinch called out orders organizing a stronger resistance. Lieutenant Fanning was valiantly leading a charge pushing the Indians back into the hammock. Theodore was able to observe without having to get involved again. As the exchange of gunfire dwindled, General Clinch discovered bullet holes in his hat and sleeve. He looked at them as if surprised, "I do believe those fellows were firing at me."[11] Theodore wasn't sure if Clinch was surprised because they dared to fire at an officer or because he hadn't noticed the bullets flying past him.

About an hour after it started, the Indians disappeared, leaving the field to the soldiers. The ensuing silence lasted but a moment before it was filled with the general's orders. The regulars tended to the four dead and fifty-nine wounded on the battleground while the volunteers resumed building the bridge to make their return crossing easier. Theodore knew General Clinch would call it a victory to still have the field after the fight but all felt the demoralizing sting of Osceola's surprise attack. Only one soldier dared to inject a cheerful comment claiming to have wounded the great warrior.

While waiting for the bridge to be completed, Lieutenant Fanning sent scouts to follow the Indians and secure the area. They returned with a soldier's knapsack left behind by the Indians.

Lieutenant Fanning rifled through the contents. He finally found some letters identifying the owner of the knapsack. He looked up at his audience in dismay. "It doesn't belong to one of our men."

A corporal frowned. "What does that mean?"

Fanning said, "They must have attacked another troop."

There was much concern and speculation spoken between the men as to how the Indians had come to be in possession of it. General Clinch was called forth and shown the knapsack and letters. He looked at each of his officers. "You don't recognize this private's name?"

Each man answered, "No sir."

Speculatively Clinch said, "I haven't heard of any recent attacks on the patrols."

General Call stepped forward. "You don't suppose it could have come from an attack on the delayed reinforcements you were expecting from Fort Brooke?"

Horror passed over the faces around Theodore, likely mirroring his own. They were all thinking the same thing. Perhaps the reason the reinforcements hadn't arrived was because the Indians had attacked and defeated them. Slowly, as if trapped in a nightmare, some nodded their heads in agreement of General Call's assessment.

General Clinch dispelled the dire mood hovering over them. "Round up the men. We'll head back to where we camped last night."

The men gathered in small groups around campfires discussing the day's events in hushed tones as if fearful that speaking too loudly would bring about another attack. Theodore was about to remove his boots when movement at the camp's perimeter caught his eye. He watched as two Indians greeted one of their guides and were then led towards General Clinch's tent. Theodore stood up to follow, ignoring his comrades as they asked, "Hey, where are you going?"

Theodore caught up to them in time to hear the guide tell Clinch, "He carries a message from Osceola."

One Indian began speaking in Muscogee and the other interpreted for the general. "You have guns and so do we; you have powder and lead and so do we; you have men and so have we; your men will fight, and so will ours until the last drop of the Seminoles' blood has moistened the dust of our hunting grounds."[12]

Silence followed. The Indians turned back the way they had come, melting into the dark, before Clinch or anyone else could decide how to respond. General Clinch finally turned back to his tent mumbling under his breath what sounded to Theodore as "Damn Indians." The others turned away as well.

Theodore returned to his fire. He removed his boots but didn't lay down. His mind replayed the days' events over and over and analyzed all the ways it could have gone different or better. He didn't know how much time had passed when the dropping of his head woke him up. After about the third or fourth time, he finally laid down, succumbing to a dreamless sleep.

The following day was a somber march back to the fort gruesomely accentuated by the moans of the wounded.

Upon returning to Fort Drane on the second of January, General Clinch learned just how competent his enemy was at fighting for their homeland. Attacks continued against the plantations and last Sunday the newly built Mosquito Inlet lighthouse was destroyed, effectively putting it out of commission before it even commenced. Major Putnam was forced to abandon New Smyrna. He marched his troops to the north and commandeered Bulow Plantation, against the owner's wishes, to set up a makeshift fort awaiting further orders. Settlers were abandoning homes for the forts and from everywhere came requests for more supplies. But the General's hand trembled as he read the report from Fort Brooke received by way of Pensacola.

On the same day Osceola attacked Fort King and killed Agent Thompson, Alligator led a second band in an attack on the reinforcements making their way from Fort Brooke to Fort King. Major Dade's company of a hundred and one men were all believed to be dead except for two privates who escaped and made their way back to Fort Brooke, both severely wounded.

Clinch gathered the other officers and Theodore to read the report to them. Afterwards, the room was silent. Even though General Call had suggested they were attacked and they all agreed it was likely, it was a shock to learn nearly all were dead. Most of the men in Dade's company were familiar to them. The sorrow in the room was palpable. It was a devastating loss both personally and militarily speaking. Theodore spent many hours talking with Major Dade in Key West before his first trip to Fort King and it was Major Dade who handed him the letter from his aunt that led to his marriage to Betsy. Theodore mourned the loss of a friend; the second to be taken by the Seminoles on the same road.

Clearly they had underestimated their adversary. Even Theodore expected the army's strength to rapidly defeat the Indians. The ineptitude of Clinch's campaign was worrisome enough but Osceola's ability to attack by surprise on multiple fronts at the same time was daunting. It was clear more troops would be needed to wage war against a foe that could spread itself across the entire territory at once.

Theodore left the general's quarters to set up his tent and send a quick letter to Betsy. He was sure the general would be sending a courier to Tallahassee as soon as he could write his report. It occurred to Theodore that his last letter to her, if it left Fort King, was dated the day of the attack. She would be worried about him.

* * *

By January the Florida War, as it came to be called, swirled around both Theodore and Betsy. While those living in Key West were distant from the action, they still felt the effects. It was the second week of the New Year and Monday morning Betsy opened her door to find Robert Mason on her threshold, hat in hand, his eyes full of concern.

He greeted her with his usual. "Milady."

Betsy smiled despite her concern. He had addressed her as such since the day they met. When she asked him why, he said because she was a noble woman to put up with the likes of Theodore. She opened the door wide. "Come in, Mr. Mason."

He bowed his head and stepped into the house. "Good afternoon, Mrs. Whitmore. Can we talk? I have news I thought you should hear from me."

Betsy's throat tightened making it hard to speak. "Is it about Theodore?"

His lips thinned before he spoke. "Not directly. Word has come from Captain Anderson of the *Motto* in Tampa. On the twenty-eighth of December, Major Dade, Captain Gardiner and their entire command, 'cept for three, were massacred by the Indians. They never reached Fort King."

Betsy's hand flew to her mouth. "Oh my Lord!" She slowly lowered it to curl in a fist over her heart. Her thoughts went to their loved ones. "Poor Mrs. Dade. How tragic. Did you know her husband volunteered to go in Captain Gardiner's stead?"

"No, I wasn't aware of that."

"Mrs. Gardiner told me of his benevolence. But it seems now two good men were lost instead of one. Major Dade may yet be alive if not for that fateful gesture."

Mr. Mason's mouth thinned. "So it would seem."

"Has anyone told Mrs. Gardiner?"

"An officer was dispatched this morning to inform her."

"I must go and offer what comfort I can. Such a shame. Her children are so young. Is there any other news?"

"Plans are being made for the defense of the island."

"Surely we are too far away to be in danger."

"An attack here isn't likely but as wide spread as they have been it is only prudent to be prepared." He turned his hat in hand. "There is one more thing." He hesitated as if afraid to speak. "I cannot confirm the validity of it, but I have heard Fort King was also attacked on the twenty-eighth."

While Betsy was reeling with the portent of that news, Robert pulled a letter from his pocket. "This letter also arrived from Fort King."

She accepted it from him with hands surprisingly steadier than she felt. "At least it is in his handwriting."

"I'll leave you now to read it."

She put her hand on his arm. "Wait. Did you receive any news from Theodore?"

"No, there was only this one letter for you."

"Then wait a moment while I read it. I'm sure you are as anxious for news as I am."

He nodded.

Her eyes flew to his when she noticed the date. Her voice faltered. "It's dated two weeks ago, on the twenty-eighth." She read the letter in silence.

My darling wife,

> *It warms my heart to know you are safe from all the violence now writhing in this territory. I am sure by now you have heard of the raids on the plantations from the St. Johns down to the Halifax Rivers and even near here. The Indians are fortifying themselves not only with staples but it is also feared with liberated slaves to join their cause although there is some debate of how many are joining them willingly. I find the loss of the planters' slaves ironic as the planters were rallying for war in order to gain the Seminole slaves.*

> *I have also learned Micanopy's interpreter, Abraham, who we thought was encouraging removal, has in fact been working against it. He was holding secret meetings at the plantations to rally the slaves to their side when the time was right. In their desire for freedom, the Indians find a strong ally in the Negroes and their numbers are not small. Three hundred or more from the plantations and another two hundred free blacks living near St. Augustine are the conservative estimates.*

> *But who can blame the Black Seminoles for fighting? The slave hunters have tried to claim many blacks, some even born Seminoles, as runaway slaves even though they were free men. The price of coloured flesh is so high; those of low character saw an opportunity to gain a valuable commodity at no cost. Slavery has so many evils; one day soon it must come to an end.*

> *But let me start back at my arrival. My first priority was to renew my acquaintances at the Indian towns but I found them vacant except for those of the chiefs willing to move. It has been confirmed those planning resistance have relocated their families in a place called the Cove of the Withlacoochee.*

> *In early November, Agent Thompson was elated as the chiefs willing to move led their people to Ft. Brooke to prepare to emigrate. I fear he dismissed their plea for protection as unnecessary and it cost Chief Charlie Emathla his life. He was the first to sell his cattle as instructed by Agent Thompson and the first to pay the price. Considered a betrayal by Osceola, he killed him. This violent act is*

being considered a declaration of war. How strange then that the first strike would be Indian against Indian.

The brutality of these people often makes me question defending them. But I keep coming back to the right and wrong of it and our government is in the wrong. I have often heard two wrongs don't make a right which will surely prove to be true for both sides of this conflict.

A few weeks ago a supply wagon train was attacked. The Indians were the victor but a few days later a large cavalry force discovered Osceola's band in their camp. Close combat took place. The Indians got away but much of the supplies and papers from the wagon train were recovered.

Enough of this depressing news.

Did you perchance see the appearance of Halley's Comet the 16th ultimo? I witnessed its passing just after sunset when the upper sky was a midnight blue backdrop atop the dramatic reds and oranges of the fading sun. Quite a beautiful sight. I only wish we could have shared it together.

What do you think of Halley for a name? Perhaps not.

Beatrice, Brianna, Cassandra and Millicent. Those have recently come to mind.

Keep well my love. Another month and I will return to you.

Your abiding husband,

Theodore

Betsy handed the letter to Mr. Mason, rather than relay the information.

She was struck by the irony of the delay in mail. He was telling her things she already knew while she knew of things he had yet to experience when he penned the letter. His letter was from Fort King on the very day Osceola attacked it which must have occurred after he finished writing it. This could be the last letter she ever received from him. Fear made her heart skip.

She took a breath, rubbing a hand over their child. She had to think positive. He could have survived the attack or he may have been somewhere else. Maybe he was even now on his way home to keep his promise.

Mr. Mason handed the letter back to her. "Nothing we didn't already know. I'll be sure to tell you if I do hear anything concerning Mr. Whitmore."

Betsy nodded. "Thank you."

Mr. Mason showed himself out. Betsy donned a shawl against the winter morning chill and went to convey her condolences to Mrs. Gardiner. It was a difficult visit. The new widow was beside herself with grief. Betsy knew better than to offer vain words of comfort. She simply sat with her until Mrs. Gardiner decided to try lying down for a while.

On her return home, a crowd was gathering at Clinton Place, a triangular patch at the foot of Whitehead and Front Street. An impromptu town meeting of sorts. All the town dignitaries were present so she stopped to listen. They just finished sharing the news of Major Dade's command leaving a hushed silence over the crowd.

Mayor Fielding Browne said, "In the interest of keeping our community safe we are organizing patrols. If you are willing to volunteer please see Marshal Easton. We have secured a vessel to take a dispatch to Commodore Dallas in Havana, requesting naval support. Letters have also been dispatched to Washington. Forthwith a curfew is in place. There is to be no visible light from any home after dark to guide an Indian attack and anyone found walking the streets will be questioned by the patrol."

During the course of the week refugees with more tales of horror began to arrive fleeing from the Seminole's wrath. Over two hundred by week's end, most with nothing more than the clothes on their back. Shelter was given by those who had room to spare. Betsy opened their home to a mother with three children. They stayed for several weeks before moving on to the home of a relative.

The closer she came to her time the more Betsy felt like the world was falling apart.

Fears were somewhat allayed by the arrival of the frigate, *Constellation*, and her commander, Commodore Dallas, on Thursday. But word of the massacre of Mr. Cooley's family of New River while he was away wrecking and the arrival of Captain Dubois, the lighthouse keeper at Cape Florida, with his family plus sixty more refugees from the mainland again unsettled the town.

The following week, fifty-seven Marines were dispatched from Key West to reinforce Fort Brooke while a smaller detachment from the *Constellation* was sent to Cape Florida to secure the lighthouse.

Daily, Betsy worried about Theodore. After that first brief moment of doubt, she refused to consider he wasn't alive. She learned others had been slain besides Agent Thompson and his lieutenant but she was sure Theodore was not one of them. She also heard the refugees at the forts put a strain on supplies so at every meal she prayed he was safe and getting enough to eat.

* * *

One bright morning in mid-January, Betsy bit the thread from sewing the last bit of lace on the last piece of the layette. She shook out the gown to admire the finished piece then laid it against her rounded belly trying not to notice it didn't quite reach her lap. She felt huge and cumbersome these days. The only good thing about Theodore's absence was he couldn't see her all swollen like this. She put the dress aside to take upstairs later. It was one of several dresses she made. She also sewed layers of cotton cloth together to make nappies. Theodore's parents sent them a cradle from Austria. She used the softest cloth she had on hand to make the bedding. Aunt Agatha was almost finished crocheting a light blanket of white to be trimmed in white satin ribbon. With that, she would be as ready for this baby as she could be.

Carefully pushing her unwieldy self out of the chair, Betsy rolled her back to try and relieve the ache before heading to the outhouse—again. Outside, she could clearly hear the sounds of the work party clearing the woods further down Whitehead Street. That morning, a large group of sailors from the *Constellation* and other citizens walked past her house on a mission to make a clear path to the lighthouse, in case there was need of escape from an attack. It seemed to her a sound idea considering one lighthouse had already been destroyed by Indians.

Returning to the parlor, Betsy stopped at Aunt Agatha's chair. "Would you care for a stroll?"

Agatha inwardly grimaced. She would rather not but knowing the exercise made Betsy feel better she agreed with a nod and laid her crocheting aside.

Betsy paused at the door to give brief consideration of a shawl to cover her girth but quickly discarded the idea. She was not going to encourage the foolishness of hiding a natural God given condition.

Leaving the porch steps, she turned to the left to walk past the half dozen or so houses extending down Whitehead Street coming to the newest, Caroline Street, running perpendicular to the left and behind the pond. She could remember a time when her little shop was the last house on Whitehead. The town was growing fast. To the right was the new jail on Jackson Square and work was progressing nicely on the new Courthouse. They walked past a few more small buildings on the right to reach the former end of the road where this morning there had been trees and a footpath.

Now they gingerly picked their way through the fresh debris of perhaps a quarter mile of newly cleared road. When they reached the men, Betsy and Agatha lingered to watch the progress. The men were efficiently working in teams to cut and remove the trees and brush. Unmarried ladies brought them water and switchel reminding her of the late summer day five years ago when she did the same for Theodore.

She secretly smiled recalling how new their relationship was then. A budding friendship she hoped would be more but he was trying to discourage. Oh, how she longed for him that day and now she was his wife, about to give birth to his child. She absently caressed her belly. Oh, the joy of life! She had no idea then how happy she could be now, well, except for one flaw—his absence. Her musings were interrupted by Aunt Agatha.

"Are you ready to go back now? The matrons will be along soon with dinner for the men and I have promised to help serve."

"Then you should stay. I can return alone."

"I believe I'll walk back and rest a bit on the porch. There is no place here to sit."

Betsy looked around but she was right. "You should have Henry bring a chair when you return so you'll have a place to rest."

Agatha smiled. "I believe I will."

When they reached the house, Robert Mason was waiting for them on the porch. The site of him made Betsy panic. The last time he visited he brought bad news.

He held his hand out to assist Betsy first. "Milady." Encumbered with child, Mr. Mason grasped her elbow as well to steady her. When they reached the top he turned to assist Aunt Agatha and found her only a step behind. He held his hand out to assist her the rest of the way. "Mrs. Pary, how are you today?"

She ignored his hand. "As well as can be expected at my age."

Betsy eased her girth into one of the wicker chairs on the porch and warily asked Mr. Mason, "Is something wrong?"

"Not necessarily. We received mail from your husband. He writes little to me of what is happening with him. He mostly sends me instructions but I find his latest article disturbing."

"How so?"

"Apparently, he was with a detachment engaged in battle. Here. I thought you should read it before anyone else."

Betsy read the neatly written lines of his article with growing horror. She never imagined he would voluntarily march into battle with soldiers. She now knew he survived the attack at Fort King and at least she could assume he survived the battle for he wrote the story in past tense. He only briefly told of the events. The article was more about military mistakes and the brilliance of Osceola's strategy. While he did so very eloquently, without putting down the generals, nevertheless, his meaning was clear. When she was done, she quietly handed it back to Mr. Mason.

He sighed heavily. "I can't print this story here. It would upset too many."

Her feelings towards the Indians were not so benevolent these days, but she couldn't thwart Theodore's mission for the paper. "You must print it. You know how Mr. Whitmore feels about it. He wants a fair and balanced paper."

Mr. Mason sighed heavily. "But I fear you will suffer the wrath, not him."

"I thank you for your concern. I have known these people a long time. I will have the support of friends against those who would mean mischief. Print it as is. He will be home soon enough to defend it." She hoped it was true.

Mr. Mason nodded. "This also came for you."

She accepted the letter and held it to her heart. She was afraid to open it. Would she learn he was injured, unable to come home?

Aunt Agatha placed an arm along her shoulder as if reading her thoughts. "You won't know until you open it."

Betsy knew she was right. She took a deep breath and broke the seal. It was dated January third. His normally structured letters were skewed and meshed together, obviously the letter was penned in haste.

> *Dearest Love,*
>
> *I am safe and whole. By now you know of the attack on Fort King and in reading this you also know I followed General Clinch into battle. In both, I was not in harm's way.*
>
> *On further consideration, I really like the name Brianna but as I've said before I will defer to your choice.*
>
> *Give my love to Henry and Aunt Agatha.*
>
> *Your adoring husband,*
> *Teddy*

She let out the breath she hadn't realized she was holding as she clutched the precious letter to her heart. "He's safe." Tears of joy slipped down her cheeks. It brought great relief to the burden she carried upon her shoulders.

Aunt Agatha said, "Praise be."

Mr. Mason smiled. "I'm glad it is good tidings. If you'll excuse me ladies, I have work to do. Good afternoon."

They both returned his greeting before heading inside; Agatha to find Henry and Betsy to take her morning nap.

* * *

The January mail brought letters and a package from Betsy's family. Henry carried the wooden box wrapped in paper and tied with string home and set it on the dining room table. Betsy savored the anticipation of opening it.

Agatha came into the room. "What do you have there, Betsy?"

"Something from my family."

Henry eyed the string on the package. "Aren't 'cha going to open it?"

Betsy looked over at her ten year old son and wrinkled her nose at him. "You think I should?" He rolled his eyes in response to her teasing making her laugh. Betsy had a little trouble undoing the knot. Henry impatiently shuffled from one foot to the other. Finally, it came loose. Betsy held the twine out to Henry. "Do you think you could find a use for this?"

"Yes ma'am." He had lots of ideas of how to put it to use.

Next, she undid the brown paper wrapping and held it out to him. "And would you also like this for your drawings?" She didn't think she had ever seen him grin so widely.

"Yes, thank you."

Betsy opened the box and removed several letters placed on top. She put them aside to read later. Beneath them were baby gifts from her family. She and Agatha oohed and aahed over each piece she removed. First were blue and yellow knitted booties and a hat made by her mother, followed by a pair of hand-me-down walking shoes, linen diapers and wool diaper coverings and a rattle passed on from her sisters. Last was a pin cushion made by her little sister, Vertiline. It was embroidered with 'Welcome Baby' entwined with vines and flowers. Betsy was moved by the thoughtful gifts. She was on the cusp of long awaited motherhood and knowing her family shared in her joy made it that much sweeter. If only Theodore would come home, all would be perfect.

Henry and Agatha returned to their pursuits while Betsy read her letters. Mostly they contained news from home, but her parents also voiced their concerns for her safety. They obviously believed she was located in the midst of danger. She did her best in her return letter to assuage their fears.

* * *

January 18th brought sad news from Indian Key of the death of Dr. Waterhouse and his son. They had gone out fishing the day before and it was believed they were caught in the bad squall that passed over the keys. The doctor's body was discovered near the overturned boat but his son could not be found. Betsy and her family sailed to Indian Key with Max and Abby to pay their final respects to a lost friend.

By the end of January, most white settlers had abandoned the Florida peninsula south of St. Augustine. As head of the household, Betsy felt it her duty to keep the family safe. In so doing, she kept a loaded rifle on the clothes pegs in her room. She learned many years ago from Max's crew how to use it, hoping to never need it.

Her condition was now so far advanced as to make sleep difficult at best. It was one of those nights she was tossing and turning when she heard a distant repetitive thumping. It would cease for a moment only to resume again. She crept to the window of her bedroom the better to hear. The strangeness of the sound gave rise to fear that rational thought was unable to temper. She quietly made her way to the corner to retrieve her loaded rifle. Holding on to the weapon made her feel somewhat better. It was not long before she heard the approach of men on patrol obviously alarmed by the noise. She remained tense, waiting, not knowing what would happen. Was this an attack? Was it a war drum?

She listened carefully as the voices faded in the distance. Now that she had her immediate fear under control, reason prevailed. If it was an attack, why would they announce themselves? Theodore often said the Indians used stealth. She pulled on a light wrap, never letting go of the gun, and made her way downstairs to peer out of the front windows. The street was bathed in the light of a nearly full moon. Not a good night for a sneak attack and another reason this didn't make sense. No shouting, no voices. She began to relax a little more but kept her vigil waiting for the patrol to return to its post.

Twenty minutes later, the patrol passed by her window. She couldn't hear what they said but their tone was very relaxed and jovial. She breathed a sigh of relief and tiptoed back to her bedroom. She returned the gun to its place and crawled under the covers. She tried to relax, waiting for the rush of excitement to pass. It seemed like hours later before she fell into a fitful slumber.

The following day the tale was regaled with much sport for the officer on duty who first sounded the alarm. For it was not a drum but the sound of a hound scratching his fleas atop of a cistern cover. However, such was their high alert, one of the patrol wives packed up her children and her bags prepared to flee the island before the source was discovered.

All of this, Betsy relayed in her letters to Theodore. She continued to send him letters even into February. With the outbreak of war, she really didn't expect him to be on his way home. At the very least, the roads were likely unsafe to travel, preventing his return.

Chapter 30

Key West, February 17th, 1836

It wasn't supposed to be like this....

It was too soon.

Betsy was breathing hard when the constricting pain finally eased. Days ago, Abby assured her most times the first baby was late but this one was coming early. She feared it was a bad omen and so she prayed ever more devoutly between the pains, holding tight to her rosary. Besides, Theodore was supposed to be here to comfort her for this ordeal. He was not supposed to be trapped in middle Florida.

She had no idea of the hour, other than it was before sunrise. The pains awakened her from a fitful slumber and for a while she dozed in between them with hope that morning was close enough she could wait till then to alert the household.

Betsy felt uncomfortable all day yesterday. The pressure on her back took a turn towards intolerable in the afternoon but she struggled through the day anyway. By evening, her burden seemed too heavy to bear any longer so she betook herself to bed early. She fell asleep before dark, briefly waking when Aunt Agatha checked on her before retiring to bed.

The strength of the next pain caught her by surprise and she involuntarily cried out. Her hands clenched and twisted the bedding for support. She wanted to laugh when she recalled doing the same thing while planting this child, but the pain robbed her of breath.

A moment later Aunt Agatha was in the room, a cloud of stormy gray hair trailing down her back. In her delirium, the sight amused Betsy. Amazing that in all this time she had never seen Agatha's unbound hair and for once her brusque demeanor was actually calming. "Is it time?"

Betsy could only nod in response. Her jaw was clenched tight holding in her cry of agony.

Agatha turned to light an oil lamp. As the room filled with the soft glow, Henry appeared in the doorway. Agatha quickly stepped in front of him, blocking his view of the bed. "I need you to go get Mrs. Eatonton." Henry started for the stairs. "Get dressed first." As he passed back down the hall to return to his room she added, "Be sure to answer, if you encounter the patrols. And walk with Mrs. Eatonton on the way back, don't run ahead of her." Agatha turned back to the room. "What do you need, Betsy?"

"I don't know. I've never done this before."

Agatha grimaced. "Neither have I. What I meant was do you need water or a cold compress or something?"

Betsy was resting in between the contractions. "A compress please."

Agatha retrieved a clean cloth and poured water in the basin. She brought them to Betsy's bedside. As she leaned over to apply the cloth to her forehead, Betsy asked, "What time is it?"

"Just after two."

For a half hour, they waited. Agatha applied compresses and wiped her brow while Betsy did her best not to show her pain.

They both were relieved to hear the front door open and Abby's soothing voice calling out, "Hold on Betsy, dear, I am here." Moments later she cheerfully breezed into the room as if arriving for a visit and tea instead of midwifery in the wee hours of morning. First she checked Betsy's progress. She smiled when she looked at her patient. "You have not long now." Next she and Agatha helped make Betsy more comfortable, then she sent Agatha to retrieve a list of items.

By this point, Betsy was feeling tired and cranky. She wanted it to be over so she could go back to sleep. When the next pain took her, her spirit weakened. She was near tears as she cried out to Abby, "I don't want to do this without him." She knew she was being ridiculous when she said it but the words flowed uncontrolled from her mouth. "I've never even witnessed a birth. How am I supposed to do this?"

Abby wiped her brow again. "You need not worry, dear. Your body knows what to do."

Another contraction gripped her closer and stronger than the last and with it anger flashed through her. When she could speak again it was to scream, "Why isn't he here? He promised me. I'm not doing this without him." She continued yelling unknowing and uncaring of what she was saying, nearly becoming hysterical.

Abby used a firm tone to reel her back in. "You are going to have to do it alone. Even if Theodore were here only you can birth this baby, but I am right here to help."

And then the tears came. Betsy sobbed. "I can't."

Abby smiled. "Yes you can. You are the strongest woman I know. You amaze me."

Betsy looked at Abby, surprised by her words. Then her eyes flew open wide and she rose up on her elbows. "Where's Henry?" She hoped he hadn't heard her wailing.

Abby casually put her hand on Betsy's shoulder. "He is not here. He was set on coming back with me, but I convinced him he would be most helpful watching over Emily, Christoff and Hawthorne since Captain Max is away at sea."

Betsy settled back into the pillows only to rise up again. This wave of pain demanded she push.

She didn't recall much after that. It was a blur of Agatha returning to the room, Abby giving her instructions, pushing, breathing, and finally released pressure. She collapsed against the pillows barely registering Abby's words.

"You have a girl."

Her trance like state was broken by the sound of her baby's first cry bringing to mind her earlier worry. "Is she healthy? Is everything as it should be?"

Abby looked up from tending Betsy. "Your daughter is fine."

Aunt Agatha was cleaning the baby's face. "She looks as well as any other babe I've seen."

Betsy impatiently waited for Aunt Agatha to let her see her child.

Joy overwhelmed her as she accepted the infant wrapped in a towel. She touched a finger to the tiny cheek and smiled when her daughter opened blue eyes like hers. Tears streamed down Betsy's face. She was truly a mother. Her baby lay safe in her arms as worn out as she was from the ordeal. She kissed her tiny forehead.

She had a daughter!

Brianna. Theodore liked the name and so did she.

Betsy was so focused on her daughter it was some time before her awareness returned to Agatha and Abby's presence. Her smile for them was radiant. "Thank you."

Abby's eyes were soft. "You are welcome."

Out of respect for family, Betsy offered first to Aunt Agatha. "Would you like to hold her?"

Aunt Agatha gently lifted her grandniece. "Do you have a name?"

Betsy relaxed her tired body but her gaze never strayed from her daughter. "Brianna Kate."

The ladies smiled. It was a good name.

Betsy's thoughts strayed to Theodore. He missed the birth and being first to hold her.

Abby ran her finger across the tiny down covered head. "Her hair is dark like yours."

Agatha said, "She has Theodore's nose."

A moment later, Abby said, "You should try to nurse before you both fall asleep. Do you know how?"

Betsy nodded, a wistful smile in her eyes as she recalled watching her mother nurse her youngest sister, Vertiline, while patiently answering Betsy's timid questions. She wished her mother could be here now to share this moment with her.

Abby and Agatha quietly left the room giving the new mother and daughter time alone to get acquainted as the sun appeared to greet the new day.

Later that morning in the Eatonton's sitting room, Henry shyly approached Abby. "Is my momma sick?" Her broad smile instantly settled the churning in his stomach.

"No, she is perfectly fine and you now have a sister."

"I do?" Her answer surprised him. Momma said he would be getting a brother or sister soon, that she was holding it in her tummy till it was big enough to be in the world, but he didn't expect it to be today. He wondered how the baby got out of her tummy but he didn't want to ask Mrs. Eatonton. He didn't want Emily to know that he didn't know. It would be embarrassing. She was only six but she had two brothers so he was sure she must know how it happens.

Mrs. Eatonton added, "Her name is Brianna."

Poppa told him since he was the older brother, that boy or girl, he was expected to be the baby's protector, but he didn't know how he was supposed to go about it. Mrs. Eatonton squeezed his shoulder. He liked that she didn't ruffle his hair like most adults. Touching his shoulder made him feel more grown up, and he stood a little taller as she left the room. Emily came up beside him and pushed against his shoulder with both hands knocking him a step sideways. It was her way of getting his attention but only when there wasn't any adults around to see. He turned his head and looked down at her.

"You just wait and see Henry Whitmore. Everything will be about the baby. Your new momma won't have time for you anymore."

Henry wanted to wipe the smug smile off Emily's face. "No she won't. She promised she would still love me just the same."

"She'll still love you but she won't spend time with you. That baby's gonna keep her too busy."

Henry frowned. He hated it when Emily acted smarter than him. Especially when he had a feeling she was right.

The following afternoon, Henry returned home. He ran up the stairs to peak in Betsy's room and loudly whisper, "I want to see the baby."

Betsy had just put a sleeping Brianna in her cradle. She motioned Henry forward and put a finger to her lips. She smiled as he made an exaggerated effort to cross the floor without making a sound. It was amusing but also appreciated. It had taken her a while to get the baby to sleep after her feeding.

When he reached the foot of the cradle Betsy whispered, "This is your sister, Brianna Kate."

"Poppa told me I'm a big brother now, and I have to protect my new sister."

Betsy smiled. "That's right."

"Protect her from what?"

"She'll need you to watch out for her and make sure she doesn't get hurt."

"Can I hold her?"

Betsy didn't want to discourage Henry but she also didn't want to wake Brianna. She knew there would be times their needs would conflict and she would have to choose between them but not so soon. Henry looked so excited; she couldn't tell him to wait. "Go sit on the bed." Betsy picked up Brianna and placed her in Henry's lap, showing him how to support her head. Then she sat next to him.

"Momma?"

When he hesitated she prompted him. "What is it Henry?"

"Is it bad that I was... disappointed when Mrs. Eatonton told me I had a sister?"

Betsy put her arm around his shoulders and her other hand against Brianna's side to make sure he didn't drop her. "No. Disappointment doesn't make you bad unless you harm another because of your disappointment. A good person has disappointments the same as anyone else. The difference is they find a way to overcome it because it is selfish and displeases God." She lifted his chin to look at her while she gently said, "And pouty boy is unpleasant to be around."

"Oh."

"Were you disappointed because you wanted a brother?"

Henry shook his head. "Emily said she wished she didn't have any brothers."

"So you were upset because you have a sibling not because it was a girl?"

Henry nodded.

Betsy looked at Brianna contentedly sleeping. "She likes you. Do you know how I know?"

He shook his head.

"She's still sleeping. If she didn't like you she would cry. Why does Emily wish she didn't have brothers?"

"Because they get all the attention."

"Are you afraid we'll love you less because of Brianna?"

He shrugged.

She squeezed his shoulder. "I promise we will always love you."

"I know but Emily said babies need lots of attention."

"They do. Brianna is tiny and helpless, and she will depend on us for everything, especially me. But it won't be forever, Henry. Only for a little while until she gets bigger. I promise I will make time for you, if you promise to be understanding when your sister's needs have to come first."

Half-heartedly he said, "I promise." He half turned pushing Brianna towards her. "Can I go play outside now?"

The baby whimpered as she was awkwardly transferred from brother to mother. Betsy called after him, "Be sure to be back by suppertime."

Henry ran off leaving Betsy alone to once again wish Theodore had been there to witness the touching moment and to help Henry cope. Theodore was missing so many little moments already.

* * *

Betsy gently towel dried little Brianna after her first bath. She was still overwhelmed by the newness of motherhood and the depth of her love for this little being. She was thankful her younger siblings gave her experience with babies; the alternative would have been truly daunting indeed.

She folded one of the nappies into a triangle and laid Brianna down pulling the three corners together over her tiny belly, she pulled a straight pin from the pin cushion to fasten it using her fingers as a barrier to protect Brianna from an accidental prick. She forgot how much she hated the pins. They inevitably worked loose to stick one or both of them. Betsy had an alternative idea she wanted to try as soon as she had a free moment and could keep her eyes open longer than it took to thread a needle.

It wasn't going to be today. She fed and burped Brianna then laid her down looking forward to a nap herself. Instead her sweet little baby wailed. She checked the pin first, then tried patting her back hoping to quiet her. It didn't work. Betsy picked her up and began pacing the floor. So much for taking a nap. An hour later she was still pacing. On the sixth or seventh attempt to put her down, Betsy got as far as lying down before Brianna started crying again.

Swaddling. She hadn't tried that yet. Betsy got a clean linen towel and wrapped Brianna up tight. After another twenty minutes of pacing to get her back to sleep, Betsy was finally able to lay her down. They both slept for an hour and a half before Brianna started whimpering. It was time to feed her again. Betsy fell asleep several times during the process. Afterwards the wailing started again.

Betsy was at her wits' end. She didn't understand it. She could easily calm Abby's children when they were fussy. Why could she not do the same for her own baby?

Downstairs, Agatha answered the knock on the door. She waved their guests upstairs with impatience. "*Please,* see what you can do to satisfy that child."

Betsy had never felt so relieved to see someone as when Abby appeared in her bedroom doorway with six year old, wide-eyed, Emily behind her.

Abby raised her voice to be heard over Brianna. "I've come to check on the new mother and baby."

Betsy voiced her frustration. "Why can I calm your babies but not mine?"

It wasn't difficult for Abby to surmise the problem. "Because you are too tired."

Abby held her arms out for Brianna. She began walking with the baby's head over her shoulder and patting her back much harder than Betsy had been doing. In a few moments they heard her burp and the wailing reduced to a whimper.

Betsy was horrified. "I'm sure I heard her burp."

"Maybe she needed a second one."

Betsy sat on the bed, shoulders slumped, head in her hands. "I thought I would be a good mother."

Abby knew exactly how Betsy felt; exhausted, and incompetent. "When did you last feed her?"

"I just did, she's can't be hungry."

"Perfect. Let me take her out for a stroll and you can get some rest. I'll bring her back when it's time for her next feeding."

Betsy tried to protest but Abby cut her off.

"Do not argue with me. Off to bed." Abby placed necessary baby items in a basket and handed it to Emily. "You'll soon learn as the mother of a newborn to take sleep when you can."

Betsy said, "But I just took an hour nap with her." She didn't want Abby to think she was weak.

"And I say you need more. Sleep. She'll be back before you know it. Come along Emily."

In a blink, Betsy was standing alone in a bedroom that was suddenly too quiet. Not knowing what else to do, she laid down as Abby suggested and was instantly asleep. The sun was setting when she woke again. At first she wasn't sure what had awakened her but then she felt the heaviness in her breasts. The cradle was empty. Reminding herself Abby was perfectly capable of taking care of a newborn, she ran her hands over her dress and a brush through her hair before twisting it in a loose bun and went in search of her daughter. At the bottom of the stairs she could hear Abby's voice on the porch. She walked outside to find Aunt Agatha and Abby rocking on the porch enjoying the evening breeze while Henry and Emily played a game in the yard and Christoff entertained Thorn on the porch. Abby held a swaddled Brianna in her lap who was sucking on Abby's little finger.

Abby smiled, "I'm glad you're awake. This wasn't going to pacify her much longer. Do you feel better?"

"Yes, I feel rested. Thank you."

Abby stood up. "Mrs. Baxley did the same for me after each one of mine. Those few hours really help get your feet back under you."

Betsy sighed, "Yes, they do. Thank you so much, for everything Abby. What would I do without you?"

Abby leaned over Brianna to kiss her friend on the cheek. "You are welcome, and if I have not told you before, you have a beautiful daughter."

* * *

Sunday, February 21st, 1836

Four days after Brianna's birth, Betsy was feeling a bit more like herself. During Brianna's morning nap she finally worked on her diaper idea. She sewed pieces of ribbon around the triangle edge like belt loops and then took a strip of ribbon and sewed the center to the point of the triangle. Putting the diaper on Brianna, she fed the ribbon through the loops around to her back, crossed it, and came back around to the front to tie it. It seemed to be secure but it was cumbersome working the ribbon around her body. Betsy made a second one and this time when she changed her diaper, Betsy ran the ribbon through the loops ahead of time and then slipped it on Brianna like pants and tied it. Other than having to straighten the corners over her belly it worked pretty well.

Midday she had to take a nap too but in the afternoon she had just enough time to fashion a sling from a remnant of dress fabric. The outcome was more serviceable than she imagined. She was now able to carry Brianna close to her chest and have her hands free to work. She tried it out that evening while writing letters. The mail ship was due in tomorrow so there was no time to waste. Of course the first letter was to Theodore. She had so much to share with him.

> *My dearest love,*
> *We have a daughter! She arrived just before sunrise on the 17th inst. I have named her Brianna Kate taking her middle name from your mother's. She has your full lips and nose and my eyes and dark hair. She is beautiful. I thank God every day for so richly blessing our union.*
> *Not having received any letters from you since the beginning of January, I am assuming the mail is running poorly so I will take the liberty of sending your parents a letter announcing her birth.*

At least she prayed it was the mail run delaying his letters and not the unthinkable. She looked down at the sweetly sleeping face peeping out of the sling. "Your father is delayed getting home. That's all."

She finished his letter and then one for his parents and hers before it was feeding time again. She visited with Aunt Agatha while she nursed. Afterwards, she paced the room with Brianna on her shoulder to burp her when she noticed the family Bible. Here was another task a husband would normally do; recording the birth. For perhaps the hundredth time today she wondered where he was and what was keeping him.

After she laid Brianna down to sleep, she took the Bible from the shelf. It was just a little thing, recording a name, but being tired and overwhelmed Betsy was not thinking clearly. She opened it to the family history page and was about to dip the pen in the ink when she realized the recordings were of the Wheeler family line. She must have made a sound for Aunt Agatha asked, "What is it dear?"

Dismayed and a little lost as to what to do, she looked to Aunt Agatha. "I don't know where to write Brianna's birth. This Bible belonged to Ben. I suppose I should return it to his family."

Aunt Agatha came to look over her shoulder and being a practical woman she suggested, "Write it on a piece of paper and slip it into the Good Book for now. I will write to our solicitor to have the Whitmore Bible sent to us. It is likely still in the library at my brother's estate."

Betsy did as she suggested and then turned in for the evening. It was early by her standards but she still tired easily.

* * *

Fort King, February 22, 1836

Theodore stood outside the Indian agent's office to see the latest arrivals to Fort King and more importantly, the first to travel the road from Fort Brooke since Dade's fateful attempt in December. A sentry brought word of their approach an hour ago exciting the whole fort. It had been weeks since anyone new had come or gone through the gates. The fort was currently manned by fifty men under Lieutenant Colonel Crane.

His promise to Betsy weighed heavy on Theodore's mind during the march back to Fort Drane with General Clinch in January. It prompted him to leave for Fort King in the company of the courier. His plan was to find his way to Fort Brooke and home. It turned out to be a bad decision. He became trapped at the now isolated Fort King since the road south was declared unsafe for travel and he was not allowed to return to Fort Drane with Clinch's courier.

The mail was also severely delayed as well since it was now being rerouted from Tampa to Tallahassee and had to travel overland to Fort Drane. He was long past due for heading home and Betsy had no way of knowing. The letter he sent in January was hopeful of his imminent departure. His letters of February still sat in the outgoing mailbox. The last courier had orders to carry only military correspondence. Fortunately, he dispatched a quick note to Betsy of his safety and delay along with his last article about the battle from Fort Drane. He hoped Betsy wouldn't worry too much.

Perhaps this troop's arrival would provide a means of safe travel for him. He was growing desperate to return home.

As the commander came into view he recognized General Edmund Gaines from the Black Hawk war. A gaunt and weathered man with course gray hair, he was known for his confrontational attitude. Theodore wondered what he was doing here. His command stretched from the border of Texas to the western panhandle of Florida, not this far east. Worse, Theodore knew President Jackson placed General Scott in charge of the Florida War. He witnessed Gaines and Scott clash in Illinois. They held the same rank, militarily speaking, but Old Hickory favoured Scott which probably explained why he was given command. Gaines' presence did not bode well.

The general was followed by twenty or so 'friendly' Indian guides, about a thousand men, a full band, and a one-pounder cannon. Their arrival overwhelmed the small garrison.

One could only imagine what they must have seen as they passed the site of the massacre. Theodore knew this man was on a mission and likely would not stay long. If he could not travel with them, the next priority was to interview the men.

It wasn't long before General Gaines was heard loudly complaining. Apparently he expected to find ample supplies for his troops at Fort King. The best they could provide was seven days' worth of rations. Theodore soon learned the lack of supplies would force Gaines to return to Fort Brooke. Hope rushed through him. He had to gain an audience with the general. Here was his way home.

Theodore finished interviewing the fourth private. Their descriptions of the death scene they encountered were enough to create nightmares in the stoutest of souls. Images of a multitude of buzzards creating a black mass as they flew away, the bodies of friends left to rot where they fell, noticeably parallel to each other and so grotesquely decayed they had to be identified by their belongings. One interviewee was part of the burial detail. His words were so graphic, Theodore was thankful to be interrupted by his call to duty.

A captain approached Theodore while he was finishing his notes before looking for the next candidate. "Would you be Mr. Theodore Whitmore?"

Theodore looked up to find a man close to his age with the telltale mannerisms of a West Point graduate. "Yes, sir."

"My name is Captain Ethan Allen Hitchcock."

Theodore shook his hand. "Any relation to General Ethan Allen?"

The captain betrayed no emotion with his straightforward answer. "My grandfather."

Theodore let himself get carried away on the excitement of meeting the grandson of a war hero. "He was a good man. One of my favourite Revolutionary stories is how he and the Green Mountain Boys captured Fort Ticonderoga. Did he ever speak of his exploits?"

"I'm afraid he died before I was born."

Contrite, Theodore murmured his apology having forgotten that detail of the general's history.

"I hear you asked to interview officers?"

Theodore nodded. "Yes, sir. Are you offering your account?"

"I am. But first, I believe I have something of yours." He pulled a letter from his pocket that looked to have been trampled in the mud and handed it to Theodore.

To see Betsy's handwriting was a surprise. "Thank you, sir. Where did you find it?"

"Lying on the ground near Major Dade. It must have fallen out of his coat pocket when it was taken by the Indians."

Theodore reverently held the letter. Several others arrived in the mail brought with the troops from Fort Brooks but this one was special knowing how close he had come to never receiving it. It was hard to contain his impatience to read it but he wanted this interview and hopefully this man's help gaining passage back to Tampa.

The captain smiled in understanding. "Our talk can wait. Go. Read your letter. Feel free to seek me out when you are done."

Theodore nodded then gestured with the letter. "Thank you, sir. Words are not enough."

"My pleasure."

The captain turned away. Theodore headed for the privacy of his tent. He turned the letter in his hand. The outside of it was stained with water, dirt and blood. Major Dade's blood. His heart ached for the loss of his friend. The weight of it told him Betsy used two sheets of paper, something his frugal wife never did. It was written too soon to be about their child, unless... He broke the seal and unfolded the sheets to reveal a pencil drawing that would have brought him to his knees if he hadn't already been sitting down. Henry faithfully captured Betsy in a beautiful moment Theodore had longed to see. She was standing in silhouette, looking down, caressing her rounded belly which pulled her dress tight delineating her middle. The details were so true it was as if Theodore was seeing her with his own eyes. He stared for long moments unable to move or think of anything except how much he missed his family.

He already broke his promise to her. It was nearing the end of February and he was a month late and still trying to leave this frontier. He wanted to be there when her time was due but she was so close, he could have already missed it. He may even now have a new son or daughter.

He read the short note included with the drawing now anxious to get to the other letters in case there was news.

20th December, 1835

My dearest husband,

I pray this letter finds you in good health. I write in haste as the Gardiner's are leaving early in the morning for Fort Brooke and have promised to carry this letter to you.

We are all well. Henry has hit another growth spurt. In the last two months, he has increased vertically as much as I have horizontally.

I miss you so much and pray every day you come home safe to me.

In my dreams, dear, I hold your hand over the place where our child grows, basking in your loving gaze which leads to other intimacies. I long for the day you are home to turn this dream into reality. Be prepared, for I fear, I will scarcely be able to let you out of my sight.

Yours always,
Betsafina

Her words would likely invade his dreams as well. And his frustration grew. He had to find a way to leave this place. He quickly read the other letters containing random news, and more baby name suggestions but nothing significant. He promptly left his tent in search of Captain Hitchcock only to find him waiting nearby and ready to resume their conversation as if there hadn't been a break.

"I have read your articles in the *New York Weekly*. You boldly write of the noble defense of the Indians against our Government and a fraudulent treaty and yet you do so without exaggeration. Neither side is portrayed as villain or hero, only men doing what they feel compelled to do. A rare find in a journalist, not to mention a rarity of papers to print it. Most are timid when it comes to speaking ill of war heroes."

"Thank you. Your sincerity leads me to believe you feel similarly."

"I do."

"Does that not make it difficult to do your duty on occasion?"

The captain grimaced. "It does, on occasion. I hear you are desirous of making your way to Fort Brooke."

"Hmm."

"If we are to return, I'll ask the general for his permission on your behalf."

In Ethan Hitchcock, Theodore found a friend. The interview turned into a sharing of personal lives and they talked long into the night. They spoke of why and how they got to this place, the tragedy of Dade's command and their plans for the future.

Because of this camaraderie, Captain Hitchcock admitted he wasn't supposed to be in Florida. Secretary Cass ordered him to Texas but when General Gaines took it upon himself to move the troops from New Orleans to Fort Brooke, Hitchcock felt compelled to stay with the volunteers. And when Gaines arrived at Fort Brooke and learned General Scott was in charge, he still pushed forward. "Gaines considers Scott his nemesis."

Theodore nodded. "I witnessed as much at the Black Hawk incident when Scott was sent in to direct Gaines's command."

"The President playing favourites doesn't help. Well, I suppose it is time to call it a night. You will need to be ready to leave first thing in the morning, in case your request is granted. Good evening to you, sir."

Theodore was packed and ready when Captain Hitchcock approached the next morning. "We are returning to Fort Brooke, rations being what they are here, and General Gaines granted permission for you to come along." Theodore's enthusiasm was noticeable. "However, I must warn you, he plans to detour along the Withlacoochee to try and engage the enemy."

Theodore's spirits fell. What was he to do? Getting caught up in another battle could be more of a risk than traveling on his own.

Chapter 31

Key West February 27th, 1836

The second Sunday after giving birth, Betsy, Agatha and Henry attended Church services. She carried Brianna in her sling making more than just the new baby the center of attention. Monday morning, orders were pouring in for a sling like hers and diapers too once they learned of her idea. Life was going well for Betsy and would be perfect as soon as Theodore returned.

The following week Abby dropped by Betsy's shop for a visit. Her ladies had the work in hand so Betsy decided to take the afternoon off. She led Abby across the street to her home to join Aunt Agatha for afternoon tea. As they walked up the porch steps Abby said, "I do not mean to be rude Betsy but how do you do it? I can barely keep up with myself and the children with the help of Max and the Baxleys. You are managing the household, raising a child, tending a newborn, and running a business all on your own."

Betsy stopped at the door and turned to her friend, she hadn't given it much thought before Abby pointed out the fullness of her responsibilities. "I suppose one finds a way to do what must be done."

Betsy ushered her guest into the parlor and her jaw dropped. Across the room, Aunt Agatha waited beside the table already set for tea.

Abby smiled. "We wanted to surprise you."

The thoughtful gesture had Betsy close to tears. "You certainly succeeded."

"It was nice of you to willingly cooperate by leaving the shop early. I thought perhaps I was going to have to manipulate you into doing so."

Betsy removed the sling and placed Brianna in the cradle before turning to Abby with a quirky smile. "And if I refused?"

They took their seats around the table as Abby teased. "We are too good of friends for you to ever deny me anything."

Betsy laughed. "I suppose you're right."

Brianna quietly napped allowing Betsy to relax for what felt like the first time in months. The tea was delicious and the company companionable. They discussed Theodore's continued absence, Max's latest merchant sailing, and of course their children, before moving on to community events. Abby poured herself a second cup of tea. "Did you hear we have a minister visiting us this week?"

Aunt Agatha said, "Yes, and I heard he is Episcopalian."

Abby looked to Betsy. "As Brianna's Godmother, I wondered if you planned to have her baptized while he was here." It was common for the islanders to take advantage of visiting clergy, no matter the denomination, to perform weddings and baptisms since they were again in between permanent pastors.

Betsy's thoughts were pulled to Theodore. It was the beginning of March and he was more than a month overdue with no word of his whereabouts. Some of her neighbors even dared to suggest he wasn't going to return. Betsy refused to give up hope and this was one event in his daughter's life she was going to make sure he didn't miss. "No. We will wait for her father's return."

Abby nodded. "I understand, but it could be a year before you get another chance."

Betsy pressed her lips together before answering. "It doesn't matter. This is one thing I am not doing without him. It will just have to wait until his return."

The mood of the day changed with Betsy's declaration and as if feeling the tension, Brianna awoke from her nap and was fussy the rest of the day.

In the wee hours of the morning, Betsy caressed the downy soft head of her nursing daughter. She enjoyed the hush of the sleeping world. It was just the two of them in the rocking chair bathed in the soft light of the nearly full moon. The fresh spring breeze floated in from the open window, embracing mother and child. She closed her eyes and imagined the one thing that would make the moment perfect—Theodore standing behind her with his warm hand resting on her shoulder.

* * *

It was the first of April and a beautiful sunny morning with puffy white clouds dotting the bright blue sky. Betsy carried the basket of wet laundry to the clothesline enjoying the pleasant temperature. As usual Brianna was in the sling across her chest and as had become her habit, Betsy often spoke to her. "How can such a little being create so much extra laundry?" Putting the basket down, Betsy went to work, humming as she hung the clothes to dry.

Henry was playing stick ball next door with the neighbor's boys.

Agatha happened to look out an upstairs window in time to see her nephew set down his gear at the corner of the house on the way to the backyard where she knew Betsy to be. She quietly entered the back balcony to watch the scene unfold in the yard below.

Theodore paused at the rear of the house to watch Betsy hanging laundry and listen to the sweet musical voice he missed so much. The sunlight glistened off her dark unbonneted hair, smoothed back from her face, the length of it braided and coiled into a bun. Her dress was a simple design the color of butter but around her neck and draped halfway down her middle she wore a brightly colored floral print. He noticed she held her hand to the material every time she leaned down to pick up another piece of laundry, as if to keep it from swinging with her movements. He puzzled over it until he realized it must be the babe. His breath hitched. He was about to meet his child. Was it a boy or a girl? He was sure somewhere in Florida there must be a lost letter telling him.

He was about to call out to her when a squeal off to his left made him turn his head to find Henry running toward him. A quick embrace and Henry pulled back embarrassed to have done something so childish.

Theodore ruffled his hair, then looked again toward his wife.

Betsy dropped the sheet she was hanging at the sound of Henry's scream. Fear shivered down her spine as she turned to see what caused it, her mind whirling through all the possible reasons he could be in distress. She saw him running towards a fully bearded man. The two hugged but it wasn't until the man looked her way and she recognized his eyes that she accepted what she was seeing.

Theodore was home!

He stepped forward narrowing the distance between them and softly called out to her. "My darling, Betsafina." He cherished the way her face lit up with a beautiful smile. She walked into his arms joyfully weeping. They were so intent to feel the other's embrace they nearly forgot the delicate bundle between them. Theodore rained kisses over Betsy's face, uncaring of who might see. After what he had been through, appearances held no import in this moment.

Betsy pulled back from him to run her fingers along his bearded cheeks, needing reassurance his presence was real, and for the moment ignoring Brianna's cry.

Reluctantly parting, Betsy lifted the baby to her shoulder to remove the sling. A few pats on her tiny back quieted Brianna's crying. Betsy gently handed her over to Theodore. "Say hello to your daughter." She watched a look of wonder cross his face as he snuggled the tiny being to his chest.

Theodore was immediately fascinated with the tiny cherub in his arms. A rush of love for this miniature creature with his wife's coloring flowed over him. His voice hushed with wonder, he said, "We have a daughter."

Betsy's brow furrowed. "Did you not get my letter telling you so?"

Theodore looked sorrowfully at her. "No. What did you name her?"

Betsy laid a hand on her daughter's head thankful to finally see her securely held in her father's arms. "Brianna Kate. Kate being short for Katarina."

"A good name. My mother will be honored."

Betsy smiled. "She did say so in her letter." At Theodore's questioning look she defensively added. "I hadn't received any letters from you so I took the liberty of writing to your parents."

He nodded once. "Hmm."

She smiled to herself. It had been too long since she played this game. *Understanding.* At least, that is what she hoped his sound signified.

Theodore turned to look for Henry standing off to the side and was reminded they were on public display. He ushered his family into the house where they could continue their homecoming in private.

"Henry, come over here and let me look at you. You've grown."

"You were gone a long time."

His sarcastic response made Theodore frown putting a damper on the happy homecoming.

Henry looked to Betsy. "May I go back outside?"

Betsy knew Henry was lashing out to protect his feelings. She hoped Theodore didn't react too strongly to his rudeness. She looked to Theodore to answer his son forcing Henry to do so as well. Theodore gave him a curt nod and watched his son race out the door as if he couldn't get away fast enough.

Betsy saw the hurt in Theodore's eyes. She stepped closer to lay her hand on his arm. "Don't think too much of it. Naturally he needs to adjust to your return and I'm sure his insolence stems from missing you. Now if you don't mind, I'm going to leave you to get acquainted with your daughter while I finish hanging the laundry."

He frowned again. "What happened to the laundress?"

Betsy smiled at Brianna. "Oh, we still employ her but this little one creates extra."

"So have her do more."

Betsy shrugged. "It works well this way and I don't mind."

Theodore dropped the subject and watched Betsy walk out the door. He had been home all of ten minutes and already had disagreements with his wife and son. He looked down at the tiny face in his arms; at least his daughter seemed content with his presence.

A creak on the stairs drew his attention. "Hello, Aunt Agatha."

"About time you returned, nephew. I see you've met your daughter."

Theodore walked forward to give her a kiss on the cheek, relishing and at the same time ignoring her sarcasm. "Good to see you too Aunt."

"How long do you plan to stay?"

As old as he was, her directness could still surprise him. "I don't know."

Aunt Agatha gave him a reprimanding look. They silently returned to the parlor and waited for Betsy's return.

Betsy walked into the room to find Theodore in a chair with his eyes closed still holding Brianna. At her approach, they opened.

Theodore looked to his daughter's sweetly sleeping face resting against his shoulder. "If you'll take her, I'll head to the barber for a cut and shave."

Her soft smile was intimate and inviting. "There's no need. You have a wife who can do that for you."

Theodore swallowed hard. It had been too long since he was alone with her. "You can cut my hair?"

Her gentle tone enticed him. "Aye."

Brianna began to stir. Betsy didn't have to look at the clock to know it was feeding time. She picked up the baby. "Why don't you heat some water to bring up to our room while I feed her."

Thirty minutes later, a freshly washed Theodore carried a pitcher of hot water and a fresh towel up to their room. He arrived just as Betsy put the baby in the cradle. She turned and silently directed him to the chair she placed near the washstand.

Without a word passing between them, Betsy lifted his loose shirt over his head and laid it on the bed. She then placed a towel around his neck to catch the trimmings so they wouldn't irritate him. She was glad she recently sharpened her medium sized sewing shears as she began trimming his hair.

Theodore sat still enjoying her nearness; the light sweep of her fingertips against his nape, the tantalizing brush of her breasts as she moved around him and the sweet smell of her verbena scented skin. However, the longer she worked, the more attune to her he became and the harder it was for him to sit still. When she removed the towel and lightly blew the hair from his neck he nearly jumped out of his skin. Then she set to work shaving him and he learned deeper depths of anticipation. Knowing he would soon be enjoying the pleasures hidden beneath her dress added another layer to his self-torture. As she stood in front of him running the sharp blade across his cheek, he placed his hands on her hips to steady him, not her. He closed his eyes to control his response to the sensation but it only made it worse. He was breathing hard by the time she finished and the warm towel she used to wipe his face didn't help.

Impatiently he took the cloth from her, briskly wiped his face, and tossed it aside. Betsy didn't have time to react before he pulled her to him, kissing her senseless. She was as eager as he to renew the intimacies of their marriage. Neither cared that it was still the middle of the day. She only prayed they did not wake Brianna.

Afterwards she lay on his chest, secure in the comfort of his arms, running a finger over his freshly shaven cheek, and memorizing again the contours of his face which were a bit thinner now. He was home and he was safe. She could put her days of worry behind her, at least for a while. She closed her eyes and peacefully slept.

An hour or so later they returned downstairs, both feeling refreshed.

The Eatonton's were invited over to celebrate Theodore's homecoming. Supper was a lively event. Afterwards, the adults conversed on the front porch enjoying the pleasant evening and watching the children play. Henry and Emily led the two younger boys in a made up game amusing the adults with the way Christoff tried to imitate Henry and little sixteen month old Hawthorne tried to keep up with his chubby little legs. Of course it wasn't long before he fell down and skinned his palms and knees and, being past his bedtime, he fussed more than was necessary. Abby picked him up and brought him back to the porch with her. In no time she rocked him to sleep. Meanwhile Betsy's arms felt empty but her heart was full. Beside her,

Theodore held a sleeping Brianna. A short time later they were forced to call it a night.

Throughout the day, Betsy wanted to ask Theodore the reason for his delay but she felt his reluctance to speak of it. When others asked, his answer was reporting on the war but he refused to elaborate. Something happened since December to upset him.

Betsy awoke that night to the usual sound of Brianna letting her know it was time to nurse. She nearly screamed when Theodore bolted upright in bed beside her, frightened not only by his sudden movement but she also momentarily had forgotten his presence. While she retrieved their daughter, Theodore sat on the edge of the bed with his head in his hands.

She whispered, "I'm sorry she woke you. I should have thought to warn you of her nightly feedings." Theodore didn't respond. She moved to the rocking chair which happened to face him and the window and set Brianna to her breast. The suckling noises seemed overloud in the quiet room bringing Theodore's intense gaze to its source. Betsy's heartbeat quickened beneath his stare. Unnerved despite their earlier intimacy, she watched him watching them but his eyes seemed unfocused. A minute passed. Her beating heart steadied. He finally lifted his gaze to hers. He looked haunted.

"Teddy, what is it?" He blinked and it was gone.

Theodore tilted his head and smiled at Brianna as her fisted hand moved against her mother's flesh. He stood up and walked over to them, placing a hand on his daughter's head. He leaned down to kiss the top of Betsy's. "Nothing. It's just been a long time since I've heard a baby's cry."

Betsy knew his excuse was a deflection but she kept her silence.

The following night it happened again only this time, in the light of the full moon, she could see what she had not the night before; Theodore was in a cold sweat. It was not the noise alone that disturbed him. The baby's cry was triggering a nightmare. As soon as Brianna was quiet, Betsy looked to her husband. "Theodore, something's upsetting you. What is it?"

He shook his head. "It's nothing of concern. I just need to adjust to being home. It will pass."

Betsy nodded in understanding. She hoped in time, he would share whatever was bothering him.

The third night she did the only thing she could. She slept lightly trying to reach Brianna before she started crying. At the first whimper, she picked her up fast prepared to leave the room in an effort to prevent him from reliving whatever was haunting him.

He called her back at the door. "Please stay."

She turned to him. His eyes beseeched her. She couldn't refuse him so each night he watched as she nursed. It seemed to calm him, so if in some small measure the tranquility of the nightly ritual helped him, Betsy was thankful for it.

* * *

April 3rd

Easter Sunday was overcast and threatened rain but fortunately waited till evening to do so. The Episcopal minister was persuaded to stay long enough to preside over Easter services and baptize Brianna. A picnic was held afterwards to celebrate the most holy of holidays. The community also welcomed Theodore's return. Betsy was so happy her cheeks ached from smiling.

Monday, Theodore threw himself into his work at the paper. He wrote letters of inquiry for an update on General Scott's campaign against the Seminole. For now he was content to learn the news from afar. Robert Mason and he spent a good part of the morning at the Court House piazza discussing Texas' bid for independence from Mexico, especially the siege at the Alamo, with the other men of the island. Theodore mostly listened.

He could well imagine what those men must have suffered, having recently gone through something similar. He was thankful his fate was not the same but he was not ready to speak of it; not even with these men he considered friends. When they asked about his published article featuring his campaign with General Clinch, he answered as shortly as possible and turned the conversation.

He knew he needed to write about General Gaines' campaign but he was reluctant to relive the events. Perhaps he could write instead of dual sieges. Gaines' campaign and the Alamo occurred nearly simultaneously, ending on the same day. A story of comparisons sounded easier than relaying the events of those nine hellish days. Normally, after coming up with an idea he couldn't wait to start writing. This one, he put off until tomorrow.

He started reading through the papers Robert published in his absence. When he was done he sought out his partner. "Well done, sir. Were they well received?"

"Yes, sir. Subscriptions have increased significantly since December."

"War tends to do that. We'll enjoy it while we can."

Robert pointed to a stack of papers on the nearby counter. "There's the *New York Weekly* copies you requested I hold for you."

"Thank you, I appreciate that." Theodore picked up the five months of papers. He skimmed through most of them stopping here and there to read articles of interest and of course his contributions. He noticed some editing in all his submissions but the article on Clinch's campaign raised his ire. He knew it was perhaps too emotional due to his presence in the battle but Bob didn't edit out the emotion. Instead he practically reversed Theodore's opinions of the army's incompetence and Osceola's brilliant strategy. He thought back to an obscure reference in one of Bob's letters of that morning. Now it made sense. He spoke of controversy in exploiting ineptitude of leaders.

Theodore felt betrayed. Bob's philosophy had always been the same as his. Print the truth and both sides of it as much as possible. Now his mentor had done just the opposite. Bob did what he swore never to do—subvert the truth. Theodore was so angry he needed to share it. He showed the paper to Robert and waited for him to read it. When he was done he gave Theodore a sheepish look.

"I have to admit, Betsy kept me from doing something similar. Although my reasons were to protect her."

Theodore's expression didn't change but he was shocked by Robert's admission. "Why would she need protection from my article?"

Robert shrugged. "I thought the people might take issue with you for disparaging our war heroes and because you were not here, they might take it out on her."

"Did they?"

"No."

"Hmm."

Theodore returned to his desk. He spent the next two hours trying to draft a letter to Bob that wasn't blistering with his anger.

Tuesday he started his article and it was every bit as difficult as he anticipated. He had to mention Clinch's troop finding and honoring Dade's command. Everyone on the island knew a good many of those men. But it brought to mind the candid images shared by the soldiers. Images that haunted his mind as if they were his own. Even writing as a comparison piece he still had to replay the events that followed in his mind.

What bothered him as much as the images was his inability to deal with his emotions. He was a grown man. He understood both sides of this fight. He knew the horrors he saw existed and they were not the worst men could do to each other. He considered himself a stable and rational person but in this matter he was anything but stable and he was growing impatient with himself for being so sensitive. Witnessing the results of war as an outsider was much easier than being caught in the middle of it. Clinch's campaign was bad. Being part of Gaines' gave him a new perspective he would rather have avoided.

It took him all day to shape his mangled thoughts into a readable piece. When he was done, he gladly handed it over to Robert to finish prepping for the paper. The darkness lingered in his spirits long afterwards. He was poor company that evening and his nightmares were more vivid than usual. He wondered if he would ever find peace again.

* * *

Seven weeks later...

Abby repeated her question a second time with no response. "Betsy?"

Deep in thought she hadn't heard a word Abby said to her. "I beg your pardon." Betsy was embarrassed. She had come to her friend for a visit and to seek solace, not to be poor company.

Abby gave her a sympathetic smile and nudged the cup of tea closer to her. "I asked how you are doing but I can see you are distracted with troubles. Care to share them with a friend?"

Betsy hesitated. Sharing her problems was one thing, sharing her husband's felt like a betrayal but she had long since run out of ideas of how to help him. "Something is bothering Theodore. Something happened to him while he was away that is giving him nightmares." Betsy shook her head. "I can't get him to tell me what it is. The best I can determine it has to do with his return trip with General Gaines."

Abby nodded. "When I read his article I got the impression there was more to it than he wrote. Sometimes the best we can do for the ones we love is simply be there for them."

"Do you think I should push him to talk about it?"

"They say time heals all wounds so perhaps it is best to wait until he is ready to talk."

"It's hard to wait for answers but I came to the same conclusion as well." Betsy idly played with the handle of her teacup. "Theodore means to leave again soon. I'm really surprised he has stayed as long as he has. It seems every day there is another skirmish with the Indians and I know he feels he should be there to report on it."

"Is that all that's bothering you?"

Betsy tightened her lips trying to keep her emotions controlled. "I think I'm with child."

Abby's eyebrows lifted. "And that is not a good thing?"

"I suppose so but... for heaven's sakes, Brianna's only three months old! I should be happy after waiting so long to have a family but I feel so overwhelmed. I'm not ready for another baby."

"When are such things ever our choice?"

Betsy lifted the corner of her lip, "Never."

Walking back home, Betsy tried to think of something else she could do to help Theodore. Low hanging gray clouds hovered over the island. The gathering gloom of darker clouds against a lighter gray backdrop fed her despondent mood. It was difficult to know how to help when she wasn't sure of the problem's source. Returning home she did the only thing she was sure would help. She took a moment to pray.

That evening, Aunt Agatha retired early, going to bed shortly after Henry, leaving Betsy and Theodore alone in the parlor. Betsy covertly watched Theodore. He stared blankly at the paper in his hands.

"A penny for your thoughts."

Slowly Theodore brought his attention to her, "Hmm?"

"I was wondering what you were thinking about."

He lifted his weary gaze to her concerned one. Betsy rose from her seat to join him on the sofa. "Tell me."

Theodore shook his head. "This war is ugly. I consider myself a patriot but I disagree with why we declared war on the Seminole and yet they took out a whole regiment of men and attacked innocent women and children on plantations. I sympathize with the Seminole cause but their atrocities are indefensible." He paused, compressing his lips, "But then so are ours. Some days I want nothing to do with either side. Other days, I find myself defending both. Worse, I don't know if I am even making a difference other than adding fuel for the abolitionists." He turned and looked at her. "And is any of this worth the time spent away from you and the children?"

"I think only you can answer that." They sat in silence for several moments before Betsy ventured to add, "I know there is more bothering you than you have said. I think you have lost your way, perhaps because you have lost Him."

She stood abruptly and left the room leaving Theodore to wonder if he upset her and if he should follow.

Betsy returned with the Bible. She stood in front of him and let him see the tears in her eyes. "Theodore, I can't give you the answers you seek. You have to find them for yourself and the Good Book is the best place to start looking." She placed the Bible in his hands. "When you are hurting, I am hurting." She smiled a little and swallowed. "I find comfort in these words. Perhaps you will too."

He saw her distress. She slowly turned and walked out of the room leaving him fighting back his tears. The last thing he wanted to do was hurt his family. He blinked till his eyes cleared. She was right. He needed to let God in to heal his heart. That night he spent several hours reading various passages and praying in solace. When he finally joined a sleeping Betsy he lay awake for hours. The words he read, while comforting spiritually, made him further question his motives and beliefs.

* * *

In the end it was Henry who managed to get his father to open up one night in June as they were finishing supper.

"Poppa, may I ask you a question?"

"Of course, Henry." Theodore was pleased he was engaging in conversation. He made a point every evening of spending time with Henry to make up for their lost time together. He hoped this was an indication of Henry's acceptance.

"Did you fight against the Indians? Momma said you did but I thought you were on their side."

"Son, I'm not on either side and I didn't fight against anyone."

"But you were with the soldiers."

"Yes, I was but not to fight with them. I was there to observe so I can tell the story of what happened."

"You didn't fire your rifle? What was it like in battle? Were you scared?"

Theodore inwardly cringed. His son sure knew how to ask the hard questions. He would make a good reporter one day.

Betsy wanted the answers to those same questions but she didn't think Henry needed to hear them and Theodore's hesitation made her think he still wasn't ready to speak of it. "Henry, perhaps this isn't a suitable conversation for the supper table."

Theodore cast a probing glance at Betsy. Did she believe what she said or was she trying to protect Henry? Maybe she was trying to protect him. He decided she was protecting both of them and ironically her protection made him feel the need to expose them both. He didn't want her to coddle Henry and he knew he needed to face the haunting images in his mind if he was ever going to be able to get past them. Perhaps the telling could help him put it all in perspective.

He could do so for his son.

Theodore placed his hand on Betsy's arm to reassure her. "I think tonight we will make an exception." Ignoring the first two questions in favour of the last, Theodore looked to Henry. "Yes, I was scared. I think nearly every man involved in a battle has some amount of fear but that is not necessarily a bad thing as long as you don't let fear dictate your actions."

Betsy held her breath waiting. Was he finally able to speak of what happened?

"In December, I chose to go with General Clinch's forces. I wanted to understand what happens in battle and the hardships endured on a campaign."

Henry interrupted. "What was it like?"

"Poor food and lots of walking while carrying a heavy pack."

"Why weren't you on a horse?"

"I wanted to travel with the soldiers." They didn't need to know he wore out his horse carrying a message in the dark from Fort King to Fort Drane. "We walked for two days when we came to the Withlacoochee River. Half of the men were across waiting in a field on the other bank when we heard the war cry. The Seminole opened fire on the men from the trees."

Betsy swallowed hard. "Where were you?"

Theodore took hold of her hand and squeezed. "I was watching from behind a tree on the opposite bank with the mounted volunteers behind me." He intentionally led her to believe he was safer than he really was without actually lying.

Henry asked, "Did the soldiers get 'em?"

"The Indians caught us by surprise but eventually the soldiers chased them away. We marched back to Fort Drane arriving on January second.

Well by now, I'm really anxious to get home so I traveled with the courier to Fort King. I hoped to leave promptly for Fort Brooke but the road was closed. I was stuck waiting for a way out. It was almost a month before General Gaines arrived with a thousand men, a full band, a cannon, and twenty-seven Indian guides. It was a sight to see and filled the fort beyond capacity. There were men everywhere and not enough food for them to stay.

"General Gaines wanted to fight the Indians but with the road closures and all the citizens fleeing to the forts for protection supplies were low. There were only enough rations to supply his troops for a week. It was not enough to supply a campaign that could take many weeks. General Gaines was forced to return to Fort Brooke so on the twenty-sixth of February I was finally able to start the journey home."

Theodore looked around the table to find a captive audience. Even his aunt was interested. He didn't mention the planned detour to fight the Seminole. For some reason he thought it better if Betsy believed it was an accidental engagement.

He brought his gaze to rest on Henry. "Do you know what General Gaines likes when he is on a march?"

Henry mutely shook his head.

"He likes to have his band play. So there we are a bunch of men walking through the swampland to the beat of a drummer and dragging a heavy cannon behind. It must have been a sight to behold."

"Really, he had a whole band playing?"

"Hmm."

Aunt Agatha muttered under her breath. "The man must be a fool."

Theodore silently agreed. "The next day we arrived at the Withlacoochee River at a place the Indian guides promised was only a few feet deep but it was wide and the opposite bank high so there was doubt. Gaines ordered a squad of unarmed soldiers to test the depth. Their comrades lined the bank hoping for some entertainment if the water proved to be swift and deep. I stayed in the trees being the only one concerned of an attack. The men no sooner set foot in the water when Osceola's war cry was heard from the opposite side. Rifle shots were fired at those lined up along the bank and some were wounded. General Gaines called everyone back into the tree line. We exchanged musket fire for nearly an hour with neither side gaining any ground. Gaines finally issued a cease fire and we withdrew deeper into the hammock. We setup our bivouac in the same place I camped two months earlier with General Clinch. That day we lost one man and seven others were wounded."

Henry piped up, "How many Indians got hurt?"

Theodore shook his head. "We don't know. If any did, they carried away their dead and wounded."

"You didn't go ask them?"

"No son."

"Why not? I thought you were their friend?"

"I am but since I was with the people shooting at them I'm not sure they would understand and besides I promised your mother I would not do anything foolish enough to get shot."

Betsy was glad he remembered his promise because his story certainly made her wonder if he had forgotten.

Henry asked, "Did you find the man who got lost?"

Theodore was puzzled. Betsy understood his question but hesitated to explain. Aunt Agatha had no such compunction. "No Henry. Your father means he was lost as in lost his life. He was dead."

Henry's mouth formed the word "Oh," but no sound came out.

Theodore resumed his tale to move past the uncomfortable moment. "The next day we moved down river to the place the guides promised would be a suitable crossing. We had no idea Osceola's band was stealthily keeping pace on the other side of the river. In hindsight we realized the guides may have been leading us to him. This time there were clearings on either side of the river and pine barrens beyond. With better visibility, Gaines decided to risk the crossing. First Lieutenant James Izard moved his mount to the edge of the river and ordered his squad forward to check the crossing. A single shot was fired from the trees striking Lieutenant Izard followed by their war cry. The soldiers scrambled for the trees. Lieutenant Izard's men dragged him into cover. He was gravely wounded but alive."

Of course he wouldn't tell them about the injury or that he knew this man from the Black Hawk war. How could he put the thought in their head of a bullet passing through the side of the man's face, of ragged, seared flesh oozing blood?

"Bullets and arrows flew for several hours until midday when again General Gaines ordered a retreat from the river. We lost one officer and several more were wounded besides Lieutenant Izard. General Gaines set men to work felling trees for fortification, a bridge and rafts. He still had intentions of crossing the river to fight the Seminole much to my dismay. I only wanted to get home to all of you and here I was caught in the middle of another fight. But since I was stuck there I used my hatchet to help cut down trees.

"I worked with three other soldiers to build a quadrangular breastwork three and in places four logs high. We dubbed it Camp Izard because he was still valiantly clinging to life. It became my job to protect the wounded." Listening to the lieutenant's suffering haunted him still. "General Gaines dispatched an express of ten men to Fort Drane asking General Clinch to come to our aide.

"The next morning which was the twenty-ninth of January, the men rose, ate and went back to work cutting timber and building. We had no idea the Indians had crossed the river and surrounded our camp until we heard Osceola's war cry echoed by his warriors and followed by thousands of shots fired simultaneously. They had patiently waited until most of the men were at work outside the fortification to attack. Our men had to scramble for weapons and return fire as they raced back to the safety of the breastwork. The Seminole retreated but they set fire to the grass. We watched as the flames licked their way towards our camp. Soldiers tried to put out the fire but it spread too fast. The smoke grew thick and then the Indians used it for cover enabling them to get deadly close. General Gaines, oddly sitting in a chair inside the fortress, deployed men to fight the fire and to repel the attack. Bullets were flying close by. One hit the general in the mouth knocking out two teeth." Theodore looked to Henry. "Do you know what he said?"

Henry shook his head.

Theodore did his best to mimic the general. "It is mean of the redskins to knock out my teeth when I have so few!"[13]

It did as Theodore hoped, lightening the mood of his audience. The ladies smiled and Henry laughed.

"Just when we thought all was lost, the wind shifted turning the fire back on itself to die out. Although the Indians were forced to retreat back into the trees they still fired upon us for another two hours. You can imagine our relief when they finally left. When it was over we had another man dead and thirty-three wounded including the general. The Indians returned again in the afternoon but the fire burned away their concealment so they could not get as close to shoot."

Aunt Agatha asked, "How many warriors did the Indians have?"

Theodore shook his head. "We couldn't tell. They were hidden in the trees."

Henry frowned. "Do you know if any of them got shot?"

"We didn't know how many but it must have been a few because that night the warriors were arguing so loudly we could hear them across the river.

"Gaines sent another dispatch to Fort King. He decided not to lead a charge because he didn't want to risk dispersing the Indians before General Clinch could arrive with reinforcements. For the next three days any of us who dared to leave the breastwork was shot at and usually twice a day they would fire upon us just to remind us they were there; fortunately without much success for we were running low on ammunition too.

"The rain of bullets was bad enough but the war cries made it worse. The shrill sound was enough to make all but the most hardened soldiers cringe. And we were running out of food." He looked at the innocent faces surrounding him. They didn't need to know that after the rations were gone they ate the corn meant for the animals and then they ate the horses, mules and camp dogs. Some refused, choosing to starve, but Theodore was more practical. Those were dark days. The smell of the unclean, the dead and the wounded, and the excrements were yet another hardship to be endured. Lieutenant Izard finally passed away on March 5th after eight days of suffering. No, these were things they didn't need to hear. Theodore took a deep cleansing breath before continuing the story.

"General Gaines was out of options. I overheard him discussing the situation with his officers. They were waiting on General Clinch to bring them relief but he may not have received the messages. If we stayed we would likely starve to death and if we tried to retreat, the warriors were waiting to shoot at us. The Indians, on the other hand, not only had provisions and could move about as they pleased; they were close enough to their camps to make visits and possibly even get rest if taken in shifts. They easily could have waited us out. Fortunately, on March fifth, about ten o'clock that night, Osceola sent John Caesar, a black interpreter, to arrange a parley."

Henry frowned. "You mean like to arrange a truce? Why would he do that? Wasn't he winning?"

"Hmm. But his scouts told him General Clinch was on his way with six hundred men."

"Oh, so he wanted to arrange a truce and leave before the army got bigger."

"Yes. The problem was General Gaines was not authorized to negotiate a truce so he decided to stall them. Mind you, we didn't know General Clinch was on the way but it was hoped he was close. The Indians agreed to meet at ten o'clock in the morning on the sixth. General Gaines sent Captain Hitchcock, Lieutenant Alvord and other officers in his stead."

Henry interrupted him. "Is that the same Lieutenant Alvord I met here?"

"Yes."

Henry smiled as if he just met someone famous.

"One of the officers knew Osceola at Fort King so the meeting was cordial. The Seminoles wanted a permanent end to hostilities and a promise they could remain in their homeland. Captain Hitchcock told them he didn't have the authority but he would pass the message to his superior. The peace talks continued for two days while they waited for the return of Micanopy. On the eighth they were meeting again and Osceola had just agreed to Gaines' request to abandon the Withlacoochee, never attack whites again, and attend formal treaty talks to settle the matter when General Clinch and his troops arrived. His lead men didn't realize there was a parley going on and started shooting. Of course the Indians fled. The siege was over but there was no celebrating. Osceola thought he had just gained peace only to be chased away by bullets and we were tired and hungry. Although, Gaines declared it a victory.

"We stayed two more days to eat and rest finally leaving that horrifying place on the tenth. We marched north three days through terrible weather to Fort Drane and I was now further away from you than when I started."

Betsy asked, "How did you get home?"

"I'll tell you in a moment. General Scott was at Fort Drane and he made it clear General Gaines was not welcome. There was so much animosity between those two, they couldn't even be civil to each other. It grew worse when we discovered Scott ordered Clinch not to come to our aide. Thank goodness Clinch eventually disobeyed those orders.

"I followed Gaines when his troops departed Fort Drane the following morning. It was the fourteenth of March. We rode a hundred and fifty miles by horseback to Tallahassee, arriving six days later. We spent the night. The people met us *en masse* to welcome the general but he declined a public dinner. The following day we left for Pensacola, another two hundred miles, where we parted ways on March twenty-seventh. Once I found passage on a ship headed home it was only a few more days' sail to get here.

"And Henry, do you know how I got through that ordeal?"

Henry shook his head.

"By repeating over and over again every day the verse you picked out from the Book of Joshua. Do you remember it?"

Proudly Henry repeated it from memory. "Have not I commanded Thee! Be strong and of a good courage: be not afraid, neither be thou dismayed: for the Lord thy God is with thee whithersoever thou goest."

"That's right."

Betsy gave Theodore a tight smile as she held her emotions in check. "We are so very thankful to have you home." His story revealed a lot. He had every reason to have nightmares. He faced a hostile enemy not once but twice and one of those engagements lasted over a week under constant threat of being shot not to mention nearly being burned by the fire. But for him, the enemy was considered a friend. How did he reconcile his benevolent feelings with their actions? But most of all there was something in his manner when he mentioned Osceola's war cry that let her know it likely sparked his nightmares.

Henry had dozens of questions he wanted to ask but after only a few it was declared to be his bedtime.

Much to Betsy's dismay, from that day forward Henry was fascinated with soldiering.

A few hours later, Theodore was laying on his side in their bed on the sleeping porch. Henry was already asleep in his bed at the other end. Aunt Agatha was still sleeping in her room. Only the hottest days of summer would induce her to move out to the porch. Betsy was preparing for bed leaving a bright-eyed and wide awake Brianna in his care. A light breeze stirred the air, bringing a bit of relief to the humid night air. The last of the daylight was fading from the evening sky, leaving just enough light to see his daughter's face. She was lying next to him and he was doing his best to coax a smile from the four month old. It was his favourite part of the day, these few moments he spent with his tiny little girl.

He randomly touched her cheeks, nose and belly to tease Brianna into smiling for him. Her arms flailed toward him and her feet kicked but tonight he was going to have to work harder for his prize. He grasped a foot and leaned over her to bring it to his lips. As soon as her sensitive skin brushed his mouth she not only grinned, he heard her giggle for the first time. It was such a sweet soft gurgling sound. He had to hear it again so he kissed her foot again and was rewarded. He turned her so he could kiss the other foot and then both feet which made her giggle even louder just as Betsy returned to the room.

She whispered, "Do it again."

Theodore obliged and Brianna laughed. Theodore looked to Betsy and saw the same awestruck wonder he felt. "Is this her first laugh?"

Betsy nodded.

Theodore kissed Brianna's feet again. It thrilled him to not only witness her first laugh but to also experience the novelty of being the one to bring it about. Betsy stepped closer to the bed catching Brianna's attention and she began to whimper. It was time for her feeding so Betsy scooped her up and settled on the bed. Theodore pulled the mosquito netting in place for protection and offering a little more privacy should Henry wake. He then climbed in next to Betsy and pulled her to rest against his shoulder.

He looked down at his wife and daughter and smiled. Tonight his mood was buoyant and his heart felt lighter than it had been in a very long time. He looked over to his sleeping son and thanked God for his blessings. If not for Henry's prodding, Theodore would not have spoken of the traumatic events and he would not have experienced the cathartic effect it had on his soul.

For the first night in months, Theodore experienced a dreamless sleep.

Chapter 32

June 1836, Key West

Betsy would never have believed she could find a reason to be thankful for yellow fever. Theodore received word the army was calling a halt to hostilities for the summer due to the high number of sick within the troops in addition to supply problems. War required men and weapons and the military was running low on both. She couldn't help but be grateful to have more moments like this one.

She and Theodore were working late at the dining room table; he on a special article for the New York paper which needed to go in the post tomorrow and she was reworking a skirt promised to a client in the morning. The curtains were drawn tight to conceal the light since the island was still under a dark curfew; although there was talk of ending the practice since there was doubt it would do any good if they were attacked. The only sounds to be heard in the room were the scratching of Theodore's quill pen against the paper and the slide of thread as she pulled it through the fabric.

Betsy paused to study Theodore's visage. The light from the oil lamp on the table illuminated one side of his face bringing into focus the lines of concentration on his forehead. Idly she noticed he needed another haircut.

Her emotions were fluid through her mind and heart. Her marriage to Ben was good but marriage with Theodore was so much more; at times it overwhelmed her. She was ever thankful to have such a wonderful, kind, honest man for her husband. He was attentive to her needs and often exceeded her expectations as he so aptly demonstrated last week with the unexpected gift of a sewing machine purchased from one of Max's salvage auctions. Even now, she couldn't help smiling as she recalled his unconcealed excitement as he revealed it. Her normally serious husband displayed a rare boyish charm more precious to her than the actual gift.

The past months were so enjoyable it was going to be especially hard to let him go when the fighting resumed. She closed her eyes against the creeping shadow of worry hovering over her heart. She couldn't bear to think of all the ways he could come to harm. The thought of losing him made her shiver. She quickly clamped down on the wayward thought. She wouldn't be able to let him go if she focused on her needs and feelings. Instead she focused on the good he was doing by recording the events of the war and especially being a voice for those who were being treated so unfairly. She couldn't say cruelly because as far as she was concerned the cruelty of this war was on both sides. Theodore quit sharing the worst of what he saw when he realized how profoundly it affected her.

His leaving was never far from her mind. It was only a matter of time before something happened to pull him away from them again. She was going to have to tell him soon. She bit her lip chagrined by the secret she was keeping. He deserved to know there was another baby on the way but she couldn't bring herself to tell him. Perhaps because she still struggled to accept her reality. She wanted more children. She should be happy but even after weeks to get used to the idea of another baby she still couldn't embrace it. She was overwhelmed with caring for Brianna and simply wasn't ready to have another baby and she felt guilty for feeling that way.

Theodore caught her staring at him and raised an eyebrow. She let another opportunity to tell him pass by. Instead she asked, "What are you working on for Bob?"

Theodore knew there was something else on her mind but he trusted her to tell him when she was ready. "He asked for an editorial on the Indians."

"What's an editorial?"

"A fancy term for an article containing the opinions and perspectives of an editor."

"But I thought you both wanted to print only the facts."

"Hmm, so did I. Apparently, my stories have helped make Osceola an overnight sensation in the North. They see him as a hero so Bob wants me to give them more details; more than just the facts."

Betsy smiled. "At least you don't have to leave home to write such an article."

Theodore smiled back. "No, I don't."

They returned to their work in silence. When the skirt was finished Betsy stood and stretched the kinks from her shoulders. She placed a hand over his heart as she kissed his temple.

He gave her hand a squeeze. "I'll be up shortly."

Betsy fell asleep nearly as soon as her head hit the pillow.

She was caught in a strange fog. It didn't make sense to her. They didn't have fog in Key West. She was blindly searching for Theodore. He was somewhere just ahead of her with Henry and Brianna but she couldn't reach them. She couldn't see where she was going. Then she caught a glimpse of Theodore only to lose him again in the gray swirling mist. She had to catch up to her family. She quickened her pace trying to reach him, fearful of what she might run into, but determined to find them. She was running so fast she couldn't breathe. And then it happened. She ran right into a fence post. Pain exploded across her midsection.

Betsy sat up in the bed on a sharply indrawn breath covered in a cold sweat. The moonlight filtering onto the porch was enough to see her family peacefully sleeping, including Brianna, assuring her it was just a dream. She felt an urgent need to visit the outhouse. Quietly she extricated herself from the bed and mosquito netting to make her way out of the room and down the stairs while holding a hand against the cramp in her middle.

When she reached the outhouse, now fully awake, she realized what the cramping signified. Her bottom lip trembled. She pulled it between her teeth.

Not wanting to disturb the others, Betsy walked the few steps to the kitchen rather than return to bed. She stoked the fire, filled the tea kettle and waited; waited for the water to boil and waited for Nature to decide her fate.

For all her previous feelings of not being ready for another baby conversely she did not want to lose it. Tears fell. Impatiently she wiped them away. When the tea kettle whistled she filled her cup but then found she really didn't want the drink. The physical pain was bearable but the heartache brought her to her knees.

Brianna's cry woke Theodore. He turned to see if Betsy was going to tend to her only to find an empty pillow beside him. Assuming she must have needed more than a chamber pot and would return soon, he retrieved Brianna from her cradle and set about soothing her as best he could. After a few moments he walked to the balcony on the back side of the house. His eyes searched the darkness of the yard below for signs of Betsy's return. Instead he heard movement in the kitchen. Brianna whimpered again. She tried to suckle on his little finger. He was going to have to take her to her mother. As quietly as he could, he descended the stairs in search of Betsy. He didn't expect to find her huddled on the kitchen floor, weeping.

"Betsy?" He crouched down in front of her holding Brianna to his chest. He reached out to touch her arm. "Darling, what's wrong?" The sight of her distress tore at his heart.

Betsy lifted her tear streaked face to see her husband's concern. The need for comfort outweighed her embarrassment that he should find her like this. She spoke between sobs. "Oh, Teddy. I'm sorry I didn't tell you."

Theodore moved to sit beside her and gathered her to his right side while he cradled a whimpering Brianna on his left. He stroked Betsy's head and kissed her temple trying to offer comfort. "Tell me what? That you are with child?" Her head came up so fast, he almost didn't get his chin out of the way in time.

"You knew?"

"Hmm." He noticed the subtle changes in her body the last few weeks and wondered why she was keeping the news from him but he thought it best to let her tell him in her own time. He couldn't understand why she wasn't happy about it when he knew she wanted more children. He was waiting for her to choose the time to confide in him and he was disappointed when she let the opportunity slip again earlier in the evening.

Brianna chose that moment to remind them she was hungry. Theodore passed the baby to Betsy and then lifted both of them onto his lap, cradling Betsy as she cradled Brianna, wanting to give Betsy more comfort. He unabashedly watched as she set the babe to suckle. Betsy laid her head against his broad shoulder. The tears started falling again when another spasm tightened around her abdomen.

Theodore lifted his hand from her knee to caress her face. "Why didn't you tell me?"

She shut her eyes and squeezed her lips against another sob. "I was ashamed."

"Why?" The silence stretched so long he didn't think she would answer him.

"Because, I didn't want it."

Theodore realized it was a good thing she couldn't see his face. He would not have been able to hide the shock and disbelief her statement produced. He had no idea how he should respond other than to acknowledge he heard her. "Hmm."

Betsy was afraid he wouldn't understand and even more afraid he would think badly of her. She looked down at the tiny being nursing at her breast, taking sustenance and growing stronger while beneath another struggled for life. Her breathing became ragged as she fought to control her emotions. "I wasn't ready. It was too soon, but I don't want to lose it." Her distress transmitted to Brianna who started fussing so she tried to calm down. "I'm sorry."

"Shh." He squeezed her shoulders to his chest.

Another cramp, stronger than before made her press her free hand against her middle. She tried to keep calm so Brianna could finish nursing.

For the first time, Theodore realized there was more going on than emotional affliction. "You're in pain! Do I need to get Abby?"

He was going to set her aside to get up. She put her hand on his arm to stay him. "No. There's nothing to be done." It was odd. but his distress calmed hers. She transferred Brianna to the other breast which was hard to do pressed as they were against Theodore's chest. "All we can do is wait and see what happens."

"Are you sure?"

She nodded her head against his shoulder. "I've been through this before."

They sat in silence for many moments.

He knew when the pain came and passed by the way she tensed and would exhale sharply through her mouth. He lost count how many times it happened.

All three of them had fallen into a fitful slumber when Betsy felt the moisture seeping between her legs. She pushed herself off Theodore but not before it soaked through her nightclothes and into his. The sorrow and guilt hit her so hard she could only stand there trembling, Brianna in one arm, her free hand covering her face, trying not to cry. Theodore stood and gathered her to his chest. In silence, they shared the pain of their loss and gained strength from each other. When Betsy calmed a little, he led them upstairs to their room. He put Brianna back in her cradle on the porch then returned to help Betsy change into a fresh gown.

Betsy held out her arms desperately needing his comfort and Theodore gathered her close as fresh tears began to fall. "I feel so guilty." Her breath hitched. "For not wanting it and because some small part of me is relieved but at the same time..." She swallowed as the hot tears scalded her cheeks. "It hurts. Why do I have such a hard time carrying babies? What if Brianna is the only one? What if I can't have any more? I want more children, I just didn't want one so soon." She tilted her head up beseeching him with her eyes. "Will God understand? Can you understand? I didn't mean this baby harm. I would have loved it. I would have found a way to handle two babies. Why did He take this one away?" She bowed her head and her shoulders trembled. "Please forgive me." It was a plea to her husband and to her God.

Theodore placed a hand on either cheek and gently tilted her head so she would look at him. She noticed his eyes shimmered with unshed tears.

Quiet and firm he said, "There's nothing to forgive." He kissed her forehead and each of her closed eyes and finally her closed lips. They stood there embraced in silence for many moments before he asked, "Are you ready to go back to bed?"

She nodded.

As they settled into bed, despite the heat, Theodore pulled Betsy close offering the only comfort left for him to give. While she fell into an exhausted slumber, he first said a prayer for Betsy's health and well-being. He then lay awake overwhelmed by the myriad of emotions he experienced in the last few hours. In the midst of the crisis he suppressed his feelings to tend to Betsy's needs but now in the quiet of the early morning hours before sunrise they swirled like a gathering storm in his heart and mind—fear, sorrow, regret, relief. He didn't try to suppress them. He allowed the feelings to ebb and flow so he could face tomorrow stronger for it.

The helpless fear he felt as he watched Betsy suffer another miscarriage swelled inside him. He squeezed his eyes tight and he swallowed hard to suppress any outward sound of his distress not wanting to disturb the others. His arm tightened around his wife's shoulders and he kissed the top of her head. She was still with him. Losing Margaret was hard. Losing Betsafina... Just the idea of it was too much to bear.

He had not given much thought before to the risks of childbirth. He did now. He loved being a father. He wanted to give Betsy the large family she craved. Honestly, he wanted it too. But could they face the heartbreak of more miscarriages, or worse, was he willing to risk losing her? No. If it were up to him, there would be no more children. He would do what he must to protect her from conception. But he also knew he would give her anything she asked and she still wanted more children so he would have to put his trust in the Lord to keep her safe.

* * *

The weeks of summer slipped by much too fast for Betsy. Physically she recovered quickly from the miscarriage. Emotionally it took time to forgive herself. Theodore's support and understanding eventually helped her to work through her guilt and sorrow.

The summer rains brought an end to the nightly patrols and some of the other precautions but the Indian conflict was still on everyone's mind, especially hers knowing any day it would take Theodore away from them. One evening in late July Theodore came home in an ill mood. Betsy confronted him after Henry went to bed.

Theodore sighed. "Do you remember the editorial I wrote for Bob?"

She poured him another cup of coffee. "Yes."

"It was well received up North. I didn't print it here because I knew it was too controversial, but I failed to consider that the Northern papers eventually make their way here."

Betsy resumed her seat across from him. "And now there are many upset with you?"

He nodded. "Several men came by the paper today to take issue with my conclusions and one asked to pull his subscription. They don't want to hear of Indians and Blacks fighting with courage and skill to protect their home. They're too darn prejudiced to give them the credit they deserve. Some even accused me of working for the abolitionists."

"Surely you can understand how hard it is to ascribe the Indians with courage and skill when they attack women and children and scalp the vanquished." Betsy meant to help him understand the others' point of view but her own feelings came to the surface. "How can you still support them when they killed your friends and could have killed you?"

Theodore was surprised by her anger. "They are courageous when facing a larger force of men and skillful to attack in such a way they suffer few casualties while inflicting many. I certainly didn't mean it the way you say. And yes, I still support them. You didn't like the north villainizing the wreckers as pirates because they were angry over the financial losses. It's the same thing. The Indians are misunderstood too. They have been tricked and coerced into signing terrible treaties and so they fight to keep their homes, the land of their ancestors, and the burial grounds of their people. Same as we would do if the situation were reversed."

"But the wreckers don't scalp people or kill innocent women and children."

"The Indians are not the only ones who have perpetrated such atrocities. I'm not saying it makes it right, only that it has been done on both sides."

Betsy's frown deepened. "Our men have scalped and killed innocents?"

Theodore nodded and then shook his head. "But people won't believe it. Pride won't let them."

"Still, the Indians are not the only ones fighting for their homes. What about the devastating loss of plantations? The livelihood of many families and communities are gone."

"I know and I write of them not that anyone wants to remember it right now. It was easier to defend the other articles when they confronted me because I was careful to include the good and bad on both sides. This editorial only presents the Indians' point of view."

"So write one to represent the other side."

Theodore gave the idea some consideration and saw the value in it. He could include not only the military counterpoint and survivors from the attacks on the plantations, but it would be the perfect way to bring attention to the plight of the militia wives left alone and vulnerable to manage farms and families on their own.

Betsy interrupted his thoughts. "Will this hurt your business?"

He shook his head. "I don't know. It's too soon to tell." He picked up her hand on the table and gave it a gentle squeeze. "More importantly, do you still support me and what I am doing?"

"Of course, I support you and if you feel what you are doing is important enough to risk your life and livelihood then I will continue to support what you are doing."

Theodore would accept it as enough. He lifted her hand to his lips to press a kiss. "Thank you."

The next week was a rough one for Theodore. Some subscriptions were cancelled and he often faced accusing questions whenever he went into town. He did his best to assure these citizens he was not against the military, which inevitably led to a disagreement over the Government policy to remove the Indians as most of the islanders were for removal. At this point he would try to bow out gracefully from the conversation and, since most he considered friends, it usually worked. One man, a recent plantation owner who lost everything, approached Theodore intent on provoking a fight. His hostility escalated the more Theodore tried to disengage. It would have come to blows if not for the timely appearance of the sheriff and marshal.

* * *

It was the last Wednesday in July and muggy. Morning showers added more humidity to the building heat of afternoon. All the doors and windows were open to catch any breeze that might stir the thick air. Theodore, Betsy and Aunt Agatha had just finished their mid-day meal of fish, fruit and bread when Henry burst into the house.

"Poppa!"

The urgency in his son's voice made Theodore get up and walk to Henry. Betsy and Aunt Agatha followed on his heels. "What is it, son?"

Henry was out of breath having run all the way from the docks making it hard to speak. "Indian attack."

Theodore's calm voice, "Where?" was overlapped by Aunt Agatha's incredulous one, "Here?"

Henry shook his head. "Lighthouse. Up North."

Betsy and Aunt Agatha visibly relaxed. Theodore moved past Henry to retrieve his hat from a peg by the door. "Where did you hear this?"

Henry turned and followed his father. "Revenue Cutter came from there. They brought the keeper." He turned to Betsy. "He's injured real bad."

Theodore took a step back to Betsy and kissed her on the cheek. "I best go see what this is about. Maybe I can talk to the keeper, get his account."

Henry looked up at his father. "May I go with?"

Theodore looked down at his son and was surprised he didn't have to look so far anymore. *When did he get so tall?* Henry was growing fast. Theodore inclined his head towards the door silently giving his permission.

At the same time Betsy said, "I don't think so Henry."

Not sure what to do, Henry looked from one parent to the other.

Betsy's eyes pleaded with Theodore but his questioning look made her add, "Don't you think he's a bit young to hear what this man might have to say?"

Theodore looked at Henry's upturned face imploring him with eagerness and hope. "He's old enough to handle it."

Henry's grin beamed with pride. Theodore put his hand on Henry's back and ushered him out the door. Neither one noticed Betsy's flabbergasted stare.

The clean, sweet smell of the witch hazel trees, always strong after it rains, surrounded father and son as they walked to town. When they rounded the corner onto Front Street they could see a group of men headed towards the Marine Hospital carrying a man on a board. Theodore recognized some of the sailors from the navy schooner *Motto*, bearing the injured man. They were led by Captain Dubose, the light keeper of the Cape Florida lighthouse, located on an island above the Florida Keys and directly off the mainland. Theodore knew the captain arrived in Key West a week ago to visit his family so the injured man must be his assistant.

Theodore fell in step with the captain. "It was your lighthouse? I thought the navy secured it?"

"So did I or I wouldn't have left. The lower windows were boarded up and the door was reinforced so those savages couldn't get in."

"What happened?"

Captain Dubose gestured to the men behind him. "They say it was set on fire. John Thompson was rescued from the upper galley. He has been in and out of consciousness ever since so we don't know what happened yet."

Theodore helped transfer Mr. Thompson from the board to a bed causing the injured man to moan in pain from the bullet wounds and burns covering his body. Theodore wasn't sure it was possible he would recover. They may never know what happened during the attack.

The doctor dispelled them from the room so he could tend to his patient. Theodore joined the men gathered outside the building. Henry trailed behind him.

Captain Dubose asked the sailors, "Do you know what became of Aaron Carter?"

One man said, "If that be the negro, he was already dead when we got there. Shot through the head, he was. We thought they both were goners with the explosion and all but then Thompson waved at us."

Captain Dubose said, "Explosion?"

Theodore said, "Would you mind starting at the beginning? What brought you to the lighthouse?"

The sailor looked at him funny. "The explosion."

The eldest of the four sailors took over. "We were running our patrols on Saturday afternoon about twelve miles away from the lighthouse when we heard the blast. Of course it was our duty to investigate. It took us until Sunday afternoon to reach the light. By then the Indians were long gone. The lighthouse was all burned out and blackened. We guessed the tanks of lamp oil must have been the explosion we heard. Some of the other buildings were still smoldering though like they had finished looting them that morning. We looked around for survivors." He nodded toward one of the blond sailors. "Nelson noticed the two bodies at the top of the tower. Didn't see any way they could be alive. The stairs were completely burned away so we were trying to figure out how to get up there to check them when we saw Thompson move. Now we had to get up there but we still couldn't figure out how. We had some rope on the ship but none of us was able to throw it high enough to catch up there. Sir, sixty feet is a long ways up."

Captain Dubose nodded his agreement. "So what did you do?"

"We had to leave him to go find help. Hated to do it, sir, but there was no way around it. It takes all of us to sail the *Motto* so we left in search of the wrecker *Pee Dee*. We knew they were running the reef nearby. We didn't get back till the next day and we were sure we'd be burying two corpses instead of one but Thompson was still alive. The wreckers, they fired a ramrod with a small line up to Thompson so they could haul up a heavy rope which they used to pull two men up to the top. Don't know how they could stand all Thompson's screaming while they attached the rope. He was burnt all over. Thank goodness he passed out before he reached bottom. We got him on the ship as careful as we could. The wreckers buried the other man so we could make straight away for Key West. And here we are."

Captain Dubose shook hands and thanked each of them for saving his assistant.

With nothing more to learn until Thompson recovered, Theodore and Henry left the hospital. Henry asked, "Poppa, are the soldiers going to go kill the Indians who did this?"

"I don't know, son. Do you think they should?"

The question surprised Henry. He wondered what his father expected him to say. "I think they should but you told me two wrongs don't make a right but the lighthouse keeper had nothing to do with taking away their land. They shouldn't have hurt him and they might hurt someone else so the soldiers should stop them."

Theodore gave him a wry grin. "And that Henry is why war is never easy. There is guilt and innocence on both sides."

Several days later, word reached Theodore that John Thompson was awake and able to talk. Theodore, Captain Dubose and Navy Lieutenant Bache gathered around Thompson's bedside to hear his tale of the harrowing events of Saturday, July twenty-third. They found him bandaged from head to toe much like Theodore imagined a mummy would look. His voice was hoarse so he spoke slowly and often paused to request a sip of water.

"Me and Aaron were working in the garden. Never heard them approach. They just all of a sudden stood up and started shooting at us. We ran for the lighthouse it being the closest building. Rifle balls were flying past us. Some went through my clothes and hat but I don't think I was injured until later. We made it through the door and I got it locked just as the Injuns tried to open it. They started shooting through the wood. Some of the balls hit the oil tanks so we took the rifles, a keg of gunpowder and balls and climbed the stairs to the upper window. The rest of the day we took turns shooting at the Injuns to keep them away. We hoped they would go away but they didn't. After dark, they were able to sneak up and set the boarded up window and door on fire. Didn't take long for the oil to catch and then the stairs. We took our stuff and climbed up to the light. I cut away the top part of the stairs to keep the fire away from us but the flames got so high we had to go outside on the platform. Some of the oil got on my clothes earlier and they caught fire. The Injuns kept shooting at us from below. We both got hit several times. Doc removed lead from both my feet."

He paused to catch his breath and another sip of water. "Where was I? Oh yes, we're on fire, the Injuns are shooting and then the lantern explodes from the heat, hitting us with shards of hot glass. It looked like the end for us and I decided to make it quick so I dropped the keg of gunpowder down the tower. I thought it would bring down the lighthouse and put an end to our misery. It exploded all right, even dampened the fire for a second, but darned if that tower didn't stay standing and then the fire flared up even bigger. When it died down again I called out to Aaron but he didn't answer. After a while I figured he was dead. I guess at least my idea worked for one of us."

There was a moment of silence given for his companion.

"I must have slept all night. I awoke the next day to sounds of the Injuns looting the other buildings. I remember being angry they were taking the food. I guess 'cause I was so hungry. They must have assumed I was dead. They never checked or fired at me. I watched them burn the other buildings filling the air with smoke. Had a hard time not coughing when the wind blew in my direction. If I had, they would have shot me dead for sure. When they left I crawled back into the tower to try and get down. It was a wasted effort. The stairs were completely gone. I think I slept again for a while. The next thing I saw was the navy schooner. Never was so relieved to see sails."

Captain Dubose said, "In the end, the explosion likely saved your life rather than ended it. If not for that, you wouldn't have been found for days."

Every head in the room nodded in agreement. The telling of his story wore Thompson out. He fell asleep before they could take their leave.

On the way out, Captain Dubose commented to Theodore, "Flooded out by a hurricane last year and burned out by Indians this year. I think I'm done being a light keeper. I prefer being able to move when danger comes."

News of the attack on the lighthouse brought more refugees to Key West being the largest settlement and the furthest point from the latest war activity. Once again the Islanders were called upon to provide shelter. Betsy and Theodore took in a family with eight children turning the parlor into a temporary bedroom for several weeks.

Betsy felt time with Theodore growing short. Privacy no longer existed in their house so in order to get her husband alone she had to invite him to join her for a private sail. They had such an enjoyable afternoon that once a week afterwards all it took was for her to whisper, "Want to sail?" in his ear and he would drop everything. They continued the ritual even after their house guests departed.

They had just returned from one of these excursions when Theodore found Henry sulking behind the house. "What's wrong, son?"

"Nothing."

Theodore gave him a stern look. Henry knew he didn't like that non-answer.

Henry shrugged. "Emily was right. Brianna takes a lot of Momma's attention so I have to get used to sharing her just like I had to get used to sharing you with Momma after you got married. But sometimes it's hard to share."

Theodore planned to return to the office for the afternoon. How could he now when his son needed him? "Let's you and I go for a sail."

Henry's face brightened. "Really?"

"Should we catch some conch for supper?"

"Yes, we should."

Father and son enjoyed a pleasant sail out to the reef. The water was choppy enough to give a thrill without being too difficult for them to handle. The sky was a deep cerulean dotted with puffy white balls of cotton. They dropped anchor over the reef to swim for a while, admiring all the different fish until a large shark came in looking for food. They scrambled into the boat breathing hard and laughing now that they were safe. Theodore peered over the side scanning the depths for the predator. "Did you see how big he was?"

"I think he was longer than you are tall, Poppa."

"Maybe so. Are you ready to catch some supper?"

Henry nodded. He directed Theodore to a place with lots of sea grass where he often found conch. In less than fifteen minutes Henry found three to Theodore's one.

Theodore was proud of his son. "Well done. What a fisherman you are!"

Henry frowned at him. "Conch aren't fish."

"No they're not but I think it's still considered fishing even though it's more like hunting."

"Oh. How many do you think we need?"

"Four of us plus eight of them and their eldest son can eat a lot. We need at least six."

They found three more to make it seven. On the way home Theodore sailed close to a large well established mangrove island.

Henry pointed to it. "Look at those long pods. I've never noticed them before. They look like giant green beans with brown tips."

"Mr. Audubon told me those are young seedlings and when they fall they can take root under the parent tree and help create a bigger island or they can float on the water to a new place and be the first to take root creating a new island. It makes me think of family. Some children are content to stay where they were raised but others wander and find a place of their own. I wonder which you will be."

Henry looked to his father. "I rather think the first kind. I like this island and I can't imagine not being near you and Momma and Aunt Aggie and even Brianna. She's finally getting interesting. She doesn't just sleep and eat any more. I like making her laugh."

Theodore smiled. "I do too." He caught Henry playing with Brianna a few days ago. It was a memory he would cherish always. At five months old his baby girl was getting to be adorable. The thought of leaving made his throat tighten.

Since coming home in March, he kept up with the war through correspondence. He knew of General Scott's failed three prong attack in an attempt to capture the warriors, followed by a failed two line attack that was supposed to capture the women and children in order to bring the warriors to submission. Osceola, on the other hand, was operating a very successful hit and run campaign. Theodore thought of it as bee sting attacks; not enough to do serious harm but dangerous enough to make a man run. And run the army, militia and citizens did. The interior of the peninsula was pretty well emptied of all but the Seminole. It was even believed Osceola and his band had taken up residence at Fort Drane—General Clinch's former plantation. Theodore wasn't surprised by the warrior's success. The large bodies of army and militia were easily detected by Osceola's scouts while his warriors could move stealthily into position ahead of them to attack and leave before a successful counter attack could be organized.

General Scott failed time and again using the wrong tactics. Secretary of War Cass reassigned him to Alabama in May. General Clinch was next in line for command but he decided to resign instead so President Jackson appointed his friend, Brigadier General Richard Keith Call, to take command until Major General Thomas Jesup could take over. Jesup was currently fighting the Creeks in Alabama. General Call spent most of the summer recovering from the same sickness plaguing the troops but he was pulling together provisions and men to start a new campaign.

The summer break was coming to an end.

Theodore watched Henry. It was hard to believe he was ten now. The last few years had flown by and, in this moment, he keenly felt the loss of time with his son. The sacrifice seemed greater than the cause and again he questioned his purpose. Henry must have felt his stare. He turned with a questioning look. Theodore smiled and turned his thoughts to the moment at hand. He must enjoy this precious time today and not waste it with regrets. As his father would say, 'what's done is done.'

When they reached the shore and pulled the boat out of the water, Theodore placed a detaining hand on his son's shoulder. "Henry, the war is going to resume again and I'll be leaving soon."

"How soon?"

"In a few weeks."

"I knew you would when the Indians attacked the lighthouse."

Theodore ruffled his hair. "You're pretty smart. Will you look after the ladies while I'm gone?"

Henry's chest puffed with pride. "Yes, sir."

* * *

Betsy looked back on September as a month of comings and goings. The displaced family left them to stay with relatives in the Carolinas. Reverend Robert Dyce, appointed by the Board of Missions, arrived to fill their vacant clergy position. Theodore departed for Fort Brooke leaving a hallow emptiness in the house felt by all of them, even little Brianna. Last month their house was home to thirteen souls. It was now down to four but she had to admit four was better than three. Brianna's needs helped to fill the loneliness of his previous absences. Still there were some moments for Betsy when the silence was deafening.

A week after Theodore's departure they were visited by a hurricane. Fortunately it was a mild one but it reminded her to count her blessings. It was a reminder she often needed. Every day there were tiny heartaches from the little things Theodore was missing especially with Brianna. Betsy had to settle for sharing their daughter's florescence in letters.

A letter from Theodore in October told her he planned to stay in Fort Brooke rather than follow General Call into battle. Having witnessed the general's actions leading the volunteers in last December's skirmish with General Clinch, Theodore had no intentions of participating in the next campaign much to Betsy's relief.

October also brought word of another Indian attack in the Upper Keys. This time it was a garden on Key Largo used by the nearby lightship *Florida* stationed on Carysfort Reef. Those men were feeling the strain of being the last remaining inhabitants between Saint Augustine and Indian Key.

The citizens of Key West were not concerned of an attack but they were feeling the effects of the war in another way. Captains, fearing Indian attacks, were willing to stray closer to the Bahamian reef reducing the number of shipwrecks along the Keys. This in turn reduced the revenue coming into Key West. Everything was becoming high priced and scarce. Earlier in the year, Betsy considered selling her business or hiring a tailor to properly tend to the men's needs. Now she was glad she had done neither one. The sewing machine helped keep up with the demands and when one of the ladies suddenly left her employ, Betsy took on the extra work often staying up late to get it done. She wondered how much longer the war could go on.

In December, without a word to Betsy, Henry hired on with a sponge fisher. After his schooling he would go down to the docks to clean the sponges harvested that morning. His clothes reeked something awful when he got home but Betsy could hardly complain when at the end of the week he so proudly handed her his earnings to contribute to the household expenses. She didn't remember saying anything about money in his presence but she must have or why else would he do this. For now, his money wasn't really needed and not wanting to hurt his pride she put it away for his future.

Later in the month, Robert Mason received an article from Theodore describing the progression of the war. Betsy's letter had a more candid recounting.

> *My dearest Betsafina,*
>
> *I hope this letter finds my family doing well. I miss you terribly and if I could be a selfish man I would leave this place and return to you.*
>
> *I am glad I didn't follow General Call. The fool started off in October and tried again to cross the Withlacoochee River. This time it was swollen with rain water. He lost men to Seminole sharpshooters firing from the other side and then continued south trying other places to cross only to lose more men and horses to the river. He continued moving south trying to reach a new supply depot to be setup by Major Read, losing more horses along the way to starvation. When scouts told him the depot wasn't there (Major Read eventually got it set up later) he was forced to abandon the march and return to Ft. Drane without ever engaging the Indians.*
>
> *In November, he gathered a force of 2500 men including Tennessee Volunteers, Florida Militia, regular army soldiers and a band of Creek warriors. The Creeks were made to wear white turbans so they wouldn't be mistaken as the enemy. Would you believe our government, in exchange for Creek help, has promised them they can keep any black prisoners to sell as slaves regardless of status? By my reckoning that violates laws of piracy and slave trade.*

This time they managed to cross the Withlacoochee only to find the Cove abandoned. I was told Call was so enraged he torched the empty villages. He then split the troops into two wings marching towards the sight of Dade's massacre. Two skirmishes along the way resulted in forty-five dead warriors and only four dead soldiers. Encouraged, General Call pushed forward even though they were running low on rations and ammunition. He allowed Osceola to draw them into an ambush in the Wahoo Swamp where the soldiers got bogged down wading through marsh water expending energy the starving men didn't have. They engaged in extensive gunfire but in the end General Call retreated, leaving the field to Osceola. He returned to Fort Drane and to a letter from President Jackson with a dismissal condemning his actions.

We now await the arrival of General Jesup.

I am sure President Jackson is quite upset with the lack of progress made in the course of this year. No one would have believed it would last this long much less have been this ineffectual. Osceola and his warriors are proving to be a worthy opponent.

The Florida militia reported recognizing a runaway slave from one of the plantations leading men in the battle. Old prejudices make it hard for them to believe a black man could be so capable. There is much concern with how many blacks are fighting with the Seminole. It was estimated in the beginning there were only fifteen hundred warriors. How many are there now?

I am sorry dear if I have said too much and made you worry. Please don't fear for my safety. For the foreseeable future I plan to stay right here. This fort is the main point of all ingress and egress of troops and I have friends supplying information so I feel no compunction whatsoever to venture into the field. I have every intention of returning to you hale and whole and if I have my way—very soon.

Your loving husband,

Teddy

She was glad Theodore was staying out of the war but the events he described didn't bode well for a quick end. Even more disconcerting to her was Henry's avid interest in reading every paper he could find with news of the war. She would never understand the fascination of men and boys with war.

Chapter 33

Key West, April 1837

White dust rose from the limestone street, coating Theodore's worn out boots as he walked the last half mile home, not that he noticed. His thoughts were firmly focused on reuniting with his family after another long six months of separation. He needed so desperately to see them he made this trip uncaring of the expense only thankful for the break in hostilities that gave him the opportunity.

The morning sun cast a warm glow over the whitewashed wood of his home. He was so entranced with the view it was several moments before he noticed Henry on the front porch. His son had yet to notice him. A smile hovered on his lips as he had an idea.

He approached the steps and placed a finger against his lips when Henry looked up. Theodore softly walked up the stairs to the porch.

Henry finished tying his shoe and stood up. Obeying his father's command, he whispered, "Welcome home, Poppa."

Warmth spread over Theodore to see the joy in his son's eyes. He placed a hand on his shoulder in greeting. "Hello, Henry." He reached into his pocket and pulled out a letter. "Take this to your mother, but don't tell her I'm here."

Henry reached for the letter, puzzled.

"I want to surprise her."

"Oh." Henry nodded then disappeared into the house.

Theodore quietly followed him careful to keep out of sight. Aunt Agatha and Betsy were in the dining room and appeared to have just finished their morning meal. He ducked into a doorway on the other side of the hallway to have a clear view of Betsy's face. Her eyes lit up when she recognized his handwriting and he wasn't sure but he thought there was the slightest tremble as she broke the seal and unfolded the paper. He impatiently waited as she read the letter.

Betsy was surprised by the unexpected letter and so excited to receive it she forgot to ask Henry how he had come by it. The sight of her husband's script always affected her so.

> *My darling Betsafina,*
>
> *It has been so long since I held you in my arms. It is to the point I cannot stand to be away from you a moment longer and now I may actually have the opportunity to come home, albeit for a short visit.*
>
> *I am a man torn by gladness for the recent military successes and sadness for the Seminoles. I am truly a patriot at heart but these people deserve better than they will receive at the hands of our government. While I applaud their heroic efforts to save their homeland*

my heart cries out at the uselessness of it. Our side will win, it is only a matter of how many lives it will cost.

In the last two years there have been many skirmishes with military losses greater than Seminole despite generals declaring victory where there was none but there have been many more casualties from sickness and hardship. The troops have been demoralized. Soldiers and officers know it is a duty to be avoided. But in the last few months General Jesup has turned the tide and so I rejoice with them even as I know their victory means Seminole defeat. Such is now the case. The chiefs have capitulated to save their starving homeless people. Large numbers of chiefs and tribesmen have gathered at Fort Brooke and Fort King awaiting deportation. Osceola and his band have not agreed but still General Jesup is pleased with his accomplishments thus far. He has certainly done more to advance this war than his predecessors—Clinch, Gaines, Scott and Call—were able to achieve.

I am as anxious as any to see this war come to an end and this turn of events is the most hopeful chance of that to date. While there is a break in these hostilities I am coming home to you even if I can only stay for a week it will be worth it to hold you in my arms again. I have been away for far too long. I cannot wait to hold my precious little girl or to go fishing and play chess with Henry. I even look forward to waging silent battles with Aunt Agatha.

I'm coming home, my darling.

All my love,

Teddy

Betsy looked up to see Theodore standing across the hall with a boyish grin. The tears clouding her eyes made her doubt what she saw but only for a moment. "Teddy!" She rose from the table and ran into his embrace throwing her arms around his shoulders, laughing and crying at the same time. Then she leaned back, put her hands against his cheeks to unabashedly rain kisses all over his face.

Agatha and Henry watched the couple in stupefied amazement. Betsy stepped back, embarrassed by her open display of affection.

Theodore left her side to greet his aunt with a kiss on her cheek.

Betsy could barely stand to break physical contact with her beloved. "Are you hungry?"

Theodore captured Betsy's hand needing her touch. "I wouldn't mind eating again so long as it's something you don't have to cook."

Betsy smiled. "Will fresh bread and cheese do?"

"Immensely." He kissed the back of her hand before letting it go and watched her leave the room with a noticeable bounce in her step. He was still smiling when he turned to Henry. "How are your studies?"

"Progressing."

His smile faded. "Your mother tells me you are working too."

"Yes, sir." Henry couldn't tell if his father was pleased or disappointed.

"Cleaning sponges, is that right?"

"Yes, sir."

"Do you like the work?"

Henry breathed a little easier. His father was only making conversation. "Cleaning them is smelly work but whenever I am caught up to him Mr. McHugh takes me out and shows me how to harvest them. I enjoy that part. He says I'm good at finding them."

"I'm proud of you, son."

Henry couldn't help the smile his father's praise generated.

Betsy returned and placed a plate of bread, cheese and fruit in front of Theodore. "Coffee's brewing." She placed a hand on his shoulder and waited while he prayed before eating, "What are your plans for today?"

"I need to make a brief visit to the office and then I want to spend the rest of the day with my family. Perhaps we could take a sail. I've missed the water."

Betsy couldn't help laughing. "But you just got off a ship."

"True. But I wasn't sailing with you nor was it a pleasure cruise over a reef just to watch the fish swim and catch some dinner."

"Ah, I see what you're about Mr. Whitmore, angling for some of my famous conch chowder, are you now?"

Theodore laughed. "You know I am, Mrs. Whitmore. But first, where is my daughter?"

"Taking her morning nap. She'll be awake soon." Betsy grabbed his hand and tugged. "Come, you must see her sleeping. She is so sweet I want to kiss her, but I learned the hard way waking her up too soon is not sweet at all."

Theodore followed her upstairs to look in on his chubby one year old little girl sweetly sleeping beneath a draping of mosquito netting. Her head was covered in short silky dark curls. He wondered if she still had her mother's blue eyes as well. They quietly left the room returning to the dining table and Theodore's meal. While he ate, the four of them talked, catching up on news too small or too recent to be in letters.

Theodore was warmly greeted by all those he passed on his way to the newspaper office. It was nice to be so welcome in one's own community. A few of the faces were unknown but that was not uncommon with all the transient visitors arriving in their port. Stepping into the front room of his newspaper shop he was assailed with the musty smells of paper and ink and the comforting rhythmic sounds of the press. The bell on the door alerted Robert Mason to his presence and the sounds presently ceased.

Robert came out of the backroom wiping his hands on his work apron. He readily greeted his employer. "How goes the war, sir? Is it true what I hear; the chiefs have surrendered?"

"Several chiefs have surrendered including Micanopy. God be willing it is almost over." Theodore handed him the article he had ready to print.

Robert scanned the first few lines then excitedly shook the pages in front of Theodore. "It will be refreshing to print some good news. Most of the stories have been about the plummeting cotton prices, specie payments, and the banking legislation." He turned and placed the pages on his desk to typeset later.

"Hmm." Theodore's mouth tightened. He wasn't looking forward to reading the letters piled on his desk from his solicitor. He likely had lost money on some of his holdings.

Robert turned back to Theodore. "Any news not in your article?"

"There is a rumor Osceola is sick and still bothered by the injury he received last January. I wish I could visit his camp and ascertain for myself."

"Why can't you?"

"He stays on the move to avoid being captured. I believe he is now deep in the swamps."

"Is General Jesup doing better than the previous commanders?"

Theodore grimaced. He did not consider the capture of Indians better but he knew what Robert meant. "He has had more success than the others at rounding up Indians. I am impressed with the way he has not only bolstered his forces but he has also recruited help from the revenue-marines and the navy to patrol the coast and inland rivers and streams capturing all the Indians they can for deportation."

"No wonder the chiefs surrendered with our forces coming at them from all directions."

"Yes, I suppose so. Is there anything else we might need to discuss today?"

Realizing he must be anxious to return to his family, Robert said, "No, nothing that cannot wait."

"I'll see you tomorrow then."

Theodore hastily returned to the house. He was greeted at the door by Betsy holding Brianna who was awake from her nap and was clinging to her mother's neck. She hid her face when Theodore tried to make eye contact.

Betsy gave him a sympathetic look. "Give her a few moments to wake up and she'll warm up to you."

He laid a hand on Brianna's back. "She has grown so much."

Betsy smiled proudly. "Yes, she has."

Theodore followed behind as Betsy led the way to the parlor. Brianna lifted her head and shyly looked his way. He smiled and she hid her face again. It was a half hour later before Brianna was moving comfortably about the room. It took a lot of encouragement from Betsy before she finally coached their daughter to take a few wobbly steps to her father. His heart lifted with joy when she reached out her arms towards him. He picked her up and kissed her cheek as she tried to squirm her way loose.

Betsy softly giggled. "She doesn't like to be contained. I'm surprised she let you pick her up, but she is more open to strangers than most babies."

Theodore drew his brows together. "Are you calling me a stranger? I'm her father." Betsy gave him that look. The one which said surely he was aware of the fallacy in his words. "Hmm."

She never realized how much facial features and inflection helped one to understand another's meaning until she had to depend on it to decipher the various meanings of his guttural response. This time she wasn't sure what he meant. She was distracted from figuring it out when Brianna grew fussy. A glance at the clock told Betsy her daughter was hungry.

Theodore smiled when Henry entered the room. "Are you ready to go for a sail, son?"

Henry's eyes lit up. "Yes, sir."

Theodore looked to Betsy.

"You two should go without me. I need to attend to Brianna and then make our midday meal."

Theodore was disappointed but tried not to let it show. He kissed Betsy then followed Henry out the door. Hunger brought them home two hours later. After their meal, Theodore settled into the chair at his desk to go through his mail.

There were several letters from his solicitor and one from Aunt Agatha's as well. They had some losses from speculating but the news was not as bad as he feared.

* * *

Sunday morning they walked to the Custom House for church service. Betsy hummed a joyful hymn. Having Theodore home made her so happy she couldn't contain the feeling. Life felt whole again with Theodore seated next to her worshiping the Lord. Their family was complete.

After services, they met up with Max and Abby and their three children. It was now a long standing custom to have dinner with the Eatontons after service so Henry and Emily went running ahead followed by Christoff. Thorn tried to toddle after them but Max swooped him up to his shoulder. At two and a half he wasn't fast enough yet to keep up with his siblings.

The two men ended up walking ahead of the ladies by virtue of their longer strides. It was no surprise their conversation immediately turned to money and politics.

"If the price of cotton goes much lower, Abby's uncle will lose his plantation."

"I hope it doesn't come to that but I'm afraid it will for many. After so many years of growth I suppose it was bound to happen."

"Between the war and the drop in cotton prices the wrecking business is taking a hard hit which affects every other business on this island. I read your article. It is good news the chiefs have surrendered. The sooner this war is over the better for everyone."

"I agree."

Betsy and Abby, by mutual consent, walked in silence, blatantly eavesdropping on their husbands. Sometimes it was the only way they could gain such knowledge. Men, often under the misguided notion they were protecting their wives or because they didn't think ladies would understand, didn't share financial information with them. The losses were news to Betsy. Theodore hadn't mentioned them to her. She wondered how much it amounted to and did they need to worry. It bothered her enough to keep her distracted all through the meal and on the walk home. She was deep in thought when Theodore whispered, "You didn't tell me Abby was increasing again."

"It seemed too delicate to mention in writing, even to you."

"When is the baby due?"

"Mid-summer."

Theodore looked at her carefully. "Does it bother you?"

Betsy met his gaze. "I hadn't given it much thought. I suppose I have been too busy taking care of Brianna." She bit her lower lip wondering if she should ask him about their finances.

Theodore noticed the tell-tale worry habit. "What is bothering you?"

"Something I overheard you say to Max."

"Hmm?"

"You told him you had some losses. Should I be concerned?"

Wanting to be honest with her he said, "Not yet but if this panic—I believe that's what they are calling it—if it continues it could seriously limit our funds." He winked at her. "It's a good thing I'm married to a frugal wife with her own business."

Betsy was oddly comforted more by his teasing than his assurances.

Despite the rampant bad news in the world, it was a blissful few weeks for the Whitmore family. While the world around them was spinning out of control, they coalesced in happiness and joy. Betsy and Theodore celebrated their second anniversary together and with a rare treat. Theodore was able to procure beef for their meal and so they grilled steaks with the Eatontons and toasted the first two years of their marriage and prayed for many years to come.

Wednesday evening of the following week the family was gathered in the parlor, Theodore brought home the monthly mail having arrived that afternoon. They each were enjoying their part of the mail except Henry who was contentedly drawing.

"The bastard."

Betsy, Aunt Agatha and Henry all looked to Theodore in shock.

Theodore felt the weight of their stares, and realized he must have said his thought out loud. "My apologies, ladies." He gave his son a stern look. "You are never to repeat that word."

Henry solemnly nodded and resumed his work.

Betsy asked, "What is it, Teddy?"

Theodore stood up and began pacing the room only to stop suddenly. "It's a letter from Gad Humphries."

Betsy interrupted him. "He's the former Indian Agent?"

"Yes. General Jesup went back on his word. He promised the Indians their 'allies', meaning the runaway slaves that joined their cause, and their 'possessions', referring to the black slaves they held, would be allowed to move west with them. Now he has decided that determining previous possession is impossible and the runaways must be returned to their former owners. This puts all of the Black Seminoles in jeopardy. Doing so may very well cost Jesup any chance of holding this capitulation. Surely he must know it was the primary reason the chiefs agreed to it in the first place."

Betsy's heart fell. It was written all over his face. He was leaving again.

They both felt the sorrow of so little time together.

Tampa, Florida Territory, May 31st, 1837

Theodore carried the sorrow in Betsy's eyes with him all the way to Fort Brooke. The separation was taking its toll on both of them and he hated being the cause of her unhappiness. At least he forewarned her his visit would be short but it was of little consolation. When he left Fort Brooke just over a month ago it was with the hope this war would be over by the end of the year. The Seminoles were gathering as promised and each side had the concessions they wanted but General Jesup more than likely ended all hope of such a possibility.

The day following his return, Theodore arranged a meeting with General Jesup. He hoped to learn why the general changed his mind.

Thomas Jesup rose from behind his desk to greet his visitor. "Welcome back, Mr. Whitmore. I trust your travels were smooth."

"It was uneventful."

The general had a rather pointed face, especially about the nose, mouth and chin, enhancing the directness of his gaze. "I did not expect to see you again so soon."

"I did not want to miss the departure. What news is there of the Seminoles?"

"Not much has changed since you left. Their numbers increase a little each week. Not as fast as I would like."

"How many are there now?"

Jesup pursed his lips before speaking. "Roughly seven hundred here and about twenty-five hundred at Fort Mellon near Lake Monroe but I expected twice that many."

"What do you think is keeping them away?"

"There are many factors, I'm afraid. Some real and some imagined.

Would you believe I had to quell a rumor we were going to put them on boats so we could take them out to sea and throw them overboard to drown? Who thinks of these things?"

"Who indeed. Certainly someone with a vivid imagination." Theodore did his best to make the general believe he sympathized with him in the hopes of learning more. "I have read the southern newspapers condemning you for the capitulation agreement. You have the planters in quite an uproar accusing you, a Virginian, of betrayal."

He grimaced. "All because of that damn Article Five."

"The Indians would not be here without it."

"You and I know that but they don't seem to care. They only want their property returned. Slave catchers have flooded the area trying to retrieve the Negros they say belong to their employers. I had to issue an order forbidding unauthorized white people from traveling to Indian Territory or near the relocation camps."

"Bringing only further complaints against you."

"Yes. What do they expect me to do, rescind the Article? And yet, I understand. Allowing Negros to emigrate west with the Seminoles would set a troubling precedent."

Theodore knew what the general was doing but pretended otherwise. "How can you avoid it?"

"It's all a matter of interpretation. Runaway slaves will not be considered allies so we will detain any Negro they can't prove as being theirs."

"Something that is nearly impossible to prove."

The general's mouth twitched as he gave a single nod.

"If you're not allowing the slave catchers in and you have vowed not to use the army for that purpose, how are you going to round up the blacks?" Theodore noticed the general had the look of a cat who swallowed the canary. He held eye contact with Jesup and fought not to smile when the man answered his question despite himself.

"I have an agreement with Coa Hadjo to surrender the Negroes the tribe has taken in during the war. He will deliver them to posts on the St. Johns."

"I suppose that does neatly solve the problem. Would you give me permission to visit the relocation camps?" General Jesup evidently decided he would only trust Theodore so far and it did not extend to letting him visit the Indians with the knowledge he now possessed.

"I'm afraid I cannot. Only military personnel is allowed."

They talked a few more minutes but Theodore failed to learn anything else of use.

After a few days at Fort Brooke, Theodore was even more anxious to visit with Micanopy, Jumper and Abraham. He learned General Jesup broke his vow not to turn the army into slave catchers. His men were patrolling in Seminole territory under the guise of observing the tribes movement into the centers but the reality was they were rounding up blacks. He wondered how many they found and if the others were aware of this latest treachery or that of Coa Hadjo. He also wondered if they were being treated well and how they felt about their situation. Theodore was giving some serious consideration to taking his chances of going without the general's permission. He was relieved when it didn't come to that.

General Jesup received word from Lieutenant Colonel William Harney at Fort Mellon that Osceola and his band had come in. The news pleased him so much he eagerly shared it with everyone at the fort. It looked as if the war was truly over. Afterwards he surprised Theodore with a change of heart and granted him permission to visit the tribes.

Jesup confided to Theodore, "I wrote Lieutenant Harney and told him when he sees Osceola again, to let him know I intend to send exploring parties into every part of the country during the summer, and that I shall send out and take all the negroes who belong to the white people, and that he must not allow the Indians or Indian negroes to mix with them. And to tell him I am sending to Cuba for bloodhounds to trail them. I intend to hang every one of them who does not come in."[14]

The general's cocky attitude and vicious threats did not sit well with Theodore. He could well imagine how Osceola would receive them. Apparently General Jesup forgot what happened to Agent Wiley Thompson for humiliating the war leader.

A letter was waiting for Theodore when he returned to his bunk. It was from Lieutenant John Graham, also stationed at Fort Mellon.

> *I am disheartened by the unexpected arrival of Osceola. Of course, I am glad to see him as a friend but his presence means we are prevailing over the Indians and I hate to see the end come to such a proud people. I am sure if not for the lingering illness still plaguing this proud warrior he would continue to fight for his homeland.*
>
> *I will say his arrival has provided much merriment. First, my fellow comrades who have never seen him before were quite surprised to discover the savage warrior they feared was a dignified man of slim build. His lighthearted banter with us is quite a refreshing change from the drudgery of our guardian assignment. We even were treated to a Seminole ball game arranged by Osceola.*
>
> *I am ever amazed by the depth of his friendship. He presented me with one of his cherished white crane feathers and asked that I wear it in battle. I thought it very generous of him.*

Theodore folded the letter and blew out the candle. It was early for him to turn in but he had an eight mile walk tomorrow to visit the relocation camp and he planned to leave early.

It was barely dawn on the morning of June third when Theodore was awakened by shouts and the commotion of soldiers running back and forth. He hurried into his clothes and grabbed his loaded rifle from the corner of his tent. The early light of dawn greeted him as he made his way to a cluster of men in front of General Jesup's quarters. He could hear the furious commander even though he was still some distance away.

"Captain Graham, tell me how in heaven's name did seven hundred captives escape undetected under your watch? What happened to the spies? Didn't you put the Creeks in the camp like I asked?"

"Yes, sir. They did not raise an alarm." Captain Graham shrugged his shoulders and shook his head. "Can't trust any Indians."

By now Theodore had reached the group. He knew Captain William Graham (no relation to Lieutenant Graham) was assigned to guard the Seminole camp because General Jesup heard rumors of a possible raid.

General Jesup barely kept his temper in check. "Why aren't you going after them?"

"Sir, they got a twelve hour head start and we'll lose their trail in the swamp."

Jesup finished for him, "And obviously, the Creeks are no longer trustworthy for tracking. If it weren't for the dad-blamed greedy slave owners badgering me for the return of their property and the blasted measles scaring those skittish Indians away they would be headed west by now and this war would be over. You hear me Captain Graham? Because of your incompetence we're back at square one. And if I had my way about it now we wouldn't bother with emigration. The only way we'll ever get the Seminole out of Florida is by extermination."

Silence met the general's tirade.

Captain Page stepped forward. "I found one of the Creek spies. He claimed he was detained from sounding the alarm. He said the chiefs refused to leave, especially Micanopy. Osceola told him his blood would be spilt if he did not go. Micanopy threw his bosom open and told them to kill him and do it quickly. Instead, they forced him on his horse and led him away. The rest of the tribe willingly followed Osceola."

General Jesup's jaw clenched. "Osceola will pay for his betrayal."

With the embarrassment of Osceola's daring liberation of his people, General Jesup asked for reassignment. Theodore waited to learn of his replacement. Instead, the President encouraged Jesup to stay in command. He was the most successful commander thus far in the war. Under him, the Seminoles were driven from their strongholds to hide deep in the swamps away from the white population and travel throughout the northern part of the territory was relatively safe. He also came closer than any others to accomplishing his mission. Jesup realized the best way to redeem his honor was to see this war to its completion so he decided to stay.

Meanwhile, summer brought widespread sickness to the troops. Dysentery, typhus, malaria, yellow fever and other illnesses reduced five battalions to only a hundred men fit for duty. Fort Mellon had to be abandoned in June. General Jesup urged them to keep this latest crisis a secret lest the settlers panic or the enemy take advantage.

Forced to wait till fall to resume the war, Theodore could see no reason to linger in the sickly environment. After six weeks away, he was headed home. If only it were for good and not just for a few months to wait for warfare to resume. It had come so close to being over this time.

Key West, End of July, 1837

Betsy was kneading bread dough in the kitchen, her hands covered in flour, when Henry came running in so out of breath he couldn't speak. He kept gesturing towards the house. Her first thought was maybe something was wrong with Brianna or Aunt Agatha except that he was too out of breath for such a short distance and he normally would have been working at the sponge dock right now so she waited until he could get enough air to say, "Poppa's home."

She felt the grin spread across her face. Impatiently she wiped her hands on a towel not caring if they weren't completely clean. She hiked her skirts above her ankles and sprinted to the front yard and on to the street. She meant to slow to a walk but seeing Theodore in the distance spurred her onward and to the devil with appearances. She covered half the distance between them when she noticed he wasn't running to her. She thought it odd, but then she realized he was struggling to walk, and she ran even faster. Reaching his side, she saw the paleness of his face and moist brow. He greeted her with a weak smile as his eyes drooped. Afraid he would collapse in the street, she stepped under his arm to help support him and felt the radiating heat of his fever.

Fear shivered down her spine.

Together they stumbled towards the house. She wasn't really strong enough to hold him up. Henry arrived and went to Theodore's other side, but he wasn't quite tall enough. The three of them walked as a cumbersome unit back to the house without saying a word. The task was too great for Theodore to speak.

The illness began on his voyage home. He hid it from the others on the ship by claiming it was sea sickness. He didn't want their sympathy or worse to be put ashore for fear of contagion. By the time they arrived in port, it was clear to everyone he was truly sick with a fever and most went out of their way to avoid him. He was also suffering from a headache that wouldn't ease and back pain making every step a chore. One kind sailor offered to help him home but Theodore refused. He was now wishing he hadn't.

Ten minutes ago, Aunt Agatha saw Betsy run past the side window from the backyard. She guessed Theodore to be the reason but she couldn't follow since she was keeping an eye on Brianna. Instead she watched their labored progress from the open window and met them at the front door. "What's wrong with him?"

Betsy shook her head against Theodore's chest. "I don't know yet."

Inside the house, Betsy considered directing Theodore to the sofa in the parlor. He would be uncomfortable, but she wasn't sure he was strong enough to make it up the stairs. He took the decision from her. With sheer determination, one step at a time, he climbed the stairs with her support.

Aunt Agatha placed an arm around Henry's shoulder to comfort him as they looked on with concern. "Should I send Henry for Mrs. Eatonton?"

"No. She is still recovering from childbirth and this is no place for her or the baby."

"Mrs. Mallory then?"

Betsy held her temper knowing fear was making her sensitive and Aunt Agatha was only trying to help, "I can see to Theodore for now but Henry should take Brianna to the Eatonton's. Whatever this is she doesn't need to be exposed to it."

Betsy and Theodore finally reached their bedroom. Theodore crumpled on the bed. Betsy broke into a sweat trying to get him properly positioned. She was working on removing his shoes when he suddenly twisted sideways and reached toward the chamber pot. Betsy scrambled to get it to him in time. He was so weak she had to hold it for him, ignoring the splatter on her dress. How she managed not to heave her stomach was a mystery to her especially in her condition.

Theodore rolled to his back. Betsy put the pot down close by in case it was needed again and went to the washstand to get a wet cloth to wipe his face. He moaned in appreciation of her ministrations. She was struggling not to jump to conclusions but the fear of history repeating itself was strangling her heart.

She couldn't hide the concern in her voice. "Teddy, how long have you been sick?"

He didn't answer.

Panic hit her for a split second before she realized he wasn't dead; he had passed out from exhaustion. She removed his shoes and made him as comfortable as she could with her limited strength. She exchanged the chamber pot for Henry's clean one, so she could take it downstairs with her. She emptied it in the outhouse then took it to the kitchen to rinse it with water from the bucket. She tossed the rinse water in the yard and returned to the house.

Agatha met her at the stairs. "How is he doing?"

"He was insensible when I left him. I haven't been able to ask him any questions yet."

"I see it in your eyes. You're afraid it's yellow fever."

Betsy swallowed hard and nodded afraid to trust her voice. Finally she said, "I need to get back."

Agatha stepped aside. "You may want to change your dress, dear. It smells something awful."

Betsy looked down, grimacing at the sight, and then her stomach roiled. Her hand flew to her mouth, she dropped the pot and ran for the back door, only making it as far as the bushes before her stomach heaved. She caught another whiff of her dress and heaved again. Breathing hard now, she kept her face turned to the side waiting for the nausea to pass. When it did, she returned to the house, picked up the pot and went up the stairs to their room. Theodore was still asleep. She took off her dress and put on a fresh one. The laundress would have to deal with the soiled one. Just the thought of it made her queasy again.

She checked Theodore's forehead. He was overly warm to the touch but not fearfully so and he was breathing fine. She slumped in a chair already worn out and this was only the beginning of what he would need. Her eyes grew heavy.

Abby's arrival jerked Betsy awake. Judging by the light in the room she must have been asleep for an hour or so. She assured her friend she was fine when Abby questioned her.

They both moved to Theodore's bedside. Abby felt his forehead and cheeks with the back of her hand, then lay her head on his chest to listen to his breathing. "Has he vomited?"

"Once when he got here. He's been asleep since then."

Theodore heard the women's voices and forced his eyes open. He glanced at Abby and then focused on Betsy. It was so good to see her again. He wanted to hold her tight and kiss her until she swooned, if only he wasn't so sick. He opened his mouth to speak but found the effort to be too much.

Abby moved away to allow Betsy to reach him and then turned aside as husband and wife reunited as best they could under the circumstances. Abby scrutinized them both when they finally separated. Theodore's eyes were fever bright and full of pain. Betsy's were fatigued.

"Brianna?" Theodore's voice was hoarse. Betsy helped him sip some water.

Abby crossed her arms over her chest. "She and Henry are at my house which is where your wife should be too. You do not want her to risk catching what you have and lose the baby."

Theodore's eyes widened as he turned to Betsy seeking confirmation. She hadn't mentioned she was increasing in her last letter.

Betsy gave Abby a withering look before turning to Theodore. "I didn't want to worry you just yet."

"Hmm." He tried pushing her away. Abby was right. She didn't need to risk getting sick.

Betsy's lips compressed. He couldn't talk but he could still make that infuriating sound. She refused to move. Instead she looked to Abby. "I'll be fine. He probably only has a cold from sleeping so many nights on the ground." She turned back to Theodore for confirmation just as he was reaching for the chamber pot. He was violently ill this time. When it was over he laid back and Betsy wiped his face with a cool cloth. Theodore took it from her and laid it over his eyes.

Abby asked, "Do you have a headache?"

"Hmm."

Betsy looked to Abby. "It could still be just a cold, and you're one to talk. You shouldn't be here either. For Heaven's sakes, you gave birth a week ago."

Theodore removed the cloth and looked questioningly to Abby.

Abby correctly interpreted his unasked question and smiled. "A boy. Nathanial James Eatonton."

Theodore weakly smiled in response and then looked to Betsy. "Go."

Betsy shook her head. "No. You just got home and you need me."

Abby sighed. "Fine. I will check on you both in the morning and we can decide then."

The following morning Abby knocked on the bedroom door but no one replied. She peaked inside and found them both doing worse than before. Theodore was feverishly tossing and turning and Betsy was asleep beside him still wearing yesterday's dress. Abby gently shook Betsy's shoulder to wake her up.

Betsy bolted upright immediately concerned for Theodore. When she realized he hadn't disturbed her sleep she turned to find Abby standing next to the bed.

Abby whispered, "Betsy, you are worn out and need your rest. This is not good for you or the baby."

"I'm fine."

"And the baby?"

"Is fine. I can do this."

Their argument stirred Theodore from his fevered haze. He labored to put all his strength into his voice. "Betsy, you must go."

"No." Tears slipped down her cheeks but her voice was laced with determination, "Don't ask it of me. I cannot leave your side nor could I endure not knowing what is happening. You need constant care and it is my duty as your wife."

His strength was waning. "You must take care of our children too."

"Henry and Brianna are being cared for."

"The baby," he barely whispered.

"The baby will be fine. I'm strong enough for the both of you."

Heartbeats passed in silence while Theodore gathered what little wits he had left. He motioned her closer to him, fearing all the while he would spread the dreaded disease to her. "I'll not rest easy...till I know... child is safe." She started to speak but was silenced by his pleading look. With shortened breaths he said, "You are....strongest woman...I know.... must find strength now... to walk away... and stay away."

410

Abby laid a hand on Betsy's shoulder. "I brought one of the Mabrity girls with me, Mrs. Wall. She has agreed to help Agatha take care of him and Mrs. Mallory is going to come by twice a day too. He will be in good hands."

Betsy couldn't fight both of them. She leaned down to whisper in Theodore's ear, "Don't you dare put me in widow's weeds again."

The corner of his mouth lifted. "Hmm."

Betsy spent every free moment praying for Theodore's health, not that she had many of those. Nathanial was a very fussy baby taking up much of Abby's time leaving it up to Betsy to care for the other five children. At any given moment one of them needed something from her. Every night before bed she was down on her knees asking God to please spare Theodore's life and right behind it praying as she had been taught. "Let thy will be done." Only to turn around and beg that His will be to heal her husband.

In her weak moments she would recall Ben's last days and weep uncontrollably, worried that she would lose Theodore the same way, only it would be worse since she wasn't there to comfort him. If not for the needs of Hawthorne, Christoff, Emily, Brianna and Henry, she would have returned home despite the risks. Mrs. Wall and the others may be doing a good job taking care of Theodore, but they could never be as attentive to his needs as she. At least there was comfort knowing Aunt Agatha was there to oversee all.

Twice a day Henry was sent to Aunt Agatha for an update. The first two days there was no change but on the third Henry ran all the way back with the wonderful news Theodore had made a turn for the better.

Betsy was thankful but couldn't allow herself to believe it was over. Many had gotten better only to get sick again and die, including Ben and Mr. Mabrity. She waited, expecting it to happen to Theodore too but each day brought the same news. He was improving. Anxiety turned into impatience to return to her husband.

A week after Theodore's arrival the family was reunited. It was still some time before he fully recovered but all of them rejoiced in his return from war and return to health. Betsy made him promise never again to risk lingering in the warfront during the sickly summer months.

As soon as he was well enough to leave his bed, Theodore anxiously attended the mail piled on his desk. He started with the letter from his parents telling him all was well with them and ending with his mother's question if there would be more grandchildren. Theodore smiled. He pulled out a fresh sheet of paper and dipped his pen in ink. He began his return letter with the happy news another child was due to arrive in the new year.

The next letter was from Bob. It was the first Theodore received from him in quite some time that was more personal than business in nature. The Panic, as it was now termed, hit Bob hard. He lost nearly everything except for the newspaper and his family estate. He assured Theodore he would still pay for his submissions but it would be less as circulation was poor as a result of the depression. Another letter from his solicitor continued the bad news. Even with the changes they made to his personal investments he was still losing money. Theodore dashed off more instructions and prayed he was making the right decisions. He wasn't poor by any means but if the losses continued for much longer he would have to consider letting go of his family home in New York or returning to it. Keeping two houses was a large drain on his diminishing income. He hoped his aunt's finances were doing better. He would have to make a point to ask her later.

The rest of his mail was news from his contacts involved in the war. General Jesup was busy getting ready for his fall campaign; making strategic plans as well as procuring supplies. It was something he knew well how to do having served as quartermaster general before coming to Florida. Congress authorized the funds for his campaign wanting an expedient end to the war. The arrival of his requisitions was a sight to behold. Crates upon crates of shotguns, new Colt revolvers, and Cochran repeaters plus stores of ammunition and powder. He also ordered the myriad of other items needed for war such as hatchets, axes, shovels, wall tents, common tents, hospital tents, camp kettles, mess kits, canteens, horses, mules, packsaddles, halters, harnesses, hobbles, whips, saddler's tools, horseshoes, Dearborn wagons, river steamers, Mackinaw boats and rations better suited to the climate. If the amount of goods arriving in Florida was any indication, the fall campaign would be massive.

Jesup was also recruiting men. He was having trouble filling the army ranks so he recruited militia from several states. A surgeon at Fort King told Theodore that Jesup also requested hundreds of warriors from the northern tribes and bloodhounds for tracking. The general was determined to retaliate for what he considered a personal betrayal by the Indians, especially Osceola.

For Theodore, this meant he had precious little time to recover and be with his family. The next several days were spent mostly with Betsy and Brianna. Henry joined them in between his studies and work. They walked the Island, sailed, explored and visited with friends. It was peaceful for them. Eighteen month old Brianna captured his heart with her cherubic smiles and bubbly laughter. He soon found he would do anything, no matter how silly or undignified, just to make her giggle and nothing worked better than a game of chase. Theodore never grew tired of watching her chubby legs go as fast as they could. Agatha grimaced and complained of the disruption in the household but Betsy could often be found standing in a doorway watching them with a grin while one hand unconsciously caressed her belly.

Occasionally, Theodore would wander to the piazza of the Custom House in the afternoons to chat with the other men of the island. He was exuberantly welcomed to the group on his first return visit. They had much news to discuss especially concerning the deepening depression, the lingering Indian wars, and the government pouring money into the war efforts while families were starving. They sought his opinion on the banks of New York City suspending specie payments and if the President was making the situation worse by not accepting paper money for public depts. They discussed the Boston riot in June between Catholic Irish mourners and Protestant Yankee firefighters and England's newly crowned eighteen year old Queen Alexandra Victoria.

On one such visit, William Whitehead sought his council. He was considering making a bid for mayor. Theodore wholeheartedly approved.

And so the month of August passed much too quickly. Theodore immensely enjoyed the time with his family and friends but the war was never far from his mind. He would have to leave soon.

If only this war would end...

* * *

Betsy said goodbye to Theodore with as much bravery as she could muster. His illness was still fresh in her mind along with the terror of almost losing him and he was headed into harm's way again. It was hard to endure but she promised herself she would not hold him from it.

For her, life was on hold waiting for his return and yet life moved on without him. Her waistline increased with their growing child. Brianna grew and learned more every day. Henry and Aunt Agatha may not change as noticeably but they did as well. Eleven year old Henry was becoming more independent and needing her less while Aunt Agatha was slowly becoming frail and needing her more.

Chapter 34

It was a dreary afternoon in October when Betsy returned from the post office with a single letter from Theodore and several from her family. She put Brianna down for a nap, made tea for her and Aunt Agatha and then settled into the rocking chair in the parlor. She read the letters from her mother and sisters, saving Theodore's for last. Savoring the anticipation.

While he was away her life revolved around the mail; making sure her letters were posted in time and anxiously awaiting word from him. Some months there were none and it was so terribly hard to wait until the next month. Then two or three would usually be waiting to relieve the heartache. She understood it was hard for him to get mail out. His letters had to travel from wherever he was to the closest coastal town, usually Tampa, St. Augustine or Pensacola, and then wait for the next mail run to the Keys. Since the establishment of the bi-monthly mail runs from Charleston, she often received letters from her family in Philadelphia sooner than those of Theodore.

She ran a finger across her name recalling the first time she saw his handwriting. It was neat, clean and precise just as one would expect from someone who had to write clear enough for typesetters to read but on the other hand it was unexpected from one with such manly hands. There were no extra flourishes. His writing was the same as his speech—short and to the point. She did enjoy one positive side to his absence. He said more in his letters than he would have told her in person; sharing both events and feelings with more openness.

October 1st, Fort Marion, St. Augustine

My Darling Betsafina,

    Your letter of the fourteenth ultimo was very comforting. It brings me peace to know my family is doing well despite my continued absence and I owe that to you. You are my strength. I am with many men whose wives are taking care of families at home but I would wager only a few of them care for family not of their blood. You treat Henry and Aunt Agatha as though they were your blood relations and for that I cannot thank you enough. Regarding Henry, allow him to work as much as he likes so long as his studies do not suffer. Then, by all means, please do what you think best.

    This war has taken a strange turn from removal of Indians to emancipation of slaves. One of Gen. Jesup's new strategies is to separate red from black knowing that together they form a stronger resistance. He issued a proclamation that runaway slaves who turn themselves in will be allowed to move west as free men. It worked well at first bringing in a number of former slaves tired of the hardships of a rootless existence. Unfortunately, he also told his men they would be compensated for any slaves they captured. Their zeal in doing so soon chased away the slaves who were coming in voluntarily.

His next strategy may have produced results but it has surely ruined his reputation.

Early September, one of King Philip's slaves turned himself in at St. Augustine. He was questioned and revealed (possibly under threat of hanging but I cannot verify this) the location of King Philip's camp. Gen. Jesup sent Gen. Hernandez, commander of the Florida militia, to seize this band located near Dunlawton plantation. The dawn raid was so effective no blood was shed. One of the captives revealed the location of Chief Euchee Billy and his band. They were soon captured in the same manner. General Hernández paraded his forty-seven captives through the stone gate of St. Augustine and down the city street in front of a cheering crowd before taking them to Ft. Marion. Balls and dinners were held to celebrate his success.

King Philip requested permission for his family to join him which Gen. Jesup was more than willing to grant. Gen. Hernandez and his battalion were assigned to meet King Philip's son, Wild Cat, at Bulow plantation and escort them to St. Augustine. I was there to see this proud warrior dressed in scarlet finery ride into the city under a white flag followed by his family and fellow warriors. When they arrived inside the fort the unthinkable happened. The warriors were seized and imprisoned despite the flag of truce.

Gen. Jesup received censure from many directions for this uncivilized action. His defense? They broke their word first by following Osceola out of the relocation center. Apparently, his mother never taught him two wrongs don't make a right. Not that anything about this war is right or just.

I will be in St. Augustine for the foreseeable future so you may direct your letters here. For the time being I am happy to put aside my tent for a rented room. Due to the continuing depression the army stopped feeding all the civilian refugees in the forts across Florida, including me, so my mission is now more expensive. Still I feel it a worthwhile cause to pursue.

The city is cramped and full of filth. I can see why Mr. Audubon, a steward of nature, would not think favourably of it but it is not without its charms. Though the city outside the fort has been burned by invaders and rebuilt several times it is still quite old as can be seen in the coquina foundations. Fort Marion is large and, while the internal masonry structure is a typical square, it has diamond shaped points protruding from each corner giving it odd angles around the perimeter. The Spanish called it Castillo de San Marcos. I can see the fort from the window of my room. It is a pleasing site to behold in the rosy glow of sunset.

The light is fading my dear and so I must regrettably end my letter.

Give my love to all.
Your loving husband,
   Teddy

October 21st

My dearest Teddy,

I hope this letter finds you well.

Some days it is hard to be a good mother and to have confidence you are doing right by your children. Today I had to discipline our sweet little Brianna. She was chattering away, carrying on a conversation in her own private language, and then for some reason she grew distraught and threw her food at me. It was quite comical and I had trouble holding my smile in check to firmly say 'no' and then she did it again! She threw her bread right in my face and laughed. I lightly smacked her hand to reinforce my 'no' this time which of course brought tears. I felt so bad but I couldn't let her get away with this now. Later it would take so much more to instill the lesson and hopefully next time 'no' will be enough.

We have never discussed child discipline. Henry has always been such a good boy it has never come up before. I hope my actions agree with you.

You will be happy to know William Whitehead has won the bid for mayor just as we knew he would. He will do an excellent job leading our fine city.

On a sad note, I have noticed your aunt is moving a bit slower these days. She claims she feels fine but she gets up from her chair less often and goes to bed earlier in the evenings. She moves around well enough, just slower. I will keep a close eye on her.

You should see me. I feel as big as a house. I swear my belly is larger than with Brianna and if indigestion is any clue I am sure it must be a boy this time. I am thoroughly miserable in body but happy as a lark in spirit. Only three more months till we meet our child.

Stay safe my love.
Always yours,
   Betsy

Theodore folded the letter to add to the others he carried with him. As always, reading her letters made him homesick. He opened his Bible to the place where he kept the miniature painting of Betsy and Henry. He ran his finger along the edge of her face. *My how life has changed.* She was even lovelier now, if that was possible, with her face filled in and slightly rounder since giving birth to Brianna and now they were expecting another in a few short months. He was truly blessed.

November 1837

It was a chilly afternoon. Betsy pulled her shawl tighter across her shoulders as she walked home. Today she was too impatient to wait. She read his letter as she walked uncaring how rude it might seem to those she passed along the way.

My dear Betsafina,

He did it again! I am still in shock as I write to you.

General Jesup released Wild Cat as a messenger to bring in more of King Philip's people under threat of harming King Philip if he did not return, so Wild Cat brought in his uncle, younger brother and more of his tribe. He also brought word Osceola wanted to meet for a parley. The noble warrior sent the general a beaded peace pipe with a white plume as a show of good faith. Jesup told Hernandez to send gifts of food with his agreement to meet.

The night before Osceola arrived, General Hernandez held a grand ball here in St. Augustine. Wild Cat was the main attraction. I could not believe how taken the ladies were by the young warrior in his Seminole dress of bright colors with metal and white plume ornamentation. I overheard one lady ask an officer if Osceola was as handsome. The officer's reply—more so—to which she nearly swooned.

The following day Jesup received a message Osceola was waiting about a mile from Fort Peyton. General Hernandez was sent to meet Osceola with a message from General Jesup. Since this would be a parley and not a battle I deemed it safe enough to join them. We approached the camp to find a large group of Indians standing under a white flag. General Hernandez rapidly read Jesup's memorandum full of questions to Osceola and Coa Hadjo. As they struggled to respond, the general unexpectedly signaled his men to step forward with guns raised. I was dumbfounded! They took all ninety-five of these people prisoner under a flag of truce including Osceola, Coa Hadjo and John Horse.

What does it say when I seem to be more surprised by this turn of events than Osceola? He stoically accepted his fate without protest as if he expected it. I'm sure he was aware of Wild Cat's arrest in such a manner. Perhaps the deprivations they have suffered make surrender seem like a relief. Indeed, Osceola appears more sickly than the last time I saw him. It is believed he is suffering from malaria. Still his eyes revealed a soul not yet subdued.

Just as before, General Hernandez paraded his captives through the streets of St. Augustine to the cheers of the people. It seemed as if the whole town stepped from their homes to see the elusive warrior. I trailed behind, ashamed to be associated with this treachery.

Again there is an uproar over the manner in which Osceola was captured. General Jesup has surely tarnished his previous reputation of integrity serving as quartermaster general. He defends his actions with many reasons but I believe his true purpose this time is because he holds Osceola to blame as the main instigator in the embarrassing June liberation of the seven hundred tribesmen from the relocation center.

I think we, as a people, will look back on this war and indeed the removal of all the native tribes as dark days in our nation's history.

Today I am feeling very pessimistic. Perhaps tomorrow I will be more like myself.

I apologize if my feelings have brought yours down. I promise to think only of pleasant thoughts of our reunion and the arrival of our child for the rest of the evening and dream of you as I slumber. I pray you do the same until I return to you again.

Love always,
Theodore

Dearest Teddy,

My time approaches and I realize we have yet to discuss names. Do you have any suggestions?

Henry is doing well at his studies and his work. You will be prouder still to know he saves most of his earnings. He is a fine son and will become a wise man.

I miss your presence. I miss your scent on the pillow. I miss your voice. I miss your arms around me. I miss you.

I think my condition must be making me weak. I'm sure I'll be back to myself in the morning. Don't you worry, I am holding down the fort here, so to speak.

I wonder where you are tonight.

Take care my love. As always I pray for a swift end to this war so you can come home to us and roam no more.

Your loving wife,
Betsafina

December 21st

Betsy returned to the parlor with Agatha's heavy shawl. The unwieldiness of her girth made it a cumbersome task to place it on Agatha's frail shoulders. She pulled the ends together across her chest and noticed the cameo she always wore was missing.

"Aunt Agatha, have you lost your pendant?"

Agatha instinctively placed her hand over the place where the pendant should be. Her brows drew together but then her face cleared. "No dear. It's still on my dresser. My fingers were too stiff this morning to put it on." She rubbed the joints of her hand still feeling the lingering swelling.

Betsy smiled lightly. "I'll be happy to do it for you, if you like." Agatha didn't answer. "I don't believe I've ever asked how you came by the necklace."

Agatha's faded blue eyes grew wistful. "It was a gift from my husband on our wedding day."

Betsy's smile grew. "How sweet."

Agatha leaned back and closed her eyes as if to take a nap effectively dismissing Betsy but she didn't mind. She had a letter to read. Theodore could keep her company for a while. She settled on the sofa and unfolded his letter.

December 2nd, 1837

 My darling wife,

  I feel as you do. It is hard to come up with any names that are appealing. I am at a loss as well. Perhaps we must meet this one first to know the name that is right.

  I miss you too, sweetheart. I miss the sweet smell of your hair, your amazing blue eyes shining with love, your sweet voice filling the air with song. If only I could be with you tonight.

  An incredible escape was made a few nights ago by twenty of those held in the same cell as Osceola. The fort has been in an uproar ever since. Inquisitions have been made as to how it was possible. It is believed the Indians somehow obtained a file to cut the bars and they tied their bed linen to make a rope to drop to the ground. Still the opening is so small—a mere eight inches wide—it hardly seems possible it could be done. Some of the Indians claimed illness in the days prior so it is believed they were really starving themselves in order to fit through the opening. The fort was considered secure so night watches were not vigilant in their duties.

  Either from illness or the pending arrival of his family, Osceola stayed behind as did the aging King Philip. The following day Osceola's family arrived under a flag of truce, half-starved and travel weary.

  We have learned a Cherokee delegation is on the way here from the western reservation. They are traveling thousands of miles for the humane purpose of negotiating an end to this war. I pray they succeed. Enough blood has been shed over this land.

  Be well my love,
    Teddy

December 15th, 1837

My darling Betsafina,

  Much has happened since my last letter.

  Just before the arrival of the Cherokee delegation Hernandez captured fifty-three more Seminoles including twenty warriors adding to the number already being held here for deportation. The delegation, led by Chief John Ross, immediately went to visit the Seminoles. They returned to Fort Mellon to meet

General Jesup with Chief Micanopy, a dozen lesser chiefs, and a number of warriors.

A quick note about Fort Mellon, it was previously known as Camp Monroe for its location on the shores of Lake Monroe but was renamed after Captain Charles Mellon who sacrificed his life to save his men during an attack in February led by King Philip before his capture. It was abandoned in June due to sickness and as usually happens, the Seminole burned it to the ground. It was ordered reopened last month as a supply depot and as of now is still under construction with only the barest of necessities available.

They arrived under a flag of truce. Jesup treated them coldly and as though they were there to surrender instead of talk. Micanopy agreed to emigrate but said it would take time to round up his people. Jesup accused him of delaying the inevitable and then ordered his men to seize them as prisoners. Chief John Ross protested the violation of a sacred rule but Jesup didn't change his mind. He had Micanopy send out a messenger giving his people ten days to come to the fort.

I was surprised the delegation tried again to bring in more Seminoles to talk despite Jesup's actions. This time they met with Wild Cat and Sam Jones. These warriors knew well Jesup's treachery having recently escaped from Ft. Marion. They ridiculed the Cherokees for siding with Jesup. Naturally, they refused to surrender. Upon learning of the delegations failure, Jesup sent Micanopy and his people to St. Augustine (seventy-eight of them came into the fort) to await deportation. Humiliated, Chief John Ross, protested Jesup's actions in a letter to the Secretary of War.

Then something incredible happened. General Jesup sent orders to Colonel Shelburne to meet with the delegation and the Seminole prisoners. He told them if the tribe promised to turn in all the runaway slaves and defend the land against invasion they could have all the land south of Tampa Bay. Of course they agreed without hesitation. When Osceola heard of this, still a prisoner, he pulled a white plume from his turban and gave it to Colonel Shelburne to pass on to the "white father" in acceptance.

Finally, this war is over. I did not believe it possible for it to end with the Seminole being allowed to stay even if it is nothing but useless swampland. If all goes well, perhaps I can be home when your time comes. I will know more in the coming weeks. Words cannot describe the joy I feel but then it doesn't matter as I'm sure you will feel the same upon reading this.

Betsy was so overjoyed she didn't finish reading his letter. She held the paper to her chest with both hands and sent a thankful prayer heavenward. It was over! Theodore would come home soon. She wanted to share the good news but Henry wasn't home and Aunt Agatha was dozing. She dropped a hand to rub the foot kicking her from the inside. Her grin was huge. "Your father's coming home to meet you little one."

* * *

As Betsy was headed to bed, Aunt Agatha called out from her room. Betsy stepped inside her door and was beckoned to her bedside. Aunt Agatha reached out to grasp Betsy's hand for a moment then pointed to her jewelry box on the dresser. "Be a dear and bring that to me."

Betsy wondered what she could want with the box before slumber. Silently she placed it on Aunt Agatha's lap and waited.

Agatha ran a hand over the glossy mahogany box before opening it. She pulled out a gold band and handed it to Betsy. "This was Margaret's ring. I want you to make sure Henry gets it when he decides to marry."

Betsy thought it strange she would bring this up now but didn't question her. She nodded and smiled. "Of course."

Agatha reached for Betsy's empty hand and placed a necklace against her palm covering it with her bony hand. "I want you to have this for your kindness in putting up with my cantankerous ways."

Betsy looked down as Aunt Agatha pulled her hand away to reveal the cameo pendant. Betsy lifted her stricken gaze, shook her head, and tried to give it back. "Oh no. I can't accept it. You always wear it."

"Don't argue with me girl. I'm old and tired and if I want you to have it, so you shall."

Fearing she had offended her, Betsy swallowed any further protest. "Thank you."

"You're welcome dear." Agatha riffled through the other items, closed the lid, and held the box out to Betsy. "You can give the rest away as you see fit."

Betsy awkwardly took the box while she still held the ring and pendant. "You speak as though you're on your deathbed."

"Hmm."

Betsy's lips quirked. *So that was where Theodore learned it.*

"Perhaps I am. I suddenly felt the need to do this tonight."

Betsy was horrified. "Aunt Agatha, don't even jest about such a thing. You have plenty of years left in you."

"Maybe." She settled in while Betsy put the box back on the dresser and returned the ring and pendant inside.

When Betsy turned around to speak, Agatha dismissed her. "Good night."

"Good night." Betsy blew out the candle on the dresser and left the room. She tried not to let the incident bother her but it was rather strange.

The next morning Betsy arrived in the parlor to find it empty. Aunt Agatha was always there ahead of her. She often said it was hard for old bones to rest properly. She could be in the outhouse or the kitchen but Betsy was compelled to check Agatha's bedroom first. She hastily climbed the stairs and knocked lightly on her door expecting an answer. There was none. She opened the door a crack and peeked in to find Aunt Agatha still abed.

She must not feel well.

Betsy quietly entered the room and stopped half way. She felt it. Her lips quivered and she brought her hand up to rest against her rapid heartbeat. The only sound in the room was her own ragged breathing. She swallowed hard, straightened her spine, and stepped to the bed. Betsy touched the back of her hand to the pale dry cheek hoping to gently wake Aunt Agatha. The coolness of her skin made Betsy reflexively pull her hand back. She stood there for a moment staring at the woman she had come to love as family struggling to accept the truth revealed.

Aunt Agatha was gone.

She had no idea how many moments passed before she gathered her wits. What was she to do now? The thought was practical for the moment. Later, she would face the emotional loss of Aunt Agatha's stoic support. For now she should wake Henry and send him to bring help but who to send him to? The sheriff? The doctor? The undertaker? Her hand flew to her mouth, and she uttered the first sound since entering the room. "Oh!" First she had to tell Henry. Tears welled. She looked to Aunt Agatha and a most uncharitable thought crossed her mind. "Couldn't you have waited 'til Theodore was here?" It was wrong to speak ill of the dead. She would pray for forgiveness later. Right now she had to find the right words to tell Henry.

"Momma, are you angry with Aunt Aggie?"

Betsy turned her head to find Henry standing in the doorway. She must have spoken aloud without realizing it. "No, Henry. I'm not angry."

He stared at the still figure in the bed. "Is Aunt Aggie sick?"

Betsy walked to the door blocking Henry's view. She ushered him out of the room and gently closed the door behind her. She paused to listen for Brianna. Hearing only quiet from her room she guided Henry into his room. Emotional weakness hit her. She sank to the bed and bowed her head to hide her distress. She blinked away the tears and after a few more cleansing breaths, looked to Henry standing in front of her patiently waiting. She reached a hand out to him and he stepped forward to place his hand in hers. While Betsy was trying to find the words, Henry found them for her.

"She's dead, isn't she?"

Betsy could only nod. She didn't trust her voice.

Henry awkwardly patted her shoulder. "She told me she would pass away soon. She said I would need to be strong for you."

Betsy's anger flared. *How dare Agatha put such a burden on Henry!*

And then she smiled, and the smile turned into a laugh. Even in death, Theodore's aunt was overbearing and meddlesome.

Henry gave her a puzzled look. Betsy squeezed his hand and stood up. Eleven now, he was only a few inches shorter than her. She put her hands on his shoulders. Seeing how he took Aunt Agatha's words to heart she couldn't dismiss them, but she didn't want him to feel burdened either. "We will be strong for each other."

The following morning Aunt Agatha was laid to rest in the cemetery by the sea. A surprising number of islanders were in attendance. Mayor Whitehead officiated the service as Reverend Dyce was currently traveling the country soliciting donations to build their church.

Afterwards, Betsy did not feel like doing much of anything and certainly not going through Aunt Agatha's belongings. She decided to put the arduous task off for a while. Instead she chose an even harder one, at least mentally. She was trying to decide how best to tell Theodore. She ran several lines in her head but they all seemed too cold and abrupt but then perhaps it was because it happened that way. Maybe she could wait to tell him—he was expected home soon—except it was not the kind of news one should delay. In the end she kept it simple, just the way he would have if their roles were reversed.

> *Your aunt passed away in her sleep the night before last. She was not sick nor do I believe she suffered in any way. Our home is not the same without her presence.*

St. Augustine, December 17th, 1837

Theodore sat in a dark and dank tavern at the edge of the city with his haversack on the floor beside him. The atmosphere of the establishment was oppressive and the service surly at best but the food was good which is why he was currently sitting across from a mail carrier working through his second bowl of stew. Theodore ate before the arrival of his companion and was now finishing a letter to Betsy. He read what he had written so far.

> *These words are as hard to write as they are to feel. There is no treaty. The war continues. I wish now I had waited to write to you so only one of us must endure this heart-rending disappointment. Bitter does not begin to describe how everyone feels about this turn of events. Especially the Seminole. For them it is another promise broken in a long string of broken promises. I am amazed they can generate any faith at all in the white man.*
>
> *As it turns out, Jesup's offer to the Indians was not sanctioned nor was it approved afterwards. President Van Buren is cut from the same cloth as Andrew Jackson and Secretary of War Poinsett is afraid allowing the Seminole to remain will cause the tribes north of here to put up more resistance.*
>
> *As I write this General Jesup's troops are headed south prepared to fight to the bitter end.*

He was still debating if he should share with her his intentions. It would upset her and he was loath to do so when she was so close to her time. His companion pushed away his empty bowl and announced it was time to leave taking the decision from Theodore. He hurriedly signed and sealed the letter, handing it off to a page boy with a coin to take it to the St. Augustine post office where it would go on the next mail ship headed south. Theodore followed the mail carrier in the opposite direction out of the city. They passed through the tall square coquina towers marking the opening in the city wall and crossed the bridge over the moat leaving civilization behind to head into the wilds of Florida.

Earlier in the month, General Jesup ordered his men to move south in three columns to push the Seminole into battle. One of those columns was led by Colonel Zachary Taylor whom Theodore met at the Black Hawk war in 1833. He liked and respected this sensible fifty-three year old man. Taylor encouraged Theodore to follow him into battle and promised to keep him out of harm's way. It was tempting. Taylor had seventy Delaware and Shawnee Indians with him. Theodore knew these warriors to be more savage than the Creeks. Just the idea of using Indian against Indian was an intriguing story and the potential results of this mix could prove disastrous for the Seminole.

At first, Theodore declined but after learning of the false treaty, he discovered a mail carrier was on his way to Colonel Taylor's position. He was being given a second chance to join him. On impulse, he decided to take it. His other options were to follow the captured Indians to the relocation center in Tampa and report on their departure or stay at Ft. Marion. There was plenty of interest going on in St. Augustine and Osceola's continued imprisonment was still a very newsworthy subject, but he was drawn to Sam Jones and Wild Cat's continued resistance. Could they lead the fight without Osceola? Theodore believed both warriors were spirited enough to do so. He also wanted to see if Taylor could find a way to counter the Seminole's hit and run tactics. So he again decided to risk his safety to report directly from another battlefield.

A few days later Theodore stopped to rest at Fort Basinger, one of the many hastily constructed strongholds for Colonel Taylor's supplies, prisoners and wounded. It was located on the south side of the Kissimmee River about ten miles north-west of Lake Okeechobee. Shortly after his arrival, a guard of Shawnee came to the fort escorting sixty-three warriors including Jumper, the highest ranking chief left in the field, increasing the number of prisoners present at the fort to a hundred and eighty. Theodore had only moments to speak with Jumper and the other prisoners before having to leave the fort. He and the mail carrier followed the Shawnee warriors further south to Colonel Taylor's position.

As he walked the newly cleared footpath keeping a cautious eye on his surroundings, Theodore still couldn't believe he talked himself into this course of action.

December 25, 1837

Theodore was war weary. He was spending another Christmas camped in the mud away from his loved ones. He was with Taylor's troops consisting of roughly eight hundred men. The last few days they pursued the Seminoles from one camp to the next always just missing them. The rainy weather was also slowing their progress. Along the way they captured a few people left behind along with cattle and ponies but it was feeling like a wild goose chase. Then, yesterday evening Captain Sparks captured an Indian skulking around the camp. When questioned, the captive reluctantly revealed many warriors were positioned a few miles away. Today they would continue the pursuit.

It was an hour before sunrise. The sky was overcast but at least it stopped raining. The camp was stirring, preparing to move out. Theodore packed up his gear wishing he could at least have dried his socks by a fire but even if dry timber could be found, Colonel Taylor had forbidden it. A hot cup of coffee would have been nice too.

At sunrise they followed a course due south. A few miles later one of the Delaware scouts captured a Seminole crossing a nearby prairie. Colonel Taylor was nearly jubilant to learn their quarry was within a half-mile; roughly three hundred Seminole warriors with the intent to fight. Onward they marched till they reached the edge of a swamp on the north shore of Lake Okeechobee. In front of them was a half mile of shallow muddy water and sawgrass five feet high. Trails were cut through the grass presumably by the Seminoles. On the other side of the swamp was a hardwood hammock and beyond the trees, the massive lake spread out to the horizon. The Seminole, likely hiding in the hammock, chose an impressive place to make a stand.

Colonel Taylor called his officers together to convey his strategy. Theodore stood a few yards behind the colonel to listen. Taylor impatiently waited for his men to gather round and then he made his announcement. "We have the advantage in numbers so we will make a head-on assault. The Delaware will take point followed by your command, Colonel Gentry. Once you have fired, you are to fall back in a line behind Lieutenant Colonel Thompson's men, then Colonel Foster will take over and finally my men will finish cleaning them out."

Theodore could tell not a single officer agreed with Taylor's plan. It seemed foolish to him too. The interpreter finished translating for the Delaware chief. Theodore didn't need a translator. His response was clear in his steadfast tone, crossed arms and head movement. The interpreter reluctantly turned to Colonel Taylor. "The chief say they will not be your fools."

Taylor fumed. "You tell the chief he will do as I say, or he will not be returned to his family."

The chief stared down Taylor as the interpreter spoke and remained stoic and silent afterwards. The colonel was forced to concede. "Colonel Gentry, you will take the lead."

Colonel Richard Gentry was as reluctant as the Delaware chief to lead his men into a slaughter. "With all due respect sir, might I suggest we use the strength of our numbers to encircle the enemy, forcing them..."

Colonel Taylor cut him off. "Are you afraid of a direct assault? We are not going to waste time in this heat waiting on troops to hack their way around the swamps when there are paths already cut. We will be swift and we will be decisive. Are your men soldiers or not?"

The gauntlet was laid. Not willing to be called a coward, Colonel Gentry reluctantly accepted his orders to lead his hundred and thirty-two Missouri volunteers toward the hammock until fired upon and then they were to retreat and reform a line behind the regular army. The 6th Infantry commanded by Lieutenant Colonel Alexander Thompson would take up the battle followed by the 4th Infantry led by Colonel William Foster. Taylor's 1st Infantry, totaling almost half of the men present, would be held in reserve.

It was noon and the sun was bright overhead. The troops marched out on foot into the middle of the swamp. Their approach heralded by the sudden flight of squawking birds. Theodore stayed behind with the horses; they being of little use in the knee deep murky water. He lifted his spyglass and called himself all kinds of a fool for voluntarily spending Christmas at the edge of a Florida swamp watching the latest battle of this sanguinary war unfold.

He could see the Missouri militia move toward the hammock following the raised sword of Colonel Gentry, as planned. They split up into several lines following the ragged paths already cut through the sawgrass. The Indians could not be seen but all knew they were there, hiding behind the trees and brush on the other side of the swamp; waiting for the opportunity to attack. As soon as the militia was in range, muzzle flashes erupted as the Indians fired on them not just from the ground but some held vantage points within the trees.

Instead of calling for retreat as planned, Colonel Gentry led his men on a charge into the hammock. Heavy fire brought down many including Gentry. Without their leader, the militia tried to retreat but it was too late. The Indians emerged from the hammock to counterattack. Their war cries carried across the swamp raising the hair on the back of Theodore's neck bringing to mind those devastating battles on the Withlachoochee. A few warriors raised dripping scalps into the smoky air.

Theodore closed his eyes, sickened by the sight of so many men falling under the onslaught. When he opened them again he could see the 6th infantry begin their advance lined up like two hundred targets marching forward past the retreating militia much as they would if facing a British troop. These men had to make new paths through the razor sharp blades of sawgrass as the wounded and dead filled the previous ones. When they reached firing range they stopped. The Indians fired targeting officers first.

The men returned fire, reloaded and fired again in a continuing volley as if unaware of those who fell around them. The casualties were high for the 6th. Theodore breathed a sigh of relief when Colonel Foster led his men in a charge to give them aide. The Indians retreated deeper into the woods. Colonel Foster urged his men to give chase sending out a right and left wing. The gun fire was growing more distant and sporadic as both sides took cover in the trees; the soldiers advancing, the Indians retreating.

Finally, Colonel Taylor sent his reserves to flank the hammock expecting to catch the retreating enemy. It was not to be. The warriors planned their escape with waiting canoes and were safely out of range by the time the soldiers reached the lake's edge. They could only stand on the shore and watch as the enemy sailed safely away.

The battle lasted three hours. It took them until sundown to carry off the hundred and twelve wounded and to bury the twenty-six dead, many were officers. It was a high number from the five hundred soldiers who directly engaged the enemy. Only a dozen Seminole casualties were discovered.

Colonel Taylor declared the battle a victory. The military measured success as routing the enemy and holding the field not in the number of dead and wounded. Theodore silently disagreed.

He helped care for the injured men. It was an arduous task. Even those who didn't have bullet wounds had crisscrossed cuts on their skin and clothing from the unforgiving sawgrass. Theodore's conversations with the men revealed sightings of Alligator, Sam Jones, Wild Cat and John Horse leading the Seminoles. These were the strongest of the Seminole resistance having refused all negotiations. Many soldiers mentioned the Black Seminoles were at the front of the battle. Apparently General Jesup's plan to separate the blacks from the Indians failed.

The wounded were to be escorted back to Tampa while Colonel Taylor continued to lead his men down the eastern side of Lake Okeechobee. Theodore had seen enough of how the army operated. Taylor was no different than the others before him. Theodore decided to take his chances tagging along with a mail carrier on his way to the newly built Fort Pierce next to the Indian River on the eastern coast. With any luck he could find a ship sailing south. It was time he headed home.

Key West, December 29th

The end of the year was near. The approaching birth, the demands of her business, and Brianna kept Betsy too busy to dwell on the loss of Aunt Agatha. Henry seemed to be managing much the same using his studies and work to keep him occupied. The evening meal was the only time they spent together as a family but for both of them another empty chair at the dining table made it the hardest part of the day.

Just as she felt like she was regaining a sense of normalcy in her grief she received Theodore's news of the continuing war. She broke down weeping, praying and weeping some more. "Dear Lord, what more must we endure?"

* * *

Theodore arrived at Fort Pierce on January 2nd to find Brevet Lieutenant Colonel Benjamin Pierce and his small command the sole occupants of the fort still under construction. Half the men were finishing the upper level of the palmetto log blockhouse while the other half were working on the surrounding barricade. The blockhouse was of similar design to the other forts. Found to be effective in defense, the second story was built larger than the lower story. Windows and loopholes allowed the occupants to shoot at the enemy in any direction.

Behind the fort, Theodore discovered the old Ais Indian mound overlooking the coast. He climbed the twenty foot rise to stare past the tranquil harbour and barrier island to the open water of the Atlantic. There seemed little hope of a ship stopping here on the way to the Keys. Theodore spent the night pondering what he should do next. Should he wait here or head west with the mail carrier in the morning. Neither option seemed promising.

As luck would have it, the following day brought the arrival of the navy commander, Lieutenant Levin Powell. He was headed south and welcomed Theodore aboard his vessel. Powell's command included over sixty sailors, most of whom were black, and twenty five artillery and volunteer infantry. They were tasked with hunting down the Seminole in the Everglades. Traveling with Lieutenant Powell took Theodore in the direction he wanted to go and would give him a better chance of finding another ship headed to the Keys.

Travel was slow aboard the navy ship as they explored each inlet along the coast looking for signs of Seminole activity. Theodore spent his time as any good journalist would do—interviewing those on board. One of the passengers was a young German naturalist and physician, Edward Leitner. He was serving as the troops' physician.

The blond man's eyes lit up when Theodore told him where he was from. "I visited Key West once. It's a pretty little island and the folks are friendly. Especially a handsome young widow who was very interested in my work. You may know of her, Betsy Wheeler."

Theodore was at once annoyed with the man's familiarity with his wife, thrilled to have an excuse to speak of her, and proud that the woman this man admired belonged to him. "It's Mrs. Whitmore now."

Leitner's cheeks colored. "Your wife? Congratulations sir. She's a fine catch."

Theodore smiled. "Yes she is."

They soon found even more in common. Leitner spoke of his travels in the Keys and to the Dry Tortugas and was fascinated to hear of Theodore's similar adventures with a man he greatly admired, James Audubon. It felt good to speak of something other than war if only for a little while.

On January 10th, they sailed into Jupiter Inlet and weighed anchor. A smaller boat was lowered to the water and a party of four infantry and two sailors were sent to scout the river. A few hours later they returned to report finding a trail. The rest of the small boats were then lowered and Lieutenant Powell took eighty of his men with several days' provisions to further investigate. Theodore almost went with them but the echo of his wife's words to him as she left his sick bed last summer made him decide to stay behind. *Don't you dare put me in widow's weeds again.*

Strange he should think of it now when it hadn't crossed his mind when he decided to follow Colonel Taylor.

Eight days later, the ragged band of men returned to the ship. Four were dead and twenty-two were wounded; a full quarter of the men Powell took with him. Theodore learned from the officers that after five days of following the trail made by a large group of Seminoles they came to a place where they could see campfire smoke just ahead. Powell ordered a charge hoping to catch the Indians by surprise. Instead his men were ambushed and surrounded, forced to fight their way into retreat and make the long journey back to the ship. Edward Leitner came back mortally wounded. He died not long after their return.

Lieutenant Powell sent a dispatch to General Jesup giving the location of the Seminole camp. His larger force would have a better chance of taking them. Powell continued southward to New River in the hopes of finding aide for his wounded men.

Key West, February 1st, 1838

Betsy moved the rocking chair out onto the sleeping porch so she could enjoy the sound of the gentle spring shower while she nursed little Agatha. She picked up the two week old infant from her cradle before her newborn mewling could wake Brianna who was thankfully taking a morning nap. Once the baby was settled at her breast, she opened the long awaited letter from Theodore. It had been over a month since she received the last one dated the middle of December and she was surprised to see this one was written over a month ago; two weeks after his last letter.

December 27th

My darling Betsafina,
I have done what I said I wouldn't do—I followed Colonel Taylor into

battle at Lake Okeechobee. You can be reassured I was never in any danger. However, the experience was as bad as the others. The only good I suppose to come from it was a renewed respect for the bravery of the soldiers and volunteers who follow orders even knowing it will likely lead to death.

Our generals seem to have no understanding of how to conduct this war. They have learned nothing from history. Colonel Foster has followed many commands of which he disagrees and his frustrations are apparent. This latest campaign is yet another example of leadership folly. It seems to me Colonel Taylor is more interested in earning a General's star than in ending this conflict.

This letter is being sent by mail carrier to Tampa while I am taking a more direct route to the eastern coast in the hopes I will be by your side when you receive it but if I am not have no fear, the delay will be due to the lack of transportation and nothing more.

Be well my love,

Teddy

Betsy was so angry with Theodore for risking his life yet again, she was sure if he were in front of her now she would slug him. What was he thinking getting involved in another battle instead of being here for the birth of their child? And where was Lake Okeechobee? She had never heard of it.

Agatha whimpered in response to her mother's agitation. Betsy did her best to calm her emotions but she couldn't keep from worrying. Where was Theodore now? The gentle rain falling upon the island offered no answers.

Many times during the day and every night before bed she prayed for his safe return as the days and weeks passed without word from him. Now with two babies and Henry to care for and no Aunt Agatha to help, for the first time, Betsy's business was more of a burden than a comfort. She vented her frustrations and concerns into letters to her mother and sisters and on rare visits with Abby. She didn't bother writing to Theodore since he should be home before he would ever see the letters.

It took some deep soul searching but she finally decided it would be best to close her shop. With the poor economy she didn't expect to be able to sell it so it came as a great surprise when Jonathon and Esperanza made her a generous offer. It was a day of sadness and relief when she signed her former home and everything in it over to the Keats.

Agatha's birth was not as easy nor did she recover as quickly as with Brianna's. Betsy hoped one less burden would help her cope. Now if only Theodore would come home.

Chapter 35

Key West, February 1838

Word of Osceola's death on January 30th in a Charleston prison at the age of thirty-three reached Key West the middle of February but it was not the only interesting news to arrive on the mail schooner. A letter from Betsy's mother expressed concern for her daughter's situation and their intentions to gather enough money to send her youngest sister, Vertiline, to help her with the children. It was welcome news. Betsy longed to see her family again but visiting them was out of the question until this Florida War was resolved. Just the idea of Vertiline's pending visit lightened her weary soul. Her sister's energy would certainly be a blessing. There were so many things she needed to get done. It would be nice to have her sister's help. Betsy wrote a quick reply and rushed it to the post office so it would leave with the mail ship on the evening tide.

Week by week her excitement built for the pending visit. Every day was filled with tasks that would seem less burdensome with someone to share them.

The next mail run brought a letter written in Vertiline's hand. Betsy quickly tore it open anxious for news of her pending arrival. Her spirits plummeted as she read the opening lines.

Dearest sister,

Our father is ill and mother is taking it hard. She needs me now. The doctor says he will recover but I must postpone my visit until his health improves. I am sure you will understand.

Of course Betsy's concern for her parents outweighed her disappointment. She wished Vertiline had given more details as to his malady. The simple nature of her sister's wording made it clear the letter was penned in haste which explained the lack of information. Betsy's reply was full of questions but the mail ship left early and so it would wait two weeks in the post office before leaving the island. She could only hope the next letter from her family was good news. Until then she would pray for her father's health and do her best to leave her worry in God's hands. It certainly wasn't going to do her any good. The disappointment and worry were only added burdens to the great weight she already carried. She had to let them go.

Fortunately Max approached her the following afternoon with a proposition which helped to take her mind off her worries. There was a huge ball to be held in April and Max wanted to surprise Abby with a proper waltz. He asked Betsy to teach him. The secret lessons were a risk to both of their reputations but it was not the first time Betsy put herself at risk to help her friends. The clandestine meetings added a little excitement to the predictable pattern of domestic chores and babies. It was agreed they would meet once a week during morning nap time.

Betsy hummed a dance tune as Max waltzed her around the room. The furniture was pushed to the walls and the curtains were drawn against spying eyes just as it was every Wednesday for the last three weeks. Max was doing so well she was thinking today's lesson would probably be their last. Besides the dance was in two weeks.

Theodore paused at the bottom of the steps outside his home when he heard his wife humming through the open window accompanied by the sound of shuffling feet. Her sweet voice, carried on the March breeze, was a musical gift for his weary soul. He entered the house as quietly as he could, the better to listen, before she discovered his presence and stopped. His smile dropped at the sight of her in the arms of a man he considered his friend. Jealous rage overtook him. It took a few deep breaths for rational thought to return. Betsy's murmured dance instructions made him realize what was really going on and the smile returned. He couldn't resist teasing them in kind for his momentary torture so he hid the smile and in a grave voice said, "Sir, I demand you name your second."

The couple froze in mid-turn, their shocked faces swung in his direction. Betsy was first to break hold. She squealed in delight and ran straight into Theodore's arms. He caught her to him and swung her around.

Max waited not only out of politeness to allow husband and wife their reunion but also to determine Theodore's true feelings before he approached. He surely hoped the challenge issued was in jest.

Betsy leaned back in Theodore's arms searching his face for all that was familiar and all that had changed in the seven months since August. He was a bit more gaunt but nothing some home-cooked meals couldn't cure. She forgot Max's presence until she noticed Theodore's eyes cut in his direction. They stepped apart and turned toward their guest. Theodore dropped his right arm from her shoulder to reach out and offer his hand in greeting.

Max's brow smoothed as he stepped forward to take Theodore's hand. "Welcome home, mate."

"Thank you, Captain. I see you have kept my wife entertained in my absence."

Betsy could feel Max's consternation, but she heard the teasing note in Theodore's tone. She pushed against her husband's arm. "Stop making him uncomfortable."

Theodore looked down at his wife. He kept his face straight. "He should be uncomfortable and so should you entertaining a man alone in the afternoon with the shades drawn. What is a husband to think?"

Betsy saw the gleam in his eye and started to answer but Theodore held a hand for her silence.

Max swallowed, again unsure of Theodore's true feelings. "I assure you sir, there is only the best of intentions going on here."

Theodore lightly growled. "You have intentions towards my wife?"

His eyes flared in surprise, but Max stood his ground. "Certainly not."

Theodore drew his brows together. "Is she not good enough for you?"

Max's jaw dropped from the unexpected change in attack. As he was gathering his words to defend Betsy's appeal and his actions, he caught a glimpse of humor in Theodore's gaze that instantly changed his response. *Two could play this game.* "She's got nothing on Abigail."

Theodore turned to Betsy. "Cheeky fellow, isn't he?"

Betsy was getting a little worried the conversation would turn sour. She used her tone as a warning. "Teddy."

Theodore turned back to Max. "I say Betsafina has it all over your Abigail. What say you?"

Max shook his head. "Man, are you trying to pick a fight?"

Theodore finally smiled. "Forgive me. I've been too long away from civilization. Now would you two care to explain the need for secret waltzing lessons in the middle of the morning? You would think you could at least have Aunt Agatha in here as a chaperone." Betsy's sharply indrawn breath was his first clue something was amiss. He swung his gaze to her to find pain and distress in her countenance.

"You didn't receive my letter?" She realized it was a silly question as soon as she spoke it. He obviously hadn't. "Your aunt passed away in December, in her sleep." She placed a hand of comfort on his upper arm. "I'm so sorry, Teddy."

, Max was feeling decidedly out of place. He stepped towards the door. "I believe it's time for me to leave." He reached out to shake Theodore's hand adding his left hand to convey his feelings. "Theodore, welcome home and my deepest sympathies for your loss. Your aunt was a remarkable woman." He gave a nod to Betsy. "Thank you for the lessons."

Betsy and Theodore both mutely nodded in acknowledgement and waited for the front door to close behind him before stepping into each other's arms. Many moments passed without speaking as they physically rejoiced in their reunion. For Betsy, thought stopped completely as she became immersed in the flood of tactile sensations created by his hands and lips. She wanted the moment to go on forever but a small voice from the bedroom brought a sudden halt to their passions.

"Mama, awake."

Theodore grinned. "Brianna." Then remembering he glanced down at Betsy's middle belatedly realizing there should be a second child. He brought his eyes up to hers. "And the baby?" For a moment he worried something may have gone wrong, but Betsy's smile quickly reassured him.

"Sleeping."

Theodore turned to hurry towards the bedroom pulling Betsy by the hand. She loved his enthusiasm for his children and couldn't help her grin.

She lifted her free hand to run her fingertips over her kiss swollen lips loving that too. It had been too long since she felt it.

They reached the bedroom where Brianna stood in her crib waiting to be released and on the other side of the room the baby slept peacefully in the cradle. Betsy waited in the doorway to see how Brianna would react to her father. Theodore reached down to pick her up. Her face changed to one of hesitation. She didn't recognize him but her desire to leave the crib was stronger than her fear of this stranger. However, as soon as she saw her mother she reached out to Betsy leaning away from Theodore. He tried to entice her to stay but she began to fuss so he relinquished her. He knew it was to be expected, still it hurt that his child didn't recognize him.

Brianna was two already and he had spent so little time with her. It was a high personal price to pay for the mission he chose to complete. For three years their greatest generals fought against the Seminoles with little gain and no end in sight. He wondered now, if he had known at the start the war would last so long, would he still have made the choice to follow the story.

Since Brianna wouldn't allow him to hold her, he turned to the cradle and gently picked up his newborn. "I forgot how tiny they are." He settled the swathed bundle in the crook of his arm and studied the tiny features of the sleeping infant.

Betsy lifted her free hand to caress the tiny head lying on his strong arm. "She's two months old now."

He looked to Betsy. "A girl?"

She didn't realize how worried she was he might be disappointed until she heard the wonder in his voice and felt the wave of relief. "You didn't receive any of my letters?"

He sadly shook his head. "Not for the last several months."

"I named her Agatha Marie." She lifted her eyes to his. "I hope you don't mind."

Theodore's chest tightened. His aunt's passing had not settled with him yet. Apparently he lost one Agatha and gained another. He studied his wife's face, amazed by her strength. She not only dealt with the full responsibilities of the household in his absences, but she also endured the physical and emotional burdens of death and birth on her own. His jaw tightened with guilt for leaving her alone under such encumbrances. He slid a hand around her neck and rubbed his thumb along her jawline. "I'm sorry I wasn't here for you."

Betsy tilted her head into his caress. "You were doing what you needed to do to come home."

He smiled. "So you did get my letter."

She grimaced. "Yes and later we shall discuss the risks you are taking." She turned her attention to Brianna. "But right now you should spend some time getting to know your daughters."

Theodore couldn't agree more. He would worry about the mail and checking on his newspaper business tomorrow. Today was for his family.

A little while later Theodore was sitting in his chair holding Agatha when Brianna timidly approached. Betsy anxiously watched as Theodore gave her a welcoming smile and Brianna stepped forward. Her father held his arm out to her and helped her climb into his lap. He whispered something to the precocious dark-haired toddler and she giggled. He pulled her closer to him and was rewarded with his little girl snuggling into his chest. Theodore's eyes met Betsy's wanting to share his joy in the moment.

Betsy absorbed every detail of the heartwarming scene to treasure deep in her mother's heart. *My cup runneth over.*

Henry returned from working at the sponge docks in the late afternoon. He was surprised to hear his father's deep voice. He followed it to find his parents in the parlor having a make believe tea party with Brianna. He stood in the doorway, undetected, for a moment watching his father play with his little sister. It brought to mind the times they played chess—his father's way of reconnecting with him after a long absence. It was a nice memory. One he pulled out often when he was feeling lonely. But something about this scene made him feel like an outsider. It was Brianna's moment and he didn't want to intrude. He quietly exited the house intending to sit on the front porch until supper.

Betsy caught a whiff of the briny odor that clung to Henry since he started working at the sponge docks. She turned around expecting to see him in the doorway. Finding the space empty of his presence surprised and puzzled her. She turned back to Theodore. "I'll be back in a moment." She rose from her seated position on the floor and left the room following her mother's instincts and her nose.

Betsy stepped outside into the lengthening shadows of the late spring evening. She found Henry on the porch step looking lost and forlorn. "Hello Henry." She waited for his response trying to judge his mood.

Henry was caught off guard by her appearance. "Hello Mother."

"Did you just get home?"

"Yes."

"May I join you?"

He slid to the side giving her room to sit but said nothing.

"You know your father is home." She intentionally said it as a statement rather than a question.

"Yes."

Betsy half smiled. He wasn't going to make this easy. Very well then, she would just have to be blunt to get him to talk to her. "Why did you leave again instead of joining the family?"

Henry's eyes flared. *How did she know?*

Betsy quietly answered his unasked question. "A mother knows." She waited several moments for him to answer her question, hoping he would open up to her.

"I didn't want to intrude."

Betsy took that to mean he didn't feel like he belonged in his own family. Prior to today, he had not indicated any animosity towards his half-sisters and their relationship was fine this morning so his withdrawal had something to do with Theodore. The realization distressed her and she struggled with how to fix it. A simple hug and verbal reassurance was not going to be enough. "Why did you feel as if you would be intruding?" She could tell she was making him uncomfortable but this was too important to let it go.

"Poppa was playing with Brianna."

"And you didn't want to play with them?"

Henry grimaced. "Well it was a tea party."

Betsy smiled. "Yes, it was but I'm sure they would have played something else if you asked. You know Brianna adores you and would do anything you suggest."

"I know but..." He paused to consider how much he was willing to say. "I've had twelve years with Poppa. Brianna has had only a few months with him. She deserves to have her time. I remember how special it felt when I was younger and Poppa would return home. We would spend hours playing chess."

The selfless nature of his action amazed Betsy. "You are a very thoughtful brother, Henry. You make me proud. But, this is your family too, so let's go in and find something we can all do together. Besides, your father has been waiting hours to see you."

Henry's demeanor brightened with her words. Together they entered the parlor.

Theodore looked up at their appearance and quickly got to his feet to greet his son.

Brianna squealed, "Henry," and ran to hug her brother's legs. She tugged on his hand. "Come play with me."

Henry ruffled her hair, in the same manner Theodore used to do his. "In a moment, Bri." Henry looked to his father.

Betsy noticed their awkward display of affection. Henry felt he was too old to be hugging his father. Theodore wanted to do more than shake his hand. Musing up Henry's hair seemed too childish, so he settled for patting him on the upper arm. "Hello son."

"Hello, Poppa."

"How is work? Do you still like it?"

His nose wrinkled. "Its smelly work."

"Yes it is. I avoid walking downwind from the warehouses. You have to be tough to handle working around such effluvium."

Henry's chest puffed up a little at the unexpected praise.

Theodore wanted to keep Henry conversing. "How do you clean a sponge?"

His father's interest excited Henry and he readily shared his hard earned knowledge. "First they have to dry in the sun for several days. Then we beat them with wooden paddles to get off the outer coating. Then we string them on a fathom of rope according to what kind of sponge they are, keeping all the same sizes together. Those get laid up on the beach to dry some more before they go to auction."

"Sounds like a lot of hard work and explains your arm muscles."

Henry flexed his biceps. He was proud of them. His friend Billy's arms were still thin.

"How are your studies?"

His tone became defensive. "I'm keeping up."

"Anything you are struggling with?"

Henry didn't want to say but knew his father would probably ask his tutor, so he might as well confess now. "Grammar."

"Well now, that is something I can help with. I was afraid you were going to say algebra."

"I understand numbers. They make sense, but why do I have to know if a past participle is being used as a verb or an adjective in a sentence as long as I write the sentence correctly? And I'm always forgetting when to use a semi-colon instead of a comma. Math is easier."

Theodore grinned. "I on the other hand, struggled with math. Sentence structure made more sense to me."

Henry snickered. "Guess that's why you became a writer."

"Hmm."

The pause in conversation was Brianna's opening. She tugged on Henry's knickers. "Come play."

Henry gave his father a questioning look seeking his dismissal from the conversation and received a nod in response. He took his little sister's hand and led her to the yard to play before supper.

From the kitchen, Betsy stopped her humming to enjoy the sound of her children's laughter as they played outside the kitchen door. Theodore was home, the children were happy, and all was right in her world. Betsy smiled to herself thinking of the night ahead. She was more than ready to renew relations with her husband. She resumed her cheerful tune as she joyfully prepared their supper.

* * *

The following morning after breaking his fast, Theodore settled into his leather desk chair to read his accumulated mail before heading to the newspaper shop. He took a moment to appreciate the comforts of the cushioned seat and the familiar surroundings of home. He didn't think he would ever take them for granted again after spending so much time sleeping on the damp ground at the mercy of insects.

He sorted the mail and then eagerly opened a letter from one of General Jesup's junior officers first. He wrote about the battle of January twenty-fourth east of Lake Okeechobee near Jupiter Inlet. Theodore suspected it was the same group of Indians Lieutenant Powell engaged with on Theodore's trip home. Much like all the other battles, the Indians attacked, some two to three hundred warriors, and then faded away once they lost field advantage inflicting more casualties than they suffered. Dubbed the Battle of Loxahatchee for the river the Indians crossed in their retreat, there were seven dead and thirty-one wounded including General Jesup. The officer said Jesup was leading a charge when he took a bullet across his face. It broke his spectacles and will leave him with a nasty scar on his cheek. The Seminole left neither dead nor wounded behind so their casualties were unknown.

Reading the letter brought to mind images Theodore wished he could forget from the battles he witnessed. There was no two ways about it—war was ugly. He still occasionally suffered nightmares especially since the Battle of Lake Okeechobee. He hoped being home for a while would keep them at bay. His wife and children were the best cure he knew for his troubled soul.

Theodore found it ironic that on the same day as Jesup's battle, according to Bob's letter, the House of Representatives held a heated debate on further funding the war and the validity of the Fort Gibson treaty. The war department was asking for another three and half million dollars for a war the general populace no longer supported. The country already spent eight or nine million trying to move what was believed to be only a few thousand Seminoles. Theodore could well imagine how volatile a topic it had become in the Capitol. In the end, the funds were appropriated. The majority of Congress voted in favour in the hopes money could produce an expedient end to the conflict. Theodore could only shake his head. He wished they had denied the funds forcing an end and perhaps allowing those Seminoles left in Florida to live in peace.

A few letters later, he was reading one posted two weeks ago from a friend in Tampa offering hope for an immediate end to the hostilities. The letter said Chiefs Tuskegee and Halleck Hadjo met with General Jesup to negotiate a peace treaty. Jesup wrote the President asking for the request to be granted. The general who once said the army could easily vanquish the Florida Indians was now recommending they be allowed to remain in the southern half of the territory or risk dragging out the war for many years to come. The Indians, over five hundred of them, were camped near Fort Jupiter waiting in hopes of the President's approval. Once again, peace was within reach. Theodore debated sharing the news but decided against it. There was every chance it would end the same as before.

He finished going through the remaining business correspondences making a neat stack of those he would reply to later. He planned to head to the shop to catch up on the island news when Betsy appeared with Agatha nestled in the sling across her chest and carrying the newly arrived post.

Betsy handed Theodore a few more letters to read. She took a seat in one of the nearby chairs to read a letter from her mother anxious to learn of her father's health. She hoped it was good news. A few moments later, her squeal of delight disturbed both husband and daughter. She soothed Agatha, then answered Theodore's questioning gaze. "My father is restored to health and Vertiline is on her way here."

"Vertiline? She's one of your sisters?"

"Yes."

"I know you grew up on a farm in Pennsylvania and you are part of a large family but you haven't told me much about them."

"Oh my goodness, I haven't, have I?"

"No."

"Well, my parents are James and Madalyn Drake."

Theodore nodded. He remembered their names from past conversations.

"I'm the third of nine children. There's Thaddeus and Jessamine—she's a year older than me, the twins—Frederick and Roderick, Sophronia, Gabriel and Zachariah. My mother said she gave him a name starting with Z because she was done having babies. God had other plans because a few years later along came sweet Vertiline. She is by far the family favourite. We all had a hand in spoiling her." Her tone became wistful. "It was hardest leaving her behind."

"And now she's coming here to visit?"

Betsy nodded, her broad grin more than telling him how happy she was with the news.

"Hmm."

Her smile faded as she noticed his less than enthusiastic response. She briefly wondered at the cause but his preoccupied look kept her from asking and her happiness would not allow her to dwell on it. "I must go prepare a room for her."

Betsy was rushing from the room when Theodore called after her. "What's your hurry? It will be weeks before she gets here."

Betsy stuck her head back in the doorway. "Mother said she was leaving within the week..."

Theodore picked up her sentence. "And with the delay in mail she will likely be here within the week. What room do you plan to put her in?"

Betsy stepped back in the room, hesitant to answer. She wasn't sure how he would react. "Aunt Agatha's."

"Hmm." Theodore let the idea settle. Finally he said, "I suppose that is best. It wouldn't make sense to move Henry out of his room." He stood up from his chair and walked to her. "Did you say twins? Frederick and Roderick Drake? I don't suppose they have red hair and both joined the military?"

Betsy was surprised and puzzled. "How did you know?"

He chuckled. "I've met them."

Her eyebrows flew to her hairline, "Where?" then dropped, "When?"

"I believe I told you I followed the Seminole delegation when they visited the Arkansas territory in '35."

"You did."

"Fred and Rod Drake were stationed at Fort Gibson." He stepped toward her.

"Oh my. What a curious coincidence."

"Indeed." He kissed her forehead. "I'm going to the shop. I'll be home later. Be sure to get help if you need to move anything heavy."

"I will. Oh, I keep forgetting to mention we've been invited to a ball hosted by the Lambert's."

"I take it this is the reason for Captain Max's dance lessons."

"It is. He wanted to surprise Abby with a waltz."

"Well, lucky for you Mrs. Whitmore, I already know how to waltz and do so quite nicely if I do say so myself."

Betsy smiled. "I shall be the judge of that Mr. Whitmore."

Theodore kissed her full on the lips before passing by her to leave the house. "I look forward to it, Mrs. Whitmore."

Betsy turned to watch him leave, a happy smile on her face.

Theodore was feeling a bit overwhelmed by all the changes in his household; a new baby, the loss of his aunt, Henry's independence, he learned last night Betsy had sold her business, and now a pending visit from her sister. It was a lot to absorb in twenty-four hours. Vertiline's arrival gave him some concern. He was barely beginning to resume his place in the household. For some reason it was more difficult this time than before. He felt a bit like a stranger in his own home, as if he had been gone years instead of months. His family adapted to life without him, as expected. It wasn't that they weren't welcoming or intentionally making it difficult, quite the contrary, it was merely the allowances they all had to make to adjust to his return. He hoped it would smooth out before Betsy's sister arrived and the process would start all over again.

As he walked to the shop, he noticed several new houses and businesses were built since his departure. Even the town had changed a lot in six months. At least when he entered the shop it felt the same as before he left. Robert Mason was happy to see him.

"Welcome home, Mr. Whitmore. How was your journey?"

"Long and taxing. I am thankful to finally be here. I have a piece for the next run." He handed Robert the article he wrote on the ship of the attack at Jupiter Inlet and Leitner's death. "Anything of interest happening here?"

Robert nodded with a huge grin. "We certainly do. There is a tax dispute going on that has the merchants upset and Mayor Whitehead determined to resign."

"What tax are they disputing?"

"The city's expenses have increased so the council passed an ordinance levying an occupational tax for the year. The merchants, particularly Mr. Baldwin, Mr. Weaver, Mr. Sawyer and Mr. Fontaine, are protesting its enforcement. They had an understanding the tax would be levied only once which they paid year before last under the latest city charter. They also are concerned if the council is allowed to add more tax this year what is to keep them from taxing whenever they wish."

Theodore nodded. "It is a valid concern."

"Mayor Whitehead responded in writing with arguments compelling enough to reconcile Judge Marvin and Mr. Weaver to the validity of the tax. Still, the others stand firmly against him so the mayor requested the city council call a meeting of the citizens to determine if the law should be enforced or the charter dissolved. The council ignored his request."

"Hmm"

"The whole business has soured Mr. Whitehead. He refuses to stultify himself trying to uphold the law when so many citizens are determined to disobey it so he turned in his resignation. An election is currently underway. He plans to turn the office over immediately to whomever wins."

"Who are the candidates?"

"That's just it. There's only one."

"One?"

Robert grimaced as he nodded.

Theodore looked askance. "Who?"

"I'm afraid feelings have gotten the better of sense. The group against Mayor Whitehead picked Tomaso Sachetti to run for the office."

Theodore frowned. "The grog shop keeper? The one down on Front Street only the sailors will patron?"

"The very one."

"Does he even speak English?"

"Barely, and I'm pretty sure he can't read."

Theodore frowned. "Obviously they chose him as a personal insult to Mr. Whitehead. And no one else has stepped forward to oppose him?"

"No. The lower ilk are all for one of their own being mayor, and he has the support of enough prominent citizens, it would be folly to even try."

Theodore couldn't believe he was seriously considering naming himself as a candidate. He knew many would support him but would it be enough? If he was elected, was he willing to let go of the Seminole story? That question gave him great pause. On the other hand, being mayor would keep him home. "When is the election?"

"Tomorrow."

So much for that idea. It was highly unlikely he could garner enough support in a day to defeat Mr. Sachetti. "And how have you reported the story?"

"I think you will be pleased. First we ran a piece from the merchants protesting the tax with Mayor Whitehead's rebuttal. Then an article on the Mayor's decision to resign and last a very factual piece on Mr. Sachetti. You will have to let me know if I managed to write the truth without disparaging the candidate or appearing as if the paper supports him. I followed it with an advertisement calling for other candidates to join the race."

"Who paid for the advertisement?"

Robert shrunk into his shoulders not sure his boss would like the answer. "No one did." He was sure Mr. Whitmore would be sympathetic to Mr. Whitehead, but he didn't know how he would feel about the paper in essence advertising for opposition. It was not exactly an unbiased thing to do.

Theodore burst out laughing and clapped Robert on the shoulder. "Well done, Mr. Mason."

Robert lightly sighed in relief.

"Is there anything else we need to discuss today?"

"No sir."

Theodore retreated to his desk to read the last six months of the paper. He found it to be the fastest way to catch up on the other news of the island. When he was done, he decided to visit Mr. Whitehead. He went to the courthouse but was met by his secretary who informed him the mayor did not wish to be disturbed unless it was an urgent matter. Theodore shook his head.

He asked, "Would you care to leave a message, sir?"

"No thank you." Theodore turned to leave when Mr. Whitehead called to him from the doorway of his office.

"Is that you, Mr. Whitmore?"

Theodore turned back. "It is indeed."

They greeted each other heartily, and Mr. Whitehead invited him into his office.

"Have you heard of my resignation?"

Theodore nodded. "Is there anything I can do for you?"

"I'm afraid there isn't."

Theodore could see with some concern how deeply hurt his friend was by this turn of events, however, being resigned to it Mr. Whitehead didn't want to talk much about it, either. Theodore left him a short time later to finish preparing the mayor's business to be turned over on the morrow to the new custodian of the office.

Theodore returned home to find Betsy in Aunt Agatha's room.

She smiled when she spied him in the doorway watching her. "Are you hungry? Supper is almost ready."

"What are we having?"

"Your favourite; baked chicken and rice." She dusted the top of Aunt Agatha's jewelry chest and handed it to him without opening it. "Would you mind taking this to our room while I finish tidying up in here?"

Theodore took the box from her. He ran a hand over the inlaid top and wondered how long it would take before these reminders of his aunt stopped making his heart ache. *Who would have thought I could miss a cantankerous old woman so much?*

He put the box on top of his chest of drawers. Little Agatha was in her cradle. She must have just woken up from a nap. She was such a tiny little cherub. Picking up the swaddled infant, he sat on the bed and lightly ran a finger down the side of her face. Her eyes flared a little in reaction so he did it again. He unwrapped her wanting to see her tiny hands and toes. She reached for his face so he leaned down closer, surprised when she grasped his beard and tugged. The little urchin had some strength. He smiled and she let go, laid her hand flat against his cheek, and grasped again, lightly scratching him. He gently released her hand and kissed her palm. He was rewarded with a tiny smile so he did it again and heard her giggle. The musical sound enticed him to continue until Agatha decided to let him know it was time to eat.

He was amazed how fast Betsy responded to her cry. She approached him with the sling held open to receive their daughter. He watched as she opened her bodice and settled the babe to her breast then secured the sling snug around the infant with an amazing fluidity of motion. Betsy smiled as she watched the tiny face suckle and Theodore's heart skipped a beat. Leaving them again was going to be downright impossible this time. He sent a prayer heavenward for the treaty to be accepted.

Betsy looked to Theodore and her heart fluttered under the intensity of his gaze. A bit flustered she said, "Little Agatha does not like to be kept waiting when she is hungry. I made the mistake once. She may just have a bit of your aunt in her. Fortunately, she is quite patient about everything else. Are you ready to eat? I could use your help getting the chicken out of the oven. It's not an easy thing to do one-handed."

"Of course, dear."

* * *

A few days later, Betsy needed to vent her frustration. She gathered the girls and went to visit Abby because talking usually helped her to accept or to see a situation more clearly. Her daughters were given over to the care of Abby's nanny so that the ladies might visit in peace. As soon as tea was served Betsy opened the topic weighing heavy on her mind.

Actually there were two topics but she could not discuss one of them with anyone, not even Abby. If she were to speak it should be to Theodore but she couldn't get past her inhibitions to find the courage to ask him why he was avoiding intimacy. The other subject she would never speak of to her husband but she knew Abby would give her consolation. "This is Theodore's third homecoming, and it's not getting any easier. I love him but Good Lord, he is underfoot and wreaking havoc with the girls' schedule; waking them up too early or keeping them up too late and so often exciting them right before bedtime. Don't hear me wrong. I'm thrilled to have him home, and I realize it's only been a few days, but each day is getting worse instead of better. And I don't know how to tell him. Did you have this problem with Max?"

Abby nodded. "It was hard at first. I didn't think it would be. My father was away for much of my youth and not having a mother I learned to fend for myself at an early age. I thought it would make it easy to adjust to a husband who was away more than he was home, but it is different. And it's difficult, especially once there are children involved. You get used to not having him around, and then you have to adjust again when he comes home."

"So true. If I had only myself to be concerned with it would not be a problem, but at first there was always Henry and Aunt Agatha to consider and now the girls too. And always, in the back of my mind, I'm wondering if the decisions I make are what he would want."

"Exactly. You are never sure you are making the right choice and hundreds of times you wish you could have his thoughts to help make the decisions. The rest of the time you are wishing he was there to share in the moments he is missing. At least I only had to wait a few weeks between return trips. You have many months. I am sure it must magnify the problem."

"It does. We get so excited when he arrives but soon after there's conflict as he tries to turn the routine of the household around his needs."

"Max did the same thing. I assumed it was because he was a captain and at sea, life on the ship revolves around his decree. But Betsy, do not despair, eventually, we found a rhythm to it."

"Theodore, for the most part, can do as he pleases while away, so I suppose he has the same trouble adjusting to being home. I wish this war would end. It will be so much easier when he is home for good." In a rare display of anger, Betsy burst out, "Why won't those savages give up already?"

"Betsy!"

"I'm so tired of this war. I wish they would just leave. They have to know it is useless. They can't defeat our military. They can't have enough men left. And I know their women have to be as fed up with fighting as we are."

Abby stood quietly by while she expelled all of her pent up frustrations and waited for Betsy to do what she always did; her friend's truest blessing— to see the other side.

Betsy sighed. "But then I also know if I was a Seminole woman I would stand behind my man until the bitter end. I would not give up my homeland. I would stand and die for what is mine. Can you imagine what those women must be enduring right now living in a swamp, on the run, struggling for food, and a dry place to shelter? I'm sure they are saying, why won't we leave them be?"

"Be strong, Betsy. All things must pass."

"I know. Some days it's hard to keep patient." Betsy sighed then her face brightened. "I do have some good news to share; I am expecting my sister,

Vertiline, to arrive any day now."

, "That is good news and nice timing too with the ball just a week away. She will see our island at its finest."

"I quite forgot about the ball." Betsy chuckled. "Do you remember your first ball when you arrived?"

Abby smiled broadly. "Oh yes, quite different from what I was used to in England."

"Vertiline has likely only attended country dances so perhaps she will not be as disappointed as you must have been."

Abby shook her head. "I was not disappointed. There was much I found to like about an island ball."

"Did Esperanza finish your dress?"

"Yes, she did. Would you like to see it?"

"Absolutely."

"Wait here. I will bring it out." She returned in a moment with a lovely emerald gown.

Betsy couldn't help noticing Esperanza's excellent workmanship. "It's beautiful. I'm sure you can't wait to wear it."

Abby gave her a conspiratorial smile. "I have tried it on twice since she gave it to me. How is yours coming along?"

"Thankfully, I finished it a few nights ago. Now I just have some finishing touches to do on Theodore's suit."

Chapter 36

Nineteen year old Vertiline Drake stepped ashore and surveyed the small island with her sparkling blue eyes, the same color as her sister's though not as round and while Betsy's hair was dark as midnight, Vertiline's was as bright as spring sunshine. She twirled her parasol while waiting for her luggage to be unloaded. Her sprigged cotton dress was the same color as her eyes and she knew she cut an appealing figure even without confirmation in the appreciative looks sent her way by every passing male.

She scanned the scene in front of her. Betsafina so often mentioned how small the town was that Vertiline had pictured something much smaller than the active scene before her with a backdrop of hundreds of buildings. Although the ambiance was quite raw with the unpainted siding and with all the sailors and dock workers lingering about but it was not without a certain amount of charm. A moment later her thoughts were not so charitable. She delicately held her handkerchief to her nose as one of the dock workers passed in close proximity carrying her trunk on his shoulder. She kept her distance as she followed him to the shoreline where he promptly deposited it and returned to the ship.

Vertiline momentarily felt completely on her own for the first time in her life. It was another new experience in a long list of new experiences this trip provided. She had never been outside her hometown so everything from traveling to the nearest port, sailing on a large ship, and arriving on this island was bewildering. When her parents learned Betsy secured free passage for her aboard the *Abigail Rose* with a promise of Captain Bennington's protection, they were relieved not to have to spend money providing Vertiline with a traveling companion. In this moment she rather wished she had the comfort of another in her same circumstance. She supposed if she had waited until Captain Bennington had finished his duties he would have seen to the transport of her luggage but her excitement erased any patience she might have found.

It wasn't long before she spied a lad of ten years or so with a hand cart to transport her luggage. He was eager to earn a coin so she had no trouble hiring his services. In no time, her trunks were loaded and they were traveling down the white dusty street away from the harbour. With the diminished breeze of inland, the warmth of the spring morning became apparent. Vertiline felt moisture run down her back and gather in other uncomfortable places despite her vigorous efforts with her fan and the shade of her parasol. It dismayed her to note it wasn't even noon. How would she handle the heat of the afternoon? Perhaps her visit would not be as long as she hoped. Vertiline didn't think she would be able to endure summer if spring was making her this uncomfortable.

Despite her discomfort she took note of her surroundings, including the different house designs they passed, but it was the unusual trees that captivated her. They were so different from the trees in Pennsylvania. They made her think of plumes in a vase with their long thin leaves clustered on branches formed much like a feather. She asked the boy for their name but he shrugged his shoulders. Just before the end of the settlement, they stopped in front of an impressive two-story with a wide front porch. The lad dropped the cart handles, "This here's the Whitmore house." Vertiline climbed the steps and knocked on the front door. There was no answer. She tried again to no avail. The windows were open so she peaked inside. No sound was to be heard. She turned to the lad. "It appears no one is home."

He shrugged his shoulders. "Don't matter. Just open the door so I can drag your trunks inside."

Vertiline thought it was rude to enter uninvited but what else could she do. Once the luggage was inside, the lad held out his hand. As soon as he received his coin, he tipped his hat and took off running back the way they came. Vertiline shrugged her shoulders and set about exploring the objects in the room. She stopped to study the painted portrait of her sister with her husband and his son. The painter captured a good likeness of Betsafina, at least from what Vertiline remembered of her sister having been only six when she moved away.

Theodore looked up from his work to see young Joshua, one of the runners from the wharf, rush into the print shop. He met him at the counter. "What can I do for you son?"

"Thought you would want to know, sir, I just left Mrs. Whitmore's sister at yore house. Tweren't no one home to receive her."

Theodore knew it was more than concern for the lady that brought him here. The lad knew the value of information. Theodore handed him a coin for his trouble and followed Joshua out the door. He knew his wife would want to know right away her sister had arrived, and if Betsy wasn't home, the most likely place she would was the Eatonton's.

Abby and Betsy were surprised by Theodore's appearance. "Sorry to interrupt your tea ladies. Betsy, we need to head home now." Betsy's questioning look was almost comical. He knew it must seem a very odd request for him to be making. "Your sister is awaiting you there." Her face lit up like firecrackers on the Fourth of July.

"Oh Abby, please excuse me. I must run." She passed Theodore headed for the front door, then stopped and turned. "Oh my, the children!"

Abby shook her head. "Go and welcome your sister. I will bring them along shortly."

Betsy couldn't stop smiling, she was so excited. She blew a kiss to her friend. "Bless you Abby. Thank you."

Theodore's long strides easily kept up with Betsy's brisk pace. She wished she could run. The moments it took to get from one house to the other were torturous but finally she was walking through the front door.

"Vertiline?"

"In here sister."

Betsy turned left toward the voice she didn't recognize. She dashed into the parlor and if not for Theodore's timely catch of her elbow she would have collided with a pile of trunks and the lady perched on top of them. Having regained her balance, Betsy got her first look at her sister. She would have recognized her anywhere. Vertiline's face was the very image of their mother's. Betsy moved around the luggage and opened her arms. "Vertie, I'm so happy to see you." The two hugged and cried and hugged some more. Betsy stepped back. "Look at you, all grown up and so beautiful. I can't believe it has been so long. You were just a child."

"You, on the other hand, look much the same as I remember." Vertiline ran a hand along the side of Betsy's face. "Time has been kind to you, Bessie."

Betsy had to choke back tears generated by her sister's use of the almost forgotten family pet name. She grasped Vertiline's hand and pressed it to her cheek. "It's so good to see you." They hugged again. Betsy finally gave a thought to her sister's needs. "You must be tired. Let me show you to your room."

About this time Henry made an appearance, word spread quickly on the dock of the beautiful lady staying at his house. He was anxious to meet her.

Henry entered the parlor and stopped in his tracks. He was smitten before she ever said a word. Except for Betsy, he had never seen a lovelier lady.

Betsy made the introductions. "Henry this is your Aunt Vertiline. Well, I suppose she isn't truthfully your aunt."

Vertiline winked at him. "You can call me Vertie."

Henry was tongue-tied and flustered for the first time in his life. He barely managed to give her a proper bow. It took his father's nudging for him to reply. "It's nice to meet you, Vertie."

As the ladies climbed the stairs, Theodore turned to his son. "Henry, have you noticed we are now outnumbered by the females in this house? What do you say, you and I go conch fishing and let these ladies gab awhile?"

Henry didn't want to leave the pretty lady with the golden hair but the thought of perhaps finding another conch pearl to impress her got his feet moving toward the door.

Betsy paused on the upper landing to call down. "Theodore could you move Vertiline's trunks to her room before you leave?"

Anxious to do anything for Vertie, Henry rushed past Theodore to the pile of trunks. He wanted to take two at a time but his father nixed the idea. If he couldn't show off his strength at least three trips meant he was in Vertie's presence a bit longer. When they were done, Henry reluctantly followed his father out the door.

The ladies barely noticed their departure. They fell into catching up on family news while settling Vertiline in her room. Shortly after they finished, Abby arrived with the children. Brianna, seeing the strange lady in the house, shyly moved to her mother's side.

"Vertiline, I would like to introduce you to my dearest friend, Abigail Eatonton."

Vertiline said, "Mrs. Eatonton, it is a pleasure to meet you. Bessie has mentioned you often in her letters and your father was most kind to me on the voyage. I felt safe and secure on his vessel."

"Please call me Abby. Betsy has told me a lot about you as well. I believe you and I may have similar temperaments. Perhaps that is why Betsy is so fond of me."

Betsy smiled at her friend. "Perhaps you are right." She took great pleasure in introducing her daughters to their aunt. She placed a hand behind Brianna's head urging her to take a step forward. "This is Brianna Kate."

Vertiline knelt down and opened her arms to greet Brianna. Betsy gave the little girl a nudge forward. Brianna dutifully gave her aunt a hug and retreated to her mother's skirt. Betsy then gestured toward the infant in Abby's arms. "And this is Agatha Marie."

Abby transferred the sleeping babe to her aunt. Vertiline moved aside the blanket to get a better look at her niece's face. "Oh Bessie, she is darling. Look at those perfectly sweet features."

Betsy couldn't hide her proud mother's grin. She gestured toward the parlor. "Ladies shall we take a moment to visit." She and Vertiline shared the sofa. Brianna climbed into her mother's lap. Abby took one of the chairs.

Once they were all seated Abby said, "Vertiline, the timing of your arrival is fortuitous."

"How so?"

"We are to have a ball Saturday next."

Excitement colored Vertiline's voice. "Am I to take it you are inviting me to your ball?"

"Oh no, it is not my ball. It is being hosted by the Lamberts."

Vertiline's face fell. "Then isn't it rude to presume I'm invited."

Abby reassured her. "Not at all. It is the island way. All are welcome."

Betsy said, "She's right. The truth is the ladies are well outnumbered by the gentlemen and so any female, invited or not, is always welcome and a host will consider it quite a boon to have one turn up as lovely and as unknown as you."

Vertiline smiled. "So then it is my duty as a guest of the island to attend? How lovely! And this will be my first ball."

Betsy smiled. "Do not elevate your idea of a Key West ball too lofty for here it is nothing more than a country dance with a bit more elegance. Am I right, Abby?"

Abby nodded. "'Tis true but they are still a very entertaining event, and Vertiline, you will have no shortage of partners. I promise you will dance every dance. The challenge lies in the artful use of diplomacy in choosing your partner."

Agatha's movement drew Vertiline's gaze to find her rooting against her bosom. "Bessie, I believe your daughter has need of you."

Betsy looked down to find Brianna struggling to keep her eyes open. "And this one needs to be put down for her nap."

Abby took that as her cue. "It is getting late. I should probably return home. Vertiline, it was nice to meet you. I look forward to seeing you again." Betsy rose to walk her to the door but Abby held her hand up, "You take care of your girls. I can see myself out." They kissed cheeks and Abby departed.

Betsy and Vertiline took care of the children. They returned to the parlor just as Theodore and Henry returned with a bucketful of conch. Betsy took them to the kitchen to prepare them for supper.

Henry said, "I'll help. Come Vertie, you should see how Betsy fixes conch."

Vertiline found the process disgusting while Henry thought her wrinkled nose adorable. He couldn't take his eyes from her. Vertiline, having seen enough, intended to leave, but Betsy's surprised announcement made her stay.

"Henry, I believe this one has a pearl." Her audience eagerly leaned forward while she moved aside the meat to reveal a round pinkish-brown stone. She rinsed it in the bucket and handed it to Henry.

Henry examined the find. It wasn't as pretty as the first one Betsy was keeping in her jewelry box for him, but it was prettier than the others he had found since then. He turned to Vertiline and placed it in her hand, so she could examine it.

"I thought pearls were white."

Henry puffed up, proud to share his knowledge. "Those are oyster pearls. Conch pearls are pink, some with shades of brown, and I've seen some almost red ones."

Vertiline inspected the pearl between her thumb and forefinger. "This one's nice." She held it out to return to Henry.

"Naw, you keep it. I want you to have it."

She smiled. "Thank you. How sweet of you."

Henry blushed.

Betsy watched the exchange with some concern. Henry's attachment was more emotional than she thought to be appropriate. "Henry, please bring another bucket of water. Vertiline, would you mind checking on the girls for me?"

Betsy managed to keep them separated until meal time. Afterwards, Henry asked Vertie to play chess. Betsy covertly watched them while she played with the girls. Henry won the game and Betsy suggested Theodore play the winner, so she and Vertie could talk. The girls were put to bed and then she visited with her sister until it was time for them all to turn in for the night.

Betsy was lying on her back, her head on Theodore's chest, enjoying the feel of his arm holding her close. They usually spent a few moments like this at the end of the day talking before slumber overtook them. "Should we be concerned about Henry?"

"Why?"

"He's clearly smitten with my sister."

"Hmm."

There was a note of surprise in his tone. She waited. "Is that all you have to say?"

"It's a boyhood infatuation. He'll get over it when she leaves."

"You're not worried about him?"

"No and you shouldn't be either." A little softer he asked, "What are you afraid will happen?"

"He'll get his heart broken."

Theodore huffed. "And isn't learning how to deal with disappointment and heartache part of growing up? It builds character. A blissful childhood leads to a weak adult."

Betsy contemplated his words, and then she wondered about the source of his advice. "Did you have your heart broken?"

"Hmm."

That sounded like reluctant confirmation. She turned over to look him in the eye, a smile playing on her lips. "Who was she?"

He cut his eyes at her obviously wanting to avoid the question.

"Was she your age or older?" She saw the telltale reaction in his eyes and grinned. "Older. A neighbor's daughter, perhaps?"

Theodore did not want to answer her questions. He did not want his wife to think less of his younger self for coveting a neighbor's wife. Nothing came of it, of course, but he was still ashamed he had the sinful thoughts in the first place. A distraction was definitely needed so he reversed their positions and proceeded to kiss her until she forgot her question.

Wednesday, the 14th of March was a beautiful day. The crystalline blue sky welcomed all. Unfortunately, it was also the day of the election and without another candidate in the running, Tomaso Sachetti was elected the new mayor. Theodore accompanied Mr. Whitehead to formally declare Mr. Sachetti the new mayor and to make arrangements for turning the office of mayor over to him.

There was a pall cast over the day as the two men walked away from the grog shop, the sound of the patrons' celebration following them. Theodore couldn't help but notice the uncharacteristic slump of Mr. Whitehead's shoulders. He wanted to cheer him up, but there was nothing he could think to say. When it came time to part ways Theodore offered his sympathies and to print his mayoral farewell in the paper.

While there were many celebrating the day, others knew it to be a sad day in Key West history. Little did they know how great the loss would soon

451

become.

Saturday evening the house was all astir getting ready for the ball. A sitter was found for the girls which gave Betsy the opportunity to enjoy a few hours at the ball between Agatha's feedings much to her delight.

Of course, Theodore was ready first. He patiently waited downstairs with Henry for the ladies to finish their preparations. When the last curl was secured, cheeks pinched, lips bitten, and skirts smoothed they finally descended the staircase.

Betsy appeared first wearing a dress of midnight blue satin with a square neckline, high waist and three quarter sleeves. It was a simple design made to flatter her figure but not attract undo attention. Her sister loosely braided her hair on each side of her head then cleverly gathered it in silky cascading ringlets falling to her shoulders. The look of adoration in Theodore's eyes was all the compliment she needed.

Theodore was mesmerized by the sensual grace and elegance of his wife as she glided down the stairs and into his arms. Surely, none could hold a candle to her beauty. Tonight he was reminded how blessed he truly was in her.

Vertiline's yellow dress with puffy sleeves may have been the height of fashion a few years ago but Betsy assured her it would suffice. Her flaxen tresses were gathered on her head with a few strategic curls brushing her neck and temple. All Henry noticed was her bright blue eyes. He wished again he were a few years older so he could go to the ball too. He jealously watched the three adults leave the house.

As soon as they walked through the door of the Lambert's lavish home, Vertiline was recognized as the belle of the ball by every available bachelor in the room. A fist fight nearly broke out for the honor of having the first dance with her. Fortunately, Theodore, in his quiet commanding way, settled the matter by pairing her up with Robert Mason for the first dance. He then reminded the young swains how gentlemen were expected to behave at a ball.

Betsy stood in a corner quietly observing him, unaware of the charming smile on her face. Theodore caught site of it and winked at her which promptly stained her cheeks a soft shade of pink as she looked around to make sure no one else noticed his roguish flirtation. He turned his attention back to the circle of young men. "Excuse me, gentlemen. I believe my wife would like to join in the dancing."

Theodore walked to Betsy and offered his arm. "May I have this dance?"

She tried to hold a serious expression. "I thought you would never ask."

"My sincerest apologies for your wait, dearest."

They joined the rapidly filling lines of a reel followed by two more folk dances and while both enjoyed them, they eagerly smiled in anticipation upon hearing the first soft strains of the waltz. They joined the other couples pairing up in the center of the room. Betsy was pleased to find Theodore was as good as he claimed. In his arms, she floated about the room under his adoring gaze. Occasionally, in a turn she would catch a glimpse of Max and Abby, proudly noting the radiant smile Abby wore. Max must be doing well.

Betsy turned her head this way and that but could not find her sister. The room was quite crowded, perhaps she was in a group along the walls. Her brows gathered.

Theodore noticed her distraction. "What is it dear?"

"Do you see Vertiline?"

He searched the room for a vibrant splash of yellow to no avail. He shook his head.

Betsy's concern for her sister outweighed the pleasure of dancing. She broke from Theodore's hold to go in search of Vertiline giving Theodore no choice but to follow.

Knowing how much Betsy looked forward to waltzing with him, he was perturbed to have the moment ruined by her unnecessary concerns. He scanned the crowd again as they were headed to the refreshment area in an adjoining room. He fully expected to find Vertiline engaged somewhere in harmless conversation and they will have missed the rest of the dance for naught.

On the far side of the room along the outside wall there were two sets of French doors leading out to the piazza. As they were leaving the room, Theodore scanned it once more and happened to see a bright yellow dress in the fading light outside. He redirected Betsy to the French door just as Vertiline reappeared in the room. She was followed by two other ladies near in age to her. All three were vigorously fluttering their fans and laughing. Theodore pulled Betsy into his arms to enjoy what little was left of the dance. He pointed to her sister. "See her by the windows? There is no cause for concern."

Betsy smiled in way of apology for the disruption.

A few bars later the music ended.

An hour later Betsy and Theodore were walking home, arm in arm, alone under a beautiful starlit night. They left Vertiline behind to enjoy the ball a bit longer with Max's promise to escort her home. As expected, she was enjoying herself far too much to want to leave early.

Betsy understood. She would have liked to stay longer too but it was time for Agatha's feeding.

Theodore leaned his head toward Betsy. "Did you have a good time, love?"

Betsy leaned closer to him, tucking her head under his chin. "I did. It's been a long time since we've danced together. I'm thankful you made it home in time to attend."

"I've missed so much already, I'm glad I was here for this."

"Did you see Max and Abby waltz? Didn't they looked beautiful together?"

In a seductive tone he said, "I was too busy watching you to notice."

It was surprising after four years of marriage and two babies he could still make her blush.

The following morning Vertiline could speak of nothing except the ball. She relished every detail of her evening as she gushingly relayed them to Betsy. It was late morning before she ran out of things to say.

The afternoon was unseasonably warm for April. The sisters were enduring the midday warmth in quiet occupations on the front porch. Betsy stopped humming at the sound of Vertiline's muffled laughter. She looked up from her mending. "Sister dear, what are you reading?"

Unaware she had uttered a sound and absorbed in the book, it took a moment for the question to register with Vertiline. "It's an adorable story of this meddling matchmaker named Emma."

"I don't remember that story. Is it a book you brought with you?"

"No, it's one of yours."

"What is the name of it?"

Vertiline held the book up for her sister's inspection. "It's simply titled *Emma* and published anonymously."

Betsy recognized it now. "My friend Victoria sent it from England raving on and on about the characters and prose of the author. I haven't had time to read it myself."

Vertie's eyebrows rose. "Oh, you should. It is highly comical and well written. I wonder if this writer has published any other works."

"I believe Victoria was trying to answer that very question. I should ask her. I've been meaning to post her anyway. I believe I will do so now."

Betsy rose to fetch her writing desk and then remembered she was out of paper. She would have to ask Theodore for some. She walked into his office in time to hear him cursing, which was completely out of character for him. "What is it, dear?"

Theodore looked up, his brows drawn together. "I apologize. I didn't know you were there."

She noticed he didn't answer the question. "Did you receive bad news about the war?"

He sighed loudly and rubbed his hand across his brow. "Hmm."

"Do you have to leave again?" She waited with baited breath.

"Maybe." He saw her deep concern and realized there was no sense holding back from her now. "Washington has denied another request to end the war and worse, Secretary Poinsett had General Jesup seize those gathered under truce waiting for the answer." His anger burst forth again. "Does a white flag mean nothing? Where is our honor?" He sighed heavily. "Five hundred Seminoles were taken prisoner to be transported west. That's the largest number they've gathered to date."

Betsy nodded. "I certainly understand why you would curse at such news."

"I hoped the outcome would be better but didn't really believe it possible; not after the last time."

Betsy eyes narrowed. "How long have you known of this possible peace agreement?"

"Since my return. The letter was waiting on my desk."

"Why didn't you share it with me?"

"I didn't want to get your hopes up just to end in disappointment."

"Do you not think me strong enough to handle it?"

"Of course you are, but I didn't see the point in burdening you."

"Sharing your hopes and fears is not a burden, it is part of a good marriage. What else have you not told me?"

Theodore's head came up defensively. "You are just as guilty. How many things have happened here you have not shared in your letters for the same reason?"

Betsy froze. He was right. She had done the same. She tried to keep her letters cheerful and full of the good things that happened, leaving out the bad unless it was of some consequence. Why just in her last letter she wrote of Agatha's arrival and choosing her name but purposely did not mention how long it was taking for her to fully recover from her birth because she didn't want to add to his burden.

Theodore came around the desk. He put his hands on her upper arms. "We do so to protect the one we love." He ran his hands down her arms to clasp her hands and lift them to his chest. "Please don't ask me to promise to share everything with you. There is much I have seen that I will not tell you. The images I carry are too brutal to share. Let me protect you."

Betsy didn't know how to respond. She wanted to tell him she was strong enough to handle it. She was sure he would be better off for talking about it, but his last statement left her unsure. Perhaps she really didn't want to know how brutal men could be to each other in warfare.

Theodore laid his hands against her cheeks. "I see how you want to ease my burden, but I won't let you. I need your heart to be untouched by this. That is the best way you can help me."

Betsy bit her lip and nodded. "As you wish."

Theodore kissed her forehead. "Thank you."

* * *

The Whitmore household fell into a routine of days that carried the occupants in pleasant harmony from April through May and into June. Betsy breathed a little easier as the heat of summer took hold knowing any war activity was usually suspended during the "sickly season" and Theodore was not likely to return to the mainland until fall. She could enjoy these next few months.

Vertiline, on the other hand, could find nothing to enjoy in the steamy summer humidity. She could well understand why the folks of Key West moved outside to sleep as any breath of wind was welcome when the nighttime temperatures were nearly that of day. There was no escape to be found. She was almost sorry she promised to stay through the summer.

Theodore was enjoying family life. Whenever he returned home, whether for the noonday meal or for the evening, he was greeted with his wife's smile. Even more precious was Brianna, the little sprite, running to him crying out "Poppa" and holding up her arms for him to pick her up and swing her around. What man could resist such sweetness? In the evenings, after Brianna welcomed him, he would set her down and check on Baby Agatha. If she was awake he would pick her up and go to his chair in the parlor. Brianna would climb onto his lap to continue their story before supper.

This ritual began shortly after his return home. The first time Brianna climbed onto his lap of her own volition, he wasn't sure what to do with his two year old cherub. He patiently submitted to her exploration of his beard and patting his cheeks but when she started to pull he kissed her hand and turned her to sit on his knee. He tried bouncing her like he used to do Henry but she didn't care for it. He wished he had one of Henry's story books but the ones appropriate for Brianna's age were left at the house in New York. He would have to ask the caretaker to send them. Meanwhile, he had an idea. He tucked Brianna to his chest and proceeded to make up a story about a fairy who lived amidst the tiny ferns clinging to a branch of an ancient oak tree hidden deep inside a faraway forest. Brianna was enchanted with the tale and made a fuss when they were called to supper. After gently admonishing her behavior, Theodore promised to continue the tale on the morrow. And so he did adding a little bit more to the story every night since.

Shortly after supper Betsy would get the girls ready for bed. It was then he and Henry would usually share a game of chess. Later, after the others retired to the sleeping porch, he and Betsy shared a few moments alone conversing or kissing or both. They spoke of many things except for one. Ever since his return, Theodore was taking precautions to prevent another child. Betsy never asked him to stop so he assumed it was what she wanted too.

Overall, it was a blissful existence and he prayed often that one day soon he would never have to leave them again.

Theodore continued to receive correspondences from friends at the Florida forts and area traders. He learned General Jesup was recalled to his position as quartermaster general of the army and replaced by Zachary Taylor, having been promoted to brigadier general in consequence of the Battle of Lake Okeechobee. Dubbed 'Old Rough and Ready,' Taylor was now the fourth general to assume command of the Florida War and he would do so with reduced forces. Taylor's strategy was to concentrate his efforts on keeping the Seminoles out of northern Florida so the settlers could return home. He planned to build small posts at twenty mile intervals across the Florida peninsula from which he would send out larger units to search designated areas. Meanwhile, it was believed the Seminole were growing crops and gathering supplies in preparation for fall and winter fighting.

Nothing in the letters made Theodore feel as if he needed to return to the mainland just yet but neither was there any news to give him hope of an end.

* * *

One day in mid-June Theodore excused himself after the midday meal to return to work. Betsy asked, "Do you mind waiting a moment so I can walk with you? I need to stop at the mercantile."

"Not at all."

Betsy turned to Vertiline. "Would you care to accompany me?"

"I believe I'll stay here and tend to my correspondences."

Betsy donned her bonnet and picked up Agatha while Theodore helped Brianna with her shoes which were neatly waiting by the door. It brought a smile to his face as he recalled days gone by when he searched for Henry's shoes.

Betsy caught sight of his grin beneath the tawny mustache. "Something amuses you, husband?"

He straightened and winked at her. "I was just reminded how wonderful it is having you for a wife."

The unexpected compliment caught her by surprise, and her heart fluttered. She was truly blessed to have a spouse who continued to fan the flames of love.

The soft look in her eyes made Theodore wish they could take a trip upstairs instead of back to town. There were too many hours between now and when they could be alone tonight. He held out his free hand indicating she should walk in front of him out the door of the house. "Come, sweetheart."

They greeted friends and neighbors as they strolled down the street. Many complimented their lovely girls, others mentioned how nice a family they made. Betsy relished the moment. It was the fulfillment of a lifelong dream to be an accomplished wife and mother. Even though much the same happened every Sunday they walked to service it still never failed to please her.

As they made the turn onto Front Street they could see several people gathered in front of Asa Tift's warehouse. Drawing near, they noticed the onlookers staring up at the copula. Theodore shaded his eyes to look. He could see a man up there but the bright sunlight made it impossible to determine who it was. Curious they walked past the mercantile to get a closer look. The copula was designed for looking long distances but was rarely used anymore especially since wrecks rarely occurred in the waters off Key West. Theodore asked the first person he came to, an old fisherman. "Who's up there?"

"William Whitehead."

Theodore's brow pursed. "What is he doing?"

The fisherman shrugged. "Dunno. Been there for hours."

Now even more curious, Theodore walked with Betsy back to the mercantile determined to learn the answer as soon as he left her. He set Brianna down at Betsy's feet and watched her reach for her mother's hand as soon as he let her go. He gave them both a smile before turning away. Anxiously, he headed back to the warehouse to climb up to the copula and find out what was occupying Mr. Whitehead.

Betsy turned to walk up the steps and noticed Mrs. Whitehead standing on the piazza with her two children as if she was about to descend but she too was staring at Mr. Tift's copula.

"Good afternoon Mrs. Whitehead." Betsy nodded toward the warehouse. "I understand your husband has been up there for some time. Might I inquire as to what he is doing?"

Mrs. Whitehead turned a bewildered gaze to Betsy. "He informed me this morning he intended to sketch the island."

"Really, whatever for?"

Mrs. Whitehead shook her head. "To recollect on later, I suppose. He loves this island so, but as you know he took it hard losing the election. He has decided we are to move back to New Jersey. I have not been able to dissuade him, although I must admit, I haven't tried very hard."

Betsy nodded sagely. "I understand. You would like to return to the bosom of your family. We will miss you both. This community is going to lose two very important people."

"Thank you. You are kind to say so."

"I assure you it is the honest truth. When do you leave?"

"He booked our passage for Wednesday next."

Betsy's eyes and mouth flew open wide. "So soon?"

"It would have been sooner if there was a ship available to accommodate us and our belongings. If you'll excuse me, I'm afraid I must return to my packing."

"Of course, do you need any help?"

Mrs. Whitehead looked at the child on her hip and the toddler squirming at her side and shook her head. "Thank you for the offer but, no, I am managing just fine."

Betsy understood her hesitation. More little ones underfoot was not a help, what she needed was less distractions. "I could watch your children for a while."

"I couldn't ask you to do that."

Betsy smiled benevolently. "You didn't ask, I offered. Besides, you know how much Brianna and Penelope like playing together, and little William is such a sweet natured boy, he is no trouble at all."

"Are you sure you can handle all four of them?"

"Absolutely. Besides, I have my sister to help."

Mrs. Whitehead's face lit up. "That's right, you do. Bless you, Mrs. Whitmore. That would be a huge kindness."

"Bring them by the house in about an hour."

"I will."

The ladies parted company. Betsy quickly picked up the few items she needed and returned home to inform Vertiline of their pending occupation for the afternoon.

Theodore arrived home after work to a ruckus. Vertiline was in the parlor entertaining three toddlers in a game of Ring around the Rosie. The little imps took great fun in falling down and giggling. He found Betsy in the dining room trying to teach a stubborn Agatha how to eat solid food. Supper wasn't thought of much less started. Betsy wiped Agatha's mouth with a towel and handed her to Theodore. "I'll figure out something for us to eat."

He held her arm to stop her progress to the kitchen. "When are the Whitehead children going home?"

Betsy bit her lip. "I don't know. We didn't set a time. Mrs. Whitehead is packing up their household. They're leaving Key West."

Theodore grimaced. "I know. I spoke with Mr. Whitehead after leaving you."

Her face reflected her inner sorrow. "I'll miss them."

He nodded. "It is a great loss for the community."

Betsy sadly shook her head. "And all because of taxes."

"He is a man of high principles and I for one respect him for it."

"I do too. It's just sad is all."

Theodore brushed her chin. "I know."

Betsy raised her eyebrows and sighed. "So I don't know how long the children will be here. What did you have in mind?"

"Supper at the boardinghouse. You look like you are too worn out to cook."

She sighed again. "I am. Who would have guessed four was so much harder than two? But Teddy, four young children in Mrs. Mallory's dining room? We couldn't possibly keep them under control."

"Why not? There are three of us, no, four with Henry, to four of them. Surely we can manage. Go tell Vertiline."

"Well, all right, I suppose. But you tell Vertiline." Betsy reached for Agatha. "This one needs a fresh nappie."

Henry arrived home just in time to join them and despite the squirming youngsters, they had a very pleasant meal. Afterwards, they split up. Vertiline and Henry took Agatha and Brianna home. Betsy and Theodore walked to the Whitehead's to return their children. They walked back home with the sunset behind them.

Betsy leaned her head against Theodore's shoulder. "Teddy, thank you for the treat of eating out." She laughed lightly. "I think I ate too much."

Theodore patted her hand. "You deserve all the best. I'm proud to have you for my wife."

She smiled broadly. It was the second time he complimented her today. "Are you turning into a sentimental old fool on me?"

Theodore appropriately looked affronted. "I surely hope not."

Betsy laughed. "I wouldn't mind."

"Woman, I have my pride." In truth, he figured he probably had gone soft. She did it to him. His love for her surpassed anything he had ever known or thought he knew about being a husband. Every day brought him more joy, and he was humbled by the experience.

On the morning of the Whitehead family's departure, many of the townsfolk turned out to say goodbye and wish them well. The men stoically shook hands while the women did their best to hold back tears. Still many handkerchiefs were surreptitiously in use. The loss to their community would be felt ever afterwards. There was no better steward of Key West than Mr. William Whitehead. He left a legacy every bit as important as his brother, John Whitehead, or John Simonton in founding the island.

Chapter 37

As summer wound to a close, Betsy grew anxious of Theodore's departure. The family was settled into a comfortable routine. Brianna looked forward to Theodore's return every evening after work often racing to greet him at the door to be swung up in his arms with laughter and kisses. And Baby Agatha gurgled and cooed every time he picked her up. How would they ever cope when he left them again? For she knew in her heart, he would eventually have to return to the mainland. If only this silly war would end. Why couldn't the government allow the Seminoles to remain in the lower part of Florida? Surely they fought hard enough to deserve it.

Theodore learned the Seminoles were still conducting raids in the north and were thought to be responsible for a few deaths in Georgia and Tallahassee. Realizing his meager troops were spread too thin, General Taylor pulled his men out of south Florida to offer greater protection to the area north of Fort King. He asked for and received funds to continue building his forts. Meanwhile, within the nation, an outcry poured forth against the Cherokee removal. Noted author, Ralph Waldo Emerson, wrote an open letter to the president decrying the injustice of the government's actions. With public support for all the Indian wars fading and General Taylor maintaining a defensive position, Theodore had no plans to leave home just yet. For now it was more important he tend to being a husband and a father.

Vertiline, however, declared at the end of August it was time for her to return home. She promised their mother to come home in time to help with the harvest and canning of the crops. It was with great sadness and many tears the sisters said goodbye to each other. She reminded Betsy several times to forward any news from Victoria about the unknown author of *Emma*. Each time Betsy smiled and promised.

Henry was despondent for weeks after her departure.

The quietness of the house without Vertiline was hard on Betsy. To stave off the gloom, she worked on turning Vertiline's room, formerly Aunt Agatha's room, into a nursery for the girls so she and Theodore could once again have the bedroom all to themselves.

* * *

Theodore threw down his pen in mental protest. He was tired of writing doom and gloom. The Indian Wars were taking a toll on the economy, not only in Key West, but across the nation. Every day there was more bad financial news to share and now today, he was writing the obituary for Pardon C. Greene, one of Key West's founding fathers and a resident of the island since the town's inception. Following the town's custom, all the businesses closed and people lined the streets to pay their last respects yesterday as the cortege progressed from the beginning of Front Street to the end of Whitehead Street and to his interment in the southern beachside graveyard. All in all, it was a sad year for the community with the election woes of spring, William Whitehead's departure, and now the loss of a community leader.

Theodore stood up from his desk to stretch his back. Walking to the window, he looked out on the sunny afternoon, a mockery to the depressing words written on the paper behind him. He needed something good to write. The idea took a strong hold on him and resolution followed. He would find something good to report. There had to be something uplifting happening in this town. Theodore picked up his hat and walked out the door with determination. What he found, wasn't much, just the latest progress on the church building, but at least it was something positive to write about and lift his spirits.

For years the church council had been working on building an actual church. Reverend Dyce toured the country last year to raise funds. He brought back three thousand dollars for the project. This past May, the Widow Fleeming donated land at the corner of Eaton and Duval, about a block behind the tidal pond and parallel to Whitehead Street, to be used for the church with the stipulation of free pews. Two months later the church council approved plans to build the church using native limestone. Theodore found men hard at work on the site with several hundred blocks already quarried and set in place, giving a good sense of structure to the future sanctuary.

Not finding anything else more noteworthy, Theodore returned to his office to write a quick uplifting piece about the church progress and the dedication of the town in seeing this noble cause brought to fruition. When he was done, he handed both articles over to Robert Mason to work the typeset for this week's edition of the paper. Looking over the pages he laid out, Theodore noted with sadness the missing submissions from William Whitehead. His contributions always added a unique and well received perception to the paper. To Theodore, the paper wasn't the same without them.

He bid good evening to Robert and eagerly returned home to see his girls. Just the thought of them was enough to put a smile on his face.

* * *

It was late November when Theodore reluctantly announced he would be returning to the mainland even though to date there was no major activity. He told Betsy if the quiet continued he may perhaps return home by Christmas, January at the latest. Betsy prayed it was so.

Henry took his departure in stride and Betsy managed as well as she could but his daughters missed their father terribly. Betsy confessed to Abby some days she could hardly console them.

* * *

December 20th, a messenger from the wharf informed Betsy her annual Christmas barrel from her family arrived and would be delivered shortly. Some thirty minutes later a knock sounded on the door. She went to answer it with coin in hand for a tip. She opened the door to find Theodore standing behind the barrel wearing a broad grin. Betsy squealed her delight, lifted her skirts, dropping the forgotten coin, and ran around the barrel into his arms. The commotion brought Brianna running to the scene. She stopped short in stunned surprise as she witnessed her mother hugging someone on the front porch, in public. Even at her tender age she recognized the oddity of it. Then the couple turned and she saw his face, "Poppa!" She ran to him and he scooped her into his arms, kissing her cheek, relishing the sound of her laughter. "Poppa, your beard tickles."

The Whitmore family had the merriest Christmastime any of them could ever remember. Betsy secretly worked for weeks to make the children new outfits to wear to Christmas service. She took pride in the compliments their family received then repented to God for her pride and vanity.

They were invited to Christmas dinner at the Eatonton's along with the Baxley's, Jonathon and Esperanza, and Thomas and Maria. Collectively the four couples had seventeen children ranging in age from six months to Henry's twelve years making for quite a lively affair.

Abby served the most succulent turkey and roasted vegetables Betsy could ever remember eating. Afterwards, the men and older boys gathered in the kitchen to pop dry corn kernels and roast the chestnuts received in the Christmas barrel. The gathering enjoyed the treats while playing parlor games. It was late when the party ended and the friends parted ways carrying sleeping little ones home to bed.

As they walked home, Betsy thought the stars were shinning a little brighter tonight perhaps too celebrating the Savior's birth.

* * *

Theodore departed again the end of January, 1839, and it was no less stressful than it was in November. Actually, it was more so. Betsy was often frustrated with three year old Brianna's tantrums and the household demands Theodore was not there to handle. Patience and a lot of praying for patience saw her through most of it but March brought more frustration with an event she wasn't allowed to handle for the family.

Betsy closed her eyes and tried to let the Lord's peace wash over her as the minister's voice droned on in her head. She had given up trying to follow his sermon; her mind was too fatigued from a restless night's sleep.

It was the first Sunday worship with Reverend Ford, their new permanent minister replacing the beloved Reverend Dyes who recently retired. Apparently, Reverend Ford was on a mission to make a strong impression on the congregation with his overlong sermon. Betsy's girls were at their limit of being good. She tried to still Agatha from squirming in her lap and put a hand on Brianna's leg to remind her to sit still too. The longer the Reverend spoke the more rustling could be heard as even the adults grew restless. There was a collective sigh of relief when Reverend Ford said to bow their heads for the final blessing. Then before he dismissed the congregation he made an announcement.

"As you know, the new church building is almost finished on the outside. Now we must turn our considerations to the inside. Unfortunately, my predecessor, Reverend Dyce, was only able to raise half the necessary funds required to finish the church and our government is no longer providing tax money to build churches. So my fellow worshippers, we must turn inward to find the means to complete our Lord's dwelling in the fine manner it deserves. To do so, we will do as the New England churches have done which is to auction the pews to raise money to cover the building costs. The vestry has approved the idea and so we will hold an auction next Sunday after services." The reverend's last sentence was barely heard over the commotion of so many voices raised at once in question and protest. "The men of each household will bid for the pew of their choice which will then be reserved for his family hence forth."

Mrs. Fleeming, who donated the land for the church, silently left the building in protest. Mr. Lambert rose to speak and all hushed to hear what he had to say. "Reverend Ford, we appreciate your enthusiasm and genuinely welcome you to our community. Being new to the island and from what you just said I am left to surmise you may not be aware, Mrs. Fleeming specifically donated the land for the church with the express intent that the pews would be free to all."

"Good sir, I am well aware of her stipulation, and it was taken into consideration. There are thirty-six pews, four of which will remain free as in the last two rows. All others are up for auction next Sunday. I am afraid it is the only way to pay for the building. It is not up for debate."

His tone was dismissive and so the congregation collectively began exiting the building, many heatedly discussing the auction. It became the primary topic of interest for the rest of the week and it soon became clear the social implications of bidding for seats. The further back in the church the lower it was considered to be one's social standing and those occupying the free seats would be looked down upon. The pressure to bid on a pew sent Betsy into a panic. Theodore was not home to bid on a family pew and as a female she was not allowed to in his absence.

Late Thursday afternoon, Betsy and the girls were headed to the Eatonton household, not for a social visit, or at least not merely for a social visit. Betsy was in urgent need of Max's assistance. She had to wait till now for him to return from a voyage. She hated having to ask for help in a family matter but there was no other option.

Yesterday she met with the vestry to ask for an exception in her case but they were adamant no females could bid. She had a feeling they were afraid of setting a precedent. They did however suggest a proxy bidder would be acceptable. The only person she would consider for such a position was Max. If he was not able to bid on their behalf there was no telling where or if they would have a seat. She didn't expect her family to have one of the first few rows but they certainly didn't want to end up in the free seats. Socially speaking it just wouldn't do.

Max agreed to help. He then asked how much she was willing to bid. Betsy hadn't considered the money aspect and of course there was no time to seek Theodore's guidance with the auction only three days away. "Do you have any idea how much the bidding will be?"

"No, but I'll feel out some of the other men tomorrow to get an idea."

"I'll need some time to consider and pray over this decision."

"Of course."

"I'll let you know before the auction starts."

Betsy left the Eatonton's feeling better about the pew situation. Now she must focus on what to serve for supper so instead of going home she and the girls continued into town to see what was for sale at the fish market. She was fortunate to arrive in time to have first pick of the day's catch. On her return home with a nice red snapper for dinner, she saw Mrs. Mallory deep in thought standing on the edge of a newly cleared plot of land about the middle of Front Street facing the harbour. It was odd to see her outside the boarding house other than shopping and worship but it would have been odd to see anyone staring at a patch of dirt as she was now. Curiosity overcame her so Betsy approached the town's matriarch. "Good afternoon, Mrs. Mallory."

The elderly lady's hand flew to her chest as her head snapped toward Betsy. "Oh my, Mrs. Whitmore, you startled me."

"I apologize. I didn't mean to upset you."

"Tis nothing dear. Look how yer darlin' daughters are growing and such beautiful girls dey are, just like der mother."

Betsy brushed a hand over Brianna's dark hair. "Thank you." She nodded to the cleared limestone in front of them. "The view seems to have captured your attention."

Mrs. Mallory smiled and her excitement accentuated her Irish brogue. "Have ye heard de good news? The island founders have generously given me dis plot of land for a new boarding house. T'will be a bigger one so I can take in more boarders and once de new building tis paid for, I'll no longer owe rent and can be assured of me future."

"That is wonderful news, Mrs. Mallory. The Good Lord has answered your prayers."

"Yes he has and in de most unexpected way. Before he left, Mr. Whitehead gave me a letter about de goodness of me character and usefulness of me duties, and said he suggested to de council I should be given de land. I thought tis all well and good and charitable of him. I never believed dey would actually do such a thing." She gestured her hand toward the expanse in front of them. "I am working out the details in my head. I am thinking a simple two story. Perhaps sixteen rooms with a common parlor and dining room. I just can't figure out where it t'would be best to put de stairs,"

"Surely Stephen can help you figure it out."

"Ah, lass, to be sure he has made his suggestion and t'was all well and good for the guests but a mite difficult for me staff servicing de rooms."

Betsy smiled. "Something a man would not likely take into consideration on his own. Well, I'm sure you will come up with something very practical to answer both needs. I wish you much success with your new and exciting endeavor."

The ladies parted ways, each deep in their own thoughts.

The new Cocoanut Grove Inn would be open for business before the end of the year. The church on the other hand would not see its full completion until the following spring but in a few weeks' time they would begin celebrating services in the unfinished structure. In the name of raising funds, the vestry did allow Captain Eatonton to bid on the Whitmore's behalf, and so it was that Max secured the third row on the left for his family and the row behind for the Whitmore's.

* * *

Betsy felt the heat of the May afternoon sun on her back as she walked home from the post office with Theodore's letter. She let her hopes rise a little as she prayed this missive would say he was coming home soon. It was nearing the time of year when the military abandoned the battleground of the interior peninsula.

In front of her, Brianna held tightly to Little Agatha's hand taking seriously her role as protector of her little sister. The pace of Agatha's chubby legs might be agonizingly slow but Betsy gladly sacrificed the time rather than carry the sixteen month old toddler for she was getting to be quite heavy. Letting her walk had the added benefit of wearing her out so she would easily take her nap.

An hour or so later, the girls were sleeping, supper was simmering, and Betsy could take a few moments to enjoy a cup of tea and her letter. She broke the seal and unfolded the parchment to find Theodore's strong handwriting. Such were her emotions today that even his script had the power to move her.

My dearest love,

It is the first of May and I know you hope to see me home soon. For the moment, I don't know when but, same as you, I pray it will be soon.

General Taylor's blockhouse and patrol system has kept the Indians on the move but has yet to clear them completely out of north Florida. I think this frustration has softened the stance in Washington. President Van Buren pulled the Commanding General of the Army, Alexander Macomb, away from foreign concerns to come here to negotiate a new treaty with the Seminoles.

I had the opportunity to speak with General Macomb and he confided in me that he was given leeway to do whatever was necessary to end hostilities. He fully agreed with General Taylor's opinion that peace would only be achieved in allowing the Seminole to remain in Florida.

Do you realize what this means? There is actually a real chance of ending this war. But at the moment it is only a chance. However, it is ironic our government and military leaders are finally in agreement and now the Indians are slow in responding. Who can blame them after all the broken treaties and promises of the past?

Hence the delay in my return. General Macomb requested I accompany Lieutenant-Colonel Harney to meet with Chief Sam Jones near Fort Lauderdale to encourage his participation in the talks. As it turns out, Colonel Harney is a burly man easily noticed and I instantly recalled seeing him at the Black Hawk War although we didn't meet then. Now it will provide a topic of conversation as we begin our long journey tomorrow to the camp of Sam Jones. Pray, love, my words to this great warrior can bring about this peace we all so desperately desire.

I laugh at myself. Of course, by the time you read this the meeting will have long since taken place.

I miss you so. These past four years have been difficult and demanding on our marriage and our family and every month that passes it grows more wearisome. I often wonder if I had known how long this course would take if I would still have made the sacrifice. Right now, I struggle to see the balance of the good I hope I have done in this endeavor against the loss of time with all of you. I fear the scale is sadly heavier on the loss of time we can never get back. Henry is thirteen now, no longer a boy and very nearly a man. Already he has taken on much in the way of responsibilities. I missed so much of his formative years. He now seems more a stranger than my son and I am sure, though he may not be aware, he has felt the loss of his father's guidance. I pray for a swift end to this conflict so I may be there for our girls to watch them grow into the wonderful ladies I know they will be with you as their shining example.

Oh, my love, if only I could hold you in my arms tonight. This tent is a miserable and lonely place to be. If the mosquitos must feast upon my flesh I would much rather it be within the confines of our sleeping porch where we are together, whispering in the quiet, surrounded by the soft sounds of our slumbering offspring.

And now I've gone and made us both feel even more lonely and desperate for the other's company. Forgive my indulgence of the moment. I find I am not always as strong as I would like. Give my love to all and if God is smiling upon us we will be together before you receive my next letter.

    Yours eternally,

    Theodore

Betsy carefully folded the letter and held it to her heart. She didn't even try to stem the flow of tears his words created. Her soul recognized his deep and painful yearning to be reunited for it mirrored her own. She closed her eyes and succumbed to the wracking sobs as her sorrow poured out for both of them, indeed for all of them. After the tears cleansed her, she dropped to her knees and prayed and in so doing found the comfort and strength she needed to pick herself up and carry on with hope for a better and brighter tomorrow.

* * *

Theodore walked behind Halleck Tustenuggee and Chitto Tustenuggee, Sam Jones' chosen successor as chief and representative since he was too old to make the journey, as they passed through the gates of Fort King. Behind him were seven warriors. It took some doing, but Theodore finally convinced Sam Jones the desire to speak of peace was sincere. After a journey of several weeks, Theodore was dirty and tired and relieved to be back.

Across the compound another group of about forty warriors was gathered. Theodore recognized Chief Tiger Tail in their midst. Lieutenant Harney announced he was meeting with the generals and dismissed the rest of his men. Theodore trailed behind as the two tribes greeted each other. Eventually Tiger Tail acknowledged his presence and they spoke through an interpreter. After the usual greetings and inquiring after shared acquaintances the chief asked if General Macomb was to be trusted. Theodore hoped he told the truth in affirming the general's sincerity. If not, it would forever tarnish his word with the Seminole.

The following day talks began with the chiefs. There was the usual hand shaking, gift giving, and pipe smoking. If Theodore thought General Scott liked pomp and circumstance, General Macomb proved to be his superior. While the Indians sat silently passing their pipe the general's band played marching tunes with gusto and his dragoons paraded in full dress. Theodore considered it a bit much and he wasn't sure it gave the impression the general intended.

It took two days for the participants to reach an oral agreement. Within two months' time the Indians would move south of Pease Creek into the southwest corner of the peninsula and if they did so the United States would cease all military action against them.

General Macomb considered the war terminated and reported so to the President but Theodore shared the same misgivings as General Taylor. They well knew an agreement with only three chiefs would not bind the other tribes. There were at least three other tribes not represented. Theodore could only hope these chiefs would encourage the others to embrace the peace. It also had not escaped their notice that General Macomb carefully avoided promising permanent occupation of the new reservation nor was the agreement in writing, carefully leaving open the later possibility of emigration.

Over the next few weeks the territory was quiet. Those citizens who fled their farms and plantations were grateful to return home from the crowded villages where food was scarce. With the appearance of the Indians moving to the reservation, Theodore began making plans to return to his home. But the peaceful beginning in June was fleeting.

Not all were happy with this new agreement. The Florida papers denounced it and encouraged protests and retaliation. The *Tallahassee Floridian* went so far as to insist whites should shoot Indians on sight and not long afterwards a meeting was held deciding no Indians should be allowed to remain because they were not to be trusted and would always be a refuge for runaway slaves. The unfortunate printing of Secretary Poinsett's letter stating his belief that General Macomb's agreement would make the eventual removal of the Seminole easier may have pleased the whites but it infuriated the Seminoles and ended Theodore's plans of leaving the territory and any hope of peace.

The Seminole response was swift and brutal. They killed a white family near Tallahassee, ambushed an army wagon train in central Florida, and assailed travelers. The recently returned pioneers fled once again leaving all behind in their panic. But it was the massacre near Port Charlotte which truly reignited the war.

As part of the peace negotiations a trading post was opened on the Caloosahatchee River. General Taylor assigned Lieutenant-Colonel Harney to protect it with twenty-six soldiers. On July twenty-third in the hours before dawn it was attacked by Hospetarke and Chakaika, two of the chiefs not involved in the peace talks. Sixteen were killed. When word reached Fort King, Theodore hastened to Fort Brooke to interview his contact but soon learned Colonel Harney was headed to Key Biscayne. Theodore hired a sloop to sail around the Florida peninsula, afraid if he traveled overland he might miss him. Theodore caught up with Harney at Fort Russell on Key Biscayne.

Colonel Harney was only too happy to oblige Theodore with an interview. After showing his guest to his quarters where he could stow his gear, Colonel Harney led the way to the mess tent with a bottle of whiskey. Facing each other across a well-worn wooden table, Theodore pulled out his notebook and pencil. It was all the encouragement Colonel Harney needed.

"I and three others returned late the night before from a boar hunt. We were all exhausted from the chase and I retired straight to bed, it was all I could do to undress. I admit, I didn't check to make sure a guard was posted.

Rifle shots dragged me from a sound sleep. It was still dark. I stumbled out of the tent wearing only my drawers, there was no time to get dressed. It was a costly mistake for those who did. I could hear the war yells and death screams of my men in their beds. The enemy was everywhere and those who escaped were fleeing in confusion.

"Later when I pieced together the accounts of the others, we realized there were upwards of two hundred warriors to our twenty-seven men and a few civilians. Hospetarke led his band in looting the trade store while Billy Bow-Legs and Chakaika's bands led the attack against us."

Theodore looked up from his writing. "Chakaika? He leads the band of so called Spanish Indians living along the southern coastal areas, correct?"

"Yes."

Theodore tapped his pencil trying to recall the details of a long ago conversation. "I seem to remember someone once saying the Seminole considered them something like criminals and unfit to associate with."

"It wouldn't surprise me. It would almost offer some sense to what they did. What infuriates me is these same Indians visited the camp numerous times in the days prior to the attack, always friendly, and whenever I asked, they replied they were satisfied with the treaty. Their duplicity is amazing. We had no suspicion of their true intent. I suppose it's true, the only good Indian is a dead one.

"Anyway, I suppose I will be held to blame for our fate. Not only was there not a guard posted but my men were unarmed because an officer forgot to pass out ammunition for the new Colt rifles.

"Those of us who escaped fled to the river. Unfortunately, the Indians anticipated it. They were firing at us from both banks. Men were being struck all around me. We swam downstream making our way to where some fishing-smacks were known to be anchored.

"Several hours later brought the timely arrival of the sloop, *Jane*, to affect a rescue. Wanting to make sure we left no survivors behind, I entreated their crew to row us back to camp. Under cover of darkness and with only three rifles between us we made our way back up the river with muffled oars. It took all night. Just before daylight we reached the shore of the camp. I cannot tell you how it grieved me to find the bodies of my men gutted and scalped. Some were found dead under their mosquito-bars.

"The Indians made off with most of the goods, about three thousand dollars' worth and some fifteen hundred in specie along with all the rifles and two kegs of powder. It's hard to convey how relieved we were to find three kegs of pickles, a bag of corn, and some coffee. When we returned downriver, this was divided between the two sloops. I dispatched the wounded and the necessary crew to man the fishing-smack to Tampa while I stayed with the crew of the *Jane* and headed here to warn the remaining troops stationed on this coast."

Theodore looked up from his notes. "That was quite an ordeal and still in the end your first thought was to your duty. I wonder, do you think if the guard was posted and your men had ammunition the result wouldn't have been the same?"

The burly man gave his question due consideration. "I would hope we wouldn't have lost so many but then again, we would have tried harder to resist. I admit the results could have verily turned out the same."

Theodore lightened the mood by switching to a lighter conversation after tossing back a tumbler of whiskey. Before they parted ways Colonel Harney told him, "I have just received orders confirming my request to take over command of this base and institute a program to better train our men on how to survive in the swamps and jungle warfare."

"Amazing no one thought to do so sooner." Theodore clapped him on the back. "You just might be the answer this war needs."

* * *

Theodore returned to Fort King and into a political maelstrom. General Taylor's men took two hundred Indians prisoner. He said he would free them in exchange for the surrender of those responsible for the massacre of Harney's men. Governor Call vehemently objected to the idea. He demanded Taylor's resignation and he be allowed to resume command. In response Secretary Poinsett, with the President's support, removed Governor Call from his position and replaced him with Robert Reid. Call retaliated by publicly denouncing Poinsett but Theodore was sure he found little satisfaction in doing so. And of course Taylor's plan failed. The guilty Indians did not surrender, forcing Taylor to send the prisoners to Arkansas.

The war turned bitter and bloody on both sides but only in small skirmishes the military couldn't even bring themselves to call battles. General Taylor ordered no more prisoners were to be taken alive. This put a moral hardship on his officers and many were loath to obey his mandate. Theodore empathized with their predicament. The heat of summer brought a suspension to the fighting and Theodore took the opportunity to finally return home.

Chapter 38

Key West, August 9th, 1839

Theodore stepped down from the wharf the second Friday in August relieved to be moments away from reuniting with his loved ones. It was a long and turbulent six months since he left and home never looked so good. Walking across the threshold and into Betsy's arms was more endearing every time he returned. Little Agatha was shy at first but Brianna more than made up for it with her enthusiastic greeting. She only gave him a minute, before she was tugging his hand trying to pull him toward the chair in the parlor. It pleased him immensely that Brianna remembered their ritual. "Fairy story Poppa."

He allowed her to pull him into the parlor where he scooped up both girls and settled into his chair with one on each knee. Fortunately, on his journey home he had given some thought to the yarn he would spin for them. Agatha lost interest a few moments later and scooted down from his lap but Brianna listened with intent rapture. When he hesitated trying to think of a good character name his precocious little Brianna piped up with one. He smiled his approval and used it. From then on whenever he hesitated it was her cue to add something to their ever growing tale.

* * *

The heat of summer was truly upon them and the following day Betsy suggested they go swimming. Theodore expected to leave the girls with Abby but Betsy shook her head. "There's no need to leave them behind. They both know how to swim." Theodore gave her an incredulous look but didn't question her declaration.

Henry was working so it would only be the four of them. They headed out under a bright blue sky with cotton clouds across translucent turquoise waters smoothly sailing between islands of emerald mangroves. Betsy relished cutting through the water in their little sailboat, happy to be able to relax and let Theodore take control. Little Agatha was sitting on her lap and three year old Brianna was close beside her. This was the furthest and fastest the girls had ever sailed and their laughter warmed her heart. Taking them out by herself, she didn't go very far, tending to stay where it was shallow enough for Brianna to stand and close enough to shore for a quick return if necessary. This excursion was a treat for her and the little ones. They loved the rush of wind and sparkling water as much as their mother. The rest of the world melted away. For now it was only the four of them and the joy of the moment.

They anchored near a place where the edge of the coral reef began only four feet below the surface making an easy underwater swim for Brianna but they were at the edge of a ten foot drop with an outgoing current. Betsy cautioned her daughter again about being aware of the dangers. Theodore agreed to stay near the boat playing with Agatha while Betsy kept a close watch on Brianna. They began with floating on the surface, face down, looking at the world below. It wasn't long before Brianna was begging to be allowed to dive down for a closer look. She recently acquired the skill and wanted to practice it.

The first dive was short but little Brianna adjusted fast and by the third she could reach the bottom and remain there for thirty seconds or so. She was excited by her accomplishment and begged to go one more time. Betsy consented, proud of her strong little swimmer, and down they went. A green turtle swam by them and in her excitement Brianna eagerly tried to follow it. The current caught her. Already tiring, her small limbs were no match for the strength with which it pulled her into deeper water. Betsy immediately gave chase, catching her arm and back swimming against the current headed for the surface. She was so focused on saving Brianna it was with some surprise she felt her foot brush the coral. She looked down expecting to see a benign elkhorn or staghorn coral. The yellow tipped brown branches stretching out from the coral bed widened her eyes with dismay.

Betsy rushed them to the surface. "Brianna I need you to swim for the boat."

"But momma, I want to go down again."

Sternly she said, "Brianna."

The three year old recognized her mother's warning. She was in danger of being disciplined for talking back and disobedience. Brianna began swimming for the boat hoping this didn't mean they were headed home already.

Theodore saw them headed his way and smiled, ready to compliment Brianna's skill until he noticed the extreme concern on Betsy's face. "What is it? Did you see a shark?"

Brianna turned around in the water to look at her mother. "Was there a shark?"

Betsy shook her head. "No. It's something else. We must leave now." Theodore saw the urgency of her expression and reacted accordingly. He scooped up a floating Agatha and deposited her into the boat. He then reached out to Brianna to pull her in faster and likewise lifted her into the boat ignoring her protest that she could do it herself. Betsy was now beside him. He whispered, "What is it?"

"I've been stung on my foot."

Theodore tried to look below the rippling surface to see her injury. "What stung you?"

"Fire coral."

"How bad is it?"

His questions were trying her patience. "It's not yet, but it will be very soon. Please help me get in the boat."

Theodore did as she asked. He wasted no time climbing in too and raising the sail much to Betsy's relief for she was starting to feel the familiar pain. Then a terribly curious thing happened. She felt the same pain across her upper arm where she was stung years earlier by fire coral. Within minutes she was in agony in both locations. She tried cupping water from over the side of the boat in the hopes of gaining some relief for her foot, but she had a hard time holding onto the liquid and the effort was not worth the minuscule relief it provided.

She turned her left shoulder toward Theodore. "Do you see any redness?"

Theodore shook his head. "I thought you said it was your foot?"

"It is."

"Then what is wrong with your arm?"

Betsy lost her battle for patience. Her response came out harsher than she intended. "Nothing."

Theodore shook his head again. Rather than try to reason out her puzzling response he focused on getting them home. By the time they reached the beach, Betsy's face showed her struggle with the searing pain. Theodore glanced down to find angry red lines crossing the top of her right foot. Walking barefoot across the coral limestone beach would be too painful so it didn't surprise him to see Betsy trying to don her shoes. Her grimace as she attempted to slip her foot past the tongue of her boot was more than he could bear. He picked her up before she could form a protest. "Brianna, get your mother's shoes." He looked around. "Agatha, where are you?" He spied her on the other side of the boat. "Agatha stay with Brianna. Hold her hand and follow me."

Betsy hid her face in his chest embarrassed by her predicament. As soon as they reached their front porch he put her back on her feet then turned back to get Little Agatha as the girls were trailing some distance behind. When he returned to the house, he found Betsy in the dining room, her stung foot propped on a chair, inspecting her wound.

"Can I get you anything?"

She nodded, her chin tense. "Vinegar. There's some in a jar on the shelf in the kitchen."

Theodore easily found the neatly labeled jar. He brought it and a towel to Betsy. She reached for it, but he waived her off. "I'll do it." He picked her foot up so he could sit in the chair with her foot in his lap to get a better look at the injury. He could see welts forming but had no idea the severity of the wound having no experience to guide him.

He placed the towel on his leg to catch the excess before pouring a little bit of vinegar over the wound. Betsy squirmed and a small sound escaped her lips as she struggled not to show her pain. Theodore glanced around to the girls standing in the doorway watching them with concern. He set the jar on the table and carefully moved her foot so he could rise. He ushered the little ones out of the room toward the stairs with a hand behind either head.

"Your mother will be fine. Brianna, take your sister and go play in your room for a bit. We'll come get you when it's time to eat." He watched them climb the stairs before returning to Betsy.

Theodore poured a little more vinegar on the wound. Her quick intake of breath made him ask, "Is it helping at all?"

"I think so."

"Do you want some more?"

"Yes."

He poured it on two more times. "Should we wrap it?"

Betsy shook her head. "I don't think I could bear anything touching it." She limped up the stairs to their room to change out of her swim dress.

Theodore followed. He was worried. To him her wound looked pretty serious. She didn't seem to be overly concerned, so he tried not to let his distress show. It crossed his mind how much worse today could have been; how easily something truly tragic could have happened. His heart wrenched. She was this family's foundation. If he lost Betsy... Even the thought was too devastating to contemplate so he thanked God for her safety instead.

When they reached their room he asked, "Do you need any help?" She shook her head. "Then I'll check on the girls."

Betsy could hear his deep voice giving them instruction. The sound was like a cozy blanket wrapped around her heart. It was good having Theodore home to help with the house and the children. She forgot how nice it was to have someone take care of her. If only this war would end before something terrible happened to him. There were so many dangers in the Florida wilderness other than man, and the men seemed to be doing a pretty good job of hurting each other. She didn't feel it was a matter of if but when something would happen to him; a bullet, a knife, or a spear, a spider, snake, alligator, bobcat, yellow fever or malaria. The fear could drive her mad with worry if she let it. She had to leave it with God.

Losing him would devastate her in ways she was sure she couldn't even imagine and moving on would be more than she could bear but she would do it for the girls. Agatha and Brianna would give her purpose and Henry would give her strength. She could do it but while he was away she prayed every day for his safe return so she would never have to figure out how to cope without him. For now, he was here and she would rejoice in it.

Emotions overcame her when he reappeared in the doorway. She walked to him with arms open to be enveloped in his warm embrace and he welcomed her as if needing the contact every bit as much as she did.

Theodore leaned back to look at Betsy. He smoothed the wisps of air away from her temple. Hours after the incident, even knowing all was well, he still carried the fear of losing her.

Betsy saw the depths of his concern and understood his emotions. She whispered, "I know. I feel the same intense relief every time you come home. The good from today is a reminder to appreciate the moments we have together to their fullest."

"Hmm."

Concordance, and likely emotions running too deep to speak. She returned his soul searching gaze.

Theodore studied his wife's face as if seeing it for the first time. He thought he memorized it the first time he left her after their marriage but he found he had to do so all over again. The visage before him was fuller, more mature and womanly; the beautiful face of the mother of his children. He ran his fingers over her forehead smoothing out the worry lines. They were the only visible sign of the burdens she willingly carried for them. He ran his thumbs over the crescent lines bracketing her lips. He loved those indentions. They proved despite it all she still smiled. Even now under his gaze the corners of her lips lifted. He raised his eyes to hers and the clarity of her azure irises mesmerized him. The intensity of her gaze made him feel as if she saw something in him others failed to notice. And the amazing part was she still loved him despite it. He leaned down and brushed his lips across hers and then pulled her against his chest. They held tight to each other until two little voices clamored for their attention. Theodore scooped up the girls and together they all headed downstairs

Betsy intended to go to the kitchen to prepare their evening meal but Theodore blocked her path, turned her around by the shoulders, and directed her to the parlor.

"You stay here, rest your foot, and let the girls entertain you. I'll take care of our meal."

Betsy was too surprised to protest. Curiously, she watched him walk out the back door toward the kitchen wondering what he might serve for supper. She was soon distracted by Brianna and Agatha. It was nice to spend some time with her girls without the distraction of other obligations, plus focusing on them helped her cope with the burning pain of her injury.

A short while later she heard Theodore in the dining room so she went to investigate. She grinned when she found him unpacking a basket of food he obviously obtained from Mrs. Mallory's boardinghouse. Betsy quirked her eyebrows at him when he caught her watching but said nothing. He returned a sheepish grin and continued his preparations. It didn't matter to her how he provided their meal, she appreciated the thoughtful gesture. When he was done, Betsy called the girls to the table. They saved a plate for Henry knowing he would be hungry when he came home later.

Despite the lingering pain in her foot, their evening was so enjoyable spending time as a family, that even Betsy was reluctant to put her daughters to bed. Theodore's firm voice ended any protests they might have made including hers. As she tucked them in and kissed their sweet foreheads she knew this was one of those magical days she would hold dear to her heart for the rest of her life.

On her knees before bed, Betsy's prayers were thankful for all her blessings.

Theodore was thankful for the health and safety of his wife and children.

* * *

Sunday morning was overcast and drizzly. Betsy's movements roused Theodore from his slumber. He opened his eyes not surprised to find her dressed for church except for her bare feet. He sat up and swung his feet to the floor and stretched. He reached out a hand to catch her as she flitted by him and pulled her to him for a kiss. "How is your foot?" She pulled her skirt aside for him to see. If anything he thought it looked worse than yesterday. It was now blistered and weeping. He brought his gaze back to hers, his brow creased. "You cannot possibly be thinking of leaving this house."

His tone stiffened her spine. "I most certainly am. It's the Lord's day."

"How do you intend to put a shoe on that foot?"

"A little pain is not going to stop me from keeping the Sabbath."

Theodore tilted his head. "I believe the Lord would understand."

"Perhaps, but still I am going."

Theodore frowned. "No, you're not."

Firmly but without anger, she replied, "Yes, I am." She turned and left the room to help the girls dress.

Theodore was mildly angry at her obstinacy. He impatiently tugged on his pants and donned his shirt to follow her. He met Henry in the hallway on his way downstairs.

"Good morning, Poppa."

Theodore gave him a tight smile. "Good morning, son."

Henry noticed his father's ill mood and wondered if he had done something wrong but when nothing more was said he knew it was not caused by him. He couldn't imagine his sister's had earned their father's displeasure, so it must be his mother. Henry couldn't recall a single time they had ever quarreled. He was curious as to the reason but deemed it prudent to stay out of his father's way, so he continued downstairs.

Theodore walked into the nursery intending to pick up where they left off in the bedroom. Betsy was dressing Little Agatha while Brianna sat on the bed next to her sister handing her mother needed items. Theodore stood just behind Betsy's left shoulder and roughly whispered, "We are not done talking."

Betsy's neck stiffened, her head turned slightly toward him, but she didn't look at him as she archly whispered, "I am. My mind is set."

Brianna looked from one parent to the other with mild concern. Theodore noticed her distress and decided it was best to hold off until Betsy was done with the children so he left the room.

Betsy felt more than heard his departure and her shoulders drooped. This was the first time they seriously disagreed over anything and it unsettled her. She noted the gray sky outside the window and thought it matched the mood inside as well.

She smiled for Brianna's sake as she finished dressing Little Agatha then put her back in the crib while she helped Brianna. As soon as her second shoe was buckled, Brianna scampered off the bed in a hurry to get downstairs to see Henry. Betsy picked up Little Agatha from her crib and held her close for a moment seeking comfort for her troubled mind in the simplicity of a mother's love. The toddler squirmed with impatience, ending the moment. Betsy grimaced and fought off the urge to feel sorry for herself.

Still barefoot, Betsy carried her shoes, stockings, and Agatha downstairs, waiting until the last possible moment to don them knowing the agony she would suffer. Agatha nearly fell from her arms trying to get down as soon as they reached the bottom. She ran off to join Henry and Brianna in the parlor. Betsy would have chastised her for not waiting to be set down if not for Theodore standing nearby waiting for her. She walked past him headed out to the kitchen. He followed behind without saying a word. His presence unnerved her.

She gingerly crossed the yard and into the kitchen trying to ignore her husband as she set about making breakfast. She didn't want to fight while he seemed set on doing so. She pulled the pot of soaking oatmeal out of the oven and placed it on the burner. She stoked the fire and gave the oatmeal a stir. With nothing more to do for a moment, she finally turned to face him. She crossed her arms and waited.

Confronted with Betsy's beleaguered demeanor Theodore hesitated. He didn't want to fight, only to make her see reason. He didn't want her to hurt. There was no way he could walk beside her to church knowing every step would bring her pain. His anger faded, replaced by deep concern. He stepped to her and she dropped her arms in response, her eyes widened and softened as she watched him. He placed his hands on her upper arms and kissed her forehead. He pulled back and looked deep in her eyes. "My love, please stay home." He felt her stiffen. "I'm not trying to rule over you, it's just that I can't bear your needless suffering."

"You consider attending worship, needless suffering?"

"I do."

"I don't. I have never broken His commandment to keep the Sabbath holy. I am not about to now."

"What about when the girls were born?"

"That was different."

"And do you believe God understood?"

"Of course."

"Then why wouldn't He understand now?"

"Because I can walk." A burp of released heat from the oatmeal reminded her to give it a stir.

"That is yet to be seen."

She turned to him with a frown. "You don't think I can?"

Theodore huffed up. "Woman, I truly believe you can endure. My disagreement is whether or not you should."

Betsy fought not to smile. It pleased her to know he believed in her. "What would people think if we didn't go to service today?"

"It matters not what they think and the rest of us will go. Only you need to stay home."

"You have been away too long if you have forgotten how much it matters what other people think in this small community. And you are going to handle those girls all by yourself?"

"How hard can it be? And Henry will be there to help."

Betsy bit her cheek to keep from smiling. *How hard—indeed!* He may just find out. She gave the pot another stir and then said, "How about this? I will try walking in my shoes, and I promise to stay home if it is more than I can bear."

Theodore shook his head. "Promise you will stay home if it is more than *I* can bear."

She had to smile at that. "I promise."

"Thank you."

"You're welcome."

He looked around the kitchen. "Now, what can I do to help?"

He was way too sweet and generous to stay mad at him. It was unheard of, a husband helping in the kitchen. "Could you bring that tray over here and get some bowls from the cupboard behind you?"

Theodore did as she asked while she moved the pot to the table and retrieved jars of honey, almonds, and dried apples. He watched as she dished up the oatmeal and the toppings and then he carried the tray to the dining room.

After the meal, Betsy tried to don her stockings and just as Theodore suspected her pain was great. Secretly, Betsy was relieved he was forcing her to stay home. Her guilt was such she would not have otherwise.

While the others were gone to church, she read the Bible and prayed. She could keep the Sabbath even if she wasn't in fellowship. After two hours, she began anxiously watching for their return having discovered the house was too quiet to bear without them. She started singing hymns to fill the air with sound. *Wasn't that as good as praying or reading scripture?*

Theodore smiled to hear Betsy singing as they approached the house. He loved the sound of her voice. She suddenly stopped and a few moments later opened the front door in welcome as they were coming up the steps.

Betsy rushed to open the door anxious to see Theodore and the children but to her surprise behind them was Max and Abby and their children; Emily, Christoff, Hawthorne and Nathanial. Caught off guard and embarrassed, Betsy hunched her shoulders hoping her skirt touched the floor to hide her bare feet. Nervously, she smoothed her hair and skirt and welcomed their guests with a smile.

Abby moved past the rest of them and hooked her arm in Betsy's to walk to the parlor. "Theodore mentioned your plight so of course I had to come and take a look. He is quite concerned about you."

"I know. He thinks it's worse than it really is." When they reached the sofa in the parlor Abby directed Betsy to sit while she turned to take Nathaniel from Max. Theodore put Agatha down and sent her toddling over to Betsy while he followed the others outside leaving Abby to examine Betsy's wound.

Theodore stepped outside in time to hear Christoff call out, "Come on Rose and Thorn, let's play hide and seek. Henry's it first."

Theodore looked to Max. "Rose and Thorn?"

Max smiled. "Christoff came up with it one day using Emily's middle name."

"He's very creative."

"Yes, he is."

Both men chuckled. Theodore led them to the side of the yard under the shade of a lime tree.

Max said, "I heard something the other day of interest to you."

"Hmm."

"Do you know Colonel Richard Fitzpatrick?"

"Only by name. I believe he lives on the east coast of Florida now. Fitzpatrick Street is named for him, isn't it?"

"Yes, it is. I saw him a few weeks ago on his way to Tallahassee. He told me he means to propose to the Florida legislature an idea of using Cuban bloodhounds to track the Indians in the swamps. You don't think they would seriously consider it, do you?"

Theodore's eyebrows rose. "Previous generals have threatened to use them before and congress is getting so desperate to end this war I believe they would try anything."

"Fitzpatrick is convinced it is the answer since it worked so well in Jamaica with the Maroon Revolt."

Theodore grimaced at the thought of dogs chasing Indians, but he also understood the appeal. "Dogs would not only be useful in tracking, they could also give warning of surprise attacks. I'm sure the colonel will find the legislature all too agreeable."

"So you think it will work?"

"I suppose it depends on how well they can track Indians. My concern is what happens once they find them."

The men fell into silence mentally visualizing the worst outcome.

Abby looked up from Betsy's foot. "Has the redness spread any?"

Betsy looked carefully at her appendage and shook her head. "No. It's the same as yesterday."

"I think you're right then. There's nothing of concern here. Keep it clean and dry and let me know if it gets any worse. It will take some time, but it will heal, and I agree with Theodore. Stay home until you can *comfortably* wear your shoes again."

Abby walked over to the open window to check on the children's play. The men were standing off to the side of the yard deep in conversation. She shook her head. For some reason men seemed to believe children did not require close supervision no matter how young they were. Once she verified the location and health of all five youngsters she turned her attention back to her husband, enjoying an unobserved moment to look her fill.

Betsy joined her when she continued to stare. "Are the children alright?"

Belatedly, Betsy's words registered, pulling Abby from her wayward thoughts. "Oh yes. They are fine."

Betsy followed Abby's gaze curious as to what had captured her attention. Seeing the men, she looked at her friend questioningly. "Is something wrong?"

Abby shook her head. "No." She smiled. "Just appreciating the view."

Betsy grinned. "Really?"

Abby pulled her gaze away to look at her friend. "Even after ten years of marriage, I never tire of looking at him. Just looking. Surely you feel the same about Theodore."

"I do. I assumed it was more to do with not having the opportunity every day which makes it more enjoyable when he is home."

"What was it about Theodore that caught your fancy when you first met?"

"His eyes. They seemed to say so much when he hadn't said a word. What about you?"

Abby sighed. "I am a fool for Max's dimples. Even now, they make my heart flutter every time I see them which is to say every time I look at him. Have you noticed his dimples are always visible?"

Betsy looked in Max's direction for confirmation. "I can't say that I have."

Abby's grin went lopsided. "Well they are much to my chagrin."

Betsy was afraid she would never look at Max the same again. Now she would notice his dimples and always remember this conversation. "Would you care to stay for dinner? We have plenty to share."

"We would love to as long as you allow me to help prepare it and contribute dessert. I made a lovely coconut custard yesterday."

"How can I say no? Theodore favours your custard as much as Max adores my cinnamon bread."

Both women giggled.

Chapter 39

August turned into September and then to October. The storm season ended quietly and now Betsy's worries returned to Theodore's inevitable departure, for no matter how much she prayed, peace would not come. It would happen. Any day now Theodore would give her *the look*. That 'I'm sorry but I have to leave you again' look she had come to hate. And worse was the weeks of anxious dread plaguing her before he ever gave her *the look*. This year was no different. It was the second Thursday in October when it happened. She saw it in his eyes.

"When are you leaving?"

Theodore wasn't surprised she knew what he was going to say. "In a week, but I'm not going far this time. I'm meeting Lieutenant John McLaughlin at Tea Table Key. Have you heard of it?"

Betsy shook her head.

"It's close to Indian Key."

Betsy's eyes flew wide. "Has the war moved so close?"

"I suppose in a way it has though I don't believe there is any reason to fear an attack on Key West."

"Are you sure?"

"Reasonably sure. McLaughlin was given command of a joint army-navy force they're calling the Mosquito Fleet. General Taylor charged him with running a blockade against any Cuban or Bahamian traders intent on helping the Indians. He is building a base on Tea Table Key. The good news is I can make my way home as often as Jonathon sails by in the *Mystic*."

Betsy had to smile. "At least that part is good news. But it doesn't seem like much of a story to keep you there long term."

"Oh there is if McLaughlin has his way about it. Do you remember Lieutenant Powell?"

"Isn't he the one who got the German botanist killed at Jupiter Inlet?" What was his name? Ah, Edward Leitner. Such a wasteful shame."

Theodore grimaced as he recalled the vivid details of Leitner's passing. "Yes it was. I am sorry I reminded you of it." He shook his head to clear it of the sad thought. "Anyway Lieutenant Powell has this idea of taking the fight to the Indians in the Everglades. He wants to circumnavigate the unchartered area, discover the Indians' hideouts, capture the women and children, and generally harass the Seminole where they feel safest. He believes it will help end the war quickly. McLaughlin has embraced Powell's ideas."

It was Betsy's turn to frown. "If I didn't know you better I would think you were excited about such brutish tactics."

"Hmm. For the Indians this would be devastating and McLaughlin's success would be heartbreaking, but on the other hand, I am very interested in this unique concept in warfare. Of course bringing the army and navy together is a challenge in itself, so you see there is much of interest to keep me close to home."

Betsy grinned. "I am happy about that at least."

True to his word, Theodore was home every other weekend for a few days until mid-December when the latest war story arrived in Key West. Theodore happened to be home on the 14th when Henry came running home from the docks in great excitement.

"Poppa, come quick. There's a man just arrived with a bunch of dogs from Cuba. He says he's going to hunt Indians with them."

Theodore recalled his conversation with Max as he retrieved his notebook, pencil and hat. "I bet his name is Fitzpatrick."

Henry was surprised. "How did you know?"

Theodore smiled. "It's my job to know these things."

Father and son walked briskly back to town.

"Poppa, you should see them. I've never seen so many dogs all together. Five dark skinned men each led six or seven dogs from the ship right past me. Why that's more than thirty dogs!"

"Did you see where they took them?"

Henry shook his head. "They were headed toward Mr. Browne's warehouse, but I came for you, so I didn't see exactly."

Outside Mr. Browne's warehouse they found a substantial number of onlookers gathered around a man speaking from the dock so as to be slightly elevated from the crowd. Theodore assumed this to be Colonel Fitzpatrick. He noticed Max was in attendance with his son, Christoff, and his father-in-law, Richard Bennington. Theodore made his way over to them in the hopes that Max would introduce him to the colonel. Having no interest in what was being said the boys left their elders to get a closer look at the dogs. The men nodded to each other in silent greeting and returned their attention to the zealous speaker.

"I and the Florida legislature have pursued this endeavor with every confidence of it being a means to end this bloody war. Jamaica suffered under revolt for eighty years. Do you know what brought it to a swift and final end? Bloodhounds! If it can work for them, it can work for us!"

The crowd gave a cheer.

Theodore thought the thin gray-haired man missed his calling. He had all the makings of a politician rather than a military man. The speech ended and some of the people dispersed, others stayed to look at the dogs. Max, Richard and Theodore waited to speak to Colonel Fitzpatrick who soon approached Max with a broad grin and a firm enthusiastic handshake.

His excitement was palpable. "Good afternoon, Captain Bennington. Captain Eatonton, I told you when last we met, I would see this done. The end of the war is at hand gentlemen."

Max gave a nod. "Yes, you did. Colonel Fitzpatrick, let me introduce the proprietor of the *Key West Weekly*, Mr. Whitmore."

The colonel firmly shook Theodore's hand. "A pleasure to meet you, sir. I am one of your subscribers. Having an affinity for this island, it allows me to stay in touch with current events. I find it to be a quality publication."

Theodore tipped his head in acknowledgement. "Thank you. I owe much to my manager, Mr. Mason, as I have spent the majority of my time on the mainland observing the Florida war."

"Such would explain the detailed articles. So tell me, sir, having first-hand experience, do you believe our project will meet with success?"

For the sake of the hunted Theodore sincerely hoped not but he replied with diplomacy. "The end of the war would be a relief to all but having no experience with bloodhounds I couldn't say if you will meet with success."

"I on the other hand am quite confident. The man I purchased them from in Matanzas assures me they are excellent trackers."

Captain Bennington said, "If they are anything like British bloodhounds they should do you proud."

The colonel was quick to distinguish the two. "British bloodhounds are bred for tracking deer and wild boar. These are bred for tracking slaves."

Theodore hid his distaste for the idea of dogs tracking humans and focused on the task at hand. "I am interested in all the details. Would you mind making time for an interview later?"

"Why not walk with me now and ask your questions?"

Theodore was pleased by his offer. He opened his notebook as the four of them turned to walk toward the warehouse. "How many dogs did you purchase?"

"Thirty-four accompanied by five Spanish handlers."

"Where are you taking them?"

"First to the capital for the legislature to inspect them. Shortly after I expect they will be dispatched to the troops."

"What is the cost of this endeavor?"

"I haven't added it all together yet."

Theodore sensed his hesitation. "You know some of the costs though?"

"Well, yes. I purchased eighty-seven pounds of fresh beef before leaving Cuba to feed them. I believe at a very reasonable price of seven dollars."

Max laughed. "I wouldn't let word get out you have so much beef. You would discover it quite profitable to sell it and sail back to Cuba for more."

The colonel smiled. "That is a tempting idea. The expenses for this project are quite numerous and for now come from my pocket."

Theodore's gaze sharpened. "Why is that sir?"

"Politics and bureaucracy. I am confident in the success of this project so I fronted the money. I am sure I will be reimbursed upon delivery in Tallahassee."

"You didn't wait for congressional approval?" The colonel gave him a sharp look confirming Theodore's suspicion. "What other costs are there?"

"Wages for the handlers and their passports at about a hundred and sixty, six hundred to charter the sloop *Marshall* and another three hundred in other transport expenses."

"And how much for the dogs?"

The colonel knew the reaction he would receive to this number. He looked to his audience and for the first time realized Theodore was taking notes. "Are you going to print this in your paper?"

"Our readers would like to know."

"No!" Fitzpatrick vehemently shook his head. He momentarily forgot to whom he was speaking. "No, no, no. You mustn't disclose it. At least not yet. I must present this to the legislature. It certainly wouldn't do for them to get the information from your paper before I can give it to them. Promise you will not print the costs."

Theodore gave it some consideration and finally conceded. "Very well, I will not print the actual costs. But you have disclosed so much already, to satisfy my curiosity..."

Max chimed in. "And mine."

"How much did they cost?" Theodore closed his notebook to reaffirm his promise.

The nervous man looked around them and finding no one else in the vicinity quietly said, "Two thousand seven hundred."

Captain Bennington frowned. "Pesos?"

Fitzpatrick's mouth thinned. "Dollars."

Captain Bennington and Theodore were speechless. Max let out a long whistle.

Colonel Fitzpatrick's face reddened. He wondered how he had been led into this uncomfortable conversation and wished now he hadn't said a word. Their reaction reinforced his opinion it was a bad deal despite his contact's assurances otherwise. He tried to defend his actions. "These dogs are rare and have a reputation of success thereby making them more expensive than other dogs. Besides they can handle the heat. Most other tracking dogs come from colder climates."

While they were talking, the trainers led the restless dogs inside the warehouse away from the crowd and the noonday sun. The colonel held out his arm toward the warehouse entrance. "Come see for yourself."

They stepped from the bright sunlight into the dim interior of Mr. Browne's warehouse. Colonel Fitzpatrick led the way down the center isle with shipwrecked goods towering on either side to the rear of the building where makeshift pens were setup to hold the costly dogs. Henry and Christoff came running as soon as their fathers were in sight. They skidded to a halt on the dusty wooden floors speaking over top of each other in excited chatter.

Max said, "Slow down boys. One at a time."

Henry spoke first. "Mr. Rodolfo said we could both have a paying job feeding the dogs if it was alright with you. Can I Poppa?"

"Who is Mr. Rodolfo?"

Colonel Fitzpatrick pointed to one of the Spaniards. "He is the lead handler."

Theodore frowned. "Does he have authority to offer these boys pay?"

The colonel nodded. "Yes. He has funds for recruiting local assistance."

Max asked, "Is it safe for the boys?"

The colonel replied with a tight smile. "I'm sure Mr. Rodolfo would not have offered otherwise."

Theodore looked to Max and saw the same skepticism he himself felt at the colonel's hesitant assurance. Of an accord, the four men proceeded toward the pens with the boys trailing behind waiting hopefully for approval.

Theodore thought the dogs looked intimidating from a distance. Up close they were even more so.

Captain Bennington whispered to them, "English bloodhounds have long ears and are very affectionate. These are nothing of the kind."

Theodore studied the dogs before him. They were of short hair and averaged about two feet tall and three feet long with cropped ears and hind quarters somewhat resembling a greyhound while the rest made him think of a lesser-sized mastiff. A few of the dogs were mature but most looked to be yearlings. They also looked far from friendly.

Colonel Fitzpatrick called the five handlers over for an introduction. One of the dogs walked freely with them. The boys stepped forward to pet it. Theodore considered intervening until he noticed this dog was not like the others in temperament. Theodore spoke to the lead trainer, nodding to the hound. "This one is a female?"

Mr. Rodolfo nodded. "Si Señor, and the only one in the pack."

Christoff looked up at his sire. "Sir, may I accept the job?"

Just then two of the dogs in the pen began to quarrel. The viciousness with which they attacked each other settled the matter. Max sternly looked at Christoff. "No son, you may not."

Henry didn't bother asking; he saw the answer on his father's face. He wasn't disappointed. "Poppa, these dogs are nothing like Mr. Audubon's dog, Plato." Henry turned to Christoff. "Plato was bigger too and well behaved. He retrieved Mr. Audubon's kills, and he liked it all the better if he had to go swimming to do it." He turned back to Theodore. "Poppa, do you remember?"

"I do, son." Recalling Plato's behavior Theodore turned toward Colonel Fitzpatrick. "What happens when these dogs find their target?"

"What do you mean?"

Theodore had the suspicion Colonel Fitzpatrick was deliberately being obtuse so he turned to Mr. Rodolfo. "What happens when they find an Indian?"

The Spaniard proudly answered. "They will attack as they've been trained."

Max swallowed hard. "They will bite?"

Mr. Rodolfo shrugged. "And perhaps kill."

Captain Bennington turned to the colonel. "Is the legislature aware of this?"

It was the colonel's turn to swallow hard. "I believe so, yes."

Theodore thought again, this man should have been a politician.

Colonel Fitzpatrick and his pack of vicious dogs departed for Tallahassee on the twenty-fourth of December. Betsy knew before he told her Theodore planned to follow. The use of vicious dogs against a formerly peaceful people was not a story her husband would neglect to follow so it came as no surprise when he announced he would be leaving on the twenty-sixth.

It was late Christmas night. Theodore entered their bedroom after securing the house for the night to find Betsy standing at the window in her favourite cotton gown with her back to him. The moonlight streaming through the glass revealed her curvaceous silhouette. She stood on one bare foot, the other curved around her calf, one hand on the bed post for support, and the other on her chest. He knew without seeing, her thumb and forefinger would be curved around her neck as was her habit with her thumb rubbing along her pulse. Her dark tresses cascaded down her back in stark contrast to the white gown. She was not yet aware of his presence. He held still absorbing the beauty of the moment.

How can I leave her again? One would think by now he would be used to living in this state of confliction. But in some moments it was harder to accept than others and this was indeed one of them. He assumed she must be similarly deep in thought. He quietly moved forward to press against her back, slip his arms around her waist, and nuzzle the side of her neck.

Betsy inhaled deeply, savoring the pleasure of his touch knowing it would be many months before she felt it again—her mind continued the thought even though her heart shied away from it—provided nothing tragic happened. She dropped her foot to the floor, leaned back into his warmth, and wrapped both arms over his.

Theodore whispered in her ear. "You understand why I have to go, don't you?"

Betsy closed her eyes, pressed tight her trembling lips, and nodded, afraid speaking of it would reveal to him the depth of her distress. She slowly opened her dewy eyes and whispered, "I'm with child." Theodore pulled his arms away, momentarily alarming Betsy with his withdrawal, until his hands came to rest against the slight rise of her abdomen.

Theodore was surprised to feel the gentle rounding he visually hadn't noticed but should have. He turned her to face him. "How long have you known?"

"A few weeks."

He wondered why she hadn't told him sooner. "Are you happy about it?" She looked at him with her limpid eyes and nodded. "Then why the reservation?"

"I wasn't sure you would be happy."

He frowned. "Why would you think that?"

Betsy swallowed summoning the nerve to speak her mind. "For a while you were preventing another child."

Theodore's face brightened. He kissed her forehead and pulled her tight into his embrace. "I wanted to give you time after Agatha and not put you in the same situation as after Brianna's birth."

Betsy trembled and her eyes welled with the emotions his thoughtfulness invoked. She whispered, "Thank you."

Theodore stroked her head tucked under his chin. Being with child turned his normally composed wife into an emotional creature. "Did you think I didn't want any more children?"

She nodded, her cheek rubbing against his chest. The sound of his steady heartbeat comforted her. She needed him so. How was she to find the strength to let him go?

"I would be happy enough with the ones we have, but I know you have your heart set on a large family, and it is my strongest desire to give you anything you wish." He set her slightly away from him and placed a hand on either side of her head looking deeply in her eyes. "Betsafina, my love, if you ask it of me, I will stay."

She was sorely tempted to do so. She didn't want to let him go but she could never do something so selfish. The sincerity of his gaze nearly robbed her of breath and she swallowed against the burning tears.

He watched her face waver between a brave watery smile and tightly holding back her tears before she finally answered. "It is important that you expose the cruelty perpetrated on these people and their bravery in the face of adversity and the effect our nation's misguided intentions have on all of us."

"True but you and the children mean more to me than anything else. If the burdens of my absence are too great to bear, I will send someone in my stead."

Betsy smiled and lightly shook her head. "Teddy, who could you possibly send?"

He could almost physically see the strength returning to her soul.

She lifted her hands to grasp his upper arms and shook her head. "There is no one else who cares as much as you. Besides you started this and I know you want to see it through to the end. All things must end and one day; this war will too. Besides, this babe will arrive in summer. For once you will be home to welcome our child into the world."

His loins tightened as he watched her suck in and bite her lower lip; another one of her endearing habits. Unable to resist her charms a moment longer, she squealed in surprise as he swung her up in his arms and carried her to the bed. "I look forward to that day but not as much as I intend to enjoy this night."

Key West, January 1840

Betsy, feeling fatigued and gloomy, decided to take the girls and visit Abby. Her friend could always be counted on to pull her out of her despondency. They hadn't seen each other in weeks; not since Christmas dinner. Betsy rubbed a hand down the front of her skirt aware she could no longer hide her condition. She wondered what Abby would say.

As soon as the girls woke from their nap and were fed they left the house. Agatha's two year old gait made it a slow walk but Betsy did not have the energy to carry her. She breathed a sigh of relief when they finally reached their destination to be greeted by ten year old Emily who happily took charge of the toddlers.

Abby took one look at her and not only smiled broadly but laughed and hugged her as well, bewildering Betsy. When she stepped back she laid a hand on Betsy's belly. "I suspected you were with child at Christmas." She moved her hands to her own belly, smoothing her skirt to reveal the slight rounding. "I am too." Laughing together, they hugged again.

Betsy asked, "How far along are you?"

"Three months."

Betsy's smile grew. "I am too." Then she frowned. "So why am I so much bigger?"

Abby's grin broadened. "Perhaps this one is a boy."

Betsy shrugged. "Perhaps. This one does seem to be growing faster than the girls did. Maybe yours will be a girl." She laughed again. "I can't believe we are going to have babies the same age."

Abby linked arms with Betsy and turned toward the parlor to get comfortable. "They say misery loves company. It will be nice having someone to commiserate with these next six or seven months."

Central Florida, June 5th, 1840

The captain finally called a halt to the long day's march through tall pines and palmetto thickets. In short order, tents were pitched, horses fed, fires built, water hauled from the nearby river, and supper underway. The smell of frying meat teased their hungry appetites. Even after spending weeks with this regiment, Theodore was still awed by their efficiency. So different from his experience with previous commands.

A fast moving storm unexpectedly darkened the western sky preceded by strong winds whipping through the encampment carrying the smell of rain. Cooking activities were suspended as soldiers were forced to seek shelter from the sudden onslaught.

It wasn't the first time Theodore experienced the true force of nature without the barrier of a manmade structure but it was certainly the most nerve-wracking. The unmuted sound of rolling thunder and crashing lightening shook his very soul with their menace. The wind twisted trees brought another threat to bear as the crack and crash of nearby victims of the storm gave way to the reality of their vulnerable position. Trepidation kept even the most stoic eyes turned toward the overhead canopy of pines.

He couldn't help jumping at the violent cracks of thunder even with the precipitous lightening. The reaction wasn't fear so much as the unexpected closeness of the cacophony.

The first windy draughts of cooler air brought welcome relief from the heat of the day. Unfortunately, it didn't take long for it to become uncomfortably chilly in their wet clothes for the water seeped under coats no matter how snug they were pulled to the body. At least the mosquitoes were temporarily kept at bay.

An hour later the storm passed leaving behind stagnant humidity swarming with feasting insects. Now without dry wood, they couldn't finish preparing their meal or dry their wet feet. Theodore couldn't imagine a more miserable place to be. The rains were unexpected after years of drought. The settlers they encountered often told Theodore it was the wettest June in recent memory.

He shook the excess water from his head. So far it had been a miserable year. In January, he followed the dogs from Tallahassee to Saint Marks for training and testing. Initially, the results seemed effective bolstering the confidence of the army and the Florida residents. Not everyone was pleased. The Quakers, abolitionists and many other concerned citizens flooded their congressmen with complaints. Governor Reid was called to account for the project since the federal government had no prior knowledge of the territory's actions. He was given conditional approval to proceed.

In February, two trainers and ten dogs were assigned to General Taylor's 1st infantry. Theodore tagged along. In response to the criticism, Secretary Poinsett instructed General Taylor to keep the dogs muzzled and leashed while tracking and they were not allowed to disturb Indian women and children. In the end it was a moot point. While the trial proved successful in tracking slaves and Indians, when employed in finding Indian hideouts deep in the swamps the dogs failed miserably, succeeding in capturing only two Indians. Men heatedly debated if the swampy terrain was to blame or if it was because they were trained to scent slaves, not Indian. Theodore learned Lieutenant McLaughlin also acquired his own Cuban bloodhounds and met with the same result on his forays into the Everglades. By summer, all had given up using the dogs and Governor Reid was likewise forced to give up his multiple requests for reimbursement. Theodore could well imagine Colonel Fitzpatrick's disappointment.

May 5th, General Taylor was granted a transfer having the distinction of being the longest serving commander in the Florida War. He eventually was assigned to Fort Gibson in the Arkansas territory. Much to the dismay of those in the field, he was replaced by Brigadier General Walker Keith Armistead; previously second in command under General Jesup. Theodore's opinion of Armistead wasn't any better. He secretly agreed with Major Ethan Allen Hitchcock's assessment, calling the general's previous actions against the Seminole 'puerile'.

Theodore was ready to pack his bags and head home expecting the new commander to take the summer to plan his fall campaign same as his predecessors. It was a rough and rainy spring with disease running rampant through the troops. Desertion was common and there were some accused of deliberately injuring themselves to escape their duty. Theodore was looking forward to leaving the war scene for a while. Instead, Armistead wasted no time initiating a strong offensive campaign. It was with a heavy heart, knowing he would miss another child's birth, Theodore wrote Betsy to advise he would not be returning home anytime soon.

Armistead commanded an impressive thirty-four thousand men against an estimated thousand remaining Seminole, including women and children. He divided his men into patrols operating south of Fort King while he depended on the militia and volunteers to maintain control of the area north of Fort King. His patrols, comprised of a hundred men each, were sent out on search and destroy missions. They sought out hidden camps, destroyed crops, and drove off the livestock in an effort to starve the Indians into submission. By mid-summer it was estimated they destroyed over five hundred acres some of which were found in areas they believed free of Indian activity. Rarely did they encounter the Seminole on these raids. When they did, they were captured and transported west. As one soldier stated, alligators were more likely to fight than the Seminoles.

That was not to say the Seminoles weren't active. They boldly made hit and run attacks on troops and civilians and even more disturbing was their close proximity to white settlements. General Taylor's block system failed to keep the Indians south of Fort King. St. Augustine's citizens were reminded just how vulnerable they still were when Wild Cat led an attack in May against an army detachment killing six soldiers and later attacked two wagons belonging to a Shakespearean troupe killing three actors and absconding with the entire costume wardrobe. The citizens were once again unsettled and on high alert.

So here he was in June, attached to one of these patrols hoping to learn directly how the Indians were fairing after so many years of warfare. Instead, weeks later, he had discovered little about the Seminoles and too much about discomfort. Occasionally they would exchange fire with a few Indians in what could hardly be described as a skirmish much less an engagement. Troop morale was low, boredom plentiful, and desertion high. It had become a war without battles.

And he was at the mercy of this captain until they came to someplace where Theodore could safely part ways with the patrol and make his way toward some other area of interest. There were many to choose from with so much taking place these days and certainly safer places than where he was now. For starters, the army command recently moved from Tampa to St. Augustine. He could return to the comfort of a rented room. He would also like to see Colonel Harney's setup in Key Biscayne where he was training men how to survive and fight in the wetlands of Florida. Ideally, he would like to return to Tea Table Key to be near Betsy but he heard McLaughlin abandoned the base to finally act on his plans to invade the rivers and streams of the Everglades.

In reality, Theodore and everyone around him would rather be anywhere other than the rain-soaked sweltering swampland of central Florida.

* * *

Key West, June 6th, 1840

Betsy wiped the moisture from her brow with the back of her right hand still clutching a fan while she pressed the left one against the small of her back attempting to relieve the pain, hardly noticing the cool press of damp clothing against her skin. The girls skipped ahead of her, holding hands, on the way to the post office. If not for the possibility of a letter from Teddy, she would not have left the house today. Carrying this child was wearing her down. She didn't know how she would make it another six to eight weeks until it was time for his birth. She was sure it was a boy. She was so much larger than when she carried the girls. And that thought concerned her too. She worried about birthing such a large baby. But there was nothing to be gained from worry so she turned her thoughts to the letter. She hoped there wasn't one. No letter could mean Theodore was on his way home.

She took her time climbing the two steps to the post office door. The added weight made her unsteady. She smiled at the clerk despite a cramping pain around her middle, not really concerned as she had felt early pains with both of the girls.

The clerk said, "I have a letter for you Mrs. Whitmore."

She paid the postage and he slid it to her. Her smile faded when she recognized Theodore's script. She nodded to the clerk and turned to leave. "Come on girls."

Theodore's letters made her anxiously excited and this one even more so. She was always excited to hear from him. They were like having a part of him near to her again but she was always anxious in case they contained bad news as she strongly suspected this one to hold.

Progress home was slow and cumbersome. She vigorously fanned herself against the oppressive heat. She could feel the flush of her cheeks and for a second her vision wavered. She paused for a moment and took as deep a breath as the foot pressing against her lung would allow and immediately grew concerned by the rapidly developing need for an outhouse. She opened her eyes to look for the closest one to avail herself to with no concern if the owner would mind.

Long moments later with that need momentarily taken care of she called the girls back to her side and continued home holding her back and fanning her face. Halfway there they met Abby, Emily, and three year old Nathaniel. As it was Saturday, Christoff and Hawthorne were off somewhere with Henry and the rest of their friends.

Betsy couldn't help the little twinge of jealousy to see Abby looking fresh and energetic despite the heat and being with child.

Abby took one look at Betsy and knew her friend was in trouble. She let go of Nathaniel's hand. "Go to Brianna, son." She then turned to Emily. "I need you to go to Mrs. Mallory for help then hurry back and take the little ones to our house. Tell her we may need someone who can carry Mrs. Whitmore." Emily turned to walk in the direction of the boardinghouse. Abby called out after her. "Run."

The urgency in her mother's voice sent Emily racing for help.

Abby spoke soothingly to Betsy not wanting to cause her any further concern. She slipped her arm around Betsy's waist. "Shall we get you home? You look to be in need of a glass of water and a cool towel on your neck."

Betsy's voice wobbled much to her embarrassment. "I'd like that very much." Betsy thought they must have made a sight, two heavily burdened women, walking together. She looked down at their protruding bellies.

Abby followed her gaze. She and Betsy had often noted the difference in their size but standing this close the degree of difference made Abby think Betsy's time was at hand despite her belief otherwise. There was no way they conceived at the same time.

Betsy's moan confirmed her thinking. "How far apart are the pains?"

Betsy shook her head. "They're not regular and it's not time anyway."

Abby bit her lip but said nothing. She would discover the truth soon enough.

Hours later, Abby sat back in the chair to wipe her own brow and rest her back. Mrs. Mallory returned to the boardinghouse to handle supper but promised to come back later to relieve her. Betsy lay barely covered on the sweat soaked bed moaning as another pain hit her. Abby leaned forward to grasp her hand for comfort, concerned that her friend was barely conscious of her doing so. Betsy's other births had progressed normally. This one seemed to have stalled leaving her in a state of limbo with continued birthing pains but no progress toward an actual birth. Abby prayed there was nothing wrong with the baby. She pressed her hand against Betsy's abdomen and was reassured by the baby's movement inside.

Abby carefully noted the protrusions against Betsy's rounded belly and a suspicion grew. She stood up and placed both hands against the mound carefully feeling all over with her eyes closed the better to picture in her mind what her hands felt. She straightened and put a hand to her own aching back and held the other hand to her head pondering her conclusion.

She dropped it when Mrs. Mallory walked in anxious to share her discovery and see if the more experienced matron agreed.

Betsy was too tired to open her eyes. She heard the low murmuring and frowned. It felt like hands were pressing uncomfortably against her belly inside and out but it was the heat that bothered her most. It robbed her of any strength to protest. She whimpered as the fiery pain wrapped around her again. She breathed through it, thankful to rest when it was over. She felt the darkness creeping in on her again. The concern in Abby's voice made her fight to stay in the moment.

"There is something wrong."

It was no use. She was slipping again. "Teddy" *Where are you?* There was so much she wished she could have told him.

Chapter 40

The same day, somewhere in middle Florida

Theodore poured the gritty remains of his strong morning coffee over the embers of his campfire and adjusted the pack on his back. The resulting sizzle and musky vapor were part of the morning ritual of life on patrol. In front of him, the sun was peeking between the pines, the light catching on the dew moistened leaves of the palmettos. All around him, the rest of the patrol was doing the same knowing the captain would expect to move out shortly. A scout brought news last night of a nearby hideout believed to be Wild Cat's and the patrol captain was anxious to investigate.

Theodore fell in line as they marched away from their campsite. His mind drifted to thoughts of Betsy and his children as he followed the soldier in front of him along the edge of another swamp, one of the endless many dotting the Florida landscape. Absently his gaze tracked the flight of a white egret fleeing between the cypresses. Losing sight of it, his eyes drifted down to the water looking for more birds instead he saw a movement behind a tree. He focused on the spot and soon saw the face of a warrior looking in the captain's direction at the head of their line. A rifle came into view. Theodore opened his mouth to issue a warning but it was too late. The shot was fired and the trees erupted with the Indian war cry. The soldiers immediately raised their loaded rifles to return fire. Men fell all around him and then the warriors rushed from the trees to execute a close attack on those soldiers still standing.

Theodore instinctively fired his gun at the young brave charging him with knife raised ready to kill. When the smoke cleared, the blood splattered body lay before him. It was the son of a warrior Theodore knew well and respected. For a moment he stood there, hearing nothing, seeing only the terrible deed he had done. He looked at the lifeless face. Without the snarl of battle twisting his features, Theodore could only see a boy close in age to Henry.

What have I done?

With an effort, Theodore tore his eyes away from the body. He scanned the smoke shrouded scene around him, seeing but not hearing. Soldiers were firing and reloading from the cover of trees. The Indians were retreating, having lost the element of surprise. Theodore saw all of this but heard nothing. A young warrior he didn't recognize cautiously approached to grab the arm of the boy and drag him away. Theodore's gaze followed the marks left in the loamy soil. They disappeared into the greenery along with the odd silence. The report of gunfire and yelling assailed his consciousness pulling Theodore back into the moment. He glanced down again at the earth before him to see the only visual evidence of his action but he knew somewhere beyond him a lifeless boy would be returned to his mother.

Kill or be killed.

It was a solid defense but it still did not in his mind atone for taking the boy's life. In all these years he avoided doing anything more than wounding an Indian in the first battle on the Withlacoochee. He considered his hands clean. He knew he was guilty by association but not by deed.

Not until this day.

Key West

The searing pain around her abdomen pulled Betsy from the dark void into the light of reality. She opened her eyes to see Abby's concerned face hovering over hers. She sighed as a cold compress helped ease her burning skin. She wanted to thank Abby but the effort to speak was too great. *Dear Lord, please take this pain from me. I cannot bear it...*

The slant of sunlight across the bedroom floor told Betsy it was late afternoon. She must have slept. She was surprised she could have slept and in the middle of the thought a strong contraction made her raise up and scream with the strength of it. Mrs. Mallory was quickly there to support her. Betsy was unsure how long she had been in labor. Fear assailed her mind. Something was wrong. This birth was different. The pain ebbed and flowed but there was a constant to it unlike her other deliveries. Weakness followed the contraction. She felt wetness touch her lips before she slipped away again.

The next time she opened her eyes it was dark. At first she didn't see anyone in the room. A small panic took hold until she saw Abby in the corner chair. She lifted her hand, thankful, when the small movement was enough to bring Abby to her side to give her a sip of water and wipe her brow. Betsy felt feverish with the pain and hazy all around. The edges blurred and faded again.

The urgent necessity to push brought her back to awareness. Relief washed over her to know the end was near. She opened her eyes to see Abby and Mrs. Mallory on either side of her. The room was now well lit with several oil lamps. Betsy knew she needed strength. *The Lord is my shepherd. I shall not want...*

Mrs. Mallory leaned close while holding her hand. "Tis time, Betsy. Dat's it lass. Give it all you got. Push dear."

So weak. So tired. She pushed with what little strength she had left. Not enough.

Her eyes drifted closed.

She lost time.

Burning pain made her wearily open her eyes to find Mrs. Mallory pushing on her stomach adding another layer of torture to the already unbearable pain. Betsy moaned in agony and tried to do her part. Finally she felt the release of the head followed by the slide of the shoulders. She fell back on the pillow with a sigh of relief. She closed her eyes only intending to rest. She tried to stay awake waiting for her baby to cry. She couldn't do it. The darkness claimed her once again.

When next she surfaced, she thought she must be dreaming. She felt contractions again. *Why?* Why were there still birthing pains? Surely she hadn't imagined the birth she felt a while ago. She wanted to ask someone. Her eyelids were too heavy to open. Frustration surged and faded as the darkness took over again.

Betsy slowly woke to Abby urgently rubbing her arm.

"Betsy dear. You have to wake up, love. You need to push one more time."

She didn't understand what she was feeling. More pushing? She was so tired of the pain. She wanted it to end; wanted to sleep. *Please Lord, take this pain from me.* She must have only dreamed of giving birth earlier. She turned beseeching eyes to the ladies in the room going back and forth between each one searching for answers to unasked questions plaguing her mind. From her dry parched lips she croaked, "Baby?"

Abby smiled and brushed the hair from her damp forehead. "You have a daughter, but you are not done. You need to push again." The ladies now on either side of her lifted her shoulders.

Betsy could not make sense of Abby's words. They wouldn't register in her mind. She didn't understand why she must push again when she had already given birth. So confusing. She felt her body's urging and did as it commanded but she felt even weaker than before. There wasn't any strength left. The darkness enveloped her mind. She tried to fight it, to stay in the moment, but it wouldn't allow her to stay awake. In her weakness, she was forced to succumb.

She opened her eyes to the dimly lit room. A lamp turned low provided the only illumination but it was enough to see she was alone. What happened? Where was her baby? Where was Abby? Most of all, where was Theodore? She needed him and his comforting presence. She felt the tears slipping down her cheeks. She closed her eyes. Her body was sore all over, like she had been put through the washer ringer.

So weak.

She couldn't even lift her hand to her head. While she was assessing her condition, she heard the door move and footsteps. She opened her eyes to see Abby hovering over her looking tired and concerned.

Abby smiled. "How are you feeling?"

Betsy's parched throat made her voice sound scratchy, "Sore. Thirsty."

She only had strength for the two words. She wanted to say so much more.

Abby brought a glass of water and lifted her head. She urged her to drink slowly. "If you can keep this down I will bring you some beef broth. You need to get your strength back. You have two hungry daughters to feed."

Betsy blinked. She couldn't have heard right. Why two? Agatha wasn't nursing anymore.

Abby saw her friend's puzzled look and realized Betsy, having been unconscious and delusional with pain during most of the delivery, wasn't aware of what happened. Her smile broadened. "Dear, you have twins." She lightly laughed at Betsy's blank stare and nodded in confirmation. "Two more daughters."

Betsy's feeble mind was having trouble absorbing the news.

"Are you ready to meet them?"

Betsy gave what she hoped was a smile.

Abby helped her sit up, fluffed her pillows, and then helped prop Betsy on them. She left the room and came back with a wrapped little bundle in each arm. Betsy lifted her arms to take one but they were so weak she was forced to let them fall back to the bed. Abby understood. She placed a sleeping bundle on either side of Betsy's legs.

Betsy put her left hand against the cheek of the baby on her left. Her right hand brushed across the downy hair of the other and then ran her finger down the soft cheek.

Thoughts scampered across her mind. They were so tiny! She didn't remember Agatha or Brianna being this small. They had red hair just like her twin brothers. She remembered how hard it was helping her mother with them. How was she to care for two of them by herself? The thought overwhelmed her, so she tried not to dwell on it. Instead she focused on the perfect little cherubs sleeping peacefully.

Abby sat down in the chair with a sigh. "They have been fed." Betsy looked to her for explanation. "You have been asleep for more than a day. I had to get them a wet nurse."

"Oh." Betsy wasn't sure how she felt about someone else nursing her babies; grateful, ashamed, concerned.

Abby looked at her gravely. "We thought we lost you a few times. You cannot imagine how frightened I was or how happy I am to see you on the mend." Abby impatiently brushed aside a tear. "Enough of that." She smiled again. "What are you naming them?"

Betsy shook her head. She was having trouble keeping up with her own flying thoughts much less Abby's. When her last question finally registered, Betsy shook her head again. "We only picked one name for a girl. Emmaline Grace." Betsy looked down at the two babies.

Abby said, "The one on the right was born first." She smiled. "We were having trouble keeping up with which one was which so we tied a piece of yarn to her ankle."

Betsy returned her smile. "We did the same when my twin brothers were born."

Abby's eyebrows flew up. "You have twin brothers?"

Betsy nodded. "And they have red hair too."

Abby bit her bottom lip. "I might have guessed you were having twins sooner if I had known."

"I'm not sure why it never occurred to me either. Both my grandmothers are twins. They happen a lot in my family." She looked down again still in awe-struck wonder to have two more little ones. Four daughters. She secretly smiled. What was Teddy going to think of all these girls? "Well, I guess the first one will be Emmaline. Theodore should be home soon. Perhaps we can wait till then to name the other one." And then she remembered. "Where's my letter?"

Abby retrieve it from the dresser handing the badly crumpled parchment to Betsy. "You didn't want to let it go."

Betsy accepted it. "Thank you, Abigail. For everything." She shook her head as her eyes welled with hot tears. "I think you likely saved all three of us."

Overwhelmed, Abby leaned down and hugged her dear, dear friend, knowing how easily it could have turned out different. She stepped back. "Would you like me to give you a moment to read your letter?"

"There's no need for you to leave however you do look as if you should go home and rest. How long have you been here?"

Maria happened to walk in with a tray of food and her six month old son on her hip. "She has not left your side for more than a few hours at a time, Mrs. Betsy, no matter how much I've tole her she needs to go home. I can stay here with you. Thomas won't mind."

Betsy looked to Abby. "I fully agree with Maria. You need to go home and rest. You've done enough for me. Take care of yourself."

Abby threw her hands up. "All right, I will now that I know you are safe. Nothing was going to pull me from your side until then."

Betsy looked to Maria. "I owe you a debt of gratitude. I assume you are the wet-nurse Abby mentioned."

Maria shook her dark head. "No need ma'am. It was my pleasure to hold your little ones. They are strong like their mammy."

Betsy grinned. "Thank you." She looked from one lady to the other, so opposite in looks and yet so similar in heart. She held out her hands and they both stepped forward to take them. "I am so blessed to have you both as friends. And Mrs. Mallory."

Abby laughed. "Betsafina, you are NOT going to make me cry again." She squeezed Betsy's hand. "I think my children have missed me long enough. I will go home, give them all a kiss, and take a very long nap."

Betsy smiled and reluctantly let her go.

At the door, Abby turned around. "I will come by tomorrow to check on you."

Maria placed the tray on the table beside the bed, handed Betsy the mug of broth from it, and followed Abby out of the room leaving her and the babies alone. Betsy inhaled the rich aroma. She took a careful swallow then returned it to the table. She took a piece of cheese from the tray, her need for nourishment as strong as her need to read the letter.

She broke the wax seal and unfolded the paper with shaking hands. She smoothed it against her leg then took a deep breath and began reading. She pressed her lips tightly together but it didn't help. He wasn't coming home. She held his heartbreaking words against her chest as the wracking sobs escaped her control. It didn't matter how tight she squeezed her eyes shut, the scalding tears still slipped down her cheeks and under her chin. She cried so hard her throat grew tight and she could hardly breathe.

Downstairs, Maria wavered between giving her friend the privacy she deserved or the comfort she so desperately needed. She put herself in Betsy's place and settled on giving her space.

Four weeks later, Abby brought her children to meet the newest members of the Whitmore family. The two ladies shared the divan in the parlor as they watched over their children, now nine in total and soon to be ten.

Abby absently rubbed her thumb over the unborn bottom pushing against her side. "Can you believe all these children belong to us? Can you remember the last time you had a hot cup of tea uninterrupted by a thousand questions?"

Betsy snickered. "I remember dreaming and hoping for these days."

"Even the tepid tea?"

Betsy shrugged. "It's too warm here for hot tea anyway."

Abby laughed. "You are nothing if not practical."

"Speaking of being practical, I have finally come up with a name for Baby Jane." Brianna dubbed the second twin Baby Jane until a proper name could be decided upon. Theodore's letter said not only was he not coming home, but he would likely be out of touch most of the summer. Betsy hated not having his input but neither did she want to leave her poor child unnamed for months on end.

Abby's face showed her eagerness. "And?"

"I am naming her after my mother, Madalyn Claire."

Abby smiled. "Emmaline Grace and Madalyn Claire. They are both beautiful names."

"Thank you."

Christoff nudged Hawthorne forward who sheepishly looked from his mother to Betsy. "May we be 'scused now?"

Betsy smiled. "Certainly."

The older boys made a rapid exit from the room leaving behind Agatha and Nathanial playing with blocks while Brianna and Emily were holding the newborns. Emily was more interested in tagging along with the boys, especially Henry. She handed Madalyn back to her mother, sedately walked to the door, and as soon as she cleared her mother's sight, sprinted after them.

Key Biscayne, Thursday, August 6th

In the rosy light of evening, Theodore stood on the deserted beach of Cape Florida facing the Atlantic Ocean puffing on a cigar purloined from Lieutenant McLaughlin. He arrived on the island over a week ago thankful to put the wilds of the Florida mainland behind him. The only thing worse than trekking through swampland was trekking through rainy flooded swampland, so for the first few days on this island, it was enough to be clean, dry, and able to enjoy the fresh breeze off the open water. But now he was getting restless waiting for some kind of transportation bound for Key West. Home was just a two day sail away. It frustrated him to be so close yet unable to move forward.

The faint sounds of Colonel Harney and his recruits returning from field training drifted to him, along with the aroma of cooking meat from the mess tent. Life on a military post was a predictable routine. The rhythmic crunch of seashells beneath the soldier's boots heralded the second lieutenant's approach; a young red head, newly graduated from West Point, on his first assignment.

"May I join you sir?"

"Hmm." Theodore didn't care one way or the other.

The young man lit his cigar trying to act like he knew what he was doing, the coughing spell that followed his first drag proved otherwise. Ruefully he nodded to Theodore as if unaware he was disturbing his peace.

Theodore cut his eyes at the young man. "What was your name again, son?"

"Sherman, W. T., sir. Folks call me Cump."

Theodore frowned. "Why?"

"On account of my middle name is Tecumseh."

Theodore half smiled. "And how did you come by that moniker?"

"My father admired the Shawnee chief."

"My name's Theodore Whitmore."

Sherman eagerly shook his hand and smiled. "I know. I've read your stories in the paper. Did you ever meet him?"

"Who?"

"Tecumseh."

"No."

"Too bad. I would have liked to hear you describe him. You've met Osceola, right?"

"Hmm."

"What was he like?"

"Thoughtful, inquisitive, dignified. Often silent."

"He seemed like a fascinating man."

"Hmm."

Sherman lapsed into silence at the lack of encouragement. Theodore idly watched an arriving schooner anchor offshore in the hopes that here finally may be his way home. A launch was lowered and filled with a half dozen men. As they progressed to shore, he wondered if he might know any of them.

Sherman ground out his half smoked cigar under his boot heel. "I'm putting together a card game later. Thought you might be interested."

Theodore absently said, "Maybe."

The second lieutenant walked away. A short while later the launch made it to shore. Theodore was pleased to see Captain Maloney of Indian Key disembark. The two greeted each other warmly.

"Mr. Whitmore. I must say you do travel far and wide. I should not be surprised to find you here, but I am."

"I'm making my way home after too many months spent walking across the peninsula."

"Between the savages, alligators, snakes, mosquitos and rain it's a wonder you made it out of there at all."

"It was tortuous at times."

"Guess you're waiting here for a boat home."

"I am sir."

Captain Maloney clapped him on the back. "I'm headed back day after tomorrow. You're welcome to join me."

"Sir, that's the best news I've had in months."

"There something left to eat around here? I'm starving."

"You have just enough time to clean up before mess is served."

The two men sat together for their meal.

Captain Maloney smiled at him. "I just moved my family back to Key West a few weeks ago."

"Your family?"

"Yes, I have a son, Walter Jr, almost a year old now. By the way, congratulations..."

Eager for news of his family, Theodore interrupted him. "Boy or girl? Have you seen Mrs. Whitmore? Is she well?"

Captain Maloney laughed. "Slow down. I take it you have been out of touch for quite a while."

Theodore's face tightened. "Yes."

Captain Maloney inwardly grinned. He wasn't going to be the one to spoil Theodore's surprise. "Your wife is doing well last I heard and you still have only one son."

Theodore smiled. "Another daughter. What is her name?"

Captain Maloney shook his head. "I'm afraid I don't know."

The men talked for hours that evening sharing news. When he finally retired to his tent, Theodore slept peacefully knowing soon he would be home. Soon he would hold his new daughter. Soon he would sleep in a comfortable bed, with his wife. The smile lingered as he drifted off to sleep.

Friday, August 7th, late morning

The occupants of Key Biscayne were enjoying a pleasant morning until the arrival of Charles Stuart from Indian Key. He barely pulled his small vessel ashore before he went running for the command tent. The commotion brought Theodore and Lieutenant McLaughlin outside. The sailor skidded to a halt in front of them breathing hard from his exertions.

"Indian Key is under attack, sir."

McLaughlin's inquisitive lighthearted look instantly sobered. "How long ago?"

"It started a couple hours after midnight. I was returning from a hunting trip and was about to land when I heard the war cries and gunfire. I pushed off before they could see me and headed here for help."

McLaughlin's voice thundered. "Damn savages. They must have been lying in wait."

Theodore turned to him. "What do you mean?"

"It cannot be a coincidence they attacked the same night after Lieutenant Rogers left with every able-bodied man and ship that could be spared."

Theodore knew McLaughlin dispatched Lieutenant Rogers to Cape Romano where he would lead a west to east expedition across the Everglades seeking out Indian hideouts. He must have ordered him to stop at the base on Tea Table Key for reinforcements and supplies.

McLaughlin turned to Second Lieutenant Sherman. "Gather some men to take a dispatch recalling Lieutenant Rogers." Then he ordered the other men nearby to prepare for immediate departure to lend aide if needed and to investigate if it be too late to render assistance to the occupants of Indian Key. Theodore asked and received permission to join him.

It was late afternoon when they sailed past Upper Matecumbe. Tea Table Key was just ahead with a navy post and hospital. A half mile further south lie the settlement of Indian Key. Both were tiny islands between Upper and Lower Matecumbe Keys. McLaughlin ordered his crew to circle the area then anchor near Tea Table Key.

The acrid smell of smoke and ash lingered on the breeze as they approached Indian Key. They sailed past as close as the shoals would allow. All seemed quiet. The men were silent as they faced the still smoldering devastation. The once beautiful island lay in ruins. Gone was the lavish home of Jacob Housman, his hotel, his store and the warehouse. His losses were substantial. Gone too was the unusual house Theodore visited last summer to interview Dr. Perrine. The house interested Theodore more than the botanist for during high tide three sides were surrounded by water. The once beautiful two story with copula and double porch was now nothing more than a pile of debris filling the cellar. Only Mr. Howe's residence and a few outbuildings were left standing.

The ship circled back to Tea Table Key and anchored near the naval schooner, *Medium*. Anxious for news, Lieutenant McLaughlin wasted no time making his way over to the other vessel. He surveyed the displaced residents scattered around the deck before turning to his junior officer. "Midshipman Murray, what is your report?"

Theodore listened carefully, rapidly taking notes of their exchange.

"Sir, the Indians left the area a few hours ago. They retreated towards Lower Matecumbe. I dispatched a boat in search of survivors. It returned with two men severely burned from the fire and two ladies and a child badly sunburned. We have forty something souls on board with varying degrees of injury and as you can see most are lacking proper dress. There was an attempt made in a smaller boat at daybreak to block the Indians' escape but it failed. One soldier was shot in the leg."

Concern flooded Theodore. He looked to the messenger. "And Key West? Was it attacked as well?"

Murray shook his head. "I don't know, sir."

McLaughlin gave Theodore a stern look warning him not to interrupt again then turned back to Murray. "Start at the beginning and tell me what happened?"

"Just after the moon set, around two a.m. The carpenters, Glass and Bieglett, discovered more than a dozen canoes pulled up on the south beach and perhaps two hundred Indians sneaking towards the warehouse. On the way to sound the alarm they were spotted by the Indians. Gun fire and yelling commenced waking the residents and fortunately giving them time to escape. The savages looted and burned for roughly twelve hours. They were mostly loaded and gone when the arrival of wreckers from Tavernier sent the rest of them fleeing. They took all the small boats kept at the island except those the residents used to escape."

"Is everyone accounted for?"

"No sir."

"How many are missing?"

"Mrs. Johnson, Mrs. Elliott Smith's nephew, Joseph Sturdy, and a few slaves."

"Have you looked for them?"

"Not yet."

McLaughlin scanned those on the deck. "Where is Captain Housman?"

"He and his family are on Tea Table Key."

"And Dr. Perrine?"

Murray's face stiffened. "We don't believe he made it, sir."

Theodore's gut tightened to hear this.

McLaughlin kept his emotions hidden. "And his family?"

"They are below deck, sir, in the main quarters."

McLaughlin nodded. "Have two boats made ready with armed men and lanterns to look for survivors."

Theodore was not the only one anxious to join the search party. Young Henry Perrine begged to be allowed to join them along with Charles Howe and his son Ralph. Theodore's heart tore at the lad's bravery. At thirteen, this Henry was a little younger than his son, Henry.

Twenty minutes later in the growing twilight they stepped ashore of the eerily quiet island. Theodore realized one didn't notice the sounds of birds or insects until they were conspicuously missing. The men fanned out searching the island for survivors. Theodore and McLaughlin followed Mr. Howe to his unburnt house.

McLaughlin turned to Theodore. "You understand these savages better than most. Why do you think one house was spared?"

"I can only speculate, but it most likely would be out of respect for the owner or perhaps they ran out of time."

McLaughlin raised his lantern as he climbed the steps. "I'm curious to see if anything is missing."

The house was thoroughly ransacked. All the food and valuables taken, mattresses torn apart and the ticking removed, debris strewn everywhere inside and out. The general disorder made the careful display of Masonic items on a small table seem odd.

Mr. Howe frowned as he walked to the table. "I kept these in a trunk in my room. I haven't looked at them in years."

Some speculation was made as to the emblem of the all-seeing eye being the reason the house was not burned. Perhaps the Indians were superstitious. Whatever the reason, Mr. Howe was grateful to still have a place to live.

The men left the house to greet the others returning with the missing Mrs. Johnson who stood silent obviously suffering from shock.

The captain reported to McLaughlin. "We found her hiding in the bathhouse at the end of Mr. Maloney's wharf. We also found the Mott family."

McLaughlin said, "Where are they?"

"Down by the beach, shot and scalped, the baby drowned, and the other child bludgeoned to death."

The news broke Mrs. Johnson's silence. She began a keening wail and was escorted away. The men were silently taking in the horror he described. Finally McLaughlin said, "They will need to be buried."

"We covered them in a sheet for now."

"What of the Sturdy boy?"

The captain shook his head. "No one has answered our calls."

McLaughlin nodded. They could only assume he was dead or worse, taken. "It's too dark now. We'll resume the search tomorrow."

A few men were left to guard the island, the rest of them returned to the *Medium* where McLaughlin began interviewing everyone, each story more harrowing than the last. Some hid behind rocks on the beach to escape the Indians but there was no hiding from the blistering summer sun. Others hid under houses until they were torched then made their escape to the sea. Several made their way to boats to seek refuge on the *Medium*.

The fate of Joseph Sturdy was finally learned when McLaughlin interviewed Mr. Bieglett. The boy was hiding with him and a sailor in the cistern of the warehouse when it was set fire. The boy suffocated in the dense smoke. Mr. Bieglett and the sailor had blistering burns about their arms and shoulders and scorched hair testifying to their narrow escape. McLaughlin promised the boy's distraught aunt and mother they would retrieve his body on the morrow.

Having interviewed all those on deck, McLaughlin proceeded to those given solace in the cabins below deck, starting with the Perrine family. His knock was answered by Henry whose posture revealed, despite being the youngest member of the family, he was already assuming his father's role as protector.

McLaughlin addressed the son, but his question was directed towards Mrs. Perrine. "I wondered if I could have a few moments of your time to ask a few questions."

Henry looked to his mother for a response and receiving none decided for himself to allow them entry. Mrs. Perrine and her daughters reflexively gathered the sheets they were wearing tighter around their shoulders. Ash and soot had been washed from their faces but still clung to their hair. Mrs. Perrine's hollow countenance tore at Theodore's heart. He could well imagine Betsy wearing the same expression if something happened to him.

Mrs. Perrine tended her eldest daughter Sarah who lay prostrate on the small bunk. Her back remained to the room leaving Henry to relate their story with occasional comments from his sister, Hester.

Taking his cue from Mrs. Perrine, McLaughlin directed his questions to Henry. "Son, can you tell me what happened?"

"We was attacked by Indians."

"Yes, I know, but how did you escape?"

"Through the turtle crawl and in a boat."

"Can you tell me everything starting from when you woke up?"

"Yes sir. My sister, Hester, woke me up. The Indians were all around our house. We could hear them yelling and whooping, breaking glass and making mischief. Father led us downstairs to the bathing room."

"Bathing room?"

Theodore wondered about that too. He had never heard of such a thing.

"There's a trap door to get under the house and when the tide comes in its deep enough to take a bath so we bathe there."

"I see. Go on."

"Father sent us under the house but he didn't come too. He left us saying 'he would see what he could do.'" Emotions got the better of him so Hester took over.

"We could hear father speaking to the Indians in Spanish telling them he was a physician. For a while they went away. We could hear them looting the other houses around us. Father came back and told us to hide. Then he closed the trap door and slid the heavy chest over it, concealing it, I suppose." She bit her lip and frowned. "That was the last time we saw him." She sobbed as she said the last.

Henry took up the story. "It was still dark outside and even darker under the house. The water was high too. We had to feel along the wall with our hands to find the passageway between the house and the turtle kraal. We waited there in water up to our necks for the Indians to leave the island and for father to tell us it was safe but at dawn the Indians returned. They took wood from the pile on the dock and used it to break into the house because father locked them out. We could hear them searching and smashing things. I heard one of them speak plain as could be in English, 'They are all hid. Old man upstairs.' Then they beat down the door to the copula where father was hiding."

Henry swallowed hard. Theodore thought he wouldn't be able to finish but he gathered himself and continued. "They were taking everything and walking right over our heads to load it into the boats. We were under the dock behind the kraal by then and we were almost discovered. The turtles started splashing and one of the Indians opened the trap door to look inside. Thank goodness he didn't look towards us or we would have been found and killed. When they were done taking everything they set fire to the house. Ma made us keep waiting. She was afraid they would come back. Eventually the house collapsed and the deck planks above us caught fire. By now, the tide was out and the smoke was thick so we were forced to put our faces down where there was just a few inches of water left."

Hester said, "The smoke grew so thick even though we were clasped together we couldn't see each other's face. We tried using the water and marl to put out the fire and covered ourselves with it to keep from getting burned."

In a thin voice, as if he was reliving it, Henry said, "I wanted out but mother wouldn't let me."

Hester grimaced. "He started screaming and we were afraid the Indians would return so mother covered his mouth and I held his arms."

Anger surged in the lad. "I told them I'd rather be killed by Indians than burn to death. I was stronger than them too. I pulled away and squeezed through the posts into the turtle pen and climbed out the trap door."

Hester shook her head. "We thought for sure he would be killed. We kept waiting but no sound came. We couldn't get out the way he did so mother started digging out the marl around a post with her bare hands while

I held Sarah."

Theodore grimaced. He had noticed Mrs. Perrine's hands were cut and raw. That she had inflicted the wounds upon herself to save her girls was testament to a mother's love.

Hester sadly shook her head. "My sister's been deathly sick for weeks and she was too weak to hold herself above the water. It seemed like it took a very long time but mother finally got the post out and we made our way to the end of the pen with the trap door. A pile of wood on the dock was burning too and the embers were dropping on us. Sarah's shoulder is badly burned. We almost waited too late to get out, but once we did I saw Henry had reached shore. There was a beached boat near him. I signaled to him to meet us there."

Henry said, "I ended up having to help them get to the boat because they were carrying Sarah."

Hester nodded. "She thought she was dying and told us to leave her right there in the water. Of course we wouldn't do it. When we did reach the boat we had to tumble her in it then drag it off the beach. Twice we grounded," she smiled at her brother, "but Henry managed to get us free."

Henry shrugged off her praise. "We got a little bit away when we saw two Indians coming after us from Lower Matecumbe so we paddled faster. They gave up and landed at the beach we just left. It turned out there were still some Indians looting the store and we took their boat loaded with plunder so they had to be rescued." He said the last with a smile, pleased he had caused trouble for their foe.

McLaughlin smiled at both children. "I'm glad you made it away safely. So many things might have prevented your escape." McLaughlin turned to their mother. "Mrs. Perrine, you have very brave children. This room is quite small for the four of you and your daughter needs rest to recover. If you would like, tomorrow we could move you to my state-room aboard the *Flirt* where you will be more comfortable."

She nodded her agreement and they bid the family good night. As McLaughlin and Theodore stepped into the passageway they looked at each other.

McLaughlin said, "Theirs is a most harrowing experience as ever I heard. Nearly murdered, drowned, and burned to death in their escape."

Theodore knew he would carry their horrific interviews in his mind same as Captain Hitchcock's telling of the Dade Massacre battlefield. To McLaughlin he said, "The bitter irony is Dr. Perrine brought his family to Indian Key to wait out the war in safety before taking up his land grant near Key Biscayne." It occurred to him Dr. Perrine had tried to remain safe only to perish at the hands of the Indians while he repeatedly put himself in harm's way over the last five years. It was a sobering reminder of how easily the worst could happen to him and leave his family hurting like this one. Instead of ending, this war kept moving closer to home and once again he was questioning his determination to see it through to the end.

Saturday morning, at first light they headed to Tea Table Key to interview the soldiers and Captain Housman. Theodore was impressed with the thoroughness of Lieutenant McLaughlin's investigation and his concern for the displaced citizens.

At dawn the morning of the attack, Housman, Midshipman Murray, and five soldiers sailed a barge between Indian Key and Tea Table Key with the thought of preventing the Indians' escape. Theodore thought it a strange thing to do but said nothing since McLaughlin didn't question their motives. They soon found themselves fired upon from every vantage point on the island. One soldier was severely wounded in the thigh. Misfortune continued when they ran aground forcing them to fire the two four-pounder cannons from athwart ship instead of from the bow or stern. The recoil from the discharge sent the cannons overboard. It was later discovered in their rush they picked up six-pound bags of powder instead of four-pound thereby overloading the guns, resulting in their loss. Meanwhile, the Indians loaded musket balls into Housman's six-pounder cannons on the island and fired back at them. They now had no choice but to retreat back to base. McLaughlin's displeasure in their performance was clear to be seen, but he held his tongue for now, perhaps due to Theodore's presence.

After the interviews, they returned to Indian Key where McLaughlin had some of the men walk him through the events of the previous morning so he could better understand the incident as a whole, specifically, where Glass and Bieglett discovered the Indians. He was also shown where the Motte family perished. Mr. & Mrs. Motte found lying together, their clothes burned from their bodies and scalped. McLaughlin assigned a detail to inter them with their girls at a place of Mrs. Johnson's choosing as the surviving family member. Then he kept his promise to search for Joseph Sturdy's body. He and several other men including Theodore began sifting through the rubble of the warehouse.

Late in the afternoon, Theodore was knee deep in the cistern when he removed a piece of wood siding uncovering the boy's boiled body. He turned his head away and nearly retched from the horror of the blackened and crackled skin covering the corpse. At least Joseph hadn't died that way, although Theodore couldn't imagine suffocating from smoke to be any better. He shook his head mentally wanting to erase one more scene added to the macabre collection of them he had gathered over the course of the war. He called out to McLaughlin to send down a towel to wrap the poor boy. It was the only way he could find the mental fortitude required to get him out of the cistern.

Theodore wasn't the only one taking care of the deceased. Mr. Howe helped Henry Perrine gather what bones they could find of his father and place them in a box which was handed over to Hester as Mrs. Perrine could not be persuaded to take it. Hester requested they be interred under his prized sisal hemp plant on Lower Matecumbe.

Some clothing, mostly dresses, were found strewn about the island. Mr. Howe thoughtfully collected them much to the relief of the ladies on board the *Medium*.

Captain Maloney arrived in the afternoon. He too explored the devastation before meeting up with Theodore and McLaughlin. "Do you know what I find strange?"

McLaughlin frowned. "There are many oddities in this attack, what particularly have you noted?"

"There is not the usual ferociousness of the attack, other than the Motte family and Dr. Perrine. They did not give chase. The motive seems to be supplies rather than death. If it were retaliation, more would have been killed. Do you agree?"

Theodore nodded. "I've been thinking it likely our summer campaign of destruction created the need for supplies, forcing them into this bold action. I wonder where else they have targeted?"

"Nowhere else in the keys or we would have heard by now."

A gust of wind had the men turning their eyes skyward. Captain Maloney grimaced. "Looks like we may have a storm this evening."

McLaughlin agreed. "Aye."

Captain Maloney said, "Mr. Whitmore, I believe we will stay here for the night and set sail for Key West tomorrow."

Theodore knew it to be a wise decision but still the delay frustrated him. Before returning to the *Medium* to gather his belongings, Theodore stood on the wall that once supported the Perrine home looking at the collapsed house filling the cellar and the burned wood of the dock over the family's hiding place. Through the gaping hole he could see the missing post allowing the ladies to escape. It was truly by the grace of God they survived.

From the evidence gathered, McLaughlin determined the Indians, perhaps a hundred and fifty in number, arrived in seventeen or eighteen canoes. Their departure added nearly the same number of stolen boats filled with plunder. They were believed to be the so called Spanish Indians living in south Florida as many described seeing a very large Indian—a description which could only apply to Chief Chakaika. McLaughlin also surmised they received some kind of intelligence suggested not only by the timing of the attack but also as their landing was an obscure part of the island farthest from their starting point. The supplies in the warehouse and the store seemed to be their primary objective.

Several things were different about this attack compared to others made by the Indians. It was done at night after crossing over thirty miles of water. It seemed not to be motivated by revenge and it was the first Theodore ever heard of Indians using cannons to counter attack.

In all, seven of the forty-five residents lost their lives but no known Indian casualties.

Fear was prevalent among the survivors and it grew rather than diminished as Saturday progressed. They were all leery of another attack and didn't feel safe even aboard the ship. It didn't help when the guards posted on Tea Table Key sounded a false alarm Saturday night. Some of the survivors begged Captain McClure to let them leave the ship but fortunately he denied their plea as the overnight storm would surely have drown them.

It was with great relief, Theodore sailed away with Maloney early Sunday morning, not just in leaving behind the ghastly nightmare of the attack but also to be only hours away from home.

Chapter 41

Key West, August 7th, 1840

The same Friday as the Indian Key massacre, Betsy was at Abby's bedside for the arrival of Jacob Gabriel Eatonton. Their fourth son was as hale and hearty as his brothers and quick to use his strong lungs to announce his presence in the world. The joy of his birth was soon overshadowed by news of the early morning attack. Key West residents were vigilant once again.

Slaves of Charles Howe and Jacob Housman arrived that afternoon with word of victims escaping with nothing but their nightclothes prompting Mrs. Gordon and Mrs. Mallory to gather donated clothing and pack it in a large trunk to be taken to Indian Key.

Theodore stood at the rail of Captain Maloney's ship on Sunday evening, August 9th, as they sailed into Key West harbour. It was a joyful sight having been away since December 26th. It wasn't just the length of time he was gone that made this absence worse but the lack of letters he was able to send and receive.

Anxiously he waited for the ship to dock and the gangway to be put in place. He didn't wait for an invitation but sprinted toward the wharf, skirting around a large trunk as he doffed his hat to Mrs. Mallory and Mrs. Gordon, making his way to shore. The setting sun was at his back as he approached the front steps of his home. He could hear his family conversing from the open window of the dining room and knew they were eating supper. He smiled mischievously as an idea came to mind. He crept up the porch steps and quietly put down his bags. Knowing the louvered front door would give him away, he tiptoed to the parlor window. Not seeing any obstacle in his way, he scanned the streets for onlookers and seeing none of those either, he moved aside the mosquito netting and entered the house. He stepped carefully across the wood floor so it wouldn't alert them to his presence. He made it undetected to the dining room doorway and took in the scene.

His empty chair was across the room from him, next to it on the far side facing him was Henry. How in the world did his boy get to be fourteen? It seemed like just yesterday he was Brianna's age. She sat across from Henry, her back to Theodore. Next to her was Little Agatha. Both girls were sitting on their legs in order to reach the table. He leaned forward just a bit in order to see Betsy wearing the well-remembered sling holding his newest daughter.

He watched them in silence for some moments before Henry discovered his presence.

"Poppa!"

Three more heads swiveled in his direction as he stepped fully into the room and opened his arms. As one they stood up from the table and raced to him, gleefully laughing and giggling, including him. How good it felt to be surrounded by such love. He kissed Betsy first and heard the mewling cries of the infant they disturbed. He kissed each of his children in turn, picking up Agatha for hers. Brianna was not to be outdone and lifted her arms as well. Theodore leaned down sideways to grasp her and groaned as he straightened. "Good Lord child, how you have grown. You know you are too big to pick up. You're not a baby anymore."

Little Agatha pointed towards her mother. "New babies."

Theodore frowned trying to figure out her words. He decided she must have said 'new baby'. He gave her a very serious look. "Yes, there is a new baby."

Brianna twitched from excitement. "Its girls!"

Theodore turned his head to her. "You have another sister?"

Brianna shook her head and held up two fingers. "Two sisters."

Theodore smiled. "That's right you have two sisters now."

Betsy's grin turned into a giggle. The other children laughed with her but only Henry understood what was so funny. Theodore cocked his head in Betsy's direction and silently questioned her with raised eyebrows. She tried to speak but laughter overtook her again until she heard both babies whimpering from inside the sling. She took a deep breath and said with a bright smile. "What Brianna is trying to tell you is she has two *new* sisters. You, my dear, now have four daughters."

"Four?" Theodore's eyes went to the sling. He slowly let the girls slip to the floor and stepped forward before lifting his eyes to Betsy's face. She pulled the strap away from her chest so he could see inside. Sure enough there were two tiny beings inside.

Betsy took his hand and led the way to the parlor, supper all but forgotten. She took a seat on the sofa pulling him down next to her. She then removed the sling from her neck, opening it up to reveal two swaddled babies on her lap. Overwhelmed, Theodore gently picked up the one closest to him.

Brianna and Agatha stood in front of them with Henry lounging off to the side. Brianna proudly said, "You have Emmaline." She pointed to the pink ribbon sewn to her blanket.

Betsy smiled and showed her the pink ribbon on the other blanket as well.

Brianna's eyes went wide. "Then which one is Emmaline?"

Betsy studied both little faces. "I believe I have her." She looked at Theodore. "And you would have Madalyn."

He looked down at the tiny being barely bigger than his hand and tested the name. "Madalyn. It's a good name."

Betsy nodded. "It's my mother's."

Theodore winked at her. "I know."

Brianna put her hands on her hips. "Are you sure?"

Betsy nodded as sagely as she could manage while suppressing her laughter. "There is one way to be sure. We will have to unwrap her." Betsy undid the swaddled blanket while all watched with rapt attention. She couldn't help her proud mother's smile when she revealed the ribbon bestowed ankle."

Brianna frowned. "How did Madalyn get into the wrong blanket?"

"I ran out of clean ones for her." Betsy turned to Theodore. "Madalyn seems to have a sensitive stomach."

Brianna pointed toward Theodore. "Momma, there she goes again making those faces."

Sure enough, Madalyn was rooting for her meal. Betsy efficiently wrapped Emmaline up again and switched babies with Theodore to discreetly set Madalyn to feed. "But she does love to eat."

Theodore shook his head in wonder. "Woman, you amaze me."

Betsy looked to her husband, surprised by the unexpected compliment.

Theodore read the question in her eyes and answered it. "You manage everything while I'm away with grace and without complaint and now you have adjusted beautifully to adding not one but two more babies." Feeling the need to touch her, he brushed the back of his fingers across her cheek. "I know it is a heavy burden I have placed on you."

The lovers locked gazes silently sharing all they were feeling; love, joy, gratitude and thankfulness.

Brianna, seeing she lost her parents' attention, walked over to her brother and tugged on his pant leg. "Come Henry. Let's play tea party."

Henry turned his attention to Brianna. "Very well little sister. I will play tea party if you hold to your agreement to play chess afterwards."

Brianna turned up her little button nose and begrudgingly said, "I promise."

Henry leaned down to loudly whisper, "If you get Poppa to help, you just might beat me this time." Henry winked at her.

Brianna looked to her father in wonder. "Will you help me beat Henry?" Belatedly she added, "Please."

Theodore had never been so thrilled in his life. How could something as simple as his children wanting his attention have such power over his emotions? The strength of it was amazing. "I certainly will, sweetheart."

Forgetting all about her tea party, Brianna eagerly pulled her father by the hand to the chess table set up in the corner and happily climbed into his lap. With Theodore's coaching Brianna won, bouncing up and down on Theodore's knee in her excitement of winning for the first time. Theodore belatedly remembered his bags on the front porch. He retrieved them while Henry reset the board for another game. The three of them played until bedtime. Brianna would have raised a fuss but Theodore's firm voice quickly put an end to her complaint. Betsy appreciated not having to be the disciplinarian. It was good to have Theodore home.

Theodore was sure it had been years since he enjoyed such an insouciant evening.

* * *

Three weeks later they were invited to supper at the Eatonton's. Max proudly showed Theodore his fourth son then looked contrite as he realized how it might appear to Theodore now having four daughters. Theodore tried to look hurt but couldn't manage it. He saw the irony. "You do realize I have one son and four daughters to perfectly match your one daughter and four sons." In a deadly serious voice Theodore said, "What do you say we go ahead and draw up the marriage contracts right now?"

Max searched Theodore's face for any sign of humor and finding none began to sputter. "But they're only babies. Don't you want to let them choose for themselves?"

The corner of Theodore's mouth gave the slightest twitch and Max let the air rush from his lungs. "Mate you had me going there for a minute. I thought you were serious."

Theodore looked around the nicely appointed room. "I am serious. You're a rich man."

Abby and Betsy stood by enjoying the exchange until, fearing it might get out of hand, Betsy laid a hand on Theodore's shoulder. "He's teasing you Max." She gave her husband a sharp look in case he had thoughts of contradicting her.

Abby said, "Shall we have our supper?"

They were almost done with the meal when Theodore said, "Abby I want to thank you for helping Betsy in her time of need. She told me she couldn't have done it without you."

"Of course, you are welcome. I am thankful it was a happy outcome. She gave me quite a fright." The look of horror on Theodore's face surprised her. Betsy's look of anguished betrayal made Abby wish she hadn't spoken.

Betsy turned to Theodore with an apologetic look. "I'm sorry. I couldn't bring myself to tell you. You always have such little time at home." Her voice faded away. "I didn't want to spoil it."

Theodore was angry. He mentally counted how many times over the last few weeks they may have created another child putting her life at risk again. She should have told him. He should have realized. Of course this time would have been more difficult. Twins had to be harder to carry and birth.

The congenial mood of the evening was ruined and by mutual consent they parted ways early. As they said their goodbyes, Abby whispered another apology to Betsy.

Betsy shook her head. "It's not your fault."

Theodore promised Betsy he wasn't angry with her only with the situation but he avoided intimacy in the bedroom which led to an emotional strain on their relationship. She tried not to take it personally for she could see something more was bothering him. Something happened to change him, but it affected her. The only time she truly felt close to him was the few times when he allowed her to hold him after waking from one of his nightmares. Their tempers were short. She hoped they could work past it but as usual time ran out.

In October, Theodore learned the two main chiefs requested a parlay with General Armistead. Once again peace was at hand. Betsy neatly folded his two freshly laundered shirts and slipped them into his haversack. The back of her hand brushed against the Bible. She pulled it out and opened it to the small painted miniature of her and Henry. *My, how he has grown.* He was closer to manhood than boyhood now. She studied her own face. Time may not have changed her looks as much as Henry's but she was sure the passage of time had left as much a mark on her internally as it had for him. Her soul felt older now. Her thumb rubbed across the edge before she replaced it in the Bible, returning it to his bag.

Theodore spoke from the doorway startling her. "You are as beautiful now as the day that portrait was made; perhaps more so." He approached her. "I wish we had more time. If I've made you feel unloved, nothing is further from the truth." He looked deep into her eyes, "I love you so much, I couldn't risk losing you. It may be selfish of me, but I need you Betsafina."

Her tears burned to be released. She swallowed them back. "In my heart I know that but I missed the comfort of your embrace. I waited so long for you to be here and you wouldn't let me touch you." Her breath hitched. "And now you're leaving again."

Theodore roughly pulled her to him in hindsight wishing he had not kept her at a distance. "I should have put my trust in the Lord and been a husband to you. I promise it will be different when I return."

She looked at him through watery eyes. "I will hold you to that promise." Softly she kissed him.

* * *

Dearest Maman,

I hope this letter finds you and Papa well. It's the end of summer here and Theodore has returned to the warfront, leaving me and the children alone again. The war still continues unabated and feels as if it will never end. I do my best to keep life normal while he's gone but it seems as all we are doing is waiting till he comes home. Our life is on hold until he returns and yet we must carry forward without him. I know he is disappointed in all the time he has missed watching his children grow. The few months he is here during the summer are hardly enough to get to know his girls and Henry becomes more distant with each passing year. It would be hard to say which loss he feels more; the relationship he had with his son or the ones he is yet to have with his daughters.

Brianna is five now and such a help around the house with the twins. I don't know what I would do without her. Little Agatha is two and quite a handful. Ever since she learned to walk it has been hard to keep up with her. Brianna never strayed far from me while Agatha likes to wander. I pray these twins are more like their older sister.

I am writing to you in case you have heard of the massacre in the keys. The Indians attacked a nearby island called Indian Key sending the refugees to Key West. I wanted you to be assured we are not in any danger. All is well. It seems to be an isolated event but still precautions are being taken to ensure our safety. It is truly a tragic thing. Many of the victims are dear friends of residents here. This war needs to end and it cannot be soon enough. We have all grown weary. Perhaps this new general will find a way to bring us peace. Let the remaining Indians live in the swamps. The land they occupy now is only hospitable to alligator and birds. They call it the Everglades. Theodore tells me it is nothing but grassy marshland covered in water part of the year with a few islands of trees called hammocks that the fugitives can nest in somewhat like birds. Why must we chase them down and kill them? Let them have it.

My faith keeps me strong. Some days it is all that keeps me going but I know I must stay strong for the children and for myself and even for Theodore. Though he is far away, knowing I have the home covered allows him to focus on what he needs to do. Some days are much harder than others. Your faith is my example and I lean on it heavily just as I watched you do when Papa was away serving our country.

Give my love to my brothers and sisters and the rest of the family. I dream we will one day see each other again. Perhaps when this war is over.

You're loving daughter,
Betsafina

Fort King, November 14th, 1840

Theodore could only shake his head in dismay. Two chiefs, Tiger Tail and Halleck Tustenuggee, and their warriors met with General Armistead four days ago. They asked for two weeks to consider the general's proposal but here it was four days later and they had all disappeared. Why? Because Armistead failed to suspend field operations. The chiefs considered it more treachery and feared being captured. After all, the white generals had proven time and again the white flag in the hands of an Indian meant nothing.

Actually, Theodore didn't know why he was upset over their departure. They wouldn't have agreed to Armistead's terms anyway. He was offering bribes to get them to move west. Halleck Tustenuggee was even more adamant than Osceola about not leaving Florida. He was rumored to have killed his own sister for wanting to emigrate. More likely their visit was a way to get his men fed, rested and resupplied.

General Armistead, of course, took it as a personal insult and issued orders to ignore any future truce flags. It was in this same mood of betrayal that he finally granted Colonel Harney permission to hunt down Chief

Chakaika in the Everglades.

Harney wasted no time exacting his revenge for Chakaika's attack on his trading post last year and the Indian Key attack four months earlier. With a runaway slave promised his freedom to be a guide and ninety men in canoes borrowed from the Mosquito Fleet, Harney was led to Chakaika's hideout deep in the Everglades. Against Armistead's orders otherwise, Colonel Harney had his men dress like Indians so as not to raise an alarm as they traveled through the enemy's territory. Along the way they overtook some Seminoles in canoes. The women and children were captured and the warriors hanged.

It was a moonless night and their guide, John, lost his way. The fleet was forced to wait while he regained his bearings. Harney tried to get the captured women to help by threatening to hang the children but they refused knowing it was an idle threat. Finally, John found his way again and just after sunrise Colonel Harney and his men surprised the chief while he was chopping wood. Their unexpected appearance left Chakaika with no escape and rather than try to run he smiled and held out his hand. A nervous soldier shot him on sight starting a fierce gun fight. It didn't last long before the Indians surrendered. Colonel Harney instructed his men to hang the two captured warriors along with Chakaika's body.

The following day, Harney tried to find the nearby camps of Hospetarke and Sam Jones but some of Chakaika's warriors escaped the previous day's battle and warned them of his approach.

Harney returned to Fort Dallas victorious having killed nine warriors and only losing one soldier. The Florida Legislature overlooked his previous mistakes and less than honorable methods in favour of his results. They presented him with a commendation and a sword. He was also given command of the Second Dragoons.

* * *

December 28th, exactly five years after the Dade Massacre, the Seminoles proved once again they were not ready to give up. A thirteen man army detail was escorting an officer's wife to Fort Wacahoota when they were attacked. Five were killed including the wife; their bodies scalped and mutilated. The attack was believed to have been led by Coosa Tustenuggee and Halleck Tustenuggee.

* * *

As 1840 came to a close, Theodore despaired of the conflict ever ending. In a letter to Betsy he debated giving up his cause. He was finding it hard to find the good in any actions. Both sides were getting desperate and both were just as set on their course. Neither would declare victory continuing on as they were. Besides, there were others now to report the battles and because of the public's strong empathy for Osceola there were even others reporting for the Indians. Perhaps it was time for him to give up. If the generals could be exchanged and reassigned, why couldn't he?

* * *

It was a lovely January afternoon in Key West. Sunny and in the seventies with a refreshing breeze; a day to enjoy before the return of spring heat and summer humidity. Betsy was sitting on the front porch watching her girls play in the yard while the twins were blessedly napping at the same time. In her hand was an unopened letter from Theodore. She was savoring the anticipation of reading it but knowing this peaceful moment wouldn't last long she finally slid her finger under the wax seal.

Her heart grew heavy as she read of his discouragement and despair. While part of her would like nothing more than to encourage him to come home she knew she couldn't. He had to see this to its end or it would haunt him the rest of his days. And she still felt the same now as she did in the beginning, she would not be the reason he didn't finish what he started.

Reading it again she could see the letter for what it was—a plea for understanding, a need for emotional reinforcement from her, and permission to continue even though the immediate outlook was grim. She smiled. It felt good to be needed by her husband despite the distance between them and especially after the emotional strain of their parting. She could do this for him. She wanted to start her reply right away but Madalyn began stirring. In a moment she would be demanding to be fed. The letter was folded and tucked in her skirt pocket to answer later.

A few hours later, the twins were changed and fed and sitting on a blanket in the middle of the parlor floor being entertained by Agatha. Betsy was tapping her finger on the writing desk, staring at the clean sheet of paper, trying to find the words she wanted to say to Theodore. She finally uncorked the ink, dipped the quill pen, and hoped if she started writing the words would come.

My dearest love,

It didn't work. She shook her head in dismay. So much she wanted to say but she couldn't find the words.

Little Agatha abruptly stood up, "Momma, privy!"

Betsy nodded as Agatha left the room at a run. A second later the back door slammed. Betsy shook her head again. Agatha had a bad habit of waiting till it was almost too late. Now she kept watch on the twins as she tried to figure out what to say to Theodore. Maybe she should open with how the girls were doing.

It's hard to believe the twins are six months old already. The time has flown in a whirlwind of soiled nappies and what sometimes felt like constant feedings but I wouldn't trade a moment of it. They are so precious and their bond is unique. They seem to have their own private way of communicating that is fascinating to watch. I cannot take one from the room without the other one crying out in distress. Whatever one does the other will invariably follow.

They are crawling now and have learned to use the furniture to pull up to a standing position. So much movement means the girls and I must keep a vigilant watch over them. Heaven help us when they start walking!

Out of the corner of her eye she saw Madalyn rapidly crawl away from the blanket. Betsy put aside the lap desk and hurried to retrieve her. Madalyn suddenly stopped, sat up, and lifted her hand to her face. Betsy rushed to catch the baby's hand before she put whatever she was holding in her mouth.

"Madalyn give that to Momma." Betsy kept her from putting her hand to her mouth but waited for her to voluntarily give up the object. "Madalyn, give it to me." It took another moment but she finally released her prize to Betsy's hand. It was a button much smaller than Betsy would have ever given her to play with. "Thank you sweetheart." Betsy picked Madalyn up and frowned. She was sure she checked this room thoroughly this morning for choking hazards. It was normal for babies to put everything in their mouth as a way of exploring their world but Madalyn was especially good at finding the smallest of items.

A glance around the room revealed her button tin left open on a side table. She closed her eyes in a bid for patience and then called out. "Brianna, come here please."

Her eldest daughter's light tread could be heard across the upper floor boards, down the stairs, and across the foyer to the doorway. "Yes, Momma?"

Betsy held out the button between two fingers. "Did you forget to put something away?"

Brianna stepped forward with her hand extended to receive it, curious as to what it might be. Betsy placed the button on her open palm. Brianna's guilty eyes flew to the open tin. "I'm sorry Momma."

"Please put it away. You must be careful to keep small things out of reach. Madalyn found this and almost had it in her mouth. She could have choked to death on it."

Brianna hung her head. "Yes, Momma."

"Please put the button tin back where it belongs."

"Yes ma'am."

Betsy put Madalyn back on the blanket and handed her a rattle just as Agatha returned. Betsy resumed her letter writing. Over the next hour all she managed to add was some community news. Nothing personal. A glance at the clock revealed it was time to start supper. She sighed as she put the writing away. Perhaps after the girls were in bed she would be able to finish.

Noticing the darkening room, Betsy glanced at the clock on the mantle and frowned. It was time to put the girls to bed and Henry still wasn't home. He did not come home for supper; a common occurrence these days but he was usually home an hour or two later having eaten at a friend's house. She hoped nothing was wrong. She couldn't search for him for she couldn't leave the girls alone. *Should she raise an alarm with the neighbor?* Perhaps she would wait a bit longer.

Brianna and Agatha said their prayers and Betsy tucked them in giving each a kiss on one cheek from her and on the other from their poppa. She picked up the candlestick from the dresser and held it over the twins. Satisfied they were sleeping peacefully, she left the nursery. She paused a moment in the doorway looking from one daughter to the next thankful for the blessing of her children.

Now with some time to herself she returned to the parlor and retrieved her writing desk. It was getting late. *Where is Henry?* She would give him twenty minutes more and then she was going to ask the neighbor to look for him and when he did get home, they were going to have a talk. She had let this go on long enough. She turned her thoughts back to her letter.

Betsy crumpled the third sheet of wasted parchment; another irritation in addition to not finding the right words and worry over Henry. She was working on the second page of Theodore's letter and her first attempt sounded too needy, the second was preachy and the last was complaining about Henry. None of these were helpful to Theodore. He needed her reassurance, not added burdens. She pulled out a fresh sheet and again stared at the blankness trying to find the words.

The ringing of the city bell startled her. She held the candle aloft to cast light on the mantle clock confirming it was half-past nine. An hour had passed. *Where is Henry?* She stood up and began pacing the room unsure what to do next. Relief washed over her when she heard the front door open. She rushed to the hall to confront him. "Henry, where have you been? You had me worried sick about you."

Henry's head jerked as if she had slapped him and the smile slipped from his face. He didn't understand her concern. "I'm grown up now. You don't need to worry about me."

"It doesn't matter how old you are. I will always worry about you."

"You don't need to." He started for the stairs.

Betsy moved to intercept him. She modified her tone to elicit his reply. "Where were you?"

"If you must know, my friends and I were helping Crazy Jim get home."

Betsy frowned. "Don't call him that." *At least, he was out late doing something noble.*

Henry frowned. "Why not? Everyone else does."

"It doesn't make it right."

"But he is crazy, roaming the streets like he does hollering 'The Indians are coming'."

"Don't judge him. He has been through something you cannot understand." It was a sad sight to see James William, on his bad days, wandering aimlessly, uttering harsh cries, and at times, screaming. Obviously, he suffered more than he could bear when the Indians attacked his home on Indian Key. They all felt sorry for him and no one knew how to help him overcome it.

Henry frowned. "Like Poppa."

Betsy knew Henry was thinking of all the times when Theodore was home but his mind was elsewhere and his face seemed haunted. Her lips thinned and she nodded. "Yes, like your father."

"Will this war ever end? We wait and wait and more people get hurt. It's so pointless."

His was a frustration they all felt. "You must keep praying for it to end."

Henry moved past her. "It's late, Mother. I'm going to bed. Good night." He paused to kiss her cheek before climbing the stairs. Under his breath he said, "I want to do more than just pray."

Betsy watched him for a moment. She didn't hear what he said but didn't feel the need to question him about it either. She returned to the parlor and while debating about going to bed or trying to finish Theodore's letter she realized she failed to say anything to Henry about not coming home late again. Maybe she could catch him in the morning.

With her mind clear of worry for Henry, she was able to finish the letter.

> *Hold fast, dearest. It seems to me both sides are growing weary and the end must be near. You are where you are needed most at the moment. See this through to the end. If the Indians lose the country needs to know of their suffering and if they win you can best describe their hard won victory for others to understand what it means to them.*
>
> *We are doing fine here and look forward to your return even if it is for a few weeks and as always we pray, even the girls, that one day soon it will be for good.*
>
> *Henry is becoming quite the man of the house. He has willingly taken on more chores while keeping up with his studies and working longer hours at the sponge docks. And tonight, he was late coming home because he was helping to get Mr. William's son home. You should be very proud of him. I know I am.*
>
> *Good night my love. I'll see you in my dreams.*
>
> *Betsafina*

She folded the letter, sealed it with wax, addressed it and left it on the table for Henry to drop off at the post office tomorrow. A soft rain began to fall as she climbed the stairs. She checked on the girls, changed her clothes, said her prayers, and slid into bed; her last thoughts before slumber as always were of Theodore. The patter of raindrops on the wooden shingles soon lulled her fast asleep.

Chapter 42

A few nights later it happened again. Betsy was alone in the parlor doing needlepoint by candlelight and watching the clock, waiting for Henry to come home. Over the last few days she tried several times to broach the subject with Henry of his late homecomings and how they made her worry. Each time he was in too much of a hurry to give her time to speak.

She knew he was likely having some harmless fun with his friends and as hard as he worked he deserved it but still her mother's inclination was to worry. Was he hurt? What if he needed her?

She was tired tonight and would like to have gone to bed early but there was no way she could turn in for the evening until her son was home safe.

There was the city bell. Where was Henry? She paced the floor for another quarter hour before he was heard entering the house.

"Henry! Where have you been? You've got to stop coming home so late. I worry about you." He brushed her concern aside, frustrating her.

"I am fifteen years old. I don't need you to mother me anymore. I can take care of myself."

"It's not about being able to take care of yourself; it's about being respectful to me. From now on I expect you to be home before the city bell rings. There is no reason for you to be out so late."

Henry's eyes widened. "My reasons are my own. I don't have to justify them to you. I am the man of the house."

Betsy's jaw dropped. She couldn't disagree with his last point. Theodore had told him so often enough over the years. While she struggled for words, he walked past her up the stairs. She turned and called out to him. "Henry." He stopped but didn't turn around. "Being man of the house doesn't give you the right to disregard my request. You are to be home when the city bell rings."

With his back still to her, he stiffened and in a tight voice said, "Yes ma'am. Is that all?"

"Yes."

He silently continued up the stairs. Feeling as if she had just destroyed something precious in their relationship, Betsy turned to retrieve the candle from the parlor and then climb the stairs to bed. She was sure if Theodore were home she would not be in this predicament.

The conversation haunted her all night long but she knew not how to resolve it with Henry. She could only hope he would come around to accept her rule. She woke the next morning having slept poorly. Mentally, she prepared herself to be strong when she faced him over the breakfast table but to her dismay he had already left the house.

Feeling out of sorts all day, Betsy took the girls to visit Abby for tea. Abby noticed her friend's distress right away and promptly delegated the care of the children to give them uninterrupted time to speak. Mrs. Baxley volunteered to watch the twins and baby Jacob. Twelve year old Emily took charge of Agatha, Brianna, Thorn and Nathanial ranging in age from three to six. Nine year old Christoff was down the street playing with friends.

Abby poured her friend a strong cup of tea and handed it to her. "Is something bothering you, Betsy?"

Betsy was not surprised when Abby bypassed the small talk to go straight to the problem. As busy mothers they both knew quiet moments were rare and fleeting and not to be squandered. "It's Henry. He's rarely home for dinner anymore and I never know when he will return. Twice now it has been after the city bell."

Betsy sighed and Abby waited sensing there was more she wanted to say.

"I'm tired of worrying about him so last night in a fit of anger I told him he had to be home before the bell."

Abby's brow raised. "That is a reasonable request. What did he say?"

"Nothing." Betsy shook her head. "Abby, I don't know what I'm going to do if he directly disobeys me in coming home late again. I fear any discipline will drive a deeper wedge between us yet to not discipline at all would remove any respect. Not to mention, what could I possible do to punish him?"

Abby sighed. "If Max were here I am sure he could talk to Henry and help him understand."

"That would be nice. Where is he?"

"He is sailing the *Abigail Rose* to England with a load of cotton for father. I do not expect him to return for at least another fortnight."

"Does he like being a merchant sailor rather than a ship salvager?"

"He will not say so because he knows my father needs him but—no—he would much rather salvage."

Betsy turned her head to the stairs as she heard one of her babies crying. She rose to go to her.

Abby said, "I am sure Mrs. Baxley can handle it."

Betsy walked faster to the stairs. "That is a distress cry. Something's wrong." She flew up the stairs with Abby trailing behind when they heard Mrs. Baxley's urgent call. "Abigail!"

They entered the room to find Jacob and one of the twins in the playpen crying. Jacob's nappie was only half secure. Mrs. Baxley held the other twin to her chest her open palm rapidly patting her back. Something in the baby's limp posture made Betsy's heart squeeze mercilessly tight. She pulled the baby from the elderly lady into the cradle of her arms, so she could see her face. Madalyn's eyes were closed, her skin pale, and her lips were blue.

Betsy laid her hand on Madalyn's chest and shook it but there was no response. Emmaline began crying even harder. Betsy lifted her frightened eyes to Abby pleading for help. "She's not breathing!"

Abby reached out. "Give her to me.'"

Betsy reluctantly handed Madalyn over to Abby praying she could save her and retrieved Emmaline to try and comfort her. Abby cleared off the top of the dresser and laid her down. She put her ear to the baby's chest, then straightened.

Mrs. Baxley picked up Jacob. "The girls were right here in the playpen. I was over there changing Jacob's nappie. I found her like that when the other one started crying."

Betsy looked at Abby. "She must have swallowed something."

Abby swept her finger inside the baby's mouth. "I don't feel anything." Abby picked her up and walked to the rocking chair. She sat down and laid Madalyn face down on her knees and began pounding her back in what looked to Betsy as a violent manner.

Betsy hugged Emmaline tighter to her as she prayed out loud. "Please, Lord, please save my baby. Don't take my baby." As the seconds ticked by tears choked her but still she repeated her desperate plea over and over. Absently she could hear Mrs. Baxley from the other side of the room praying the Hail Mary while tears streaked down her cheeks.

Abby again listened for breath and checked Madalyn's throat before turning her over and pounding some more. She felt panic fraying the edges of her conscience and tried to push it back. The baby was limp and lifeless and she was helpless to change it. Every second robbed her of hope. She turned the baby over again and blew in her face carefully watching for any signs of life. She checked her throat again with her finger and visually but still found nothing. She didn't know anything else to do.

Brianna came running to the door followed by Thorn in what appeared to be a game of chase. Seeing all the adults in the room and feeling the tension, Brianna stopped in mid-flight. Thorn careened into her back. Mrs. Baxley quickly stepped forward to block their view and usher them downstairs.

Abby lifted sad defeated eyes to Betsy. She was having trouble accepting the child was lost, how could Betsy?

Betsy saw the finality in her friend's sorrowful gaze. She felt the need to take Madalyn in her arms but couldn't forsake Emmaline who needed her. Abby rose from the rocker and gestured Betsy forward. Once seated, Betsy repositioned a sobbing Emmaline over her right shoulder and then accepted Madalyn's still form from Abby. She kissed the tousled curls and set the chair in motion.

Abby reached for Emmaline, but Betsy shook her head, so she silently slipped from the room leaving her friend to come to terms with her sudden loss.

Twenty minutes later Emmaline finally cried herself to sleep. Betsy continued to rock. Her emotions were numb. Her eyes were hot and dry. The initial shock wore off but she knew she had yet to absorb the full reality of what happened. She wanted to pretend Madalyn was asleep rather than deal with what came next; telling her other children, a funeral with a tiny coffin, writing Theodore. Betsy leaned her head back against the chair and closed her eyes. *How am I going to get through this? Dear Lord, please help me!*

She looked down at her sleeping daughters; one would soon wake for she could feel the wetness seeping through her nappie and the other would never be hers to hold again once she let her go. Betsy choked on her anguish, struggling to breathe as hot tears poured down her cheeks. She fought back her sobs, so Emmaline would continuing sleeping. She didn't want to let go of the moment. Her precious little Madalyn was about to be taken from her and all too soon placed underground. Already she heard Abby's light tread on the stairs coming to coax her to do what must be done.

Betsy squeezed her eyes shut trying to control her emotions. Denial and anger warred within her making her breath shallow, her head hurt, and her heart felt as if it could shatter into a million tiny pieces.

Abby slowly entered the room not sure how Betsy would react. Seeing the eerie calmness worried Abby more than if Betsy was screaming in rage. "I have made arrangements for Brianna and Agatha to stay here tonight and I sent word to Henry." She tried to gage Betsy's emotional state. Remembering the overwhelming grief she felt for the loss of her daughter, Abby tried to guess what her friend might need. "Do you want me to keep Emmaline too?"

Betsy wasn't sure of her voice, so she shook her head in reply.

Abby's lips thinned and she nodded. "Very well. Is there anything else I can do for you?"

"Give me a little more time before you take her away."

Abby nodded and left the room.

The next few days were a blur of moments for Betsy. The space between those moments was filled with hollow emptiness, unending tears, and caring for an inconsolable Emmaline. There was the heart-wrenching moment she released Madalyn to Abby to prepare her for burial. She must have made decisions, but she couldn't recall doing so. She vaguely remembered leaving Abby's house and being thankful she didn't see Mrs. Baxley on the way out for she might have said something she didn't really mean. It was hard not to blame the elderly woman who likely went home burdened in guilt. Betsy knew she would forgive Mrs. Baxley in ti,me but she was glad to not see her then.

The next moment was a blustery overcast morning on the southern beach, holding onto Emmaline while Abby and Mrs. Mallory supported her. Seeing the tiny box placed in the small limestone hole nearly collapsed her carefully held emotions, only pride kept Betsy from falling apart.

Somehow, she got from the grave to her house to be surrounded by a sea of faces belonging to the caring neighbors who came to offer their condolences. Emmaline was fussy and clingy the whole day and Betsy eventually used her as an excuse to escape to the quiet of the nursery.

Abby came to check on her a while later waking her from a sorely needed nap in the rocking chair. She then sent everyone away and promised to bring supper and the other children home in a few hours. Betsy nodded, then took Emmaline to her room where they napped together in her bed.

When Abby arrived with Agatha, Brianna, Henry and a basket of fried chicken, Betsy felt a little more capable of handling the next ordeal. Henry was aware of what happened, but Abby kept the news from the two girls. Betsy thought she would have to paste a smile on her face for them, but she was able to give them a genuine smile of happiness to see them. She knelt down and opened her arms. Her girls came running to fill them. It did her heart good. She held them a little longer and tighter than they liked, finally letting go when they started squirming. She stood up and held out her hands to take theirs and lead them to the parlor where the three of them were seated on the sofa.

"Girls, you know something is wrong, don't you?"

They both solemnly nodded, Agatha mimicking Brianna.

"Madalyn has gone to be with the angels." They frowned at her so she added, "She is in heaven now."

Agatha asked, "When is she coming back?"

Betsy swallowed hard and shook her head. "She's not coming back." Betsy was having trouble thinking of a way to explain it so they could understand.

Brianna looked at her little sister. "She's dead. People in heaven are dead. Isn't that right, Momma?"

Betsy's throat was too tight to answer so she nodded. Brianna, having inherited her practical nature, was handling it well. She looked to Little Agatha and found her demeanor accepting and unconcerned. She knew it was likely because she was too young to fully understand and the days to come would bring more questions.

Henry stepped forward and held out his hands. "Sisters, come outside and I'll swing you around."

Betsy gave him a grateful look.

As they left the room, Abby stepped forward and joined her on the sofa. She picked up Betsy's hand and squeezed it, conveying her sympathy and support. "How are you doing?"

Betsy lightly shrugged. "As well as can be expected, I suppose. I wish Theodore was here."

"Have you written him yet?"

Betsy shook her head.

Abby wasn't surprised by her answer. "Can I make you some tea?"

Betsy gave her a weak smile. "That would be nice."

No sooner had Abby left the room, Emmaline could be heard whimpering, awake from her nap. Betsy left the room to retrieve her. For now, mother and daughter needed the comfort of each other to console their loss.

Abby returned to find Betsy pacing the floor with Emmaline. When she tried to take the child, Emmaline clung tightly to her mother's neck surprising Abby for before Emmaline had always eagerly come to her. Betsy took a seat in the wingback chair so she could drink her tea. Abby offered Emmaline a biscuit but she turned her head away again. She hoped the child's behavior was temporary. It would be a double tragedy if losing her twin permanently changed Emmaline's sweet, open and joyful nature.

The ladies sipped tea in companionable silence occasionally broken by Abby with odd bits of news. After a while, Abby stood up to leave. "Is there anything else I can do for you?"

"I can't think of anything. I'm sorry I am such poor company."

Abby smiled. "Nonsense. You have nothing to apologize for."

Later in the evening, Betsy laid a sleeping Emmaline in her crib and arranged the netting around her having spent the last hour nursing and then walking the floor with her before she finally succumbed to slumber. Madalyn's empty place beside her sister brought fresh tears to Betsy's eyes. She turned away to check the covers on Agatha and Brianna. She had her hands full caring for Emmaline and the poor darlings put themselves to bed. She was giving Emmaline her way for now, trying to console both of them in their grief but it could not continue this way much longer. Brianna and Agatha needed her too. Tomorrow she would think of something to help Emmaline.

She slipped out of the nursery and made her way to the sleeping porch. Wishing she could lean into Theodore and feel his arms around her, she looked up at the moon and recalled his words. It gave her a feeling of connection knowing the same moon was shining down on him and he likely was looking at it and thinking of her too. Tomorrow she would have to write him but she would worry about that tomorrow too. She was exhausted from walking the floor with Emmaline. Tonight she needed rest but it was not to be as Emmaline was whimpering again. Rather than keep the other girls awake too, Betsy retrieved her from the nursery. She laid down in her bed with the child, keeping a hand on her and humming. It wasn't long before they were both asleep.

The following day she somehow managed to write brief letters to Theodore and her parents while experimenting with letting Emmaline soothe herself which meant listening to her cry for as long as she could stand it. It left Betsy feeling overwhelmed and inadequate and sick of tears, her own and Emmaline's. She prayed throughout the day for the strength and wisdom to bring her family through this tragedy.

It was finally bedtime for the girls after the long and stressful day. Brianna and Agatha were irritable and fussy. Betsy closed her eyes reaching for the patience to deal with her girls. Earlier, she moved Emmaline's crib to her room. Now she put her in it and closed the door to mute her cry. Betsy listened to Brianna and Agatha's prayers, not surprised when they both prayed for Emmaline to be happy again. She tucked them in, kissed their cheeks, one for her and one from their poppa, and then left the room closing the door behind her.

Betsy returned to her room and picked up the tear streaked, hiccupping toddler. "Baby girl, I'm so sorry. Momma didn't mean to let you cry so hard." Once she calmed her down again she tried returning her to the crib but Emmaline immediately began fussing again. Betsy picked her up. "Oh Emmaline, what are we going to do?" Exhausted, Betsy looked at her bed feeling ready to sleep herself. Remembering how easily Emmaline went to sleep the night before, Betsy laid down with her in the bed, gently running her hand over the downy head and humming softly. Her crying eased. Betsy breathed a sigh of relief and then it made sense. Emmaline was used to the constant closeness of her twin so of course she would be uncomfortable sleeping alone. All her baby needed was a sleeping companion. Betsy yawned and a moment later she slumbered as well.

Fort Cumming, Florida, March 3, 1841

Theodore was visiting with Colonel William Worth currently stationed at the two year old fort in middle Florida about fifty miles east of Tampa nestled on dry ground between several small lakes. The two men were discussing the current situation in Florida under General Armistead's command.

Colonel Worth sighed. "I don't have a problem with bribing the chiefs to surrender and bring in their people except when it comes to Coosa Tustenuggee." His tone escalated with his frustration. "For goodness sakes, he murdered an officer's wife and now they want to give him five thousand dollars to move west and his warriors thirty dollars each and a rifle. Why that's better pay than my soldiers get for doing honest work. Even General Jesup and all his underhanded dealings would not have given money to a murderer of women."

Theodore grimaced. "I agree with you but it matters little. Congress gave Armistead plenty of money to bribe these chiefs and as long as it works, integrity matters little. With Coosa Tustenuggee gone, Wild Cat is now the leading chief."

Colonel Worth exhaled a ring of tobacco smoke. "Capturing him could really mean the end of this. I have scouts looking for him to persuade him to come to me for a parley."

Theodore smirked. "You're hoping to bring him in so you can get your promotion."

"A long overdue promotion."

The mail carrier arrived handing Colonel Worth a stack of correspondence to deal with before turning to Theodore with three letters.

Theodore stood. "I'll leave you to your work. It was good talking to you, sir." The colonel absently dismissed him having already become absorbed in his mail.

Theodore sat on the edge of the elevated wooden boardwalk between one of the blockhouses and the supply depot to read his letters. The sun was almost at its zenith and the day was comfortably warm.

He opened Bob's letter first with news of Congress approving General Armistead's request for another thirty thousand in funds to bribe the chiefs.

> *Your Florida War has become such a nuisance Congress approves money for any scheme presented that might bring it to a close; bloodhounds, forts, troops, and now bribes.*

Theodore smiled. It was old news. He was already aware of the increase and how Armistead was spending it. However, the next part of Bob's letter was news to him.

> *The debate in the House to increase the funds was heated with representative Giddings, an abolitionist from Ohio, insisting the cause of the war should be examined, particularly the slave issue. Mr. Cooper and Mr. Black of Georgia responded in kind, demanding the standing gag order prevent such discussion. The ensuing argument turned into a fistfight. When all settled down, the bill was passed but the conflict remains and adds fuel to the abolition movement.*

The second letter was from McLaughlin celebrating his successful expedition across the Everglades from east to west having failed to do so last October. He was disappointed to not encounter any Indians but he was sure it was more likely they were avoiding him than because they weren't there.

Theodore folded the letter and was now anxious to read Betsy's but he was distracted by a commotion at the fort gate. He slipped the letters into his pocket and pushed himself off his perch on the boardwalk to investigate.

Several soldiers hurried ahead of him. As he rounded the last building blocking his view, Theodore was shocked to see the unexpected visitor. Proudly standing at the gate entrance was Wild Cat and seven of his warriors. The young chief would create excitement in the fort just because of who he was but it was his appearance dressed as Hamlet that made today's visit so distressingly memorable. One of the warriors wore the royal purple robe of Richard III and a third seemed to be dressed as Horatio. The others all sported something shiny and colorful from the theater wardrobe. It was obvious to all they were in possession of the stolen trunks from the Shakespearean troupe ambushed last year.

One of Wild Cat's warriors carried a white flag of truce and despite General Armistead's orders otherwise and the flaunting of their dastardly deeds, Colonel Worth honored it. The Indians were allowed to enter the fort. A child ran past Theodore and right up to the chief. It was Wild Cat's daughter. She was one of the prisoners being held for transport west. Theodore watched in amazement as the brave little girl emptied her pockets, handing her father items she had pilfered around the fort; musket balls, packets of powder, and anything else she thought was valuable for weapons. Her father was brought to tears. Theodore couldn't say if it was seeing his daughter or her thoughtful gift that moved him so; likely it was both. The unbidden moment touched all who were present and helped to temper the simmering anger brought on by the reminder of past transgressions.

A talk was held that afternoon. Theodore sat next to Lieutenant Sprague who was also vigorously taking notes of the meeting. Wild Cat gave an opening speech eloquently describing his attachment to the land and how the white man came and befriended him only to later deceive, lie, and steal. The chief spoke with such calm honesty, he earned the sympathy, if not the forgiveness, of his listeners.

After the council meeting, Theodore was allowed to interview the chief. He learned the reason for the emotional reunion with his daughter was because Wild Cat believed her to be dead and was overcome with joy to hold her again. The warrior's emotions deeply moved Theodore.

Just before turning in for the night, Theodore opened his letter from Betsy. He read it three times finding it difficult to accept the truth in her words.

Dear Theodore,

I write you with a very heavy heart. Tragedy has struck our family in the sudden loss of Madalyn. We were visiting Abby for tea and for some reason she stopped breathing. Abby tried everything she knew but nothing could save her. She was laid to rest next to Aunt Agatha.

I am coping but Emmaline misses her twin terribly. She clings to me, crying, whenever she is awake. She gets especially upset whenever I am not with her. I suppose it is understandable and I hope it is something she will overcome in time. Henry and Brianna have accepted the loss while Little Agatha is too young to understand.

Be safe my love.
Your loving wife,
Betsafina

Theodore slowly folded the letter with a heavy sigh. He felt so helpless. Betsy was hurting more than she would say. It was in the stilted tone of her letter and her pride would not allow her to ask him to come home because in her mind there was nothing he could do. She wouldn't consider her emotional support reason enough to ask it of her.

The twins were four months old when he left in October. He only shared a few months of her life but he supposed he should be thankful he had that much time with Madalyn.

He stepped outside his tent and looked to the stars shining in between the moss covered oak branches. He was disappointed the moon wasn't high enough yet to be seen. He needed the connection tonight to his beloved. His jaw clenched. *What am I doing here?* Nothing was going to change. Wild Cat wasn't ready to surrender. He saw it in the young chief's eyes when he interviewed him earlier. Nothing was likely to come from this latest negotiations any more than in all the others before it. He should go home. His family needed him more than this war. Betsy patiently waited five years for this conflict to end and even though her previous letter eloquently assured him she would wait as long as it took that was before this latest hardship fell on her shoulders. Even if he didn't stay long he at least could offer her some comfort and share the burden for a little while.

Across the fort there was a low murmur of voices from the chief and his people gathered around their campfire. Theodore watched the darkened silhouette of a little girl in her father's arms and was struck by life's sad irony. Tonight Wild Cat held the daughter he believed to be dead this morning while Theodore now grieved for the loss of his child he thought to be safe and healthy just twenty minutes ago.

* * *

Two weeks later Theodore stepped off the wharf onto the white limestone street of Key West. Ten minutes later he walked through the front door of his house and set his haversack on the floor. His gaze traveled left to right enjoying all the familiarities of home. Hearing footsteps approaching the stairs on the second floor he turned his eyes upward.

"Henry, is that you?" Betsy heard the sound of the front door and since the girls were all in the room with her, she could only surmise it was Henry home early. The sight of Theodore was such an unexpected surprise she squealed in delight bringing Brianna and Agatha running from the room as she flew down the stairs to be welcomed in her husband's strong embrace.

Theodore swung her around then each of the girls in turn before asking, "Where's Emmaline?"

Betsy held her hand out to him. "Napping."

Theodore followed her up the stairs to the crib in their bedroom instead of the nursery.

Betsy gave him an apologetic look. "I had to move her back in here. She was keeping the other two awake with her crying. She often falls asleep lying beside me and with the crib in here it is easier to transfer her."

He looked down at the peacefully sleeping cherub. "She's still crying all the time?" When Betsy didn't immediately answer, he turned to look and found tears pooling in her eyes. Words were inadequate. He opened his arms and Betsy walked into his embrace with a vulnerability she rarely displayed. He pulled her to his chest and tucked her head under his chin. It felt good to be needed, but the heartbreak of it was almost more than he could bear. He kissed the crown of Betsy's head and ran a hand up and down her back trying to give her comfort. His unfocused gaze drifted out the window to the palm fronds dancing under the afternoon sunshine. He blinked back his tears and held her a little tighter.

For a moment, Betsy couldn't speak. She was engulfed in her grief. She fought against the sobs threatening to choke her. It felt good to share her heartache with someone who didn't just sympathize but shared the depth of it with her. She needed the comfort and security of his arms but it made it too easy to fall apart. She swallowed hard and leaned back in his arms to see his face. She wiped away her tears and finally answered his question. "Not as much as at first. She still cries herself to sleep every night. We all try to keep her entertained during the day and there are moments we can even coax a smile out of her."

Theodore's heart wrenched to see Betsy's grief stricken face and his throat tightened to hear of Emmaline's suffering. When he left she was such a happy baby. The connection between the twins amazed him. It was tragic she should experience such a devastating loss at barely nine months old. It took him back to those dark days dealing with Henry after Margaret's death. How much harder was it for Emmaline to grieve than for Henry?

"I am so sorry I wasn't here when you needed me."

She swallowed the tears burning the back of her throat. "No matter. You are here now. I didn't mean for you to come."

"I know. You didn't ask it but I had to come home."

She tried to smile. "I'm glad you did."

He tipped her chin up and gave her the healing kiss they both needed. He wanted to deepen it but two little girls burst into the room. Betsy instantly stiffened and pushed away from him returning to her stoic self not wanting the girls to see her weakness.

"Poppa come play with us."

Betsy angrily turned to them. "Hush! You'll wake Emmaline." Too late, she turned to the crib as the whimpering started.

Theodore intercepted Betsy. "You need to go spend time with them." He saw the hurt on Brianna and Agatha's faces before they turned from the room. "Let me see if I can quiet Emmaline. Is it time for her to be up?"

"No, I just got her to sleep before you arrived."

Theodore's heart constricted to see the exhaustion in her eyes. "Go." She cast a doubtful glance between him and Emmaline.

He turned her toward the door. "They need you and you need to spend time with them."

He was right. She did need to spend time with Agatha and Brianna and she hated to admit a break from Emmaline was welcome. Conceding to his request, Betsy quietly left the room.

Theodore moved aside the netting and talked softly to his daughter the way he did before he left hoping she would remember and be comforted.

"Hello there baby girl. Poppa's home now. Everything's going to be alright." She quieted at first as if fascinated by his voice but as soon as he picked her up she started crying. "Shh. I know baby. It hurts doesn't it? I miss your sister too." Theodore paced the floor trying to cuddle Emmaline but she began struggling, pushing against his chest and crying in tired frustration. "Shh. Now, now, Em. Your momma needs a break. Let me take care of you."

What he needed was something to distract her. He walked to the nursery in search of a book. He smiled when he saw Henry's *Puss 'n Boots*. He knew the story by heart but it had pictures for Emmaline to look at while he read. He sat in the rocking chair and settled her back against his stomach. She was crying less; distracted by curiosity. He opened the book and started reading, changing his voice with the characters like he used to do for Henry. He smiled when her crying ceased and a chubby little hand reached out to touch the page.

Betsy was tidying up the parlor when she realized all was quiet upstairs. Curious as to how Theodore managed what she thought would be impossible for him, she quietly crept up the stairs. Reaching the landing, she heard his voice from the nursery and peeked in the door to find Theodore reading to a quietly occupied Emmaline. It hurt a little that he could do in a few moments what she struggled with for weeks but mostly she was relieved and it was a beautiful sight to see Theodore nurturing his baby girl.

He glanced her way, smiled and winked, making Betsy's heart flutter even after seven years of marriage. Perhaps that was because if one added up all the time they actually spent together it wouldn't amount to two years. She shook off the bitter thought and smiled in return. He was home today and she was thankful. He hoicked his head indicating she should return to the other girls. He was right; they needed her attention. She nodded, took one more moment to appreciate the scene before her, then turned to descend the stairs.

A short time later, Betsy looked up from the paper dress she was cutting out for Brianna's paper doll to see Theodore enter the room. "Is she asleep?"

"Hmm."

My, how she missed that sound and all its various meanings. "You must be hungry from traveling." She rose from the chair and smoothed her skirt. "Shall I fix you something to eat?"

"No, I'm fine till supper."

His gaunt frame made her think otherwise. "Speaking of which, I need to get started on it."

Agatha came running up to him, pulling on his pant leg. "Story, Poppa. Tell us a story."

Theodore swung her up in his arm. "What kind of story?"

"A fairy story."

Brianna abandoned her paper dolls to follow them to a chair. Theodore settled both girls on his lap and began weaving a tale to entertain them.

Betsy picked up the scissors and quickly finished cutting out the dress she was working on so she could put the scissors away. She took a moment to enjoy the sweet blessing of watching Theodore and his girls before leaving the room to start their meal.

Henry came home just before supper was served just as he had done every night since Madalyn's passing knowing Betsy needed him. He greeted his father warmly. The last few weeks he felt the burden of being the man of the house and was happy to return the mantle where it belonged. The meal was a joyful celebration of Theodore's return.

Betsy kneeled beside the bed in her white cotton nightgown. She had a lot to be thankful for today. Finished with her prayers she climbed into bed and waited for Theodore to join her. She wasn't sure what to expect tonight considering how it was between them when he left. She wondered what was taking him so long since she assumed he was only checking the doors, windows, candles and kitchen fire. Never mind it was something she had already done out of habit since it was her responsibility while he was gone.

When he finally entered the room, his hair was damp and she caught a whiff of the clean scent of soap. She gave him a tentative smile hoping he had taken the time to bathe with amorous intentions in mind. She impatiently waited for him to join her. He combed his hair and emptied his pockets on the dresser. The bed dipped as he sat down to remove his socks and shoes and decompressed as he stood up to remove his pants and shirt. And all the while she nervously waited, anxious to feel him next to her and run her hands over his skin assuring herself he was really here. He neatly folded his clothes and placed them at the end of the bed. But her hopes fell when he blew out the candle and slid into the sheets next to her sure now that he meant to go straight to sleep. She couldn't blame him. He had to be tired after traveling over a week to get home. Perhaps tomorrow.

She closed her eyes and turned over feeling dejected until he did the same, pulling her close and nuzzling her ear. Eagerly she turned in his arms and welcomed him home.

* * *

Several idyllic weeks passed in which Betsy's only worry was how it would affect Emmaline when Theodore left again. He shared her concern but neither could bring themselves to limit his interaction with her. Betsy would just have to cross that bridge when she came to it.

One day Theodore received a letter from Colonel Worth exciting him so much he couldn't wait to share the news with Betsy. He found her in the garden tending her potted herbs. He waved the letter as he approached her. "We have good news!"

Betsy brushed her hands on her skirt. "What is it?"

"Wild Cat has agreed to emigrate with his people."

She tilted her head. "How is that good news?"

"It's not for Wild Cat but it does bring this conflict closer to an end and to me staying home for good."

Betsy nodded. She knew Theodore would want to be there when the chief sailed. "When has he agreed to leave?"

"He will gather his people at Fort Pierce on the Atlantic coast after the Green Corn dance."

"And when is that?"

"In a month or two."

Betsy breathed again. She had a little more time with her husband. "Are you sure he will follow through with it; it's not just a ploy to keep the peace?"

Theodore nodded. "He left his daughter with Colonel Worth as a show of good faith."

Betsy's surprise was apparent. "How could he do that?"

Theodore shook his head. "I don't know but it gives me hope this may really be the end this time."

* * *

In May, Theodore learned General Armistead asked to be reassigned. During his year in command 450 Indians were sent west and another 236 were waiting for transport in Tampa. Colonel Worth now assumed command of the Florida War and he was leading a charge of 'search and destroy' missions during the summer intended to put pressure on any remaining Indians to surrender by making it difficult to feed themselves. It was a brutal tactic but it seemed to be working as small groups were turning in for relocation.

Still, Theodore was reluctant to leave his family preferring instead to help Brianna beat Henry in nightly chess matches, weave stories to amuse Little Agatha, watch as Emmaline learned to walk and talk, and make love to his wife as often as they could find time alone and the energy.

In June, Theodore received an unusual letter from Colonel Worth venting his frustration.

It seems Wild Cat was making a nuisance of himself at Fort Pierce. I was told he was being obnoxious and demanding; first a horse and then large amounts of food and liquor supposedly for a meeting with Sam Jones, Billy Bowlegs and Hospetarke. Some upstart second lieutenant named Sherman got worried the chief was building his forces and had him seized along with fourteen warriors and three blacks. They were escorted to Tampa where another second lieutenant shipped them off to New Orleans without consulting me. I have since ordered Wild Cat's return. I need him to bring in his people.

Reluctantly Theodore decided he must return to the war. Too much was happening now for him to stay away. He left them a few days after Emmaline's first birthday and arrived in Tampa a week before the ship bearing Wild Cat returned.

On the fourth of July, Theodore followed Lieutenant Sprague and Colonel Worth onto the transport ship at anchor in Tampa Bay. The sun was climbing in the clear blue sky casting radiant heat to rapidly turn the humid air oppressive. The bay breeze stirred the sultry air as they waited on deck for the Indians to be brought up from the hold. Theodore could only imagine how miserable it must get in the belly of the ship by late afternoon.

The sound of clanking iron brought Theodore's attention to the passageway. It was a tragic sight to see the noble young chief and his proud warriors shuffling forth in leg shackles. Occasionally, Theodore saw one or another of them glance toward shore with longing in their eyes. They were seated on a bench before Colonel Worth in weary silence with heads hung and hands placed upon their knees. Theodore was struck by their dignity even in their disgrace.

Colonel Worth stepped forward and took Wild Cat by the hand and proceeded to praise the chief as a strong and brave warrior. He understood why the chief fought so hard but now the time had come to realize the war must end and as a respected leader he was being called upon to encourage his people to emigrate.

"I wish you to state how many days will be required to effect an interview with the Indians in the woods. You can select five of these men to carry your talk; name the time, it shall be granted; but I tell you, as I wish your relatives and friends told, that unless they fulfill your demands, yourself and these warriors now seated before us shall be hanged from the yards of this vessel, when the sun sets on the day appointed, with the irons upon your hands and feet."[15]

A collective gasp rose from those gathered around but no reaction was seen from the Indians.

Worth continued. "I tell you this, that we may well understand each other. I do not wish to frighten you, you are too brave a man for that; but I say what I mean and I will do it. It is for the benefit of the white and red man. This war must end, and you must end it."[15]

Silence ensued before Wild Cat stood to answer him. "I was once a boy, then I saw the white man afar off. I hunted in the woods, first with a bow and arrow, then with a rifle. I saw the white man, and was told he was my enemy. I could not shoot him as I would a wolf or bear; yet like these he came upon me; horses, cattle and fields, he took from me. He said he was my friend; he abused our women and children and told us to go from the land. Still he gave me his hand in friendship; we took it; whilst taking it, he had a snake in the other, his tongue was forked; he lied, and stung us. I asked but for a small piece of these lands, enough to plant and to live upon far south, a spot where I could place the ashes of my kindred, a spot only sufficient upon which I could lay my wife and child. This was not granted me. I was put in prison; I escaped. I have been again taken; you have brought me back; I am here; I feel the irons in my heart.

"It is true I have fought like a man so have my warriors; but the whites are too strong for us. I wish now to have my band around me and go to Arkansas. I never wish to tread upon my land unless I am free."[15]

As Wild Cat spoke it brought to mind for Theodore all he witnessed and had written since coming to Florida; of meeting the Indians before the war and the wrongs done on both sides leading up to it; cheating, stealing, murder and retaliations, imprisonments and humiliations, burned plantations and death, fleeing citizens, stealth attacks and scalping; his first experience in battle, the bravery of soldiers and incompetence of generals; the chilling sound of Osceola's war cry. It was long years of heat, mosquitoes, rain, swamps, sickness and bloodshed and so many dead. So many deaths on both sides. Followed by desperation and deceit, daring escapes and an ignoble death of a great leader. General after general failing to understand and conquer the remarkable fortitude of the Seminole warriors. And men like him and John Graham, forced to do the unthinkable against those they would rather call friend, to kill or be killed.

And even though he knew in the beginning it would end in their defeat it hurt to see it in the young chief's eyes. Micanopy and the older chiefs' defeat bothered him but not as much as Osceola and Wild Cat. After so many times of false hope and betrayal they all could sense the end was at hand.

Wild Cat promised Colonel Worth his people would be gathered in forty days. Five of his warriors were sent out to tell his people while the rest remained imprisoned on the ship awaiting their fate.

Chapter 43

Key West, August 1841

"Emily, can you keep a secret?" Henry waited for her response as they walked side by side down Front Street. He happened to see her enter the mercantile a little while ago on an errand for her mother and offered to carry her package home.

She looked up at the blond-haired boy who used to be her playmate but now they rarely saw each other. He was always busy with work and schooling and she with helping her mother care for her little brothers and the house. He had turned into quite the dashing young man. All the young ladies wanted his attention and she was no different. It sent a thrill through her when he offered to carry her purchase and walk her home. Wouldn't her friends be jealous if they were to see her now? "I suppose it would depend on what the secret is."

"The kind you don't tell."

She frowned at his harsh tone but not wanting to lose his attention she quickly agreed. "Alright, I promise not to tell." She held her chest out hoping he would notice she was starting to develop her womanly parts.

He frowned down at her. "Why are you walking like that?"

"Like what?"

"Like a strutting rooster."

Darn, that wasn't the image she wanted to give him. She straightened her shoulders. "Am not. What's your big secret anyway?"

"I'm going to be leaving soon."

This news surprised her so much she stopped walking. When he did too and turned to look at her all she could think to say was, "Why?" Indeed, it was all that mattered.

"I'm tired of this tiny place and of carrying obligations that aren't mine. I want to see the world Em and if I wait until this bloody war is over for my father to return for good... Well I'll be waiting forever."

"You're too young to go out on your own."

His frown darkened. "Am not. I'm almost sixteen. There's lots of men who left home at my age." He turned and started walking again.

She ran a few steps to catch up to him. "What will you do?"

"Join the army. They will take care of bed and meals until I can figure out what I want to do." He shrugged his shoulders. "If I can make rank, I just might stay in it."

"They don't take boys. You have to be eighteen."

"I can lie about my age. I've been told I pass for older many a time."

Emily frowned. "Why are you in such a hurry to leave? I thought you liked it here."

He shrugged. "I used to." He looked around as if he could see the horizon beyond the houses. "But there's so much more world out there I want to see," he looked down at her, "and I want to fight. I already missed the Texas War. I don't want to miss the next big one."

"What about the war your father writes about?"

"Father sympathizes with the Indians." He shook his head. "It wouldn't be good if I joined up to kill them. Besides, he would find me and have me sent home. He knows too many of the officers."

"So you're really planning on running away from home?"

He stopped walking, angry she would suggest such a thing. "I'm not running away."

"You are too! It's a secret isn't it? And you're not old enough. And you're supposed to be the man of the house while your father is gone. That's running away."

Her accusation bothered him but still he defended his decision. "I've been working since I was thirteen and I'm into college studies now. So, I've got my own money to leave and more education than I need to join the military. That makes me old enough to make my own decisions." He humped. "Now I wish I never told you. You're probably going to tell."

Emily didn't want to disappoint him. "No of course not. I promised not to and besides it's your business what you do." They walked a moment in silence. They were getting close to her house and she knew the private moment would end as soon as they reached her doorstep. She wanted something to bind him to her. "Henry, will you make me a promise?"

"Hmm."

She would take that as a yes. "Promise you'll write to me."

He hesitated to make such a commitment.

"I'll make sure I always get the mail and keep your letters a secret." When still he hesitated she added, "Please."

The way she said it got to him every time. Since they were children, he hadn't been able to deny her anything when she added her eloquent 'please' with her pleading gray eyes. "I promise." And just like every time before he was rewarded with her sparkling smile that never failed to make him smile in return.

They were almost at her doorstep. "When will you leave?"

"Soon."

"Will you say goodbye?"

He handed her package to her. "If I can." He turned on his heel and left before she made him promise to do that as well.

Emily's accusation of running away bothered Henry like a canker sore. He didn't want to admit it but he knew she was right so he finally mailed a letter to his father. He was finding it a lot harder to tell his mother. He was frustrated and felt trapped because he couldn't just leave like he wanted and he was worried what his father's reply would say. Would he let him go or insist he wait? These thoughts consumed him and the distraction slowed him down cleaning the sponges forcing him to work late to finish up. He walked home, tired and sweaty in the late August heat. When he reached the front yard, he went around back to the washstand next to the kitchen to clean up for supper.

Betsy wiped the moisture from her brow as she placed their food on the tray to carry in the house. Henry was late again but she couldn't hold supper any longer. Off and on all day she worried over their strained relationship and his disregard for coming home in a timely manner. The fighting wasn't working. Tonight she would try to get him to talk about his thoughts and feelings. Hearing sounds outside, she wiped her hands on her apron as she stepped outside. "Henry, where have you been?" Her tone was a little harsher than she intended, nor was it what she meant to say. It must be the heat getting the better of her.

Henry's temper flashed. He wiped the towel down his face and threw it at the washstand. "I had to work late."

"You promised you wouldn't be late anymore."

"I said I would be home for supper and I'm here aren't I?"

His anger escalated hers. "You should have been here a half hour ago. Your sisters are hungry and so am I."

"Well soon you won't have to put up with my tardiness."

His words were ominous. "What does that mean?"

"I've been meaning to tell you something. I'm tired of this place and I plan on leaving it very soon."

"You can't leave. You're not old enough."

"Old enough to work and earn my own keep, aren't I?"

Betsy frowned. "Well yes but..." She was hot, tired and frustrated and ill prepared to handle this conversation. "You, sir, are not leaving." She knew as soon as it rolled off her tongue it was the worst thing she could say.

Henry's jaw clenched. "You are not my mother."

Betsy's jaw dropped. Of all the things he could say that hurt the most. She was left standing there speechless as he left the yard and walked down the street back towards town.

It felt like *deja vu*. She was walking the floor of the parlor, the city bell about to ring, waiting on Henry. He walked in the door just before the first chime. She met him in the foyer.

His troubled eyes met hers. "I'm sorry for saying you weren't my mother. I didn't mean it." He rapidly climbed the stairs not giving her a chance to beg him to change his mind. He still planned to leave. He just meant to tell her better than he did.

Betsy didn't get a chance to talk to Henry in the morning either. Worry kept her awake all night and in the morning she felt hopelessly inadequate as his mother. Not knowing what else to do she cleaned up breakfast and wrote a hasty and emotional letter to Theodore. She rushed to the post office with all three girls in tow knowing the mail ship was due to leave today.

By mid-afternoon she was second guessing her words to Theodore and after a restless night's sleep she was regretting having done what she promised herself she wouldn't do. She penned another letter from a much calmer state to go out the following week. It was the best she could do to fix it.

* * *

In the early light of a September dawn, as the ship pulled away from the dock, Henry cast one final look at the island he called home for the last nine years. He was headed to New Orleans and from there to Arkansas. Unwilling to fight in a war his father was against, he decided to go to the western reservation and enlist in the army for guard duty. It was the furthest he could get out of reach of his father. He wasn't proud of the way he was leaving but he felt it was the only way he could get away. They were all trying to hold him back—except his father. He was surprised to receive his sire's blessings although he did ask Henry to wait until he was at least sixteen. His birthday wasn't for another five months so Henry was actually disappointing him too but what was done, was done.

Henry turned around and walked to the bow of the ship to face a future of his own making with excitement and a hint of trepidation.

* * *

Betsy picked up the letter on the dining room table knowing what it would say. She felt the emptiness of the room upstairs as she walked past so the letter was no surprise. Still, she didn't have the heart to read it. If only he had given her more time maybe she could have convinced him to wait.

In the days that followed Henry's departure she found herself crying at odd moments for what seemed like no reason until she realized that even when he wasn't in her immediate thoughts her heart ached for her son. She also hadn't realized how much she depended on him since Aunt Agatha's death. Perhaps too much. Her dependency may have attributed to some of his rebellion, adding guilt to her grief and worry. Often times through the day she would pray to God to help her let it all go and to watch over her boy. And when she recited their family verse for Theodore, it now was for Henry too.

"Have not I commanded Thee! Be strong and of a good courage: be not afraid, neither be thou dismayed: for the Lord thy God is with thee whithersoever thou goest."

* * *

The following week's mail brought a letter from Theodore written before her fateful one to him. His words were a comfort for he knew her so well. They were exactly what she needed to hear.

Dearest Love,

I know you are struggling. Have faith in God and yourself.

Do not fret over Henry. He is angry with me and taking it out on you. He has written me of his intentions. Do not try and hold him. It will only lead to bitterness. You must have the courage to let him go. I have faith God will watch over our son. You have raised him well and he knows more of self-reliance having grown up in Key West than he would ever have learned in New York. He is no longer our little boy and if he really leaves then he is ready to face the world. I know it will be one of the hardest things you ever have to do, but let him go.

I am unsure when I will be with you. I intended to head home with the summer heat but other events have intervened. Perhaps soon I will be able to let you know when to expect my return.

Faithfully yours,

Teddy

Tears slid down her cheeks for Henry and Theodore, for her, and for all the families torn apart.

If only this war would end...

Fort Brooke, August 1841

The mail carrier handed Theodore a letter from Betsy. He knew she continued to struggle at home without him, leaving Theodore in a constant state of guilt. Daily he wavered between staying and leaving especially after receiving the disturbing letter from Henry. Standing under the shade of a large oak in the center of the fort he opened the folds of her letter.

Dearest Theodore,

We are losing him!

You must come home!

His heart and throat constricted. Theodore noticed the water droplets marring the letter when he opened it. He assumed they were from rain but now he realized they were her tears. He took a deep breath and looked at the soldiers around him. They were not paying attention. He was already looked down upon for 'sympathizing with the savages'. He did not need to add the weakness of tears to their derision. He refolded the letter and went in search of a modicum of privacy to finish reading it.

Henry has become an angry young man. Last night he told me he plans to leave. We argued and he left. His parting words were, "You are not my mother!" He later apologized but his words still echo in my heart.

He doesn't understand why you sympathize with the Seminoles against your country. He has read your articles but only listens to the stories of Indian savagery oft repeated by frightened citizens. He does not believe we have hurt them every bit as much as they have hurt us. He has not tried to understand their reasons for fighting. In the innocence of youth, his world is black and white.

Please come home!

I never intended to utter these words but I know not how to keep him with us. He is but fifteen. Not yet man enough to face the world. He will not listen to me. You must come home and talk to your son. Sooner, rather than later. I fear he will be gone before too long.

Otherwise, all is well. The girls are growing as fast as the mangroves.

Your always love,

Betsafina

He wanted to run to her. For almost six years she endured managing the house and children by herself, handling all that came her way, birth and death, time and again without complaint, never once begging him to come home. Until now. How could he not go to her?

He looked at the date and realized her letter was written before the one he sent telling her to let him go. He hoped it would comfort her guilt for he knew much of her distress was in feeling she failed him and Henry. But the letter would do nothing for the loss of support Henry provided her. Theodore doubted even she knew how much she depended on Henry. Now she was left to carry the burden alone. She needed him home.

Theodore assessed the current situation. The forty days passed and most of Wild Cat's band was gathered at Fort Brooke awaiting transport. Inspired by his success with Wild Cat, Colonel Worth requested Alligator be brought back from Arkansas to encourage more of the Tallahassee bands to surrender. The troops were working through the summer chasing small bands of Indians and destroying any camps, huts or crops they came across. They were seldom able to capture any but they made it difficult for the Indians to sustain themselves being afraid to hunt by rifle for fear of being captured. And perhaps even more devastating to their morale, for the first time they were not able to perform the Green Corn Ceremony. As the days of summer passed, those weary of running surrendered.

So much was happening, it was a bad time to leave. At this rate it would be over soon and Theodore wanted very much to witness the final declaration or truce. He looked down at the letter in his hand. *Please come home!* He couldn't ignore her plea. Betsafina was more important. He headed to the wharf to find his way home.

He booked passage on a schooner headed to Key West in three days. While waiting to leave two things happened to change his plans. The first was another letter from Betsy telling him to ignore her rash plea to return as it was merely a moment of weakness on her part and assuring him he should stay. Theodore still intended to return home until Colonel Worth captured Chief Hospetarke and fifteen of his warriors. He decided to postpone his return to interview the latest captives and then his departure became indefinite as Alligator was soon to arrive. From him, Theodore could learn how the Seminoles were faring in their new home.

* * *

No sooner was Alligator taken off the transport ship, Wild Cat, Hospetarke and nearly three hundred of their followers were loaded on board headed for Arkansas. The night it sailed Colonel Worth and his officers quietly celebrated over drinks.

Lieutenant Sprague raised his glass. "Tracks seen, fields destroyed, country waded, troops exhausted, Indians gone."[16]

Colonel Worth clinked glasses with him. "Here, here."

Alligator's emissaries were soon dispatched and succeeded in bringing in two chiefs and a hundred and sixty-two of their people. The chiefs still at large banded together swearing to kill any messengers from the whites. They made good on that promise killing two of them as they tried to persuade Halleck Tustenuggee to surrender. Colonel Worth was disappointed at the loss of this particular chief as he was the most ardent one against leaving and was believed to be responsible for the burning, looting and death plaguing the settlers Colonel Worth promised to protect.

Throughout the winter months, his troops chased Halleck Tustenuggee but his warriors made tracking difficult by walking backward, crisscrossing their paths, and it was even believed they were jumping stumps in the swamps to elude the soldiers. More than once the army thought they were about to capture him only to find their prey had vanished.

Theodore, weary of waiting for an end that would never come, returned home in November.

Key West

The first few months after Henry's departure were emotionally difficult. Especially since he did not give them a chance to say goodbye, instead leaving a simple letter on the dining room table letting Betsy know he left on a ship sailing at dawn for New Orleans.

Of course in the first few weeks, Brianna and Agatha missed Henry something terrible. He was good about giving his little sisters attention, often playing with them when he was home. They moped about the house until Betsy took pity on them often inviting Abby's children to come over to play. Abby's visits helped comfort Betsy as well. With the resiliency of children,

Brianna and Agatha soon adjusted. It took Betsy longer as she came to realize in how many subtle ways she depended on Henry's support and companionship much as she had done with Aunt Agatha.

Her worry for him only increased with his absence. She knew full well she needed to hand it over to God but she struggled daily to do so. He was often in her thoughts knowing he was traveling in lands unknown to him, facing all kinds of dangers, and meeting people who could mean him harm. Not knowing what was happening to him was the worst. She didn't even know which direction he was headed after landing in New Orleans. He neglected to mention it to either her or his father.

Five long worrisome weeks after Henry's sudden departure, Betsy finally received a letter from Fort Gibson, Arkansas Territory.

Dear Mother,

These weeks of travel gave me a lot of time to think about—and regret—the way I left. You have always been loving and kind to me and I in return was thoughtless and cruel leaving the way I did and even in telling you I was planning to leave. I was feeling trapped in a cage and in the end quite desperate to escape. I am sorry I hurt you in doing so. Please forgive me.

As you will see by the postmark, I have made my way to the Indian reservation. There is so much land and space here, I no longer feel trapped but instead sometimes I feel lost and small and insignificant. I can't believe how much I miss the ocean and the salt water breeze across the island. I know I will one day return but for now, I need to wander and explore the world.

The army commander at Fort Gibson is very astute. He knew I was lying about my age and either liked me despite it or took pity on me because of it. Either way, he hired me as an errand boy and gave me a place to sleep in the barracks for I know not what I would have done otherwise. There are not many jobs to be had here.

This place is very much as father described it and like him my favourite spot is under the hardwoods by the river. I go there almost every evening to fish and think.

I have made friends with many of those stationed here and even with some of the Indians who visit the fort regularly. I am often surprised how many know father but I am not surprised they think of him kindly.

Thank you for all you taught me and for your love and kindness. You are the best mother a son could ask for.

Give my love to Brianna, Agatha and Emmaline.

Your son,

Henry

Betsy found comfort in knowing Henry's whereabouts and that someone, even if it was a stranger, was looking out for him. It lessened her worry and made it easier to manage on her own for the following six weeks before Theodore's return. She felt even better when Theodore admitted to her, he had entreated a general to have her brothers, Frederick and Roderick, reassigned to Fort Gibson so they could look out for Henry. Knowing he likely would need it, Betsy mailed Henry a bank draft equal to his earnings from cleaning sponges that she saved for him.

* * *

Thanksgiving, Christmas and New Year's flew by in rapid succession. Betsy enjoyed every moment of the past two and a half months with Theodore. There were only two dark shadows to mar her happiness. The loss of Madalyn and Henry's absence were vividly felt by all in the family. They took turns entertaining Emmaline trying to keep her from dwelling on her missing twin. She smiled a little more often now and anyone who succeeded in making her laugh was championed by the family.

It was now the end of January, 1842, and Betsy looked upon every day as a gift to be enjoyed. Her children were growing fast. Agatha turned four last week and the toddler tantrums finally diminished but now she questioned everything. Betsy would wager she heard 'why' at least a hundred times a day. Brianna was turning six next month and daily surprised Betsy with her sweet and thoughtful generosity and her patience with eighteen month old, Emmaline. Betsy was very thankful to have Brianna's energy in keeping up with the roaming toddler.

Every day with Theodore was a blessing too. The war still continued and it was only a matter of time before news or a letter pulled him away again. She especially enjoyed their conversations in the evenings, after the girls were put to bed. Not having an adult—or almost adult—in the house to converse with was perhaps the hardest to endure between Henry's leaving and Theodore's return. They talked of everything. The war, their hopes for the future, the girls, and it was funny after all this time they finally discussed their differing ideas on parenting. She was a little dismayed to realize she could not get him to take on more of the role of disciplinarian for his beliefs were more lenient than hers. Betsy thanked Aunt Agatha for that disappointment. She was sure it was the starchy old lady's treatment of Theodore in his early years that kept him from being strict with his girls.

Otherwise, all was smooth between them. Especially in the bedroom. He was ardent and affectionate and made her feel not only desirable after bearing four children but cherished as well. She in turn did all she could to take care of him in every way a wife should. She wanted to make it hard for him to leave so perhaps he would continue to delay doing so.

There was one other thing clouding their happiness. Theodore still suffered nightmares and sometimes she would find him brooding, his face reflecting the dark thoughts plaguing him. And once she saw a shadow cross his eyes that made her shudder. Something dreadful was bothering him. He would dismiss it whenever she asked, assuring her it was nothing to worry about but she could tell there were things haunting him.

This war had to end soon....

* * *

Theodore put off leaving long enough. Colonel Worth wrote him a few weeks ago to let him know another group of Seminoles was ready to ship west and he estimated not more than three hundred could be left in the territory. Worth wrote Congress asking to end the war and allow the remaining Seminoles to settle on a reservation far south of the settlers. Theodore wrote the article but didn't believe it would happen. Almost every general before Worth tried to declare an end to this war and one side or the other always managed to mess it up.

Sure enough, Theodore now held a letter from Colonel Worth letting him know the request was denied. Congress wasn't ready to concede. They still felt they had the men and the means to rid Florida of all Indians. Instead Worth was instructed to offer the soldiers $100 for every Indian captured. Theodore shook his head contemplating the ill effects such an action could create. He had to go back.

He hung his head in defeat. The last few months were a wonderful balm on his soul. He hated bringing it to an end but, once again, duty called. With a bounty placed on them, the Seminole were going to be hunted down such as they never had before. Greedy men were unscrupulous.

Key West, March 28th, 1842

Betsy sat alone in the dark parlor by the open front window listening to the sound of a soft spring shower, bathed in the shifting light of a hurricane lantern on a nearby table as the breeze flickered the flame. She inhaled deeply the fresh scent of rain. The girls were asleep and she was finally writing some long overdue letters. She shifted the lap desk and freshened her ink. She couldn't help smiling as she added the next line to her mother's letter.

> *Despite Theodore's return to the war, I can't help smiling in happiness for I am increasing again. I prayed it would happen one more time and He answered. This little one will arrive around harvest time.*

Betsy absently rubbed her left hand over her secret joy as she considered her next words. Her mother's letter was easy. It was the letter to Theodore that concerned her. She hoped he would be happy there was another child on the way.

Chapter 44

Fort Brooke, April 5th, 1842

Theodore decided to take a walk after spending hours working on his latest article. He stepped out following the edge of the barracks to keep his distance from the passing troops engaged in field practice. Afternoon sunlight caught and sparkled in the lingering raindrops clinging to the oak leaves from the recent shower. In the distance, the bay glistened as the sunlight played upon the rippling water. All was bright and beautiful in God's world. If only the same could be said for man.

He stopped when he noticed Lieutenant Sprague headed in his direction bearing a letter. The officer stepped up to him. "I thought you might like to have this right away. It's from your wife."

Theodore accepted the letter. "Yes, thank you."

Lieutenant Sprague tipped his hat. "I'll leave you to read it. Good evening, sir."

Absently, Theodore replied, "Hmm," while he impatiently broke the seal.

> *My dearest love,*
>
> *The girls and I miss you deeply but we are doing fine. They of course, send their love as do I.*
>
> *I have news to tell you and I hope it brings you as much joy as it does for me. Our family will grow again in the fall. I am thankful for this blessing. I am sure it will worry you but rest assured so far I feel wonderful. Even the morning sickness is less this time. I am feeling confident in my ability to carry this child despite my years.*
>
> *Every night I pray for you and Henry and look forward to the day we are all reunited again.*
>
> *It is late now. The girls put to bed long ago. I should go to my slumber for Emmaline rises early as well you know. I need all my energy to keep up with her little legs.*
>
> *I'll see you in my dreams, love. Be well.*
>
> *Your adoring wife,*
>
> *Betsafina*

Theodore folded the letter and looked out to the bay feeling a little more homesick than he had moments ago. Some days he despaired of ever being able to stay home for good.

How did he feel about another child? He would love another one, boy or girl. Wanting was never the issue. It was Betsy's health that mattered. He hoped she was telling the truth about feeling good. They both were guilty of writing the words they thought the other one needed instead of the truth. He had no choice but to believe she was being honest. Under that assumption, he was happy about another baby which is what he would write to her later.

He watched another worn out battalion enter the fort gates returning from a three day hunt for Halleck Tustenuggee and his warriors. Colonel Worth was determined to catch the thirty-five year old chief who was attacking the settlers and rousing the others to kill Alligator's messengers. Worth believed the chief's capture was the key to ending the war. Theodore was skeptical they could catch him and at this point he was having a hard time believing anything short of rounding up every single Indian in the territory would end the war.

He felt locked in an unending nightmare.

* * *

Week after week the soldiers hunted the Indians bringing in a few here and there but Halleck Tustenuggee continued to elude them.

One afternoon, Colonel Worth came to Theodore all excited because his scouts assured him this time they had found Halleck's ca.p.

"Tomorrow I am leading my men and we are going to bring in this chief. Do you want to come along to see me put an end to this war?"

Theodore wanted to laugh but knew better than to offend his host. Even if he didn't believe the colonel, he was bored sitting around the fort. The exercise alone would do him good. As evidenced by the last few weeks, the danger of being involved in an engagement was slim, "Thank you for the offer. I believe I will."

"Very well. We leave at dawn."

* * *

Theodore stepped in line behind four hundred soldiers led by Colonel Worth and several black and Indian guides as they marched out of the gates of Fort Brooke. They were headed northeast to Lake Apopka. After two days of hard travel, they arrived at a hammock near Pilarklikaha Swamp, about thirty miles south of Fort King. The area was also known as Abraham's Old Town. They stopped early to rest, for tomorrow, the 19th of April, they hoped to engage the enemy where he slept.

Theodore was awake before dawn anxious to get this expedition over with and return to civilization. He sipped a second cup of heavy coffee from a tin cup as dawn lightened the inky sky to gray. Clouds hung low and the humidity climbed. Everyone was anxious for battle. It had been a long time coming to this.

The scouts led them out, their pace quick through the swampy land sending birds and animals scurrying out of the way. An hour later the scouts suddenly halted in front of a hammock surrounded by a bog of rotting vegetation the stench of which had all of them covering their mouth and nose.

Colonel Worth ordered the dragoons to go around to the other side of the hammock to encircle their foe. He did not want this opportunity to slip away. The foot soldiers were ordered to move forward. The men waded into the mud hacking down the thick botany before them.

The fetor of decay was so overwhelming soldiers could be heard retching. Theodore remained behind holding a handkerchief to his face though it did little good. His stomach churned and bile rose giving him a second unwelcome taste of his morning coffee. Worth showed no signs of such discomfort as he eagerly followed his men into the bog. Theodore could well imagine in his excitement of the moment the colonel was oblivious to any discomfort.

A half hour later, Theodore heard a shot fired and yelling followed by a large volley of gunfire. Birds rose from the trees flying away in all directions. It didn't last long before all was quiet again.

Curiosity made Theodore brave the mud and the stench to see the warriors' camp. Just inside the tree line was a barricade of logs. Behind it, the soldiers were milling around rummaging through the belongings left behind by the fleeing Indians. One soldier was guarding a captured warrior being interrogated by Colonel Worth with the aid of an interpreter.

Theodore stepped up to First Lieutenant George McCall. "What happened?"

"They were waiting for us behind the logs."

"How many?"

"About forty warriors. They fired and we returned fire and then the dragoons charged in and fired from the rear. They realized quickly enough they were outnumbered. Left everything behind and fled into the swamps." He nodded his head to the left. "We lost one man, four more are injured."

"And the Indians?"

"They left one dead behind and we captured another. Don't know how many of them were wounded."

Colonel Worth turned away from his prisoner and headed to a cluster of his officers. McCall and Theodore joined him. Disappointment made the colonel brusk. "Burn it. We'll make camp at Warm Springs and send out the scouts. Maybe we can get another run at 'em."

Collectively his men replied, "Yes sir."

* * *

Several disappointing days later they were still waiting for the scouts to return with news of Halleck's whereabouts when a junior officer came running into Colonel Worth's makeshift office. "Sir, you need to come see this."

"What is it?"

"We think it's him."

"Him?"

"Halleck, sir, and his wives."

Theodore had never seen the colonel move as fast as he did now to get out the door. Theodore and the lieutenants followed just as excited by this turn of events. Reaching the yard, Theodore recognized the tall lean warrior he characterized as modest and unassuming. It was definitely Halleck Tustenuggee.

The colonel stopped in the center of the camp and waited for the warrior to come to him. Halleck held a white flag and behind him were two women believed to be his wives and two children. Excited energy filled the camp. The colonel welcomed the chief as a guest.

Several days followed of talking but Colonel Worth was frustrated for although both men agreed the war must end, he couldn't get the chief to promise to emigrate. Frustrated, yet determined, he decided to follow in the footsteps of General Jesup. Colonel Worth devised a scheme to get what he wanted.

He invited Halleck to visit Fort King. Theodore followed them more than ready to leave the wilderness. The morning after their arrival a messenger sped into Fort King with urgent news for Colonel Worth. Lieutenant Sprague, Theodore, Halleck Tustenuggee and an interpreter patiently waited for him to read the message. When Worth finished he looked directly at Halleck Tustenuggee.

"Last night, my men offered a feast for your band during which, under my orders, all were seized and loaded into wagons. They are now on their way to the embarkation center in Fort Brooke." Four soldiers entered the room unnoticed. At his signal, they stepped forward with their guns at the ready. "And you Chief Halleck are now my prisoner as well."

Halleck's chest heaved and his eyes flashed in silent rage. It was apparent he wanted to fight but saw the futility of it. He ran his hands through his hair and suddenly sank to the floor, unconscious. The soldiers picked him up and carried him off to the same cell in which Agent Thompson once imprisoned Osceola.

Theodore could only stare at Colonel Worth in silent shock, never suspecting he was planning such underhanded treachery. The Colonel smiled as he read from the message still in his hand. "Forty-three warriors, thirty-seven women, and thirty-four children." He looked up with a huge grin. "That should please the War Department."

* * *

Indeed it did. On May 10th, President John Tyler told Congress he was now agreeable to ending the war. He authorized Colonel Worth to do so any way he saw fit. Theodore wrote the facts but didn't believe them. He was waiting for the other shoe to drop, so to speak. Worth revived his plan from January. He offered peace to those who agreed to remain in an assigned area in the southwest portion of the peninsula. All others would be forced to emigrate.

Worth shipped Halleck and his band west in July. There were small bands scattered about the territory. In the north were Creeks led by Octiarche. Tiger Tail and his Muskogee band were near Tallahassee. Chipco and his Muskogee band were north of Lake Okeechobee. Billy Bowlegs had a larger band near Charlotte Harbour and Sam Jones led a band of Mikasukis in the Everglades near Fort Lauderdale. Worth offered these chiefs and their warriors each a new rifle, money, and a year's worth of rations to move west. A few accepted the offer right away. He gave the others time to decide—accept or move to the Florida reservation.

August 4th, Congress passed the Armed Occupation Act encouraging settlement of Florida by offering 160 acres to each new settler with the stipulation they must build a house and cultivate five acres in the first year and they were expected to protect themselves. It was the government's way of trying to ensure the Indians were kept out of upper Florida.

On August 14th, Colonel Worth officially declared an end to the hostilities assuming those remaining would move or agree to leave. Theodore wanted to believe it was over but it had been declared before only to resume again. He refused to get his hopes up. Just because their side was done fighting didn't mean the Seminoles would hold to it.

It wasn't until Worth started reducing the army's presence in Florida that he allowed himself to consider the possibility of it truly being over but still he didn't believe it. Not to mention it was a bit anti-climactic after seven years of fighting. There was no treaty signed. No meeting with the chiefs to agree to end it. There was no finality to it. It was as if both sides were simply done fighting and went their separate ways.

Colonel Worth received his long awaited promotion to Brigadier General and was granted a ninety day leave. He wasted no time making good on his departure. Theodore decided to follow his example.

His last thought as he sailed away from Fort Brooke was to marvel that somehow he had managed to be involved in the first and last military engagement of this odd Florida War.

Chapter 45

Key West, Wednesday, September 7th, 1842

Betsy wanted to run but her girth would not allow it. She was forced to wait on the front porch watching Theodore in the distance making his way home to her. She heard rumors the war was over. She didn't believe them but it was hope enough for her to find every excuse to be out on the porch, day after day, watching for his return. Joy leapt in her breast when moments ago she saw a lone man walking. She knew it was him before she could make out his features and now, impatiently she stood waiting at the top step.

The girls were on the porch with her entertaining themselves. Brianna, curious as to what had captured her mother's attention, moved to stand beside her. "What is it Momma?"

Betsy laid a hand on her chest as if it would steady her racing heart. Breathily she answered Brianna. "Your father." She knew the moment he saw her for his pace quickened to nearly a run. Agatha and Emmaline came to wait on her other side.

Theodore dropped his bags without breaking stride and raced up the stairs. Betsy took a step back to give him room and another step as his momentum demanded.

Theodore pulled his wife to him getting as close as her burden would allow. He buried his bearded face in her neck. "It's over Betsy. I'm home for good." The strength of his emotion nearly brought him to tears.

She pulled back to look him in the eye. "The rumors are true? It's really over?"

He solemnly nodded. "It is really over this time. I'll not be leaving you again Betsafina; at least not these long absences." He said the words but he didn't believe them. Not truly. He was waiting for something to happen. It always did.

He held her as she laughed and cried. The emotions of the moment were overwhelming. Brianna and Agatha began pulling on his trousers to be included. He knelt down and opened his arms to them. Emmaline hesitated but seeing her sisters rush to him she followed suit.

Agatha pulled away a little to say, "Story, Poppa."

Emmaline mimicked her. "Story, Poppa."

Betsy and Theodore's shared laughter mingled on the late summer breeze. He smiled broadly and ruffled Agatha's hair. "Of course, sweetheart. As soon as I wash up." How was he going to fit all three of his girls on his lap? He didn't know but it was a delightful problem to have.

He and his daughters were inseparable the rest of the day. He told stories, played games, and was even invited to their tea party. He didn't mind a bit. He had a lot of missed time to make up for with them.

In the parlor before supper he approached Betsy with his hand held out. Curious she placed her hand in his and rose from the chair. Theodore tucked a wayward tendril behind her ear. "Would you sing us a song? I want to dance with you."

Betsy's heart fluttered just as it did a long ago December evening when he asked her to dance at Esperanza's wedding party. She sang a flowing song of courtship as he waltzed her around the room.

Agatha clapped her hands. "I want to dance." She held her hands up to her father. "Dance with me Poppa."

As they twirled past, Theodore said, "Patience little one."

One more turn about the room and Betsy pulled away winded. Dancing, singing, and breathing were a bit much all at once in her delicate condition. While she caught her breath, Theodore hummed a tune as he twirled Brianna about the room. When Betsy was able to sing again, he danced with Agatha but her little legs had trouble keeping up, so he swept her up in his arms. Her giggling laughter put joy in his heart. The next song was for Emmaline but first he had to coax her into his arms.

While Theodore waltzed their daughters she studied the changes in him. The lines around his eyes and lips were deeper, his face tanned a bit darker, and his brown hair was now streaked with gray at the temples. His smile was as bold and his laughter as infectious as always. He was the man she married, albeit older and travel weary, and behind his eyes she could see a shadow of the horrors he had witnessed. She wondered if it would fade with time or was it now a part of him.

As they sat down to their meal, Theodore looked at Henry's empty chair. It was the only flaw in an otherwise perfect day. He looked across the table and saw the same thought reflected in Betsy's eyes.

At bedtime they both listened to the girls' prayers and tucked them in. Betsy kissed each of her curly haired pixies on one cheek then left to clean up downstairs while Theodore read them a familiar story. The excitement of the day wore them out and they were all sound asleep before he finished. He kissed their cheeks and thanked the good Lord for blessing him with each one of them. He also said a prayer for Madalyn's soul and Henry's safety.

Theodore found Betsy outside on the sleeping porch watching the sun set. He quietly walked up behind her and slipped his arms atop hers crossed above her protruding belly. Gathering her close, he nuzzled the side of her neck and wondered at how naturally they fit together. They stood still watching the radiant orb drop towards the horizon across the water. Moments later he realized they were swaying slightly back and forth in unison. He guessed she must have started it; an innate result of motherhood. He whispered in her ear sending a shiver down her spine. "Are you ready for bed?" She turned in his arms and the corners of her kissable lips lifted in a seductive smile more than answering his question.

* * *

The following morning over breakfast Betsy surprised him with an announcement. "Let's have a cookout to celebrate the war's end. We can invite everyone."

Theodore's brow furrowed. "Everyone?"

"Yes, the end of war is good for everyone, so everyone should celebrate with us."

Her laugh enchanted him and so he found himself agreeing even when he would rather not. "And when do you plan to have this cookout?"

"I was thinking this Saturday."

Brianna asked, "What's a cookout?"

Betsy smiled. "It's when friends and family share food and eat together outside."

"Will Thorn and Nathaniel be there?"

"Yes, of course. All the Eatonton children will be there and many of your other friends too."

In a petulant voice she asked, "How long do I have to wait till Saturday?"

Betsy gave her an admonishing look. "You tell me. Today is Thursday."

Brianna scrunched her nose and forehead but did as she was told. "All of today and tomorrow's Friday. Two days. No." She looked to her mother. "What time on Saturday?"

Theodore was impressed and quite proud of her reasoning skills.

Betsy considered. "Hmm, should we have it for dinner or supper?"

Brianna said, "Dinner! Please, let's have it for dinner."

Betsy smiled. "Alright, Dinner it is."

"Then I have to wait two and a half days."

Theodore grinned and Betsy nodded.

* * *

Those two and a half days flew in a flurry of plans and preparations. Word spread to everyone living on or near the island and almost all were planning to be there. It had been too long since they really celebrated anything other than holidays. The gathering would be so large, it was moved to the open ground of Jackson Square. The men put together a large makeshift grill to cook the meat. Theodore surprised Betsy by purchasing a whole cow to be butchered, promising to cook her the best steak she would ever eat. Betsy made a dozen loaves of her famous cinnamon bread for her contribution. Others would bring side dishes to share and the navy commander ordered his men to set up open tents to offer shade.

The weather was perfect the day of the party. There was still the heat of summer to contend with for the afternoon meal but puffy clouds filled the sky and the breeze from the ocean was prevalent keeping the guests from overheating. Much like Washington's 100th birthday celebration years ago, tables and chairs, dishes and food were bought by all who joined. Spirits flowed freely, food was plentiful, toasting was boisterous, children scampered everywhere playing their games, and all were having a good time.

Theodore wasn't enthused about the cookout when Betsy first mentioned it but he had to admit he was enjoying it and it was a very efficient means of reconnecting with everyone on the island after spending so much time away these last seven years. He had fun joshing around with Max and Jonathon as they worked over the grill. And as people began to gather, he made the rounds greeting Mayor Alexander Patterson, Judge Marvin, the marshal, numerous lawyers, shop keepers, sailors and the like but he really appreciated the time spent with friends.

He saw Betsy standing under the shade of a lone palm tree. She looked beautiful in her blue gingham dress and white apron. He lovingly took in her profile, heavy with child, recalling how badly he wanted to see her like this with their first one and how pleased he was to receive Henry's thoughtful drawing. As good as it was, Henry hadn't done her justice. In the flesh, she was breathtaking. Drawn to her, Theodore made his way to her side and slipped his arm behind her. She turned slightly leaning into him and slipped her arm behind his back as well. He leaned down to softly say, "Are you enjoying yourself?"

She nodded in reply.

"Do you need to sit down and rest?"

"Not just yet. Soon."

"Impressive, isn't it?"

She looked up at him. "What is?"

"What you can manage in just two and half days."

She smiled.

They watched their girls run past chasing the Eatonton boys along with the six Keats children and several others he couldn't place. Betsy scanned the crowd for Emmaline. It wasn't uncommon for babies to be passed around in a crowd like this. She relaxed when she found her in Abby's arms standing next to Max who held Jacob. The two toddlers appeared to be holding their own happy conversation. Betsy nodded her head in their direction drawing Theodore's attention to the pleasant scene.

Theodore kissed Betsy's temple. "It's good to see Emmaline happy."

Betsy nodded and leaned into him again. "There are moments now she is like she was before..." She couldn't finish the sentence.

Theodore squeezed her waist in understanding.

To their left, Mrs. Mabrity was surrounded by her children and grandchildren. Earlier she told them this event was worth losing her afternoon shut-eye and the light just might have to take care of itself tonight. They knew she wasn't serious for as long as she had breath she would not fail in her duties. Not far away Jonathon and Esperanza were conversing with Mr. and Mrs. Sanchez. Clusters of folks were everywhere visiting with each other.

Thomas and Maria were two of the many free blacks present. Cubans and other immigrants mingled in the crowd as well. It was a nice reminder to Theodore after so many years of reporting on whites against the black and red man that it was possible they could all get along. He wondered how different it might have been if Andrew Jackson lost the 1828 election. It likely would have spared the Choctaw and Cherokee their ordeal. Without Jackson's Indian Removal Act there would have been no reason for the Trail of Tears. But would it only have delayed the inevitable? With certainty Theodore knew it would have only been a delay for the Seminole. The runaway slaves would have created the Florida War regardless.

Betsy felt the tension in her husband. "What is it?"

Theodore looked down and saw the concern etched on her face and made a point of lightening his spirits. He shook his head. "It's nothing dear. Just brooding for a moment. Have I thanked you for doing this?" He inclined his head toward their guests.

"I don't believe you have."

He kissed the top of her head. "Thank you."

"I know you didn't really want to and you did it for me so thank you."

"You're right." He grinned. "But as it turned out I am really glad we did."

Mr. and Mrs. Baxley came to bid them farewell. Theodore overheard her say to Betsy, "Dear, you really need to sit down. You are too old to be in your condition much less standing for so long. Your ankles are going to look like tree trunks when you get home." When they moved on Theodore gave Betsy a critical look, surprised he had not considered her age before. He turned forty this year which would make her thirty-seven. Many were grandparents at their ages. Worry made him speak harshly. "Let's find a chair for you. Or better yet, perhaps we should go home."

Betsy's frown deepened. Mrs. Baxley's comment hurt her feelings but Theodore's angered her. "We have to clean up and we are the hosts; we can't leave until all our guests do."

Theodore bit out, "I think they will understand." Theodore waved Abby over to them. Max followed her. "I'm taking Betsy home. She's been on her feet too long. Would you mind taking over as hosts and seeing to the cleanup? I'll be back shortly to help."

Abby saw the sparks in Betsy's eyes but agreed with Theodore. "We would not mind at all. Betsy you do look a bit flushed. You really should cool down and take a nap..." Betsy opened her mouth to protest. "...for the baby's sake."

Betsy's lips pressed together. She couldn't argue against Abby's wisdom and her child's welfare. Begrudgingly she said, "Of course."

Abby looked to Max and receiving his nod turned back to them. "We will take the children home with us and to church tomorrow. You two deserve a night of rest. Do not worry about anything here, either. We can manage the rest of this too."

Before Betsy could protest, Theodore eagerly accepted their offer. He shook Max's hand. "Thank you." She let Theodore usher her home and fuss over her. She reminded herself his overbearing way was a small price to pay for having him home.

* * *

Helping Betsy prepare for the party kept Theodore busy his first few days home and then it was Sunday with church service and bible studies and Sunday dinner at the Eatonton's. Monday he was busy catching up on shop business and reading the past issues of the paper. Robert Mason, as usual, had done an excellent job keeping the business going without him. Now it was Tuesday afternoon and with time to settle in he was coming to realize he had lost his sense of purpose. Publishing a paper in a small town felt mundane compared to writing articles of war.

At a loss for what to do, Robert finally suggested he should work on a summary article of the war. It was a good idea and time consuming as there were many facts to be gathered. And so work for Theodore finally fell into a routine.

Home was another matter. Being with his family was easy and enjoyable except for the rare times discipline was required. For the most part, his daughters were well behaved and despite his worry the weeks passed and Betsy continued to do well. He knew he was abundantly blessed and therein lie the problem.

His biggest regret was not being home much while Henry was growing up. He vowed to do better for his other children. He had some comfort in knowing where Henry was and what he was doing even though it was in a dangerous place. He hoped one day he and his son would be able to find peace with each other. For now, he needed to find peace within himself; a way to return to a normal life and accept the rich blessings he had even though he felt unworthy with the Indians suffering so.

He was warm and safe and dry in his home surrounded by his loved ones while those Seminoles who remained in Florida were forced to build a new life in the wetlands with alligators, snakes, and the constant insects. They were forced to find shelter in the isolated hammocks. How would they survive? How does a mother raise her child in such conditions? How does a father provide for his family and keep them safe when harm is all around? And those in the west suffered as well trying to establish a new community in a foreign land.

His family was intact. The Indians, not just the Seminole but all the tribes forced to relocate, lost family members and some were even now divided between those who stayed and those who left.

He was surrounded by friends. They were now settled among their former enemy; a peaceful people in the midst of warring tribes in the west or land greedy whites in Florida.

Every moment of joy he felt was tempered by guilt for having so much when they had so little.

His articles and those of other journalists eventually turned the tide of opinion in favour of the Seminoles. The nation found much to admire in warriors like Osceola, eventually rallying for the Seminoles to keep their homeland. Theodore often wondered if he had tried harder in the beginning could he have saved the needless suffering. The obvious answer should have been no but it was the doubt that plagued him.

But one guilt outweighed all the others, haunting his sleep, tainting his soul, and making him feel unworthy. Often he woke up in a cold sweat reliving that fateful moment when he ended the life of a boy wanting to be a man. In his dreams he never saw the blade descending towards his neck, only the face of a respected warrior's son whose name he couldn't recall.

October 2nd

Betsy moved to stand between Theodore's legs wearing only her cotton nightgown. He was sitting on the bed in his trousers having just removed his shoes and shirt preparing for bed. Lamplight from the dresser flickered around her silhouette. Theodore placed a hand against her protruding belly, caressing the taught skin surrounding his sixth child whose birth was imminent.

Betsy placed her hands on either side of Theodore's head. She ran her fingers through his soft hair and caressed his face before nudging his chin upward to lift his face and look at her. Her lips softened, the edges lifted but in her eyes were sadness and concern. "Teddy, I've watched you struggle these past weeks and I've waited for you to figure it out on your own... but you haven't. Your melancholy only increases. It is time you talk about it." When he moved to dismiss her she pleaded. "Let me help you."

"You can't help with this."

"Then at least share the burden. Tell me what is bothering you."

He was silent. They looked at each other a long time. When he finally moved she thought he might leave but instead he moved over so she could sit beside him. He picked up her hand, caressing it as he so often did before they fell asleep each night. "I don't..." He frowned and tried again, "I have everything. I have too much."

Understanding dawned on her. "You feel guilty for having so much knowing the Indians suffer."

His brow creased as he turned his head to the side to look at her. "Hmm. They were a peaceful people before we moved in and took away everything. I am thankful for my blessings, I truly am, but I can't enjoy them

561

when they are facing such hardships."

Betsy grasped his hand with both of hers. "Is there anything you can do or didn't do to change their fate?"

A smile flickered. His wife was always practical. But then he grew serious. "I could have tried harder before the war."

"To do what, sway opinion?" He nodded. Betsy tilted her head to better look at him. "No, Theodore. Your words and your passion were not enough. It was who you were writing about that made people take notice. They changed their mind about the war because you gave them someone to care about. Osceola made them want to leave the Seminoles in peace." She smiled at him. "But Osceola couldn't have done that without you. You gave him a voice and emotion and in doing so you gave your readers a man to be respected and admired. I'm proud of you." Tears welled in her eyes and she kissed him. She took a deep breath to clear the emotions. "Now, I ask you again, was there anything you could have done to change their fate?"

Reluctantly, Theodore conceded, "No."

"Then it is not your fault nor is it your responsibility. However, this family is your responsibility. You need to take care of *this* family, which includes giving us the best of you. Your children need you. I need you. All of you. You have to find a way to accept what you cannot change and be truly thankful for what God has blessed upon you. He wants you to enjoy his gifts the same as we want those we bestow gifts upon to enjoy them."

Theodore frowned. "You know I am thankful."

"Yes but part of honoring God is also accepting his blessings and living in the fullness of them. Think of it like this; if you gave me a pearl necklace and I refused to wear it because I felt unworthy it would diminish the value of the gift for both of us."

He quietly took in her words.

Betsy grimaced. She didn't like the potential repercussions her next thought might bring. "But then again there is another way to look at it. Perhaps your guilt is God's way of making sure you continue your work."

Theodore frowned looking at her askance. Surely she didn't think he should leave again. "What are you suggesting?"

Betsy took a deep fortifying breath. "The war is over but as you said their struggles continue. Perhaps it is up to you to help us as a nation keep them in mind. You have Henry and my brothers in Arkansas to keep you informed and you've made enough contacts on the mainland to keep you posted. You have the motivation and the means to write updates as needed and still keep your promise of staying home more than you are away."

Theodore couldn't help his grin. His brave and steady, practical Betsafina was also wise. He never wanted to leave her side again.

Betsy returned his smile but then hers faded. There was one more thing she wanted to resolve and it had to be now in this moment of open honesty. "Teddy, tell me what is in your nightmares?"

The question shouldn't have surprised him. Theodore knew he would eventually have to tell her his deed of two summers past. Betsy would accept him but could he accept himself? His reluctance was not because he had any doubt of her. It was because she was so full of light and good. He didn't want to taint her soul with the darkness he had seen and done.

She felt his hesitation. "Please, open up to me."

"Are you sure?"

She lifted her steadfast chin. "Yes."

He reminded himself again she was brave and steady and strong. "I took a life."

Betsy's gasp was audible. She had no idea he was harbouring something so tragic.

Once started, Theodore rushed to finish the telling. "Early on the nightmares were from engagements I witnessed and my imaginings taken from interviews with soldiers, especially of the Dade massacre but now I am haunted by my own sin."

Betsy quietly waited for more.

"I could hardly believe it when you told me... The same day you gave life to our twin girls, I took the life of a boy almost the same age as Henry." His voice remained steady. "I met his father a few times. He was respected and honorable. He was killed early on in the war." Theodore took a deep breath. "I wish I could remember his name."

Betsy whispered, "How did it happen?"

"It was instinctual. He would have killed me if I hadn't reacted. We weren't even expecting the attack. We were ambushed. I know I shouldn't feel guilty but I still do." His tone changed with the clenching of his jaw. "I was not there to kill or take sides. I only wanted to tell people the unbiased truth."

He turned to her, and she saw the anger in his eyes.

"I did not want to answer to God for the blood of another man. Do you understand? I didn't want to kill but he gave me no choice."

She steadily looked at him. "And you're angry with this boy for putting blood on your hands."

He hissed, "Yes."

With one eyebrow lifted, she waited for this revelation to sink in.

Theodore couldn't believe all this time, beyond the guilt, he was holding on to anger. Now that it was released he felt drained. Somehow acknowledging the anger removed it from his soul. For the first time, he felt it was possible to move past that fateful moment and live his life.

They sat in silence for a few minutes and then, without a word, he stood up and walked to the dresser to turn down the wick, extinguishing the light. Methodically, he removed his trousers and laid them on the back of a chair. Betsy climbed into her side of the bed, respecting his silence. He slid into the sheets and moved to hold her against him. In her ear, he whispered, "Thank you," knowing she would hear all he meant by those simple words.

Theodore made a conscious effort from that day forward to live in the fullness of his blessings. He still felt guilty for having so much but he no longer allowed it to keep him from enjoying that which he had been given. He also discovered giving his time and talents to the island community, more than money, helped alleviate his guilt. And in this new awareness, he began to find peace. But one event would seal his salvation.

October 21st

Theodore woke suddenly in the dark of night. He wasn't sure why at first until he heard the shuffling noise again and realized Betsy was pacing the room. He sat up, "Is everything all right, love?"

Her terse reply came out of the darkness. "Yes."

Instantly he was fully awake. "Is the baby coming?"

"Not yet."

She sounded as if her teeth were clenched. "But you're having pains. I can hear it in your voice."

"You can go back to sleep. These things take time."

"Is there anything I can get you?"

"Someone else to birth this child would be nice."

The flame of a match flared and faded as Theodore lit the lantern. "I would gladly take your pain if I could."

"Oh Teddy. I know you would, but I suppose there's a reason God gave women this burden."

He crossed the room to her, taking her in his arms, and kissing her moist forehead. "How about a cool wet cloth?"

"That would be lovely." As Theodore approached the door she added, "And could you bring the rocker from the nursery?"

"Certainly." He took the stairs two at a time on his way down to the kitchen to retrieve cool water from the cistern. He was out of his depth in this situation. He never witnessed a birth, not even an animal. He had no idea what to expect or how long it would take or what kind of ordeal she would face. All he knew was from the few stories he overheard—and most of those were of the horrible things that had gone wrong. Being away from home for all the other births, not only was he distant but his worries were kept distant too which is probably why he acted so poorly when he learned the twins birth was difficult. And now Betsy was older...

Worry shot through him like arrows to the heart. He stopped at the bottom of the stairs breathing hard. He couldn't return to her like this. He had to remain calm. Calmer than her. He laughed. That was not possible. But he had to allay his fears somehow so he did the only thing he could, he dropped to his knees at the bottom step and prayed for his wife and baby. Feeling a bit better, he resumed his errands, retrieving the rocker from the nursery.

Betsy sat down while he wrung out a cloth. Seeing her physically in pain increased his mental agony for leaving her to endure it alone the previous three deliveries. When he turned to hand the cloth to her she was struggling to get up again. He reached out to help her.

She panted. "Sitting is no good." More panting.

"I'm going to get Abby."

She grasped his arm so tight he flinched. "No. Not yet." She was breathing easier now. "The pains are still too far apart. There's no need for another to lose sleep just yet."

Over the next several hours he watched her flit about the room, walking, sitting and lying in numerous positions trying to find a moment's respite. He tried rubbing her back, caressing her shoulders, and just holding her but the longer it went the less anything helped. His eyes went to the clock on the dresser whenever she tensed in pain.

The night dragged on.

He must have dozed off in the rocking chair because Betsy had to nudge him awake. "Teddy, it's time."

Grogginess clouded his thinking. "Time?"

Another pain hit and she bit out the words. "Time to get Abby."

Theodore jumped out of his seat and flew towards the door.

Betsy called after him. "Pants!"

He halted in mid-step, looked down in surprise at his undress, and turned around to pull on shirt and trousers as fast as he could nearly ripping seams in the process. He pulled his boots on without concern for socks then sprang for the door. He stopped in his tracks and turned to look at her. "Maybe I shouldn't leave you alone. I'll wake Brianna."

"No. I'll be fine. Just go. Now!"

He would have argued but one look at her strained face sent him flying down the stairs and out the front door. The stars shined brightly in the deep of night. Moonlight reflected off the white limestone street illuminating his way as he ran for help.

He reached the Eatonton's out of breath and in record time. He banged loudly on the door, a little harder than was needed. He heard movement in the house and waited. The seconds seemed interminable.

Max opened the door and grinned. One look at Theodore's haggard and worried face told him all he needed to know. "I'll get Abby. No need to wait. Go home. I'll walk her over."

Theodore forgot to thank him in his haste to return to Betsy's side.

Abby took control as soon as she entered the bedroom and Theodore was happy to let her. He never felt as helpless in his entire life as he did watching Betsy endure her pain. Abby took in the situation and promptly gave him a list of things to gather. He overheard her tell Betsy, as he left the room, "You waited till the last minute to send for me." Concern sent him flying through the house to gather the requested items, nearly colliding with

Max in the dark foyer.

Max laughingly whispered, "Whoa there! I know you've missed the last few, but these things tend to take a lot of time."

"It's been hours already."

"And likely hours yet to go. Abby suggested I take the girls back to our house."

"That's a good idea." Betsy quietly suffered through the pain so far but he knew it was an effort for her to do so. "Let me get the rest of this and then I'll wake them."

"Let the little ones sleep. We can carry them."

Moments later, Theodore met Abby at the bedroom door and transferred the items. "Here's the towels, scissors and string. There are two pots of water heating on the stove. If that's all you need, Max and I will take the girls to your house now."

"Thank you." Abby glanced at Betsy then turned back to Theodore. "Hurry back. I will need your assistance."

Theodore blanched. "My assistance? Isn't there another mid-wife?"

"No. She is busy with another birth. I need you to come back."

He swallowed hard. "All right. I'll be back as soon as I can."

Twenty minutes later after tucking his girls in bed with Emily to watch over them, Theodore returned. Hearing Betsy's screams from the front porch, he took the stairs three at a time. He came to a halt in the bedroom doorway surprised to see Abby calmly sitting at the head of the bed wiping Betsy's brow. His wife was lightly panting after this latest pain. She weakly smiled and held her hand out to him.

He rushed to her side. "I'm here sweetheart."

Abby handed Theodore the water bowl and cloth, then moved to the foot of the bed to check her progress. She looked up and smiled at them. "Almost there."

When the next wave of pain crossed Betsy's face, she cried out as she tightly squeezed his hand. He winced, surprised by her strength and then frowned. He hated to see her suffer so. Surely something must be wrong. It was on the tip of his tongue to ask for reassurance all was well when Abby nonchalantly removed the sheet covering Betsy.

Theodore's eyes were drawn to the crowning head. No longer was he aware of Betsy clinging to his hand or of supporting her as she pushed. Mesmerized, he watched as his child came into the world. As if in a dream he heard Abby say, "It's a boy!" In slack jawed wonder his eyes met Betsy's. Her beautiful smile broke his trance. His face split into a grin, and he leaned down to kiss his lovely wife. Love and joy flooded and overwhelmed him. Betsy's tears made his eyes well. For a moment, he forgot Abby was in the room until the mewling cries of the newborn pulled his eyes in their direction.

Abby efficiently cut and tied the cord then swaddled the babe and offered him to Theodore. "Would you like to hold your son?"

Awestruck, he accepted the bundle. He gazed for a moment at the tiny face with sleepy eyes before sitting next to Betsy and transferring the babe to her waiting arms. Neither paid any attention to Abby as she finished her duties as midwife. When she was done she stood before them smiling. "Congratulations. What are you naming him?"

Betsy looked to Theodore for confirmation and receiving his nod of approval said, "James Lawrence after our fathers."

Abby smiled and nodded. "A good strong name and a good birth."

Something in her tone brought Theodore to awareness. "You never needed me."

Abby shrugged. "Betsy insisted you should stay."

Theodore turned his puzzled gaze on his blissfully smiling wife. "Why?"

"I thought it would do you good."

"Hmm." Wise. He shook his head in wonder. She was definitely wise. He kissed her and cupped his son's head. He may have failed to be around for Henry but he would be there for James. Here was his second chance to be the father he wanted to be for his son and he wasn't going to take it for granted.

Another joyful tear slipped down Betsy's cheek knowing in this moment her life was perfect; healthy children, a comfortable living and the love of a good man who was finally home to stay. She whispered to God, "My cup runneth over."

Theodore squeezed her shoulders and kissed her temple. "Mine too."

Abby quietly slipped from the room as always moved by the miracle of birth. Today, she was also amazed by the healing power of love for Theodore seemed to be a man made whole again and she saw many happy years ahead for her friends.

Epilogue

Key West, April 1843

It was a Thursday afternoon and Theodore came home early hoping for some peace and quiet to work on his article for next week's paper. The office was too noisy with Robert running the presses to get out this week's edition. After months of gathering details he was ready to put this story on paper and close that chapter of his life but he soon discovered home was not quiet either.

Within minutes of walking in the door, Betsy was asking for his assistance, James was squalling in need of attention, and the girls were arguing. He sighed realizing it was too late to escape. Work was going to have to wait. He suddenly smiled. He wouldn't trade his life for anything. He kissed a surprised Betsy and sent her off to see to James while he waded in to settle the girls' argument.

Hours later when the children were finally in bed, he settled down at his desk. Staring at the blank sheet of paper before him, he contemplated where to start. There was so much to say but where to begin? Then he recalled last Sunday overhearing Brianna defending the Indians to Christoff and Hawthorne after church. He smiled now as he did then. Her defense validated the sacrifice he made so the Seminoles would be understood.

In the months since he left the forts of Florida, it wasn't entirely quiet. Some of the northern bands were still attacking pioneers. Colonel Worth decided he had given them long enough to decide for themselves to move to the reservation. Upon his return from leave, he rounded up all those he could find and shipped them west, including Tiger Tail who was so ill he had to be carried. Theodore received word the great warrior died in New Orleans.

They all waited for retaliation to reopen the war but it didn't come. Instead the troops were further reduced from three regiments down to one. The remaining Seminoles were mostly staying on the reservation or avoiding whites. It seemed as though peace had finally come to Florida. Theodore wondered how long it would last.

He turned his mind from the disturbing thought to the task at hand. He became so involved he worked on it into the wee hours of the morning, barely acknowledging when Betsy kissed him goodnight and only stopping to note the time when he was forced to find a replacement for the empty oil lamp. It was close to dawn when he finally laid his pen down and stretched his cramped shoulder and neck muscles.

It wasn't a grand piece or even his best work. It was more of a bold statement of facts to bring awareness and closure to the last seven years. Seeing it in print the following week gave him the sense of finality he needed.

Key West Weekly   April 27th, 1843   Number IX, Volume XVII

My fellow citizens, as April comes to a close and we look forward to the summer rains, if not the summer heat, I know you rejoice with me in the improvement of our economy. The cloud of war we have lived under has finally parted and while we look forward to improvement and prosperity, allow me one final moment to take stock in all that transpired over the last seven years.

The end of the Seminole's peaceful existence began with President Andrew Jackson's Indian Removal Act but it was fueled by slave owners desperate to retrieve runaways across the Florida border. Secret meetings and broken treaties, skirmishes and theft, trust was lost on both sides and war became inevitable with plenty of blame to share on both sides.

We demanded they move and they demanded the right to keep their homeland.

After the first battle in 1836, Osceola sent a message to General Duncan Clinch predicting the war would last at least five years. It seemed laughable at the time. How could a paltry number of warriors and ignorant Negros win against an army ten times their size? Twice we beat Brittan. The Seminole were the smallest and least organized band of Southern Indians. They didn't stand a chance.

Seven years later no one is laughing and we all paid dearly for our folly with the long, deadly, expensive war that didn't end in victory or even a treaty. It ended with both sides walking away likely to face each other another day.

Congress approved over thirty million in funds for the "suppression of Indian hostilities" over the course of the war. To put such a large number in perspective, the annual Federal budget is twenty-five million. For what was this grand amount spent? To move thirty-eight hundred Indians west and return some five hundred blacks to slavery many of whom it is believed were free men before the war.

At the start of our Florida war, the army was a little over seven thousand strong spread over the entire nation. By its conclusion, over ten thousand enlisted men and another thirty thousand militiamen and volunteers faced fifteen hundred warriors. Astounding odds and yet the mighty were defeated. Six generals, all of them seasoned war heroes, could not defeat these black and red men fighting for freedom and their homeland.

The war claimed the lives of a known 1466 of our men in army uniform, though only three hundred or so were killed in action; disease claimed the rest. The navy lost more than forty men and the volunteers fifty-five in actual battles. Many more succumbed to fevers. The number of civilians, Seminoles and Blacks killed is unknown. There were an estimated five thousand Indians at the start of the war, only a few hundred remain in Florida.

Untold suffering was endured on all sides. By the men carrying out their duties far from family in an inhospitable environment unlike any they had ever known. By the Indians, forced to flee their homes and to live on the run in constant fear of discovery. By the families who lost loved ones due to the conflict. By the settlers living in fear of attack and those who survived the devastating destruction of their homes.

There are no winners in this war but some good has come from it. The army and navy learned how to work together and both developed new strategies that will serve them well in battles to come. It gave rise to great men on both sides but one man was admired above all and by all. Osceola rose from obscurity to lead his people in a great battle. His loyalty was unquestionable. He promised his black brethren protection and to the peril of his people he kept his word. He rallied his tribe to fight even when his chief was ready to surrender. He led his warriors against some of the most notable generals in our army and though our rules of war did not declare him the victor, he often inflicted more loss than he sustained.

His spirit was indomitable to the very end and because of that this country found a hero, someone to look up to and admire and to champion. Many cried out against our government to leave him in peace. But even more amazing to this writer was Osceola's compassion and love of people. Except when angered, he was always friendly to the white man. He even entertained his visitors while imprisoned in Fort Marion and Fort Moultrie. He was able to look past the enemy to hold a lasting friendship with Lieutenant John Graham.

A man like Osceola is rare in this world and if not for this war we would have never known him and I for one am a better person for having met him.

Theodore carefully folded the paper and slipped it into his desk drawer to share with his children years from now when they were older. He breathed deeply feeling as though a burden was lifted. Now that this task was done, he had a new and exciting one to work on with lots of planning to do. He promised Betsy they would take their children to meet their grandparents. First they would visit her parents in Pennsylvania and then his in Austria.

Betsy appeared in the doorway with a smile on her lips and James on her hip. "He woke up from his nap asking for his da-da."

Theodore rose from the desk, gave his wife a kiss, and took his son from her arms lifting him up over his head before bringing him down to his chest. "How's my boy today?"

Three girls came running into the room circling their parents. Brianna trailed behind trying to feign propriety as she approached the room. Agatha reached her father first. "Poppa tell us a story, please." Emmaline came up behind her. "Poppa. Story."

Theodore smiled at Betsy. "Thank you."

Betsy gave him a lopsided smile and a questioning look with her head adorably tilted.

He answered her unasked question. "For waiting on me and giving me another chance to be the father I want to be."

"It is I who should thank you for choosing me to be the mother of your children."

They gazed lovingly in each other's eyes for the two seconds their squirming youngsters allowed before Theodore herded them all into the parlor. He settled on the sofa, Emmaline and James held secure on his lap while Brianna and Agatha snuggled close on either side of him. He soon had them enthralled as he began weaving an adventurous tale of a wee prince and three princesses searching for a lost prince in a faraway land.

Little Agatha looked up at her father. "Poppa, you're telling a story about us."

Theodore gave a hearty chuckle. "Perhaps I am." Brianna's question sobered his mirth.

"Is Henry lost?"

Theodore's eyes met Betsy's before he turned to Brianna. "No sweetheart. He is looking for his place in the world."

"His place is with us."

"He will always have a place here, but you'll understand when you get older. Each of you will have to decide what kind of mangrove seedling you want to be—one that drops where they are and adds to the existing island or one that starts a new island in a new spot of sand." Both girls said they would stay. It warmed his heart. Although he knew they were too young to know their path, he intended to be there to guide his children and to avoid ever leaving his beloved Betsafina again.

I hope you enjoyed reading **Love Again**.
Please consider posting an honest review on
Amazon and/or Goodreads
Your recommendation is the highest compliment.

Read on to catch a sneak peek of

Enduring Love

The next installment of the Key West series coming in 2019

Author's Notes

All the places referenced in this book are real although some have changed names over time. You probably also noticed my characters "met" a lot of real people. Of course the conversations are all a product of my imagination except for the ones citied below.

Did you recognize those real people from the Civil War era? I didn't seek them out, rather, I chose places and events that fit Theodore's story and in researching the details discovered these future leaders in their early careers so of course I had to include them. I find it fascinating that the Seminole Wars were led by well-known men (at least in that time period) from the War of 1812 and supported by men who would become famous in the Civil War. One surprise that stands out from my research was discovering a softer side of General Sherman's character through Hester Perrine's words (see my website for her story). Growing up in the South, I only knew him for his devastating march through Georgia.

A bit about Yellow Fever and Cholera—In the early 19th century no one knew the cause of these diseases. Treatment was limited to making the patient feel better, not actually curing the illness. Although the treatments used by some doctors were worse than the disease. Bloodletting and purging were widely accepted during this time. Dr. Ben Strobel (you may remember him from early chapters in the book) published a study on Yellow Fever in 1839. And speaking of medical knowledge, the Heimlich maneuver and CPR, things we take for granted now, were unknown in this time period making it difficult to save infants in Madalyn's situation.

Although I prefer to keep real events true to their dates, I must admit I took literary license with the timeline of Osceola's imprisonment before the war. There are many different accounts of why he was imprisoned and if it happened once or twice but it most likely occurred in June. I placed it in April to fit into the events of my story.

I used the *Pride of Baltimore* for the Whitmore's first trip to Key West as a tribute to the *Pride of Baltimore II* which still sails today. www.pride2.org

Please visit my website for more details, photos, history, a list of resources, a character list of who is real and who's not, and many other behind the scenes extras.

www.susanblackmonauthor.com/behind-the-scenes.html

Quote sources:

1. Peters, Thelma (editor). 1965 "William Adee Whitehead's Reminiscences of Key West." *Tequesta* (25:3-42[January]).
2. *Key West Gazette*, 7 Dec 1831.
3. *Key West Gazette*, 7 March 1832.
4. Peters, Thelma (editor). 1965 "William Adee Whitehead's Reminiscences of Key West." *Tequesta* (25:3-42[January]).
5. *The Bible. King James Version*, Joshua 1:9.
6. Potter, Woodburne. *The War in Florida*. Kindle ed., Location No. 1805.
7. Potter, Kindle Location No. 1556.
8. http://www.johnhorse.com/trail/02/a/10.htm Quotations attributed to Osceola from military reports.
9. Sprague, John. *The Origin, Progress, and Conclusion of the Florida War*, Kindle Location No. 1871.
10. Potter, Kindle Location No. 1498.
11. Potter, Kindle Location No. 2109.
12. Cohen, Myer M. (1836). *Notices of Florida and the Campaigns*, Gainesville: University Press of Florida, page 125-6.
13. Hitchcock, Ethan Allen. (1909) (*Fifty Years in Camp and Field*, New York: Putnam, page 93.
14. Coe, Charles H. (1898) *Red Patriots: The Story of the Seminoles*. Cincinnati: Editor Publishing, page 78.
15. Sprague, Kindle Location No. 6117.
16. Sprague; Kindle Location No. 9331.

ENDURING LOVE

Key West, Florida, September 2nd, 1846

Apprehension made Henry James Whitmore fluff his cravat and smooth the lapel of his new suit with his free hand. In his other, he carried a carpet bag with all his worldly possessions; a shave kit, trousers, two shirts, small clothes, a bundle of oft read letters from home, a ragged bible, a sketch pad nearly full of drawings, a small bundle of charcoal pencils, and his prized Patterson Colt revolver. The salty island breeze ruffled the fullness of his dark blond hair and long sideburns cut in the latest style according to the New Orleans barber he visited before leaving the mainland. His tanned, normally clean shaven face, was scruffy with three days growth. Most of the trip they sailed through stormy weather. He may not have been seasick like many of the other passengers but even so his sea legs were not worthy of taking a blade to his face. The first thing he planned to do when he got home was shave.

Home.

He wondered if his parent's house would still feel like home. Four years had passed since he left Key West. Four years had wrought a lot of change in his body and soul but in this moment he felt younger than his twenty years. He remembered the day he fled the island leaving only a letter behind to say goodbye to his family. He was not quite sixteen then but he recalled the foolishly confident feeling he had of being ready to take on the world. Standing here now on the busy wharf of Key West bight surrounded by the pungent odors of the dry goods being loaded and unloaded from the merchant ships he felt anxiety not unlike that of a disobedient child about to be disciplined. Their letters assured him of their acceptance. Still, he felt he had failed his parents and he would have to atone for his sins before he could feel at home again.

He thought he was satisfied with his life and content to be a soldier on the Texan frontier. But two months ago he got a strong feeling God wanted him to return to Key West. He didn't understand why but the feeling persisted and nagged until he finally requested his resignation from the army and headed towards the coast to find a ship sailing east. The solitary and dangerous trek across lower Texas to New Orleans was easier than taking this next step off the dock.

He stood at the end of the wharf looking at the town of Key West, unsure if he was there to visit or to stay, taking in all the ways it had grown since he left. More buildings, more people, more ships filled the harbor, their tall wooden masts too numerous to count. Stevedores and sailors passed up and down the aged and worn wooden planks not paying him any attention. There was a time he knew the names of every man who worked the docks.

Today he recognized none of them. At least the huge warehouses flanking the bight still bore the painted names of Tift, O'Hara, Browne and Greene giving him a small measure of familiar comfort.

As he neared the end of the dock, a putrid odor drew his attention upward to the sponges drying in the sun on the roof of a small work shack. It brought to mind long summer afternoons spent cleaning the sponges before climbing up on a scorching hot roof to lay them out to dry. He would come home smelling every bit as awful as the air around him did now. He smiled as he recalled his mother, other than reminding him to wash up before supper, never complained.

He shifted the carpetbag to his other hand and walked toward shore noting again the new buildings added over the past few years. Where once there were wide spaces between structures there was now in some cases only alley ways. It made him feel even more like an intruding stranger.

Henry stepped off the dock onto the crushed white limestone street. He made his way between Asa Tift's salvage warehouse on his left and, judging by the rich earthy smell, a cigar factory on his right. From inside he could hear the low murmur of men talking as they went about their repetitive task of rolling cigars. He stepped from the shade between the buildings onto Front Street. Across from him were familiar weathered gray buildings mixed with many new ones of butter colored fresh cut lumber. All around him were signs of the town's prosperity. Besides the new buildings and the thriving business with their neatly kept store fronts, it was evident in the number of businessmen and well-dressed ladies going about their day.

Coming from the open frontier it made him feel hemmed in reminding him of the last time he returned to New York when he was a child. He hated the closed in feeling of the city streets after leaving the carefree summer days of roaming the undeveloped woods of this island. For a moment, he wished again to be on the wide open range of Texas but a few steps further and he was once again in the path of the ocean breeze and its gentle caress filled him with reminders of his youthful summers. A glimpse of the open tidal pond behind Front Street and the uncleared woods beyond the town also brought him comfort. At least some things hadn't changed.

One might consider his roots to be in New York. It was where he was born, where his father and grandfather grew up, and where the family's ancestral estates and trust were still located. But for Henry, home was Key West. He was seven when his father moved them to the island. The salty air and ocean breezes were not to be compared with icy winter winds or shiftless summer air that held all the rank odors of city life. He reveled in the warm tropic sun and swimming in the turquoise waters surrounding the island. It was paradise and thinking back on those sunny days of his youth, it was hard to remember why he felt so desperate to leave.

He turned to his right and worked his way down Front Street away from the wharfs and warehouse headed towards the residential side of the small waterfront town. Few paid him any attention and as yet no one recognized him. His progress was arrested when he saw Abigail Eatonton exiting the mercantile across the street, her daughter behind her. At least for a moment he thought it was Emily, but then he realized it couldn't be. Emily was sixteen now and this girl was several years younger. It must be her cousin, Laura, visiting from Montgomery. My how they favored each other. Catching up to the cousin on the steps was another girl nearly the same age. He knew right away the blue eyes and raven hair belonged to his half-sister Brianna. The two girls had their heads together whispering and giggling as girls often do.

Next to appear was his mother, Betsy. Truthfully she was his step-mother but he could only recall vague images of his real mother having lost her at the tender age of four. Betsy's raven hair now had strands of gray, a sad reminder of how time marches on, but her blue eyes were as round and as bright as ever.

All of the homesickness he had not allowed himself to feel since he left this island suddenly engulfed him. He could only stand there staring at the ladies who were as yet oblivious to him.

In the next moment, his mother's eyes met his. She searched his face. He could tell she had not yet placed him. He missed the moment of her recognition for his eyes were drawn above her to the enchanting young lady appearing last in the doorway and his heart skipped a beat.

Emily.

It had to be her; his childhood friend now all grown up and unexpectedly beautiful.

Heartstoppingly so.

Waves of red-gold hair cascaded about her shoulders and caressed her ample bosom. Those were a surprise. She was still flat-chested the last time he saw her. His gaze traveled further past her narrow waist to gently flaring hips. Guiltily his gaze shot upwards in search of eyes the light gray of a summer squall over the Keys.

She must have felt his regard for she looked his way. Her recognition was immediate. He could flatter himself that she would have known him anywhere, even after the changes of four years, but in fairness she had the advantage of a miniature drawing done by a fellow soldier he sent to her on a whim.

Both his mother and Brianna were leading the ladies coming towards him as fast as they could walk. He moved to intercept them in the street catching his mother about the waist. He twirled her as she held his neck in a tight hug; tears of joy streamed down her face. He put her down and she stepped back but kept both hands on his cheeks, obviously looking for signs of her boy in the man before her.

He was first to break eye-contact as he looked to Emily, but could do no more than a glance before Brianna launched herself into his arms. He twirled

4

her too before moving them all out of the middle of the road to give way to a heavily loaded milk cart pulled by a donkey.

His gaze was drawn back to Emily. Up close, her beauty hit him like a load of bricks. The skinned-knee tomboy who bravely followed him on his escapades around the island was gone. She had grown into a lovely lady who probably had no interest in the returning proverbial prodigal son. More than likely she had a beau. The thought of her affection being given to another hurt. He was having trouble breathing and didn't hear his mother's question. He was aware she was speaking but failed to pull his attention away from Emily until she forcefully called his name.

"Henry."

Reluctantly he turned his gaze away from luminesce eyes, radiant complexion, and auburn hair catching fire from the sun. His mother's lips were pursed in displeasure. He hoped it was due to his inattention and not because she knew his thoughts although he suspected it was the latter. If so, was it the object of his desire she objected to or the thoughts in general? Surely she didn't object to the daughter of her best friend. Whatever it was she had pushed it aside to smile broadly.

"Are you home for good?" He heard the excitement in her voice drop. "Or is this just a visit?"

He hated the disappointment he would see in his mother's eyes but he could not be less than honest with her. "I am not sure." She accepted his words as if they were expected. "Where are Agatha, Emmaline, and the boys?" He was surprised his two little sisters and baby brother, James, were not with his mother nor were Emily's four younger brothers with Mrs. Eatonton.

"The older boys are playing with their friends. Agatha is helping Mrs. Baxley watch the younger ones at Mrs. Eatonton's house. Are you anxious to see them or would you rather go home first and freshen up from your journey?"

"I suppose a wash cloth and a change of clothes would not be remiss."

Betsy grinned as she nodded in agreement.

Emily stepped forward to greet Henry. With unaccustomed shyness she said, "Hello."

Henry had said no more than, "Hello," in return when his mother took his arm and turned him away anxious to get him home. He cast a disappointed glance over his shoulder and noticed Emily was disappointed as well. Surely, there would be a chance later to speak with her.

As a group they headed down Front Street gaining attention as they passed the open shops and bars. All who knew Henry greeted him warmly and welcomed him home. Some joined in their walk turning it into more of a parade as they approached Clinton Place, a triangular patch of ground at the bend of Front Street and the beginning of Whitehead Street. Henry's heart was warmed by all the fond greetings of remembered names and faces, fortunately he was often able to put one with the other.

As they turned on Whitehead Street he noticed there were many more houses built between Whitehead and the beach and barely visible just beyond them was the large two story Marine Hospital. Someone pointed out the large pier past the hospital docks leading far out into the water and all the activity traveling across it to the beginnings of a new fort under construction in the harbour. It peaked Henry's curiosity. He had never known a structure other than bridges to be built in the water. To his left, there were now two streets instead of one spreading out behind the pond. He would guess nearly two hundred more buildings had been added while he was away. In his mind the island had remained unchanged. It was disconcerting to see how much really had progressed since last he walked these streets.

He paused in front of the house he considered home. Being here was almost surreal. He had woken up from many a dream at the moment of opening the front door and here he was walking up the steps. If not for all the friends and family gathered behind him, he could easily believe this moment wasn't real and he would wake up any minute to feel alone and bereft. He paused as he touched the door handle. As if she understood, his mother placed her hand against his back for support.

Taking a deep breath, Henry turned the handle and opened the door. He stepped into the foyer and as his gaze took in all he could see, he was suddenly assaulted by memories. He could almost hear the echo of his sisters' laughter as they played hide-and-seek on a rainy afternoon. Brianna's triumphant smile as she won her first game of chess against him with their father's help. Agatha and Emmaline begging him to play tea party or swing them around in the backyard. His father's chair where he gathered the girls in his lap and would make up a story to entertain them. He turned to the stairs and remembered all the times his sisters raced down them to greet him in the morning. Just behind the staircase, he and little Emily had a pretend wedding the day his father wed Betsy. He remembered panicking for a moment when her father caught them but Captain Max simply picked Emily up and tickled her as he admonished that weddings of any kind could wait. The sweet memories gave way to the more bitter moments of when he disappointed his mother and he would escape the hurt look on Betsy's face by turning his back on her and climbing the stairs to his room. And the worst memories were of all the times he watched his father walk out the door leaving them for months on end as he reported on the Indian wars. Especially when they were left to handle the deaths of Aunt Agatha and his sister Madalyn with his support.

His reverie was broken as his mother slipped her arm around his waist.

"Welcome home, Henry. We left your room much as it was other than making room for James to share it. I don't believe he has bothered any of your things. Why don't you go on up and get settled in. I'll find you something to eat."

Henry glanced down into the beloved face of his step-mother and teased, "I don't suppose you have any cinnamon bread."

She gently admonished him. "If I had known you were coming I would have had a whole loaf waiting for you, as it is you'll just have to wait till I can have some ready to bake tomorrow."

It shouldn't surprise him but it did. "You would do that for me?"

"Of course."

He then realized none of the others had followed them into the house. He really wanted to see Emily again. At his questioning look, Betsy said, "I sent them on to the Eatonton's. We'll join them as soon as you're ready."

He bit back his temporary disappointment. "Of course. I'll be but a moment." He left her standing in the foyer to take the stairs two at a time. He entered the first room on the left and saw his neatly made bed and nightstand looking just as he left it but the wash stand was gone and the chest of drawers was moved to a corner by the door to allow room for the small child's bed. He knew he had a little brother from his mother's letters but this was the first time he was faced with the reality of it. The knowledge was only superficial while he was living out west. He was curious as to how he would feel when they actually met. Would he feel the same sibling bond he felt for his little sisters?

He placed his satchel on his bed and removed his clean shirt. He was in the process of unbuttoning his cuffs when *Betsy* appeared in the doorway with a pitcher and bowl. "Pardon me. I remembered you didn't have water so I brought you these." She turned and placed them on the chest of drawers with a washcloth. "I'll wait for you downstairs."

Henry pulled the suspenders from his shoulders and unbuttoned his travel stained shirt letting it slip from his shoulders. The sea breeze whispering past the curtains of the open window brushed across his bare back drying the heat drawn moisture gathered there. It was as refreshing as the cool water he now splashed across his face. The heat didn't bother him so much as the humidity and he was grateful for the moment's respite from it. He washed his face, neck and armpits and then stood a moment in the breeze of the open window before slipping into his clean shirt. He brushed the dust from his trousers and used his dirty shirt to wipe the dust from his boots. He then combed his hair. He was now as presentable as he could be without a bath and pressed clothes.

He walked down the stairs and found Betsy waiting for him on the front porch. He offered her his arm. As they walked down the steps together, Henry asked, "Should we go see father and let him know I am home?"

Betsy patted his arm. "I'm afraid he is in Tallahassee. He should be home in a day or two."

Henry was unexpectedly disappointed. He didn't realize how much he yearned to see his father until now when he was forced to wait longer to do so.

Silently, he and his mother walked past the next two houses to reach the Eatonton's. As they approached, Mrs. Baxley who was rocking on the front porch called into the house and soon his dark-haired, eight year old sister, Agatha, came running to greet him. She was followed by six year old, red-headed Emmaline. They squealed in delight and launched themselves into his open arms. Henry was sure Emmaline likely was mimicking her sister more than she actually remembered him. He lifted them to his chest and swung them around much to their delight before placing them back on the ground. Over their heads he could see Briana and Emily descend the porch steps and behind them Emily's four rambunctious brothers. The girls stepped aside for the eldest, Christoff, to approach with hand outstretched. Henry warmly grasped the proffered hand of the fifteen year old who once tagged along after him and his friends as they trolled the island. It suddenly occurred to him Christoff was now the age he was when he left the island. He seemed so young. No wonder his mother had been so desperate to keep him from leaving.

Henry greeted the other brothers in turn. He did some quick math to come up with Hawthorn, better known as 'Thorn', was eleven and Nathanial was nine. Emily's youngest brother was Jacob was only two when Henry left and would soon turn six, the same as Emmaline. Jacob had no recollection of him. Henry was surprised Nat did being only five when he left. Christoff and Thorn often trailed after Henry and now offered good natured teasing of his former efforts to dislodge them and acknowledging how burdensome they must have been to a teenage boy.

The parade of boys ushered Henry up the steps of the porch where Mrs. Eatonton waited in the doorway holding the hand of a brown-haired toddler with features similar to his own. When their eyes met, the little boy timidly moved behind her skirt. Henry felt an instant kinship to the youngster despite his expectations otherwise.

Betsy stepped forward to pick up her youngest child and straddle him on her right hip. When he buried his face in her neck, she grasped his right hand to gain his attention. "Jamie, this is your brother Henry. Remember? We've told you about him and how he lived far away. Now he has come home and he wants to meet you. Be a good boy and shake his hand."

Henry watched in fascination as the toddler overcame his apprehension to dutifully hold his little hand out to him. Henry grasped the small hand with what he hoped was a friendly smile. "Hello little brother."

James pulled his hand away and once again hid his face in Betsy's neck.

Betsy patted the little back indulgently as she smiled at Henry. "Give him time. He'll warm up to you. He's shy at first with strangers."

Stranger. The word hurt but it was the truth. He was a stranger in his own family and he had only himself to blame. He and James were family by blood and though he was aware he had a little brother, James was too young to be aware of him until now. The look on his mother's face told him she felt his pain and regretted her choice of words. He let the moment pass with a self-deprecating smile before turning his attention back to the face peeping out from Betsy's shoulder. As they moved into the house, he said, "Do you know we share the same name? My middle name is James, same as yours."

He belligerently raised his head and in all seriousness said, "My name James Lawrence, not yours." He then stuck his thumb in his mouth and turned his face away.

Henry wasn't sure how to respond so he remained silent.

A short while later, Emily's father, Captain Max Eatonton, returned home. He firmly shook Henry's hand and clapped him on the back in greeting. "Welcome home. I heard you've been soldiering out west. Did you like it?"

"Yes sir."

"Were you fighting the Indians or the Mexicans?"

"Both sir."

He made small talk with their parents for a few moments before Christoff pulled him away with some relief. He and the three Eatonton boys made their way outside. At the bottom of the steps, Henry turned and was surprised to see the empty doorway having expected Emily to trail after them as she had always done. Recalling the drastic change in her appearance from tomboy to young lady he was saddened to realize she was too grown up to tag along with the boys.

* * *

Emily stared at the closed front door wishing she dared to follow Henry as in days of old. She wanted him to notice she was all grown up but she hated that it meant she could no longer run freely about the island. She was now forced to return to the parlour and sit quietly pretending to enjoy stitching flowers on a handkerchief while her mother and Mrs. Whitmore visited instead of having fun traipsing after the boys. How odd that she hadn't missed such things while Henry was gone.

She thought back to the moment this afternoon when she stepped from the musky dry goods store into the bright sunshine to see Henry across the street standing still as if a figment of her imagination. She knew it would happen unexpectedly. One day he would return without warning. She imagined the moment hundreds of times but always they were alone and could speak freely of their feelings for one another. Of course, reality was far from her dreamed reunion. Today, at the moment of their meeting, four other females stood between them and his mother and sister had first rights to his attention. Social proprieties gave her none of the freedom to express her true emotions and she supposed it was just as well considering she had no idea how he might really feel about her after all this time. His letters were few and far between and mentioned only matter of fact details of his life in the west. Sending the miniature likeness of himself was the closest he had come to anything personal and she would be foolish to construe its meaning as anything more than friendship.

At least while everyone else was distracted by the familial greetings, she had been free to study the changes in him. The tiny portrait hardly did justice to the breadth of his shoulders. His overall physique was now that of a man and it intimidated her. The harshness of life and the Texas sun added planes and lines to his face removing the last vestiges of boyhood. The scruffy new growth on his cheeks and chin enhanced rather than distracted from his pleasing appearance. All traces of the childhood playmate she knew were gone except in his eyes. His piercing blue gaze skipped to hers and she noticed they still held a glimmer of youthful insecurity. His voice was deeper and the pleasing sound of it as he greeted her sent shivers down her spine.

They barely exchanged pleasantries before Brianna pulled him away. Nor had they a chance since then to speak which explained her frustration of the moment. She spent the last four years secretly pinning for him and she was impatient to have a chance to get reacquainted.

In recent years, many boys had expressed interest in her though few had made it past her over-protective younger brother. Christoff was her self-proclaimed guardian much to her chagrin. Those few suiters brave enough to face off against him usually wavered under her father's scrutiny. Only one or two had made it as far as daring to walk her home from school and they only did so once for in the end she found the poor lads, although brave, a poor substitute for her former companion. None of them could make her laugh the way Henry did or challenged her mentally. At any rate, their appeal was not enough to encourage their pursuit.

Her mind was brought back to the present when she overheard her mother inviting Mrs. Whitmore for supper. It brought a secret hopeful smile to Emily's lips.

* * *

Henry had forgotten how spirited meals could be at the Eatonton's. Soldiers ate swift and quiet and meals at his home growing up were sedate affairs with his well-behaved younger sisters. In this house, with Emily's four brothers, conversation was lively and hands were always reaching for something. It was a good thing the Eatonton's had a large table as there were fourteen of them dining together consisting of himself, his mother, three sisters, baby brother, Emily, her parents, four brothers, and her cousin, Laura. He watched the proceedings in fascination from his position next to Emily's father at the head of the table. Every once in a while he caught her speculating look from across the table despite trying to keep his attention from her for fear he would be caught staring. He couldn't get over the changes in her. She was the most beautiful creature he had ever seen.

Christoff mentioned earlier, in an offhand manner, how the local boys started buzzing around her at fourteen and he had his hands full discouraging them. Henry could well imagine his difficulties. It was a brave lad who dared to discourage much older boys. Henry asked him how often it had come to fisticuffs. Christoff replied with a proud smile, "only a few," which Henry took to mean he had prevailed and in doing so discouraged others from trying to best him. Christoff was not a strapping lad by any means but he was scrappy and in a fight that often mattered more. Henry certainly wasn't about to challenge him or get into trouble with Captain Max so he kept his gaze adverted from Emily as much as possible.

Captain Max pulled Henry from his musings. "I suppose you've noticed all the changes?"

For a panicked moment, Henry thought he had read his thoughts but Captain Max's calm demeanor and common sense suggested he was referring to the town and not his daughter. "Yes sir. A lot of new buildings and judging by the citizens I passed on the street and the number of specialty stores I gather business has been prosperous."

"It certainly has. My wrecking ships have brought in three times the money of the merchant line."

"You have more than one wrecker now?"

"I own two and have shared interests in three more. I would be out on the reefs now if I hadn't made a promise."

Henry noticed his indulgent smile at Mrs. Eatonton sitting at the foot of the table. He supposed it was to take the sting out of the complaint. Captain Max's desire to be out wrecking was easy to see. Henry supposed he could understand the draw of challenging a storm versus the necessity of avoiding one on a merchant ship. It was something similar to his need to join the Texas Rangers versus doing odd jobs around a fort as an errand boy.

Captain Max smiled broadly. "Indeed, the wrecking business is so lucrative I hear it has made us the richest city in the entire country."

Henry returned his smile. "Impressive."

Max raised his glass of wine. "Yes, indeed."

Looking around the Eatonton home, one would have to blind not to realize Captain Max was doing well. The furnishings, while of a practical nature, were of high quality. Nothing was too ostentatious but the house lacked for nothing. It reflected Mrs. Eatonton's excellent taste and Captain Max's humble beginnings. The dining room, for instance, was richly appointed with silk covered chairs, silver candelabras, fine oil paintings, and on the table, crystal stemware, delicate bone china, and fine linens but one felt comfortable enough to lean back in the chair and enjoy each other's company.

The Eatonton's lived their life in much the same way. They employed only the minimum number of servants and treated them more like family than employees. It was also not unusual for the family members to help with the chores. Captain Max treated his crew the same way and Abby treated all her patients, rich or poor, the same as she would her friends and family. It was why the Eatonton's were so widely accepted and liked among all the classes in Key West society.

When the meal was over, they adjourned to the parlour where the ladies gathered at one end to discuss feminine interests and the men at the other end with cigars and brandy while the older boys listened in and the younger children played their own games in between the two groups. Christoff and Max were soon deep in discussion of their upcoming sailing. It was to be the first time Max was taking his son on a merchant run from Mobile to New Orleans, Savannah, and Charleston before returning home. They expected to be gone two to three weeks. Christoff was rightfully excited by the prospect and Thorn was sick of hearing about it. He soon pulled Henry into a game of chess.

Emily soon came over to watch. "I want to play the winner."

Henry glanced at her eager smile while he waited for Thorn to make his move. It was obvious Henry was about to win the game. He hoped her smile was as much for the prospect of her opponent as for the game itself. A few moves later, Henry declared check mate and Thorn relinquished his seat to his grinning sister. Henry started resetting the pieces with the white on her side of the board trying to ignore his rapidly beating pulse. Emily settled the full skirt of her green stripped taffeta dress and then began helping him. When their hands brushed, he felt a spark and his eyes flew to her wide-eyed dove-gray gaze. The corner of her lip quirked upward before her eyes demurely returned to the task at hand. He knew she had felt it too.

When the pieces were all in place, Emily raised her eyes to his in question. He gestured to the white pieces on her side of the board. "Ladies first."

Emily moved her e-pawn. Henry answered with his d-pawn. Next she moved her knight to block him. He smiled. Her strategy had improved while he was away. The moves continued closely matched and he was forced to admit she was now a worthy opponent. They soon garnered more attention. Christoff and Thorn supported Henry. Brianna and Laura were in support of Emily. The spectators participated in good natured ribbing but Henry and Emily remained focused and silent. When he realized the game was a draw, he lifted his gaze to find Emily watching him with twinkling eyes and a very self-satisfied grin as if she had done something better than winning the game. Perhaps she had in proving his equal without embarrassing him with a loss. And in that moment he knew without a doubt he was smitten with her.

He rose from his seat and held his hand out to her. "Your skills have greatly improved." She placed her warm hand in his and the connection sparked as before surprising them both.

Emily smiled demurely. "Thank you."

They moved off to the side allowing Christoff and Brianna to take their places at the board. Henry positioned them close enough to spectate but a pace away giving them a chance to converse without disrupting the players. Emily's first question was true to her nature and direct.

"How long do you plan to visit?"

"I'm not sure." Curiosity made him ask, "What if I planned to stay?"

"Then you would need a job."

He laughed. Of course she would give him a practical answer instead of a hint of her feelings which he had been fishing for. "True. But what kind of job?"

She waited for him to answer is own question.

"I suppose I could go back to cleaning sponges."

Her pert nose wrinkled in distaste. "Oh please no. You smelled horrible."

"Ah, true, cleaning them is an odorous task, but I was thinking of fishing for them."

"Well then, I suppose that will do."

He laughed again. "What do you have in mind for me then?"

"Hmm. The fort is always hiring construction help. They would probably take you on without hesitation."

He frowned. "Why is that?"

"Your army background, of course." She paused a moment before very softly adding, "And your broad shoulders."

She blushed becomingly and his gut tightened. His gaze dropped to her mouth as her tongue swept across her bottom lip leaving it shiny with moisture. Suddenly the only thought in his head was how much he wanted to kiss her, to find out how her lips felt pressed beneath his. A surprising revelation and a first for him. He had only kissed one girl before now outside his family and the experience had been anything but pleasant.

He had just turned eighteen and had been with the Texas Rangers long enough to establish friendships with the older men. Upon learning how innocent he truly was in the ways of women and men, they made it their mission to initiate him. The next town they passed had a bordello so they convinced Captain Hays a rest was required. That night, they snuck Henry into town and straight into a seedy room and the arms of a Spanish barmaid wearing only her underclothes, with rolls of exposed flesh, red lips, powdered face, and reeking of heavy perfume. When he hesitated on the threshold, they pushed him into the room and pulled the door closed.

The woman - he couldn't bring himself to call her a lady - pulled him forward. She said, "You don't have to worry about a thing, Carmelita is going to take care of you." In the middle of the room, she stopped their momentum and then stepped to him, running a hand over his head before bringing his mouth to hers. She licked his lips while her other hand brushed much lower. The revulsion he felt was full and immediate. That certainly was not the way his father kissed his mother. Wanting nothing further of this experience, he rushed to the door jerking it open and was dismayed to find it barricaded by his so-called friends. Desperate to get out of the cloying room, he peered out the window relieved to find a balcony beneath it. Without a backward glance, he raised the sash and slipped from the room. He didn't have any trouble finding his way down to the ground or to his mount. He rode for camp without any concern for his companions and what they might think of him.

It was Captain Walker who calmed his anger and assuaged his shame. He explained that while some men only needed a warm body others preferred meaning in their relationships with women and there was nothing wrong with that. In his opinion, it made him more of a man, not less, and Henry would know when the time was right for him.

Staring into the dove-gray eyes before him, Henry finally understood what Captain Walker was trying to explain.

ABOUT THE AUTHOR

Susan Blackmon has enjoyed reading historical novels all her life. With a talent for writing it was only natural for her to try her hand at creating one of her own. All that was missing was inspiration. An unexpected cruise ship detour to Key West and a few history tours later, Max and Abby's story began.

When Susan isn't writing, she enjoys being with her family, hiking waterfalls, reading, scrapbooking, and escaping to the coast every chance she gets.

Visit www.susanblackmonauthor.com to learn more about her books or to find your favorite way to connect via social media.

Made in the
USA
Columbia, SC